Praise for Harlan Coben

'It is always satisfying to discover a new crime writer – and this is the business . . . this book will keep you up until 2 A.M.' *The Times*

'Harlan Coben. He's smart, he's funny, and he has something to say' Michael Connelly

'An increasingly frightening conspiracy with an unguessable ending . . . hard to put down' *Sunday Telegraph*

'At last a British publisher has given British readers the chance to discover something every US mystery fan already knows – that Harlan Coben is one of the most entertaining and intriguing crime writers around'
Val McDermid, *Manchester Evening Guardian*

'What sets Harlan Coben above the crowd are wit and . . . an entertaining plot'
Los Angeles Times Book Review

'Fast action, snappy dialogue and plenty of insider hoops material make this a fast, enjoyable read' *Toronto Star*

'Coben . . . scores a hole in one! The characters are deftly etched and the details keenly observed'
Publishers Weekly

Harlan Coben is one of the most exciting talents in crime writing. His most recent novels, *The Woods, Promise Me, Hold Tight* and *Long Lost*, were all international bestsellers, hitting the charts of the *Sunday Times*, the *New York Times, Le Monde* and many others throughout the world. His books are published in forty languages in over thirty countries. Harlan's breakthrough novel, *Tell No One*, has been adapted into an award-winning and hugely successful feature film. He was the first ever author to win all three major US crime awards, and established a bestselling series of crime novels starring his powerful creation, Myron Bolitar, before turning to stand-alone books. Harlan lives in New Jersey with his wife and four children. Visit his website at www.harlancoben.com.

Harlan COBEN

Fade Away

Back Spin

Fade Away
First published in Great Britain by Hodder & Stoughton in 2000

Back Spin
First published in Great Britain by Orion in 2002

This omnibus edition published in 2010
by Orion Books Ltd
Orion House, 5 Upper St Martin's Lane
London WC2H 9EA

An Hachette UK company

A CIP catalogue record for this book is available
from the British Library.

ISBN 9781407230160

Printed in Great Britain by CPI Mackays, Chatham ME5 8TD

www.orionbooks.co.uk

Fade Away

For Larry and Craig, the coolest brothers a guy
could ever have. If you don't believe me,
just ask them.

Acknowledgements

The author wishes to thank the following for their help: Anne
Armstrong-Coben, MD; James Bradbeer, Jr, of Lilly Pulitzer;
David Gold, MD; Maggie Griffin; Jacob Hoye; Lidsay Koehler;
David Pepe of Pro Agents, Inc.; Peter Roisman of Advantage
International; and, of course, Dave Bolt. Any errors – factual or
otherwise – are totally their fault. The author is not to blame.

Chapter 1

'Just behave.'

'Me?' Myron said 'I'm always a delight.'

Myron Bolitar was being led through the corridor of the darkened Meadowlands Arena by Calvin Johnson, the New Jersey Dragons new general manager. Their dress shoes clacked sharply against the tile and echoed through empty Harry M. Stevens food stands, Carvel Ice Cream carts, pretzel vendors, souvenir booths. The smell of sporting-event hot dogs – that sort of rubbery, chemically, yet nostalgically delicious aroma – wafted from the walls. The stillness of the place consumed them; there is nothing more hollow and lifeless than an empty sports arena.

Calvin Johnson stopped in front of a door leading to a luxury box. 'This may all seem a bit strange,' he said. 'Just go with the flow, okay?'

'Okay.'

Calvin reached for the knob and took a deep breath.

'Clip Arnstein, the owner of the Dragons, is in there waiting for us.'

'And yet I'm not trembling,' Myron said.

Calvin Johnson shook his head. 'Just don't be an ass.'

Myron pointed to his chest. 'I wore a tie and everything.'

Calvin Johnson opened the door. The luxury box faced midcourt. Several workers were putting down the basketball floor over the hockey ice. The Devils had played the night before. Tonight was the Dragons' turn. The box was cozy. Twenty-four cushioned seats. Two television monitors. To the right was a wood-paneled counter for the food – usually fried chicken, hot dogs, potato knishes, sausage and pepper sandwiches, that sort of stuff. To the left was a brass cart with a nicely stocked bar and minifridge. The box also had its own bathroom – this so the corporate high rollers would not have to urinate with the great unwashed.

Clip Arnstein faced them, standing. He wore a dark blue suit with a red tie. He was bald with patches of gray over both ears. He was burly, his chest still a barrel after seventy-some-odd years. His large hands had brown spots and fat blue veins like garden hoses. No one spoke. No one moved. Clip glared hard at Myron for several seconds, examining him from head to toe.

'Like the tie?' Myron asked.

Calvin Johnson shot him a warning glance.

The old man made no movement toward them. 'How old are you now, Myron?'

Interesting opening question. 'Thirty-two.'

'You playing any ball?'

'Some,' Myron said.

'You keep in good shape?'

2

'Want me to flex?'

'No, that won't be necessary.'

No one offered Myron a seat and no one took one. Of course the only chairs in here were the spectator seats, but it still felt weird to stand in a business setting where you're supposed to sit. Standing suddenly became difficult. Myron felt antsy. He didn't know what to do with his hands. He took out a pen and held it, but that didn't feel right. Too Bob Dole. He stuck his hands in his pockets and stood at a weird angle, like the casual guy in the Sears circular.

'Myron, we have an interesting proposition for you,' Clip Arnstein said.

'Proposition?' Always the probing interrogatory.

'Yes. I was the one who drafted you, you know.'

'I know.'

'Ten, eleven years ago. When I was with the Celtics.'

'I know.'

'First round.'

'I know all this, Mr Arnstein.'

'You were a hell of a prospect, Myron. You were smart. You had an unbelievable touch. You were loaded with talent.'

'I coulda been a contenda,' Myron said.

Arnstein scowled. It was a famous scowl, developed over some fifty-plus years in professional basketball. The scowl had made its first appearance when Clip played for the now-defunct Rochester Royals in the forties. It grew more famous when he coached the Boston Celtics to numerous championships. It became a legendary trademark when he made all the famous trades ('clipping' the competition, ergo the nickname) as team president. Three years ago Clip had become majority owner of the New

3

Jersey Dragons and the scowl now resided in East Rutherford, right off Exit 16 of the New Jersey Turnpike. His voice was gruff. 'Was that supposed to be Brando?'

'Eerie, isn't it? Like Marlon's actually in the room.'

Clip Arnstein's face suddenly softened. He nodded slowly, giving Myron the doelike, father-figure eyes. 'You make jokes to cover the pain,' he said gravely. 'I understand that.'

Dr Joyce Brothers.

'Is there something I can do for you, Mr Arnstein?'

'You never played in a single professional game, did you, Myron?'

'You know very well I didn't.'

Clip nodded. 'Your first preseason game. Third quarter. You already had eighteen points that game. Not bad for a rookie in his first scrimmage. That was when fate took over.'

Fate took the form of big Burt Wesson of the Washington Bullets. There had been a collision, a searing pain, and then nothing.

'Awful thing,' Clip said.

'Uh huh.'

'I always felt bad about what happened to you. Such a waste.'

Myron glanced at Calvin Johnson. Calvin was looking off, arms crossed, his smooth black features a placid pool. 'Uh huh,' Myron said again.

'That's why I'd like to give you another chance.'

Myron was sure he'd heard wrong. 'Pardon?'

'We have a slot open on the team. I'd like to sign you.'

Myron waited. He looked at Clip. Then he looked at Calvin Johnson. Neither one was laughing. 'Where is it?' Myron asked.

4

'What?'

'The camera. This is one of those hidden camera shows, right? Is this the one with Ed McMahon? I'm a big fan of his work.'

'It's not a joke, Myron.'

'It must be, Mr Arnstein. I haven't played competitive ball in ten years. I shattered my knee, remember?'

'All too well. But as you said, it was ten years ago. I know you went through rehabilitation to rebuild it.'

'And you also know I tried a comeback. Seven years ago. The knee wouldn't hold up.'

'It was still too early,' Clip said. 'You just told me you're playing again.'

'Pickup games on weekends. It's a tad different than the NBA.'

Clip dismissed the argument with a wave of his hand. 'You're in shape. You even volunteered to flex.'

Myron's eyes narrowed, swerving from Clip to Calvin Johnson, back to Clip. Their expressions were neutral. 'Why do I have the feeling,' Myron asked, 'that I'm missing something here?'

Clip finally smiled. He looked over to Calvin Johnson. Calvin Johnson forced up a return smile.

'Perhaps I should be less' – Clip paused, searched for the word – 'opaque.'

'That might be helpful.'

'I want you on the team. I don't much care if you play or not.'

Myron waited again. When no one continued, he said. 'It's still a bit opaque.'

Clip let loose a long breath. He walked over to the bar, opened a small hotel-style fridge, and removed a can of

5

Yoo-Hoo. Stocking Yoo-Hoos. Hmm. Clip had been prepared. 'You still drink this sludge?'

'Yes,' Myron said.

He tossed Myron the can and poured something from a decanter into two glasses. He handed one to Calvin Johnson. He signaled to the seats by the glass window. Exactly midcourt. Very nice. Nice leg room too. Even Calvin, who was six-eight, was able to stretch a bit. The three men sat next to one another, all facing the same way, which again felt weird in a business setting. You were supposed to sit across from one another, preferably at a table or desk. Instead they sat shoulder to shoulder, watching the work crew pound the floor into place.

'Cheers,' Clip said.

He sipped his whiskey. Calvin Johnson just held his. Myron, obeying the instructions on the can, shook his Yoo-Hoo.

'If I'm not mistaken,' Clip continued, 'you're a lawyer now.'

'I'm a member of the bar,' Myron said. 'I don't practice much law.'

'You're a sports agent.'

'Yes.'

'I don't trust agents,' Clip said.

'Neither do I.'

'For the most part, they're bloodsucking leeches.'

'We prefer the term "parasitic entities,"' Myron said. 'It's more PC.'

Clip Arnstein leaned forward, his eyes zeroing in on Myron's. 'How do I know I can trust you?'

Myron pointed at himself. 'My face,' he said 'It screams trustworthiness.'

6

Clip did not smile. He leaned a little closer. 'What I'm about to tell you must remain confidential.'

'Okay.'

'Do you give me your word it won't go any farther than this room?'

'Yes.'

Clip hesitated, glanced at Calvin Johnson, shifted in his seat. 'You know, of course, Greg Downing.'

Of course. Myron had grown up with Greg Downing. From the time they had first competed as sixth graders in a town league less than twenty miles from where Myron now sat, they were instant rivals. When they reached high school, Greg's family moved to the neighboring town of Essex Fells because Greg's father did not want his son sharing the basketball spotlight with Myron. The personal rivalry then began to take serious flight. They played against each other eight times in high school, each winning four games. Myron and Greg became New Jersey's hottest recruits and both matriculated at big-time basketball colleges with a storied rivalry of their own – Myron to Duke, Greg to North Carolina.

The personal rivalry soared.

During their college careers, they had shared two *Sports Illustrated* covers. Both teams won the ACC twice, but Myron picked up a national championship. Both Myron and Greg were picked first-team All-American, both at the guard spots. By the time they both graduated, Duke and North Carolina had played each other twelve times. The Myron-led Duke had won eight of them. When the NBA draft came, both men went in the first round.

The personal rivalry crashed and burned.

Myron's career ended when he collided with big Burt Wesson. Greg Downing sidestepped fate and went on to become one of the NBA premier guards. During his ten-year career with the New Jersey Dragons Downing had been named to the All-Star team eight times. He led the league twice in three-point shooting. Four times he led the league in free-throw percentage and once in assists. He'd been on three *Sports Illustrated* covers and had won an NBA championship.

'I know him,' Myron said.

'Do you talk to him much?' Clip Arnstein asked.

'No.'

'When was the last time you spoke?'

'I don't remember.'

'Within the last few days?'

'I don't think we've spoken in ten years,' Myron said.

'Oh,' Clip said. He took another sip. Calvin had still not touched his drink. 'Well, I'm sure you heard about his injury.'

'Something with his ankle,' Myron said. 'It's day to day. He's in seclusion working on it.'

Clip nodded. 'That's the story we gave the media anyway. It's not exactly the truth.'

'Oh?'

'Greg isn't injured,' Clip said. 'He's missing.'

'Missing?' Again the probing interrogatory.

'Yes.' Clip took another sip. Myron sipped back, not an easy task with Yoo-Hoo.

'Since when?' Myron asked.

'Five days now.'

Myron looked at Calvin. Calvin remained placid but he had that kind of face. During his playing days, his nickname had been Frosty because he never displayed emotion. He was living up to his name now.

Myron tried again. 'When you say Greg is missing—'

'Gone,' Clip snapped. 'Disappeared. Into thin air. Without a trace. Whatever you want to call it.'

'Have you called the police?'

'No.'

'Why not?'

Clip gave him the wave-off again. 'You know Greg. He's not a conventional guy.'

The understatement of the millennium.

'He never does the expected,' Clip said. 'He hates the fame. He likes to be on his own. He's even disappeared before, though never during a playoff drive.'

'So?'

'So there's a good chance he's just being his usually flaky self,' Clip continued. 'Greg can shoot like a dream, but let's face facts: the man is a couple of sandwiches short of a picnic. You know what Downing does after games?'

Myron shook his head.

'He drives a cab in the city. That's right, a goddamn yellow taxi cab in New York City. Says it keeps him close to the common man. Greg won't do appearances or endorsements. He doesn't do interviews. He doesn't even do the charity thing. He dresses like something out of a seventies sitcom. The man is a nut job.'

'All of which makes him immensely popular with the fans,' Myron said. 'Which sells tickets.'

'I agree ,' Clip said, 'but that just underlines my point. If we call the cops it could damage both him and the team. Can you imagine the media circus if this got out?'

'It would be bad,' Myron admitted.

'Exactly. And suppose Greg is just hanging out in French Lick or whatever hickville town he goes to in the off-season, fishing or something? Christ, we'd never hear the end of it. On the other hand, suppose he's up to something.'

'Up to something?' Myron repeated.

'Hell, I don't know. I'm just talking here. But I don't need a goddamn scandal. Not now. Not with the playoffs coming up, you know what I'm saying?'

Not really, but Myron decided to let it go for now. 'Who else knows about this?'

'Just the three of us.'

The work crew rolled in the baskets. Two extras were kept in storage in case someone pulled a Darryl Dawkins and shattered a backboard. They then began putting down additional seats. Like most arenas, the Meadowlands holds more seats for basketball than hockey – in his case around a thousand more. Myron took another sip of Yoo-Hoo and let it roll around his tongue. He waited until it slid down his throat before he asked the obvious question. 'So how do I fit in?'

Clip hesitated. His breathing was deep, almost labored. 'I know something of your years with the FBI,' he said finally. 'No details, of course. Not even vagaries really, but enough to know you have a background in this kinda stuff. We want you to find Greg. Quietly.'

Myron said nothing. His 'undercover' work for the feds, it seemed, was the worst kept secret in the continental United States. Clip sipped his drink. He looked at Calvin's full glass, then at Calvin. Calvin finally took a sip. Clip turned his attention back to Myron. 'Greg's divorced now.' Clip went on. 'He's basically a loner. All his friends – hell, all his acquaintances – are teammates. They're his support group, if you will. His family. If anyone knows where he is – if anyone's helping him stay hidden – it's got to be one of the Dragons. I'll be honest with you. These guys are a major pain in the ass. Spoiled, pampered prima donnas who think our purpose in life is to serve them. But they all have one thing in common: They see management as the enemy. Us against the world and all that crap. They won't tell us the truth. They won't tell reporters the truth. And if you approach them as some, uh, "parasitic entity," they won't talk to you either. You have to be a player. It's the only way to get on the inside.'

'So you want me to join the team so I can find Greg.'

Myron heard the echoes of hurt in his voice. It was unintentional, but he saw that both men heard it too. His face flushed in embarrassment.

Chip put a hand on his shoulder. 'I meant what I said, Myron. You could have been great. One of the greatest.'

Myron took a deep swig of his Yoo-Hoo. No more sipping. 'I'm sorry, Mr Arnstein. I can't help you.'

The scowl was back. 'What?'

'I have a life. I'm a sports agent. I have clients to tend to. I can't just drop it all.'

'You'll get the player's minimum prorated. That's two hundred thousand dollars less whatever. And there's only a couple of weeks left until the playoffs. We'll keep you on till then no matter what.'

'No. My playing days are over. And I'm not a private investigator.'

'But we need to find him. He could be in danger.'

'I'm sorry. The answer is no.'

Clip smiled. 'Suppose I sweeten the pot.'

'No.'

'Fifty-thousand-dollar signing bonus.'

'I'm sorry.'

'Greg could show up tomorrow and you'd still get to keep that. Fifty grand. Plus a share of playoff money.'

'No.'

Clip sat back. He stared at his drink, dipped his finger into it, stirred. His voice was casual. 'You say you're an agent, right?'

'Yes.'

'I'm very friendly with the parents of three guys that will go in the first round. Did you know that?'

'No.'

'Suppose,' Clip said slowly, 'I guarantee you that one of them signs with you.'

Myron pricked up. A first round draft pick. He tried to keep his expression cool – to do like Frosty – but his heart was thumping. 'How can you do that?'

'Don't worry about how.'

'It doesn't sound ethical.'

Clip made a scoffing noise. 'Myron, don't play choirboy with me. You do me this favor and MB SportsReps gets a first round draft pick. Guaranteed. No matter how this thing with Greg plays out.'

MB SportsReps. Myron's company. Myron Bolitar, ergo MB. Representing sports people, ergo SportsReps. Add it together: MB SportsReps. Myron came up with that name on his own but still no offers came in from major advertising companies to use his services.

'Make it a hundred-thousand-dollar signing bonus,' Myron said.

Clip smiled. 'You've learned well, Myron.'

Myron shrugged.

'Seventy-five thousand,' Clip said. 'And you'll take it so don't bullshit a bullshitter.'

The two men shook hands.

'I have a few more questions about the disappearance,' Myron said.

Using both armrests Clip rose and stood over Myron. 'Calvin will answer all your questions,' he said with a nod toward his general manager. 'I have to go now.'

'So when do you want me to start practicing?'

Clip looked surprised. 'Practicing?'

'Yeah. When do you want me to start?'

'We have a game tonight.'

'Tonight?'

'Of course,' Clip said.

'You want me to suit up tonight?'

'We're playing our old team, the Celtics. Calvin will make sure you have a uniform by game time. Press conference at six to announce your signing. Don't be late.' Clip headed toward the door. 'And wear that tie. I like it.'

'Tonight?' Myron repeated, but Clip was already gone.

Chapter 2

After Clip left the box, Calvin Johnson allowed himself a small smile. 'I warned you it would be strange.'

'Serious strange,' Myron agreed.

'Finished with your nutritious chocolate beverage?'

Myron put down the can. 'Yeah.'

'Come on. Let's get you ready for the big debut.'

Calvin Johnson walked fluidly, back straight. He was black, six-foot-eight, thin but not gawky or disproportionate. He wore an olive Brooks Brothers suit. Perfectly tailored. Perfectly knotted tie. Perfectly shined shoes. His tightly kinked hair was receding, making his forehead overly prominent and shiny. When Myron matriculated at Duke, Calvin had been a senior at North Carolina. That made him around thirty-five years old, though he looked older. Calvin had enjoyed a solid pro career over eleven seasons. When he retired three years ago, everyone knew he'd end up in the front office. He started off as an assistant coach, moved to player personnel, and just recently was promoted to vice president and general manager of the New Jersey Dragons. These however were just titles. Clip ran the show. General managers, vice presidents, player personnel, trainers, even coaches all bent to his will.

'I hope you're all right with this,' Calvin said.

'Why wouldn't I be all right?'

Calvin shrugged. 'I played against you,' he said.

'So?'

'You were the most competitive son of a bitch I ever faced,' Calvin said. 'You'd stomp on someone's head to win. Now you're going to be a pissant bench-warmer. How's that going to sit with you?'

'I can handle it,' Myron said.

'Uh huh.'

'I've mellowed over the years.'

Calvin shook his head. 'I don't think so.'

'No?'

'You may think you've mellowed. You may even think you've got basketball out of your system.'

'I have.'

Calvin stopped, smiled, spread his arms. 'Sure you have. Just look at you. You could be the poster child for life after sports. A fine example to your fellow athletes. Your whole career crashed down around your ears, but you rose to the challenge. You went back to school – at Harvard Law nonetheless. You started up your own business – a growing company in the field of sports representation. You still dating that writer?'

He meant Jessica. Their togetherness seemed to always be an iffy thing but Myron said, 'Yes.'

'So you got the education, the job, and the gorgeous

girlfriend. Yep, on the outside you're happy and well adjusted.'

'On the inside too.'

Calvin shook his head. 'I don't think so.'

Everyone's Dr Joyce Brothers. 'Hey, I didn't ask to be put on the team.'

'No, but you didn't argue much either – except to up your price.'

'I'm an agent. That's what I do. I up the price.'

Calvin stopped and looked at Myron. 'Do you really think you have to be on the team to find Greg?'

'Clip seemed to think so.'

'Clip is a great man,' Calvin said, 'but he often has ulterior motives.'

'Like what?'

Calvin did not respond. He started walking again.

They reached the elevator. Calvin pressed the button and the doors immediately slid open. They stepped inside and began to descend. 'Look me in the eye,' Calvin said. 'Look me in the eye and tell me you never think about playing again.'

'Who doesn't *think* about it?' Myron countered.

'Yeah, but tell me you don't take it one step further. Tell me you never drift off and dream about making a comeback. Even now, when you're watching a game on TV, tell me you don't sit there and do a slow burn. Tell me you never watch Greg and think about all the adulation and fame. Tell me you never say, "I was better than him," because it's the truth. Greg is great. One of the top ten players in the league. But you were better, Myron. We both know that.'

'Long time ago,' Myron said.

Calvin smiled. 'Yeah,' he said. 'Right.'

'What's your point?'

'You're here to find Greg. Once he's found, you're gone. The novelty will be over. Clip will be able to say he gave you a chance, but you weren't up to the challenge. He'll still be the good guy with the good press.'

'Good press,' Myron repeated, remembering the upcoming press conference. 'One of his ulterior motives?'

Calvin shrugged. 'Doesn't matter. What does matter is that you understand you don't have a chance. You're only going to play during scrub time and we rarely win or lose by a lot so that doesn't happen and even if it does, even if you play spectacularly, we both know it's scrub time. And you won't play well because you are such a competitive son of a bitch, you need the points to mean something to the outcome of the game or you don't play your best.'

'I understand,' Myron said.

'I hope you do, my friend.' Calvin looked up at the numbered lights. The lights flickered in his brown eyes. 'Dreams never die. Sometimes you think they're dead, but they're just hibernating like some big old bear. And if the dream has been hibernating for a long time, that bear is going to wake up grumpy and hungry.'

'You should write country songs,' Myron said.

Calvin shook his head. 'Just giving a friend fair warning.'

'Much obliged. Now why don't you tell me what you know about Greg's disappearance?'

The elevator stopped and the doors opened. Calvin led the way. 'Not much to tell,' he said. 'We played against the Sixers in Philly. After the game Greg got on the bus with everybody else. When we got here, he got off the bus with everybody else. The last time anyone saw him he was getting into his car. The end.'

'How did Greg seem that night?'

'Fine. He played well against Philly. Scored twenty-seven points.'

'And his mood?'

Calvin thought about it. 'Nothing I noticed,' he said.

'Anything new going on in his life?'

'New?'

'Changes, that kind of thing.'

'Well, the divorce,' Calvin said. 'It's been nasty. I understand Emily can be quite difficult.' He stopped walking again and smiled at Myron. The Cheshire cat smile. Myron stopped but did not return the smile.

'Something on your mind, Frosty?'

The smile spread a bit farther. 'Weren't you and Emily an item at one time?'

'A lifetime ago.'

'College sweethearts, if I recall.'

'Like I said, a lifetime ago.'

'So,' Calvin said, starting to walk again, 'you were even better with the women than Greg.'

Myron ignored the comment. 'Does Clip know about my so-called past with Emily?'

'He's very thorough.'

'So that explains why you chose me,' Myron said.

'It was a consideration, but I don't think it's too important.'

'Oh?'

'Greg hates Emily. He'd never confide in her. But since this whole custody battle started there's definitely been a change in Greg.'

'How so?'

'For one thing, he signed a deal with Forte sneakers.'

Myron was surprised. 'Greg? An endorsement deal?'

'It's very hush-hush,' Calvin said. 'They're supposed to announce it end of the month, right before the playoffs.'

Myron whistled. 'They must have paid him a bundle.'

'A bundle and a half, I hear. Upwards of ten million a year.'

'Makes sense,' Myron said. 'A popular player who has refused to endorse any products for more than a decade – it's an irresistible draw. Forte does well with track and tennis shoes, but they're fairly unknown in the basketball world. Greg gives them instant credibility.'

'That he does,' Calvin agreed.

'Any idea why he changed his mind after all these years?'

Calvin shrugged. 'Maybe Greg realized he wasn't getting any younger and wanted to cash in. Maybe this whole divorce thing. Maybe he got whacked on the head and woke up with an iota of sanity.'

'Where's he been living since the divorce?'

'In the house in Ridgewood. It's in Bergen County.'

Myron knew it well. He asked for the address. Calvin gave it to him. 'What about Emily?' Myron asked. 'Where's she staying?'

'She and the kids are with her mother. I think they're in Franklin Lakes or thereabouts.'

'Have you done any checking yet – Greg's house, his credit cards, bank accounts?'

Calvin shook his head. 'Clip thought this thing was too big to trust to an agency. That's why we called you. I've driven past Greg's house a few times, knocked on the door once. No car in the driveway or garage. No lights on.'

'But no one's checked inside the house?'

'No.'

'So for all you know he slipped in the bathtub and hit his head.'

Calvin looked at him. 'I said, no lights on. You think he bathed in the dark?'

'That's a good point,' Myron said.

'Some hotshot investigator.'

'I'm a slow starter.'

They arrived at the team room. 'Wait here,' Calvin said.

Myron took out his cellular. 'Mind if I make a call?'

'Go ahead.'

Calvin disappeared behind the door. Myron turned on the power and dialed. Jessica answered on the second ring. 'Hello?'

'I'm going to have to cancel dinner tonight,' Myron said.

'You better have a good excuse,' Jessica said.

'A great one. I'll be playing professional basketball for the New Jersey Dragons.'

'That's nice. Have a good game, dear.'

'I'm serious. I'm playing for the Dragons. Actually, "playing" is probably not the right word. Might be more accurate to say I'll be getting fanny sores for the Dragons.'

'Are you for real?'

'It's a long story, but yes, I'm now officially a professional basketball player.'

Silence.

'I've never boffed a professional basketball player,' Jessica said. 'I'll be just like Madonna.'

'Like a virgin,' Myron said.

'Wow. Talk about a dated reference.'

'Yeah, well, what can I say. I'm an eighties kinda guy.'

'So, Mr Eighties, you going to tell me what's going on?'

'No time now. Tonight. After the game. I'll leave a ticket at the window.'

Calvin stuck his head back in. 'What's your waist? Thirty-four?'

'Thirty-six. Maybe thirty-seven.'

Calvin nodded and withdrew. Myron dialed the private line of Windsor Horne Lockwood III, president of the prestigious investment firm of Lock-Horne Securities in midtown Manhattan. Win answered on the third ring.

'Articulate,' Win said.

Myron shook his head. 'Articulate?'

'I said articulate, not repeat.'

'We have a case,' Myron said.

'Oh yippee,' he drawled in that preppy, Philly Main-Line accent of his. 'I'm enthralled. I'm elated. But before I completely wet myself, I must ask but one question.'

'Shoot.'

'Is this case of your customary charity persuasion?'

'Wet away,' Myron said. 'The answer is no.'

'What? No moral crusade for brave Myron?'

'Not this time.'

'Heavens be, do tell.'

'Greg Downing is missing. It's our job to find him.'

'And for services rendered we receive?'

'At least seventy-five grand plus a first-round draft pick as a client.' Now was not the time to fill Win in on his temporary career change.

'My, my,' Win said happily. 'Pray tell, what shall we do first?'

Myron gave him the address of Greg's house in Ridgewood. 'Meet me there in two hours.'

'I'll take the Batmobile,' Win said and hung up.

21

Calvin returned. He held out a purple-and-aqua Dragon uniform. 'Try this on.'

Myron did not reach for it right away. He stared at it, his stomach twisting and diving. When he spoke his voice was soft. 'Number thirty-four?'

'Yeah,' Calvin said. 'Your old number at Duke. I remembered.'

Silence.

Calvin finally broke it. 'Go try it on.'

Myron felt something well up in his eye. He shook his head. 'No need,' he said. 'I'm sure it's the right size.'

Chapter 3

Ridgewood was a primo suburb, one of those old towns that still calls itself a village, where ninety-five percent of the students go on to college and no one lets their kids associate with the other five percent. There were a couple of strips of tract housing, a few examples of the mid-sixties suburban explosion, but for the most part Ridgewood's fine homes dated from an earlier, theoretically more innocent time.

Myron found the Downing house without any problem. Old Victorian. Very big but not unwieldy, three levels with perfectly faded cedar shingles. On the left side there was one of those rounded towers with a pointy top. Lots of outdoor porch space with all the Rockwellian touches: the kind of double swing where Atticus and Scout would share a lemonade on a hot Alabama night; a child's bicycle tipped on its side; a Flexible Flyer snow sled, although it hadn't snowed in six weeks. The required basketball hoop hung slightly rusted over the driveway. Fire Department 'Tot Finder' stickers glistened red and silver from two upstairs windows. Old oak trees lined the walk like weathered sentries.

Win hadn't arrived yet. Myron parked and rolled down a window. The perfect mid-March day. The sky was robin-egg blue. The birds chirped in cliché. He tried to picture Emily here, but the picture would not hold. It was far easier to see her in a New York high rise or one of those nouveau-riche mansions all done in white with Erté sculptures and silver pearls and too many gaudy mirrors. Then again he hadn't spoken to Emily in ten years. She may have changed. Or he may have misjudged her all those years ago. Wouldn't be the first time.

Funny being back in Ridgewood. Jessica had grown up here. She didn't like coming back anymore, but now the two loves of his life – Jessica and Emily – had something else in common: the village of Ridgewood. That could be added to the list of commonalities between the two women – stuff like meeting Myron, being courted by Myron, falling in love with Myron, crushing Myron's heart like a tomato under a stiletto heel. The usual fare.

Emily had been his first. Freshman year of college was late to lose one's virginity, if one were to listen to the boasts of friends. But if there had indeed been a sexual revolution among American teenagers in the late seventies/early eighties, Myron had either missed it or been on the wrong side. Women had always liked him – it wasn't that. But while his friends discoursed in great detail on their various orgylike experiences, Myron seemed to attract the wrong girls, the nice girls, the ones who still said no – or would have had Myron had the courage (or foresight) to try.

That changed in college when he met Emily.

24

Passion. It's a word bandied about quite a bit, but Myron thought it might apply here. At a minimum, unconfined lust. Emily was the type of woman a man labels 'hot,' as opposed to 'beautiful.' See a truly 'beautiful' woman and you want to paint or write a poem. See Emily and you want to engage in mutual fabric-ripping. She was raw sexuality, maybe ten pounds bigger than she should have been but those pounds were exquisitely distributed. The two of them made a potent mix. They were both under twenty, both away from home for the first time, both creative.

In a word: *kaboom*.

The car phone rang. Myron picked it up.

'I assume,' Win said, 'that you plan on having us break into the Downing residence.'

'Yes.'

'Then parking your car in front of said residence would not be a sound decision, would it?'

Myron glanced about. 'Where are you?'

'Drive down to the end of the block. Make a left, then your second right. I'm parked behind the office building.'

Myron hung up and restarted the car. He followed the directions and pulled into the lot. Win leaned against his Jaguar with his arms crossed. He looked, as he always did, as if he were posing for the cover of *WASP Quarterly*. His blond hair was perfectly in place. His complexion slightly ruddy, his features porcelain and high and a little too perfect. He wore khaki pants, a blue blazer, Top-Siders *sans* socks, and a loud Lilly Pulitzer tie. Win looked like what you'd picture a guy named Windsor Horne Lockwood III to look like – elitist, self-absorbed, wimpy.

Well, two out of three ain't bad.

The office building held an eclectic mix. Gynecologist. Electrolysis. Subpoena delivery service. Nutritionist. Women-only health club. Not surprisingly Win was standing near the entrance to the women-only health club. Myron approached.

'How did you know I was parked in front of the house?'

Keeping his eye on the entranceway Win motioned with his head. 'Up that hill. You can see everything with a pair of binoculars.'

A woman in her early twenties wearing a black Lycra aerobics suit walked out carrying a baby. It hadn't taken her long to get her figure back. Win smiled at her. The woman smiled back.

'I love young mothers,' Win said.

'You love women in Lycra,' Myron corrected.

Win nodded. 'There's that.' He snapped on a pair of sunglasses. 'Shall we begin?'

'You think breaking into that house will be a problem?'

Win made his I'll-pretend-you-didn't-ask-that face. Another woman exited the health club; sadly, this one did not warrant a Win smile. 'Fill me in,' Win said. 'And move away. I want to make sure they can see the Jag.'

Myron told him all he knew. Eight women came out in the five minutes it took to tell the story. Only two of them were awarded The Smile. One wore a tiger-striped leotard. She was treated to the Full-Wattage Smile, the one that almost touched Win's eyes.

Win's face did not seem to register anything Myron said. Even when he told him about taking Greg's temporary slot on the Dragons, Win went on staring hopefully at the health club door. Normal Win behavior. Myron finished up by asking, 'Any questions?'

Win bounced a finger against his lip. 'Do you think the one in the tiger-striped leotard was wearing any under-wear?'

'I don't know,' Myron said, 'but she was definitely wearing a wedding band.'

Win shrugged. Didn't matter to him. Win didn't believe in love or relationships with the opposite sex. Some might take this for simple sexism. They'd be wrong. Women weren't objects to Win; objects sometimes got his respect.

'Follow me,' Win said.

They were less than half a mile from the Downing house. Win had already scouted it out and found the path with the least chance of being seen or arousing suspicion. They walked in the comfortable silence of two men who had known each other a long time and very well.

'There's one interesting aside in all this,' Myron said.

Win waited.

'Do you remember Emily Shaeffer?' Myron asked.

'The name rings a bell.'

'I dated her for two years at Duke.' Win and Myron had met at Duke. They had also been roommates for all four years. It had been Win who had introduced Myron to the martial arts, who had gotten him involved with Feds. Win was now a top producer at his Lock-Horne Securities on Park Avenue, a securities firm that had been run by Win's family since the market had first opened. Myron rented space from Win, and Win also handled all money-matters for MB SportsReps' clients.

Win thought a bit. 'Is she the one who used to make the little monkey noises?'

'No,' Myron said.

Win seemed surprised. 'Who was the one who made the little monkey noises?'

'I have no idea.'

'Maybe it was someone I was with.'

'Maybe.'

Win considered this, shrugged. 'What about her?'

'She used to be married to Greg Downing.'

'Divorced?'

'Yep.'

'I remember her now,' Win said. 'Emily Schaeffer. Built.'

Myron nodded.

'I never liked her,' Win said. 'Except for those little monkey noises. They were rather interesting.'

'She wasn't the one who made monkey noises.'

Win smiled gently. 'The walls were thin,' he said.

'And you used to listen in?'

'Only when you pulled down the shade so I couldn't watch.'

Myron shook his head. 'You're a pig,' he said.

'Better than a monkey.'

They reached the front lawn and proceeded to the door. The secret was to look like you belonged. If you scurried around back, hunched over, someone might take notice. Two men in ties approaching the door does not normally lead one to think thief.

There was a metal keypad with a little red light. The light was on.

'Alarm,' Myron said.

Win shook his head. 'Fake. It's just a light. Probably bought it at Sharper Image.' Win looked at the lock and made a tsk-tsk noise. 'A Kwiktight brand on a pro basketball player's salary,' he said, clearly disgusted. 'Might as well use Play-Doh.'

'What about the dead bolt?' Myron asked.

'It's not locked.'

Win already had out his strip of celluloid. Credit cards are too stiff. Celluloid worked much better – known as 'loiding the lock. In no more time than it would take with a key, the door was open and they were inside the front foyer. The door had a chute and the mail was all over the place. Myron quickly checked some postage dates. No one had been here in at least five days.

The decor was nice in a fake-rustic, Martha Stewart sort of way. The furniture was what they called 'simple country' where the look was indeed simple and the price outrageous. Lots of pines and wickers and antiques and dry flowers. The smell of potpourri was strong and cloying.

They split up. Win went upstairs to the home office. He turned on the computer and began to download everything onto floppy disks. Myron found the answering machine in a room that used to be called a 'den' but now went by such lofty titles as the 'California room' or 'great room.' The machine announced the time and date of each message. Awfully convenient. Myron pressed a button. The tape rewound and started playing. On the first message, which according to the digital voice was received at 9:18 P.M. the night Greg vanished, Myron hit bingo.

A shaky woman's voice said, 'It's Carla. I'll be in the back booth until midnight.' Click.

Myron rewound and listened again. There were lots of noises in the background – people chatting, music, glasses clinking. The call had probably been placed from a bar or restaurant, especially with that back-booth reference. So who was this Carla? A girlfriend? Probably. Who else would call that late to set up a meeting for even later that night? But of course this had not been just any night. Greg Downing had vanished sometime between the time this call was made and the next morning.

Strange coincidence.

So where did they meet – assuming Greg had indeed made their back-booth liaison? And why did Carla, whoever she might be, sound so shaky – or was this just Myron's imagination?

Myron listened to the rest of the tape. No other messages from Carla. If Greg hadn't shown up at said back booth, wouldn't Carla have called again? Probably. So for now, Myron could safely assume that Greg Downing had seen Carla sometime before his disappearance.

A clue.

There were also four calls from Martin Felder, Greg's agent. He seemed to grow more perturbed with each message. The last one said, 'Jesus, Greg, how can you not call me? Is the ankle serious or what? And don't go incommunicado on me now, not when we're wrapping up the Forte deal. Call me, okay?' There were also three calls from a man named Chris Darby who apparently worked for Forte Sports Incorporated. He too sounded panicked. 'Marty won't tell me where you are. I think he's playing a game with us, Greg, trying to up the price or something. But we had a deal, am I right? Let me give you my home number, okay, Greg? How bad's this injury anyhow?'

Myron smiled. Martin Felder's client was missing, but he was doing all he could to turn it into a positive lever. Agents. He pressed the mode button on the answering machine several times. Eventually the LCD screen scrolled to reveal the code number Greg had set to call in for messages: 317. A fairly new trick of the trade. Now

Myron could call in anytime, press 317, and hear what messages had been left on the machine. He hit the redial button on the phone. Another fairly new trick. Find out who Greg called last. The phone rang twice and was picked up by a woman saying, 'Kimmel Brothers.' Whoever they were. Myron hung up.

Myron joined up with Win in the upstairs office. Win continued copying onto computer disks while Myron went through the drawers. Nothing particularly helpful.

They moved on to the master bedroom. The king-size bed was made. Both night tables were cluttered with pens and keys and papers.

Both.

Curious for a man who lived alone.

Myron's eyes swept the room and landed on a reading chair that doubled as a dressing dummy. Greg's clothes were strewn over one arm and the back. Normal enough, Myron guessed – neater than Myron, in fact, though that wasn't saying much. But looking again, he noticed something a tad strange on the other arm of the chair. Two articles of clothing. A white blouse and a gray skirt.

Myron looked at Win.

'They might belong to Miss Monkey Noises,' Win said.

Myron shook his head. 'Emily hasn't lived here in months. Why would her clothes still be on a chair?'

The bathroom, too, proved interesting. A large Jacuzzi on the right, a big steam shower with a sauna, and two vanities. They checked the vanities first. One contained a can of men's shaving cream, a roll-on deodorant, a bottle of Polo after-shave, a Gillette Atra razor. The other vanity had an open make-up case, Calvin Klein perfume, baby powder, and Secret Roll-On. A sprinkling of baby powder was on the floor near the vanity. There were also two disposable Lady Schick razors in the soap dish next to the Jacuzzi.

'He's got a girlfriend,' Myron said.

'A professional basketball player shacking up with some nubile lass,' Win remarked. 'Quite a revelation. Perhaps one of us should cry out, "Eureka."'

'Yes, but it raises an interesting question,' Myron said. 'If her boyfriend had suddenly vanished, wouldn't said lover have reported it?'

'Not,' Win said, 'if she were with him.'

Myron nodded. He told Win about the cryptic message from Carla.

Win shook his head. 'If they were planning on running away,' he said, 'why would she say where they were meeting?'

'She didn't say where. Only in a back booth at midnight.'

'Still,' Win said. 'It's not exactly the kind of thing you do before you disappear. Let's say that for some reason Carla and Greg decide to vanish for a little while. Wouldn't Greg know where and when to meet her before the fact?'

Myron shrugged. 'Maybe she was changing their meeting place.'

'From what? Front booths to back booths?'

'Damned if I know.'

They checked the rest of the upstairs. Not much doing. Greg's son's bedroom had racing-car wallpaper and a poster of Dad driving past Penny Hardaway for a layup. The daughter's room was done in Early American Barney – dinosaurs and purple. No clues. In fact there were no other clues until they reached the basement.

When they turned on the lights, Myron saw it right away.

It was a finished basement, a brightly colored playroom for the kids. There were lots of Little Tikes cars and big Legos and a plastic house with a sliding board. There were scenes from Disney movies like *Aladdin* and *The Lion King* on the wall. There was a television and a VCR. There was stuff too for when the kids got a little older – a pinball machine, a jukebox. There were small rocking chairs and mattresses and knock-around couches.

There was also blood. A fair amount of it in drips on the floor. Another fair amount smeared on a wall.

Bile nestled in Myron's throat. He had seen blood many times in his life, but it still left him queasy. Not so with Win. Win approached the crimson stains with something akin to amusement on his face. He bent to get a better look. Then he stood back up.

'Look at the bright side,' Win said. 'Your temporary slot on the Dragons may become more permanent.'

Chapter 4

There was no body. Just the blood.

Using Glad sandwich bags he found in the kitchen, Win collected a few samples. Ten minutes later they were back outside, the lock on the front door reengaged. A blue Oldsmobile Delta 88 drove past them. Two men sat in the front seat. Myron glanced at Win. Win barely nodded.

'A second pass,' Myron said.

'Third,' Win said. 'I saw them when I first drove up.'

'They're not exactly experts at this,' Myron said.

'No,' Win agreed. 'But of course, they hadn't known the job would require expertise.'

'Can you run the plates?'

Win nodded. 'I'll also run Greg's ATM and credit card transactions,' he said. He reached the Jag and unlocked it. 'I'll contact you when I have something. It shouldn't take more than a few hours.'

'You heading back to the office?'

'I'm going to Master Kwon's first,' Win said.

Master Kwon was their tae kwon do instructor. Both of them were black belts – Myron a second degree, Win a sixth degree, one of the highest ranking Caucasians in the world. Win was the best martial artist Myron had ever seen. He studied several different arts including Brazilian jujitsu, animal kung fu, and Jeet Kun Do. Win the Contradiction. See Win and you think pampered, preppy panty-waist; in reality, he was a devastating fighter. See Win and you think normal, well-adjusted human being; in reality, he was anything but.

'What are you doing tonight?' Myron asked.

Win shrugged. 'I'm not sure.'

'I can get you a ticket to the game,' Myron said.

Win said nothing.

'Do you want to go?'

'No.'

Without another word, Win slipped behind the wheel of his Jag, started the engine, peeled out with nary a squeal. Myron stood and watched him speed away, puzzled by his friend's abruptness. But then again, to paraphrase one of the four questions of Passover: why should today be different than any other day?

He checked his watch. He still had a few hours before the big press conference. Enough time to get back to the office and tell Esperanza about his career shift. More than anyone else, his playing for the Dragons would affect her.

He took Route 4 to the George Washington Bridge. There was no waiting at the tolls. Proof there was a God. The Henry Hudson however was backed up. He swung off near Columbia Presbyterian Medical Center to get on Riverside Drive. The squeegee guys – the homeless men who 'cleaned' your windshield with a mixture of equal parts grease, Tabasco sauce, and urine – were no longer at the light. Mayor Giuliani's doing, Myron guessed. They had been replaced by Hispanic men selling flowers and something that looked like construction paper. He asked once what it was and had gotten an answer back in Spanish. As much as Myron could translate, the paper smelled nice and spruced up any home. Maybe that was what Greg used as potpourri.

Riverside Drive was relatively quiet. Myron arrived at his Kinney lot on 46th Street and tossed Mario the keys. Mario did not park the Ford Taurus up front with the Rolls, the Mercedes, Win's Jag; in fact, he usually managed to find a cozy spot underneath what must have been a nesting ground for loose-stooled pigeons. Car discrimination. It was an ugly thing, but where were the support groups?

The Lock-Horne Securities building was on Park Avenue and 46th, perpendicular to the Helmsley building. High-rent district. The street bustled with the doings of big finance. Several stretch limos double-parked illegally in front of the building. The ugly modern sculpture that looked like someone's intestines stood pitifully in its usual place. Men and women in business attire sat on the steps, eating sandwiches too hurriedly, lost in their own thoughts, many talking to themselves, rehearsing for an important afternoon meeting or rehashing a morning mistake. People who worked in Manhattan learned how to be surrounded by others yet remain completely alone.

Myron entered the lobby and pressed the button for the elevator. He nodded to the three Lock-Horne Hostesses, known to everyone else as the Lock-Horne Geishas. They were all model/actress wanna-bes, hired to escort high rollers up to the offices of Lock-Horne Securities and look attractive while doing it. Win had brought the idea home after a trip to the Far East. Myron guessed this could be more blatantly sexist, but he wasn't sure how.

Esperanza Diaz, his valued associate, greeted him at the door. 'Where the hell have you been?'

'We need to talk,' he said.

'Later. You've got a million messages.'

Esperanza wore a white blouse – an absolute killer look against her dark hair, dark eyes, and that dark skin that shimmered like moonlight on the Mediterranean. Esperanza had been spotted by a modeling scout when she was seventeen, but her career took a few weird turns and she ended up making it big in the world of professional wrestling. Yes, professional wrestling. She'd been known as Little Pocahontas, the brave Indian Princess, the jewel of the Fabulous Ladies of Wrestling (FLOW) organization. Her costume was a suede bikini, and she was always cast as the good guy in the morality play that was professional wrestling. She was young, petite, tight-bodied, gorgeous, and though of Latin origin, she was dark enough to pass for Native American. Racial backgrounds were irrelevant to FLOW. The real name of Mrs Saddam Hussein, the evil harem girl in the black veil, was Shari Weinberg.

The phone rang. Esperanza picked it up. 'MB Sports-Reps. Hold on a moment, he's right here.' She flashed the eyes at him. 'Perry McKinley. It's his third call today.'

'What does he want?'

She shrugged. 'Some people don't like dealing with underlings.'

'You're not an underling.'

She looked at him blankly. 'You going to take it or not?'

Being a sports agent was – to use computer terminology

– a multitasking environment with the capability of performing a variety of services with but a click of a button. It was more than simple negotiating. Agents were expected to be accountants, financial planners, real estate agents, hand-holders, personal shoppers, travel agents, family counselors, marriage counselors, chauffeurs, errand boys, parental liaisons, lackeys, butt-kissers, you name it. If you weren't willing to do all that for a client – to be what is known as a 'full service agency' – the next guy would be.

The only way to compete was to have a team, and Myron felt he had assembled a small yet extremely effective one. Win, for example, handled all the finances for Myron's clients. He set up a special portfolio for each player, met with them at least five times a year, made sure they understood what their money was doing and why. Having Win gave Myron a big leg up on the competition. Win was a near-legend in the financial world. His reputation was impeccable (at least in the financial world) and his track record unmatched. He gave Myron an instant 'in,' instant credibility in a business where credibility was a rare and heady concoction.

Myron was the JD. Win was the MBA. Esperanza was the all-purpose player, the unflappable chameleon who held it all together. It worked.

'We need to talk,' he said again.

'So we'll talk,' she said in a dismissing tone. 'First take this call.'

Myron entered his office. He overlooked Park Avenue in midtown. Great View. On one wall he had posters of Broadway musicals. On another there were movie stills from some of Myron's favorites: the Marx Brothers, Woody Allen, Alfred Hitchcock, and a potpourri of other classics. On a third wall were photographs of Myron's clients. The client wall was a bit sparser than Myron would have liked. He imagined what it would look like with an NBA first rounder in the middle.

Good, he decided. Very good.

He strapped on his headset.

'Hey, Perry.'

'Jesus Christ, Myron, I've been trying to reach you all day.'

'Good, Perry. And you.'

'Hey, I don't mean to be impatient but this is important. You get anything on my boat?'

Perry McKinley was a golfer on the fringe, no pun intended. He was a pro. He made some money, but he wasn't a name anyone but big golf fans would recognize. Perry loved to sail and was in need of a new vessel.

'Yeah, I got something,' Myron said.

'What company?'

'Prince.'

Perry did not sound thrilled. 'Their boats are just okay,' he whined. 'Nothing great.'

'They'll let you trade in your old boat for a new one. You have to do five personal appearances.'

'Five?'

'Yep.'

'For a Prince eighteen-footer? That's too many.'

'They originally wanted ten. But it's up to you.'

Perry thought about it a moment. 'Ah, shit, okay the deal. But first I want to make sure I like the boat. A full eighteen-footer, right?'

'That's what they said.'

'Yeah, all right. Thanks, Myron. You're the best.'

They hung up. Bartering – an important component in

the agent's multitasking environment. No one ever paid for anything in this business. Favors were exchanged. Trading products for some form of endorsement. Want a free shirt? Wear it in public. Want a free car? Shake hands at a few car shows. The big stars could demand serious payments in exchange for their endorsements. The lesser-known athletes happily seized the freebies.

Myron stared at the pile of messages and shook his head. Playing for the Dragons and keeping MB Sports-Reps afloat – how the hell was he going to pull it off?

He buzzed Esperanza. 'Come on in here please,' he said.

'I'm in the middle—'

'Now.'

Silence.

'Gosh,' she said, 'you're so macho.'

'Give me a break, huh?'

'No, really, I'm very frightened. I better drop everything and immediately do your bidding.'

Her phone fell. She sprinted in, feigning fear and breathlessness. 'Fast enough?'

'Yes.'

'So what is it?'

He told her. When he came to the part where he'd be playing for the Dragons, he was once again surprised to see no reaction. This was strange. First Win, now Esperanza. The two of them were his closest friends. They both lived for ridiculing him. Yet neither one of them had taken advantage of the obvious opening. Their silence on the subject of his 'comeback' was a tad unnerving.

'Your clients aren't going to like this,' she said.

'*Our* clients,' he corrected.

She made a face. 'Does it make you feel better to be patronizing?'

Myron ignored the comment. 'We have to turn this into a positive,' he said.

'How?'

'I'm not sure,' he said slowly. He leaned back in his chair. 'We can say that the publicity of all this will help them.'

'How?'

'I can make new contacts,' he said, the ideas coming to him even as he spoke. 'I can get closer to sponsors, learn more about them. More people will hear about me and indirectly my clients.'

Esperanza made a scoffing sound. 'And you think that's going to fly?'

'Why not?'

'Because it's bullshit. "Indirectly my clients." Sounds like trickle-down economics.'

She had a point. 'What's the big deal really?' he asked, palms to the ceiling. 'Basketball will only be a couple of hours a day. I'll be here the rest of the time. I'll have the cellular phone with me all the time. We just have to emphasize that I won't be there long.'

Esperanza looked at him skeptically.

'What?' he asked.

She shook her head.

'No, I want to know. What?'

'Nothing,' she said. She looked him straight in the eye, her hands resting on her lap. 'What does the bitch say about all this?' she asked sweetly.

Her pet name for Jessica. 'Will you please stop calling her that?'

She made a suit-yourself face, for once not arguing.

41

There had been a time – long, long ago – when Jessica and Esperanza had at least tolerated each other. But then Jessica left, and Esperanza saw what it did to Myron. Some people held grudges. Esperanza internalized them. It didn't matter that Jessica had come back.

'So what does she think?' Esperanza asked again.

'About what?'

'About the prospects for peace in the Middle East,' she snapped. 'What do you think I mean? Your playing again.'

'I don't know. We haven't had a chance to talk about it much. Why?'

Esperanza shook her head again. 'We're going to need help in here,' she said, closing the subject. 'Someone to answer the phones, do some typing, that kind of thing.'

'You have someone in mind?'

She nodded. 'Cyndi.'

Myron blanched. 'Big Cyndi?'

'She could answer the phone, do some odd jobs. She's a good worker.'

'I didn't even know she could talk,' Myron said. Big Cyndi had been Esperanza's tag-team wrestling partner, fighting under the name of Big Chief Mama.

'She'll take orders. She'll do shit work. She's not ambitious.'

Myron tried not to wince at the thought. 'Isn't she still working at the strip joint as a bouncer?'

'It's not a strip joint. It's a leather bar.'

'My mistake,' Myron said.

'And she's a bartender now.'

'Cyndi's been promoted?' Myron said.

'Yes.'

'Well, I'd hate to sidetrack her burgeoning career by asking her to work here.'

'Don't be an ass,' Esperanza said. 'She works there nights.'

'What,' Myron said, 'Leather and Lust doesn't do a big lunch crowd?'

'I know Cyndi. She'll be perfect.'

'She scares people,' Myron said. 'She scares me.'

'She'll stay in the conference room. No one will see her.'

'I don't know.'

Esperanza rose smoothly. 'Fine, you find somebody. I mean, you're the boss. You know best. Me, I'm just a pissant secretary. I wouldn't dare question how you handle *our* clients.'

Myron shook his head. 'Low blow,' he said. He leaned forward, his elbows on his desk, his hands holding up his head. 'All right,' he said finally, releasing a deep breath. 'We'll give her a try.'

Myron waited. Esperanza stared back at him. After several seconds passed, she said, 'Is this the part where I jump up and down and say thank you, thank you?'

'No, this is the part where I leave.' He checked his watch. 'I got to talk to Clip about those bloodstains before the press conference.'

'Have fun.' She headed for the door.

'Hold up,' he called out. She turned and freed him. 'Do you have class tonight?' Esperanza took night classes at NYU Law school.

'No.'

'You want to go to the game?' He cleared his throat. 'You can, uh, bring Lucy, if you'd like.'

Lucy was Esperanza's latest love. Before Lucy she had

dated a man named Max. Her sexual preference seemed to vacillate. 'We broke up,' she said.

'Oh, I'm sorry,' Myron said, not knowing what else to say. 'When?'

'Last week.'

'You didn't say anything.'

'Maybe because it's none of your business.'

He nodded. True enough. 'Well, you can bring a new, uh, friend, if you'd like. Or you can go yourself. We're playing the Celtics.'

'I'll pass,' she said.

'You sure?'

She nodded again, left the room. Myron grabbed his jacket and headed back to the lot. Mario tossed him his keys without looking up. He took the Lincoln Tunnel and hopped onto Route 3. He passed a huge and fairly famous appliance and electronics store called Tops. The billboard featured a giant nose jutted out over Route 3. The caption: Tops Is Right Under Your Nose. Very lifelike. The only thing missing were the giant nose hairs. He was only a mile or so from the Meadowlands when the car phone rang.

'I have some preliminaries,' Win said.

'Go ahead.'

'None of Greg Downing's accounts or credit cards have been accessed in the past five days.'

'Nothing?'

'Nothing.'

'Any cash withdrawals from his bank?'

'Not in the past five days.'

'How about earlier? Maybe he grabbed out a lot of money before he vanished.'

'It's being worked on. I don't know yet.'

Myron took the Meadowlands exit. He considered what this all meant. So far, not much, but it wasn't really good news. The blood in the basement. No sign of Greg. No financial activity. It wasn't really promising. 'Anything else?' Myron asked.

Win hesitated. 'I may soon have an idea where dearest Greg had that drink with fair Carla.'

'Where?'

'After the game,' Win said. 'I'll know more then.'

Chapter 5

'Sports is folklore,' Clip Arnstein told the room full of reporters. 'What captures our imagination is not simply the winning and losing. It's the stories. The stories of perseverance. The stories of sheer will. The stories of hard work. The stories of heartbreak. The stories of miracles. The stories of triumph and tragedy. The stories of comebacks.'

Clip looked down at Myron from the podium, his eyes properly moist, his smile his most grandfatherly. Myron cringed. He fought back an intense desire to duck under the conference table and hide.

After a proper pause Clip turned back to the front. The reporters were silent. An occasional flashbulb burst forth. Clip swallowed several times as though summoning some inner resolve he'd need to continue. His throat slid up and down. He raised his moist eyes to the audience.

A little hammy, Myron thought, but all in all a fine performance.

The press conference was more crowded than Myron would've thought. Not a free seat and many reporters standing. Must have been a slow news day. Clip took his time, regaining his seemingly lost composure. 'A little over a decade ago, I drafted an exceptional young man, a player I believed was destined for greatness. He had a great jumper, a well-honed court sense, mental tenacity, and on top of all that was a fine human being. But the gods had other plans for that young man. We all know what happened to Myron Bolitar on that fateful night in Landover, Maryland. There is no reason to dredge up the past. But as I said when I opened this press conference, sports is folklore. Today the Dragons are giving that young man a chance to weave his own legend into the lush tapestry of sports. Today the Dragons are allowing that young man to try and recapture what was so cruelly snatched away from him all those years ago.'

Myron started squirming. His cheeks flushed. His eyes darted about, seeking a safe haven and finding none. He settled for looking at Clip's face, as per the media's expectations. He zeroed in on a cheek mole, staring so hard his vision began to mercifully blur.

'It won't be easy, Myron,' Clip said, turning now and addressing Myron directly. Myron kept his vision locked on the mole; he couldn't meet the gaze. 'No promises have been made to you. I don't know what happens from here. I don't know if this is the culmination of your story or the commencement of a brave new chapter. But those of us who love sports can't help but hope. It is in our nature. It is in the nature of all true combatants and fans.' Clip's voice started to crack.

'This is reality,' he went on. 'I have to remind you of that, Myron, much as I'd rather not. On behalf of the

New Jersey Dragons I welcome you, a man of class and courage, to the team. We wish you nothing but the best. We know that no matter what happens to you on the court, you will bring honor to the entire Dragon organization.' He stopped, tightened his lips and managed a quick, 'Thank you.'

Clip held out a hand to Myron. Myron played his part. He stood to shake Clip's hand. Clip however had other ideas. He put his arms around Myron and pulled him toward him. The flashbulbs increased to the point of being a disco strobe. When Clip finally pulled back, he wiped his eyes with two fingers. Sheesh, the man put Pacino to shame. Clip held out an arm, ushering Myron to the podium.

'How does it feel to be back?' one reporter yelled out.

'Scary,' Myron replied.

'Do you really think you have what it takes to play at this level?'

'No, not really.'

The moment of honesty stopped them for a second. But only a second. Clip laughed and everyone else in the room followed suit. Figuring it was a joke. Myron didn't bother correcting them.

'Do you think you still have three-point shooting range?' another asked.

Myron nodded. 'I have the shooting range,' he said. 'I'm just not sure I have the making range.' A stolen joke but what the hey.

More laughs.

'Why the comeback so late, Myron? What convinced you to come back now?'

'The Psychic Friends Network.'

Clip stood and warded off further questions with a

raised hand. 'Sorry, gang, that's it for now. Myron has to get suited up for tonight's game.'

Myron followed Clip out. They hurried down the corridor and into Clip's office. Calvin was already there. Clip shut the door. Before he sat down Clip asked, 'So what's the matter?'

Myron told him about the blood in the basement. Clip visibly blanched. Frosty's fingers tightened against the armrest.

'So what are you trying to say?' Clip snapped when he finished.

'Say?'

Clip gave an elaborate shrug. 'I don't get it.'

'There's nothing to get,' Myron said. 'Greg is missing. No one has seen him for five days. He hasn't used his ATM or credit card. And now there's blood in the basement.'

'In his kids' playroom, right? That's what you said before. The kids' playroom.'

Myron nodded.

Clip looked a question at Calvin then turned his palms to the sky. 'So what the hell does that mean?'

'I'm not sure.'

'It doesn't exactly add up to foul play, now does it?' Clip continued. 'Think it through, Myron. If Greg were murdered, for example, where is his body? Did the killer or killers take it with them? And what do you think happened here? The killers – what? – surprised Greg? Alone? In his kids' playroom where, I guess, Greg was playing with his little dolly? Then what happened? They killed him down there and dragged him out of the house without leaving traces of blood anywhere but in the basement?' Clip spread his hands. 'Does that make sense?'

The scenario had bothered Myron too. He sneaked a glance at Calvin. Calvin seemed deep in thought. Clip stood.

'For all we know,' Clip went on, 'one of Greg's kids cut himself playing down there.'

'Hell of a cut,' Myron said.

'Or a bloody nose. Christ, those things gush like mad. Could be nothing but a bloody nose.'

Myron nodded. 'Or maybe they were slaughtering chickens,' he said. 'Could be that too.'

'I don't need sarcasm, Myron.'

Myron waited a beat. He glanced at Calvin. Nothing. He glanced at Clip. Nada. 'It's getting opaque in here again.'

'Pardon?'

'You hired me to find Greg. I'm tracing down a major lead. Yet you don't want to hear it.'

'If you mean I don't want to hear that perhaps Greg has met with foul play—'

'No, that's not what I mean. You're afraid of something and it's not just that Greg may have met with foul play. I'd like to know what.'

Clip looked over at Calvin. Calvin nodded almost imperceptibly. Clip sat back down. His fingertips drummed the desktop. The grandfather clock in the corner ticked an imitating echo. 'Understand,' Clip said, 'that we have Greg's best interests at heart. We really do.'

'Uh huh.'

'You know anything about hostile takeovers?'

'I was alive in the eighties,' Myron said. 'In fact, someone recently remarked on what an eighties kinda guy I am.'

'Well, I'm undergoing one now.'

'I thought you were a majority owner.'

Clip shook his head. 'Forty percent. No one else owns more than fifteen percent. A couple of the minority shareholders have gotten together and are trying to oust me.' Clip made two fists and put them on his desk like paperweights. 'They say I'm too much a basketball mind and not enough a business mind. I should only be handling players and the on-court affair. They vote in two days.'

'So?'

'So right now the vote is very close. A scandal and I'm done.'

Myron looked at both men and waited a beat. Then he said, 'You want me to sit on this.'

'No, no, of course not,' Clip said quickly. 'I'm not saying that at all. I just don't want the press going berserk over what might be nothing. I can't afford to have anything unsavory uncovered now.'

'Unsavory?'

'Right.'

'Like what?'

'Hell if I know,' Clip said.

'But Greg might be dead.'

'And if that's the case, a day or two isn't going to help – cold as that might sound. And if something did happen to Greg, there might be a reason.'

'A reason?'

Clip threw up his hands. 'Hell, I don't know. You lift up a corpse or even a man in hiding and worms start to crawl out. You know what I mean?'

'No,' Myron said. But Clip went on.

'I don't need that, Myron. Not now. Not till after this vote.'

'Then you are telling me to sit on this,' Myron said.

'Not at all. We just don't want an unnecessary panic. If Greg is dead, we can't do him any good now anyway. If he's vanished, well, then you are his best hope to avoid media glare or to save him.'

They were still not telling him everything but Myron decided not to press it just now. 'Do you have any idea why someone would be watching Greg's house?'

Clip looked puzzled. 'Someone is watching his house?'

'I think so, yes.'

Clip looked over to Calvin. 'Calvin?'

'No idea,' Calvin said.

'I don't know either, Myron. Do you have any thoughts?'

'Not yet. One more question: did Greg have a girl-friend?'

Again Clip looked toward Calvin.

Calvin shrugged. 'He played around a lot. But I don't think there was anyone special.'

'Do you know any of the women he played around with?'

'Not by name. Some groupies, stuff like that.'

'Why?' Clip asked. 'You think he ran off with a broad?'

Myron shrugged and stood. 'Guess I better get to the locker room. It's almost game time.'

'Wait.'

Myron stopped.

'Please, Myron, I know it sounds like I'm being cold, but I really do care about Greg. Very much. I want him found alive and well.' Clip swallowed. The wrinkles in his skin looked more pronounced, like someone had just pinched them out a bit. His color was not good. 'If you can honestly tell me that revealing what we know to the public is best, I'll go along with it. No matter what the costs. Think about it. I want to do what's best for Greg. I care about him very much. I care about both of you. You're both fine young men. I mean that. I owe you both a great deal.'

Clip looked like he was about to cry. Myron wasn't sure what to make of all this. He decided to nod and say nothing. He opened the door and left.

As he approached the elevator Myron heard a familiar, husky voice say, 'If it isn't the Comeback Kid?'

Myron looked over at Audrey Wilson. She was wearing her customary sports-reporter garb: dark blue blazer, black turtleneck, what they called 'stone-washed' jeans. Her makeup was either light or nonexistent, her nails short and unpolished. The only splash of color could be found on her sneakers – bright aqua Chuck Taylor Cons. Her looks were completely unspectacular. There was nothing wrong with her features but nothing particularly right about them either. They were just there. Her straight black hair was cut short in a pageboy with bangs. 'Do I detect the scent of cynicism?' he asked.

Audrey shrugged. 'You don't really think I buy all this, do you?'

'Buy what?'

'Your sudden desire to' – she checked her notes – 'weave your own legend into the lush tapestry of sports.' She looked up, shook her head. 'That Clip can sure talk some shit, huh?'

'I have to get dressed, Audrey.'

'How about giving me the lowdown first?'

'The lowdown, Audrey? Gee, why not ask for a "scoop"? I love it when you reporters say that.'

She smiled at that. It was a nice smile. Full and open. 'Kinda defensive, aren't we, Myron?'

'Me? Never.'

'Then how about – to coin yet another cliché – a statement for the press?'

Myron nodded, put his hand to his chest in dramatic fashion. 'A winner never quits, and a quitter never wins.'

'Lombardi?'

'Felix Unger. It was on *The Odd Couple*, the one where Howard Cosell guest starred.'

He turned and walked toward the locker room. Audrey followed. She was probably the top female sports reporter in the country. She covered the Dragons for the East Coast's biggest newspaper. She had her own radio show on WFAN in a coveted time slot with huge ratings. She had a Sunday morning round-table talk show called *Talking Sports* on ESPN. And yet, like almost every other female in this male-dominated profession, there was something tenuous about her station, her career always a half-step from toppling over no matter how big she became.

'How's Jessica?' Audrey asked.

'Good.'

'I haven't spoken to her in a month,' she said with a singsong tone. 'Maybe I should give her a call. Sit down and have a heart-to-heart, you know.'

'Gee,' Myron said, 'that won't be transparent.'

'I'm trying to make this easier on you, Myron. There's something strange going on here. You know I'm going to find out what it is. Might as well just tell me.'

'I really don't know what you're talking about.'

'First Greg Downing leaves the team under mysterious circumstances—'

'What's mysterious about an ankle injury?'

'—then you, his old nemesis, takes his place after being

54

out of commission for the better part of eleven years. You don't find that strange?'

Great, Myron thought. On the job five minutes and already someone was voicing suspicion. Myron Bolitar, master of the undercover. They reached the door to the locker room.

'I gotta go, Audrey. We'll talk later.'

'Count on it,' she said. She smiled at him with a gentle mocking sweetness. 'Good luck, Myron. Knock them dead.'

He nodded, took a deep breath, and pushed open the locker-room door.

Show time.

Chapter 6

No one greeted Myron when he entered the locker room. No one broke stride. No one even looked at him. The room did not go quiet like something out of an old Western where the sheriff pushes open the creaking door and sashays into the saloon. Maybe that was the problem. Maybe the door needed to creak. Or maybe Myron had to work on his sashay.

His new teammates were sprawled about like socks in a college dorm. Three of them were draped over benches, semidressed and seminapping. Two were on the floor, a leg being held in the air by assistants, stretching quads and calves. A couple others were dribbling basketballs. Four were hobbling back to their lockers after getting taped. Almost all were chewing gum. Almost all were also listening to Walkmans, the tiny speakers jammed in their ears and blaring so loudly that they sounded like competing floor models at a stereo store.

Myron found his dressing area pretty easily. All the

other lockers had bronze plaques with a player's name engraved on it. Myron's did not. It had a piece of white adhesive tape above it, the kind used to tape ankles, with the letters M. BOLITAR scrawled in black marker. It hardly inspired confidence or spoke commitment.

He glanced around for someone to talk to, but the Walkmans were the ideal room dividers. Everyone was in their own private space. Myron spotted Terry 'TC' Collins, the team's famed whining superstar, sitting alone in a corner. TC was the media's newest poster boy for the spoiled athlete, the guy 'ruining' the genteel world of sports 'as we know it,' whatever that meant. TC was a hell of a physical specimen. Six-ten, muscular, wiry. His cleanly shaven head glistened in the fluorescent light. Rumor had it TC was black though it was hard to see any trace of skin through the work of his tattoo artist. The obscure ink images blanketed almost all available somatic sites. Body piercing too appeared to be more of a lifestyle with TC than a hobby. The man looked like a nightmare version of Mr Clean.

Myron caught TC's eye, smiled, and nodded a hello. TC glared daggers and turned away. Making chums already.

His uniform was hung where it should be. His name had already been sewn on the back in block letters. BOLITAR. He stared at it for a moment or two. Then he quickly snatched it off the hanger and put it on. Everything caused bouts of déjà vu. The feel of the crumbly cotton. The shoelacelike tie-string on his shorts. The slight elastic tug at the waist when he put them on. The slight tightness of the top as it went over his shoulders. The practiced hands tucking in the tail. The lacing up of his high-tops. It all caused pangs. It was getting harder to breathe. His eyes blinked something back. He sat and waited until the feeling went away.

Myron noticed very few of the guys wore jock straps anymore, preferring those tight, Lycra shorts. Myron stuck with old dependable. Mr Old Fashioned. Then he strapped a contraption onto his leg that was loosely labeled a 'knee brace.' Felt more like a metal compressor. The last thing he put on was his warm-ups. The bottoms had dozens of snaps up and down the legs, so a player could dramatically rip them off when called to go into a game.

'Hey, kid, how's it going?'

Myron stood and shook hands with Kip Corovan, one of the team's assistant coaches. Kip wore a plaid jacket that was about three sizes too small. The sleeves inched up to the forearms. The gut jutted out with great defiance. He looked like a farmer at the semiannual square dance. 'I'm doing fine, coach.'

'Great, great. And call me Kip. Or Kipper. Most people call me Kipper. Sit down, relax.'

'Okay.' Kipper?

'Great, happy to have you with us.' The Kipper pulled over a chair, turned it so the back faced Myron, and straddled it. His pants inseam didn't look happy with the move. 'I'll be honest with you, Myron, okay? Donny wasn't thrilled about this. Nothing personal, you understand. Just Donny likes to pick his own players. He don't like interference from upstairs, you know what I'm saying?'

Myron nodded. Donny Walsh was the head coach.

'Great, good. Donny's a straight guy though. He remembers you from the old days, liked you a lot. But we got a team heading for the playoffs. With a bit of luck we can lock up home-court advantage throughout the playoffs. It took a while to get the ducks all in a row. It's a balance, you know. Got to keep the ducks on an even keel. Losing Greg really knocked the wind from our sails, but we finally got those ducks back up. Now you come along, see. Clip doesn't tell us why, but he insists we add you to the roster. Fine, Clip is the big chief, no question. But we worry about getting our ducks back sailing straight, you see?'

The mixing of metaphors was making Myron dizzy. 'Sure. I don't want to cause any problems.'

'I know that.' He stood, put the chair back with a sweeping motion. 'You're a good guy, Myron. Always were a straight arrow. We need that now. A team-comes-first kinda guy, am I right?'

Myron nodded. 'A straight-sailing duck.'

'Great, fine. See you out there. And don't worry. You're not going to get in unless it's a blowout.' With that the Kipper hoisted his belt up over the gut and sauntered – almost sashayed – across the room.

Three minutes later, the Kipper shouted out, 'Gather round the board, boys.' No one paid any attention. He repeated this several times, tapping Walkman-entranced players on the shoulders, so that they would hear. It took a full ten minutes to get twelve professional athletes to move less than ten feet. Coach Donny Walsh strode in with great self-importance, took center stage, and began spilling out the tired clichés. This didn't mean he was a bad coach or anything. You play over a hundred games a season it's hard to come up with anything new.

The pep talk lasted a full two minutes. Some of the guys never bothered turning off their Walkmans. TC was busy taking off his jewelry, a task that took great concentration and a team of well-trained technicians. Another minute or two passed and then the locker-room door opened. Everyone removed their Walkmans and headed out. Myron realized they were heading for the court.

Game time.

Myron stood at the end of the line. He swallowed deeply. A cold rush swept through him. As he made his way up the ramp he heard a voice over the loudspeaker scream, 'And nowwwwww, your New Jersey Dragons!' Music blared. The jog quickened into a full trot.

The ovation was thunderous. The players automatically split into two makeshift lines for the lay-up drill. Myron had done this a zillion times before, but for the first time he really thought about what he was doing. When you were a star or a starter, you warmed up casually, loosely, unhurriedly. There was no reason to press it. You had the whole game to show the crowd what you could do. The scrubs – something Myron had never been – handled the warm-ups in one of two ways. Some went all out, slamming reverse dunks, doing windmill moves. In a phrase: showing off. Myron had always found this behavior sort of desperate. Others hung around the superstars, feeding them the ball, playing the mock defender like a boxer with a sparring partner. Cool by association.

Myron got to the front of the lay-up line. Someone passed him the ball. When you're warming up, you are subconsciously convinced that all eyes in the arena are on you, though in point of fact, most people were settling in or chatting or getting food or checking out the crowd and those that were watching couldn't care less what you did. Myron took two dribbles and laid the ball against the glass and in. Sheesh, he thought. The game hadn't started yet and already he didn't know what to do.

Five minutes later the lay-up lines disintegrated and players began to free shoot. Myron glanced into the stands for Jessica. She was not hard to spot. It was like a beacon hit her, like she came forward and the rest of the crowd stepped back, like she was the Da Vinci and the rest of the faces were but a frame. Jessica smiled at him and he felt a warmth spread through him.

With something close to surprise, he realized that this would be the first time Jessica had seen him play in anything but pickup games. They'd met three weeks before Myron's injury. The thought made him pause. And remember. For a brief moment his mind dragged him back. Guilt and pain washed over him until a ball careened off the backboard and smacked him in the head. But the thought remained:

I owe Greg.

The buzzer sounded and the players moved to the bench. Coach Walsh blurted out a few more clichés and made sure each player knew whom they were covering. The players nodded, not listening. TC still glared. Game face, Myron hoped, but didn't really believe it. He also kept an eye on Leon White, Greg's roommate on the road and closest friend on the team. The huddle broke. The players from both sides approached the center circle, greeting one another with handshakes and hand slaps. Once out there, the players on both teams started pointing around, trying to figure out who was covering whom since no one had listened thirty seconds earlier. Coaches from both sides were up, yelling out the defensive assignments until the ball was mercifully tossed in the air.

Basketball is normally a game of momentum shifts,

keeping things fairly close until the final minutes. Not tonight. The Dragons cruised. They led by twelve after one quarter, twenty points by halftime, twenty-six by the end of the third period. Myron started getting nervous. The lead was big enough for him to get in. He hadn't really counted on that. Part of him silently cheered on the Celtics, hoping they could stage enough of a comeback to keep his butt on the aluminum chair. But it was a no-go. With four minutes remaining the Dragons led by twenty-eight points. Coach Walsh shot a glance down the bench. Nine of the twelve players had already gotten in. Walsh whispered something to the Kipper. The Kipper nodded and walked down the bench, stopping in front of Myron. Myron could feel his heart beating in his chest.

'Coach is going to clear the bench,' he said. 'He wants to know if you want to go in.'

'Whatever he wants,' Myron replied, while sending out telepathic messages of no, no, no. But he couldn't tell them that. It wasn't in his nature. He had to play the good trooper, Mr Team-First, Mr Dive-On-The-Grenade-If-That's-What-The-Coach-Wants. He didn't know how else to do it.

A time-out was called. Walsh looked down the bench again. 'Gordon! Reilly! You're in for Collins and Johnson!'

Myron let loose a breath. Then he got mad at himself for feeling such relief. What kind of competitor are you? he asked himself. What kind of a man wants to stay on the bench? Then the truth rose up and smacked him hard in the face:

He was *not* here to play basketball.

What the hell was he thinking? He was here to find Greg Downing. This was just undercover work, that's all.

62

Like with the police. Just because a guy goes undercover and pretends he's a drug dealer doesn't make him a drug dealer. The same principle applied here. Just because Myron was pretending to be a basketball player didn't make him one.

The thought was hardly comforting.

Thirty seconds later, it started. And it filled Myron's chest with dread.

One voice triggered it. One beer-infested voice rising clearly above all others. One voice that was just deep enough, just different enough, to separate it from the usual cacophony of fandom. 'Hey, Walsh,' the voice cried out. 'Why don't you put in Bolitar?'

Myron felt his stomach plummet. He knew what was coming next. He had seen it happen before, though never to him. He wanted to sink into the floor.

'Yeah!' another voice crowed. 'Let's see the new guy!'

More shouts of agreement.

It was happening. The crowd was getting behind the underdog, but not in a good way. Not in a positive way. In the most blatantly patronizing and mocking way possible. Be-Nice-To-The-Scrub time. We've won the game. We want a few laughs now.

A few more calls for Myron and then . . . the chant. It started low but built. And built. 'We want Myron! We want Myron!' Myron tried not to slouch. He pretended not to hear it, feigning intense concentration on what was happening on the court, hoping his cheeks weren't reddening. The chant grew louder and faster, eventually disintegrating into one word, repeated over and over, mixed with laughter:

'Myron! Myron! Myron!'

He had to defuse it. There was only one way. He

checked the clock. Still three minutes to go. He had to go in. He knew that wouldn't be the end of it, but it would at least quiet the crowd temporarily. He looked down the bench. The Kipper looked back. Myron nodded. The Kipper leaned over to Coach Walsh and whispered something. Walsh did not stand up. He simply shouted, 'Bolitar. In for Cameron.'

Myron swallowed and rose to his feet. The crowd erupted in sarcasm. He headed for the scorer's table, ripping off his sweats. His legs felt stiff and cramped. He pointed to the scorer, the scorer nodded and sounded the buzzer. Myron stepped on the court. He pointed at Cameron. Cameron jogged off. 'Kraven,' he said. The name of the man Myron would defend.

'Now reporting for Bob Cameron,' the loudspeaker began. 'Number 34. Myron Bolitar!'

The crowd went absolutely wild. Hoots, whistles, screams, laughs. Some might think they were wishing him well, but that was not really the case. They were wishing him well the same way you wish a circus clown well. They were looking for pratfalls and darn gone-it, Bolitar was their man!

Myron stepped on the court. This was, he suddenly realized, his NBA debut.

He touched the ball five times before the game ended. Each time it was met with cheer/jeers. He shot only once, from just inside the three point line. He almost didn't want to, knowing the crowd would react no matter what happened, but some things are just too automatic. There was no conscious thought. The ball went in with a happy swish. By now there were only thirty seconds left and thankfully most everyone had had enough and were heading to their cars. The sarcastic applause was minimal. But for those brief seconds when Myron caught the ball, when his fingertips found the groove, when he bent his elbow and cradled the ball half an inch above both palm and forehead, when the arm smoothed into a straight line, when the wrist flowed into a front curl, when the fingertips danced along the ball's surface and created the ideal backspin, Myron was alone. His eyes were focused on the rim, only the rim, never glancing at the ball as it arched its way toward the cylinder. For those few seconds there was only Myron and the rim and the basketball and it all felt very right.

The mood in the locker room was far more animated after the game. Myron managed to meet all of the players except TC and Greg's roommate Leon White, the one man he wanted to get close to most. Figures. He couldn't push it either; that would just backfire. Tomorrow maybe. He'd try again.

He stripped down. The knee began to tighten up, as though somebody had pulled all the tendons too taut. He slapped on an ice pack and fastened it with a stretch wrap. He limped to the showers, dried off, and was just finishing dressing when he realized TC was standing over him.

Myron looked up. TC had his various pierce-jewelry in place. Ear, of course. Three in one, four in the other. One in his nose. He wore black leather pants and a black cut-off mesh tank top, giving one an excellent view of the ring on his left nipple and the one in the belly button. Myron couldn't make out what the tattoos were. They just looked like swirls. TC wore sunglasses now, the wrap-around kind.

'Your jeweler must send you a hell of a Christmas card,' Myron said.

TC replied by sticking out his tongue and revealing another ring near the tip. Myron almost gagged. TC looked pleased by his reaction.

'You new, right?' TC said.

'Right.' Myron held out his hand. 'Myron Bolitar.'

TC ignored the hand. 'You gots to get thumped.'

'Excuse me?'

'Thumped. You the new guy. You gots to get thumped.'

Several other players started chuckling.

'Thumped?' Myron repeated.

'Yeah. You the new guy, right?'

'Right.'

'Then you gots to get thumped.'

More chuckling.

'Right,' Myron said. 'Thumped.'

'There you go.' TC nodded, snapping his fingers, pointed at Myron, left.

Myron finished dressing. Thumped?

Jessica was waiting for him outside the locker-room door. She smiled as he approached, and he smiled back, feeling goofy. She hugged him and gave him a brief kiss. He smelled her hair. Ambrosia.

'Ah,' a voice said. 'Now ain't this just too sweet?'

It was Audrey Wilson.

'Don't talk to her,' Myron said. 'She's the Antichrist.'

'Too late,' Audrey said. She put her hand through Jessica's arm. 'Jess and I are going out now to have a few drinks, talk over old times, that kind of thing.'

'God, you are shameless.' He turned to Jessica. 'Don't tell her anything.'

'I don't know anything.'

'Good point.' Myron said. 'So where are we going?'

'*We* are going nowhere,' Jessica said. She made a motion behind her with her thumb. Win was leaning against the wall, completely still and at ease. 'He said you'd be busy.'

'Oh.' Myron looked over at Win. Win nodded. Myron excused himself and made his way over.

Without preamble, Win said. 'The last cash transaction Greg made was at an ATM machine at eleven oh three P.M. the night he vanished.'

'Where?'

'Manhattan. A Chemical Bank near Eighteenth Street on the West Side.'

'It makes sense,' Myron said. 'Greg gets a call at nine eighteen P.M. from Carla. Carla tells him to meet her in the back booth. So he drives himself to the city and picks up cash before he sees her.'

Win looked at him with flat eyes. 'Thank you for that analysis of the obvious.'

'It's a gift really.'

'Yes, I know,' Win said. 'Moving right along, there are eight saloons within a four block radius of this particular ATM. I limited my search to those. Of the eight only two have what one might term a "back booth." The others had tables or dining facilities sans booths in the rear. Here are the names.'

Myron had long since gotten past asking how Win did it. 'You want me to drive?'

'I can't go,' Win said.

'Why not?'

'I'm going away for a few days.'

'When?'

'I leave from Newark airport in an hour,' Win said.

'This is sudden.'

Win didn't bother responding. The two men headed out the players' entrance. Five kids ran up to Myron and asked for his autograph. Myron obliged. One kid who looked to be around ten years old took back the paper, squinted at Myron's scrawl, and said, 'Who the hell is he?'

Another kid said, 'Some scrub.'

'Hey!' Win snapped. 'That's Mr Scrub to you.'

Myron looked at him. 'Thanks.'

Win made an it's-nothing gesture.

The first kid looked at Win. 'You anybody?'

'I'm Dwight D. Eisenhower,' Win replied.

'Who?'

Win spread his hands. 'Our blessed youth.' He walked away then without saying another word. Win was not big on good-byes. Myron reached his car. When he put the key in the door, he felt a slap on the back. It was TC. He pointed at Myron with a finger holding more jewelry than a Gabor-family reunion. 'Remember,' TC said.

Myron nodded. 'Thumped.'

'Exacto.'

Then he, too, was gone.

Chapter 7

Myron arrived at MacDougal's Pub, the first bar on Win's list. The back booth was empty so he grabbed it. He sat there for a moment, hoping a psychic force would tell him if this was the place where Greg had met up with Carla. He felt nothing – positive or negative. Maybe he should hold a séance.

The waitress came over slowly, as if the effort of crossing the floor was synonymous with wading through deep snow and she should be rewarded for it. Myron warmed her up with one of his patented smiles. The Christian Slater model – friendly yet devilish. Not to be mistaken for the Jack Nicholson model which was devilish yet friendly.

'Hi,' he said.

She put down a Rolling Rock cardboard coaster. 'What can I get you?' she asked, trying to toss up a friendly tone and falling way short. You rarely find a friendly barmaid in Manhattan, except for those born-again waitresses at chains like TGI Friday's or Bennigan's where they tell you their name and that they'll be your 'server' like you might mistake them for something else, like your 'legal consultant' or 'medical advisor.'

'Got any Yoo-Hoo?' Myron asked.

'Any what?'

'Never mind. How about a beer?'

She gave him flat eyes. 'What kind?'

Subtlety was not going to work here. 'Do you like basketball?' he asked her.

Shrug.

'Do you know who Greg Downing is?'

Nod.

'He told me about this place,' Myron said. 'Greg said he was here the other night.'

Blink.

'Did you work last Saturday night?'

Nod.

'Same station? I mean, this booth?'

Quicker nod. Getting impatient.

'Did you see him?'

'No. I got tables. Michelob okay?'

Myron looked at his watch, faked shock. 'Whoops, look at the time. I gotta go.' He gave her two dollars. 'Thanks for your time.'

The next bar on the list was called the Swiss Chalet. Not even close. A dive. The wallpaper was supposed to trick you into believing that the place was wood paneled; the effect may have worked better had the wallpaper not been peeling in so many spots. The fireplace had a flickering, Christmas-light log in it, hardly giving the place the desired ski-lodge warmth. For some reason there was one of those disco mirrored balls in the middle of the bar. No dance floor. No lights. Just the disco mirrored ball – another staple of authentic Swiss chalets, Myron surmised. The place had the stale smell of spilled beer mixed with just a hint of what might have been vomit, the kind of smell only certain bars or frat houses held, the kind where the odor had seeped into the walls like rodents that ended up dying and rotting.

The jukebox blared 'Little Red Corvette' by Prince. Or was it by the Artist Formerly Known As Prince? Wasn't that what he called himself now? But of course when 'Little Red Corvette' had been released he had been Prince. So which was it? Myron tried to reconcile this crucial dilemma, but it began to confuse him like one of those time paradoxes in the *Back to the Future* movies so he gave up.

The place was pretty empty. A guy with a Houston Astros baseball cap and bushy mustache was the sole patron seated at the bar. There was a man and woman semi-necking at a table in the center of the room – the most conspicuous table in the place, as a matter of fact. No one seemed to mind. Another male patron skulked around the back like he was in the adult movie area at his local video store.

Again Myron took the back booth. Again he struck up a conversation with a far more animated waitress. When he reached the part about Greg Downing telling him about the Swiss Chalet, she said, 'Yeah, no kidding? I only seen him in here once.'

Bingo.

'Would that have been Saturday night?'

She scrunched up her face in thought.

'Hey, Joe,' the waitress shouted to the bartender. 'Downing was in here Saturday night, right?'

71

'Who the fuck wants to know?' Joe shouted back from his spot behind the bar. He looked like a weasel with mousy hair. Weasel and mouse. Nice combination.

'This guy and me, we was just talking.'

Joe Weasel squinted with beady, ferret eyes. The eyes widened. 'Hey, you're the new guy, right? On the Dragons? I saw you on the news. With the dorky name.'

'Myron Bolitar,' Myron said.

'Yeah, right, Myron. That's it. You guys gonna start hanging out here?'

'I don't know.'

'We get a pretty exclusive celebrity clientele,' Joe said, wiping the bar with what looked like a gas station rag. 'You know who was in here once? Cousin Brucie. The disc jockey. Real regular guy, you know.'

'Sorry I missed that,' Myron said.

'Yeah, well we've had other celebs, right, Bone?'

The guy with the Astros hat and bushy mustache pepped up and nodded. 'Like that guy who looked like Soupy Sales. Remember him?'

'Right. Celebrities.'

'Except that wasn't really Soupy Sales. Just someone who looked like him.'

'Same difference.'

Myron said, 'Do you know Carla?'

'Carla?'

'The girl Greg was with.'

'That her name? No, never got a chance to meet her. Didn't meet Greg either. He just kinda ducked in, cognitolike. We didn't bother them.' He sort of puffed out his chest like he was about to salute. 'At the Swiss Chalet, we protect our celebrities.' He pointed at Myron with the dishrag. 'You tell the other guys that, okay?'

72

'Will do,' Myron said.

'Fact, we weren't even sure it was Greg Downing at first.'

'Like with Soupy Sales,' Bone added.

'Right, like that. Except this was really him.'

'Guy looked like Soupy though. Great actor, that Soupy.'

'And what a nickname.'

'Talent all the way round,' Bone agreed.

Myron said, 'Had he ever been in here before?'

'The guy who looked liked Soupy?'

'Moron,' Joe said, snapping the rag at Bone. 'Why the fuck would he want to know about that? He's talking about Greg Downing.'

'How the fuck was I supposed to know? I look like I work for one of those psychic networks or something?'

'Fellas,' Myron tried.

Joe held up a hand. 'Sorry, Myron. Believe me, this don't normally happen here at the Swiss Chalet. We all get along, right, Bone?'

Bone spread his arms. 'Who's not getting along?'

'My point exactly. And no, Myron, Greg isn't one of our regulars. That was his first time here.'

'Same with Cousin Brucie,' Bone added. 'He only came in that one time.'

'Right. But Cousin Brucie liked the place, I could tell.'

'He ordered a second drink. That shoulda told you something.'

'Right you are. Two drinks. Coulda just had one and left. Course, they were only Diet Cokes.'

Myron said, 'How about Carla?'

'Who?'

'The woman Greg was with.'

'What about her?'

'Had she been here before?'

'I never seen her here before. Bone?'

Bone shook his head. 'Nope. I woulda remembered.'

'What makes you say that?'

Without hesitation, Joe said, 'Serious hooters.'

Bone cupped his hands and stuck them in front of his chest. 'Major Charlies.'

'Not that she was good looking or anything.'

'Not at all,' Bone agreed. 'Kinda old for a young guy.'

'How old?' Myron asked.

'Older than Greg Downing, that's for sure. I'd say late forties. Bone?'

Bone nodded. 'But a first-rate set of ta-tas.'

'Humongous.'

'Mammoth.'

'Yeah, I think I got that,' Myron interrupted. 'Anything else?'

They looked puzzled.

'Eye color?' Myron tried.

Joe blinked, looked at Bone. 'Did she have eyes?'

'Damn if I know.'

'Hair color?' Myron said.

'Brown,' Joe said. 'Light brown.'

'Black,' Bone said.

'Maybe he's right,' Joe said.

'No, maybe it was on the lighter side.'

'But I'm telling you, Myron. That was some rack. Major guns.'

'Guns of Navarone,' Bone agreed.

'Did she and Greg leave together?'

Joe looked at Bone. Bone shrugged. 'I think so,' Joe said.

74

'Do you know what time?'

Joe shook his head.

'Bones, you know?' Myron tried.

The bill of the Astros hat jerked toward Myron like a string had been pulled. 'Not Bones, dammit!' he shrieked. 'Bone! No S at the end. Bone! B-O-N-E! No S! And what the fuck do I look like, Big Ben?'

Joe snapped the dishrag again. 'Don't insult a celebrity, moron.'

'Celebrity? Shit, Joe, he's just a scrub. Not like he's Soupy or something. He's a nobody, a zero.' Bone turned to Myron. The hostility was completely gone now. 'No offense, Myron.'

'Why would I take offense?'

'Say,' Joe said, 'you got a photograph? We can put your picture on the wall. You could autograph it to your pals at the Swiss Chalet. We should start like a celebrity wall, you know?'

'Sorry,' Myron said. 'I don't have one on me.'

'Can you send us one? Autographed, I mean. Or bring it next time you come.'

'Er, next time.'

Myron continued to question them but learned nothing more except Soupy Sales's birthday. He left and headed up the block. He passed a Chinese restaurant with dead ducks hung in the window. Duck carcasses, the ideal appetite whetter. Maybe Burger King should hang slaughtered cows in the window. Really draw the kids in.

He tried putting the pieces together a bit. Carla calls Greg on the phone and tells him to meet her at the Swiss Chalet. Why? Why there of all places? Did they not want to be seen? Why not? And who the hell is Carla anyway? How does all this fit into Greg's vanishing act? And what about the blood in the basement? Did they go back to Greg's house or did Greg go home alone? Was Carla the girl he lived with? And if so, why meet here?

Myron was so preoccupied he didn't spot the man until he almost bumped into him. Of course calling him a man might be a bit of an understatement. More like a brick wall doubling as a human being. He stood in Myron's way. He wore one of those pectoral-displaying ribbed T-shirts under an unbuttoned flower-patterned semi-blouse. A gold horn dangled between his near-cleavage. Muscle-head. Myron tried to pass him on the left. The brick wall blocked his path. Myron tried to pass him on the right. The brick wall blocked his path. Myron went back and forth one more time. Brick Wall followed suit.

'Say,' Myron said, 'you know the cha-cha?'

The brick wall showed about as much reaction as one might expect from a brick wall. Then again it wasn't one of Myron's better quips. The man was truly enormous, the size of your average lunar eclipse. Myron heard foot-steps. Another man, this one on the large size but at least of the human variety, came up behind Myron. The second man wore fatigue camouflage pants, a popular new urban fashion trend.

'Where's Greg?' Camouflage Pants asked.

Myron feigned startled. 'What? Oh, I didn't see you.'

'Huh?'

'In those pants,' Myron said. 'You just blended into the background.'

Camouflage didn't like that. 'Where's Greg?'

'Greg?' Snappy retort.

'Yeah. Where is he?'

'Who?'

'Greg.'

'Greg who?'

'You trying to be funny?'

'What, you think this is funny?'

Camouflage looked over at Brick Wall. Brick Wall remained completely silent. Myron knew that there was a very real possibility of a physical altercation. He also knew he was good at such things. He also knew – or at least figured – that these two goons were probably good too. Despite Bruce Lee movies, one man defeating two or more quality opponents was nearly impossible. Experienced fighters were not stupid. They worked as a team. They never rushed one at a time.

'So,' Myron said. 'You guys want to catch a beer? Chat this through.'

Camouflage made a scoffing noise. 'We look like guys who like to chat?'

Myron motioned to Brick Wall. 'He does.'

There were three ways to get out of a situation like this unharmed. One was to run, which was always a good option. Problem was, his two adversaries were close enough yet spaced far enough to tackle and/or slow him down. Too risky. Second option: your opponents underestimate you. You act scared and cower and then whammo, you surprise them. Unlikely for Myron. Goons rarely underestimate a guy six-four, two-twenty. Third option: you strike first and hard. By doing this you increase the likelihood of putting one out of commission before the other one can react. This action however required a delicate balance. Until someone strikes, you really cannot say for sure that a physical altercation could not be avoided altogether. But if you wait for someone to strike, this option becomes null and void. Win liked option three. Then again Win liked option three even if there was only one opponent.

Myron never got the chance to make a selection. Brick Wall slammed a fist into the small of Myron's back. Myron sensed the blow coming. He shifted enough to avoid both the kidney and serious damage. At the same time he spun and delivered an elbow strike to Brick Wall's nose. There was a satisfying, crunching noise like a fist closing over a bird's nest.

The victory was short-lived. As Myron had feared, these guys knew what they were doing. Camouflage Pants struck at the same time, connecting where his comrade had failed. Pain erupted in Myron's kidney. His knees buckled but he fought it off. He doubled over toward Brick Wall and threw a back kick, his foot snapping out like a piston. His lack of balance threw off his aim. The blow landed on Camouflage's thigh. It didn't do much damage but it was powerful enough to push him away. Brick Wall was starting to recover. He groped blindly and found Myron's hair. He grabbed and pulled up. Myron pinned the hand with one of his own, digging his fingernails into the sensitive pressure points between the joints. Brick Wall screamed. Camouflage Pants was back. He punched Myron straight in the stomach. It hurt. A lot. Myron knew he was in trouble. He went down to one knee and bounced up, a palm strike at the ready. It connected with Brick Wall's groin. Brick Wall's eyes bulged. He dropped like somebody had pulled a stool out from under him. Camouflage Pants connected with a solid shot to the side of Myron's head. Numbness flowed into Myron's skull. Another blow landed. Myron's eyes began to lose focus. He tried to stand up but his legs wouldn't let him. He felt a kick land on a rib. The world began to spin.

'Hey! Hey, what you doing? Hey, you!'

'Stop it! What the fuck!'

In his haze Myron recognized the voices. Joe and Bone from the bar. Myron took the opportunity to scramble away on all fours. There was no need. Camouflage Pants had already helped Brick Wall to his feet. Both men ran.

Joe and Bone quickly came over and looked down at Myron.

'You okay?' Joe asked.

Myron nodded.

'You won't forget about sending us that autographed picture, will you? Cousin Brucie never sent one.'

'I'll send you two,' Myron said.

Chapter 8

He convinced Joe and Bone not to call the cops. They didn't take much convincing. Most people do not like activities that involve law enforcement. They helped Myron into a taxi. The driver wore a turban and listened to country music. Multiculturalism. Myron spit out Jessica's Soho address and collapsed into the ripped cushions. The driver wasn't interested in conversation. Good.

Myron mentally checked over his body. Nothing broken. The ribs would be bruised at worst. Nothing he couldn't play through. The head was another matter. Tylenol with codeine would help tonight, then he could move down to Advil or something in the morning. There was nothing much you could do for head trauma but give it time and control the pain.

Jessica met him at the door in her bathrobe. He felt, as he often did around her, a little short of breath. She skipped admonishments, drew a bath, helped him undress, crawled in behind him. The water felt good against his skin. He leaned back on her as she wrapped washcloths around his head. He let loose a deep, totally content breath.

'When did you go to medical, school?' he asked.

From behind him Jessica kissed his cheek. 'Feeling better?'

'Yes, Doctor. Much better.'

'You want to tell me about it?'

He did. She listened in silence, her fingertips gently massaging his temples. Her touch was soothing. Myron imagined there were better things in life than being in this tub leaning back against the woman he loved, but for the life of him he couldn't think of any. The pain began to dull and slacken.

'So who do you think they were?' she asked.

'No idea,' Myron said. 'I imagine they're hired goons.'

'And they wanted to know where Greg was?'

'Seems so.'

'If two goons like that were looking for me,' she said, 'I might disappear too.'

The thought had crossed Myron's mind too. 'Yes.'

'So what's your next step?'

He smiled and closed his eyes. 'What? No lectures? No telling me it's too dangerous?'

'Too cliché,' she said. 'Besides, there's something else here.'

'What do you mean?'

'Something about all this you're not telling me.'

'I—'

She put a finger over his lips. 'Just tell me what you plan on doing next.'

He settled back down. Scary how easily she read him. 'I have to start talking to people.'

'Like?'

'His agent. His roommate, a guy named Leon White. Emily.'

'Emily. That would be your old college sweetheart?'

'Uh huh,' Myron said. Quick subject change before she started reading him again. 'How was your evening with Audrey?'

'Fine. We mostly talked about you.'

'What about me?'

Jessica began to stroke his chest. The touch slowly drifted away from being merely soothing. Her fingertips caressed his chest with a feather touch. Gently. Too gently. She was strumming him like Perlman on a violin.

'Uh, Jess.'

She shushed him. Her voice was soft. 'Your ass,' she said.

'My ass?'

'Yep, that's what we talked about.' To emphasize the point her hand cupped a cheek. 'Even Audrey had to admit it was edible, running up and down the court like that.'

'I have a mind too,' Myron said. 'A brain. Feelings.'

She lowered her mouth toward his ear. When her lips touched the lobe, he felt a jolt. 'Who cares?'

'Uh, Jess . . .'

'Shhh,' she said as her other hand slid down his chest. 'I'm the doctor here, remember?'

82

Chapter 9

The ringing phone jabbed at the base of nerves in the back of his skull. Myron's eyes blinked open. Sunlight knifed through the slit in the curtain. He checked next to him in the bed – first with his hands, then with his eyes. Jessica wasn't there. The phone continued to blare. Myron reached for it.

'Hello.'

'So this is where you are.'

He closed his eyes. The ache in his head multiplied tenfold. 'Hi, Mom.'

'You don't sleep in your home anymore?'

His home was the basement of his parents' house, the same house in which he'd been raised. More and more he was spending his nights at Jessica's. It was probably a good thing. He was thirty-two; he was fairly normal; he had plenty of money. There was no reason to still be living with Mommy and Daddy.

'How's your trip?' he asked. His mother and father

were on some tour of Europe. One of those bus tours that hit twelve cities in four days.

'You think I called at the Vienna Hilton's long distant rates to chitchat about our itinerary?'

'Guess not.'

'You know how much it cost to call from a hotel in Vienna? With all their surcharges and taxes and everything?'

'A lot, I'm sure.'

'I have the rates right here. I'll tell you exactly. Hold on. Al, what did I do with those rates?'

'Mom, it's not important.'

'I had it a second ago. Al?'

'Why don't you tell me when you get home?' Myron suggested. 'It'll give me something to look forward to.'

'Save the fresh remarks for your friends, okay? You know very well why I'm calling.'

'I don't, Mom.'

'Fine, then I'll tell you. One of the other people on this tour – the Smeltmans, very nice couple. He's in the jewelry business. Marvin, his name is. I think. They have a shop in Montclair. We used to drive by it all the time when you were a kid. It's on Bloomfield Avenue, near that movie theater. Remember?'

'Uh huh.' He had no idea what she was talking about but it was easier.

'So the Smeltmans talked to their son on the phone last night. He called them, Myron. He had their itinerary and everything. Just called his parents to make sure they were having a nice time, that kind of thing.'

'Uh huh.' Mom was in decompensation mode. There was no way to stop it. She could go in a heartbeat from the modern, intelligent woman he knew her to be to

84

something out of summer stock *Fiddler on the Roof*. Right now she was Golda heading toward Yenta.

'Anyway the Smeltmans brag how they're on the same trip with Myron Bolitar's parents. Big deal, right? Who knows you anymore? You haven't played in years. But the Smeltmans are big basketball fans. Go figure. Their son used to watch you play or something, I don't know. So anyway the son – I think his name is Herb or Herbie or Ralph, something like that – he tells them you're playing professional basketball. That the Dragons signed you. He says you're making a comeback or something, what do I know? Your father is so embarrassed. I mean, complete strangers are talking about it and your own parents don't even know. We thought the Smeltmans were crazy.'

'It's not what you think,' Myron said.

'What's not what I think?' she countered. 'You shoot around in the driveway a little. Okay, no big deal. But I don't understand. You never even mentioned you were playing again.'

'I'm not.'

'Don't lie to me. You scored two points last night. Your father called Sports Phone. You know what it cost to call Sports Phone from here?'

'Mom, it's no big deal.'

'Listen to me, Myron, you know your father. The man pretends it doesn't mean anything. He loves you no matter what, you know that. But he hasn't stopped smiling since he heard. He wants to fly home right now.'

'Please don't.'

'Don't,' she repeated, exasperated. 'You tell him, Myron. The man is loo-loo, you know that. A crazy person. So tell me what's going on.'

'It's a long story, Mom.'

'But it's true? You're playing again?'

'Only temporarily.'

'What does that mean, "only temporarily"?'

Jessica's Call Waiting clicked in. 'Mom, I gotta go. I'm sorry I didn't tell you earlier.'

'What? That's it?'

'I'll tell you more later.'

Surprisingly she backed off. 'You be careful with your knee.'

'I will.'

He changed over to the other line. It was Esperanza. She didn't bother with hello.

'It's not Greg's blood,' she said.

'What?'

'The blood you found in the basement,' she said. 'It's AB positive. Greg's blood type is O negative.'

Myron had not expected to hear this. He tried to reconcile it in his head. 'Maybe Clip was right. Maybe it was one of Greg's kids.'

'Impossible,' she said.

'Why?'

'Didn't you take basic biology in high school?'

'Eighth grade. But I was too busy staring at Mary Ann Palmiero. What?'

'AB is rare. In order for a kid to have it, his parents have to be A and B or it's impossible. In other words, if Greg is O, then his kids can't be AB.'

'Maybe it's a friend's,' Myron tried. 'Maybe one of the kids had a friend over.'

'Sure,' Esperanza said. 'That's probably it. The kids have some friends over. One of them bleeds all over the place and nobody cleans it up. Oh and then by a strange coincidence Greg vanishes.'

Myron threaded the phone cord through his fingers like his hand was a loom. 'Not Greg's blood,' he repeated. 'Now what?'

Esperanza didn't bother responding.

'How the hell am I supposed to investigate something like this without getting anyone suspicious?' he went on. 'I have to ask people questions, right? They're going to want to know why.'

'I feel very sorry for you,' Esperanza said in a tone that made clear she was anything but. 'I got to get to the office. You coming in?'

'Maybe this afternoon. I'm going to see Emily this morning.'

'Is that the old girlfriend Win told me about?'

'Yes,' Myron said.

'Don't take any chances. Put on a condom now.' She hung up.

Not Greg's blood. Myron didn't get it. As he drifted off to sleep last night he had worked up a neat little theory that went something like this: the hoods were searching for Greg. Maybe they had roughed him up a bit, made him bleed a little. Just to show him they meant serious business. Greg had reacted by running away.

It all sort of fit. It explained the blood in the basement. It explained why Greg suddenly took off. Yep, all a very nice and neat equation: One beating plus one death threat equaled a man on the run.

Problem was, the blood in the basement was not Greg's. Kinda put a damper on the theory. If Greg had been beaten in the basement, then it would have been his blood. Greg would have bled his own blood, not someone else's. In fact, it was very difficult to bleed someone else's blood. Myron shook his head. He needed a shower. A bit more deducing like this and the slaughtered-chicken theory would begin to pick up steam.

Myron soaped himself up, then turned his back to the shower and let the water cascade over his shoulders and down his chest. He toweled off and got dressed. Jessica was on the word processor in the other room. He had learned never to disturb her when the keyboard was clacking. He left a quick note and slipped out. He grabbed the 6 train up to midtown and walked to the Kinney lot on 46th Street. Mario tossed him the keys without glancing up from his paper. He picked up the FDR north at 62nd Street and took it to the Harlem River Drive. There was a slow down for right lane construction, but he made it to the George Washington Bridge in pretty good time. He took Route 4 through a place called Paramus, which was actually a giant mall pretending to also be a township. He veered to the right and passed the Nabisco building on Route 208. He was hoping for a factory Ritz-whiff, but today he got nothing.

As he pulled up to Emily's house, déjà vu swatted him in the back of the head like a father's warning blow. He had been here before, of course, during college breaks in their courting days. The house was brick and modern and fairly huge. It sat in a well-groomed cul-de-sac. The backyard was fenced. He remembered that there was a swimming pool in the back. He remembered that there was also a gazebo. He remembered making love with Emily in the gazebo, their clothes wrapped around ankles, the humidity coating their skin with a thin layer of sweat. The sweet bird of youth.

He parked the car, pulled the key out of the ignition, and just sat there. He had not seen Emily in more than ten years. Much had happened in the ensuing years, but he still feared her reaction to seeing him. The mental image of Emily opening the door, screaming 'Bastard,' then slamming it in his face was one of the reasons he hadn't worked up the nerve to call first.

He looked out the car window. There was no movement on the street. Then again there were only ten houses. He debated his approach and came up with nothing. He checked his watch, but the time didn't register in his head. He sighed. One thing was for sure: he couldn't sit here all day. This was a nice neighborhood, the kind where someone would spot him and call the police. Time to get a move on. He opened the door and stepped out. The development was at least fifteen years old but it still looked new. All the yards were just a little too sparse. Not enough trees and shrubbery yet. The grass looked like a guy with a bad hair transplant.

Myron walked up the brick path. He checked his palms. They were wet. He rang the doorbell. Part of him flashed back to earlier visits, his mind playing along with the long, still-familiar chime of the bell. The door opened. It was Emily.

'Well, well, well,' she said. Myron could not tell if the tone was one of surprise or sarcasm. Emily had changed. She looked a little thinner, a bit more toned. Her face was less fleshy too, accentuating the cheekbones. Her hair was cut shorter and styled. 'If it isn't the good one I let get away.'

'Hi, Emily.' Mr Big Opening.

'Here to propose?' she asked.

'Been there, done that.'

'But you didn't mean it, Myron. I wanted sincerity back then.'

'And now?'

'Now I realize sincerity is overrated.' She flashed him a smile.

'You look good, Emily,' he said. Get Myron on a roll and it's one good line after another.

'So do you,' she said. 'But I'm not going to help you.'

'Help me what?'

She made a face. 'Come on in.'

He followed her inside. The house was full of skylights and cathedral ceilings and white painted walls. Airy. The front foyer was done in some expensive tile. She led Myron to the living room. He sat on a white couch. The floors were beechwood. It was exactly the same as it was ten years ago. Either they had gotten the exact same couches again or their house guests had been exceptionally well behaved. There wasn't a spot on them. The only mess was a pile of newspapers in the corner. Mostly daily tabloids, from the looks of it. A *New York Post* front-page headline read SCANDAL! in huge 72 point print Specific.

An old dog traipsed into the room on rigid legs. It looked like he was trying to wag his tail, but the result was a pitiful sway. He managed to lick Myron's hand with a dry tongue.

'Look at that,' Emily said. 'Benny remembers you.'

Myron stiffened. 'This is Benny?'

She nodded.

Emily's family had bought the overactive puppy for her younger brother Todd when Myron and Emily had first started dating. Myron was there when they brought the puppy home from the breeder. Little Benny had stumbled around with blinking eyes and then peed on this very floor. No one cared. Benny quickly got used to people. He greeted everyone by jumping on them, believing in a way only a dog could that no one would ever do him harm. Benny was not jumping now. He looked very old. He looked a brief step away from death. A sudden sadness swept through Myron.

'You looked good last night,' Emily said. 'It was nice seeing you back on the court.'

'Thanks.' The quips never stop.

'Are you thirsty?' she asked. 'I could make you some lemonade. Like in a Tennessee Williams play. Lemonade for the gentleman caller, except I doubt Amanda Wingfield used a Crystal Light mix.' Before he could answer she disappeared around the corner. Benny looked up at Myron, straggling to see through milky cataracts. Myron scratched the dog's ear. The tail picked up a bit of velocity. Myron smiled sadly at Benny. Benny moved closer, as if he understood how Myron felt and appreciated the sentiment. Emily returned with two glasses of lemonade.

'Here,' she said. She handed him a glass and sat down.

'Thank you.' Myron took a sip.

'So what's next on your agenda, Myron?'

'Next?'

'Another comeback?'

'I don't understand.'

Emily gave him the smile again. 'First you replace Greg on the court,' she said. 'Maybe next you'll want to replace him in the bedroom.'

Myron almost gagged on his lemonade, but he managed to smother the sound. Going for the shock. Classic Emily. 'Not funny,' he said.

'I'm just having a little fun,' she said.

'Yes, I know.'

She put her elbow on the back of the couch and

propped up her head with her hand. 'I see you're dating Jessica Culver,' she said.

'Yep.'

'I like her books.'

'I'll tell her.'

'But we both know the truth.'

'What's that?'

She leaned forward now and took a slow sip from her glass. 'Sex with her isn't as good as it was with me.'

More classic Emily. 'You're sure about that?' he said.

'Very sure,' she replied. 'I'm not being immodest. I'm sure your Ms Culver is quite skilled. But with me it was new. It was discovery. It was impossibly hot. Neither of us can ever recapture that rapture with anyone else. It'd be impossible. It would be like going back in time.'

'I don't compare,' Myron said.

With a smile and a tilt of the head, she said, 'Bullshit.'

'You don't want me to compare.'

The smile was unfazed. 'Come, come now, Myron. You're not going to give me that spiritual crap, are you? You're not going to tell me it's better because you share a deep and beautiful relationship and thus the sex is beyond something physical? That line would be so unbecoming on you.'

Myron did not respond. He didn't know what to say and he didn't feel very comfortable with the conversation. 'What did you mean before?' he asked, shifting gears. 'When you said you wouldn't help me.'

'Exactly what I meant.'

'What won't you help with?'

Again the smile. 'Was I ever stupid, Myron?'

'Never,' he said.

'Do you really think I believed that comeback story? Or

the one about Greg being' – she made quote marks in the air – ' "in seclusion" for an ankle injury? Your visit here just confirms my suspicion.'

'What suspicion?'

'Greg is missing. You're trying to find him.'

'What makes you think Greg is missing?'

'Please, Myron, don't play games with me. You owe me that much at least.'

He nodded slowly. 'Do you know where he is?'

'No. But I hope the bastard is dead and rotting in a hole.'

'Stop mincing words,' Myron said. 'Tell me how you really feel.'

The smile was sadder this time. Myron felt a pang. Greg and Emily had fallen in love. They'd been married. They had two children. What had torn that all apart? Was it something recent . . . or was it something in their pasts, something tainted from the beginning? Myron felt his throat go dry.

'When was the last time you saw Greg?' he asked.

'A month ago,' she said.

'Where?'

'In divorce court.'

'Are you two on speaking terms?'

'I meant what I said before. About him being dead and rotting.'

'I'll take that as a no.'

Emily nodded a suit-yourself.

'If he was hiding, do you have any idea where?'

'Nope.'

'No summer house? No place he liked to get away?'

'Nope.'

'Do you know if Greg had a girlfriend?'

'Nope. But I would pity the poor woman.'

'Have you ever heard the name Carla?'

She hesitated. Her index finger tapped her knee, an old gesture so familiar to him it almost hurt to watch. 'Wasn't there a Carla who lived on my floor at Duke?' she asked. 'Yes, Carla Anderson. Sophomore year, wasn't it? Pretty girl.'

'Anything more recent?'

'No.' She sat up, crossed her legs. 'How's Win?'

'The same.'

'One of life's constants,' she said. 'He loves you, you know. I wonder if he's a latent homosexual.'

'Two men can love each other and not be gay,' Myron said.

She arched an eyebrow. 'You really think so?'

He was letting her get to him. Bad mistake. 'Are you aware that Greg was going to sign an endorsement deal?' he asked her.

That got her attention. 'Are you serious?'

'Yes.'

'A big one?'

'Huge from my understanding,' Myron replied. 'With Forte.'

Emily's hands tightened. She would have made fists had her nails not been so long. 'Son of a bitch.'

'What?'

'He waited until the divorce had been finalized and I got squat. Then he signs the deal. That son of a bitch.'

'What do you mean, squat? Greg was still wealthy.'

She shook her head. 'His agent lost it all. Or so he claimed in court.'

'Martin Felder?'

'Yep. Didn't have a penny to his name. Son of a bitch.'

94

'But Greg still works with Felder. Why would he stay with a guy who lost his money?'

'I don't know, Myron.' Her voice was clipped and annoyed. 'Perhaps the son of a bitch was lying. It wouldn't be the first time.'

Myron waited. Emily looked at him. Tears welled in her eyes but she bit them back down. She stood and walked to the other side of the room. Her back was now to him. She looked out the sliding glass doors into the fenced-in yard. The pool was covered with a tarp; random sticks and leaves clung to the aqua. Two children appeared. A boy of about ten chased a girl who looked to be eight. They were both laughing with faces wide and open and a little rosy from either cold or exertion. The boy stopped when he saw his mother. He gave her a big smile and wave. Emily raised her hand and gave a small wave back. The children ran on. Emily crossed her arms like she was hugging herself.

'He wants to take them away from me,' she said in a remarkably calm voice. 'He'll do anything to get them.'

'Like?'

'Like the sleaziest things you can imagine.'

'How sleazy?'

'None of your goddamn business.' She stopped. She still had her back to him. Myron could see her shoulders quake. 'Get out,' she said.

'Emily . . .'

'You want to help him, Myron.'

'I want to find him. There's a difference.'

She shook her head. 'You don't owe him,' she said. 'I know you think you do. It's your way. I saw the guilt in your face back then, and I could still see it the second I

95

opened the front door. It's over, Myron. It had nothing to do with what happened to us. He never found out.'

'Is that supposed to make me feel better?' he asked.

She spun toward him. 'It's not supposed to make you feel better,' she snapped. 'It's not about you. I'm the one who married him. I'm the one who betrayed him. I can't believe you're still beating yourself up about it.'

Myron swallowed. 'He visited me in the hospital. After I got injured. He sat and talked with me for hours.'

'And that makes him a swell guy?'

'We shouldn't have done it.'

'Grow up,' she said. 'It was more than ten years ago. Gone and forgotten.'

Silence.

After some time had passed, Myron looked up at her. 'Could you really lose your kids?' he asked.

'Yes.'

'How far would you go to keep them?'

'As far as I had to.'

'Would you kill to keep them?' Myron asked.

'Yes.' No hesitation.

'Did you?'

'No.'

'Do you have any idea why some goons would be looking for Greg?'

'No.'

'You didn't hire them?'

'If I did,' she said, 'I wouldn't tell you. But if these "goons" want to hurt Greg, I'll do all I can to help them locate him.'

Myron put down the lemonade. 'I guess I better get going.'

She showed him to the door. Before she opened it, she

put a hand on his arm. Her touch burned right through the material. 'It's okay,' she said gently. 'Let it go. Greg never found out.'

Myron nodded.

She took a deep breath and smiled again. Her voice returned to its normal tone. 'It was good to see you again, Myron.'

'Same here,' he said.

'Come back again, will you?' She was trying so hard to be casual. Myron knew it was just an act, one he had seen before. 'Perhaps we can have a quick fling for old times' sake. Couldn't hurt, right?'

One last grasp at the shock. Myron pulled away. 'That's what we said last time,' he said. 'And it still hurts.'

Chapter 10

'It was the night before they got married,' Myron began. He was back at his office. Esperanza sat in front of him. Her eyes were on him, but he didn't know that. He stared at the ceiling, his fingers laced and resting on his chest. He had his chair tilted far back. 'Do you want the details?'

'Only if you want to tell me,' Esperanza said.

He told her. He told her how Emily had called him. He told her how she came to his room. He told her that they'd both had too much to drink. He said that last one as a sort of trial balloon, but a quick glance at Esperanza blew that particular old balloon out of the sky. She interrupted with one question.

'How long after the draft did all this take place?'

Myron smiled at the ceiling. She was so damned perceptive. There was no reason to answer.

'I assume,' Esperanza continued, 'that this little tryst occurred sometime between the pro draft and your injury.'

'You assume correctly.'

'Ah,' she said with a small nod. 'So let me see if I got the true picture now. It's your senior year of college. Your team won the NCAA finals – a point for you. You end up losing Emily and she ends up engaged to Greg – a point for him. The draft comes. Greg is the seventh overall pick; you are the eighth – a point for Greg.'

Myron closed his eyes and nodded. 'You're wondering if I was trying to even the score.'

'Not wondering,' Esperanza corrected. 'The answer is obvious.'

'You're not helping.'

'You want help, go to a shrink,' she said. 'You want the truth, come to me.'

She was right. He took his hands off his chest. Keeping the fingers laced, he placed them behind his head. He put his feet on the desk.

'Did she cheat on you with him?' she asked.

'No.'

'You're sure?'

'Yes. They met after we broke up.'

'Too bad,' she said. 'It would have given you a nice out.'

'Yeah, Pity.'

'So this is why you feel obligated to Greg? Because you slept with his fiancée?'

'That's a big part of it, but there's more to it than that.'

'Like?'

'It's going to sound corny, but there's always been a bond between us.'

'A bond?'

Myron's line of vision traveled from the ceiling to his movie-still wall. Woody Allen and Diane Keaton were enjoying a Manhattan moment in *Annie Hall*. Bogie and

Bergman leaned on Sam's piano back in the days when Paris had been theirs. 'Greg and I were once-in-a-lifetime competitors,' he said. 'And there is a special bond between competitors. Kinda like Magic Johnson and Larry Bird. You become defined by one another. It was like that with Greg and me. It was unspoken, but we both knew the bond was there.'

He stopped. Esperanza waited in silence. 'When I hurt my knee,' Myron continued, 'Greg visited me in the hospital. He showed up the very next day. I woke up from some pain medication and there he was. Sitting with Win. And I instantly understood. Win must have understood too, otherwise he would have thrown him out.'

Esperanza nodded.

'Greg stayed around too. He helped with rehab. That's what I mean by a bond. He was devastated by the news because when I got hurt, it was like a part of him was gone too. He tried to tell me why it meant so much to him, but he couldn't put it into words. It didn't matter. I knew. He just had to be there.'

'And you hurt your knee how long after you'd slept with his new bride?'

'About a month.'

'Did seeing him all the time help or hurt?'

'Yes.'

She said nothing.

'Do you understand now?' he asked. 'Do you see why I have to pursue this? You're probably right. Sleeping with Emily was probably nothing more than payback for not getting drafted before Greg. Just another stupid battle. But what kind of way was that for a marriage to start? I owe Greg Downing. It's that simple.'

'No,' she said. 'It's not that simple.'

'Why not?'

'Because too much of your past is resurfacing. First Jessica—'

'Don't start with that.'

'I'm not,' she said calmly. Her voice was rarely calm when it came to Jessica. 'I'm just stating a fact. Jessica crushed you when she left. You never got over her.'

'But she's back now.'

'Yes.'

'So what's your point?'

'Basketball also crushed you when it left. You never got over it.'

'Sure I did.'

She shook her head. 'First you spent three years trying every possible remedy to fix your knee.'

'I just tried to get better,' he interjected. 'Nothing wrong with that, is there?'

'Nothing. But you were a pain in the ass. You pushed Jessica away. I'm not forgiving her for what she did to you. You didn't ask for that. But you played a part in her leaving.'

'Why are you bringing this all up?'

She shook her head. 'You're the one who's bringing it all up. Your entire past. Jessica and now basketball. You want us to watch you go through all this again, but we won't.'

'Go through what?'

But she didn't answer. Instead she asked, 'Do you want to know why I didn't go see you play last night?'

He nodded, still not facing her. His cheeks felt flush and hot.

'Because with Jessica, at least there's a *chance* you won't get hurt again. There's a chance the witch smartened up.

But with basketball, there is no chance. You can't come back.'

'I can handle it,' he said, hearing those words yet again.

She said nothing.

Myron stared off. He barely heard the phone ring. Neither one of them moved to answer it. 'You think I should drop this?' he asked.

'Yes. I agree with Emily. She's the one who betrayed him. You were just a handy tool. If what happened somehow poisoned their relationship, it was her doing. It was her decision. You don't owe Greg Downing a thing.'

'Even if what you're saying is true,' he said, 'that bond is still there.'

'Bullshit,' Esperanza said. 'That's just a load of pedantic, macho bullshit. You're just proving my point. There's no bond anymore, if there ever was one. Basketball hasn't been a part of your life for a decade. The only reason you think the bond is still there is because you're playing again.'

There was a loud pounding on the door. The frame shook and almost gave way. Myron startled upright. 'Who's manning the phones?' he asked.

Esperanza smiled.

'Oh no.'

'Come in,' Esperanza said.

The door opened. Myron's feet fell to the floor. Though he had seen her many times before, his jaw still dropped open. Big Cyndi ducked in. She was mammoth. Six-five and over three hundred pounds. Cyndi wore a white T-shirt with the sleeves ripped off at the biceps. Her arms were the envy of Hulk Hogan. Her makeup was more garish than it had been in the ring. Her hair was purple spikes; her mascara was also purple though a darker shade than her hair. Her lipstick was a red smear. Cyndi looked like something out of Rocky Horror Picture Show. She was the single most frightening sight Myron had ever seen.

'Hi, Cyndi,' Myron tried.

Cyndi growled. She held up her middle finger, turned, stepped back through the door, closed it.

'What the—'

'She's telling you to pick up line one,' Esperanza said.

'Cyndi's answering phones?'

'Yes.'

'She doesn't talk!'

'In person. On the phone she's very good.'

'Jesus Christ.'

'Pick up the phone and stop whining.'

Myron did so. It was Lisa, their contact at New York Bell. Most people think that only the police can get phone records. Not true. Almost every private eye in the country has a contact at their local phone company. It's just a matter of simply paying someone off. A month's phone record can cost you anywhere from one thousand to five thousand dollars. Myron and Win had met Lisa during their days with the feds. She didn't take money, but they always took care of her in some way or another. 'I got what Win wanted,' Lisa said.

'Go ahead.'

'The call at nine eighteen P.M. came from a public phone located in a diner near Dyckman Street and Broadway,' she said.

'Isn't that up near Two Hundredth Street?'

'I think so. You want the phone number?'

Carla had called Greg from a diner on 200th Street? Weirder and weirder. 'If you have it.'

She gave it to him. 'Hope that helps.'

'It does, Lisa. Thanks.' He held up the paper to Esperanza. 'Lookie what I got,' he said. 'A real live clue.'

Chapter 11

To be fair, the Parkview Diner lived up to its name. You did indeed have a view of Lieutenant William Tighe Park across the street; it was smaller than the average backyard with shrubs so high you really couldn't see the landscaped garden within. A wire-mesh fence enclosed the grounds. Hung on the fence in several places were signs that read in big, bold letters: DO NOT FEED THE RATS. No joke. In smaller print the warning was repeated in Spanish: *No Des Comida a Las Ratas*. The signs had been placed there by a group calling itself the Quality of Life Zone. Myron shook his head. Only in New York would this be a problem – people who could not contain themselves from the seductive lure of feeding vermin. Myron glanced again at the sign, then the diner. Rats. Quite the appetite-enhancer.

He crossed the street. Two levels above the Parkview Diner, a dog squeezed his head through the grates of a fire escape and barked at passing pedestrians. The Parkview's green overhang was ripped in several spots. The letters were faded to the point of unintelligibility, and the support pole was bent so far that Myron had to duck to get to the door. There was a poster of a gyro sandwich in the window. Today's specials, according to a blackboard in the same window, included eggplant parmigiana and chicken à la king. The soup was beef consommé. There were permits from the City of New York Department of Buildings stuck on the door like car-inspection decals.

Myron entered and was immediately greeted by the familiar yet nonspecific smell of a Manhattan diner. Fat was in the air. Taking a deep breath felt as if it would clog an artery. A waitress with hair bleached to the point of straw offered him a table. Myron asked her for the manager. Using her pencil she pointed over her shoulder at a man behind the counter.

'That's Hector,' she said. 'He owns the place.'

Myron thanked her and grabbed a soda-fountain stool at the counter. He debated spinning himself in the seat and decided the act might be viewed as immature. Two stools to his right, an unshaven, perhaps homeless man with black Thom McAn sneakers and a tattered overcoat smiled and nodded. Myron nodded and smiled back. The man went back to his coffee. He raised his shoulders and huddled into the drink as though he suspected someone might try to swipe it in mid-sip.

Myron picked up a vinyl menu with cracked binding. He opened it but didn't really read it. There were a lot of worn index cards jammed into protective plastic cases announcing various specials. Worn was an apt description of the Parkview Diner, but it didn't fairly convey the overall impression. There was something welcoming and even clean about this place. The counter gleamed. So did the utensils and the silver milkshake maker and the soda fountain. Most patrons read a newspaper or gabbed with one another as if they were eating at home. They knew their waitress's name, and you could bet your last dollar she didn't introduce herself and tell them she was going to be their server when they first sat down.

Hector the owner was busy at the grill. Almost two P.M. It wasn't the height of the lunch hour, but business was still pretty brisk. He barked out some orders in Spanish, his eyes never leaving the food. Then he turned around with a polite smile, wiped his hands on a rag, and asked Myron if he could help him. Myron asked if he had a pay phone.

'No, sir, I'm sorry,' Hector answered. The Hispanic accent was there, but Hector had worked on it. 'There's one on the street corner. On the left.'

Myron looked at the number Lisa had given him. He read it out loud. Hector did several things at the same time. He flipped burgers, folded over an omelette, checked the french fries. His eyes were everywhere – the cash register, the clientele at both the tables and the counter, the kitchen to his left.

'Oh that,' Hector said. 'It's in the back. In the kitchen.'

'The kitchen?'

'Yes, sir.' Still polite.

'A pay phone in the kitchen?'

'Yes, sir,' Hector said. He was on the short side, thin under his white apron and polyester black pants. His nose had been broken several times. His forearms looked like steel cords. 'It's for my staff.'

'Don't you have a business phone?'

'Of course we do.' His voice spiked up a bit now, as if the question was an insult. 'We do a big takeout and delivery business here. Lots of people order lunch from us. We have a fax machine too. But I don't want my staff tying up the lines, you know? You get a busy signal, you give your business to someone else, yes? So I put a pay phone in the back.'

'I see.' An idea came to Myron. 'Are you telling me customers never use it?'

'Well, sir, if a customer truly insists, I would never refuse him.' The practiced politeness of a good business-man. 'The customer must come first at the Parkview. Always.'

'Has a customer ever insisted?'

'No, sir. I don't think any customers even know we have it.'

'Can you tell me who was using the pay phone at nine eighteen P.M. last Saturday?'

That question got his attention. 'Excuse me?' Myron started to repeat the question but Hector interrupted him. 'Why would you want to know that?'

'My name is Bernie Worley,' Myron said. 'I'm a pro-duct supervising agent with AT&T.' *A product what?* 'Somebody is trying to cheat us, sir, and we are not happy about it.'

'Cheat you?'

'A Y511.'

'A what?'

'A Y511,' Myron repeated. You start tossing the bull, your best bet is to just keep tossing. 'It's an electronic monitoring device built in Hong Kong. It's new on the market, but we're onto it. Sold on the streets. Somebody used one on your phone at nine eighteen P.M. on March eighteenth of this year. They dialed Kuala Lumpur and spoke for nearly twelve minutes. The total cost of the call is twenty-three dollars and eighty-two cents, but the fine for using a Y511 will be at least seven hundred dollars with the potential for up to one year in prison. Plus we'll have to remove the phone.'

Hector's face became a mask of pure panic. 'What?' Myron wasn't thrilled with what he was doing – scaring an honest, hard-working immigrant like this – but he knew that the fear of government or big business would work in a situation like this. Hector turned around and shouted something in Spanish to a teenager who looked like him. The teenager took over the grill. 'I don't understand this, Mr Worley.'

'It's a public phone, sir. You just admitted to a product supervising agent that you used the public phones for private use; that is, for your employees only and denying public access. This violates our own code, section one twenty-four B. I wouldn't report it normally, but when you add in the use of a Y511—'

'But I didn't use a Y511!'

'We don't know that, sir.' Myron was playing Mr Bureaucrat to the hilt; nothing made a person feel more impotent. There is no darker pit than the blank stare of a bureaucrat. 'The phone is on your premises,' Myron continued in a bored singsong voice. 'You just explained to me that the phone was only used by your employees—'

'Exactly!' Hector leaped. 'By my employees! Not me!'

'But you own this establishment. You are responsible.' Myron looked around with his best, bored expression – the one he learned while waiting on line at the Division of Motor Vehicles. 'We'll also have to check out the status of all your employees. Maybe we can find the culprit that way.'

Hector's eyes grew big. Myron knew this would hit

home. There wasn't a restaurant in Manhattan that didn't employ at least one illegal alien. Hector's jowls slackened. 'All this,' he said, 'because someone used a pay phone?'

'What someone did, sir, was use an illegal electronic device known as a Y511. What you did, sir, was refuse to cooperate with the product supervising agent investigating this serious matter.'

'Refuse to cooperate?' Hector was grasping at the possible life preserver Myron had offered up. 'No, sir, not me. I want to cooperate. I want to very much.'

Myron shook his head. 'I don't think you do.'

Hector bit down and set his polite meter on extra-strength now. 'No, sir,' he said. 'I want to help very much. I want to cooperate with the phone company. Tell me what I can do to help. Please.'

Myron sighed, gave it a few seconds. The diner bustled. The cash register dinged while the guy who looked homeless with the Thom McAn sneakers picked out greasy coins from a dirty hand. The griddle sizzled. The aroma from the various foods battled each other for dominance with none winning outright. Hector's face grew more and more anxious. Enough, Myron thought. 'For starters, you can tell me who was using the pay phone at nine eighteen P.M. last Saturday.'

Hector held up a finger imploring patience. He shouted something in Spanish to the woman (Mrs Hector maybe?) working the cash register. The woman shouted something back. She closed the drawer and walked toward them. As she drew closer, Myron noticed that Hector was suddenly giving him an odd look. Was he starting to see through Myron's rather husky load of bull-dooky? Perhaps. But Myron looked back at him steadily and Hector quickly backed down. He might be suspicious, but not suspicious enough to risk offending the all-powerful bureaucrat by questioning his authority.

Hector whispered something to the woman. She urgently whispered back. He made an understanding 'ah' noise. Then he faced Myron and shook his head.

'It figures,' he said.

'What?'

'It was Sally.'

'Who?'

'At least I think it was Sally. My wife saw her on the phone around then. But she said she was only on for a minute or two.'

'Does Sally have a last name?'

'Guerro.'

'Is she here now?'

Hector shook his head. 'She hasn't been here since Saturday night. That's what I mean by, figures. She gets me in trouble and then she runs out.'

'Has she called in sick?'

'No, sir. She just up and left.'

'You got an address on her?' Myron asked.

'I think so, let me see.' He pulled out a big carton that read 'Snapple Peach Iced Tea' on the side. Behind him, the griddle hissed when fresh pancake batter touched down upon the hot metal. The files in the box were neat and color coded. Hector pulled one out and opened it. He shuffled through the sheets, found the one he was looking for, and frowned.

'What?' Myron prompted.

'Sally never gave us an address,' Hector said.

'How about a phone number?'

'No.' He looked up, remembering something. 'She said

she didn't have a phone. That's why she was using the one in the back so much.'

'Could you tell me what Ms Guerro looked like?' Myron tried.

Hector suddenly looked uncomfortable. He glanced at his wife and cleared his throat. 'Uh, she had brown hair,' he began. 'Maybe five-four, five-five. Average height, I guess.'

'Anything else?'

'Brown eyes, I think.' He stopped. 'That's about it.'

'How old would you say she was?'

Hector checked the file again. 'According to this, she was forty-five. That sounds about right.'

'How long has she worked here?' he asked.

'Two months.'

Myron nodded, rubbed his chin vigorously. 'It sounds like an operative who goes by the name Carla.'

'Carla?'

'A notorious phone fraud,' Myron continued. 'We've been after her for a while.' He glanced left, then right. Trying to look conspiratorial. 'Have you ever heard her use the name Carla or hear someone call her Carla?'

Hector looked at his wife. She shook her head. 'No, never.'

'Did she have any visitors? Any friends?'

Again Hector checked with his wife. Again the head shook. 'No, none that we ever saw. She kept to herself most of the time.'

Myron decided to push a little further and confirm what he already knew. If Hector balked at this stage, so what? Nothing ventured, nothing gained. He leaned forward; Hector and his wife did likewise. 'This may sound insensitive,' Myron whispered, 'but was this woman large chested?'

Both nods were immediate. 'Very large,' Hector said.

Suspicion confirmed.

He asked a few more questions, but any useful information had already been culled from these waters. Before leaving, he told them that they were in the clear and could continue to violate code section 124B without fear. Hector almost kissed his hand. Myron felt like a louse. *What did you do today, Batman? Well, Robin, I started off by terrorizing a hard-working immigrant's livelihood with a bunch of lies. Holy Cow, Batman, you're the coolest!* Myron shook his head. What to do for an encore – throw empty beer bottles at the dog on the fire escape?

Myron exited the Parkview Diner. He debated going to the park across the street, but suppose he became overcome by a lustful need to feed rats? No, he couldn't risk it. He'd have to stay away. He began to head to the Dyckman Street subway station when a voice stopped him.

'You looking for Sally?'

Myron turned. It was the homeless-looking man with the Thom McAns from the diner. He sat on the pavement, his back leaning against the brick building. He had an empty plastic coffee cup in his hand. Panhandling.

'You know her?' Myron asked.

'She and I . . .' He winked and crossed his fingers. 'We met because of that damn phone, you know.'

'Really.'

Using the wall for support the man stood. His facial hair was whiteish, not full enough to be a beard yet past the stage of a Miami Vice wanna-be. His long hair was black as coal. 'Sally was using my phone all the time. It pissed me off.'

'Your phone?'

'The pay phone in the back,' he said licking his lips. 'It's right by the back door. I hang out in the back alley a lot so I can hear it, you know? It's kind of like my business phone.' Myron couldn't guess his age. His face was boyish but leathered – from the passing years or hard living, Myron couldn't say. His grin was missing a couple of prominent teeth, reminding Myron of that beloved Christmas classic 'All I Want for Christmas Is My Two Front Teeth.' Such a nice song really. No toys, no Sega Genesis video game. The kid just wanted teeth. So selfless really.

'I used to have my own cellular,' the man continued. 'Two of them, as a matter of fact. But they got stolen. And the damn things are so unreliable, especially around the high buildings. And anyone can listen in with the right equipment. Me, I need to keep what I do secret, you see. Spies are everywhere. And they also give you brain tumors. The electrons or something. Brain tumors the size of beach balls.'

Myron kept his face blank. 'Uh huh.' Speaking of tossing the bull.

'So anyway Sally started using it, too. It pissed me off, you know? I mean, I'm a businessman. I got important calls coming in. I can't have the line tied up. Am I right?'

'As rain,' Myron said.

'See, I'm a Hollywood screenwriter.' He stuck out his hand. 'Norman Lowenstein.'

Myron tried to remember the fake name he used with Hector. 'Bernie Worley.'

'Nice to meet you, Bernie.'

'Do you know where Sally Guerro lives?'

'Sure. We used to be . . .' Norman Lowenstein crossed his fingers.

'So I heard. Could you tell me where she lives?'

Norman Lowenstein pursed his lips and used his pointer finger to scratch a spot near his throat. 'I'm not real good with addresses and stuff,' he said. 'But I could take you there.'

Myron wondered how big of a waste of time this was going to be. 'Would you mind?'

'Sure, no problem. Let's go.'

'Which way?'

'The A train,' Norman said. 'Down to One Hundred Twenty-fifth Street.'

They walked toward the subway.

'You go the movies much, Bernie?' Norman asked.

'Much as the next guy, I guess.'

'Let me tell you something about movie-making,' he began, growing more animated. 'It's not all glamour and glitz. It's a dog-eat-dog business like no other, making dreams for people. All the back-stabbing, all that money, all that fame and attention . . . it makes people act funny, you know? I got this screenplay with Paramount right now. They're talking to Willis about it. Bruce Willis. He's really interested.'

'Good luck with it,' Myron said.

Norman beamed. 'Thanks, Bernie, that's real nice of you. I mean it. Real nice. I'd like to tell you what my flick is about, but well, my hands are tied. You know how it is. Hollywood and all the theft out there. The studio wants it kept hush-hush.'

'I understand,' Myron said.

'I trust you, Bernie, it's not that. But the studios insist. I can't blame them really. They got to protect their interests, right?'

'Right.'

'It's an action-adventure flick, that much I can tell you. But with heart too, you know? Not just a shoot-em-up. Harrison Ford wanted in, but he's too old. I guess Willis is okay. He's not my first choice, but what can you do?'

'Uh huh.'

One Twenty-fifth Street was not the nicest stop in the city. It was safe enough during the day, Myron surmised, but the fact that he was now carrying a gun made him feel a tad more secure. Myron did not like 'packing heat' and rarely did so. It was not that Myron was particularly squeamish; it had more to do with comfort. The shoulder holster dug into his armpit and made it itch like he was wearing a tweed condom. But after last night's soiree with Camouflage Pants and Brick Wall, it would be foolhardy to walk around unarmed.

'Which way?' Myron asked.

'Downtown.'

They headed south on Broadway. Norman regaled him with tales of Hollywood. The ins and outs. Myron nodded and kept walking. The farther south they headed, the better the area became. They passed the familiar iron gates of Columbia University, then turned left. 'It's right up here,' Norman said. 'Toward the middle of the block.'

The street was lined with low-rise apartments that were mostly used by Columbia's grad students and professors. Strange, Myron thought, that a diner waitress would live here. But then again nothing else about her involvement in all this made sense – why should where she lived? If she lived here at all, and not, say, with Bruce Willis in Hollywood.

Norman interrupted his thoughts. 'You're trying to help her, right?'

'What?'

Norman stopped walking. He was less animated now. 'All that stuff about being from the phone company. That was all crap, right?'

Myron said nothing.

'Look,' he said, putting his hand on Myron's forearm, 'Hector is a good man. He came to this country with nothing. He works his ass off in that diner. He and his wife and son – they slave there every day. No days off. And every day he's scared someone's going to take it all away from him. All that worry . . . it clouds the thinking, you know? Me, I got nothing to lose so I'm not afraid of anything. Makes it easier to see some stuff. Know what I mean?'

Myron gave a slight nod.

Norman's bright eyes dimmed as a bit of reality swept through him. Myron looked at him, really looked at him, for the first time. He made his eyes stop sweeping by him with barely a notice of age or height or even species. Myron realized that behind the lies and self-delusion lay the dreams of any man, the hopes and wants and needs that are the sole reserve of the human race.

'I'm worried about Sally,' Norman went on. 'Maybe that's clouding my thinking. But I know she wouldn't just up and leave without saying good-bye to me. Sally wouldn't do that.' He stopped, met Myron's eyes with his own. 'You're not from the phone company, are you?'

'No, I'm not.'

'You want to help her?'

'Yes,' Myron said. 'I want to help her.'

He nodded and pointed. 'In here. Apartment two E.'

Myron walked up the stoop while Norman stayed on the street level. He pressed the black button reading 2E. No one answered. No surprise there. He tried the entrance door, but it was locked. You had to be buzzed in.

'You better stay there,' he told Norman. Norman nodded, understanding. These buzzer-protected doors were mild deterrents to crime, but their true purpose was to prevent vagrants from coming in and setting up camp in the lobby. Myron would just wait. Eventually an occupant would leave or enter the building. While said occupant opened the door, Myron would enter as though he belonged. No one would question a man dressed in khakis and a button-down BD Baggies shirt. If Norman stood next to him, however, that same occupant might react differently.

Myron moved down two steps. When he saw two young women approach the door from the inside, he slapped his pockets as though looking for keys. Then he walked purposefully up to the door, smiled, and waited for them to push it open. He need not have bothered with the dramatics. The two young women – college students, Myron guessed – went through the portal without looking up or decelerating their oral activities. Both were talking nonstop, neither listening. They paid absolutely no attention to him. Amazing restraint really. Of course from this angle they couldn't see his ass, so their self-control was not only admirable but somewhat understandable.

He looked back at Norman, who thankfully waved him off. 'You go yourself,' he said. 'I don't want to cause a problem.'

Myron let the door close.

The corridor was pretty much what he expected. It was

painted off-white. No stripes or designs. There were no wall-hangings other than a huge bulletin board that read like a schizophrenic political manifesto. Dozens of leaflets announced everything from a dance sponsored by the Native American Gay and Lesbian Society to poetry readings by a group calling itself the Rush Limbaugh Review. Ah, the college life.

He ascended a stairway lit by two bare bulbs. All this walking and stair climbing were starting to take a toll on his bad knee. The joint tightened up like a rusted hinge. Myron felt himself dragging the leg behind him. He used the railing for support and wondered what the knee would be like when he reached arthritis age.

The floor plan of the building was far from symmetrical. Doors seemed to be placed in the wall as though at random. Off in a corner, a good distance from the other apartments, Myron found the door marked 2E. The positioning made the apartment look like an afterthought, as if someone had spotted some extra space in the back and decided to add an extra room or two. Myron knocked. No answer. No surprise. He checked the corridor. No one in sight. He was thankful that Norman was not here because he wouldn't want someone to witness him breaking in.

Myron was not great at the lock-picking game. He had learned a bit over the years, but picking locks was a bit like playing a video game. You work at it enough, and eventually you move up levels. Myron hadn't worked at it. He didn't like it. He really didn't have much natural talent for it. In most cases, he relied on Win to handle the mechanical stuff, like Barney used to do on *Mission: Impossible*.

He examined the door and felt his heart sink. Even for

New York the dead bolts were nothing short of impressive. Three of them stacked intimidatingly from six inches above the knob to six inches below the top frame. Top of the line stuff. Brand new, judging by the gleam and lack of scratches. This was a tad odd. Was Sally/Carla the extracautious type, or was there a more aberrant reason for such security? Good question. Myron looked at the locks again. Win would have enjoyed the challenge; Myron knew that any effort he made would be fruitless.

He debated kicking in the door when he noticed something. He moved closer and squinted into the door crack. Again something struck him as being odd. The dead bolts were not engaged. Why buy all these expensive locks and not use them? He tried the knob. It was locked, but that one would be easy to get through with the 'loid card.

He took out the card. He couldn't remember the last time he had used it. It looked pristine. Maybe never. He jammed it into the opening. Despite being an old lock it still took Myron almost five minutes to find the right spot to push the lock back. He gripped the knob. The door began to swing open.

It was open barely six inches when the odor attacked.

The bloodcurdling stench popped out into the hallway like pressurized gas. Myron felt his stomach dive and swoop. He gagged a little and felt a weight on his chest. He knew the smell, and dread filled him. He searched his pockets for a handkerchief and came up empty. He blocked his nose and mouth with the crook of his elbow, as if he were doing Bela Lugosi in *Dracula*. He didn't want to go in. He wasn't good at this type of thing. He knew that whatever image lay behind the door would stay with him, would haunt his nights and too often his days too. It would stay with him like a dear friend, tapping him on the shoulder every once in a while when he thought he was alone and at peace.

He pushed the door all the way open. The rancid smell permeated his meager protection. He tried to breathe through his mouth, but the thought of what he was sucking in made that option unbearable.

Fortunately, he didn't have to travel far to find the source of the odor.

Chapter 12

'Whoa, Bolitar, new cologne?'

'Funny, Dimonte.'

NYPD homicide detective Roland Dimonte shook his head. 'Christ, what a stink.' He was out of uniform, but you wouldn't ever call him 'plainclothes.' He wore a green silk shirt and jeans that were too tight and too dark blue. The bottoms were tucked into purple snakeskin boots; the color faded in and out with any angle change, like some psychedelic Hendrix poster from the sixties. Dimonte gnawed on a toothpick, a habit he picked up, Myron surmised, when he spotted himself doing it in the mirror and decided it looked tough. 'You touch anything?' he asked.

'Just the doorknob,' Myron said. He had also checked the rest of the apartment to make sure there weren't any other gruesome surprises. There weren't.

'How did you get in?'

'The door was unlocked.'

'Really?' Dimonte raised an eyebrow and looked back at the door. 'The door is set to lock automatically when you close it.'

'Did I say unlocked? I meant, ajar.'

'Sure you did.' Dimonte did a bit more gnawing, shook his head. He ran his hand through greasy hair. Ringlets clung to his forehead, refusing to give ground. 'So who is she?'

'I don't know,' Myron said.

Dimonte scrunched up his face like a closed fist. Displaying very skeptical. Subtle body language was not Dimonte's forte. 'Little early in the day to be pulling my hardware, ain't it, Bolitar?'

'I don't know her name. It might be Sally Guerro. Then again it might be Carla.'

'Uh-huh.' Toothpick chew. 'I thought I saw you on TV last night. That you were playing ball again.'

'I am.'

The coroner came over. He was tall and thin and his wire-rim glasses looked too big on the elongated face. 'She's been dead awhile,' he pronounced. 'At least four days.'

'Cause?'

'Hard to say for sure. Someone bludgeoned her with a blunt object. I'll know more when I get her on the table.' He looked at the corpse with professional disinterest, then back at Dimonte. 'They're not real, by the way.'

'What?'

He vaguely motioned toward the torso. 'Her breasts. They're implants.'

'Jesus Christ,' Dimonte said, 'you fiddling with dead bodies now?'

The elongated face sagged, his jaw dropping to

somewhere around his navel. 'Don't even joke about that,' the coroner said in a stage whisper. 'You know what rumors like that could do to a guy in my business?'

'Get him promoted?' Dimonte said.

The coroner did not laugh. He gave Myron a wounded look, then Dimonte. 'You think that's funny, huh? Goddamn it, this is my career you're fucking around with!'

'Calm down, Peretti, I'm just playing with you.'

'Playing with me? You think my career is some kind of fucking joke? What the hell is wrong with you?'

Dimonte's eyes narrowed. 'Kind of sensitive about all this, Peretti.'

'You have to be in my position,' he said, back straightening.

'If you say so.'

'What the hell does that mean?'

' "The lady protests too much, methinks." '

'What?'

'It's Shakespeare,' Dimonte said. 'From *Macbeth*.' Dimonte looked over to Myron.

Myron smiled. '*Hamlet*.'

'I don't give a shit who said it.' Peretti protested. 'You shouldn't mess around with a man's reputation. I don't think any of this is funny.'

'Like I give a rat's ass what you think,' Dimonte said. 'You got anything else?'

'She's wearing a wig.'

'A wig? No kidding, Peretti. The case is as good as solved now. All we need to do is find a killer who hates wigs and fake tits. This is helpful, Peretti. What kind of panties was she wearing, huh? You sniff them yet?'

'I was just—'

'Do me a big favor, Peretti.' Dimonte made himself a

little taller, hitched his pants. Signaling importance. Again the subtlety. 'Tell me when she died. Tell me how she died. Then we'll talk about her fashion accessories, okay?'

Peretti held up his hands in surrender and returned to the body. Dimonte turned to Myron. Myron said, 'The implants and wig might be important. He was right to tell you.'

'Yeah, I know. I just like busting his chops.'

'And the quote is, "Methinks the lady doth protest too much."'

'Uh huh.' Dimonte changed toothpicks. The one in his mouth was frayed like a horse's mane. 'You going to tell me what the fuck is going on, or am I going to drag you downtown?'

Myron made a face. 'Drag me downtown?'

'Don't bust my balls on this, Bolitar, okay?'

Myron forced himself to look at the bloodied corpse. His stomach did back flips. He was starting to get used to the smell, the thought of which was nearly as bad as the smell itself. Peretti was back at it, making a small slit to get to the liver. Myron diverted his gaze. The homicide crew from John Jay was setting up, taking photographs, that kind of thing. Dimonte's partner, a kid named Krinsky, quietly walked around and took notes. 'Why would she make them so big?' Myron wondered out loud.

'What?'

'Her breasts. I can understand the desire to enlarge them. All the pressures in this society. But why make them that big?'

Dimonte said, 'You're shitting me, right?'

Krinsky came over. 'All her stuff is in those suitcases.' He motioned with his hand to two bags on the floor.

Myron had met Krinsky on maybe half a dozen occasions. Talking was not the kid's forte; he seemed to do it as often as Myron picked locks. 'I'd say she was moving out.'

'You got an ID yet?' Dimonte asked.

'Her wallet says her name is Sally Guerro,' Krinsky continued in a soft voice. 'So does one of her passports.'

They both waited for Krinsky to continue. When he didn't, Dimonte shouted, 'What do you mean, one of her passports? How many does she have?'

'Three.'

'Jesus Christ, Krinsky, talk.'

'One is in the name Sally Guerro. One is in the name Roberta Smith. One is in the name Carla Whitney.'

'Give me those.' Dimonte scanned through the various passports. Myron looked over his shoulder. The same woman was in all three pictures, albeit with different hair (ergo the wig) and different Social Security numbers. Judging by the amount of stamps, the woman had traveled extensively.

Dimonte whistled. 'Forged passports,' he said. 'And good ones too.' He turned more pages. 'Plus she has a couple of visits to South America in here. Colombia. Bolivia.' The passports closed with a dramatic snap. 'Well, well, well. Looks like we got ourselves a nice, neat drug hit.'

Myron mulled over that bit of information. A drug hit – could that be part of the answer? If Sally/Carla/Roberta was dealing drugs, it might explain her connection with Greg Downing. She was his source. The meeting on Saturday night was nothing more than a buy. The waitress job was a cover. It also explained her using a pay phone and maintaining powerful door locks – tools of a drug dealer's trade. It made some sense. Of course, Greg Downing did not appear to be a drug user, but he would not be the first person to fool everyone.

Dimonte said, 'Anything else, Krinsky?'

The kid nodded. 'I found a stack of cash in the bedside drawer.' He stopped again.

Dimonte gave him exasperation. 'Did you count it?'

Another nod.

'How much?'

'A little over ten thousand dollars.'

'Ten grand in cash, huh?' That pleased Dimonte. 'Let me see it.'

Krinsky handed it over. New bills, held by rubber bands. Myron watched while Dimonte shuffled through them. All hundreds. The serial numbers were sequential. Myron tried to memorize one of them. When Dimonte finished, he tossed the packet back to Krinsky. The smile was still there.

'Yep,' Dimonte said, 'it looks like things are coming together in a nice, neat, drug-hit package.' He paused. 'Only one problem.'

'What?'

He pointed at Myron. 'You, Bolitar. You're messing up my nice, neat drug-hit. What the hell are you doing—?' Dimonte stopped himself and snapped his fingers. 'Holy shit . . .' His voice sort of drifted off. He slapped the side of his own head. A small spark in his eyes expanded. 'My God!'

Again note the subtlety. 'You have a thought, Rolly?'

Dimonte ignored him. 'Peretti!'

The coroner looked up from the body. 'What?'

'Those plastic tits,' he said. 'Myron noticed they were huge.'

127

'Yeah, so?'

'How big?'

'What?'

'How big are they?'

'You mean like cup size?'

'Yeah.'

'I look like a lingerie manufacturer? How the fuck would I know?'

'But they're big, right?'

'Right.'

'Really big.'

'You got eyes, don't you?'

Myron watched the exchange in silence. He was trying to follow Dimonte's logic – a most treacherous trail.

'Would you say they were bigger than a water balloon?' Dimonte continued.

Peretti shrugged. 'Depends on the balloon.'

'Didn't you ever make water balloons when you were a kid?'

'Yeah, sure,' Peretti said. 'But I don't remember how big the balloons were. I was a kid then. Everything looks bigger when you're a kid. A couple years ago I went back to my old elementary school to visit my third grade teacher. She still works there, if you can believe it. Her name is Mrs Tansmore. I swear to God the building looked like a goddamn dollhouse to me. It was huge when I was a kid. It was like—'

'All right, moron, let me make this simple.' Dimonte took a deep breath. 'Could they be used for smuggling drugs?'

Silence. Everyone in the room stopped moving. Myron wasn't sure if he just heard the most idiotic thing in the world or the most brilliant. He turned toward Peretti. Peretti looked up, mouth open in fly-catching pose.

'Well, Peretti? Could it be?'

'Could it be what?'

'Could she stick dope in her boobs? Smuggle drugs through customs with them?'

Peretti looked at Myron. Myron shrugged. Peretti turned back to Dimonte. 'I don't know,' he said slowly.

'How can we find out?'

'I'd have to examine them.'

'Then what the fuck you staring at me for? Do it.'

Peretti did as asked. Dimonte smiled at Myron; his eyebrows did a little dance. Proud of his deduction. Myron remained quiet.

'Nope, no way,' Peretti said.

Dimonte wasn't happy with this report. 'Why the hell not?'

'There's hardly any scar tissue,' Peretti said. 'If she were smuggling drugs in there, they'd have to rip the skin open and sew it up. Then they'd have to do it again on this side. There's no sign of that.'

'You're sure?'

'Positive.'

Dimonte said, 'Shit.' Then he glared at Myron and pulled him into a corner. 'Everything, Bolitar. Now.'

Myron had debated how to handle it, but in truth he had no choice. He had to tell. He couldn't keep Greg Downing's disappearance a secret any longer. The best he could hope to do was keep it contained. He suddenly remembered that Norman Lowenstein was waiting outside. 'One second,' he said.

'What? Where the fuck you going?'

'I'll be right back. Just wait here.'

'Like hell.'

Dimonte followed him down the stairs and out onto the stoop. Norman wasn't there. Myron looked up and down the block. No sign of Norman. This was hardly a surprise. Norman probably ran when he saw the cops. Guilty or not, the homeless learn quickly to make themselves scarce when the authorities come calling.

'What is it?' Dimonte asked.

'Nothing.'

'Then start talking. The whole story.'

Myron told him most of it. The story almost knocked the toothpick out of Dimonte's mouth. Dimonte didn't bother asking questions, though he continuously stuck in exclamations of 'Jesus Christ!' and 'Frigging A,' whenever Myron paused. When Myron finished, Dimonte sort of stumbled back and sat on the steps of the stoop. His eyes looked unfocused for a few moments. He gathered himself together, but it took some time.

'In-fuckin—' credible,' he managed.

Myron nodded.

'Are you telling me no one knows where Downing is?'

'If they do, they aren't talking.'

'He just vanished?'

'That's how it appears.'

'And there's blood in his basement?'

'Yes.'

Dimonte shook his head again. He reached down and put his hand on his right boot. Myron had seen him do this before. He liked to sort of pet the boot. Myron had no idea why. Maybe he found the feel of snakeskin soothing. Reminiscent of the womb.

'Suppose Downing killed her and ran,' he said.

'That's a pretty big suppose.'

'Yeah, but it fits,' Dimonte said.

'How?'

'According to what you said, Downing was seen with the victim Saturday night. How much you want to bet that once Peretti gets her on the table we find the time of death around then?'

'Doesn't mean Downing killed her.'

Dimonte increased the speed of his boot-petting stroke. A man on Rollerblades skated by with his dog. The dog looked out of breath, trying to keep up. New product idea: Dog Rollerblades. 'Saturday night, Greg Downing and the victim get together at some gin joint downtown. They leave sometime around eleven o'clock. Next thing we know she's dead and he's vanished.' Dimonte looked up at Myron. 'That points to him killing her and running.'

'It points to a dozen things.'

'Like what?'

'Like maybe Greg witnessed the murder and got scared and ran. Maybe he witnessed the murder and was kidnapped. Maybe he was killed by the same people.'

'So where's his body?' Dimonte asked.

'It could be anywhere.'

'Why not just leave it here with hers?'

'Maybe they killed him someplace else. Or maybe they took his body because he's famous and they didn't want that kind of heat.'

He scoffed at that one. 'You're reaching, Bolitar.'

'So are you.'

'Maybe. Only one way to find out.' He stood. 'We got to get out an APB on Downing.'

'Whoa, hold up a second. I don't think that's a good idea.'

Dimonte looked at Myron as if he were something left

unflushed in a toilet. 'I'm sorry,' he said feigning politeness. 'You must be mistaking me for someone who gives a
rat's ass what you think.'

'You're suggesting putting out an APB on a major,
beloved sports hero.'

'And you're suggesting I play favorites because he's a
major, beloved sports hero.'

'Not at all,' Myron said, his mind racing. 'But imagine
what happens when you call out this APB. The press gets
it. You start getting that OJ coverage. But there's a
difference here. You got squat on Downing. No motive.
No physical evidence. Nothing.'

'Not yet I don't,' Dimonte said. 'But it's early—'

'Exactly, it's early. Wait a little while, that's all I'm
saying. And handle this one right because the whole
world is going to look at everything you do. Tell those
bozos upstairs to videotape every step. Leave nothing to
chance. Don't let anyone come back later and say you
tampered or contaminated something. Get a warrant
before you go to Downing's house. Do everything by the
book.'

'I can do all that and still put out an APB.'

'Rolly, suppose Greg Downing did kill her. You put out
an APB, you know what happens? One, you look single-
minded. You look like you got it in your head that
Downing was the killer and that was it. Two, you got
the press in your face – watching your every move, trying
to beat you to the evidence, compromising and commenting on everything you do. Three, you drag Greg in
here now and you know what bottom-feeders are stuck to
him?'

Dimonte nodded and made a lemon-sucking face.
'Fucking lawyers.'

'A dream team's worth. Before you have anything, they're filing motions and suppressing whatever and, well, you know the routine.'

'Shit,' Dimonte said.

Myron nodded. 'You see what I mean?'

'Yeah, I do,' Dimonte said. 'But there's some stuff you forgot, Bolitar.' He gave Myron big-time toothpick gnawing. 'For example, if I issue an APB your little team investigation goes down the toilet. You lose out.'

'Could be,' Myron said.

Dimonte studied him with a small, uneven smile. 'That doesn't mean what you're saying is wrong. I just don't want you to think I don't see what you're up to.'

'You read me,' Myron said, 'like Vasco da Gama reads a map.'

Dimonte gave him hard eyes for a moment; Myron fought off the desire to roll his in return. 'So here's how we're going to play it. You're going stay on the team and you're going to continue your little investigation. I'm going to try to keep what you told me to myself as long' – he held up a finger for emphasis – 'as long as it benefits my case. If I find enough to haul Downing's ass in here, I put out the APB. And you are going to report everything to me. You are not going to hold back. Any questions?'

'Just one,' Myron said. 'Where do you buy your boots?'

Chapter 13

On the ride to practice, Myron placed a call from the car phone.

'Higgins,' a voice answered.

'Fred? It's Myron Bolitar.'

'Hey, long time, no speak. How you doing, Myron?'

'Can't complain. You?'

'A thrill a minute here at the Treasury Department.'

'Yeah, I bet.'

'How's Win?' Higgins asked.

'The same,' Myron said.

'The guy scares the piss out of me, you know what I mean?'

'Yes,' Myron said, 'I do.'

'You two miss working for the feds?'

'I don't,' Myron said. 'I don't think Win does either. It got too restrictive for him.'

'I hear you. Hey, I read in the papers you're playing ball again.'

'Yep.'

'At your age and with that knee? How come?'

'Long story, Fred.'

'Say no more. Hey, you guys are coming down to play the Bullets next week. Can you get me tickets?'

'I'll do my best.'

'Great, thanks. So what do you need, Myron?'

'The wheres and why of about ten grand in hundred dollar bills. Sequentially wrapped. Serial number B028856011A.'

'How fast you need it?'

'Soon as you can get it.'

'I'll do my best. You take care, Myron.'

'You too, Fred.'

Myron held nothing back at practice. He let it all hang out. The feeling was awesome and overpowering. He entered his own zone. When he shot, it was like an invisible hand carried the ball to the cylinder. When he dribbled, the ball became part of his hand. His senses were heightened like a wolf's in the wilderness. He felt like he'd fallen into some black hole and emerged ten years earlier at the NCAA finals. Even his knee felt great.

Most of practice consisted of a scrimmage between the starting five players and the five who saw the most bench time. Myron played his best ball. His jumper was popping. He came off screens strong and ready to shoot. He even drove straight down the lane twice – into the teeth of the big men's domain – and came away the victor both times.

There were moments he completely forgot about Greg Downing and Carla/Sally/Roberta's mangled corpse and the blood in the basement and the goons who jumped him and yes, even Jessica. An exhilarating rush like no other flooded his veins – the rush of an athlete at his peak. People talked about a runner's high, a euphoria from a gland secretion when your body was pressed to its limit. Myron couldn't relate to that, but he understood the incredible highs and plunging depths of being an athlete. If you played well, your whole body tingled and tears of pure joy came to your eyes. The tingles lasted well into the night when you lay in bed with no chance of sleep and replayed your finest moments, often in slow motion, like an overzealous sportscaster with his finger on the replay button. When you played poorly, you were surly and depressed and stayed that way for hours and even days. Both extremes were way out of proportion with the relevant importance of jamming a ball through a metallic circle or swatting a ball with a stick or throwing a sphere with great velocity. When you played poorly, you tried to remind yourself how stupid it was to get so caught up in something so meaningless. When you hit that rare high, you kept your internal big mouth shut.

As Myron dashed back and forth in the wave of basketball action, a thought sneaked in through the back door of his brain. The thought stayed on the fringes, hiding behind a couch, popping into view every once in a while before ducking back down again. *You can do this*, the thought taunted. *You can play with them.*

Myron's lucky streak continued when it came to his defensive assignment: Leon White, Greg's roomie-on-the-road and best friend. Myron and Leon bonded a bit while playing, the way teammates and even opponents often do. Whispering quick jokes in one another's ear while lined up chest-to-chest for an inbounds pass. Patting the other guy on the back when he made a nice play. Leon was a classy guy on the floor. No trash talk. Even when Myron burned his butt on a fade-away eighteen-footer, Leon offered only words of encouragement.

Coach Donny Walsh blew the whistle. 'That's it, fellas. Take twenty foul shots and go home.'

Leon and Myron exchanged a half-handshake, half-high-five the way only children and professional athletes can. Myron had always loved this part of the game, the almost soldierlike camaraderie; he hadn't had that in years. It felt good. The players partnered themselves up in groups of two – one guy to shoot, one to rebound – and went off to different baskets. Myron lucked out again and hooked up with Leon White. They each snatched a towel and a water bottle and strolled past the bleachers. Several reporters were perched up there for the practice. Audrey was there, of course. She looked at him with an amused smile. He resisted the temptation to stick his tongue out at her. Or his ass. Calvin Johnson had been watching practice too. He wore a suit and leaned against the wall like he was posing for a candid picture. Myron tried to gauge his reaction during the scrimmage, but of course Calvin's expression remained unreadable.

Myron shot first. He stood at the foul line, feet spread shoulder length, his eyes on the front rim. The ball backspun through the hoop.

'I guess we're going to be roommates,' Myron said.

'That's what I heard,' Leon said.

'Probably won't be for very long.' Myron took another shot. Swish. 'When do you think Greg will be back?'

In one motion Leon grabbed the bouncing ball and swooped it back to Myron. 'I don't know.'

'How's Greg feeling? The ankle doing okay?'

'I don't know,' he said again.

Myron took another foul shot. Another swish. His shirt, heavy with sweat, felt right. He grabbed the towel and wiped his face again. 'Have you talked to him at all?'

'No.'

'That's funny.'

Leon passed the ball to Myron. 'What's funny?'

Myron shrugged, took four dribbles. 'I heard you two were tight,' he said.

Leon gave a half-smile. 'Where did you hear that?'

Myron released the ball. Another swish. 'Around, I guess. In the newspapers and stuff.'

'Don't believe everything you read,' Leon said.

'Why's that?'

He bounce-passed the ball to Myron. 'The press loves to build up a friendship between a white player and a black player. They're always looking for that Gale Sayers-Brian Piccolo slant.'

'You two aren't close?'

'Well, we've known each other a long time. I'll say that.'

'But you're not tight?'

Leon looked at him funny. 'Why you so interested?'

'I'm just making conversation. Greg is my only real connection to this team.'

'Connection?'

Myron started dribbling again. 'He and I used to be rivals.'

'Yeah, so?'

'So now we're going to be teammates. It'll be weird.'

Leon looked at Myron. Myron stopped dribbling. 'You think Greg still cares about some old college rivalry?' There was disbelief in his voice.

Myron realized how lame he was sounding. 'It was a

pretty intense thing,' he said. 'At the time, I mean.' Extra lame. Myron didn't look at Leon. He just lined up the shot.

'I hope this don't hurt your feelings or nothing,' Leon said, 'but I've been rooming with Greg for eight years now. I've never heard him mention your name. Even when we talk about college and stuff.'

Myron stopped right before releasing the ball. He looked over at Leon, fighting to keep his face neutral. Funny thing was – much as Myron didn't want to admit it – that did hurt his feelings.

'Shoot already,' Leon said. 'I want to get out of here.'

TC lumbered toward them. He palmed a basketball in each hand with the ease most adults palm grapefruits. He dropped one of the balls and did a handshaking/slapping ritual with Leon. Then he looked over at Myron. His face broke into a big smile.

'I know, I know,' Myron said. 'Thumped, right?'

TC nodded.

'What exactly is thumped?'

'Tonight,' TC said. 'Party at my house. All will be revealed then.'

Chapter 14

Dimonte was waiting for him in the Meadowlands parking lot. He leaned out of his red Corvette. 'Get in.'

'A red Corvette,' Myron said. 'Why aren't I surprised?'

'Just get in.'

Myron opened the door and slid into the black leather seat. Though they were parked with the engine off, Dimonte gripped the steering wheel with both hands and stared in front of him. His face was sheet-white. The toothpick hung low. He kept shaking his head over and over. Yet again, the subtlety. 'Something wrong, Rolly?'

'What's Greg Downing like?'

'What?'

'You fucking deaf?' Dimonte snapped. 'What's he like?'

'I don't know. I haven't spoken to him in years.'

'But you knew him, right? In school. What was he like back then? Did he hang out with perversive types?'

Myron looked at him. 'Perversive types?'

'Just answer the question.'

'What the hell is this? Perversive types?'

Dimonte turned the ignition key. The sound was loud. He hit the gas a bit, let the engine do the rev thing for a while. The car had been jacked up like a race car. The sound was, like, totally rad, man. No women were in the nearby vicinity to hear this human mating call or they would surely be disrobing by now. Dimonte finally shifted into gear.

'Where we going?' Myron asked.

Dimonte didn't answer. He followed the ramp that leads from the arena to Giants Stadium and the horse track.

'Is this one of those mystery dates?' Myron asked. 'I love those.'

'Stop fucking around and answer my question.'

'What question?'

'What's Downing like? I need to know everything about him.'

'You're asking the wrong guy, Rolly. I don't know him that well.'

'Tell me what you do know.' Dimonte's voice left little room for disagreement. His tone was less fake-macho than usual, and there was a funny quake in it. Myron didn't like it.

'Greg grew up in New Jersey,' Myron began. 'He's a great basketball player. He's divorced with two kids.'

'You dated his wife, right?'

'A long time ago.'

'Would you say she was left-wing?'

'Rolly, this is getting too weird.'

'Just answer the goddamn question.' The tone aimed for angry and impatient, but fear seemed to overlap them. 'Would you call her politics radical?'

'No.'

'She ever hang out with perversives?'

'Is that even a word? Perversives?'

Dimonte shook his head. 'Do I look like I'm in the mood for your shit, Bolitar?'

'Okay, okay.' Myron made a surrendering gesture with his hands. The Corvette swerved across the empty stadium lot. 'No, Emily did not hang out with perversives, whatever they are.'

They headed past the racetrack and took the other ramp back toward the arena. It became apparent to Myron that they were just going to circle the Meadowlands' vast expanse of paved lots. 'Let's get back to Downing then.'

'I just told you we haven't talked in years.'

'But you know about him, right? You've been investigating him; you've probably read stuff about him.' Gear shift up. Extra rev power. 'Would you say he was a revolutionary?'

Myron could not believe these questions. 'No, Mr Chairman.'

'Do you know who he hangs out with?'

'Not really. He's supposed to be closest to his teammates, but Leon White – that's his roommate on the road – seemed less than enamored. Oh, here's something that might interest you: after home games, Greg drives a taxi in the city.'

Dimonte looked puzzled. 'You mean he picks up fares and stuff?'

'Yes.'

'Why the fuck does he do that?'

'Greg is a little' – Myron searched for the word – 'off.'

'Uh huh.' Dimonte rubbed his face vigorously, as if he were polishing a fender with a rag. He did this for several seconds, not looking at the road; fortunately, he was in the middle of an empty parking lot. 'Does it make him feel like a regular guy or something? Could that be part of it? Getting closer to the masses?'

'I guess,' Myron said.

'Go on. What about his interests? His hobbies?'

'He's a nature boy. He likes to fish and hunt and hike and boat, that goyish stuff.'

'A back-to-nature type?'

'Sort of.'

'Like maybe an outdoor, communal guy?'

'No. Like maybe an outdoor, loner guy.'

'You have any idea where he might be?'

'None.'

Dimonte hit the gas and circled the arena. He came to a stop in front of Myron's Ford Taurus and put the car in park. 'Okay, thanks for the help. We'll talk later.'

'Whoa, hold up a second. I thought we were working together on this.'

'You thought wrong.'

'You're not going to tell me what's going on?'

His voice was suddenly soft. 'No.'

Silence. The rest of the players were gone by now. The Taurus stood alone in the still, empty lot.

'It's that bad?' Myron said.

Dimonte kept frighteningly still.

'You know who she is, don't you?' Myron went on. 'You got an ID?'

Dimonte leaned back. Again he rubbed his entire face. 'Nothing confirmed,' he muttered.

'You got to tell me, Rolly.'

He shook his head. 'I can't.'

'I won't say anything. You know—'

'Get the fuck out of my car, Myron.' He leaned across Myron's lap and opened the car door. 'Now.'

143

Chapter 15

TC lived in a turn-of-the-century, red brick mansion encircled by a six-foot, matching brick fence on one of the better streets of Englewood, New Jersey. Eddie Murphy lived down the block. So did three Forbes 500 CEOs and several major Japanese bankers. There was a security post by the driveway entrance. Myron gave the security guard his name. The guard checked his clipboard.

'Please park along the drive. The party is out back.' He raised the yellow-and-black striped gate and waved him through. Myron parked next to a black BMW. There were maybe a dozen other cars, all glistening from fresh washes and waxes or perhaps they were all new. Mostly Mercedes Benzes. A few BMWs. A Bentley. A Jag. A Rolls. Myron's Taurus stood out like a zit in a Revlon commercial.

The front lawn was immaculately manicured. Perfectly pruned shrubs guarded and clung to the brick facade. In stark contrast to this majestic setting was the rap music blaring from the speakers. Awful. The shrubs looked pained by the sound. Myron didn't necessarily hate all rap. He knew there was worse music out there – John Tesh and Yanni proved it every day. Some rap songs Myron found engaging and even profound. He also recognized that rap music had not been written for him; he didn't get it all, but he suspected that he wasn't supposed to.

The party was held in the well-lit pool area. The crowd of about thirty mingled about in a fairly subdued fashion. Myron was wearing a blue blazer, a button-down pinstripe shirt, a flower tie, J. Murphy casual loafers. Bolitar the Prep. Win would be so proud. But Myron felt frighteningly underdressed next to his teammates. At the risk of sounding racist, the black guys on the team – there were only two other white players on the Dragons right now – knew how to dress with style. Not Myron's style (or lack thereof), but definitely with style. The group looked like they were readying themselves for a Milan runway walk. Perfectly tailored suits. Silk shirts buttoned to the neck. No ties. Shoes polished like twin mirrors.

TC reclined in a lounge chair by the shallow end of the pool. He was surrounded by a bunch of white guys who looked like college students. They were laughing at his every word. Myron also spotted Audrey in her customary reporter's garb. She had added pearls for the occasion. Really dressing up. He barely had a chance to step toward them when a woman in her late thirties/maybe forty approached him. 'Hello,' the woman said.

'Hi.' The Wordsmith Strikes Again.

'You must be Myron Bolitar. My name is Maggie Mason.'

'Hi, Maggie.' They shook hands. Firm grip, nice smile.

She was dressed conservatively in a white blouse, charcoal-gray blazer, red skirt, and black pumps. Her hair was down and slightly mussed, as if she'd just released her bun. She was slim and attractive and would have been the perfect choice to play the opposing attorney on *L.A. Law*.

She smiled at him. 'You don't know who I am, do you?'

'Sorry, I don't.'

'They call me Thumper.'

Myron waited. When she didn't add anything, he said, 'Uh huh.'

'Didn't TC tell you about this?'

'He mentioned something about getting thump . . .' He stopped midword. She just smiled at him and spread her arms. After some time had passed, he said, 'I don't get it.'

'Nothing to get,' she said matter-of-factly. 'I have sex with all the guys on the team. You're new to the team. It's your turn.'

Myron opened his mouth, closed it, tried again. 'You don't look like a groupie.'

'Groupie.' She shook her head. 'God, I hate that word.'

Myron closed his eyes and pinched the bridge of his nose. 'Let me see if I'm getting this.'

'Go ahead.'

'You've slept with every guy on the Dragons?'

'Yes.'

'Even the married ones?'

'Yes,' she replied. 'Anyone who has been on the team since 1993. That's when I started with the Dragons. I started with the Giants in 1991.'

'Wait a second. You're a groupie for the Giants, too? The football Giants?'

146

'I told you. I don't like the term groupie.'

'What word would you be more comfortable with?'

She tilted her head a little and kept the smile. 'Look, Myron, I'm an investment banker on Wall Street. I work very hard. I like taking cooking classes and I'm a step-aerobics nut. All in all I am pretty normal by this world's standards. I don't hurt anybody. I don't want to get married or have a relationship. But I have this one little fetish.'

'You have sex with professional athletes.'

She held up her index finger. 'Only with the guys on the Giants and Dragons.'

'Nice to see team loyalty,' Myron said, 'in this era of free agency.'

Thumper laughed. 'That's pretty funny.'

'Are you telling me you've slept with every player on the Giants?'

'Just about. I have tickets on the fifty-yard line. After every game, I have sex with two players – one from the defense, and one from the offense.'

'Sort of like the game MVPs?'

'Exactly.'

Myron shrugged. 'Beats getting the game ball, I guess.'

'Yes,' she said slowly. 'It definitely beats getting a game ball.'

Myron rubbed his eyes. *Ground control to Major Tom.* He studied her for a moment. She seemed to be doing the same thing to him. 'So how did you get the nickname Thumper?' he asked.

'It's not what you think.'

'What's not what I think?'

'How I got the nickname. Everyone assumes it has something to do with screwing like a rabbit.'

'And it doesn't?'

'No, it doesn't.' She looked up in the air. 'How do I explain this delicately?'

'You're worried about delicacy?'

She gave him a mildly disapproving look. 'Don't be like that.'

'Like what?'

'Like some right-wing, narrow-minded, Pat Buchanan-type Neanderthal. I have feelings.'

'I didn't say you didn't.'

'No, but you're acting like it. I don't hurt anyone. I'm honest. I'm forward. I'm direct. I control what I do and to whom. And I'm happy.'

'Not to mention disease-ridden,' he heard himself say and immediately regretted it. The words had just slipped out; that happened to him sometimes.

'What?'

'I'm sorry,' he said. 'That was uncalled for.'

But he had hit a nerve. 'The men I have sex with always wear condoms,' she snapped. 'I get tested frequently. I'm clean.'

'I'm sorry. I shouldn't have said anything.'

She didn't stop. 'And I don't sleep with anyone I think might be infected with something. I'm careful that way.'

Myron bit his lip this time. No point. 'My mistake,' he said. 'I didn't mean it; I'm sorry. Please accept my apology.'

Her chest heaved, but she was calm now, 'Okay,' she said with an exhale. 'Apology accepted.'

Her eyes met his again. They smiled at each other for far too long. Myron felt like a game-show contestant. A thought thankfully interrupted the semitrance. 'Did you sleep with Greg Downing?' he asked.

'In 1993,' she said. 'He was one of the first Dragons.'

How that must swell his bosom with pride. 'You still see him?'

'Sure. We're good friends. I'm friends with most of the guys afterwards. Not all, but most.'

'Do you two talk a lot?'

'Sometimes.'

'Recently?'

'Not the past month or two.'

'Do you know if he's seeing anyone?'

Thumper gave him a curious look. 'Why would you want to know about that?'

Myron shrugged. 'Just making conversation.' The Return of Mr Lame.

'It's an odd topic,' she said.

'I guess I've been thinking about him a lot. All this talk about my being on Greg's team and our history together. It just got me thinking.'

'It got you thinking about Greg's love life?' She wasn't buying it.

Myron sort of shrugged and mumbled something even he didn't understand. A laugh broke out from the other side of the pool. A group of his new teammates were enjoying a joke. Leon White was one of them. He met Myron's eye and nodded a hello. Myron nodded back. Myron realized that while no one seemed to be staring at them, all of his teammates had to know why Thumper had approached him. Again he felt like he was back in college, but this time the feeling didn't bring on the same happy nostalgia.

Thumper was busy studying him again, her eyes narrowed and focused. Myron tried to look neutral, but he felt like a doofus. Being so openly inspected did that to him. He tried to meet her gaze.

Thumper suddenly smiled widely and folded her arms. 'I get it now,' she said.

'What?'

'It's obvious.'

'What's obvious?'

'You want revenge,' she said.

'Revenge for what?'

The smile grew a bit, then relaxed. 'Greg stole Emily from you. Now you want to steal someone back.'

'He didn't steal her from me,' Myron said quickly. He heard the defensive tone in his voice and didn't like it. 'Emily and I broke up before they started dating.'

'If you say so.'

'I say so.' Mr Snappy Retort.

She let loose a throaty laugh and put a hand on his arm. 'Relax, Myron. I'm only teasing you.' She looked at him again. All of this eye contact was beginning to give Myron a headache. He stared at her nose instead. 'So are we going to do this?' she asked.

'No,' Myron said.

'If it's the fear of disease—'

'It's not. I'm involved with someone.'

'So?'

'So I don't cheat on her.'

'Who wants you to cheat? I just want to have sex with you.'

'And you think those two things are mutually exclusive?'

'Of course they are,' Thumper said. 'Our having sex should have absolutely no effect on your relationship. I don't want you to stop caring about your girlfriend. I don't want to be a part of your life. I don't even want to be intimate.'

'Gee, you make it sound so romantic,' Myron said.

'But that's just the point. It's not romantic. It's just a physical act. Sure, it feels great, but in the end it's just a physical act. Like shaking hands.'

'Shaking hands,' Myron repeated. 'You should write greeting cards.'

'I'm just telling you how it is. Past civilizations – ones far more intellectually advanced than us – understood that pleasure of the flesh was no sin. Associating sex with guilt is a modern, absurd hang-up. This whole concept of tying sex to possession is something we got from uptight Puritans who wanted to maintain control over their major possession: their wife.'

A history scholar, Myron thought. Nice to see.

'Where is it written,' she continued, 'that two people can't reach heights of physical ecstasy without being in love? I mean, think about how ridiculous that is. It's silly, isn't it?'

'Maybe,' Myron said. 'But I'll still pass, thank you.'

She shrugged a suit-yourself. 'TC will be very disappointed.'

'He'll get over it,' he said.

Silence.

'Well,' she said, clasping her hands together, 'I think I'll mingle. It was nice chatting with you, Myron.'

'A true experience,' Myron agreed.

Myron mingled a bit, too. He hooked up with Leon for a while. Leon introduced him to his wife, a blond sex-pot named Fiona. Very Playmate-like. She had a breathy voice and was one of those women who made even the most casual conversation one long double entendre – so accustomed to using her physical charms that she did not know when to turn them off. Myron chatted with them both briefly and excused himself.

The bartender informed him that they were not stocking any Yoo-Hoo. He took an Orangina instead. Not just orange soda, but Orangina. How European. He took a sip. Pretty good.

A hand slapped Myron's back. It was TC. He had foregone the *GQ*-suit look, opting for white leather pants and a white leather vest. No shirt. He wore dark sunglasses.

'Having a good time?' he asked.

'It's been interesting,' Myron said.

'Come on. I'll show you something.'

They walked in silence up a grassy hill away from the party. The incline grew steadily steeper, the music fainter. The rap had been replaced with an alternative group called the Cranberries. Myron liked their music. 'Zombie' was on right now. Dolores O'Riordan was repeatedly singing, 'In your head, in your head,' until she got tired and moved to repeating the word, 'Zombie, zombie' several hundred times. Okay, the Cranberries could work on their chorus lyrics, but the song still worked. Good stuff.

There were no lights now, but a glow from the ones by the pool provided enough illumination. When they reached the plateau, TC motioned in front of them. 'There.'

Myron looked out, and the sight nearly took his breath away. They were up high enough to get an unimpeded, spectacular view of the Manhattan skyline. The sea of lights seemed to shimmer like beads of water. The George

Washington Bridge looked close enough to touch. They both stood in silence for several moments.

'Nice, huh?' TC said.

'Very.'

He took off his sunglasses. 'I come up here a lot. By myself. It's a good place to think.'

'I would think so.'

They looked off again.

'Thumper talk to you yet?' Myron asked.

TC nodded.

'Were you disappointed?'

'No,' TC said. 'I knew you'd say no.'

'How?'

He shrugged. 'Just a feeling. But don't let her fool you. Thumper's good people. She's probably the closest thing I got to a friend.'

'What about all those guys you were hanging out with?'

TC sort of smiled. 'You mean the white boys?'

'Yeah.'

'Not friends,' he said. 'If tomorrow I stopped playing ball, they'd all look at me like I'm pinching on a loaf on their sofa.'

'Poetically put, TC.'

'Just the truth, man. You in my position, you don't have no friends. Facts of life. White or black, it don't matter. People hang around me because I'm a rich super-star. They figure they can get something for free. That's all.'

'And that's okay with you?'

'Don't matter if it's okay,' TC said. 'It's the way it is. I ain't complaining.'

'Do you get lonely?' Myron asked.

153

'Too many people around to get lonely.'

'You know what I mean.'

'Yeah, I know what you mean.' TC sort of jerked his head from side to side, like he was trying to loosen up his neck before a game. 'Folks always talking about the price of fame, but you wanna know the real price? Forget that privacy shit. So I don't go out to the movies as much. Big fucking deal – where I come from you can't afford to go anyway. The real price is you ain't a person anymore. You're just a thing, a shiny thing like one of those Benzes out there. The poor brothers think I'm a golden ladder with goodies at every step up. The rich white boys think I'm a fancy pet. Like with OJ. Remember those guys who hung out in OJ's trophy room?'

Myron nodded.

'Look, I ain't complaining. Don't get me wrong. This is a whole lot better than pumping gas or working in a coal mine or something. But I always got to remember the truth: the only thing that separates me from any nigger on the street is a game. That's it. A knee going pop, like with what happened to you, and I'm back down there. I always remember that. Always.' He gave Myron hard eyes, letting his words hang in the crisp air. 'So when some hot babe acts like I'm something special, it ain't me she's after. You see what I'm saying? She's blinded by all that money and fame. Everyone is, male or female.'

'So you and I could never be friends?' Myron asked.

'Would you be asking me that if I was just some ignorant fool pumping gas?'

'Maybe.'

'Bullshit,' he said with a smile. 'People bitch about my attitude, you know. They say I act like everybody owes me. Like I'm a prima donna. But they just mad because I see through them. I know the truth. They all think I'm some ignorant nigger – the owners, the coaches, whatever – so why should I respect them? Only reason they even talk to me is because I can slam the ball through the hoop. I'm just a monkey making them money. Once I stop, that's it. I'm just another dumb slice of ghetto shit not fit to sit my black ass on their toilet.' He stopped then, as though out of breath. He looked back at the skyline. The sight seemed to rejuvenate him. 'You ever meet Isiah Thomas?' he asked.

'The Detroit Piston? Yeah, once.'

'I heard him doing this interview one time, must have been when the Pistons won those championships. Some guy asked him what he'd be doing if he wasn't a basketball player. You know what Isiah said?'

Myron shook his head.

'He said he'd be a United States senator.' TC laughed hard and high-pitched. The sound echoed in the still night. 'I mean, is the brother crazy or what? Isiah really believe that shit. A United States senator – who the fuck is he kidding?' He laughed again, but the sound seemed more forced now. 'Me, I know what I'd be. I'd be working in a steel mill, the midnight to ten A.M. shift, or maybe I'd be in jail or dead, I don't know.' He shook his head. 'United States senator. Shit.'

'What about the game?' Myron asked.

'What about it?'

'Do you love playing basketball?'

He looked amused. 'You do, don't you? You buy all that "for the love of the game" bullshit.'

'You don't?'

TC shook his head. The moon reflected off his shaved pate, giving his head an almost mystical glow. 'It was never about that for me,' he said. 'Basketball was just a means to an end. It's about making money. It's about setting me up for life.'

'Did you ever love the game?'

'Sure, I guess I must have. It was a good place to go, you know? But I don't think it was the game – I mean, not the running and jumping and shit. Basketball was just what I was all about. Everywhere else I was just another dumb black boy, but on the basketball court, I was, well, the man. A hero. It's an incredible high, everyone treating you like that. You know what I mean?'

Myron nodded. He knew. 'Can I ask you something else?'

'Go ahead.'

'What's with all the tattoos and rings?'

He smiled. 'They bother you?'

'Not really. I'm just curious.'

'Suppose I just like wearing them,' TC said. 'That enough?'

'Yes,' Myron said.

'But you don't believe it, do you?'

Myron shrugged. 'I guess not.'

'Truth is, I do like them a little. The bigger truth is, it's business.'

'Business?'

'Basketball business. Making money. Lots of it. You know how much money I make in endorsements? A shit load. Why? Because outrageousness sells. Look at Deon. Look at Rodman. The more crazy shit I do, the more they pay me.'

'So it's just an act?'

'A lot of it, yeah. I like to shock, too, just my way. But mostly I do it for the press.'

'But the press is always ripping you apart,' Myron said.

'Don't matter. They write about me, they make me more money. Simple as that.' He smiled. 'Let me clue you in on something, Myron. The press is the dumbest animal on God's green earth. You know what I'm gonna do one day?'

Myron shook his head.

'One day I'll get rid of the rings and shit, and I'll start dressing nice. Then I'll start talking polite, you know, giving them all yes-sirs and yes-ma'ams and start spitting out all that team-effort bullshit they like to hear. You know what'll happen? These same fucks that say I'm destroying the integrity of the game will be kissing my black ass like it's the Blarney Stone. They be talking about how I went through some sort of miraculous trans-formation. How now I'm a hero. But only thing that's really changed is my act.' TC gave him a big smile.

Myron said, 'You're a piece of work, TC.'

TC turned back to the water. Myron watched him in silence. He hadn't bought all of TC's rationalizations. There was more at work here. TC wasn't lying, but he wasn't exactly telling the truth either – or maybe he couldn't admit the truth even to himself. He hurt. He truly believed no one could love him, and no matter who you are, that hurts. It made you insecure. It made you want to hide and build fences. The sad thing was, TC was at least partially right. Who'd care about him if he wasn't playing professional basketball? If not for his ability to play a child's game, where would he be right now? TC was like the beautiful girl who wanted you to look down deep to find the soul within – but the only reason you'd bother trying was because she was beautiful. Get rid of that physical beauty – become the ugly girl – and nobody gives a damn about scratching the surface to find the beauty within. Get rid of TC's physical prowess and the same thing happens.

In the end, TC was not as off-the-wall as he appeared in public nor was he as put-together as he wanted Myron to think. Myron was no psychologist, but he was sure that there was more to the tattoos and body piercing than making money. They were too physically destructive for so pat an explanation. With TC, there were a lot of factors at work. Being a former basketball star himself, Myron understood some of them; being that Myron and TC came from completely different worlds, there were others he could not so readily grasp.

TC interrupted their joint solitude. 'Now I got a question for you,' he said.

'Shoot.'

'Why you really here?' TC asked.

'Here? As in your house—'

'On the team. Look, man, I saw you play when I was in junior high. In the NCAAs. You were great, okay? But that was a long time ago. You got to know you can't do it anymore. You had to see that at practice today.'

Myron tried not to look stunned. Had he and TC been at the same practice? But of course they had, and of course, TC was right. Didn't Myron remember the days when he was the team's superstar? Didn't he remember scrimmaging against the last five guys who would play their butt off while the starting five screwed around and played with no incentive? Didn't he remember how disillusioned those last five became, fooling themselves into believing they were just as good as the first five when the first five were tired from real games and were just slacking off? And back then, Myron was in college. He played maybe twenty-five games a season – these guys played almost a hundred against vastly superior competition.

Good enough to play with these guys? Who had he been kidding?

'I'm just giving it a shot,' Myron said softly.

'Can't let go, huh?'

Myron said nothing. They fell back into a brief silence.

'Hey, I almost forgot,' TC said. 'I hear you're good friends with a big hotshot at Lock-Horne Securities. That true?'

'Yes.'

'Was he that slice of white bread you talking with after the game?'

Myron nodded. 'His name is Win.'

'You know Thumper works on Wall Street, right?'

'She told me,' Myron said.

'Thumper wants to change jobs. Think your friend could talk to her?'

Myron shrugged. 'I could ask him.' Win would certainly appreciate her outlook on the role of sex in ancient civilizations. 'Who does she work for now?'

'Small outfit. Called Kimmel Brothers. But she needs to move on, you know? They won't make her a partner, even though she busts her butt for them.'

TC said something else but Myron was no longer listening. Kimmel Brothers. Myron remembered the name immediately. When he'd hit the redial button on the phone at Greg's house, a woman had answered and said, 'Kimmel Brothers.' Yet Thumper had just told Myron she hadn't spoken to Greg in a month or two.

Coincidence? Myron thought not.

Chapter 16

Thumper was gone.

'She came for you,' TC said. 'When it didn't happen she split. She got work tomorrow morning.'

Myron checked his watch. Eleven-thirty. Long day. Time for a little shut-eye. He made his good nights and headed for his car. Audrey was leaning against the hood, her arms folded across her chest, her ankles crossed. Pure casual.

'You going back to Jessica's?' she asked.

'Yes.'

'Mind giving me a lift?'

'Hop in.'

Audrey gave him the same smile he had seen back at practice. He had thought at the time she had been impressed with his play; now it was clearer that the amusement was more akin to ridicule than appreciation. He unlocked the doors in silence. She took off her blue blazer and laid it on the backseat; he did likewise. She wore a forest green turtleneck underneath it. She adjusted the neck part, folding it back an extra time. She took off the pearls and jammed them in the front pocket of her jeans. Myron started the car.

'I'm starting to put this thing together,' Audrey said.

Myron did not like the way she said it. Too much authority in her voice. Audrey hadn't needed a lift home, he was sure of that. She wanted to talk to him alone. That worried him. He gave her the good-natured smile and said, 'This doesn't have anything to do with my ass, does it?'

'What?'

'Jessica told me you two were discussing my ass.'

She laughed. 'Well, I hate to admit this,' she said, 'but it did look pretty scrumptious.'

Myron tried not to look too pleased. 'So you doing a story on it?'

'On your ass?'

'Yes.'

'Of course,' she said. 'I was thinking we could give it a big spread.'

Myron groaned.

'You're trying to change the subject,' she said.

'There was a subject?'

'I was telling you how I was putting this thing to-gether.'

'That's a subject?'

He glanced at her. She was sitting with her left knee on the seat and her left ankle tucked under her so her entire body could face him. Audrey had a wide face and a few freckles, though he bet she had a lot more when she was a kid. Remember that tomboy who was kinda cute in your sixth grade class? Here she was all grown up. No beauty certainly. Not in the classic sense. But there was an earthy appeal to Audrey that made you want to reach out and hug her and roll in leaves on a crisp autumn day.

'It shouldn't have taken me so long to figure out,' she continued. 'It's pretty obvious in hindsight.'

'Am I supposed to know what you're talking about?'

'No,' she replied. 'You're supposed to continue to play dumb for a few more minutes.'

'My specialty.'

'Good, then just drive and listen.' Her hands were in constant gesturing motion, peaking and valleying along with her voice. 'See, I was waylaid by the whole poetic irony stuff. That's what I concentrated on. But your backgrounds as rivals is secondary in all this. It's not nearly as important as, say, your past relationship with Emily.'

'I have no idea what you're talking about.'

'You didn't play AAU. You didn't play in any summer league. You play in pickup games at the Y maybe once a week. Your major workout revolves around Master Kwon's place with Win – and they don't have a basketball court.'

'Is there a point?'

Her hands spread in disbelief. 'You haven't been honing your skills. You haven't played anyplace where Clip or Calvin or Donny would have seen you play. So why would the Dragons sign you? It doesn't make sense. Was the move strictly P.R.? Unlikely. The positive bump will be minimum, and if you fail – which, let's face it, is very likely – that good publicity will probably be nullified. Ticket sales are good. The team is doing well. They don't need a publicity stunt right now. So there has to be another reason.' She stopped and readjusted herself on the car seat. 'Enter the timing.'

'The timing?'

'Yes,' she said. 'Why now? Why sign you so late in the season? The answer is obvious really. There is only one thing about the timing that stands out.'

'And that is?'

'Downing's sudden disappearance.'

'He didn't disappear,' Myron corrected. 'He's injured. That's your precious timing. Greg got hurt. A spot opened up. I filled it.'

Audrey smiled and shook her head. 'Still want to play dumb, huh? Fine, go ahead. You're right. Downing is supposed to be injured and in seclusion. Now I'm good, Myron, and for the life of me I can't find this secluded spot of his. I've called in all my best contacts and I can't get anything. Don't you find that a bit odd?'

Myron shrugged.

'Maybe,' she went on, 'if Downing really craved seclusion to fix his injured ankle – an injury which doesn't show up on any game tape, by the way – he could find a way. But if all he's doing is working on an injury, why work so hard at it?'

'So pain in the asses like you don't bother him,' Myron said.

Audrey almost laughed at that one. 'Said with such conviction, Myron. It's almost like you believe it.'

Myron said nothing.

'But let me just add a few more points and then you can stop playing dumb.' Audrey counted them off on ringless, slightly callused fingers. 'One, I know you used to work for the feds. That gives you some background in investigative work. Two, I know Downing has a habit of vanishing. He's done it before. Three, I know Clip's situation with the other owners. The big vote is coming up. Four, I know you visited Emily yesterday and I doubt you were there to restoke the flames.'

'How did you know about that?' Myron asked.

She just smiled and put her hand down. 'Add them up and there's only one conclusion: you are looking for Greg Downing. He's missing again. This time however the timing is much more critical; Clip's ownership vote and the playoffs are coming up. Your job is to find him.'

'You got a hell of an imagination, Audrey.'

'I do at that,' she agreed, 'but we both know I got this right so let's end playing dumb and cut to the heart of it: I want in.'

'Want in.' Myron shook his head. 'You reporters and your lingo.'

'I don't want to give you up,' she continued. Her knee was still up on the seat. Her face was as bright and expectant as a school kid's waiting for the final bell in May. 'I think we should team up. I can help. I got great sources. I can ask questions without worrying about blowing my cover. I know this team inside and out.'

'And what exactly do you want for this help?'

'The full story. I'm the first reporter to know where he is, why he vanished, whatever. You promise to tell only me; I get the full exclusive.'

They passed several sleazy motels and a potpourri of gas stations on Route 4. No-tell motels in New Jersey always gave themselves lofty names that belied their social station. Right now, for example, they were driving past the 'Courtesy Inn.' This fine establishment not only gave you courteous attention, but they gave it to you by the hour at a rate, according to the sign, of $19.82. Not twenty dollars, mind you, but $19.82 – so priced, Myron guessed, because it was also the year they last changed sheets. The CHEAP BEER DEPOT, according to another sign, was the next building on Myron's right. Truth in advertising. Nice to see. The Courtesy Inn could learn a lesson from them.

'We both know I could report it now,' she said. 'It'd still be a pretty good scoop – reporting that Downing wasn't really injured and you're just here to find him. But I'd be willing to trade it in for a larger story.'

Myron thought it over as he paid the toll. He glanced at her expectant face. She looked wild-eyed and wild-haired, kind of like the refugee women coming off the boat in Palestine in the movie *Exodus*. Ready to do battle to claim her homeland.

'You have to make me a promise,' he said.

'What?'

'No matter what – no matter how incredible the story seems – you won't jump the gun. You won't report any of it until he's found.'

Audrey nearly leapt from her seat. 'What do you mean? How incredible?'

'Forget it, Audrey. Report whatever you want.'

'All right, all right, you have a deal,' she said quickly, hands raised in surrender. 'You had to know saying something like that would pique my interest.'

'You promise?'

'Yeah, yeah, I promise. So what's up?'

Myron shook his head. 'You first,' he said. 'Why would Greg vanish?'

'Who knows?' she replied. 'The man is a professional flake.'

'What can you tell me about his divorce?'

'Just that's it's been acrimonious as all hell.'

'What have you heard?'

165

'They've been battling over the kids. They're both trying to prove the other is an unfit parent.'

'Any details on how they're going about that?'

'No. It's been kept pretty hush-hush.'

'Emily told me Greg had pulled some sleazy tricks,' Myron said. 'Do you know anything about that?'

Audrey chewed on her bottom lip for a few moments. 'I heard a rumor – a very unsubstantiated rumor – that Greg hired a private eye to follow her.'

'Why?'

'I don't know.'

'To film her maybe? Catch her with another man?'

She shrugged. 'It's just a rumor. I don't know.'

'You know the P.I.'s name, or who he works for?'

'Rumor, Myron. Rumor. A pro basketball player's divorce is hardly earth-shattering sports news. I didn't follow it that closely.'

Myron made a mental note to check Greg's files for any payment to an investigation firm. 'How was Greg's relationship with Marty Felder?'

'His agent? Good, I guess.'

'Emily told me Felder had lost Greg millions.'

She shrugged. 'I've never heard anything about that.'

The Washington Bridge was fairly clear. They stayed to the left and took the Henry Hudson Parkway south. On their right, the Hudson River sparkled like a blanket of black sequins; on their left was a billboard with Tom Brokaw displaying his friendly yet firm smile. The caption under his picture read: 'NBC News – Now More Than Ever.' Very dramatic. What the hell did it mean?

'How about Greg's personal life?' Myron continued. 'Girlfriends, that kind of thing?'

'You mean a steady?'

'Yes.'

She ran her fingers through the thick, curling locks, then rubbed the back of her own neck. 'There was this one girl. He kept it kind of secret, but I think they were living together for a while.'

'What's her name?'

'He never told me. I saw them together at a restaurant once. A place called the Saddle River Inn. He didn't look happy to see me.'

'What did she look like?'

'Nothing special from what I remember. She was a brunette. She was sitting so I couldn't tell you height or weight.'

'Age?'

'I don't know. Thirty-ish, I guess.'

'What makes you think they were living together?'

It seemed like an easy question, but she stopped and raised her eyes. 'Leon let something slip once,' she said.

'What did he say?'

'I don't remember anymore. Something about the girl-friend. Then he clammed up.'

'How long ago was this?'

'Three, four months ago. Maybe more.'

'Leon implied that he and Greg weren't really that close, that the media made a bigger deal out of it than it was.'

Audrey nodded. 'There is a tension there now, but I think it's just temporary.'

'Why would there be a tension?'

'I don't know.'

'How long have you noticed the tension?'

'Not long. Within the last two weeks maybe.'

'Anything happen recently between Greg and Leon that you're aware of?'

'Nope. They've been friends for a long time. Friends have disagreements. I didn't take it too seriously.'

Myron let loose a deep breath. Friends did indeed have disagreements, but the timing was curious. 'Do you know Maggie Mason?'

'Thumper? Of course.'

'Were she and Greg close?'

'If you mean did they screw—'

'No, I don't mean that.'

'Well, they screwed. That I'm sure of. Despite what Thumper claims, not every guy on the team has gotten thumped. Some have turned her down. Not many, I admit. But some. She hit on you yet?'

'Just a few short hours ago.'

She smiled. 'I assume you joined the few, the proud, the Unthumped?'

'You assume correctly. But what about her relationship with Greg? Are they close?'

'They're pretty close, I'd say. But Thumper is closest to TC. Those two are very tight. It's not purely sexual either. Don't get me wrong. I'm sure TC and Maggie have had sex and probably still do on occasions. But they're like brother and sister too. It's weird.'

'How do TC and Greg get along?' Myron asked.

'Not bad for team superstars. Not great either.'

'Care to elaborate?'

She paused, gathered her thoughts. 'For five years now, TC and Downing have shared the spotlight. I guess there is a mutual respect for each other on the court, but they don't talk off it. At least, not very much. I'm not saying they dislike each other, but playing basketball is a job like any other. You might be able to stand one another at work, but you don't want to see the person socially.' She looked up. 'Take the Seventy-ninth Street exit.'

'You still live on Eighty-first?'

'Yes.'

Myron took the exit and stopped at a traffic light on Riverside Drive.

'Now it's your turn, Myron. Why did they hire you?'

'It's like you said. They want me to find Greg.'

'What have you learned so far?'

'Not much.'

'So why were you so concerned I'd jump the gun and tell the story early?'

Myron hesitated.

'I promised not to say anything,' she reminded him. 'You have my word.'

Fair is fair. He told her about the blood in Greg's basement. Her mouth dropped open. When he told her about finding Sally/Carla's body, he feared her heart might give out.

'My God,' Audrey said when he finished. 'You think Downing killed her.'

'I didn't say that.'

She fell back against the seat. Her head lolled against the headrest as though her neck could no longer support her. 'Christ, what a story.'

'And one you can't tell.'

'Don't remind me.' She sat back up again. 'Do you think it'll leak soon?'

'It might.'

'Why can't I be the recipient of that leak?'

Myron shook his head. 'Not yet. We got a lid on this so far. You can't be the one to blow it off.'

Her nod was grudging. 'Do you think Downing killed her and ran?'

'There is no evidence of that.' He pulled up to her building. 'One last question,' he said. 'Was Greg involved in anything unsavory?'

'Like what?'

'Like is there any reason thugs would be after him?'

Again her excitement was palpable. The woman was like an electric current. 'What do you mean? What thugs?'

'A couple of thugs were watching Greg's house.'

Her face was positively glowing. 'Thugs? You mean like professional gangsters?'

'Probably. I don't know for sure yet. Can you think of anything that would connect Greg to thugs or for that matter, the murder of this woman? Drugs maybe?'

Audrey shook her head immediately. 'It can't be drugs.'

'What makes you so sure?'

'Downing is a health nut, a real Granola head.'

'So was River Phoenix.'

She shook her head again. 'Not drugs. I'm sure of it.'

'Look into it,' he said. 'See what you can come up with.'

'Sure,' she said. 'I'll look into everything we talked about.'

'Try to be discreet.'

'No problem,' she said. She got out of the car. 'Good night, Myron. Thanks for trusting me.'

'Like I had a choice.'

Audrey smiled and closed the car door. He watched her walk into the building. He put the car back in drive and headed back to Seventy-ninth Street. He got back on the parkway and continued south toward Jessica's. He was about to pick up his cellular phone and call her when the phone rang. The dashboard clock read 12:07 A.M. It had to be Jessica.

'Hello?'

It wasn't Jessica. 'Right lane, three cars behind you. You're being followed.'

It was Win.

Chapter 17

'When did you get back?' Myron asked.

Win ignored the question. 'The automobile following you is the same one we spotted at Greg's house. It is registered to a storage facility in Atlantic City. No known mob connections, but that would seem to me to be a safe bet.'

'How long have you been following me?'

Again Win ignored him. 'The two men who jumped you the other night. What did they look like?'

'Big,' Myron said. 'One was absolutely huge.'

'Crew cut?'

'Yes.'

'He's in the car following you. Passenger seat.'

Myron didn't bother asking how Win knew about the thugs jumping him. He had a pretty good idea.

'They've been communicating on the telephone quite a bit,' Win continued. 'I believe they're coordinating with someone else. The phone activity picked up after your stop on Eighty-first Street. Hold on a second. I'll call you right back.' He hung up. Myron checked his rearview mirror. The car was still there, right where Win said it was. A minute later the phone rang again.

'What?' Myron said.

'I just spoke to Jessica again.'

'What do you mean, again?'

Win sighed impatiently. He hated explanations. 'If they are planning to jump you tonight, it is logical to assume it will be by her loft.'

'Right.'

'Ergo, I called her ten minutes ago. I told her to keep an eye out for anything unusual.'

'And?'

'An unmarked white van parked across the street,' Win answered. 'No one got out.'

'So it appears they are going to strike,' Myron said.

'Yes,' Win said. 'Should I preempt it?'

'How?'

'I could disable the car following you.'

'No,' Myron said. 'Let them make their move and see where it leads.'

'Pardon?'

'Just back me up. If they grab me, I may be able to get to the boss.'

Win made a noise.

'What?' Myron asked.

'You complicate the simple,' Win said. 'Would it not be easier to simply take out the two in the car? We could then make them tell us about their boss.'

'It's that "make them" part I have trouble with.'

'But of course,' Win countered. 'A thousand pardons for my lack of ethics. Clearly it is far wiser to risk your own life than to make a worthless goon feel momentary discomfort.'

Win had a way of putting things that made very frightening sense. Myron had to remind himself that the logical was often more terrifying than the illogical – especially where Win was concerned. 'They're just hired help,' Myron said. 'They're not going to know anything.'

Pause. 'Fair point,' Win conceded. 'But suppose they simply shoot you.'

'That wouldn't make any sense. The reason they're interested in me is because they think I know where Greg is.'

'And dead men tell no tales,' Win added.

'Exactly. They want to make me talk. So just follow me. If they take me some place well guarded—'

'I'll get through,' Win said.

Myron did not doubt it. He gripped the steering wheel. His pulse began to race. Easy to dismiss the possibility of getting shot by reasonable analysis; it was another thing to have to park a car down the street from men you knew were out to hurt you. Win would have his eye on the van. So would Myron. If a gun came out before a person, the situation would be handled.

He got off the highway. The streets of Manhattan were supposed to be a nice, even grid. Streets ran north/south and east/west. They were numbered. They were straight. But when you got to Greenwich Village and Soho, it was like a grid painted by Dali. Gone were the numerical roads for the most part, except when they twisted and turned between streets with real-live names. Gone was any pretext of straight or systematized.

Luckily Spring Street was a direct run. A bicyclist sped by Myron, but no one else was out. The white van was parked right where it was supposed to be. Unmarked, just as Jessica had said. The windows were tinted so you couldn't look in. Myron didn't see Win's car, but then again he wasn't supposed to. He moved slowly down the street. He passed the van. When he did, the van started its motor. Myron pulled into a spot toward the end of the block. The van pulled out.

Show time.

Myron parked the car, straightened out the steering wheel, turned the engine off. He pocketed the keys. The van inched forward. He took out his revolver and stuck it under the car seat. It wouldn't do him any good right now. If they grabbed him, they would search him. If they started shooting, shooting back would be a waste of time. Win would either remove the threat or not.

He reached for the door handle. Fear nestled into his throat, but he did not stop. He pulled the handle, opened the door, and stepped out. It was dark. The streetlights in Soho were nearly worthless, like pen beams in a black hole. Lights drifting out from nearby windows provided more of an eerie kindle than real illumination. There were plastic garbage bags out on the street. Most had been torn open; the odor of spoiled food wafted through the air. The van slowly cruised toward him. A man stepped out from a doorway and approached without hesitation. The man wore a black turtleneck under a black overcoat. He pointed a gun at Myron. The van stopped, and the side door slid open.

'Get in, asshole,' the man with the gun said.

Myron pointed at himself. 'You talking to me?'

'Now, asshole. Haul ass.'

'Is that a turtleneck or a dickey?'

The man with the gun moved closer. 'I said, now.'

'It's nothing to get angry about,' Myron said, but he

stepped toward the van. 'If it is a dickey, you can't tell. It's a very sporty look.' When Myron got nervous, his mouth went into overdrive. He knew it was self-destructive; Win had pointed that out to him on several occasions. But Myron couldn't stop himself. Diarrhea of the mouth or some such ailment.

'Move.'

Myron got in the van. The man with the gun did likewise. There were two more men in the back of the van and one man driving. Everyone was in black, except for one guy who looked to be in charge. He wore a blue pinstripe suit. His Windsor-knotted yellow tie was held in place by a gold tie bar at the collar. Euro-chic. He had long, bleached-blond hair and one of those tans that were a little too perfect to come from the sun. He looked more like an aging surfer boy than a professional mobster.

The van's interior had been custom designed, but not in a good way. All the seats had been ripped out except for the driver's. There was a leather couch in the back along one wall where Pinstripe sat alone. A lime-green shag carpet even Elvis would have found too garish ran along the van's floor and up the sides like a poor man's ivy.

The man in the pinstripe suit smiled; his hands were folded in his lap, very much at ease. The van started moving.

The gunman quickly searched Myron. 'Sit, asshole,' he said.

Myron sat on the carpeted floor. He ran his hand over the shag. 'Lime green,' he said to Pinstripe. 'Nice.'

'It's inexpensive,' Pinstripe said. 'That way we don't worry about bloodstains.'

'Thinking of overhead.' Myron nodded coolly, though his mouth felt very dry. 'That's smart business.'

Pinstripe did not bother with a response. He gave the man with the gun and dickey/turtleneck a look that made the man jolt upward. The man cleared his throat.

'This here is Mr Baron,' the gunman told Myron, indicating Pinstripe. 'Everyone calls him the B Man.' He cleared his throat again. He spoke like he'd been rehearsing this little speech, which, Myron surmised, was probably likely. 'He's called the B Man because he enjoys breaking bones.'

'Say, that must woo the women,' Myron said.

The B Man smiled with capped teeth as white as anything in those old Pepsodent commercials. 'Hold his leg out,' he said.

The man with the turtleneck/dickey pressed the gun against Myron's temple hard enough to leave a permanent imprint. He wrapped his other arm around Myron's neck, the inside of his elbow jammed into Myron's windpipe. He lowered his head and whispered, 'Don't even flinch, asshole.'

He forced Myron into a lying position. The other man straddled Myron's chest and pinned the leg to the floor. Myron had trouble breathing. Panic seized him, but he remained still. Any move at this stage would almost inevitably be the wrong one. He'd have to play it out and see where it went.

The B Man moved off the leather couch slowly. His eyes never left Myron's bad knee; his smile was a happy one. 'I'm going to place one hand on the distal femur and the other on your proximal tibia,' he explained in the same tone a surgeon might use with a student. 'My thumbs will then rest on the medial aspect of the patella. When my thumbs snap forward, I will basically rip off your kneecap laterally.' He met Myron's gaze. 'This will tear your medial retinaculum and several other ligaments. Tendons will snap. I fear it will be most painful.'

Myron didn't even try a wisecrack. 'Hey, wait a second,' he said quickly. 'There's no reason for violence.'

The B Man smiled, shrugged. 'Why does there have to be a reason?'

Myron's eyes widened. Fear hardened in his belly. 'Hold on,' he said quickly. 'I'll talk.'

'I know you will,' the B Man replied. 'But first you'll jerk us around a bit—'

'No, I won't.'

'Please don't interrupt me. It's very rude to interrupt.' The smile was gone. 'Where was I?'

'First he'll jerk us around,' the driver prompted.

'That's right, thank you.' He turned the white smile back to Myron. 'First, you'll stall. You'll do a song-and-dance. You'll hope we'll take you someplace where your partner can save you.'

'Partner?'

'You're still friends with Win, aren't you?'

The man knew Win. This was not a good thing. 'Win who?'

'Precisely,' B Man said. 'This is what I mean by being jerked around. Enough.'

He moved closer. Myron started to struggle, but the man jammed the gun in Myron's mouth. It struck teeth and made him gag. The taste was cold and metallic.

'I'll destroy the knee first. Then we'll talk.'

The other man pulled Myron's leg straight while the gunman took the revolver out of Myron's mouth and pressed it back against his temple. Their grips grew a bit tighter. The B Man lowered his hands to Myron's knee, his fingers spread like eagle's talons.

'Wait!' Myron shouted.

'No,' B Man replied calmly.

Myron started to squirm. He grabbed a loading handle on the floor of the van, the kind of thing used to tie down cargo. He held on and braced himself. He didn't have to wait very long.

The crash jarred them. Myron had been ready for it. No one else had. They all went flying, their grips slackening. Glass shattered. The scream of metal hitting metal filled the air. Brakes screeched. Myron held on until the van slowed. Then he curled into a ball and rolled out of harm's way. There were shouts and a door opened. Myron heard a shot being fired. Voices sounded in a cacophony of confusion. The driver ducked out through his door. The B Man followed, leaping like a grasshopper. The side door opened. Myron looked up as Win stepped in with his gun drawn. The man with the turtleneck/dickey had recovered. He picked up his gun.

'Drop it,' Win said.

The man with the turtleneck/dickey didn't. Win shot him in the face. He turned his aim toward the man who had straddled Myron's chest.

'Drop it,' Win said.

The man did. Win smiled at him. 'Fast learner.'

Win's eyes slid smoothly from side to side, never darting. Win barely moved, seeming to glide rather than walk. His movements were short and economical. He returned his eyes to his captive. The one still breathing.

'Talk,' Win said.

'I don't know nothing.'

'Bad answer,' Win said. He spoke with calm authority, his matter-of-fact tone more intimidating than any scream. 'If you know nothing, you are useless to me; if you are useless to me, you end up like him.' He vaguely motioned toward the still form at his feet.

The man held up his hands. His eyes were round and white. 'Hey, wait a sec, okay? It's no secret. Your buddy heard the guy's name. Baron. The guy's name is Baron. But everyone calls him the B Man.'

'The B Man works out of the Midwest,' Win said. 'Who brought him in?'

'I don't know; I swear.'

Win moved the gun closer. 'You're being useless to me again.'

'It's the truth, I'd tell you if I knew. All I know is the B Man flew in late last night.'

'Why?' Win asked.

'It's got something to do with Greg Downing. That's all I know, I swear.'

'How much does Downing owe?'

'I don't know.'

Win moved closer still. He pressed the barrel of the gun between the man's eyes. 'I rarely miss from this distance,' he said.

The man dropped to his knees. Win followed him down with the gun. 'Please.' His voice was a pained plea. 'I don't know nothing else.' His eyes filled with tears. 'I swear to God, I don't.'

'I believe you,' Win said.

'Win,' Myron said.

Win's eyes never left the man. 'Relax,' he said. 'I just wanted to make sure our friend here had confessed all. Confession is good for the soul, is it not?'

The man nodded hurriedly.

'Have you confessed all?'

More nods.

'You're sure?'

Nod, nod.

Win lowered the weapon. 'Go then,' he said. 'Now.'

The man didn't have to be told twice.

Chapter 18

Win looked down at the dead body as though it were a bag of peat moss. 'We best depart.'

Myron nodded. He reached into his pants pocket and took out the cellular phone. A relatively new trick of the trade. Neither he nor Win had hung up after their call. The line was left open; Win had been able to hear everything that had gone on in the van. It worked as well as any bug or walkie-talkie.

They stepped into the cool night. They were on Washington Street. During the day the place was popping with delivery trucks, but at night it was completely silent. Someone would find a nasty surprise in the morning.

Win normally drove a Jaguar, but he had smashed a 1983 Chevy Nova into the van. Totaled. Not that it mattered. Win had several such vehicles he kept out in New Jersey to use for surveillance or activities just east of legal. The car was untraceable. The plates and paperwork were all phony. It would never lead back to anyone.

Myron looked at him. 'A man of your breeding in a Chevy Nova?' He tsk-tsked.

'I know,' Win said. 'Sitting in it almost gave me a rash.'

'If anyone at the club saw you . . .'

Win shuddered. 'Do not even think such a thought.'

Myron's legs still felt shaky and numb. Even as the B Man had reached down for his knee, Myron had known that Win would find a way to get to him. But the thought of how close he'd come to being crippled for life kept plucking at the muscles in his calves and thighs. He kept bending down and touching the bad knee, as if he couldn't believe it was still there. Tears brimmed in his eyes as he looked at Win. Win saw them and turned away.

Myron followed behind him. 'So how do you know this B Man?' he asked.

'He operates out of the Midwest,' Win said. 'He is also a superb martial artist. We met in Tokyo once.'

'What sort of operation does he run?'

'The usual assorted sundries – gambling, drugs, loan sharking, extortion. A bit of prostitution too.'

'So what's he doing here?'

'It appears that Greg Downing owes him money,' Win said, 'probably from gambling. The B Man specializes in gambling.'

'Nice to have a specialty.'

'Indeed. I would assume that your Mr Downing owes them a large sum of money.' Win glanced over at Myron. 'That's good news for you.'

'Why?'

'Because it implies that Downing is on the run rather than dead,' Win said. 'The B Man is not wasteful. He wouldn't kill someone who owes him a lot of money.'

'Dead men pay no debts.'

'Precisely,' Win said. 'On top of that, he is clearly looking for Downing. If he killed him, he wouldn't need you to find him.'

Myron considered this for a moment. 'It sort of meshes with what Emily told me. She said Greg had no money. Gambling might explain that fact.'

Win nodded. 'Kindly fill me in on what else has occurred in my absence. Jessica mentioned something about finding a dead woman.'

Myron told him everything. As he spoke, new theories rushed forward. He tried to sort through them and organize them a bit. When he finished the recap, Myron went right into the first one.

'Let's assume,' he said, 'that Downing does owe a lot of money to this B Man. That might explain why he finally agreed to sign an endorsement deal. He needs the money.'

Win nodded. 'Go on.'

'And let's also assume the B Man is not stupid. He wants to collect, right? So he would never really hurt Greg. Greg makes him money through his physical prowess. Broken bones would have an adverse effect on Greg's financial status and thus his ability to pay.'

'True,' Win said.

'So let's say Greg owes them a lot of money. Maybe the B Man wanted to scare him in another way.'

'How?'

'By hurting someone close to him. As a warning.'

Win nodded again. 'That might work.'

'And suppose they followed Greg. Suppose they saw him with Carla. Suppose they figured that Greg and Carla were close.' Myron looked up. 'Wouldn't killing her be a hell of a warning?'

Win frowned. 'You think the B Man killed her to warn Downing?'

'I'm saying it's possible.'

'Why wouldn't he just break some of her bones?' Win asked.

'Because the B Man wasn't personally on the scene yet, remember? He got in last night. The murder would have been the work of hired muscle.'

Win still didn't like it. 'Your theory is improbable, at best. If the murder was indeed a warning, where is Downing now?'

'He ran away,' Myron said.

'Why? Because he was afraid for his own life?'

'Yes.'

'And did he run away immediately after learning Carla was dead?' Win asked. 'On Saturday night?'

'That would be most logical.'

'He was frightened off then? By the murder?'

'Yes,' Myron said.

'Ah.' Win stopped and smiled at Myron.

'What?' Myron asked.

'Pray tell,' Win began with a lilt in his voice, 'if Carla's body was just discovered today, how did Downing know about the murder last Saturday night?'

Myron felt a chill.

'For your theory to hold up,' Win continued, 'Greg Downing would have to have done one of three things. One, he witnessed the murder; two, he stumbled into her apartment after the murder; three, he committed the murder himself. Furthermore, there was a great deal of cash in her apartment. Why? What was it doing there? Was this money to help pay back the B Man? If so, why didn't his men take it? Or better yet, why didn't Downing take it back when he was there?'

Myron shook his head. 'So many holes,' he said. 'And we still haven't come up with what connection there is between Downing and this Carla or Sally or whatever her name is.'

Win nodded. They continued walking.

'One more thing,' Myron said. 'Do you really think the mob would kill a woman just because she happened to be with Greg at a bar?'

'Very doubtful,' Win agreed.

'So basically, that whole theory is blown to hell.'

'Not basically,' Win corrected. 'Entirely.'

They kept walking.

'Of course,' Win said, 'Carla could have been working for the B Man.'

An icy finger poked at Myron. He saw where Win was going but he still said, 'What?'

'Perhaps this Carla woman was the B Man's contact. She collected for him. She was meeting Downing because he owed a great deal of money. Downing promises to pay. But he doesn't have the money. He knows they are closing in on him. He has stalled long enough. So he goes back to her apartment, kills her, and runs.'

Silence. Myron tried to swallow, but his throat felt frozen. This was good, this talking it through. It helped. His legs were still rubbery from the incident, but what really bothered him now was how easily he had forgotten the dead man lying in the van. True, the man was probably a professional scum bag. True, the man had jammed the barrel of a gun into his mouth and had not dropped his weapon when Win told him to. And true, the world was probably a better place without him. But in the past

Myron would have still felt some remorse for this fellow human being; in all honesty, he didn't now. He tried to muster some sympathy, but the only thing he felt sad about was that he didn't feel sad.

Enough self-analysis. Myron shook it off and said, 'There are problems with that scenario too.'

'Such as?'

'Why would Greg kill her? Why not just run off before the back-booth meeting?'

Win considered this. 'Fair point. Unless something happened during their meeting to set him off.'

'Like what?'

Win shrugged.

'It all comes back to this Carla,' Myron said. 'Nothing about her adds up. I mean, even a drug dealer doesn't have a setup like hers – working as a diner waitress, hiding sequentially numbered hundred dollar bills, wearing wigs, having all those fake passports. And on top of that, you should have seen Dimonte this afternoon. He knew who she was and he was in a panic.'

'You contacted Higgins at Treasury?' Win asked.

'Yes. He's tracing those serial numbers.'

'That could help.'

'We also need to get a hold of the telephone records from the Parkview Diner. See who Carla called.'

They fell back into silence and kept walking. They didn't want to hail a taxi too close to the scene.

'Win?'

'Yes?'

'Why didn't you want to go to the game the other night?'

Win kept on walking. Myron kept pace. After some

187

time, Win said, 'You've never watched a replay of it, have you?'

He knew he meant the knee injury. 'No.'

'Why not?'

Myron shrugged. 'No point.'

'No, there is a point.' Win kept walking.

'Mind telling me what that is?' Myron said.

'Watching what happened to you might have meant dealing with it. Watching it might have meant closure.'

'I don't understand,' Myron said.

Win nodded. 'I know.'

'I remember you watched it,' Myron said. 'I remember you watched it over and over.'

'I did that for a reason,' Win said.

'For vengeance.'

'To see if Burt Wesson injured you on purpose,' Win corrected.

'You wanted to pay him back.'

'You should have let me. Then you might have been able to put it behind you.'

Myron shook his head. 'Violence is always the answer for you, Win.'

Win frowned. 'Stop sounding melodramatic. A man committed a vile act upon you. Squaring things would have helped put it behind you. It's not about vengeance. It's about equilibrium. It's about man's basic need to keep the scales balanced.'

'That's your need,' Myron said, 'not mine. Hurting Burt Wesson wouldn't have fixed my knee.'

'But it might have given you closure.'

'What does that mean, closure? It was a freak injury. That's all.'

Win shook his head. 'You never watched the tape.'

'It wouldn't have mattered. The knee was still ruined. Watching a tape wouldn't have changed that.'

Win said nothing.

'I don't understand this,' Myron continued. 'I went on after the injury. I never complained, did I?'

'Never.'

'I didn't cry or curse the gods or do any of that stuff.'

'Never,' Win said again. 'You never let yourself be a burden on any of us.'

'So why do you think I needed to relive it?'

Win stopped and looked at him. 'You've answered your own question, but you choose not to hear it.'

'Spare me the Kung-Fu-grasshopper philosophical bullshit,' Myron shot back. 'Why didn't you go to the game?'

Win started walking again. 'Watch the tape,' he said.

Chapter 19

Myron didn't watch the tape. But he had the dream.

In the dream he could see Burt Wesson bearing down on him. He could see the gleeful, almost giddy violence in Burt's face as he drew closer and closer. In the dream, Myron had plenty of time to step out of harm's way. Too much time really. But in this dream – as in many – Myron could not move. His legs would not respond, his feet mired in thick, dream-world quicksand while the inevitable approached.

But in reality, Myron had never seen Burt Wesson coming. There had been no warning. Myron had been pivoting on his right leg when the blinding collision befell him. He heard rather than felt a snap. At first there had been no pain, just wide-eyed astonishment. The astonishment had probably lasted less than a second, but it was a frozen second, a snapshot Myron only took out in dreams. Then came the pain.

In the dream Burt Wesson was almost on him now.

Burt was a huge man, an enforcer-type player, the basket-ball equivalent of a hockey goon. He did not have much talent, but he had tremendous bulk and he knew how to use it. It had gotten him far, but this was the pros now. Burt would be cut before the start of the season – poetic irony that neither he nor Myron would play in a real professional basketball game. Until two nights ago any-way.

In the dream Myron watched Burt Wesson approach and waited. Somewhere in his subconscious, he knew that he would awaken before the collision. He always did. He lingered now in that cusp between nightmare and being awake – that tiny window where you are still asleep but you know it is a dream and even though it may be terrifying, you want to go on and see how it will end because it is only a dream and you are safe. But reality would not keep that window open for long. It never did. As Myron swam to the surface, he knew that whatever the answer was, he would not find it in any nocturnal voyage to the past.

'Phone for you,' Jessica said.

Myron blinked his eyes and rolled onto his back. Jessica was already dressed. 'What time is it?' he asked.

'Nine.'

'What? Why didn't you wake me?'

'You needed the sleep.' She handed him the phone. 'It's Esperanza.'

He took it. 'Hello.'

'Christ, don't you ever sleep in your own bed?' Esper-anza said.

He was hardly in the mood. 'What is it?'

'Fred Higgins from Treasury is on the line,' she said. 'I thought you'd want it.'

'Pass it through.' A click. 'Fred?'

'Yeah, how you doing, Myron?'

'I'm okay. You got anything on those serial numbers?'

There was a brief hesitation. 'You stumbled into some heavy shit, Myron. Some very heavy shit.'

'I'm listening.'

'People don't want this out, you understand? I had to jump through all kinds of hoops to get this.'

'Mum's the word.'

'Okay then.' Higgins took a deep breath. 'The bills are from Tucson, Arizona,' he said. 'More specifically, First City National Bank of Tucson, Arizona. They were stolen in an armed bank heist.'

Myron shot up in the bed. 'When?'

'Two months ago.'

Myron remembered a headline, and his blood turned cold.

'Myron?'

'The Raven Brigade,' Myron managed. 'That was one of theirs, right?'

'Right. You ever work on their case with the feds?'

'No, never.' But he remembered. Myron and Win had worked on cases with a special and almost contradictory nature: high profile with the need for undercover. They had been perfect for such situations – who, after all, would suspect a former basketball star and a rich, Main Line prep of being undercover agents? They could travel in whatever circles they wanted to and not raise suspicion. Myron and Win didn't have to create a cover; their reality was the best one the agency had. But Myron was never full-time with them. Win was their fair-haired boy; Myron was more a utility fielder Win called in when he thought it necessary.

But of course he knew about the Raven Brigade. Most people with even a passing familiarity with sixties extremism knew about them. Started by a charismatic leader named Cole Whiteman, the Ravens had been yet another splinter group of the Weather Underground. They were very much like the Symbionese Liberation Army, the group that kidnapped Patty Hearst. The Ravens, too, attempted a high-profile kidnapping, but the victim ended up dead. The group had gone underground. Four of them. Despite the FBI's best efforts, the four escapees – including Cole Whiteman, who with his Win-like blond hair and Waspy background never looked the part of an extremist – had remained hidden for nearly a quarter century.

Dimonte's bizarre questions about radical politics and 'perversives' no longer seemed so bizarre.

'Was the victim one of the Ravens?' Myron asked.

'I can't say.'

'You don't have to,' Myron said. 'I know it was Liz Gorman.'

There was another brief hesitation. Then: 'How the hell did you know that?'

'The implants,' Myron said.

'What?'

Liz Gorman, a fiery redhead, had been one of the founding members of the Raven Brigade. During their first 'mission' – a failed attempt to burn down a university chemistry lab – the police had picked up a code name on the scanner: CD. It was later revealed that the male members of the Brigade called her CD, short for Carpenter's Dream, because she was 'flat as a board and easy to screw.' Sixties radicals, for all their so-called progressive thoughts, were some of the world's biggest sexists. Now the implants made sense. Everyone Myron had interviewed remembered one thing about 'Carla' – her cup size. Liz Gorman had been famous for her flat chest – what better disguise than oversized breast implants?

'The feds and cops are cooperating on this one,' Higgins said. 'They're trying to keep this quiet for a while.'

'Why?'

'They got her place under surveillance. They're hoping to maybe draw out another member.'

Myron felt completely numb. He had wanted to learn more about the mystery woman and now he had: she was Liz Gorman, a famous radical who had not been seen since 1975. The disguises, the various passports, the implants – they all added up now. She wasn't a drug dealer, she was a woman on the run.

But if Myron had hoped learning the truth about Liz Gorman would help clarify his own investigation, he had been sadly mistaken. What possible connection could there be between Greg Downing and Liz Gorman? How had a professional basketball player gotten enmeshed with a wanted extremist who had gone underground when Greg was still a kid? It made absolutely no sense.

'How much did they get in the bank heist?' Myron asked.

'Hard to say,' Higgins answered. 'About fifteen thousand in cash, but they also blew open the safe-deposit boxes. Over a half million in goods have been declared for insurance purposes, but a lot of it is bullshit. A guy gets robbed, all of a sudden he was keeping ten Rolexes in the box instead of one – trying to rip off the insurance company, you know how it is.'

'On the other hand,' Myron said, 'anyone keeping illegal dollars in there wouldn't declare it. They'd just have to swallow the loss.' Back to drugs and drug money. The extremists in the underground needed resources. They'd been known to rob banks, blackmail former followers who had gone mainstream, deal drugs, whatever. 'So it could have been even more.'

'Right, hard to say.'

'You got anything else on this?'

'Nothing,' Higgins said. 'It's being kept sealed tight, and I'm not in the loop. I can't tell you how hard it was to get this, Myron. You owe me big.'

'I already promised you the tickets, Fred.'

'Courtside?'

'I'll do my best.'

Jessica came back into the room. When she saw Myron's face, she stopped and looked a question at him. Myron hung up and told her. She listened. Remembering Esperanza's crack, Myron realized that he had now spent four nights in a row here – a postbreakup world and Olympic record. He worried about that. It wasn't that he didn't like staying here. He did. It wasn't that he feared commitment or any of that other drivel; to the contrary, he craved it. But part of him was still afraid – old wounds that wouldn't heal and all that.

Myron had a habit of exposing too much of himself. He knew that. With Win or Esperanza it was okay. He trusted them absolutely. He loved Jessica with all his heart, but she had hurt him. He wanted to be tentative. He wanted to hold back, to not leave himself so open, but the heart don't know from stop. At least, Myron's didn't. Two primal internal forces were at odds here: his natural instinct to give all he had when it came to love vs. the survival instinct of pain avoidance.

'This whole thing,' Jessica said when he had finished, 'is just too weird.'

'Yep,' he said. They had barely talked last night. He had assured her that he was all right and they had both gone to sleep. 'I guess I should thank you.'

'For what?'

'You were the one who called Win.'

She nodded. 'After those goons jumped you.'

'I thought you said you weren't going to interfere.'

'Wrong. I said I wasn't going to try to stop you. There's a difference.'

'True enough.'

Jessica started chewing on her bottom lip. She was wearing jeans and a Duke sweatshirt several sizes too large on her. Her hair was still wet from a recent shower. 'I think you should move in,' she said.

Her words hit him square in the jaw. 'What?'

'I didn't mean to just blurt it out like that,' she said. 'I'm not very good at beating around the bush.'

'That's my job anyway,' he said.

She shook her head. 'You pick the strangest times to be crude.'

'Yeah, I'm sorry.'

'Look, I'm not good at this stuff, Myron. You know that.'

He nodded. He knew.

She tilted her head to the side, shrugged, smiled nervously. 'It's just that I like having you here. It feels right.'

His heart soared and sung and quivered in fear. 'It's a big step.'

'Not really,' she said. 'You're here most of the time anyway. And I love you.'

'I love you, too.'

The pause lingered a bit longer than it should. Jessica jumped into it before it could do irreparable harm. 'Don't say anything now,' she said, rushing the words out in a gush. 'I want you to think about it. It was a dumb time to bring it up, with all this stuff going on. Or maybe that's why I chose now, I don't know. But don't say anything. Just think about it. Don't call me today. Or tonight. I'm going to your game, but then I'm taking Audrey out for a few drinks. It's her birthday. Sleep at your house tonight. Maybe we'll talk tomorrow, okay? Tomorrow?'

'Tomorrow,' Myron agreed.

Chapter 20

Big Cyndi sat at the reception desk. 'Sat.' was probably
the wrong word. Talk about the proverbial camel trying
to squeeze through the eye of the needle. The desk's four
legs were off the floor, the top teetering on Big Cyndi's
knees like a seesaw. Her coffee mug disappeared into
fleshy hands that resembled couch cushions. Her short
spikes of hair had more of a pinkish hue today. Her
makeup reminded him of a childhood incident involving
melted Crayola crayons. She wore white lipstick, like
something out of an Elvis documentary. Her size-3XL
T-shirt read CLUB SODA NOT SEALS. It took Myron a few
seconds to get it. Politically correct but cute.

Usually she growled when she saw Myron. Today she
smiled sweetly and batted her eyes at him. The sight was
far more frightening, like Bette Davis in *Whatever Happened to Baby Jane*, only on steroids. Big Cyndi pointed
up her middle finger and bounced it up and down.

'Line one?' he tried.

She shook her head. The up and down gesture became more hurried. She looked up at the ceiling. Myron followed her gaze but he saw nothing. Cyndi rolled her eyes. The smile was frozen on her face, like a clown's.

'I don't get it,' he said.

'Win wants to see you,' she said.

It was the first time Myron had heard her voice, and it startled him. She sounded like one of those perky hostesses on a cable shopping network, the one where people call up and describe in far too much detail how much their lives were improved by purchasing a green vase shaped like Mount Rushmore.

'Where's Esperanza?' he asked.

'Win's cute.'

'Is she here?'

'Win seemed to think it was important.'

'I'm just—'

'You're going to see Win,' Cyndi interrupted. 'You're certainly not checking up on your most valued associate.' The sweet smile.

'I'm not checking up. I just want to know—'

'Where Win's office is. It's two stories up.' She made a sound with her coffee that some might loosely label, 'slurping.' Moose in the tri-state area scattered in search of mates.

'Tell her I'll be back,' Myron said.

'But of course.' She batted her eyelashes. They looked like two tarantulas in death throes. 'Have a nice day.'

Win's corner office faced Fifty-second Street and Park Avenue. Major league view for Lock-Horne Securities' golden boy. Myron sank into one of the lush burgundy leather chairs. There were several paintings of fox hunts on the richly paneled walls. Dozens of manly men on horseback, dressed in black hats, red blazers, white pants, black boots, rode out armed with only rifles and dogs to chase down a small furry creature until they caught and killed it. Ah, gamesmanship. A tad overkill maybe. Like using a flamethrower to light a cigarette.

Win typed on a laptop computer that looked lonely on the mono-expanse he called a desk. 'I found something of interest on the computer disks we made at Greg's house.'

'Oh?'

'It appears our friend Mr Downing had an e-mail address with America Online,' Win said. 'He downloaded this particular piece of mail on Saturday.' Win spun the laptop around so Myron could read the screen:

Subj:	Sex!
Date:	3–11 14:51:36 EST
From:	Sepbabe
To:	Downing22

Meet you tonight at ten. The place we discussed. Come. I promise you the greatest night of ecstasy imaginable.
  —F

Myron looked up. 'Greatest night of ecstasy imaginable?'

'She has quite the writing flair, no?' Win said.

Myron made a face.

Win put a sincere hand to his heart. 'Even if she could not live up to such a promise,' he continued, 'one has to admire her ability to take risk, her dedication to her craft.'

'Uh huh,' Myron said. 'So who is F?'

'There is no profile for the screen name Sepbabe on line,' Win explained. 'That doesn't mean anything, of course. Many users don't have a profile. They don't want everyone knowing their real name. I would assume however that F is yet another alias for our dearly departed friend Carla.'

'We have Carla's real name now,' Myron said.

'Oh?'

'Liz Gorman.'

Win arched an eyebrow. 'Pardon?'

'Liz Gorman. As in the Raven Brigade.' He told Win about Fred Higgins's call. Win leaned back in his chair and steepled his fingers. As usual his face gave away nothing.

When Myron finished, Win said, 'Curiouser and curiouser.'

'It comes down to this,' Myron said. 'What connection could there possibly be between Greg Downing and Liz Gorman?'

'A strong one,' Win said, nodding toward the screen. 'The possibility of the greatest night of ecstasy imaginable, if one is to buy into the hyperbole.'

'But with Liz Gorman?'

'Why not?' Win almost sounded defensive. 'You shouldn't discriminate on the basis of age or implants. It wouldn't be right.'

Mr Equal Rights. 'It's not that,' Myron said. 'Let's pretend that Greg has the hots for Liz Gorman, even though nobody described her as much of a looker . . .'

'You're so shallow, Myron,' Win said with a disenchanted shake of the head. 'Did you ever consider the possibility that Greg saw beneath that? She did, after all, have large breasts.'

'As usual when discussing sex,' Myron replied, 'you've missed the point.'

'Which is?'

'How would they have hooked up in the first place?'

Win steepled his fingers again, bouncing the tips against his nose. 'Ah,' he said.

'Right, ah. Here's a woman who's been living underground for more than twenty years. She's traveled all over the world, probably never staying in one spot for very long. She was in Arizona robbing a bank two months ago. She's working as a waitress in a tiny diner on Dyckman Street. How does this woman hook up with Greg Downing?'

'Difficult,' Win allowed, 'but not impossible. There is plenty of evidence to support that.'

'Like?'

Win motioned to the computer screen. 'This e-mail is talking about last Saturday night, for one – the same night Greg and Liz Gorman met in a New York City bar.'

'In a dive bar,' Myron corrected. 'Why there? Why not go to a hotel or her place?'

'Perhaps because it is out of the way. Perhaps, as you implied, Liz Gorman would want to keep out of the public eye. Such a bar might be a good alternative.' He stopped steepling and lightly drummed his fingers on the desk. 'But you, my friend, are forgetting something else.'

'What?'

'The woman's clothes in Greg's house,' Win said. 'Your investigation has led us to conclude that Downing has a lover he was keeping secret. The question, of course is: why? Why would he work so hard to keep a love affair clandestine? One possible explanation is that the secret love was the infamous Liz Gorman.'

Myron wasn't sure what to think. Audrey had seen Greg at a restaurant with a woman that did not fit Liz

Gorman's description. But what did that mean? It might have been another date. It might have been something innocent. It might have been a side affair, who knows? Still, Myron had trouble buying a romantic entanglement involving Greg Downing and Liz Gorman. Something about it just didn't wash. 'There must be a way of tracing down this screen name and finding out the user's real identity,' he said. 'Let's make sure it checks back to Liz Gorman or one of her aliases.'

'I'll see what I can do. I don't have any contacts with America Online, but someone we know must.' Win reached behind him. He opened up the paneled door on his minifridge. He tossed Myron a can of Yoo-Hoo and poured himself a Brooklyn Lager. Win never drank beer, only lager. 'Greg's money has been difficult to locate,' he said. 'I'm not sure there is very much.'

'That would fit into what Emily said.'

'However,' Win continued, 'I did find one major with-drawal.'

'How much?'

'Fifty thousand dollars in cash. It took some time because it came out of an account that Martin Felder holds for him.'

'When did he withdraw it?'

'Four days before he disappeared,' Win said.

'Paying off a gambling debt?'

'Perhaps.'

Win's phone rang. He picked it up and said, 'Articu-late. Okay, put it through.' Two seconds later he handed the phone to Myron.

'For me?' Myron asked.

Win gave him flat eyes. 'No,' he said. 'I'm handing you the phone because it's too heavy for me.'

Everyone's a wiseass. Myron took the phone. 'Hello?'

'I got a squad car downstairs.' It was Dimonte in full bark. 'Get your ass in it now.'

'What's wrong?'

'I'm at fucking Downing's house, that's what's wrong. I had to practically suck off a judge to get the warrant.'

'Nice imagery, Rolly.'

'Don't fuck with me, Bolitar. You said there was blood in the house.'

'In the basement,' Myron corrected.

'Well, I'm in the basement right now,' he countered. 'And it's as clean as a baby's ass.'

Chapter 21

The basement was indeed clean. No blood anywhere.

'There's got to be traces,' Myron said.

Dimonte's toothpick looked like it was about to snap between his clenched teeth. 'Traces?'

'Yeah. With a microscope or something.'

'With a . . .' Dimonte flapped his arms, his face crimson. 'What the hell good is traces going to do me? They don't prove a damn thing. You can't test traces.'

'It'll prove there was blood.'

'So what?' he shouted. 'You go through any house in America with a microscope and you're bound to find traces of blood. Who the fuck cares?'

'I don't know what to tell you, Rolly. The blood was there.'

There were maybe five lab cops – no uniforms, no marked cars – going through the house. Krinsky was there too. The videocamera in his hand was off right now. He also had what looked like manila files jammed into his armpit. Myron motioned to them. 'That the coroner's report?'

Roland Dimonte stepped in to block Myron's view. 'That ain't none of your business, Bolitar.'

'I know about Liz Gorman, Rolly.'

The toothpick hit the floor on that one. 'How the hell . . . ?'

'It's not important.'

'The fuck it ain't. What else do you know? If you're holding out on me, Bolitar—'

'I'm not holding out on you, but I think I can help.'

Dimonte narrowed his eyes. Senor Suspicious. 'Help how?'

'Just tell me Gorman's blood type. That's all I want to know. Her blood type.'

'Why the hell should I?'

'Because you're not a total numb nut, Rolly.'

'Don't give me that shit. Why do you want to know?'

'Remember I told you about finding blood in the basement?' Myron said.

'Yeah.'

'I left something out.'

Dimonte gave him the glare. 'What?'

'We tested some of the blood.'

'We? Who the fuck is . . .' His voice trailed off. 'Oh Christ, don't tell me that psycho-yuppie is in on all this?'

To know Win was to love him. 'I'd like to make a little trade.'

'What kind of trade?'

'You tell me the blood type in the report. I tell you the blood type we found in the basement.'

'Fuck you, Bolitar. I can arrest your ass for tampering with evidence in a police investigation.'

'What tampering? There was no investigation.'

'I could still nail your ass for breaking and entering.'

'If you could prove it. And if Greg were around to press charges. Look, Rolly—'

'AB positive,' Krinsky said. He ignored Dimonte's renewed glare and continued. 'It's fairly rare. Four per-cent of the populace.'

They both turned their attention to Myron. Myron nodded. 'AB positive. It's the same.'

Dimonte put up both hands and scrunched his face into perplexed. 'Whoa, hold up here. Just what the fuck are you trying to say? That she was killed down here and moved?'

'I'm not saying anything,' Myron said.

'Cause we didn't see any evidence of the body being moved,' Dimonte went on. 'None at all. Not that we were looking for it. But the bleeding pattern – I mean, if she was killed down here, there wouldn't have been so much blood like that at her apartment. You saw the mess there, right?'

Myron nodded.

Dimonte's eyes darted aimlessly. Myron could practic-ally sees the gears inside his head grinding to a halt. 'You know what that means, don't you, Bolitar?'

'No, Rolly, why don't you enlighten me?'

'It means the killer came back here after the murder. It's the only explanation. And you know who all this is starting to point to? Your pal Downing. First we found his fingerprints in the victim's apartment—'

'What's this?'

Dimonte nodded. 'That's right. Downing's fingerprints were by the door frame.'

'But not inside?'

'Yeah, inside. Inside the door frame.'

'But nowhere else?'

'What the hell's the difference? The fingerprints prove he was at the scene. What more do you need? Anyway, here's how it must have happened.' He stuck a new toothpick in his mouth. New toothpick for a new theory. 'Downing kills her. He comes back to his house to pack or something. He's in a rush so he leaves a little mess in the basement. Then he runs away. A few days later he comes back and cleans it up.'

Myron shook his head. 'Why come down to the basement in the first place?'

'The laundry room,' Dimonte answered. 'He was coming down here to wash his clothes.'

'The laundry room is upstairs off the kitchen,' Myron said.

Dimonte shrugged. 'So maybe he was getting a suitcase.'

'They're in the bedroom closet. This is just a kids' playroom, Rolly. Why did he come down here?'

That stopped Dimonte for a moment. It stopped Myron too. None of this made much sense. Had Liz Gorman been killed here and dragged to her apartment in Manhattan? That didn't seem to make much sense based on the physical evidence. Could she have been injured down here?

Whoa, hold the phone.

Maybe the attack started here. Maybe there had been a scuffle in the basement. In the course of subduing or knocking her out, blood was spilled. But then what? Did the killer stick her in a car and drive to Manhattan? And then – what? – on a fairly active street, the killer parked a car, dragged her injured body up the stairs, entered her apartment, killed her?

Did that make any sense?

From the first level a voice cried down, 'Detective! We found something! Quick!'

Dimonte wet his lips. 'Turn on the video,' he told Krinsky. Videotaping all the relevant moments. Just like Myron had told him. 'Stay here, Bolitar. I don't want to have to explain your ugly mug being on the film.'

Myron followed but at a discreet distance. Krinsky and Dimonte headed up the stairs into the kitchen. They turned left. The laundry room. Vinyl yellow wallpaper with white chicks blanketed all four walls. Emily's taste? Probably not. Knowing Emily she'd probably never even seen the inside of a laundry room.

'Over here,' someone said. Myron stayed back. He could see that the dryer had been pushed away from the wall. Dimonte bent down and looked behind it. Krinsky arched over to make sure the whole thing was being filmed. Dimonte stood back up. He was trying like hell to look grim – a smile wouldn't look good on film – but he was having a rough time of it. He snapped on a pair of rubber gloves and lifted the item into view.

The baseball bat was covered with blood.

Chapter 22

When Myron got back to the office, Esperanza was at the reception desk.

'Where's Big Cyndi?' Myron asked.

'Having lunch.'

The image of Fred Flintstone's car tipping over from the weight of his Bronto-ribs flashed in front of Myron's eyes.

'Win filled me in on what's been going on,' Esperanza said. She wore an aqua-blue blouse open at the throat. A gold heart on a slender chain dangled proudly against the dark skin of her sternum. Her always-mussed hair was slightly entangled in big hoop earrings. She pushed the hair back with one finger. 'So what happened at the house?'

He explained about the cleaned-up blood and the baseball bat. Esperanza usually liked to do other things while she listened. She wasn't right now. She stared square into his eyes. When she looked at you like that, there was such intensity it was sometimes hard to look back.

'I'm not sure I understand,' she said. 'You and Win found blood in the basement two days ago.'

'Right.'

'Since then, someone cleaned up that blood – but they left behind the murder weapon?'

'So it appears.'

Esperanza considered this for a moment. 'Could it have been a maid?'

'The police already checked on that. She hasn't been there in three weeks.'

'Do you have a thought?'

He nodded. 'Someone is trying to frame Greg. It's the only logical explanation.'

She arched a skeptical eyebrow. 'By planting and then cleaning up blood?'

'No, let's start from the beginning.' He grabbed the chair and sat in front of her. He had been going over it in his mind the whole ride back, and he wanted to talk it out. In the corner on his left, the fax machine sounded its digitally primordial screech. Myron waited for the sound to subside. 'Okay,' he said, 'first I'm going to assume that the killer knew Greg was with Liz Gorman that night – maybe he followed them, maybe he was waiting for them near her apartment. Whatever, he knows they were together.'

Esperanza nodded, stood. She walked over to the fax machine to check the incoming transmission.

'After Greg leaves, the killer murders Liz Gorman. Knowing that Downing would make a good fall guy, he takes some blood from the murder scene and plants it at Greg's house. That will raise suspicion. To put the icing on the cake, the killer also takes the murder weapon and plants it behind the dryer.'

'But you just said the blood was cleaned up,' she interjected.

'Right. Here's where it gets a little tricky. Suppose, for example, I wanted to protect Greg Downing. I go into his house and find the blood. Now remember, I want to protect Greg from a murder rap. So what would I do?'

She squinted at the fax coming through. 'Clean up the blood.'

'Exactly.'

'Wow, thanks. Do I get a gold star? Get on with it already.'

'Just bear with me, okay? I would see the blood and clean it up. But – and here's the important part – the first time I was in that house I *never* saw the bat. That's not just in this example. That's real life. Win and I only saw the blood in the basement. No baseball bat.'

'Hold on,' she said. 'You're saying someone cleaned up the blood to protect Greg from a murder rap but didn't know about the bat?'

'Right.'

'Who?'

'I don't know.'

Esperanza shook her head. She moved back to her desk and hit some keys on her computer keyboard. 'It doesn't add up.'

'Why not?'

'Suppose I'm madly in love with Greg Downing,' she said, moving back to the fax machine. 'I'm in his house. For some reason I can't fathom, I'm in his kids' playroom. Doesn't matter where I am. Imagine I'm in my own apartment. Or I'm visiting your house. I could be anywhere.'

'Okay.'

'I see blood on the floor or on the walls or wherever.' She stopped, looked at him. 'What conclusion would you logically expect me to draw?'

Myron shook his head. 'I don't understand what you're saying.'

Esperanza thought a moment. 'Suppose you left here right now,' she began, 'and went back to the bitch's loft.'

'Don't call her that.'

'Whatever. Suppose when you walked in, you found blood on her walls. What would be your first reaction?'

Myron nodded slowly. Now he saw what she was getting at. 'I'd be worried about Jessica.'

'And your second reaction? After you found out she was okay?'

'Curiosity, I guess. Whose blood is it? How did it get there? That sort of thing.'

'Right,' she said with a quick nod. 'Would you think to yourself, "Gee, I better clean it up before the bitch gets accused of murdering somebody"?'

'Stop calling her that.'

Esperanza waved him off. 'Would you think that or not?'

'Not in that circumstance, no,' Myron said. 'So in order for my theory to hold water—'

'Your protector had to know about the murder,' she finished for him, back checking her computer for something. 'He or she would also have to know that Greg was somehow involved.'

Myron's head spun with possibilities. 'You think Greg killed her,' he said. 'You think he went back to his house after the murder and left behind some traces of the crime – like blood in the basement. Then he sent this protector back to the house to help cover his tracks.'

Esperanza made a face. 'Where the hell did you come up with that?'

'I just—'

'That's not what I think at all,' Esperanza said. She stapled the fax pages together. 'If Greg sent someone to get rid of the evidence, the weapon would be gone too.'

'Right. So that leaves us where?'

Esperanza shrugged, circled something on the fax page with a red marker. 'You're the great detective. You figure it out.'

Myron thought about it a moment. Another answer – one he prayed was wrong – came to him all at once. 'There's another possibility,' he said.

'What?'

'Clip Arnstein.'

'What about him?'

'I told Clip about the blood in the basement.' Myron said.

'When?'

'Two days ago.'

'How did he react?'

'He freaked, pretty much,' Myron said. 'He's also got motive – any scandal will destroy his chances of keeping control of the Dragons. Hell, that's why he hired me. To keep any trouble contained. Nobody else even knew about the blood in the basement.' Myron stopped. He leaned back and ran it through his mind again. 'Of course I haven't had a chance to tell Clip about Liz Gorman's murder. He didn't even know the blood wasn't Greg's. All he knew was that there was blood in the basement. Would he go that far just on that? Would he still risk covering it all up if he didn't know anything about Liz Gorman?'

Esperanza gave him a small smile. 'Maybe he knows more than you think,' she said.

'What makes you say that?'

She handed him the fax. 'It's the list of long distance calls made from the pay phone at the Parkview Diner,' she said. 'I already cross-checked it with my computer Rolodex. Look at the number I circled.'

Myron saw it. A call lasting twelve minutes had been made from the Parkview Diner four days before Greg's disappearance. The phone number was Clip's.

Chapter 23

'Liz Gorman called Clip?' Myron looked up at Esperanza. 'What the hell is going on?'

Esperanza shrugged. 'Ask Clip.'

'I knew he was keeping something from me,' he went on, 'but I don't get it. How does Clip fit into this equation?'

'Uh huh.' She shuffled through some papers on her desk. 'Look, we got a ton of work to do. I mean, sports agent work. You have a game tonight, right?'

He nodded.

'So ask Clip then. In the meantime, we're just going around in circles here.'

Myron scanned the sheet. 'Any other numbers jump out at you?'

'Not yet,' she said. 'But I want to talk about something else for a minute.'

'What?'

'We have a problem with a client.'

'Who?'

'Jason Blair.'

'What's wrong?'

'He's pissed off,' she said. 'He's not happy with me handling his contract negotiations. He said he hired you, not some' – she made quote marks in the air with her fingers – ' "scantily clad wrestler with a nice ass." '

'He said that?'

'Yep. Nice ass. Didn't even notice my legs.' Esperanza shook her head.

Myron smiled. 'So what happened?'

Behind them the elevator dinged. Only one hit this part of the floor. The elevator opened directly into the reception area of MB SportsReps. Classy, or so he had been told. When the doors opened, two men came out. Myron recognized them right away. Camouflage Pants and Brick Wall. They were both armed. They aimed their guns at Myron and Esperanza. B Man stepped out behind them like he'd just been introduced on the Leno show. Big smile, acknowledging-the-crowd wave.

'How's the knee, Myron?' he asked.

'Better than your van.'

B Man laughed at that one. 'That Win,' he mused. 'The man is always a surprise. How did he know when to hit us?'

No reason not to tell. 'We kept the cellular phones on.'

B Man shook his head. 'Ingenious really. I'm very impressed.' He wore one of those suits that are just a tad too shiny and a pink tie. His shirt was french-cuffed and monogrammed with four letters: B MAN. Taking the nickname thing a little far. A thick, ropelike gold bracelet encircled his right wrist.

'How did you get up here?' Myron asked.

217

'Do you really think a few rent-a-cops are going to stop us?'

'I'd still like to hear,' Myron said.

B Man shrugged. 'I called Lock-Horne Securities and told them I was looking for a new financial advisor for my millions. An anxious young peon told me to come right up. I hit the twelfth floor on the elevator instead of the fifteenth.' He spread his hands. 'So here I am.' He smiled at Esperanza. What with the too-white teeth and the tan, it looked like he switched on a night-light.

'And who is this fetching creature?' he asked with a wink.

'My,' Esperanza said, 'what woman doesn't love to be called a creature?'

B Man laughed again. 'The little lady has gumption,' he said. 'I like that. I really do.'

'Like I care,' Esperanza said.

More laughter. 'May I indulge you a moment, Miss . . . ?'

'Money Penny,' she finished for him. She said it with her best Sean Connery imitation. No Rich Little, but not bad either.

Another laugh from the B Man. The man was half-hyena. 'Would you please call Win down here? On the speakerphone if you don't mind. Tell him to come down unarmed.'

She looked at Myron. Myron nodded. She dialed. Over the speakerphone, Win offered up another, 'Articulate.'

Esperanza said, 'Some bottled blond with a bottled tan is down here to see you.'

'Ah, I've been expecting him,' Win said. 'Hello, B Man.'

'Hello, Win.'

'I assume you are in well-armed company.'

'That I am, Win,' B Man said. 'If you try anything, your friends won't make it out alive.'

'"Won't make it out alive"?' Win repeated. 'I expected better from you, B Man, really. I'll be down in a second.'

'Come unarmed, Win.'

'Not a chance. But there will be no violence. That I promise you.' The phone clicked off. For several moments everyone looked at one another as if wondering who was going to take the lead.

'I don't trust him,' B Man said. He pointed to Brick Wall. 'Take the girl in the other room. Duck down behind a desk or something. You hear any shooting, you blow her head off.'

The Brick Wall nodded.

B Man directed his attention to Camouflage Pants. 'Keep your gun on Bolitar.'

'Right.'

B Man took out his own weapon. When the elevator dinged, he squatted and aimed. The doors slid open, but it wasn't Win. Big Cyndi emerged from the elevator, not unlike a dinosaur emerging from its egg.

'Jesus Christ!' Camouflage Pants said. 'What the hell is that?'

Big Cyndi growled.

'Who is she, Bolitar?' B Man demanded.

'My new receptionist.'

'Tell her to wait in the other room.'

Myron nodded to her. 'It's okay. Esperanza's in there.'

Cyndi growled again, but she listened. She walked past the B Man on her way to Myron's office. His gun looked like a disposable lighter next to her. She opened the door, snarled one last time, and closed it.

Silence.

'Jesus Christ,' Camouflage Pants said again.

They waited approximately thirty seconds before the elevator dinged again. B Man got back into his squat and aimed. The doors slid open. Win stepped out. He looked mildly annoyed when he saw the weapon aimed his way. His voice was clipped. 'I told you there would be no violence.'

'You have information we need,' B Man said.

'I'm well aware of that.' Win replied. 'Now put that gun away and we'll talk civilly.'

The B Man kept his weapon on Win. 'You armed?'

'Of course.'

'Hand over your weapon.'

'No,' Win said. 'And it's not weapon. It's weapons. Plural.'

'I said—'

'And I heard you, Orville.'

'Don't call me that.'

Win sighed. 'Fine, *B Man*.' He shook his head as he said it. 'You are making this far more difficult than it has to be.'

'What's that supposed to mean?'

'It means that for an intelligent fellow, you too often forget that brute strength is not the only course. There are situations that call for restraint.'

Win lecturing on restraint, Myron thought. What next? Xaviera Hollander lecturing on monogamy?

'Think about what you've already done,' Win said. 'First, you have Myron roughed up by a pair of amateurs—'

'Amateurs!' Camouflage Pants didn't like that. 'Who you calling—'

'Shut up, Tony,' B Man said.

'You hear what he called me? An amateur?'

'I said, shut up, Tony.'

But Tony The Pants wasn't through yet. 'Hey, I got feelings too, B Man.'

The B Man gave him hard eyes. 'Your left femur, if you don't shut up.'

Tony closed his mouth.

The B Man looked back to Win. 'Sorry about the interruption.'

'Apology accepted.'

'Go on.'

'As I was saying,' Win continued, 'first you try to rough Myron up. Then you try to kidnap and cripple him. All for naught.'

'Not for naught,' B Man countered. 'We need to know where Downing is.'

'And what makes you think Myron knows?'

'You were both at his house. Then all of a sudden Bolitar is on Downing's team. As a matter of fact, he takes his place on the roster.'

'So?'

'So I'm not stupid. You two know something.'

'And what if we do?' Win said, hands spread. 'Why didn't you just ask? Did you ever even consider that possibility? Did you ever think that maybe the best course of action would be simply to ask?'

'I did ask!' Camouflage Pants jumped in. He was defensive now. 'On the street! I asked him where Greg was. He gave me lip.'

Win looked at him. 'Were you ever in the military?' he asked.

Pants seemed confused. 'No.'

'You are a worthless punk,' Win said in the same tone he might use when discussing a mixed stock report. 'A pitiful ectoplasm such as yourself wearing army fatigues is an affront to any man or woman who has ever experienced real combat. If I ever happen across you again donning any similar garb, I will hurt you severely. Do I make myself clear?'

'Hey—'

'You don't know this guy, Tony,' B Man interrupted. 'Just nod and shut up.'

Camouflage Pants looked hurt but he did as he was told.

Win turned his attention back to the B Man. 'We can help each other out in this situation,' he said.

'How?'

'It just so happens that we, too, are searching for the elusive Mr Downing. That is why I wish to make a proposal.'

'I'm listening.'

'First,' Win said, 'stop aiming the weapons at us.'

B Man gave him a funny look. 'How do I know I can trust you?'

'If I wanted you dead,' Win answered, 'I would have killed you last night.'

The B Man thought it over, nodded, lowered his weapon. He signaled Camouflage Pants, who then did likewise. 'Why didn't you?' B Man asked. 'I probably would have killed you in the same situation.'

'That's what I mean about brute force,' Win said. 'About being wasteful. We need each other here. If I had killed you, I wouldn't be able to make this proposal today.'

'Fair enough. The floor is yours.'

'I assume that Mr Downing owes you a rather hefty sum.'

'Very hefty sum.'

'Fine,' Win said. 'You tell us what you know. We find him, no cost to you. When we do find him, you promise not to hurt him if he pays up.'

'And if he doesn't pay up?'

Win grinned and held his hands out, palms up. 'Who are we to interfere with the way you conduct your business?'

B Man thought about it, but not for very long. 'Okay, I can live with that,' he said. 'But I don't talk with the hired help around.' He turned to Camouflage. 'Go sit in the other room.'

'Why?'

'Because if someone decides to torture you, you'll know nothing.'

That answer seemed to make perfect sense to Camouflage. He went into Myron's office without another word.

'Why don't we sit?' Win suggested.

They did so. B Man crossed his legs and started right in. 'Downing is your basic gamble-a-holic,' he began. 'He had pretty good luck for a long time. That's a bad thing when a man has the itch. When his luck changed – as it must in the long run – he kept thinking he could win it back. They all do. When they have the sort of money that Downing has, I let them go. Let them dig their own grave. It's good for business. But at the same time, you have to keep an eye out. There is a fine line working here. You don't want them to end up digging to China either.' He turned and looked at Myron. 'You know what I'm saying?'

Myron nodded. 'China.'

'Right. Anyway, Downing started losing big. I'm talking very big here. He was never a prompt payer, but he was always good for it. I sometimes let the tab run as high as two-fifty or even three.'

'Hundred thousand?' Myron asked.

'Yeah.' B Man smiled. 'You don't know any gamblers, do you?'

Myron kept silent. He wasn't about to tell this slime bucket his life story.

'It's as bad as alcohol or heroin,' B Man went on. 'They can't stop themselves. In some ways, it's even worse. People drink and do drugs to escape despair. Gambling has that element, too, but it also offers you the friendly hand of hope. You always got hope when you gamble. You always believe that you're just one bet away from turning it all around. It's a catch-twenty-two. If you got hope, you keep on gambling. But with gambling, there's always hope.'

'Very deep,' Win said. 'Let's get back to Greg Downing.'

'Simply put, Greg stops paying his tab. It runs up to half a million. I start putting some pressure on him. He tells me he's flat broke, but I shouldn't worry because he's signing some big endorsement deal that will net him zillions.'

The Forte deal, Myron thought. Greg's sudden change of heart about endorsement money made more sense now.

'I asked him when this endorsement money will be coming in. He tells me in about six months. Six months? On a half million dollar debt and growing? I told him that's not good enough. He'd have to pay up now. He said he didn't have the money. So I ask for a show of good faith.'

Myron knew where this was going. 'He shaved points.'

'Wrong. He was *supposed* to shave points. The Dragons were favored by eight over Charlotte. Downing was going to see to it that the Dragons won by less than eight. No big deal.'

'He agreed?'

'Sure he did. The game was on Sunday. I dumped a ton on Charlotte. A ton.'

'And Greg never played,' Myron finished for him.

'You got it,' B Man said. 'The Dragons won by twelve. Okay, I figure Greg got hurt. Like the papers say. A freak injury, that's not his fault. Don't get me wrong. He's still responsible for what I lost. Why should I pay for his freak injury?' He paused to see if anyone was going to argue with his logic. No one bothered. 'So I waited for Downing to call me, but he never did. I'm owed close to two million by now. Win, you know I can't just sit back with that kind of thing, right?'

Win nodded.

'When was the last time Greg made a payment to you?' Myron asked.

'It's been a while. I don't know. Five, six months maybe.'

'Nothing more recent?'

'Nothing.'

They talked a bit more. Esperanza, Big Cyndi, Camouflage, and Brick Wall came back into the room. Win and B Man changed the topic to martial art buddies they had in common. A few minutes later B Man and his entourage left. When the elevator door closed, Big Cyndi turned and smiled widely at Esperanza. Then she began to skip in a circle. The floor shook.

Myron looked a question at Esperanza.

'That big guy,' Esperanza said, 'the one who was with us in the other room.'

'What about him?'

'He asked Cyndi for her phone number.'

Big Cyndi continued skipping with childlike abandon. The occupants of the floor beneath them were probably diving for cover like it was the last day of Pompeii. He turned to Win. 'Did you catch the fact that Greg hadn't paid anything in months?'

Win nodded. 'Clearly the fifty thousand dollars he withdrew before his disappearance was not to pay off gambling debts.'

'So what was it for?'

'To run, I imagine.'

'So he knew at least four days before the fact that he was going to take off,' Myron said.

'It would appear so.'

Myron thought about that for a moment. 'Then the timing of the murder can't just be a coincidence. If Greg planned to disappear, it can't be a coincidence that the day he takes off is the day Liz Gorman gets killed.'

'Doubtful,' Win agreed.

'You think Greg killed her?'

'The clues point in that direction,' Win said. 'I mentioned to you that the money had come from an account handled by Marty Felder. Perhaps Mr Felder has an answer.'

Myron wondered about that. Big Cyndi suddenly stopped skipping. She hugged Esperanza and made a la-la noise. Young love. 'If Felder knew Greg was going into hiding,' Myron said, 'why would he leave those messages on Greg's machine?'

'Perhaps to throw us off. Or perhaps he did not know Greg's intent.'

'I'll call him,' Myron said. 'See if I can make an appointment for tomorrow.'

'You have a game tonight, do you not?'

'Yes.'

'What time?'

'Seven-thirty.' Myron checked his watch. 'But I need to leave pretty soon if I want to talk to Clip first.'

'I'll drive,' Win said. 'I'd like to meet this Mr Arnstein.'

After they left, Esperanza went through the messages on the voice mail. Then she straightened out her desk. Her two photographs – one of her bearded collie Chloe getting Best in Breed at the Westchester Dog Show; the other of her as Little Pocahontas and Big Cyndi as Big Chief Mama, holding up their FLOW (Fabulous Ladies Of Wrestling) tag-team title belts – had been knocked askew by Cyndi's knees.

As she stared at the photographs, something Myron said kept needling her. He was worried about timing. The timing of the murder. The timing of Downing's disappearance. But what about Liz Gorman's timing? What about the timing of her arrival in New York City? The bank in Tucson was robbed two months ago; Liz Gorman also started working for the Parkview Diner two months ago. A criminal on the run would want to get far away from the crime scene, yes, but to a place as populated as New York City? Why?

The more Esperanza thought about it, the more she grew bewildered. There had to be a cause and effect at work here. There had to be something about the bank heist that made Liz Gorman come out this way. Esperanza chewed on this for another minute or two. Then she picked up the phone and called one of Myron and Win's closest contacts at the bureau.

'They need everything you got on the Raven Brigade bank heist in Tucson,' Esperanza said. 'Can you send me a copy of the file?'

'You'll have it by tomorrow morning.'

Chapter 24

Win and Myron shared a somewhat unusual passion for Broadway musicals. Right now, the stereo system in Win's Jag was pumping out the soundtrack from *1776*. A Continental Congressman cried out, 'Somebody better open up a window!' This led to a fierce argument over the merits of opening said window (it was 'hot as hell in Philadelphia') vs. keeping them closed ('too many flies'). Interspersed in this argument, people were telling John Adams to sit down. History.

'Who played the original Thomas Jefferson?' Win asked. He knew the answer. Life with Myron's friends was a nonstop quiz show.

'Movie version or stage?'

Win frowned. 'I don't do movie versions.'

'Ken Howard,' Myron answered.

'Correct. What is Mr Howard's most famous role?'

'The coach on the *White Shadow*.'

'Correct again. The original John Adams?'

'William Daniels.'

'Best known as?'

'The obnoxious surgeon on *St. Elsewhere*.'

'The actress who portrayed Martha Jefferson?'

'Betty Buckley. Best known as Abby on *Eight Is Enough*.'

Win smiled. 'You are good.'

Myron stared out the window, the buildings and cars blurring into one pulsating mass, and thought about Jessica. Moving in with her. There was no reason not to. He loved her. She loved him. More than that, she had made the first move – the first time he could remember such a thing. In most relationships, one partner has more control than the other. It was just the natural order of things. Perfect balance was a hard thing to find. In their case, Jessica currently had the upper hand. Myron knew that – if he hadn't, Esperanza's constant references to his being 'whipped' would surely have made him aware. It didn't mean he loved her more or Jessica loved him less. Or maybe it did. Myron wasn't sure anymore. What he did know for sure was that moments where Jessica made the move – where she was the one exposing herself – were rare. Myron wanted to embrace it, encourage it. He had waited a long time for her to say such words to him. But something held him back. Like with TC, there were a lot of factors pushing and pulling at him.

His mind churned through the pros and cons, but no conclusions spewed forward. What he really wanted was to bounce his thoughts off someone. He deliberated best that way – by thinking out loud with a close friend. The problem was, who? Esperanza, his most dependable confidante, hated Jessica. Win . . . well, when it came to matters of the heart, Win was simply not your man;

something in that nether region had shorted out a long time ago.

Still Myron heard himself say, 'Jessica asked me to move in.'

For a moment Win said nothing. Then: 'Do you get a full share of the playoff money?'

'What?'

'You joined the team late. Have you worked out what share of the playoff money you'll be getting?'

'Don't worry. It's taken care of.'

Win nodded. His eyes remained on the road. The speedometer hovered around eighty, a swiftness Route 3 was not built to bear. Win swerved lanes constantly. Myron had gotten somewhat used to Win's driving over the years, but he still kept his eyes averted from the front windshield.

'Are you staying for the game?' Myron asked.

'That depends.'

'On?'

'On if this Thumper will be there,' Win replied. 'You said she was seeking employment. Perhaps I can interrogate her at the same time.'

'What will you say?'

'That,' Win said, 'is a dilemma we both face. If you ask her about Downing's call, you blow your cover. If I ask her, she'll want to know the whys and wherefores. Either way, unless this Thumper is brain dead, she will be suspicious. Moreover, if she knows anything significant, she will most probably lie.'

'So what do you suggest?'

Win tilted his head as though in deep thought. 'Perhaps I'll bed her,' he concluded. 'Then I can make her talk while lost in the throes of passion.'

'She only sleeps with men on the Giants or the Dragons,' Myron said. Then he frowned and added, 'Bed her?'

Win shrugged. 'Just suggesting an alternative to whipping her with a rubber hose,' he said. 'Unless, of course, she's into that kind of thing.'

'Any other suggestions?'

'I'm working on it.' They took the exit to the Meadowlands in silence. On the CD player, Abigail Adams was telling John Adams that women in Massachusetts needed pins. Win hummed along with the music for a moment. Then he spoke. 'As far as Jessica goes' – he took one hand off the wheel and sort of waved it – 'I'm not one to ask about such things.'

'I know.'

'You were miserable the first time she left,' he added. 'I don't know why you would risk going through that again.'

Myron looked at him. 'You really don't, do you?'

Win said nothing.

'That's sad, Win.'

'Yes,' he replied. 'So very tragic.'

'I'm serious,' Myron said.

Win put a dramatic forearm to his brow. 'Oh, what woe that I may never experience the depths of misery you plunged to when Jessica left. Pity this child.'

'You know there's more to it than that.'

Win put down the arm, shook his head. 'No, my friend, there is not. What was real was your pain. The rest of what you felt is the stuff of cruel delusion.'

'You really feel that way?'

'Yes.'

'About all relationships?'

Win shook his head. 'I never said that.'

232

'How about our friendship? Is that a cruel delusion too?'

'This isn't about us,' Win said.

'I'm just trying to understand—'

'There is nothing to understand,' Win interrupted. 'Do what you believe is best. As I said, I am not the one with which to have this discussion.'

Silence. The arena loomed in front of them. For years, it had been called the Brendan Byrne Arena, named for the unpopular governor who had been in office when the complex had been built. Recently, however, the sports authority needed to raise funds, so the name had been changed to the Continental Airlines Arena – not exactly musical, but then again the old name didn't exactly make you want to break out in song either. Brendan Byrne and his past lackeys cried foul over this affront. What a disgrace, they shouted with grave indignation. This was Governor Byrne's legacy. How could they sell him out like this? But Myron didn't have a problem with the name change. Which would you rather do – tax the people to collect twenty-seven million dollars or bruise a politician's ego? No contest when you thought about it.

Myron glanced over at Win. Win's eyes were on the road, his fingers tightly wrapped around the wheel. Myron's mind flashed back to the morning after Jessica left five years ago. He'd been moping around his house alone when Win knocked on the door. Myron opened it.

Without preamble, Win said, 'Come on. I'll hire you a girl. You need to get laid.'

Myron shook his head.

'Are you certain?'

'Yes,' Myron said.

'Do me a favor then.'

'What?'

'Don't go out and get drunk,' Win said. 'That would be such a cliché.'

'And what, getting laid isn't?'

Win pursed his lips together. 'But at least it's a good cliché.'

Then Win turned around and left. That had been it. They had never broached the subject of his relationship with Jessica again. It'd been a mistake to have brought it up now. Myron should have known better.

There were reasons Win was the way he was. Myron looked now at his friend and truly did pity him. From Win's vantage point, his life had been one long lesson in how to take care of himself. The results weren't always pretty, but they were usually effective. Win had not severed off his feelings or anything that dramatic, nor was he as robotic as he sometimes wanted people to think. But Win had learned not to trust or depend on others very much. There were not many people he cared about, but those he did were cherished with an intensity few ever experienced. The rest of the world meant very little to him.

'I'll get you a seat near Thumper's,' Myron said softly.

Win nodded, pulled into a parking spot. Myron gave his name to Clip's secretary and they were shown into his office. Calvin Johnson was already there, standing to Clip's right. Clip was behind his desk. He looked older today. His cheeks were grayer; and the skin around his jowls seemed looser. When he stood, it seemed to take more effort.

Clip eyed Win for a moment. 'This must be Mr Lockwood.'

He even knew about Win – again well prepared. 'Yes,' Myron said.

'He's helping us with our problem?'

'Yes.'

Introductions were made. Hands were shaken. Rear ends were seated. As was his custom in such situations, Win remained silent. His eyes slid from one side of the room to the other, taking in everything. He liked to study people for a while before speaking to them, especially in their home environment.

'So,' Clip began, forcing up a tired smile, 'what have we got?'

'When you first approached me,' Myron began, 'you were afraid I'd uncover something unsavory. I'd like to know what that something was.'

Clip tried to look amused. 'Nothing personal, Myron,' he began with a light chuckle, 'but if I knew that, I wouldn't have needed to hire you.'

Myron shook his head. 'Not good enough.'

'What?'

'Greg has disappeared before.'

'So?'

'So you never suspected anything unsavory then,' Myron said. 'Why now?'

'I told you. I have the owners' vote coming up.'

'That's your only concern?'

'Of course not,' Clip said. 'I'm worried about Greg too.'

'But you never hired anyone to find him before. What are you afraid of?'

Clip shrugged. 'Probably nothing. I'm just covering all my bases. Why? What have you found out?'

Myron shook his head. 'You never cover all your bases, Clip. You're a risk-taker. Always were. I've seen you trade popular, proven veterans for untested draft picks. I've seen you risk going for the steal rather than hoping your defense holds. You've never been afraid to lean over that edge, to risk it all.'

Clip smiled thinly. 'The problem with that strategy,' he said, 'is that you lose too. Sometimes you lose a lot.'

'What did you lose this time?' Myron asked.

'Nothing yet,' he said. 'But if Greg doesn't come back, it might cost my team a championship ring.'

'That's not what I meant. There's something more going on.'

'I'm sorry,' Clip said, spreading his hands. 'I really don't know what you're talking about. I hired you because it was the logical thing to do. Greg vanished. Now true, he's vanished before, but never this late in the season and never when we were so close to a championship. This simply isn't like him.'

Myron glanced over at Win. Win appeared to be bored.

'Do you know a woman named Liz Gorman?' Myron tried.

In the corner of his eye, Myron saw Calvin sit up a bit.

'No,' Clip said. 'Should I?'

'How about a woman named Carla or Sally?'

'What? You mean have I ever known a woman named—'

'Recently. Or any woman involved in some way with Greg Downing.'

Clip shook his head. 'Calvin?' Calvin also shook his head, but the shake was a little too lingering. 'Why do you ask?' Clip demanded.

'Because that's whom Greg was with the night he vanished,' Myron said.

Clip sat up, his words coming scattergun. 'Have you located her? Where is she now? Maybe they're together.'

Myron looked at Win again. This time, Win nodded

236

ever so slightly. He'd caught it too. 'She's dead,' Myron said.

Any traces of color on Clip's face drained away. Calvin remained silent, but he crossed his legs. A big move for ol' Frosty. 'Dead?'

'Murdered, to be more specific.'

'Oh my God . . .' Clip's eyes leapt from one face to another, as though seeking some sort of answer or solace there. He found none.

'Are you sure you don't know the names Liz Gorman, Carla, or Sally?' Myron asked.

Clip opened his mouth, closed it. No sound came out. He tried again. 'Murdered?'

'Yes.'

'And she was with Greg?'

'He's the last known person to see her alive. His fingerprints are at the murder scene.'

'The murder scene?' His voice trembled, his eyes dazed. 'My God, the blood you found in the basement,' he said. 'The body was at Greg's house?'

'No. She was killed in her apartment in New York.'

Clip looked puzzled. 'But I thought you found blood in Greg's basement. In the playroom.'

'Yes. But that blood is gone now.'

'Gone?' Clip sounded both confused and annoyed. 'What do you mean, gone?'

'I mean somebody cleaned it up.' He looked straight at Clip. 'I mean somebody entered Greg's house in the past two days and tried to snuff out an unsavory scandal.'

Clip startled up at that one. Life came back into the eyes. 'You think it was me?'

'You were the only one I told about the blood. You wanted to keep the discovery secret.'

'I left that up to you,' Clip countered. 'I said I thought it was the wrong move, but I'd respect your decision. Of course, I would want to avoid a scandal. Who wouldn't? But I would never do something like that. You know me better than that, Myron.'

'Clip,' Myron said, 'I have the dead woman's phone records. She called you four days before the murder.'

'What do you mean she called me?'

'Your office number is in the phone records.'

He started to say something, stopped, started again. 'Well, maybe she called here, but that doesn't mean she spoke to me.' His tone was far from convincing. 'Maybe she spoke to my secretary.'

Win cleared his throat. Then he spoke for the first time since entering the office. 'Mr Arnstein?' he said.

'Yes.'

'With all due respect, sir,' Win continued, 'your lies are growing tiresome.'

Clip's mouth dropped. He was used to underlings kissing his rear, not to being called a liar. 'What?'

'Myron has a great deal of respect for you,' Win said. 'That's admirable. People do not earn Myron's respect easily. But you know the dead woman. You talked to her on the phone. We have proof.'

Clip's eyes narrowed. 'What kind of proof?'

'The phone records, for one—'

'—but I just told you—'

'And your own words, for another,' Win finished.

He slowed down, his expression wary. 'What the hell are you talking about?'

Win steepled his fingers. 'Earlier in this conversation, Myron asked you if you knew Liz Gorman or a woman named Carla or Sally. Do you recall that?'

'Yes. I told him no.'

'Correct. And then he told you – and I quote his exact words because they are relevant – "that's whom Greg was with the night he vanished." Awkward phrasing, I admit, but with a purpose. Do you recall your next two queries, Mr Arnstein?'

Clip looked lost. 'No.'

'They were – and again I quote exact words – "Have you located *her* yet? Where is *she* now?" ' Win stopped.

'Yeah, so?'

'You said, *her*. Then you said, *she*. Yet Myron asked you if you knew Liz Gorman or Carla or Sally. From his wording, wouldn't it be natural to assume he was referring to three different women? A *they* rather than a she or her? But you, Mr Arnstein, immediately concluded that these three names belonged to one woman. Don't you find that odd?'

'What?' But Clip's anger was all bluster now. 'You call that evidence?'

Win leaned forward. 'Myron is being well compensated for his efforts here. For that reason, I would normally recommend that he continue working for you. I would advise him to mind his own business and take your money. If you wish to muck up your own investigation, who are we to interfere? Not that Myron would listen. He is a nosy man. Worse, he has this warped sense of doing right, even when it is not required.'

Win stopped, took a breath, leaned back again. Instead of steepling his fingers, he gently bounced the tips against one another. All eyes were on him. 'The problem is,' he continued, 'a woman has been murdered. On top of that, someone has tampered with a crime scene. Someone has also vanished and may very well be a murderer or another victim. In other words, it is now far too dangerous to remain in such a situation with blinders on. The potential costs outweigh the possible benefits. As a businessman, Mr Arnstein, you should understand that.'

Clip remained silent.

'So let us get to it, shall we?' Win spread his hands, then resteepled. 'We know the murder victim spoke to you. Either tell us what she said, or we shake hands and part company.'

'She spoke to me first.' It was Calvin. He shifted in his seat. He avoided Clip's eyes, but there was no need. Clip did not seem upset by the outburst. He sank farther down in his chair, a balloon continuing to deflate. 'She used the name Carla,' Calvin continued.

With a small nod, Win settled back into his chair. He had done his part. The reins were back in Myron's hands.

'What did she say?' Myron asked.

'She said she had some kind of dirt on Greg. She said she could destroy the franchise.'

'What was the dirt?'

Clip came back into the fold. 'We never found out,' he chimed in. Clip hesitated a moment – to buy time or gather himself, Myron wasn't sure which. 'I didn't mean to lie to you, Myron. I'm sorry. I was just trying to protect Greg.'

'You spoke to her too?' Myron asked.

Clip nodded 'Calvin came to me after she called. The next time she called we both spoke to her. She said she wanted money in exchange for silence.'

'How much?'

'Twenty thousand dollars. We were supposed to meet on Monday night.'

'Where?'

'I don't know,' Clip said. 'She was going to tell us the locale on Monday morning, but she never called.'

Probably because she was dead, Myron thought. Dead people rarely made phone calls. 'And she never told you her big secret?'

Clip and Calvin looked a question at each other. Calvin nodded. Then Clip turned back to Myron. 'She didn't have to,' Clip said with resignation. 'We already knew.'

'Knew what?'

'Greg gambled. He owed a lot of money to some very bad people.'

'You already knew about his gambling?'

'Yes,' Clip said.

'How?'

'Greg told me.'

'When?'

'About a month ago,' Clip said. 'He wanted help. I . . . I've always been something of a father figure to him. I care about him. I care about him very much.' He looked up at Myron, his eyes raw with pain. 'I care about you too, Myron. That's what makes this so hard.'

'Makes what so hard?'

But he shook it off. 'I wanted to help him. I convinced him to start seeing somebody. A professional.'

'Did he listen?'

'Greg started with the doctor just last week. A psychiatrist who specializes in gambling addictions. We also talked about him signing an endorsement deal,' he added. 'To pay off the gambling debt.'

'Did Marty Felder know about the gambling?' Myron asked.

'I can't say for certain,' Clip said. 'The doctor told me about the amazing lengths gamblers go to keep their addiction a secret. But Marty Felder handled most of Greg's money. If he didn't know, I'd be surprised.'

Behind Clip's head was a poster of this year's team. Myron looked at it a moment. The co-captains, TC and Greg, were kneeling in front. Greg smiled widely. TC sneered in typical fashion. 'So even when you first hired me,' Myron said, 'you suspected Greg's disappearance had something to do with his gambling.'

'No.' Then thinking further, Clip added. 'At least not in the way you think. I never thought Greg's bookie would harm him. I figured the Forte deal bought him time.'

'Then in what way?'

'I worried about his sanity.' Clip motioned to Greg's image on the poster behind him. 'Greg is not the most balanced person to begin with, but I wondered how much the pressure from the gambling debt weighed on his already questionable sanity. He loved his image, you know, strange as that might sound. He loved being a fan favorite more than the money. But if his fans learned the truth, who knows how they'd react? So I wondered if all of this pressure was too much for him. If maybe he had snapped.'

'And now that a woman is dead,' Myron asked, 'what do you think?'

Clip shook his head vehemently. 'I know Greg better than anyone. When he feels trapped, he runs away. He wouldn't kill anyone. I believe that with all my heart. He is not a violent man. Greg learned the dangers of violence a long time ago.'

No one spoke for several moments. Myron and Win both waited for Clip to elaborate. When he didn't, Win said, 'Mr Arnstein, do you have anything else to tell us?'

'No. That's all.'

Win rose without another word or gesture and walked out of the office. Myron sort of shrugged and started after him.

'Myron?'

He turned back to Clip. The old man was standing now. His eyes looked moist.

'Have a good game tonight,' he said softly. 'It's only a game, after all. Remember that.'

Myron nodded, discomfited yet again by Clip's demeanor. He jogged ahead and caught up with Win.

'Do you have my ticket?' Win asked.

Myron handed it to him.

'Describe this Thumper person please.'

Myron did. When they reached the elevator, Win said, 'Your Mr Arnstein is still not telling us the truth.'

'Anything concrete or just a hunch?'

'I don't do hunches,' Win said. 'Do you believe him?'

'I'm not sure.'

'You are fond of Mr Arnstein, are you not?'

'Yes.'

'Even though he has already admitted lying to you?'

'Yes.'

'Then let me present you with an interesting scenario,' Win said. 'Who, besides Greg, has the most to lose if his gambling addiction becomes public knowledge? Who, besides Greg, would have the greatest motive to keep Liz Gorman silent? And finally, if Greg Downing was about to become a terrible embarrassment to the franchise – to the point of devaluating if not destroying Clip Arnstein's chances of maintaining control – who would have the best motive to make sure Greg Downing disappeared?'

Myron did not bother answering.

Chapter 25

The seat next to Thumper was open. Win took it and gave her the full-wattage smile.

'Good evening,' he said.

She smiled back. 'Hello.'

'You must be Ms Mason.'

She nodded. 'And you are Windsor Horne Lockwood III. I recognize you from the picture in *Forbes*.'

They shook hands, their eyes meeting. Their hands released one another; their eyes didn't. 'A pleasure to meet you, Ms Mason.'

'Please call me Maggie.'

'Yes, fine.' Win upped the smile for a moment. A buzzer sounded on the court. The first quarter was over. He saw Myron stand up to let his teammates sit. Seeing him dressed in a uniform on an NBA court hit Win in a very weird, unpleasant way. He didn't like to watch. He turned back toward Thumper. She looked at him expectantly.

'I understand that you are seeking employment with my firm,' Win said.

'Yes.'

'Do you mind if I ask you a few questions?'

'Please do.' She motioned a welcome with her hand.

'You are currently employed by Kimmel Brothers, are you not?'

'Yes.'

'How many traders do they currently engage?' Win asked.

'Less than ten,' she said. 'We're very small.'

'I see.' Win did the steepling, feigning consideration of her words. 'Do you work there on weekends?'

'Sometimes.'

'Weekend evenings?'

Her eyes narrowed just slightly, then relaxed back into place. 'Sometimes,' she repeated.

'How about last Saturday night?'

'Pardon me?'

'You know Greg Downing, do you not?'

'Of course but—'

'As you are no doubt aware,' Win continued, 'he has been missing since last Saturday night. Interestingly enough, the last call Mr Downing made from his home was to your office. Do you recall that phone call?'

'Mr Lockwood—'

'Please. Call me Win.'

'I don't know what you're trying to do here—'

'It's quite simple really,' Win interrupted. 'Last night, you told my associate Mr Bolitar that you had not spoken to Greg Downing in several months. Yet, as I have just told you, I have information that contradicts your statement. So there is a discrepancy here – a discrepancy that may cause some to view you, Ms Mason, as less than honest. I cannot have that at Lock-Horne Securities. My employees must be beyond reproach. For that reason, I'd like you to explain this contradiction.'

Win took out a bag of peanuts from his coat pocket. He shelled a few in the neatest manner imaginable, swept the shells with small movements into a second bag, then placed the peanuts into his mouth one at a time.

'How do you know Mr Downing called my office?' Thumper asked.

'Please,' Win said with a side glance. 'Let us not waste time with trivialities. His call is an established fact. You know it. I know it. Let us move beyond it.'

'I didn't work last Saturday night,' she said. 'He must have been calling somebody else.'

Win frowned. 'I grow weary of your tactics, Ms Mason. As you just admitted to me, yours is a small firm. I could call your employer, if you wish. I am sure he would be glad to tell Mr Windsor Horne Lockwood III if you were there or not.'

Thumper sat back in her chair, folding her arms across her chest, looking out at the game. The Dragons were up 24 to 22. Her eyes followed the course of the ball down the court. 'I have nothing more to say to you, Mr Lockwood.'

'Ah. No longer interested in a job?'

'That's right.'

'You misunderstand,' Win said. 'I don't mean just with Lock-Horne Securities. I mean with anybody, including your current employer.'

She turned to him. 'What?'

'There are two options here,' Win said. 'Let me spell them out for you clearly, so that you choose the one most suitable for you. One, you tell me why Greg Downing called you on Saturday night. You tell me why you lied to Myron about it. You tell me everything you know about his disappearance.'

'What disappearance?' she interrupted. 'I thought he was injured.'

'Option two,' Win went on. 'You continue to either stay silent or lie to me, in which case I will begin to circulate a rumor within our industry vis-à-vis your integrity. More specifically, I will let it be known that there are federal authorities looking into serious allegations of embezzlement.'

'But . . .' she started, stopped. 'You can't do that.'

'No?' He made an amused face. 'I am Windsor Horne Lockwood III. My word on such matters will not be questioned. You, on the other hand, will have difficulty finding employment as a hat check girl in a roadside Denny's when I'm through.' He smiled and tilted the bag her way. 'Peanut?'

'You're insane.'

'And you are normal,' Win countered. He looked down at the court. 'Say, that young towel boy is wiping a player's sweat off the floor. That must be worth' – he gave a big shrug – 'oh, I don't know. Fellatio at the very least, wouldn't you say?'

Win smiled at her sweetly.

'I'm leaving.' She started to stand.

'Would you sleep with me?' he asked.

She looked at him in horror. 'What?'

'Would you sleep with me? If you're very good, I may consider employing you at Lock-Horne.'

Her teeth were clenched. 'I'm not a prostitute,' she hissed.

'No, you are not a prostitute,' Win said, loud enough so that a few heads turned. 'But you are a hypocrite.'

'What are you talking about?'

Win motioned to her seat. 'Please sit down.'

'I'd rather not.'

'And I'd rather not have to shout.' He motioned again. 'Please.'

With wary eyes she did as he asked. 'What do you want?'

'You find me attractive, do you not?'

She made a face. 'I think you are the most repulsive man I have—'

'I am just speaking only about looks here,' Win said. 'The physical, remember? As you told Myron just last night, having sex is merely a physical thing. Like shaking hands – though with an analogy like that I question your partners' prowess. Now, at the risk of appearing immodest, I know that I am not physically unattractive. When you think back over the many Giants and Dragons you've bedded in your stellar career, surely there must be at least one that was less physically attractive than *moi*.'

Her eyes squinted. She looked intrigued and horror-stricken at the same time. 'Perhaps,' she allowed.

'Yet you will not sleep with me. That, my dear, is hypocritical.'

'How so?' Thumper countered. 'I'm an independent woman. I choose.'

'So you've told me,' Win said. 'But why do you choose only Giants and Dragons?' When she hesitated a bit too long, he smiled and wagged his finger. 'You should at least be honest as to why you made that particular choice.'

'You seem to know a lot about me,' Thumper said. 'Why don't you tell me?'

'Fine. You immediately announce this bizarre rule about Dragons and Giants and whatnot. You set limits. I do not. If I find a woman attractive, that is enough. But you need this random team affiliation. You use it as a fence to separate you.'

'Separate me from what?'

'Not from what. Whom. From so-called freewheeling sluts. As you just pointed out to me, you are not a prostitute. You choose, dammit. You are no slut.'

'That's right, I'm not.'

He smiled. 'But what is a slut? A woman who sleeps around? Well, no. That's what you do. You wouldn't criticize a fellow sister to the cause. So what exactly is a slut? Well, by your definition, there is no such thing. Except, of course, you needed to deny being a slut when I questioned you. Why?'

'Don't make it out to be more than it is,' Thumper said. 'Slut carries with it a negative connotation. That's the only reason I got defensive.'

Win spread his hands. 'But why should there be any negative connotation? If a slut is, by definition, a so-called loose woman, a woman who sleeps around, why not embrace the term with both legs? Why put up these fences? Why create these artificial limits? You use your team affiliations to announce your independence. But it announces the opposite. It announces that you are unsure and insecure.'

'And that's why I'm a hypocrite?'

'Of course. Go back to my request to sleep with you. Either sex is a purely physical act, in which case my brusque behavior with you now should have no bearing on it, or sex is something more than physical. Which is it?'

She smiled, gave a quick head shake. 'You're an interesting man, Mr Lockwood. Maybe I will sleep with you.'

'No good,' he said.

'What?'

'You'll be doing it simply to prove I'm wrong. That, my dear, is as pathetic and insecure as what you are currently doing. But we are getting sidetracked. That is my fault, I apologize. Are you going to tell me about your conversation with Greg Downing, or do I destroy your reputation?'

She looked dazed. It was what he wanted.

'Of course there is option three,' Win continued, 'which closely follows option two. That is, on top of having your reputation destroyed you face a murder charge.'

That made her eyes widen. 'What?'

'Greg Downing is a serious suspect in a murder investigation. If it is discovered that you in some way helped him, that would make you an accessory.' He stopped, frowned. 'But to be frank, I don't think the D.A. will get a conviction. No matter. I'll start with your reputation. We'll see how it goes from there.'

Thumper looked at him steadily. 'Mr Lockwood?'

'Yes.'

'Go fuck yourself,' she said.

Win rose. 'Undeniably a better option than present company.' He smiled and bowed. If he had a hat, he would have tipped it. 'Good day.'

He moved away, head high. There was, of course, a method to such madness. She would not talk. He knew that almost immediately. She was both smart and loyal. A dangerous albeit admirable combination. But what he had said would jar her. Even the best amongst us would panic or at the very least act. He would wait outside and follow her.

He checked the scoreboard. Midway through the second quarter. He had no interest in watching any more of this game. But as he reached the gate, a buzz came over the loudspeaker and then a voice said, 'Now coming in for Troy Erickson, Myron Bolitar.'

Win hesitated. Then he took another step for the exit. He did not wish to watch. But he stopped again and, still standing, he faced the court.

Chapter 26

Myron sat at the far end of the bench. He knew that he wasn't going to play, but his chest was still wrapped in the steel bands of pregame jitters. In his younger days Myron had enjoyed the pressure of big-time competition, even when the jitters reached a level of near paralysis. They never lasted long after the opening tip. Once he had physical contact with an opponent or chased down a loose ball or shot a fade-away jumper, the butterflies flew off, the crowd's cheers and jeers dissolving into something akin to office background music.

Pregame jitters hadn't been a part of Myron's existence for over a decade, and he knew now what he'd always suspected: this nerve-jangled high was directly connected to basketball. Nothing else. He had never experienced anything similar in his business or personal life. Even violent confrontations – a perverted high if ever there was one – were not exactly like this. He had thought this uniquely sports-related sensation would ebb away with age and maturity, when a young man no longer takes a small event like a basketball game and blows it into an entity of near biblical importance, when something so relatively insignificant in the long run is no longer magnified to epic dimensions through the prism of youth. An adult, of course, can see what is useless to explain to a child – that one particular school dance or missed foul shot would be no more than a pang in the future. Yet here Myron was, comfortably ensconced in his thirties and still feeling the same heightened and raw sensations he had known only in youth. They hadn't gone away with age. They'd just hibernated – as Calvin had warned him – hoping for a chance to stir, a chance that normally never came in one man's lifetime.

Were his friends right? Was this all too much for him? Had he not put this all behind him? He spotted Jessica in the stands. She was watching the action, that funny look of concentration on her face. She alone seemed unconcerned by his return, but then again, she had not been a part of his life in his basketball heyday. Did the woman he love not understand, or did she—?

He stopped.

When you are on the bench, an arena can be a small place. He saw, for example, Win speaking with Thumper. He saw Jessica. He saw the other players' wives and girlfriends. And then, entering from a gate dead straight in front of him, he saw his parents. His eyes quickly fled back to the court. He clapped his hands and yelled out encouragement to his teammates, pretending to be interested in the outcome of the game. His mom and dad. They must have flown in early from their trip.

He risked a quick glance. They sat near Jessica now, in the family and friends section. His mom was staring back at him. Even from the distance he could see the lost look in her glassy eyes. Dad's eyes darted about, his jaw taut, as though he were summoning up a little extra before looking at the court straight on. Myron understood. This was all too familiar, like an old family film coming to life. He looked away again.

Leon White came out of the game. He grabbed an empty seat next to Myron. A towel boy draped his sweat top around his shoulders and gave him a squeeze bottle. Leon guzzled some Gatorade, his body glistened with sweat.

'Saw you talking with Thumper last night,' Leon said.

'Yeah.'

'You get some?'

Myron shook his head. 'I remain thump-less.'

Leon chuckled. 'Anyone tell you how she got that nickname?'

'No.'

'When she gets into it – I mean, when she gets really fired up – she's got this habit of thumping her leg up and down. Left leg. Always her left leg, you know. So she's like on her back and you're pumping her for all you're worth and then all of a sudden her left leg starts bopping up and down. You hear thump-thump, get it?'

Myron nodded. He got it.

'So if she don't do that – if a guy don't get Thumper thumping – it's like you haven't done your duty. You can't show your face. You hang your head.' Then he added, 'It's a pretty serious tradition.'

'Like lighting a menorah on Hanukkah,' Myron said.

Leon laughed. 'Well, not exactly.'

'You ever been thumped, Leon?'

'Sure, once.' Then he quickly added, 'But that was before I was married.'

'How long you been married?'

'Me and Fiona been married a little over a year.'

Myron's heart plummeted down an elevator shaft. Fiona. Leon's wife's name was Fiona. He looked up in the stands at the flashy, well-rounded blonde. Fiona began with the letter F.

'Bolitar!'

Myron looked up. It was Donny Walsh, the head coach. 'Yeah?'

'Go in for Erickson.' Walsh said it like the words were fingernail clippings he needed to spit out. 'Take the off guard spot. Put Kiley at the point.'

Myron looked at his coach as if he were speaking Swahili. It was the second quarter. The score was tied.

'What the fuck you waiting for, Bolitar? For Erickson. Now.'

Leon slapped his back. 'Go, man.'

Myron stood. His legs felt like strung-out Slinkys. Thoughts of murder and disappearances fled like bats in a spotlight. He tried to swallow but his mouth was bone dry. He jogged over to the scorer's table. The arena spun like the bed of a drunk. Without conscious thought he discarded his sweats on the floor like a snake changing skin. He nodded at the scorer. 'For Erickson,' he said. Ten seconds later, a buzzer sounded. 'Now coming in the game for Troy Erickson, Myron Bolitar.'

He jogged out, pointing to Erickson. His teammates looked surprised to see him. Erickson said, 'You got Wallace.' Reggie Wallace. One of the game's best shooting guards. Myron lined up next to him and prepared. Wallace studied him with an amused smile.

'SWB alert,' Reggie Wallace called out with a mocking laugh. 'Goddamn SWB alert.'

Myron looked at TC. 'SWB?'

'Slow White Boy,' TC told him.

'Oh.'

Everyone else was breathing deeply and coated with sweat. Myron felt stiff and unprepared. His eyes swung back to Wallace. The ball was about to be inbounded. Something caught Myron's eye and he looked up. Win stood near an exit. His arms crossed. Their eyes met for a brief second. Win gave a half nod. The whistle blew. The game began.

Reggie Wallace began the trash talk immediately. 'You got to be kidding me,' he said. 'Old-timer, I'm gonna make you my woman.'

'Dinner and a movie first,' Myron said.

Wallace looked at him. 'Lame retort, old man.'

Hard to argue.

Wallace lowered himself to a ready position. He shook his head. 'Shit. Might as well have my grandma cover me.'

'Speaking of making someone your woman,' Myron said.

Wallace looked at him hard, nodded. 'Better,' he said.

The Pacers inbounded the ball. Wallace tried to post Myron up under the basket. This was a good thing. Physical contact. Nothing unclasped those steel bands like battling for position. Their bodies bounced against one another with small grunts. At six-four, two-twenty, Myron held his ground. Wallace tried digging back with his butt, but Myron held firm, putting a knee into Wallace's backside.

'Man,' Wallace said, 'you are so strong.'

And with that, he made a move Myron barely saw. He spun off Myron's knee so quickly that Myron barely had time to turn his head. Seeming to use Myron for leverage, Wallace leaped high in the air. From Myron's vantage point, it looked like an Apollo spacecraft heading straight out of the arena. He watched helplessly as Wallace's outstretched hands grasped the lob pass at rim level. He seemed to pause in midair, then continue rising as though gravity itself had decided to freeze frame the moment. When Reggie Wallace finally began to descend, he pulled the ball behind his head before throwing it through the cylinder with frightening force.

Slam dunk.

Wallace landed with both arms spread for applause. His taunting chased Myron up court. 'Welcome to the NBA, has-been. Or never-was. Or whatever the fuck you are. Oh, man, was that pretty or what? How did I look going up? Be honest. Bottom of my sneakers look sweet, don't they? I'm so pretty. So very pretty. How did it feel when I slammed it in your face? Come on, old-timer, you can tell me.'

Myron tried to tune him out. The Dragons came down and missed a quick shot. The Pacers grabbed the rebound and headed back up court. Wallace faked going back inside and popped way out past the three point circle. He caught the pass and shot in one motion. The ball went in with a swish. Three pointer.

'Whoa, old man, did you hear that sound?' Reggie Wallace went on. 'That swish? There is no sweeter sound on earth. You hear me? No sweeter sound at all. Not even a woman crying out in orgasm.'

Myron looked at him. 'Women have orgasms?'

Wallace laughed. 'Touché, old-timer. Touché.'

Myron checked the clock. He'd been in for thirty-four seconds and his man had scored five points. Myron did some quick math. At that rate, Myron could hold Reggie Wallace to under six hundred points per game.

The boos started soon after. Unlike his youth, the crowd sounds did not fade into the background. They were not one indistinguishable blur of sound, a home-court cheer to perhaps ride upon the way a surfer picks up a wave. Or a boo in a rival's arena – something you expect and even thrive on in a perverse way. But to hear your own fans boo your specific performance, to hear your home crowd turn against you – Myron had never experienced that before. He heard the crowd now as never before, as a collective entity of derision and as distinct voices making ugly catcalls. 'You suck, Bolitar!' 'Get that stiff outta there!' 'Blow out your other knee and sit down!' He tried to ignore them but each catcall punctured him like a dagger.

Pride took over. He would not let Wallace score. The mind was willing. The heart was willing. But as Myron soon saw, the knee was not. He was simply too slow. Reggie Wallace scored six more points off Myron that period for a total of eleven. Myron scored two off an open jumper. He took to playing what he used to call 'appendix' basketball; that is, certain players on the floor are like your appendix – they're either superfluous or they hurt you. He tried to stay out of the way and hit TC down low. He kept passing and moving away from the ball. When he saw a big opening and drove the lane near the end of the quarter, the Pacers' big center swatted the shot into the crowd. The boos were thunderous. Myron looked up. His mom and dad were still as two statues. One box over, a group of well-dressed men were cupping their hands around their mouths and starting a 'Bolitar Sucks' chant. Myron saw Win move quickly toward them. Win offered his hand to the cheer's leader. The leader took it. The leader went down.

But the odd thing was, even as Myron stunk up the joint, even as he continued to get beaten on defense and play ineffectively on offense, the old confidence remained. He wanted to stay in the game. He would still look for an opening, relatively unshaken, a man in denial, a man ignoring the mounting evidence that a crowd of 18,812 (according to the loudspeaker) could plainly see. He knew his luck would change. He was a little out of shape, that was all. Soon it would all turn around.

He realized how much that sounded like B Man's description of a compulsive gambler's rationale.

The half ended not long after that. As Myron headed off the court, he looked up again at his parents. They stood and smiled down at him. He smiled and nodded back. He looked toward the group of well-dressed booers. They were nowhere to be seen. Neither was Win.

Nobody spoke to him at halftime, and Myron didn't get in the rest of the game. He suspected that Clip had been behind his playing. Why? What had Clip been trying to prove? The game ended in a two-point victory for the Dragons. By the time they got into the locker room and began changing, Myron's performance was forgotten. The media surrounded TC, who had played a brilliant game, scoring thirty-three points and grabbing eighteen rebounds. TC slapped Myron's back when he walked past him but said nothing.

Myron unlaced his sneakers. He wondered if his parents were going to wait for him. Probably not. They would figure he would want to be alone. His parents, for all their butting in, were actually pretty good at knowing when to make themselves scarce. They'd wait for him at home, staying up all night if they had to. To this day, his father stayed awake watching TV on the couch until Myron got home. Once Myron put the key in the lock, his father feigned sleep, his reading glasses still perched at the end of his nose, the newspaper lying across his chest. Thirty-two years old and his father still waited up for him. Christ, he was too old for that anymore, wasn't he?

Audrey peered tentatively around the corner and waited. Only when he signaled with a beckoning wave did she approach. She stuck her pad and pencil in her purse and shrugged. 'Look at the bright side,' she said.

'And that is?'

'You still have a great ass.'

'It's these pro shorts,' Myron said. 'They really mold and hold.'

'Mold and hold?'

He shrugged. 'Hey, happy birthday.'

'Thanks,' Audrey said.

' "Beware the Ides of March," ' Myron pronounced in dramatic fashion.

'The Ides are the fifteenth,' Audrey said. 'Today is the seventeenth.'

'Yeah, I know. But I never skip an opportunity to quote Shakespeare. Makes me look smart.'

'Brains and a good ass,' Audrey said. 'Who cares if you have no lateral movement?'

'Funny,' Myron said, 'Jess never complains about that.'

'At least not to your face.' Audrey smiled. 'Nice to see you so chipper.'

He returned the smile, shrugged.

Audrey looked around to make sure no one was in earshot. 'I got some info for you,' she said.

'On?'

'On the private eye in the divorce case.'

'Greg hired one?'

'Either him or Felder,' she replied. 'I have a source who does electronics work for ProTec Investigations. They do all of Felder's work. Now my source doesn't know all the details, but he helped set up a videotaping at the Glenpointe Hotel two months ago. You know the Glenpointe?'

Myron nodded. 'The hotel on Route 80? Maybe five miles from here?'

'Right. My source doesn't know what it was for or what ended up on it. He just knows the work was for the Downing divorce. He also confirmed the obvious: this thing is usually done to catch a spouse in *flagrante delicto*.'

Myron frowned. 'This was two months ago?'

'Yep.'

'But Greg and Emily were already separated by then,' Myron said. 'The divorce was practically finalized. What would be the point?'

'The divorce, yes,' she agreed. 'But the child custody battle was just starting.'

'Yeah, but so what? She was a near-single woman having a sexual encounter. That kind of thing hardly proves parental unfitness in this day and age.'

Audrey shook her head. 'You are so naive.'

'What do you mean?'

'A tape of a mother getting it on with some buck at a motel, doing lord-knows-what? We still live in a sexist society. It would be bound to influence a judge.'

Myron mulled it over, but it just wouldn't mesh. 'First of all, you're assuming the judge is both male and a Neanderthal. Second' – he sort of held up his hands and shrugged – 'it's the nineties for crying out loud. A woman separated from her husband having sex with another man? Hardly earth-shattering stuff.'

'I don't know what else to tell you, Myron.'

'You got anything else?'

'That's it,' she said. 'But I'm working on it.'

'Do you know Fiona White?'

'Leon's wife? Enough to say hello. Why?'

'She ever model?'

'Model?' She sort of chuckled. 'Yeah, I guess you'd call it that.'

'She was a centerfold?'

'Yep.'

'You know what month?'

'No. Why?'

He told her about the e-mail. He was fairly sure now that Ms F was Fiona White, that Sepbabe was short for September babe, the month, he bet, that she was a center-fold. Audrey listened raptly. 'I can check it out,' she said when he finished. 'See if she was a September playmate.'

'That would help.'

'It would explain a lot,' Audrey continued. 'About the tension between Downing and Leon.'

Myron nodded.

'Look, I gotta run. Jess is getting the car around back. Keep me posted.'

'Right, have fun.'

He finished up, toweled off, started dressing. He thought about Greg's secret girlfriend, the one who had been staying at his house. Could it possibly be Fiona

White? If so, that would also explain the need for secrecy. Could Leon White have found out about it? That seemed logical based on his antagonism toward Greg. So where did that leave us? And how did this all tie in with Greg's gambling and Liz Gorman's blackmail scheme?

Whoa, hold the phone.

Forget gambling for a moment. Suppose Liz Gorman had something else on Greg Downing, a revelation equally if not potentially more explosive than laying down a few bets. Suppose she had somehow found out that Greg was having an affair with his best friend's wife. Suppose she had decided to blackmail Greg and Clip with this information. How much would Greg pay to keep his fans and teammates from learning about his betrayal? How much would Clip pay to keep that particular warhead from detonating in the midst of a championship run?

It was worth looking into.

Chapter 27

Myron stopped at the traffic light that divided South Livingston Avenue and the JFK Parkway. This particular intersection had barely changed in the past thirty years. The familiar brick facade of Nero's Restaurant was on his right. It had originally been Jimmy Johnson's Steak House, but that had to be at least twenty-five years ago. The same Gulf station occupied another corner, a small firehouse another, undeveloped land on the last.

He turned onto Hobart Gap Road. The Bolitar family had first moved to Livingston when Myron was six weeks old. Little had changed in comparison to the rest of the world. The familiarity of seeing the same sights over so many years was less comforting now than numbing. You didn't notice anything. You looked but you never saw.

As he turned up the same street where his dad had first taught him to ride that two-wheeler with a Batman reflector on the back, he tried to pay true heed to the homes that had surrounded him all of his life. There had been changes, of course, but in his mind it was still 1970. He and his parents still referred to the neighboring homes by their original owners, as though they were Southern plantations. The Rackins, for example, hadn't lived in the Rackin House for over a decade. Myron didn't know anymore who lived in the Kirschner Place or the Roth House or the Parkers'. Like the Bolitars, the Rackins and the Kirschners and the rest had moved in when the construction was new, when you could still see some remnants of the Schnectman farm, when Livingston was considered the boonies, as far away from New York City at twenty-five miles as western Pennsylvania. The Rackins and the Kirschners and the Roths had lived a big chunk of their lives here. They'd moved in with infant children, raised them, taught them how to ride bicycles on the same streets Myron had learned on, sent them to Burnet Hill elementary school, then Heritage Junior High, finally Livingston High School. The kids had gone off to college, visiting only on college breaks. Not long after, wedding invitations went out. A few started displaying photos of grandchildren, shaking their heads in disbelief at how time flew. Eventually the Rackins and the Kirschners and the Roths felt out of place. This town designed to raise kids held nothing for them anymore. Their familiar homes suddenly felt too big and too empty, so they put them on the market and sold them to new young families with infant children who would too soon go off to Burnet Hill elementary school, then Heritage Junior High, and finally Livingston High School.

Life, Myron decided, was not that different from one of those depressing life insurance commercials.

Some neighborhood old-timers had managed to hang on. You could usually tell which houses belonged to them because – in spite of the fact that the children were grown – they had built additions and nice porches and kept their lawns well groomed. The Brauns and the Goldsteins were two who had done just that. And of course, Al and Ellen Bolitar.

Myron pulled his Ford Taurus into the driveway, his headlights sweeping across the front yard like searchlights during a prison break. He parked up on the blacktop not far from the basketball hoop. He turned off the ignition. For a moment he just stared at the basket. An image of his father lifting him so he could reach the basket appeared before him. If the image had come from memory or imagination, he could not say. Nor did it matter.

As he moved toward the house, outside lights came on via a motion detector. Though the detectors had been installed three years ago, they were still a source of unbridled awe for his parents, who considered this technological advance on a par with the discovery of fire. When the motion detectors were first put up, Mom and Dad spent blissful hours in disbelief testing the mechanism, seeing if they could duck under its eye or walk super-slowly so that the detector would not sense them. Sometimes in life, it's the simple pleasures.

His parents were sitting in the kitchen. When he entered, they both quickly pretended they were doing something.

'Hi,' he said.

They looked at him with tilted heads and too-concerned eyes. 'Hi, sweetheart,' Mom said.

'Hi, Myron,' Dad said.

'You're back from Europe early,' Myron said.

Both heads nodded like they were guilty of a crime.

266

Mom said, 'We wanted to see you play.' She said it gently, like she was walking on thin ice with a blowtorch.

'So how was your trip?' Myron asked.

'Wonderful,' Dad said.

'Marvelous,' Mom added. 'The food they served was just terrific.'

'Small portions though,' Dad said.

'What do you mean, small portions?' Mom snapped.

'I'm just commenting, Ellen. The food was good, but the portions were small.'

'What, did you measure it or something? What do you mean small?'

'I know a small portion when I see one. These were small.'

'Small. Like he needs larger portions. The man eats like a horse. It wouldn't kill you to lose ten pounds, Al.'

'Me? I'm not getting heavy.'

'Oh no? Your pants are getting so tight you'd think you were starring in a dance movie.'

Dad winked at her. 'You didn't seem to have any problem taking them off on the trip.'

'Al!' she shrieked, but there was a smile there too. 'In front of your own child! What's wrong with you?'

Dad looked at Myron, arms spread. 'We were in Venice,' he said in a way of explanation. 'Rome.'

'Say no more,' Myron said. 'Please.'

They laughed. When it died out his mother spoke in a hushed tone.

'You okay, sweetheart?'

'I'm fine,' he said.

'Really?'

'Really.'

'I thought you did some good things out there,' Dad

said. 'You hit TC for a couple of nice passes on the post. Real nice passes. You showed smarts.'

Count on Dad to find the silver lining. 'I bit the big one,' Myron said.

Dad gave a staunch head shake and said, 'You think I'm saying this just to make you feel good?'

'I know you're saying this just to make me feel good.'

'It doesn't matter,' Dad said. 'It never mattered. You know that.'

Myron nodded. He did know. He had witnessed pushy fathers all his life, men who tried to live hollow dreams through their offspring, forcing their sons to carry a burden they themselves could never carry. But not his father. Never his father. Al Bolitar had never needed to fill his son with grandiose stories of his athletic prowess. He never pushed him, possessing the wondrous ability to appear almost indifferent while making it clear he cared intensely. Yes, this was a direct contradiction – sort of a detached attachment – but somehow Dad pulled it off. Sadly, it was unusual for Myron's generation to admit to such wonderment. His generation had remained un-defined – shoehorned between the Beat Generation of Woodstock and the Generation X of MTV, too young when *thirty-something* had ruled the airwaves, too old now for *Beverly Hills, 90210,* or *Melrose Place.* Mostly, it seemed to Myron, he was part of the Blame Generation, where life was a series of reactions and counterreactions. In the same way those pushy fathers put everything on their sons, the sons came right back and blamed their future failures on the fathers. His generation had been taught to look back and pinpoint exact moments when their parents had ruined their lives. Myron never did. If he looked back – if he studied his parents' past feats – it was only to try to unravel their secret before he had children of his own.

'I know what it looked like tonight,' he said, 'but I really don't feel that bad.'

Mom sniffled. 'We know.' Her eyes were red. She sniffled again.

'You're not crying over—'

She shook her head. 'You've grown up. I know that. But when you ran out on the court again like that, for the first time in so long . . .'

Her voice died out. Dad looked away. The three of them were all the same. They were drawn to nostalgia like starlets to paparazzi.

Myron waited until he was sure his voice would be clear. 'Jessica wants me to move in with her,' he said.

He expected protests, at least from his mother. Mom had not forgiven Jessica for leaving the first time; Myron doubted that she ever would. Dad, as was his way, acted like a good news reporter – neutral, but you wondered what opinion he was making under those balanced questions.

Mom looked at Dad. Dad looked back and put a hand on her shoulder. Then Mom said, 'You can always come back,' she said.

Myron almost asked for a clarification, but he stopped himself and simply nodded. The three of them gathered around the kitchen table and began to talk. Myron made himself a grilled cheese. Mom didn't do it for him. Dogs were domesticated, she believed, not people. She never cooked anymore, which Myron took as a positive thing. Her doting was all verbal, and that was all right with him.

They told him about their trip. He briefly and very vaguely sketched out why he was playing pro basketball again. An hour later he headed into his room in the basement. He had lived here since he was sixteen, the year his sister had gone off to college. The basement was subdivided into two rooms – a sitting area he almost never used except for company and hence kept clean, and a bedroom that looked very much like a teenager's. He crawled into bed and looked at the posters on the wall. Most had been up since his adolescence, the colors faded, the corners frayed near the thumbtacks.

Myron had always loved the Celtics – his father had grown up near Boston – and so his two favorite posters were of John Havlicek, the Celtics star of the sixties and seventies, and Larry Bird, the team's star of the eighties. He looked now from Havlicek to Bird. Myron was supposed to have been the next poster on the wall. It had been his boyhood dream. When the Celtics drafted him, it barely surprised him. A higher power was at work. It had been preordained that he would be the next Celtics legend.

Then Burt Wesson slammed into him.

Myron put his hands behind his head. His eyes adjusted to the light. When his phone rang, he reached for it absently.

'We have what you're looking for,' an electronically altered voice said.

'Excuse me?'

'The same thing Downing wanted to buy. It'll cost you fifty thousand dollars. Get the money together. We'll call you with instructions tomorrow night.'

The caller hung up. Myron tried hitting star-six-nine to ring back, but the call was from out of the area. He lowered his head back to the pillow. Then he stared at the two posters and waited for sleep to claim him.

Chapter 28

Martin Felder's office was on Madison Avenue in midtown, not far from Myron's own. The agency was called Felder Inc., the clever name making it very apparent that Marty wasn't on Madison Avenue as a hotshot advertising exec. A sprightly receptionist was all too happy to show Myron the way to Marty's office.

The door was already open. 'Marty, Myron is here to see you.'

Marty. Myron. It was one of those kind of offices. Everyone was a first name. Everyone was dressed in that new, neat-casual look. Marty, who Myron guessed was in his mid-fifties, wore one of those blue jean shirts with a bright orange tie. His thinning gray hair was plastered down, almost a comb over but not quite. His pants were Banana Republic green and crisply pressed. His orange socks matched the tie and his shoes looked like Hush Puppies.

'Myron!' he exclaimed, pumping Myron's hand. 'Great to see you.'

'Thanks for seeing me so soon, Marty.'

He waved a dismissing hand. 'Myron, please. For you, anytime.' They'd met a few times at different sporting and sports representative events. Myron knew that Marty had a solid reputation as a guy who was – to coin a cliché – tough but fair. Marty also had a knack for getting great media coverage for both himself and his athletes. He'd written a couple of how-to-succeed books which helped enhance his name recognition as well as his rep. On top of that, Marty looked like your favorite, self-effacing uncle. People liked him instantly.

'Can I get you a drink?' he asked. 'Caffè latte perhaps?'

'No thanks.'

He smiled, shook his head. 'I've been planning on calling you for the longest time, Myron. Please, have a seat.'

The walls were bare except for bizarre sculptures twisted out of neon light. His desk was glass, the built-in shelves fiberglass. There were no visible papers. Everything shone like the inside of a spaceship. Felder gestured to a chair in front of the desk for Myron; then he took the other chair in front of the desk. Two equals chatting it up. No desk to use as a divider or intimidator.

Felder started right in. 'I don't have to tell you, Myron, that you are quickly making a name for yourself in this field. Your clients trust you absolutely. Owners and managers respect and fear' – he emphasized the fear part – 'you. That's rare, Myron. Very rare.' He slapped his palms on his thighs and leaned forward. 'Do you enjoy being in sports representation?'

'Yes.'

'Good,' he said with a sharp nod. 'It's important to like what you're doing. Choosing a profession is the most important decision you'll ever make – more important even than choosing a spouse.' He looked up at the ceiling. 'Who was it that said, you may tire of your relationship with people but never of a job you love?'

'Wink Martindale?' Myron said.

Felder chuckled and offered up a shy, caught-himself smile. 'Guess you didn't come here to hear me drone on about my own personal philosophies,' he said. 'So let me put my cards on the table. Just flat out say it. How would you like to come work for Felder Inc.?'

'Work here?' Myron said. Job Interview Rule #1: Dazzle them with sparkling repartee.

'Here's what I'd like to do,' Felder said. 'I want to make you a senior vice president. Your salary would be generous. You'd still be able to give all your clients the personal Bolitar attention they've come to expect, plus you'll have all the resources of Felder Inc. at your command. Think about it, Myron. We employ over one hundred people here. We have our own travel agency to handle all those arrangements for you. We have – well, let's call them what they are, shall we? – gofers who can deal with all those details that are so necessary in our business, freeing you up to tackle important tasks.' He raised a hand as if to stop Myron, though Myron hadn't moved. 'Now I know you have an associate, Miss Esperanza Diaz. She'd come aboard too, of course. At a higher salary. Plus I understand she's finishing up law school this year. There'll be plenty of room for advancement here.' He gestured with his hands before adding, 'So what do you think?'

'I'm very flattered—'

'Don't be,' Felder interrupted. 'It's a sound business decision for me. I know good stock when I see it.' He leaned forward with a sincere smile. 'Let someone else be the client's errand boy, Myron. I want to free you up to do what you do best – recruit new clients and negotiate deals.'

Myron had no interest in giving up his company, but the man knew how to make it sound attractive. 'May I think about it?' he asked.

'Of course,' Felder said, raising his hands in surrendered agreement. 'I don't want to pressure you, Myron. Take your time. I certainly don't expect an answer today.'

'I appreciate that,' Myron said, 'but I actually wanted to talk to you about another matter.'

'Please.' He leaned back, folded his hands on his lap, smiled. 'Go right ahead.'

'It's about Greg Downing.'

The smile didn't budge, but the light behind it flickered a bit. 'Greg Downing?'

'Yes. I have a few questions.'

Still smiling. 'You realize, of course, that I cannot reveal anything that may fall under what I consider privileged.'

'Of course,' Myron agreed. 'I was wondering if you could tell me where he is.'

Marty Felder waited a beat. This was no longer a sales pitch meeting. It was now a negotiation. A good negotiator is frighteningly patient. Like a good interrogator, he must above all else be a listener. He must make his opponent do the talking. After several seconds, Felder asked, 'Why do you want to know that?'

'I need to speak with him,' Myron said.

'May I ask what this is about?'

'I'm afraid it's confidential.'

They looked at each other, both faces open and friendly, but now they were two card sharks who didn't want to show their hands. 'Myron,' Felder began, 'you have to understand my position here. I don't feel comfortable divulging this type of information without having at least some hint as to why you want to see him.'

Time to jar something loose. 'I didn't join the Dragons to make a comeback,' Myron said. 'Clip Arnstein hired me to find Greg.'

Felder's eyebrows dropped to half mast. 'Find him? But I thought he went into seclusion to heal an ankle injury.'

Myron shook his head. 'That was the story Clip told the press.'

'I see.' Felder put a hand to his chin and nodded slowly. 'And you're trying to locate him?'

'Yes.'

'Clip hired you? He chose you himself? It was his idea?'

Myron answered in the affirmative. There was a faint smile on Felder's face now, like he was enjoying an inside joke. 'I'm sure Clip already told you that Greg had done this kind of thing before.'

'Yes,' Myron said.

'So I don't see why you should be all that concerned,' Felder said. 'Your help is appreciated, Myron, but it is really not necessary.'

'You know where he is?'

Felder hesitated. 'Again, Myron, I ask you to put yourself in my position. If one of your clients wanted to stay hidden, would you go against his wishes or respect his rights?'

Myron smelled a bluff. 'That would depend,' he said.

'If the client was in big trouble, I'd probably do whatever I could to help him.'

'What sort of big trouble?' Felder asked.

'Gambling, for one. Greg owes a lot of money to some awfully unpleasant fellows.' Still no reaction from Felder. In this case, Myron read it as a good thing. If most people had just heard that a client owed money to mobsters, they would show some sort of surprise. 'You know about his gambling, don't you, Marty?'

Felder's words were slow, as if he were weighing each one separately with a hand scale. 'You are still new in this business, Myron. With that comes a certain enthusiasm that is not always well placed. I am Greg Downing's sports representative. That gives me certain responsibilities. It is not a carte blanche to run his life. What he or any other client does on his own time is not, should not, and cannot be my concern. For all our sakes. We care about every client, but we are not parental substitutes or life managers. It's important to learn this early on.'

The Cliff Notes summary: he knew about the gambling.

Myron asked, 'Why did Greg withdraw fifty thousand dollars ten days ago?'

Again Felder showed no reaction. He was either beyond being surprised by what Myron knew or he had the ability to shut off any connection between his brain and facial muscles. 'You know I can't discuss that with you – or even confirm that such a withdrawal took place.' He slapped his palms against his thighs again and mounted a smile. 'Do us both a favor, Myron. Think about my offer and drop this other matter. Greg will pop up soon. He always does.'

'I wouldn't be so sure,' Myron said. 'He's in real trouble this time.'

'If you are talking about his alleged gambling debts—'

Myron shook his head. 'I'm not.'

'Then what?'

So far, the man had given Myron nothing. Letting on that he knew about the gambling problem was a lay-up. He had realized Myron knew about it. To deny it would make him look either incompetent for not knowing or dishonest for making a strong denial. Marty Felder was shrewd. He would not misstep. Myron tried shifting direction. 'Why did you videotape Greg's wife?'

He blinked. 'Pardon?'

'ProTec. That's the name of the agency you hired. They set up a videotape surveillance at the Glenpointe Hotel. I'd like to know why.'

Felder looked almost amused. 'Help me understand this, Myron. First you say that my client is in deep trouble. You claim you want to help him. Then you start making allegations about a videotape. I'm having trouble following you.'

'I'm just trying to help your client.'

'The best thing you can do for Greg is to tell me all you know. I am his advocate, Myron. I am truly interested in doing what's best for him – not what might be best for the Dragons or Clip or anybody else. You said he was in trouble. Tell me how.'

Myron shook his head. 'First you tell me about the videotape.'

'No.'

There you have it. Top-notch negotiating getting down to basics. Soon they'd be sticking tongues out at each other, but for now both faces remained pleasant. They were playing the waiting game. Who would be the first to crack? Myron ran down the situation in his mind. The cardinal rule of negotiating: Don't lose sight of what you want and what your opponent wants. Okay. So what did Felder have that Myron wanted? Information on the fifty thousand dollars, the videotape, and maybe some other stuff. What did Myron have that Felder wanted? Not much. Myron had made him curious when he mentioned big trouble. Felder might already know what trouble Greg was in, but he would still want to know what Myron knew. End analysis: Myron needed the information more. He would have to move. Time to up the ante. And no more delicacy.

'I don't have to be the one asking you these questions,' Myron said.

'What do you mean?'

'I could have a homicide detective ask them.'

Felder barely moved, but his pupils expanded in a funny way. 'What?'

'A certain homicide detective is this close' – Myron held up his thumb and index finger close together – 'to putting out an APB on Greg.'

'A homicide detective?'

'Yes.'

'But who was killed?'

Myron shook his head. 'First the videotape.'

Felder was not a man to jump. He refolded his hands on his lap, looked up, tapped his foot. He took his time, considering the pros and cons, the costs and benefits, all that. Myron half-expected him to start charting graphs.

'You never practiced as an attorney, did you, Myron?'

Myron shook his head. 'I passed the bar. That's about it.'

'You're lucky,' he said. He sighed and made a tired gesture with his hands. 'You know why people make all the jokes about lawyers being scum? It's because they are. It's not their fault. Not really. It's the system. The system encourages cheating and lying and basic scummy behavior. Suppose you were at a Little League game. Suppose you told the kids that there were no umpires today – that they were to umpire themselves. Wouldn't that lead to some pretty unethical behavior? Probably. But then tell the little tykes that they must win, no matter what. Tell them that their only obligation is to winning and that they should forget about things like fair play and sportsmanship. That's what our judicial system is like, Myron. We allow for deceit in the name of an abstract greater good.'

'Bad analogy,' Myron said.

'Why's that?'

'The part about no umpires. Lawyers have to face judges.'

'Not many of them. Most cases are settled before a judge sees it. You know that. But no matter, my point is made. The system encourages attorneys to lie and distort under the guise of the client's best interest. That best-interest crap has become an all-purpose excuse for anything goes. It's ruining our judicial system.'

'Fascinating, really,' Myron said. 'And all this relates to the videotape . . . ?'

'Very directly,' Felder said. 'Emily Downing's lawyer lied and distorted the truth. She did it to an unethical and unnecessary extreme.'

'Are you talking about the child custody case?' Myron asked.

'Yes.'

'What did she do?'

He smiled. 'I'll give you a hint. This particular claim is made now in one out of every three child custody cases in the United States. It has become almost standard practice, tossed about like rice was at the actual wedding, though it destroys lives.'

'Child abuse?'

Felder did not bother with an answer. 'We felt that we needed to quell these malicious and dangerous untruths. To balance the scales, so to speak. I'm not proud of that. None of us are. But I'm not ashamed either. You can't fight fair if your opponent insists on using brass knuckles. You must do what you can to survive.'

'What did you do?'

'We videotaped Emily Downing in a rather delicate situation.'

'When you say delicate, what exactly do you mean?'

Felder stood up and took a key from his pocket. He unlocked a cabinet and pulled out a videotape. Then he opened another cabinet. A TV and VCR faced them. He placed the tape in the machine and picked up the remote. 'Your turn now,' he said. 'You said Greg was in big trouble.'

It was time for Myron to give a little. Another cardinal rule of negotiation: don't be a pig and just take. It'll backfire in the long run. 'We believe a woman may have been blackmailing Greg,' he said. 'She has several aliases. Usually Carla but she may have used the names Sally or Liz. She was murdered last Saturday night.'

That one stunned him. Or at least he acted stunned. 'Surely the police don't suspect Greg—'

'Yes,' Myron said.

'But why?'

Myron kept it vague. 'Greg was the last person seen with her the night of the murder. His fingerprints were at the murder scene. And the police found the murder weapon at his house.'

'They searched his house?'

'Yes.'

'But they can't do that.'

Already playing the ready-to-distort lawyer. 'They got a warrant,' Myron said. 'Do you know this woman? This Carla or Sally?'

'No.'

'Do you have any idea where Greg is?'

'None.'

Myron watched him, but he couldn't tell if he was lying or not. Except in very rare instances, you can never tell if a person is lying by watching their eyes or their body language or any of that stuff. Nervous, fidgety people tell the truth too, and a good liar could look as sincere as Alan Alda at a telethon. So-called 'students of body language' were usually just fooled with more certainty. 'Why did Greg take out fifty thousand dollars in cash?' Myron asked.

'I didn't ask,' Felder said. 'As I just explained to you, such matters were not my concern.'

'You thought it was for gambling.'

Again Felder didn't bother responding. He lifted his eyes from the floor. 'You said this woman was blackmailing him.'

'Yes,' Myron said.

He looked at Myron steadily. 'Do you know what she had on him?'

'Not for sure. The gambling, I think.'

Felder nodded. With his eyes looking straight ahead, he

pointed the remote control at the television behind him and pressed some buttons. The screen brightened into gray static. Then a black and white image appeared. A hotel room. The camera seemed to be shooting from the ground up. No one was in the room. A digital counter showed the time. The setup reminded Myron of those tapes of Marion Barry smoking a crack pipe.

Uh oh.

Could that be it? Having sex would hardly be grounds to show unfitness as a parent, but what about drugs? What better way to balance the scales, as Felder had put it, than to show the mother smoking or snorting or shooting up in a hotel room? How would that work on a judge?

But as Myron was about to see, he was wrong.

The hotel room door opened. Emily entered alone. She looked around tentatively. She sat on the bed, but then got back up. She paced. She sat down again. She paced again. She checked the bathroom, came right back out, paced. Her fingers picked up whatever object they could find – hotel brochures, room services menus, a television guide.

'Is there any sound?' Myron asked.

Marty Felder shook his head no. He was still not looking at the screen.

Myron watched transfixed as Emily continued to go through her nervous ritual. Suddenly she froze in place and turned to the door. Must have heard a knock. She approached tentatively. Looking for Mr Goodbar? Probably, Myron surmised. But when Emily turned the knob and let the door swing open, Myron realized he was wrong again. It was not Mr Goodbar who entered the hotel room.

It was Ms Goodbar.

The two women talked for a bit. They had a drink from the room's minibar. Then they began to undress. Myron's stomach coiled. By the time they moved to the bed, he had seen more than enough.

'Turn it off.'

Felder did so, still not looking at the screen. 'I meant what I said before. I'm not proud of that.'

'What a guy,' Myron said.

So now he understood Emily's ferocious hostility. She had indeed been taped in *flagrante delicto* – not with another man, but with a woman. Certainly no law against it. But most judges would be influenced. It was the way of the world. And speaking of the way of the world, Myron knew Ms Goodbar by another nickname:

Thumper.

Chapter 29

Myron walked back to his office, wondering what it all meant. For one thing, it meant that Thumper was more than a harmless diversion in all this. But what exactly was she? Had she set up Emily or had she, too, been taped unaware? Were they steady lovers or participants in a one-night stand? Felder claimed he didn't know. On the tape, the two women hadn't appeared to be all that familiar with each other – at least, not in the small portion he had watched – but he was hardly an expert on the subject.

Myron cut east on 50th Street. An albino wearing a Mets cap and yellow boxer shorts on the outside of ripped jeans played an Indian sitar. He was singing the seventies classic 'The Night Chicago Died' in a voice that reminded Myron of elderly Chinese women in the back of a laundromat. The albino also had a tin cup and a stack of cassettes. A sign read 'The Original Benny and His Magical Sitar, only $10.' The original. Oh. Wouldn't want that imitation albino, sitar, AM seventies music, no sir.

Benny smiled at him. When he reached the part of the song where the son learns a hundred cops are dead – maybe even the boy's fathers – Benny began to weep. Moving. Myron stuffed a dollar into the cup. He crossed the street, his thoughts reverting back to the videotape of Emily and Thumper. He wondered now about the relevance. He'd felt like a dirty voyeur for watching the tape in the first place, and now he felt that way for rehashing it in his mind. It was, after all, probably no more than a bizarre aside. What possible connection could there be in all this to the murder of Liz Gorman? None that he could see; then again he still had trouble seeing how Liz Gorman fit in with Greg's gambling or how she fit in at all.

Still, the video undoubtedly raised a few fairly major issues. For one thing, there was the abuse allegations made against Greg. Was there anything to them, or as Marty Felder had indicated, was Emily's attorney just playing hardball? And hadn't Emily told Myron she would do anything to keep her kids? Even kill. How did Emily react when she learned about the videotape? Spurred on by this awful violation, how far would Emily go?

Myron entered his office building on Park Avenue. He exchanged a brief elevator smile with a young woman in a business suit. The elevator reeked of drugstore cologne, the kind where some guy decides that taking a shower is too time-consuming so he opts for sprinkling himself with enough cologne to glaze a wedding cake. The young woman sniffed and looked at Myron.

'I don't wear cologne,' he said.

She didn't seem convinced. Or perhaps she was condemning the gender in general for this affront. Understandable under these circumstances.

'Try holding your breath,' he said.

She looked at him, her face a seaweed green.

When he entered his office, Esperanza smiled and said, 'Good morning.'

'Oh no,' Myron said.

'What?'

'You've never said good morning to me before. Ever.'

'I have, too.'

Myron shook his head. '*Et tu*, Esperanza?'

'What are you talking about?'

'You heard about what happened last night. You're trying to be – dare I say it? – nice to me.'

The fire in her eyes flamed up. 'You think I give a shit about that game? That you got your butt burned at every turn?'

Myron shook his head. 'Too late,' he said. 'You care.'

'I do not. You sucked. Get over it.'

'Nice try.'

'What, nice try? You sucked. S-U-C-K-E-D. A pitiful display. I was embarrassed to know you. I hid my head in shame when I came in.'

He bent down and kissed her cheek.

Esperanza wiped it off with the back of her hand. 'Now I got to get a cootie shot.'

'I'm fine,' he said. 'Really.'

'Like I care. Really.'

The phone rang. She picked it up. 'MB SportsReps. Why yes, Jason, he is here. Hold on a moment.' She put a hand over the receiver. 'It's Jason Blair.'

'The vermin who said you had a nice ass?'

She nodded. 'Remind him about my legs.'

'I'll take it in my office.' A photograph on the top of a stack of papers on her desk caught his eye. 'What's this?'

'The Raven Brigade file,' she said.

He picked up a grainy photo of the group taken in 1973, the only shot of the seven of them together. He quickly found Liz Gorman. He hadn't gotten a good look at her, but from what he saw, there was no way anyone would ever imagine that Carla and Liz Gorman were one and the same. 'Mind if I keep this for a few minutes?' he asked.

'Suit yourself.'

He moved into his office and picked up the phone. 'What's up, Jason?'

'Where the fuck have you been?'

'Not much. How about you?'

'Don't play smart guy with me. You put that little lady on my contract and she fucked it all up. I got half a mind to leave MB.'

'Calm down, Jason. How did she fuck it up?'

His voice cracked with incredulity. 'You don't know?'

'No.'

'Here we are, hot in the middle of negotiating with the Red Sox, right?'

'Right.'

'I want to stay in Boston. We both know that. But we have to make a lot of noise like I'm leaving. That's what you said to do. Make them think you want to switch teams. To up the money. I'm a free agent. This is what we got to do, right?'

'Right.'

'We don't want them to know I want to be on the team again, right?'

'Right. To a degree.'

'Fuck to a degree,' he snapped. 'The other day my neighbor gets a mailing from the Sox, asking him to renew his season tickets. Guess whose picture is on the brochure saying I'm gonna be back? Go ahead. Guess.'

'Would that be yours, Jason?'

'Damn straight mine! So I call up little Miss Nice Ass—'

'She's got great legs too.'

'What?'

'Her legs. She's not that tall, so they're not very long. But they're nicely toned.'

'Will you quit fucking around here, Myron? Listen to me. She tells me the Sox called up and asked if they could use my picture in the ad, even though I wasn't signed. She tells them to go ahead! Go right fucking ahead! Now what are those Red Sox assholes supposed to think, huh? I'll tell you what. They think I'm gonna sign with them no matter what. We lost all our leverage because of her.'

Esperanza opened the door without knocking. 'This came in this morning.' She tossed a contract on Myron's desk. It was Jason's. Myron began to skim through it. Esperanza said, 'Put the pea brain on the speakerphone.'

Myron did.

'Jason.'

'Oh Christ, Esperanza, get the fuck off the line. I'm talking to Myron here.'

She ignored him. 'Even though you don't deserve to know, I finalized your contract. You got everything you wanted and more.'

That slowed him down. 'Four hundred thou more per year?'

'Six hundred thousand. Plus an extra quarter million on the signing bonus.'

'How the . . . what . . . ?'

'The Sox screwed up,' she said. 'Once they printed your picture in that mailer, the deal was as good as done.'

'I don't get it.'

'Simple,' she said. 'The mailer went out with your picture on it. People bought tickets based on that. Meanwhile I called the front office and said that you'd decided to sign with the Rangers down in Texas. I told them the deal was almost final.' She shifted in the chair. 'Now, Jason, pretend you are the Red Sox for a moment. What are you going to do? How are you going to explain to all those ticket holders that Jason Blair, whose picture was on your latest mailer, won't be around because the Texas Rangers outbid them?'

Silence. Then: 'To hell with your ass and legs,' Jason said. 'You got the most gorgeous set of brains I ever laid eyes on.'

Myron said, 'Anything else, Jason?'

'Go practice, Myron. After the way you played last night, you need it. I want to talk over the details with Esperanza.'

'I'll take it at my desk,' Esperanza said.

Myron put him back on hold. 'Nice move,' he said to her.

She shrugged. 'Some kid in the Sox marketing department screwed up. It happens.'

'You read it very well.'

Her tone was exaggerated monotone. 'My heaving bosom is swelling with pride.'

'Forget I said anything. Go take the call.'

'No, really, my goal in life is to be just like you.'

Myron shook his head. 'You'll never have my ass.'

'There's that,' she agreed before leaving.

Left alone, Myron picked up the Raven Brigade photo. He located the three members still at large – Gloria Katz, Susan Milano, and the Raven's enigmatic leader and most famous member, Cole Whiteman. No one had drawn the press's attention and ire more than Cole Whiteman. Myron had been in elementary school when the Ravens went into hiding, yet he still remembered the stories. For one thing, Cole could have passed for Win's brother – blond, patrician-featured, well-to-do family. While everyone else in the picture was scraggly and long haired, Cole was fresh shaven with a conservative haircut, his one sixties concession being sideburns that went down a tad too far. Hardly your Hollywood-cast, radical leftist. But as Myron had learned from Win, looks could often be deceiving.

He put down the photograph and dialed Dimonte's line at One Police Plaza. After Dimonte snarled a hello, Myron asked him if he had anything new.

'You think we're partners now, Bolitar?'

'Just like Starsky and Hutch,' Myron said.

'God, I miss those two,' Dimonte said. 'That hot car. Hanging out with Fuzzy Bear.'

'Huggy Bear,' Myron said.

'What?'

'His name was Huggy Bear, not Fuzzy Bear.'

'Really?'

'Time's short, Rolly. Let me help if I can.'

'You first. What have you got?'

Another negotiation. Myron told him about Greg's gambling. Figuring that Rolly had the phone records too, he also told him about the suspected blackmail scheme. He didn't tell him about the videotape. It wouldn't be fair, not until he spoke to Emily first. Dimonte asked a few questions. When he was satisfied, he said, 'Okay, what do you want to know?'

'Did you find anything else at Greg's house?'

'Nothing,' Dimonte said. 'And I mean, nothing.

Remember how you told me you found some feminine doodads in the bedroom? Some woman's clothes or lotions or something?'

'Yes.'

'Well, someone got rid of them too. No sign of any female apparel.'

So, Myron thought, the lover theory rears its ugly head once again. The lover comes back to the house and cleans up the blood to protect Greg. Then she covers her own tracks too, making sure that their relationship remains a secret. 'How about witnesses?' Myron asked. 'Anybody in Liz Gorman's building see anything?'

'Nope. We canvassed the whole neighborhood. No one saw nada. Everybody was studying or something. Oh, another thing: the press picked up the murder. The story hit the morning editions.'

'You gave them her real name?'

'You crazy? Of course not. They think it's just another breaking and entering homicide. But get this. We got an anonymous tip called in this morning. Someone suggested we check out Greg Downing's house.'

'You're kidding.'

'Nope. Female voice.'

'He's being set up, Rolly.'

'No shit, Sherlock. By a chick nonetheless. And the murder didn't exactly make a big news splash. It was stuck in the back pages like every other unspectacular homicide in this cesspool. Got a little extra juice because it was so close to a college campus.'

'Have you looked into that connection?' Myron asked.

'What connection?'

'Columbia University being so close by. Half of the sixties movements started there. They must still have some sympathizers in the ranks. Maybe someone there helped Liz Gorman.'

Dimonte gave a dramatic sigh. 'Bolitar, do you think all cops are morons?'

'No.'

'You think you're the only one who thought of that?'

'Well,' Myron said, 'I have been called gifted.'

'Not in today's sports section.'

Touché. 'So what did you find out?'

'She rented the place from some whacko, fanatic, leftist, commie, pinko so-called Columbia professor named Sidney Bowman.'

'You're so tolerant, Rolly.'

'Yeah, well, I lose touch when I keep missing those ACLU meetings. Anyway, this pinko won't talk. He says she just rented from him and paid in cash. We all know he's lying. The feds grilled him, but he got a team of faggot, liberal lawyers down here to spring him. Called us a bunch of Nazi pigs and stuff.'

'That's not a compliment, Rolly. In case you don't know.'

'Thanks for clueing me in. I got Krinsky tailing him right now, but he's got nothing. I mean, this Bowman's not a retard. He's got to know we're watching.'

'What else have you got on him?'

'Divorced. No kids. He teaches a class in existential, worthless-in-the-real-world bullshit. According to Krinsky he spends most of his time helping the homeless. That's supposed to be his daily ritual – hanging out with hobos in parks and shelters. Like I said, a whacko.'

Win entered the office without knocking. He headed straight for the corner and opened the closet door, revealing a full-length mirror. He checked his hair. Patted it though every strand was perfect. Then he spread his legs a bit and put his arms straight down. Pretending to be gripping a golf club. Win slowly began to turn into a backswing, watching his motion in the mirror, making sure the front arm remained straight, the grip relaxed. He did this all the time, sometimes stopping in front of store windows while walking down the street. This was the golf equivalent, Myron surmised, to the weight lifters who flex whenever they happen past their reflection. It was also annoying as all hell.

'Got anything else, Rolly?'

'No. You?'

'Nothing. I'll talk to you later.'

'Can hardly wait, Hutch,' Dimonte said. 'You know something? Krinsky's so young he doesn't even remember the show. Sad, ain't it?'

'Today's youth,' Myron said. 'They got no culture.'

Myron hung up. Win continued to study his shot in the mirror. 'Fill me in please,' he said. Myron did. When he finished, Win said, 'This Fiona, the ex-playmate. She sounds like a perfect candidate for a Windsor Horne Lockwood III interrogation.'

'Uh huh,' Myron said. 'But why don't you first tell me about the Windsor Horne Lockwood III interrogation of Thumper?'

Win frowned at the mirror, adjusted his grip. 'She is rather closed mouthed,' he said. 'So I took a distinctive tack.'

'What tack is that?'

Win told him about their conversation. Myron just shook his head. 'So you followed her?'

'Yes.'

'And?'

293

'And there is not much to report. She went to TC's house after the game. She slept over. No calls of any consequence were made from his residence. Either she was not rattled by our conversation, or she doesn't know anything.'

'Or,' Myron added, 'she knew she was being followed.'

Win frowned again. He either didn't like Myron's suggestion or he'd spotted a problem with his swing. Probably the latter. He turned away from the mirror and glanced at Myron's desk. 'Is that the Raven Brigade?'

'Yes. One of them looks like you.' Myron pointed to Cole Whiteman.

Win studied it for a moment. 'While the man is indeed handsome, he lacks both my sense of style and my striking, debonair good looks.'

'Not to mention your humility.'

Win put out his hand. 'Then you understand.'

Myron looked at the picture again. He thought again about what Dimonte said about Professor Sidney Bowman's daily routine. Then it came to him all at once. Ice flooded his veins in a gush. In his mind he changed around Cole's features a bit, imagined distortions from plastic surgery and twenty years of aging. It didn't fit exactly, but it was close enough.

Liz Gorman had disguised herself by perverting her most distinguishing characteristic. Wouldn't it make sense to assume that Cole Whiteman had done the same?

'Myron?'

He looked up. 'I think I know where to find Cole Whiteman.'

Chapter 30

Hector was not thrilled to see Myron back at the Parkview Diner.

'We think we found Sally's accomplice,' Myron said.

Hector cleaned the counter with a rag.

'His name is Norman Lowenstein. Do you know him?'

Hector shook his head.

'He's a homeless man. He hangs out in the back and uses your pay phone.'

Hector stopped cleaning. 'You think I'd let a homeless man in my kitchen?' he said. 'And we don't even have a back. Take a look.'

The answer did not surprise Myron. 'He was sitting at the counter when I was here the other day,' he tried. 'Unshaven. Long black hair. Tattered beige overcoat.'

Still working the rag over the Formica, Hector nodded. 'I think I know who you mean. Black sneakers?'

'Right.'

'He comes in a lot. But I don't know his name.'

'Did you ever see him talk to Sally?'

Hector shrugged. 'Maybe. When she was his waitress. I really don't know.'

'When was he here last?'

'I haven't seen him since the day you came in,' Hector said.

'And you never met him?'

'No.'

'Or know anything about him?'

'No.'

Myron wrote down his phone number on a scrap of paper. 'If you see him, please call. There's a thousand dollar reward.'

Hector studied the phone number. 'This your work number? At AT&T?'

'No. It's my personal phone.'

'Uh huh,' Hector said. 'I called AT&T after you left last time. There's no such thing as Y511 and there's no employee named Bernie Worley.' He did not look particularly upset, but he wasn't dancing the hula either. He just waited, watching Myron with steady eyes.

'I lied to you,' Myron said. 'I'm sorry.'

'What's your real name?' he asked.

'Myron Bolitar.' He gave the man one of his cards. Hector studied it for a moment.

'You're a sports agent?'

'Yes.'

'What does a sports agent have to do with Sally?'

'It's a long story.'

'You shouldn't have lied like that. It wasn't right.'

'I know,' Myron said. 'I wouldn't have done it if it wasn't important.'

Hector put the card in his shirt pocket. 'I have

customers.' He turned away. Myron debated explaining further, but there was no point.

Win was waiting for him on the sidewalk. 'Well?'

'Cole Whiteman is a homeless man who calls himself Norman Lowenstein.'

Win waved down a taxi. A driver in a turban slowed down. They got in. Myron told him where to go. The driver nodded; as he did, his turban buffed the taxi's ceiling. Sitar music blew forth from the front speakers, plucking at the air with razor-sharp nails. Awful. It made Benny and His Magical Sitar sound like Itzhak Perlman. Still it was preferable to Yanni.

'He looks nothing like that old picture,' Myron said. 'He's had plastic surgery. He grew his hair and dyed it jet black.'

They waited at a traffic light. A blue TransAm pulled up next to them, one of those souped up models that hip-hopped up and down while playing music loud enough to crack the earth's core. The taxi actually started shaking from the decibel level. The light turned green. The Trans-Am sped ahead.

'I started thinking about how Liz Gorman had disguised herself,' Myron continued. 'She'd taken her defining attribute and stood it on its head. Cole was the well-bred, clean-cut, rich boy. What better way to stand that on its head than to become an unkempt vagrant?'

'A *Jewish*, unkempt vagrant,' Win corrected.

'Right. So when Dimonte told me that Professor Bowman liked to hang out with the homeless, something clicked.'

The turban barked, 'Route.'

'What?'

'Route. Henry Hudson or Broadway.'

'Henry Hudson,' Win replied He glanced over at Myron. 'Continue.'

'This is what I think happened,' Myron said. 'Cole Whiteman suspected Liz Gorman was in some kind of trouble. Maybe she hadn't called him or met up with him. Something. The problem was, he couldn't check it out himself. Whiteman hasn't survived underground all these years by being stupid. He knew that if the police found her, they'd set a trap for him – the way they're doing right now.'

'So,' Win said, 'he gets you to go in for him.'

Myron nodded. 'He hangs around the diner, hoping to hear something about "Sally." When he overhears me talking to Hector, he figures I'm his best bet. He gives me this weird story about how he knows her from using the phone at the diner. Claimed they were lovers. The story didn't really mesh, but I didn't bother questioning it. Anyway, he takes me to her place. Once I'm inside, he hides and waits to see what happens. He sees the cops come. He probably even sees the body being taken out – all from a safe distance. It confirms what he probably suspected all along. Liz Gorman is dead.'

Win thought about it a moment. 'And now you think Professor Bowman may be contacting him when he visits with the homeless?'

'Yes.'

'So our next goal is to find Cole Whiteman.'

'Yes.'

'Amongst the wretched unbathed in some godforsaken shelter?'

'Yes.'

Win looked pained 'Oh, goodie.'

'We could try to set a trap for him,' Myron said. 'But I think it'll take too long.'

'Set a trap how?'

'I think he's the one who called me on the phone last night,' Myron said. 'Whatever blackmail scheme Liz Gorman was running, it's natural to think that Whiteman was in on it too.'

'But why you?' Win asked. 'If he has dirt on Greg Downing, why would you be the target of his extortion?'

It was a question that had been gnawing at Myron too. 'I'm not sure,' he said slowly. 'The best guess I can come up with is that Whiteman recognized me at the diner. He probably figures that I'm closely connected to Greg Downing. When he couldn't reach Greg, he decided to try me.'

Myron's cellular phone rang. He flicked it on and said hello.

'Hey, Starsky.' It was Dimonte.

'I'm Hutch,' Myron said. 'You're Starsky.'

'Either way,' Dimonte said, 'I think you'll want to get your butt over to the precinct pronto.'

'You got something?'

'Only if you call a picture of the killer leaving Gorman's apartment something,' Dimonte said.

Myron almost dropped the phone. 'For real?'

'Yep. And you'll never guess what.'

'What?'

'It's a she.'

Chapter 31

'Here's the deal,' Dimonte said. They were threading their way through a veritable United Nations of cops, witnesses, and whatnots. Win was waiting outside. He didn't like cops, and they didn't exactly feel like taking him out for ice cream. Best for all if he kept his distance. 'We got a partial image of the perp on a videotape. Problem is, it's not enough to make an ID. I thought maybe you'd recognize her.'

'What kind of videotape?'

'There's a shipping garage on Broadway between One Hundred Tenth and One Hundred Eleventh streets, east side of the block,' Dimonte said. He remained a pace ahead of Myron, moving briskly. He kept turning behind him to make sure Myron was keeping up. 'They handle home electronics. You know how that is – every worker steals like it's a Constitutional right. So the company set up surveillance cameras all over the place. Videotape everything.' Still moving he shook his head, awarded

Myron a toothpick-less smile and added, 'Good old big brother. Every once in a while somebody tapes a crime instead of a bunch of cops beating up a perp, you know what I'm saying?'

They entered a small interrogation room. Myron looked into a mirror. He knew it was one-way glass – so did anybody with even a passing knowledge of cop shows or movies. Myron doubted anybody was on the other side, but he stuck his tongue out just in case. Mr Mature. Krinsky was standing by a television and a VCR. For the second time today, Myron was going to watch a video. He trusted this one would be more tame.

'Hey, Krinsky,' Myron said.

Krinsky barely nodded. Mr Loquacious.

Myron looked over at Dimonte. 'I still don't see how a shipping garage camera could have gotten the killer on tape.'

'One of the cameras is by the truck entrance,' Dimonte explained. 'Just to make sure nothing falls off the truck as it's leaving, if you know what I mean. The camera catches part of the sidewalk. You can see people walking by.' He leaned up against the wall and motioned Myron to sit in a chair. 'You'll see what I mean.'

Myron sat. Krinsky hit the play button. Black and white again. No sound again. But this time the shot was from above. Myron saw the front end of a truck and behind it, a glimpse of the sidewalk. Not many people walked by; the ones that did were barely more than distant silhouettes.

'How did you come up with this?' Myron asked.

'With what?'

'This tape.'

'I always check for this stuff,' Dimonte said, hitching

up his pants by belt loops. 'Parking garages, storage houses, any of those places. They all have surveillance cameras nowadays.'

Myron nodded. 'Good work, Rolly. I'm impressed.'

'Wow,' Dimonte said, 'now I can die happy.'

Everyone's a wiseass. Myron turned his attention back to the screen. 'So how long is each tape?'

'Twelve hours,' Dimonte replied. 'They change them at nine A.M. and P.M. Eight camera set-up. They keep each tape for three weeks. Then they tape over them.' He pointed his fingers. 'Here she comes now. Krinsky.'

Krinsky pressed a button and the tape froze.

'The woman who just entered the picture. On the right. Heading south, which would be away from the scene.'

Myron saw a blurry image. He couldn't see a face or even gather much about her height. She wore high heels and a long overcoat with a frilly neck. Hard to tell much about her weight either. The hair however was familiar. He kept his tone neutral. 'Yeah, I see her.'

'Look at her right hand,' he said.

Myron did. There was something dark and long in it. 'I can't make it out.'

'We got it blown up. Krinsky.'

Krinsky handed Myron two large black and white photographs. The woman's head was enlarged in the first one, but you still couldn't see any facial features. In the second picture, the long, dark object in her hand was clearer.

'We think it's a plastic garbage bag wrapped around something,' Dimonte said. 'Kind of an odd shape, wouldn't you say?'

Myron looked at the photo and nodded. 'You figure it's covering up a baseball bat.'

'Don't you?'

'Yeah,' Myron said.

'We found plastic garbage bags just like that one in Gorman's kitchen.'

'And probably half the kitchens in New York City,' Myron added.

'True enough. Now look at the date and time on the screen.'

On the top left-hand side of the screen, a digital clock read 02:12.32 A.M. The date was early Sunday morning. Just hours after Liz Gorman had been at the Swiss Chalet bar with Greg Downing.

'Did the camera get her coming the other way?' Myron asked.

'Yeah, but it's not too clear. Krinsky.'

Krinsky hit the rewind button. Several seconds later, he stopped and the picture came back on. The time now read 01:41.12. A little more than thirty minutes earlier.

'Coming now,' Dimonte said.

The image almost flew past. Myron only recognized the woman by the long overcoat with the frilly neck. This time, she was carrying nothing in her hand. Myron said, 'Let me see the other part again. All the way through.'

Dimonte nodded at Krinsky. Krinsky found it and hit play. While Myron still couldn't see the woman's face, her walk was another matter. And a person's walk could be fairly distinctive. Myron felt his heart crawl up into his throat.

Dimonte was studying him through squinting eyes. 'You recognize her, Bolitar?'

Myron shook his head. 'No,' he lied.

Chapter 32

Esperanza liked to make lists.

With the Raven Brigade file in front of her, she jotted down the three most important factors in chronological order:

1) The Raven Brigade robs a bank in Tucson.

2) Within days, at least one of the Ravens (Liz Gorman) was in Manhattan.

3) Soon after, Liz Gorman made contact with a high profile professional basketball player.

It didn't flow.

She opened the file and briefly scanned the 'brigade's' history. In 1975 the Ravens had kidnapped Hunt Floot-worth, the twenty-two-year-old son of publishing giant Cooper Flootworth. Hunt had been a classmate at San Francisco State of several of the Ravens, including both Cole Whiteman and Liz Gorman. The famous Cooper Flootworth, never one to sit around idly and let others handle his affairs, hired mercenaries to rescue his son.

During their raid, young Hunt was shot at point-blank range in the head by one of the Ravens. No one knew which one. Of all the brigade members at the scene, four managed to escape.

Big Cyndi skipped into the office. The vibrations rolled Esperanza's pens off the desk.

'Sorry,' Cyndi said.

'It's okay.'

'Timmy called me,' Cyndi said. 'We're going out Friday night.'

Esperanza made a face. 'His name is Timmy?'

'Yeah,' Cyndi said. 'Isn't that sweet?'

'Adorable.'

'I'll be in the conference room,' Cyndi said.

Esperanza turned back to the file. She flipped ahead to the Tucson bank heist – the group's first in more than five years. The robbery took place as the bank was closing. The feds believed one of the security guards was in on it, but so far they had nothing more than the guard's left-leaning background. About $15,000 in cash was taken, but the robbers took the time to blow the safe deposit boxes. Risky. The feds theorized that the Ravens had somehow found out that drug money was stored there. The bank cameras showed two people dressed head to toe in black with black ski masks. No fingerprints or hairs or fibers. Nada.

Esperanza read through the file again, but nothing new exploded from the pages. She tried to imagine what the past twenty years had been like for the surviving Ravens, constantly on the run, never sleeping in the same place very long, leaving and reentering the country, relying on old sympathizers you were never sure you could completely trust. She grabbed her piece of paper and made some more notes:

Liz Gorman ──⟶ Bank Robbery ──⟶ Blackmail

Okay, she thought, follow the arrows. Liz Gorman and the Ravens needed funds, so they robbed the bank. That worked out. It explained the first arrow. That was a gimme anyway. The real problem was that second connection:

Bank Robbery ──⟶ Blackmail.

Simply put, what about the bank robbery had led her to the East Coast and her scheme to blackmail Greg Downing? She tried to write down possibilities.

1) Downing was involved in the bank robbery.

She looked up. It was possible, she surmised. He needed the money for gambling debts. He might do something illegal. But this hypothesis still did not answer the biggest question in all this: how did they meet? How did Liz Gorman and Greg Downing hook up in the first place?

That, she felt, was the key.

She wrote a number two. And waited.

What other link could there be?

Nothing came to mind so she decided to try it from the opposite end. Start with the blackmail and go back. In order to blackmail Downing, Liz Gorman had to have stumbled across something incriminating. When? Esperanza drew another arrow:

Bank Robbery ⟵──⟶ Blackmail

Esperanza felt something like a tiny pinprick. The bank robbery. Something they found at the bank robbery led to the blackmail scheme.

She quickly shuffled through the file, but she already knew that it wasn't there. She picked up the phone and dialed. When the man answered, she said, 'Do you have a list of the people who were renting safe-deposit boxes?'

'Somewhere, I guess,' he replied. 'Why, you need it?'

'Yes.'

Deep sigh. 'All right, I'll start looking. But tell Myron he owes me for this. Owes me big.'

When Emily opened the door, Myron said, 'Are you alone?'

'Why, yes,' she replied with a coy smile. 'What do you have in mind?'

He shoved past her. Emily stumbled back, her mouth an open circle of surprise. He headed straight for the foyer closet and opened it.

'What the hell are you doing?'

Myron did not bother answering. His hands pushed hangers left and right in a frenzy. It didn't take long. He pulled the long overcoat with the frilly neck into view. 'Next time you commit a murder,' he said, 'dispose of the clothes you wore.'

She took two steps back, her hand fluttering toward her mouth. 'Get out,' she hissed.

'I'm giving you one chance to tell the truth.'

'I don't care what you're giving. Get the fuck out of my house.'

He held up the coat. 'You think I'm the only one who knows? The police have a videotape of you at the murder scene. You were wearing this coat.'

Her body slackened. Her face looked like she'd been on the receiving end of a palm strike to the solar plexus.

Myron lowered the coat to his side. 'You planted the murder weapon at your old house,' he said. 'You smeared blood in the basement.' He turned and half-pounced into the living room. The pile of tabloids was still there. He pointed at it. 'You kept searching the papers for the story. When you read about the body being found, you made an anonymous call to the police.'

He glanced back at Emily. Her eyes were unfocused and glazed.

'I kept wondering about the playroom,' Myron said. 'Why, I kept asking myself, would Greg go down there of all places after the murder? But of course that was the point. He wouldn't. The blood could remain undetected for weeks if need be.'

Emily made two fists at her sides. She shook her head, finally finding her voice. 'You don't understand.'

'Then tell me.'

'He wanted my kids.'

'So you framed him for murder.'

'No.'

'This isn't the time to lie, Emily.'

'I'm not lying, Myron. I didn't frame him.'

'You planted the weapon—'

'Yes,' she interrupted, 'you're right about all that. But I didn't frame him.' Her eyes closed and reopened, almost like she was doing a minimeditation. 'You can't frame somebody for something they did.'

Myron stiffened. Emily stared at him stone faced. Her hands were still tightened into small balls. 'Are you saying Greg killed her?'

'Of course.' She moved toward him, taking her time, using the seconds the way a boxer uses an eight count after a surprise left hook. She took the coat from his hands. 'Should I really destroy it, or can I trust you?'

'I think you better explain first.'

'How about some coffee?'

'No,' Myron said.

'I need some. Come on. We'll talk in the kitchen.'

She kept her head high and walked the same walk Myron had watched on the tape. He followed her into a bright white kitchen. The kitchen gleamed in tiled splendor. Most people probably thought the decor was to die for; Myron thought it resembled a urinal at a fancy restaurant.

Emily took out one of those new coffee presses people were using. 'You sure you won't have some? It's Starbucks. Kona Hawaiian blend.'

Myron shook his head. Emily had regained her senses now. She was back in control; he'd let her stay there. A person in control talks more and thinks less.

'I'm trying to figure out where to begin,' she said, adding hot water to the press. The rich aroma immediately filled the air. If this was a coffee commercial, one of them would be saying 'Ahhhh' right about now. 'And don't tell me to begin at the beginning or I'll scream.'

Myron held up his hands to show he would do no such thing.

Emily pushed a little on the plunger, met resistance, pushed again. 'She came up to me one day in the supermarket of all places,' she said. 'Out of the blue. I'm reaching for some frozen bagels, and this woman tells me she has uncovered something that could destroy my husband. She tells me that if I don't pay up, she's going to call the papers.'

'What did you say?'

'I asked her if she'd need a quarter for the phone.' Emily chuckled, stopped pressing, stood upright. 'I figured it was a joke. I told her to go ahead and destroy the bastard. She just nodded and said she'd be in touch.'

'That was it?'

'Yep.'

'When was this?'

'I don't know. Two, three weeks ago.'

'So when did you hear from her next?'

Emily opened a cabinet and took out a coffee mug. The mug had a picture of some cartoon character. The words WORLD'S GREATEST MOM was emblazoned on the side. 'I'm making enough for two,' she said.

'No thank you.'

'You sure?'

'Yes,' Myron said. 'What happened next?'

She bent down and peered into the coffee press like it was a crystal ball. 'A few days after this, Greg did something to me . . .' She stopped. Her tone was different now, the words coming slower and with more care. 'It's like I told you last time you were here. He did something awful. The details aren't important.'

Myron nodded but said nothing. No reason to raise the videotape now and knock her off stride. Facilitate her – that was the key.

'So when she came back and told me Greg was willing to pay big for her silence, I told her I'd pay more to make her talk. She told me it would cost a lot. I told her I didn't care how much. I tried to appeal to her as a woman. I went so far as to tell her about my situation, how Greg was trying to take my kids away from me. She seemed to sympathize, but she also made it clear that she couldn't afford to be philanthropic. If I wanted the information, I'd have to pay up.'

'Did she tell you how much?'

'One hundred thousand dollars.'

Myron held back a whistle. Serious double dipping. Liz

Gorman's strategy was probably to keep collecting from both of them, bleeding them both for as long as she thought it was safe. Or maybe she was hitting hard and fast because she knew she would have to go underground again. Either way, it made sense from Liz Gorman's perspective to collect from all interested parties – Greg, Clip, and Emily. Take money for silence. Take money to sing. Blackmailers have the loyalty of election-year politicians.

'Do you know what she had on Greg?' he asked.

Emily shook her head. 'She wouldn't tell me.'

'But you were prepared to pay her a hundred grand?'

'Yes.'

'Even though you didn't know what it was for?'

'Yes.'

Myron gestured with both hands. 'How did you know she wasn't just a crackpot?'

'The truth? I didn't know. But I was going to lose my kids, for chrissake. I was desperate.'

And, Myron thought, Emily had shown that desperation to Liz Gorman who, in turn, took full advantage of it. 'So you still have no idea what she had on him?'

Emily shook her head. 'None.'

'Could it have been Greg's gambling?'

Her eyes narrowed in confusion. 'What about it?'

'Did you know Greg gambled?'

'Sure. But so what?'

'Do you know how much he gambled?' Myron asked.

'Just a little,' she said. 'A trip to Atlantic City once in a while. Maybe fifty dollars on a football game.'

'Is that what you thought?'

Her eyes moved over his face, trying to read it. 'What are you saying?'

Myron looked out the back window. The pool was still

covered, but some of the robins had returned from the yearly aliya to the south. A dozen or so crowded a bird feeder, heads down, wings flapping happily like dog tails. 'Greg is a compulsive gambler,' Myron said. 'He's lost away millions over the years. Felder didn't embezzle money – Greg lost it gambling.'

Emily gave him a little head shake. 'That can't be,' she said. 'I lived with him for almost ten years. I would have seen something.'

'Gamblers learn how to hide it,' Myron said. 'They lie and cheat and steal – anything to keep on betting. It's an addiction.'

Something in her eyes seemed to spark up. 'And that's what this woman had on Greg? The fact that he gambled?'

'I think so,' Myron said. 'But I can't say for sure.'

'But Greg definitely gambled, right? To the point where he lost all his money?'

'Yes.'

The answer kindled Emily's face with hope. 'Then no judge in the world would award him custody,' she said. 'I'll win.'

'A judge is more likely to give the kids to a gambler than a murderer,' Myron said. 'Or someone who plants false evidence.'

'I told you already. It's not false.'

'So you say,' Myron said. 'But let's get back to what happened with the blackmailer. You were saying she wanted a hundred grand.'

Emily moved back to her coffee press. 'That's right.'

'How were you to pay her?'

'She told me to wait by a pay phone outside a Grand Union supermarket on Saturday night. I was supposed to

312

get there at midnight and have the money ready. She called at midnight on the dot and gave me an address on One Hundred Eleventh Street. I was supposed to get there at two in the morning.'

'So you drove to One Hundred Eleventh Street at two in the morning with one hundred thousand dollars?' He tried not to sound too incredulous.

'I could only raise sixty thousand,' she corrected.

'Did she know that?'

'No. Look, I know this all sounds crazy, but you don't understand how desperate I was. I would have done anything at this point.'

Myron understood. He had seen up-close how far mothers would go. Love twists; maternal love twists absolutely. 'Go on,' he said.

'When I turned the corner, I saw Greg come out of the building,' Emily said. 'I was stunned. He had his collar up, but I could still see his face.' She looked up at Myron. 'I was married to him a long time, but I've never seen his face like this.'

'Like what?'

'So filled with terror,' she replied. 'He practically sprinted toward Amsterdam Avenue. I waited until he turned the corner. Then I approached the door and pressed her apartment button. Nobody answered. I started pressing other buttons. Somebody finally buzzed me in. I went upstairs and knocked on her door for a while. Then I tried the knob. It was unlocked. So I opened the door.'

Emily stopped. A trembling hand brought the cup up to her lips. She took a sip.

'This is going to sound awful,' she went on, 'but I didn't see a dead human being lying there. I only saw my last hope of keeping my kids.'

'So you decided to plant evidence.'

Emily put down the cup and looked at him. Her eyes were clear. 'Yes. And you were right about everything else, too. I chose the playroom because I knew he'd never go down there. I figured that when Greg got back home – I didn't know he'd run – the blood would be safe. Look, I know I went too far, but it's not like I was lying. He killed her.'

'You don't know that.'

'What?'

'He might have stumbled across the body the same way you did.'

'Are you serious?' Her tone was sharp now. 'Of course Greg killed her. The blood on the floor was still fresh. He was the one who had everything to lose. He had motive, opportunity.'

'Just as you do,' Myron said.

'What motive?'

'You wanted to set him up for murder. You wanted to keep your children.'

'That's ridiculous.'

'Do you have any proof your story is true?' Myron asked.

'Do I have what?'

'Proof. I don't think the police are going to buy it.'

'Do you buy it?' she asked him.

'I'd like to see proof.'

'What do you mean, proof?' she snapped 'Like what? It's not like I took pictures.'

'Any facts that back up your story?'

'Why would I kill her, Myron? What possible motive could I have? I needed her alive. She was my best chance of keeping my kids.'

314

'But let's assume for a moment that this woman did indeed have something on Greg,' Myron said. 'Something concrete. Like a letter he wrote or a videotape' – he watched for a reaction – 'or something like that.'

'All right,' she said with a nod. 'Go ahead.'

'And suppose she double-crossed you. Suppose she sold the incriminating evidence to Greg. You admit Greg was there before you. Maybe he paid her enough so that she'd back out of your agreement. Then you go into her apartment. You find out what she's done. You realize your one chance at keeping your kids is gone. So you kill her and pin it on the man who had seemed to have the most to gain from her death: Greg.'

Emily shook her head. 'That's nuts.'

'You hated Greg enough,' Myron continued. 'He played dirty with you; you'd play dirty back.'

'I didn't kill her.'

Myron took another look at the robins, but they were gone. The yard looked barren now, stripped of any life. He waited a few seconds before he turned back toward her. 'I know about the videotape of you and Thumper.'

A quick bolt of anger hit Emily's eyes. Her fingers clutched the coffee mug. Myron half-expected her to throw it at him. 'How the hell . . . ?' Then her grip suddenly slackened. She backed away. She sort of shrugged into a slouch. 'It doesn't matter.'

'It must have made you furious,' he said.

She shook her head. A small sound like a chuckle escaped from her lips. 'You just don't get it, do you, Myron?'

'Don't get what?'

'I wasn't looking for revenge. The only thing that mattered was that the tape could take away my kids.'

'No, I do get it,' Myron countered. 'You'd do anything to keep your kids.'

'I didn't kill her.'

Myron shifted gears. 'Tell me about you and Thumper,' he said.

Emily snorted a derisive laugh. 'I didn't think you were that type, Myron.'

'I'm not.'

She picked up her coffee mug and took a deep sip. 'Did you watch the whole tape from beginning to end?' she asked in a tone somewhere between flirtatious and furious. 'Did you hit the slow motion button a few times, Myron? Rewind and replay certain parts over and over? Drop your pants to your knees?'

'No to all of the above.'

'How much did you see?'

'Just enough to know what was going on.'

'Then you stopped?'

'Then I stopped.'

She regarded him from behind the mug. 'You know something? I actually believe you. You're that kind of goody two-shoes.'

'Emily, I'm trying to help.'

'Help me or Greg?'

'Help get to the truth. I assume you want that too.'

She shrugged noncommittally.

'So when did you and Thumper . . . ?' He made vague coming-together motions with his hand.

She laughed at his discomfort. 'It was the first time,' she replied. 'In all respects.'

'I'm not judging—'

'I don't care if you are or not. You want to know what

happened, right? It was my first time. That little whore set me up.'

'How?'

'What do you mean, how?' she countered. 'You want me to go into details – how many drinks I had, how I was feeling lonely, how her hand started up my leg?'

'I guess not.'

'Then let me give you the quick capsule: she seduced me. We'd flirted innocently a few times in the past. She invited me to the Glenpointe for drinks. It was like a dare on myself – I was drawn and repelled, but I knew I wouldn't go through with it. One thing led to another. We went upstairs. End of capsule.'

'So you're saying Thumper knew you were being filmed?'

'Yes.'

'How do you know? Did she say anything?'

'She didn't say anything. But I know.'

'How?'

'Myron, please stop asking so many goddamn questions. I just know, okay? How else would anyone know to set up a camera in that room? She set me up.'

That made sense, Myron thought. 'But why would she do it?'

Her face registered her exasperation. 'Christ, Myron, she's the team whore. Didn't she fuck you yet? Or no, let me guess. You refused, right?'

Emily stormed away into the living room and collapsed on a couch. 'Get me the aspirin,' she said. 'They're in the bathroom. In the medicine chest.'

Myron shook out two tablets and filled a cup with water. When he came back, he said, 'I have to ask you about one more thing.'

She sighed. 'What?'

'I understand you made allegations against Greg,' he said.

'My attorney made allegations.'

'Were they true?'

She put the pills on her tongue, took some water, swallowed. 'Some of them.'

'How about the ones about him abusing the children?'

'I'm tired, Myron. Can we talk more later?'

'Were they true?'

Emily looked into Myron's eyes, and a cold gust of air blew across his heart. 'Greg wanted to take my kids away from me,' she said slowly. 'He had money, power, prestige on his side. We needed something.'

Myron broke the eye contact. He walked toward the door. 'Don't destroy that coat.'

'You have no right to judge me.'

'Right now,' he said, 'I don't want to be near you.'

Chapter 33

Audrey was leaning against his car. 'Esperanza told me you'd be here.'

Myron nodded.

'Jesus, you look like hell,' she said. 'What happened?'

'Long story.'

'And one that you will soon tell me in riveting detail,' Audrey added. 'But I'll go first. Fiona White was indeed a Miss September in 1992 – or as that particular rag calls it, the September Babe-A-Rama.'

'You're kidding.'

'Nope. Fiona's turn-ons include moonlit walks on the beach and cozy nights by a fireplace.'

He smiled in spite of himself. 'My, what originality.'

'Her turn-offs include shallow men who only care about looks. And men with back hair.'

'Did they list her favorite movies?'

'*Schindler's List*,' Audrey said. 'And *Cannonball Run II.*'

He laughed. 'You're making this up.'

'All except the part about being the September Babe-A-Rama in 1992.'

Myron shook his head. 'Greg Downing and his best friend's wife,' he sighed. In a way, the news sort of buoyed him. Myron's ten-year-old indiscretion with Emily no longer seemed quite so bad. He knew that he shouldn't find comfort in such logic, but man takes solace where he can find it.

Audrey motioned toward the house. 'So what's up with the ex?'

'Long story.'

'You said that already. I got time.'

'I don't.'

She held up her palm like a cop directing traffic. 'Not fair, Myron. I've been a good girl. I've been running your errands and keeping my big mouth shut. Not to mention the fact that I got zippo from you for my birthday. Please don't make me start with the exposure threats again.'

She was right. Myron gave her an abbreviated update, leaving out two parts: the Thumper videotape (no reason anyone had to know about that) and the fact that Carla was the infamous Liz Gorman (it was simply too big a story; no reporter could be trusted to keep it off the record).

Audrey listened intently. Her page-boy cut had grown a little too long in the front. Hairs dangled close to her eyes. She kept sticking out her lower lip and blowing strands off her forehead. Myron had never before seen this particular gesture done by anybody over the age of eleven. It was kind of sweet.

'Do you believe her?' Audrey asked, motioning again to Emily's house.

'I'm not sure,' he replied. 'Her story sort of makes sense. She had no motive to kill the woman, except to frame Greg and that's reaching.'

Audrey tilted her head as if to say, maybe yes – maybe no.

'What?' he asked.

'Well,' she began, 'isn't there a chance that we're looking at this from the wrong perspective?'

'What do you mean?'

'We assume that this blackmailer had dirt on Downing,' Audrey said. 'But maybe she had dirt on Emily.'

Myron stopped, looked back at the house as though it held some answers, looked back at Audrey.

'According to Emily,' Audrey went on, 'the blackmailer approached her. But why? She and Greg aren't together anymore.'

'Carla didn't know that,' Myron replied. 'She figured Emily was his wife and would want to protect him.'

'That's one possibility,' Audrey agreed. 'But I'm not sure it's the best one.'

'Are you saying that they were blackmailing her, not Greg?'

Audrey turned her palms skyward. 'All I'm saying is that it could work the other way too. The blackmailer might have had something on Emily – something Greg would want to use against her in the child custody case.'

Myron folded his arms and leaned against the car. 'But what about Clip?' he asked. 'If they had something on Emily, why would he be interested?'

'I don't know.' Audrey shrugged. 'Maybe she had dirt on both of them.'

'Both of them?'

'Sure. Something that could destroy them both. Or

maybe Clip thought whatever it was – even if it was about Emily – would distract Greg.'

'Any guesses?'

'Not a one,' Audrey said.

Myron mulled it over for a few seconds, but nothing came to him. 'There's a chance,' he said, 'we'll find out tonight.'

'How?'

'The blackmailer called. He wants to sell me the information.'

'Tonight?'

'Yep.'

'Where?'

'I don't know yet. He's going to call. I got my home line forwarded to the cellular.'

As if on cue, the cellular rang. Myron took it out of his pocket.

It was Win. 'The dear professor's schedule was posted on his office door,' he said. 'He is in class for another hour. After that, he has open office hours so the kiddies can whine about grades.'

'Where are you?'

'On Columbia's campus,' Win replied. 'By the way, Columbia women are fairly attractive. I mean, for the Ivy Leagues and all.'

'Glad you haven't lost your powers of observation.'

'Indeed,' Win said. 'Have you finished speaking to our girl?'

Our girl was Emily. Win did not trust cellular phones with names. 'Yes,' he said.

'Goodie. What time should I expect you then?'

'I'm on my way.'

Chapter 34

Win was sitting on a bench near the Columbia gate on 116th Street. He was wearing Eddie Bauer khakis, Top-Siders without socks, a blue button-down Oxford, and a power tie.

'I'm blending in,' Win explained.

'Like a Hasid at Christmas mass,' Myron agreed. 'Is Bowman still in class?'

Win nodded. 'He should be exiting that door in ten minutes.'

'Do you know what he looks like?'

Win handed him a faculty handbook. 'Page two ten,' he said. 'So tell me about Emily.'

Myron did. A tall brunette dressed in a black, skintight cat suit strolled by with her books pressed up against her chest. Julie Newmar on Batman. Win and Myron watched her closely. Meow.

When Myron finished, Win didn't bother with any

questions. 'I have a meeting at the office,' he said as he stood. 'Do you mind?'

Myron shook his head and sat down. Win left. Myron kept his eye on the door. Ten minutes later students began to file out the door. Two minutes after that, Professor Sidney Bowman followed suit. He had the same unkempt, academic beard as in the photo. He was bald but kept his fringe hair ridiculously long. He wore jeans, Timberland boots, and a red flannel shirt. He was either trying to look like a working stiff or Jerry Brown on the campaign trail.

Bowman pushed up his spectacles and kept walking. Myron waited until he was out of sight before following. No rush. The good professor was indeed heading for his office. He crossed the grassy commons and disappeared into yet another brick building. Myron found a bench and sat down.

An hour passed. Myron watched the students and felt very old. He should have brought a newspaper. Sitting for an hour without reading material meant he had to think. His mind kept conjuring up new possibilities and then dismissing them. He knew he was missing something, could see it bobbing in the distance, but every time he reached out it ducked back down below the surface.

He suddenly remembered that he had not checked Greg's answering machine today. He took out his cellular phone and dialed the number. When Greg's voice came on, he pressed 317, the code numbers Greg had programmed into the machine. There was only one message on the tape, but it was a doozy.

'Don't fuck with us,' the electronically altered voice said. 'I've spoken to Bolitar. He's willing to pay. Is that what you want?'

End of message.

Myron sat very still. He stared at a brick, ivyless wall. He listened to a tone for a few seconds and did nothing. What the hell . . . ?

'. . . *He's willing to pay. Is that what you want?*'

Myron pressed the star button to have the message replayed. Then he did it again. He probably would have listened for a fourth time, had Professor Bowman not suddenly appeared at the door.

Bowman stopped to chat with a couple of students. The conversation grew animated, all three displaying fervent, academic earnest. College. Continuing their undoubtedly weighty discourse, they walked off campus and down Amsterdam Avenue. Myron pocketed the phone and kept his distance. At 112th Street, the group separated. The two students continued south. Bowman crossed the street and headed toward the Cathedral of St John the Divine.

St John the Divine's was a massive structure and interestingly enough, the largest cathedral in the world in terms of cubic square feet (St Peter's in Rome is considered a basilica by this statistic, not a cathedral). The edifice was like the city that housed it: awe-inspiring yet worn. Towering columns and gorgeous stained-glass windows were surrounded by signs like HARD HAT AREA (though it dated back to 1892, St John the Divine's has never been completed) and THE CATHEDRAL IS PATROLLED AND ELECTRONICALLY MONITORED FOR YOUR PROTECTION. Wooden planks plugged holes in the granite facade. On the left side of this architectural wonder were two prefab aluminum storage barracks that brought back memories of the opening credits of *Gomer Pyle*. On the right was the Children's Sculpture Garden featuring the Peace Fountain, an enormous sculpture that inspired several moods, none of them peaceful. Images of severed heads and limbs, lobster claws, hands reaching out from the dirt as though trying to escape hell, a man twisting the neck of a deer all whirled together to create an atmosphere that was more Dante meets Goya than languid tranquillity.

Bowman headed down the driveway on the cathedral's right. Myron knew that there was a homeless shelter down that way. He crossed the street and tried to keep his distance. Bowman passed a group of apparently homeless men – all dressed in threadbare synthetics and pants with plunging butt-lines. Some waved and called out to Bowman. Bowman waved back. Then he disappeared through a door. Myron debated what to do. There was no choice really. Even if it meant blowing his cover, he had to go in.

He passed the men, nodded, smiled. They nodded and smiled back. The shelter entrance was a double black door with chintzy lace curtains. Not far from it were two signs – one reading SLOW CHILDREN AT PLAY and the other CATHEDRAL SCHOOL. A homeless shelter and a children's school side by side – an interesting yet working combo. Only in New York.

Myron entered. The room was packed with frayed mattresses and men. A smell like a used bong after an allnighter singed his nostril hairs. Myron tried not to make a face. He spotted Bowman talking to several men in one corner. None of them was Cole Whiteman aka Norman Lowenstein. Myron glanced about the unshaven faces and hollow eyes, his gaze swinging left to right.

They spotted each other at exactly the same time.

From across the room, their eyes locked for perhaps a second, but that was long enough. Cole Whiteman turned and ran. Myron followed, threading his way through the throngs. Professor Bowman spotted the disturbance. Eyes afire, he jumped in Myron's path. Myron lowered his shoulder and flattened him without breaking stride. Just like Jim Brown. Except Jim Brown had to do it against guys like Dick Butkus and Ray Nitschke opposed to a fifty-year-old college professor who probably didn't weigh 180 even with the soft gut. Still.

Cole Whiteman disappeared out a back door, slamming it behind him. Myron went through it not long after. They were outside now, but only briefly. Whiteman disappeared up a metal stairway and back into the main chapel. Myron followed. The inside was very much like the outside – spectacular examples of art and architecture mixed in with the tattered and tacky. The pews, for example, were cheap folding chairs. Lush tapestries hung upon granite walls with seemingly no organization. Ladders were melded into thick columns.

Myron spotted Cole heading back out a nearby door. He sprinted after him, his heels echoing up through the giant arched ceiling. They were back outside. Cole headed down below the cathedral and through heavy fire doors. A sign read A.C.T. PROGRAM. It looked like a basement school or daycare center. Both men raced down a hallway lined with beat-up, metallic lockers. Cole turned right and disappeared behind a wooden door.

When Myron pushed the door open, a darkened stairway greeted him. He heard footsteps below him. He trotted down, the light from above dwindling with each step. He was descending deep into the cathedral's subdwelling now. The walls were cement and clammy to the touch. He wondered if he was entering a crypt or tomb or something equally creepy, if indeed there was equally creepy. Did American cathedrals have crypts, or was that only in Europe?

By the time he reached the bottom step, Myron was bathed in darkness, the light from above little more than distant glint. Great. He stepped into a black hole of a room. He cocked his head, listening for a sound like a dog on a hunt. Nothing. He felt for a light switch. Again nothing. The room had a bone-chilling, windless cold. A damp smell permeated his surroundings. He didn't like it down here. He didn't like it at all.

He inched forward blindly, his arms outstretched like Frankenstein's monster. 'Cole,' he called out. 'I just want to talk to you.'

His words echoed hard before fading out like a song on the radio.

He kept going. The room was still as . . . well, as a tomb. He had moved about five feet when his outstretched fingers hit something. Myron kept his hand on the smooth, cold surface. Like marble, he thought. He traced down. It was a statue of some sort. He felt the arm, the shoulder, to the back, down a marble wing. He wondered if it was some kind of tombstone decoration and quickly withdrew his hand.

He stayed perfectly still and tried to listen again. The only sound was a rushing in his ears, like seashells were pressed against them. He debated going back upstairs, but there was no way he could do that. Cole knew now that his identity was in danger. He would go into hiding again and not resurface. This was Myron's only chance.

He took another step, leading now with his foot. His toe hit something hard and unyielding. Marble again, he figured. He circled around it. Then a sound – a scurrying sound – made him freeze in his tracks. It had come from the ground. Not a mouse. Too big for a mouse. He cocked his head again and waited. His pulse raced. His eyes were just beginning to adjust to the darkness, and he could make out a few shadowy, tall figures. Statues. Lowered heads. He imagined the serene expressions of religious art on their faces, looking down at him with the knowledge they were embarking on a journey to a better place than the one in which they dwelled.

He took another step, and cold fingers of flesh grabbed his ankle.

Myron screamed.

The hand pulled and Myron fell hard against the cement. He kicked his leg loose and scrambled backward. His back slammed into more marble. A man giggled madly. Myron felt the hairs on the nape of his neck stand up. Another man giggled Then another. Like a group of hyenas were encircling him.

Myron tried to get to his feet, but midway up, the men suddenly pounced. He didn't know how many. Hands dragged him back to the floor. He threw a blind fist and connected square into a face. Myron heard a crunching sound and a man fell. But others reached their target. He found himself sprawled on the wet cement, fighting blindly and frantically. He heard grunts. The stench of body odor and alcohol was suffocating, inescapable. The hands were everywhere now. One ripped off his watch. One grabbed his wallet. Myron threw another punch. It hit ribs. Another grunt and another man fell.

Somebody turned on a flashlight and shone it into his eyes. It looked like a train heading toward him.

'Okay,' a voice said, 'back off him.'

The hands slid off like wet snakes. Myron tried to sit up.

'Before you get any cute ideas,' the voice behind the flashlight said, 'take a look at this.'

The voice put a gun in front of the flashlight.

Another voice said, 'Sixty bucks? That's fuckin' all? Shit.'

Myron felt the wallet hit him in the chest.

'Put your hands behind your back.'

He did as the voice asked. Someone grabbed the forearms, pulling them closer together, tearing at the shoulder tendons. A pair of handcuffs were snapped on his wrists.

'Leave us,' the voice said. Myron heard the rustling movements. The air cleared. Myron heard a door open, but the flashlight in his eyes prevented him from seeing anything. Silence followed. After some time passed, the voice said, 'Sorry to do this to you, Myron. They'll let you go in a few hours.'

'How long you going to keep running, Cole?'

Cole Whiteman chuckled. 'Been running a long time,' he said. 'I'm used to it.'

'I'm not here to stop you.'

'Imagine my relief,' he said. 'So how did you figure out who I was?'

'It's not important,' Myron said.

'It is to me.'

'I don't have any interest in bringing you down,' Myron said. 'I just want some information.'

There was a pause. Myron blinked into the light 'How did you get involved in all this?' Cole asked.

'Greg Downing vanished. I was hired to find him.'

'You?'

'Yes.'

Cole Whiteman laughed deep and hearty. The sound bounced around like balls of Silly Putty, the volume

330

reaching a frightening crescendo before mercifully fading away.

'What's so funny?' Myron asked.

'Inside joke.' Cole stood, the flashlight rising with him. 'Look, I have to go. I'm sorry.'

More silence. Cole flicked off the flashlight, plunging Myron back into total blackness. He heard footsteps receding.

'Don't you want to know who killed Liz Gorman?' Myron called out.

The footsteps continued unimpeded. Myron heard a switch and a dim lightbulb came on. Maybe forty watts. It didn't come close to fully illuminating the place, but it was a hell of an improvement. Myron blinked away black spots left over from the flashlight assault and examined his surroundings. The room was jammed with marble statues, lined and piled up without reason or logic, some tilted over. It wasn't a tomb, after all. It was some bizarre, church-art storage room.

Cole Whiteman came back over to him. He sat cross-legged directly in front of Myron. The white stubble was still there – thick in some spots, completely missing in others. His hair jutted up and out in every direction. He lowered the gun to his side.

'I want to know how Liz died,' he said softly.

'She was bludgeoned with a baseball bat,' Myron said.

Cole's eyes closed. 'Who did it?'

'That's what I'm trying to find out. Right now, Greg Downing is the main suspect.'

Cole Whiteman shook his head. 'He wasn't there long enough.'

Myron felt a knot in his stomach. He tried to lick his lips but his mouth was too dry. 'You were there?'

'Across the street behind a garbage can. Like Oscar the fucking Grouch.' His lips smiled, but there was nothing behind it. 'You want no one to notice you? Pretend you're homeless.' He stood up in one fluid motion, like some kind of yoga master. 'A baseball bat,' he said. He pinched the bridge of his nose, turned away, and lowered his chin to his chest. Myron could hear small sobs.

'Help me find her killer, Cole.'

'Why the fuck should I trust you?'

'Me or the police,' Myron said. 'It's up to you.'

That slowed him. 'The cops won't do shit. They think she's a murderer.'

'Then help me,' Myron said.

He sat back down on the floor and inched a bit closer to Myron. 'We're not murderers, you know. The government labeled us that and now everyone believes it. But it's not true. You understand?'

Myron nodded. 'I understand.'

Cole gave him a hard look. 'You patronizing me?'

'No.'

'Don't patronize me,' Cole said. 'You want me to stay and talk, don't you dare patronize me. You stay honest – I'll stay honest.'

'Fine,' Myron said. 'But then don't hand me the "we're not killers, we're freedom fighters" line. I'm not in the mood for a verse of "Blowin' in the Wind."'

'You think that's what I'm talking about?'

'You're not being prosecuted by a corrupt government,' Myron said. 'You kidnapped and killed a man, Cole. You can dress it up in all the fancy language you want, but that's what you did.'

Cole almost smiled. 'You really believe that.'

'Wait, don't tell me; let me guess,' Myron said. He

feigned looking up in thought. 'The government brain-washed me, right? This whole thing has been a CIA plot to crush a dozen college students who threatened to undermine our government.'

'No,' he said. 'But we didn't kill Hunt.'

'Who did?'

Cole hesitated. He looked up and blinked back what looked like tears. 'Hunt shot himself.'

His reddening eyes looked to Myron for a reaction. Myron remained still.

'The kidnapping was a hoax,' Cole went on. 'The whole thing was Hunt's idea. He wanted to hurt his old man so he figured what better way than to take his money and then embarrass the shit out of him? But then those assholes surprised us and Hunt chose another revenge.' Cole's breathing grew deep and erratic. 'He ran outside with the gun. He screamed, "Fuck you, Dad." Then he blew his own head off.'

Myron said nothing.

'Look at our history,' Cole Whiteman said, his voice a semiplea. 'We were a harmless group of stragglers. We protested at antiwar rallies. We got stoned a lot. We never committed one act of violence. None of us even had a gun, except for Hunt. He was my roommate and best friend. I could never hurt him.'

Myron didn't know what to believe; more to the point, he didn't have time now to worry about a twenty-year-old homicide. He waited for Cole to continue, to let him talk out the past, but Cole remained still. Finally, Myron tried to update the subject. 'You saw Greg Downing go into Liz Gorman's building?'

Cole nodded slowly.

'She was blackmailing him?'

'Not just her,' he corrected. 'It was my idea.'

'What did you have on Greg?'

Cole shook his head. 'Not important.'

'She was probably killed over it.'

'Probably,' Cole agreed. 'But you don't need to know the specifics. Trust me.'

Myron was in no position to push it. 'Tell me about the night of the murder.'

Cole scratched at his stubble hard, like a cat on a post. 'Like I said,' he began, 'I was across the street. When you live underground, you have certain rules you live by – rules that have kept us alive and free for the last twenty years. One of them is that after we commit a crime, we never stay together. The feds look for us in groups, not individuals. Since we've been in the city, Liz and I have made sure we were never together. We only commun- icated by pay phone.'

'What about Gloria Katz and Susan Milano?' Myron asked. 'Where are they?'

Cole smiled without mirth or humor. Myron saw the missing teeth and wondered if they were part of the dis- guise or something more sinister. 'I'll tell you about them another time,' he said.

Myron nodded. 'Go on,' he said.

The lines in Cole's face seemed to deepen and darken in the bare light. He took his time before continuing. 'Liz was all packed and ready to go,' he said finally. 'We were going to score the cash and get out of the city, just like I planned. I was just waiting across the street for her signal.'

'What signal?'

'After all the money was collected, she'd flicker the lights three times. That meant she'd be down in ten minutes. We were going to meet at One Hundred Six-teenth Street and take the One train out of here. But the signal never came. In fact, her light never went off at all. I was afraid to go check on her for obvious reasons. We got rules about that, too.'

'Who was Liz supposed to collect from that night?'

'Three people,' Cole said, holding up the pointer, middle man, and ring man. 'Greg Downing' – he dropped ring man – 'his wife what's-her-name—'

'Emily.'

'Right, Emily.' The middle finger went down. 'And the old guy who owns the Dragons.' His hand made a fist now.

Myron's heart contracted. 'Wait a second,' he said. 'Clip Arnstein was supposed to show up?'

'Not supposed to,' Cole corrected. 'He did.'

A black coldness seeped into Myron's bones. 'Clip was there?'

'Yes.'

'And the other two?'

'All three showed up. But that wasn't the plan. Liz was supposed to meet Downing at a bar downtown. They were going to make the transaction there.'

'A place called the Swiss Chalet?'

'Right.'

'But Greg showed up at the apartment too?'

'Later on, yeah. But Clip Arnstein arrived first.'

Win's warning about Clip came back to him. You like him too much. You're not being objective. 'How much was Clip supposed to pay?'

'Thirty thousand dollars.'

'The police only found ten thousand in her apartment,'

Myron said. 'And those bills were from the bank robbery.'

Cole shrugged. 'Either the old man didn't pay her or else the killer took the money.' Then, thinking it through a little more he added, 'Or maybe Clip Arnstein killed her. But he seems kind of old, don't you think?'

Myron didn't answer. 'How long was he inside?'

'Ten, fifteen minutes.'

'Who came by next?'

'Greg Downing. I remember he had a satchel. I figured it had the money in it. He was in and out fast – couldn't have been more than a minute. And he still had the satchel on him when he came out. That's when I started to worry.'

'Greg could have killed her,' Myron said. 'It doesn't take long to hit someone with a baseball bat.'

'But he wasn't carrying a bat,' Cole said. 'The satchel wasn't big enough for one. And Liz had a bat in her apartment. She hated guns, so she kept it for protection.'

Myron knew that no bat had been found at Gorman's apartment. That meant the killer must have used Liz's. Could Greg have gone upstairs, entered her apartment, found the bat, killed her with it, ran out – all in such a short time?

It seemed doubtful.

'What about Emily?' Myron asked.

'She came in last,' Cole said.

'How long was she there?'

'Five minutes. Something like that.'

Time enough to gather the evidence to plant. 'Did you see anybody else go in and out of the building?'

'Sure,' Cole said. 'Lot of students live there.'

'But we can assume that Liz was already dead by the time Greg Downing arrived, right?'

'Right.'

'So the question is, who do you remember going in between the time she got back from the Swiss Chalet and the time Greg arrived? Besides Clip Arnstein.'

Cole thought about it and shrugged. 'Mostly students, I guess. There was a real tall guy—'

'How tall?'

'I don't know. Very.'

'I'm six-four. Taller than me?'

'Yeah, I think so.'

'Was he black?'

'I don't know. I was across the street and the light wasn't too good. I wasn't watching that closely. He might have been black. But I don't think he's our man.'

'Why do you say that?'

'I watched the building until the next morning. He never came back out. He must have lived there or at least stayed with someone overnight. I doubt the killer would've hung around like that.'

Tough to argue, Myron thought. He tried to process what he was hearing in a cold, computerlike way, but the circuits were starting to overload. 'Who else did you remember seeing? Anybody stand out?'

Cole thought again, his eyes wandering aimlessly. 'There was one woman who went in not long before Greg got there. Now that I think of it, she left before he got there too.'

'What did she look like?'

'I don't remember.'

'Blond, brunette?'

Cole shook his head. 'I only remember her because she

wore a long coat. The students all wear windbreakers or sweatshirts or something like that. I remember thinking she looked like an adult.'

'Was she carrying anything? Did she—'

'Look, Myron, I'm sorry. I gotta get moving.' He stood and looked down at Myron with a hollow, lost expression. 'Good luck finding the son of a bitch,' he said. 'Liz was a good person. She never hurt anyone. None of us did.'

Before he could turn away, Myron asked, 'Why did you call me last night? What were you going to sell me?'

Cole smiled sadly and began to walk away. He stopped before he reached the door and turned back around. 'I'm alone now,' he said. 'Gloria Katz was shot in the initial attack. She died three months later. Susan Milano died in a car crash in 1982. Liz and I kept their deaths a secret. We wanted the feds searching for four of us, not two. We thought it would help us stay hidden. So you see, there is only one of us left now.'

He had the bone-weary look of a survivor who wasn't so sure the dead weren't the lucky ones. He rambled back over toward Myron and unlocked the handcuffs. 'Go,' he said.

Myron rose, rubbing his wrists. 'Thank you,' he said.

Cole merely nodded.

'I won't tell anyone where you are.'

'Yeah,' Cole said. 'I know.'

Chapter 35

Myron sprinted to his car and dialed Clip's number. Clip's secretary answered and told him that Mr Arnstein was not in at the moment. He asked her to transfer the call to Calvin Johnson. She put him on hold. Ten seconds later, the call was put through.

'Hey, Myron,' Calvin said, 'what's up?'

'Where's Clip?'

'He should be here in a couple of hours. By game time anyway.'

'Where is he now?'

'I don't know.'

'Find him,' Myron said. 'When you do, call me back.'

'What's going on?' Calvin asked.

'Just find him.'

Myron disconnected the call. He opened the car window and took deep breaths. It was a few minutes after six. Most of the guys would already be at the arena warming up. He headed up Riverside Drive and crossed the George Washington Bridge. He dialed Leon White's number. A woman answered.

'Hello?'

Myron disguised his voice. 'Is this Mrs Fiona White?' he asked.

'Yes, it is.'

'Would you like to subscribe to *Popular Mechanics*? We have a special going on for a limited time.'

'No, thank you.' She hung up.

Conclusion: Fiona White, the Sepbabe and promisor of night ecstasy, was home. Time to pay her a little visit.

He took Route 4 and got off at Kindermack Road. Five minutes later, he was there. The house was a semi-nouveau ranch with orange-tinged brick and diamond-shaped windows. This particular architectural look was all the rage for maybe a two-month span in 1977, and it had aged about as well as the leisure suit. Myron parked in the driveway. On either side of the cement walkway were low-rise iron fences with plastic ivy snaked through them. Classy.

He rang the bell. Fiona White opened the door. Her green, flower-print blouse hung open over a white leotard. Her bleached-blonde hair was tied in a bun that was falling apart, spare strands dangling down over her eyes and ears. She looked at Myron and frowned. 'Yes?'

'Hi, Fiona. I'm Myron Bolitar. We met the other night at TC's house.'

The frown was still there. 'Leon isn't here.'

'I wanted to talk to you.'

Fiona sighed and crossed her arms under the ample bosom. 'What about?'

'Can I come inside?'

'No. I'm busy right now.'

'I think it would be better in private.'

'This is private,' she said, her face unyielding. 'What do you want?'

Myron shrugged, conjured up his most charming smile, saw it would take him nowhere. 'I want to know about you and Greg Downing.'

Fiona White's arms dropped to her side. She suddenly looked horror-stricken. 'What?'

'I know about your e-mail to him. Sepbabe. You were supposed to meet last Saturday for the' – Myron made quote marks with his fingers – ' "greatest night of ecstasy imaginable." Do you recall that?'

Fiona White went to close the door. Myron stuck his foot in the way.

'I've got nothing to say to you,' she said.

'I'm not trying to expose you.'

She pushed the door against his foot. 'Get out.'

'I'm just trying to find Greg Downing.'

'I don't know where he is.'

'Were you having an affair with him?'

'No. Now leave.'

'I saw the e-mail, Fiona.'

'Think what you want. I'm not talking to you.'

'Fine,' Myron said, moving back and throwing up his hands. 'I'll talk to Leon instead.'

Her cheeks flushed. 'Do whatever you want,' she said. 'I did not have an affair with him. I did not see him last Saturday night. I don't know where he is.'

She slammed the door.

Gee, that went well.

Myron headed back to his car. As he reached the door, a black BMW with tinted windows rocketed up the street and screeched to a halt in the driveway. The driver's door opened and Leon flew out like an escaped bird.

'What the fuck you doing here?' he snapped.

'Take it easy, Leon.'

'Fuck take it easy,' he shouted. Leon ran up and stuck his face within an inch of Myron's. 'What the fuck you doing around here, huh?'

'I came by to see you.'

'Bullshit.' The spittle hit Myron's cheeks. 'We're supposed to be at the arena in twenty minutes.' He pushed Myron in the chest. Myron stumbled back. 'Why you here, huh?' Leon pushed again. 'What are you sniffing after?'

'Nothing.'

'You think you'd find my wife alone?'

'It's nothing like that.'

Leon lined himself up for another push. Myron was ready. When Leon's hand reached him, Myron's right forearm shot across his body, pinning Leon's hands helplessly against Myron's chest. Myron bent at the waist, bending Leon's wrists back the wrong way. The pressure forced Leon to drop to one knee. Myron's right hand slid until it met Leon's left. He grabbed it and quickly executed an elbow lock. Leon winced.

'You calm?' Myron asked.

'Motherfucker.'

'That doesn't sound like calm, Leon.' Myron applied a little pressure to the elbow. Joint locks were about controlled pain. They worked by bending joints in ways they were never intended to bend. The more the bend, the more the pain. But go too far and the joint dislocated or a bone broke. Myron was careful.

'Greg is missing again,' Myron said. 'That's why I'm on the team. I'm supposed to find him.'

Leon was still on his knees, his arm locked and upright. 'So what does that have to do with me?'

'You two have had a falling out,' Myron said. 'I want to know why.'

Leon looked up at him. 'Let go of me, Myron.'

'If you attack me again—'

'I won't. Just let go already.'

Myron waited another second or two, then did as Leon asked. Leon rubbed his arm and stood. Myron eyed him.

Leon said, 'You're here because you think Greg and Fiona were getting it on.'

'Were they?'

He shook his head. 'Not from a lack of trying though.'

'What do you mean?'

'He's supposed to be my best friend. But he's not. He's just another fucking superstar who takes what he wants.'

'Including Fiona.'

'He tried. Tried like hell. But she's not like that.'

Myron said nothing. Not his place.

'Guys are always hitting on Fiona,' he went on. 'Because of the way she looks. And the whole racial thing. So when I saw you here when you figured I wouldn't be around . . .' He shrugged into silence.

'Did you ever confront Greg?' Myron asked.

'Yeah,' he said. 'A couple of weeks ago.'

'What did you say to him?'

Leon's eyes narrowed, suddenly wary. 'What does this have to do with finding him?' he asked, suspicious now. 'You trying to pin this on me?'

'Pin what on you?'

343

'You said he's disappeared. You trying to pin that on me?'

'I'm just trying to find out where he is.'

'I got nothing to do with it.'

'I didn't say you did. I just want to know what happened when you confronted him.'

'What do you think happened?' Leon countered. 'The motherfucker denied it. He made this big point of swearing he'd never sleep with any married woman – especially his best friend's wife.'

Myron sort of gulped at that one. 'But you didn't believe him.'

'He's a superstar, Myron.'

'That doesn't make him a liar.'

'No, but it makes him something different. Guys like Greg and Michael Jordan and Shaq and TC . . . they ain't like the rest of us. They got their own thing going. Everyone else is a fucking underling to them. The whole planet is set up to cater to their whims, you know what I'm saying?'

Myron nodded. In college he had been one of those who got to breathe the rarefied air of superstardom. He thought again about the bonds superstars shared. He and Greg had not exchanged more than five words before Greg visited him in the hospital, but there had been a bond. They both knew. Superstars share that rarefied air with very few. As TC had told him, it does indeed isolate in a very bizarre, often unhealthy way.

And with that thought came something of a revelation. Myron took a step back.

He'd always thought that if Greg was in trouble, he'd go to his closest friend for help. But that wasn't the case. If Greg had indeed stumbled across the dead body and panicked, if he had seen all his problems – the gambling debts, the threat of exposure, the divorce, the child custody case, the blackmail, the probability of being a suspect in a murder – closing in on him, who would he go to for help?

He'd go to the guy who understood him best.

He'd go to the guy who could best relate to the unique troubles of superstardom.

He'd go to the guy who shared that rarefied air with him.

Chapter 36

Myron wasn't sure what to do next.

In truth, he had nothing more than a suspicion. There was no proof. No real evidence. But it could potentially answer a lot of questions. Why, for example, had Thumper helped set up Emily on videotape? By all accounts, she was not particularly close to Greg.

But she was to TC.

Again the superstar bond. Greg had feared losing his kids in a custody battle. That's about as big a worry as a person can have. So whom did he turn to for help?

TC.

When Win had leaned on Thumper last night, letting her know that he was searching for Greg, whom had she warned?

TC.

No proof, of course. But it felt very right.

Myron could now put a lot of it together. Greg was under incredible strain – not the best situation for a man of his questionable mental fortitude to be ensnared. What had gone through his mind when he saw Liz Gorman dead on the floor? He'd have to have known that he would be the prime suspect in her murder. As Emily had pointed out, Greg had motive, opportunity, and was at the murder scene. Emily saw that. It was why she set him up. Greg must have seen it too.

So what did he do?

He ran.

Seeing Liz Gorman dead had been the final straw. But Greg had also known that he could not do it alone. People would be looking for him this time. He needed help. He needed time and space.

So whom did Greg reach out to?

The guy who understood him best. Who could relate to the unique troubles of superstardom. Who shared that rarefied air with him.

Myron stopped at a red light. He was close, so god-damn close. TC was helping Greg hide; he was sure of it. But of course, TC was only part of the solution. None of this answered the central question in all this:

Who killed Liz Gorman?

He put his mind on rewind and reviewed the night of the murder. He thought about Clip being the first of the three to arrive. In many ways, Clip was now his best suspect. But Myron still saw big problems with that scenario. What was Clip's motive, for example? Yes, Liz Gorman's information may have been detrimental to the team. The information may have even been potent enough for him to lose the vote. But would Clip pick up a baseball bat and murder a woman over that? People kill for money and power all the time. Would Clip?

But there was still a larger problem at work here, one

that Myron could not get around no matter how hard he tried. Emily was the one who planted the blood and murder weapon at Greg's house. That was established and that made sense. Okay, fine. We know who planted the evidence . . .

. . . but who cleaned it up?

There were only three logical choices: 1) Greg Downing, 2) someone trying to protect Greg, or 3) the killer.

But it couldn't have been Greg. Even if you accept the semi-impossible premise that Greg went back into his house after going into hiding, how did he find the blood? Did he just happen to go down into the playroom? No. It was too ridiculous. The only way Greg would have gone down there was if he'd known the blood had been planted.

Myron froze.

That was it. Whoever had cleaned up the blood had known what Emily had done. They didn't just stumble across it by accident. So how did they find out? From Emily? Uh uh, no way. Emily would be the last person to say anything. Could she have been spotted in the act? Again, the answer was a resounding no. If that had been the case, the bat would have been removed too. More to the point, the blood would have been cleaned up right away – *before* Myron and Win found it. The timing of the clean-up was crucial – it'd happened after Myron and Win had revealed their discovery. That meant Myron and Win were the leak.

So who had they told?

The finger pointed back to Clip.

He turned on Route 3 and entered the Meadowlands complex. The arena loomed before him like a large UFO on a white landing pad. Did Clip Arnstein murder Liz

Gorman and clean up the blood? Myron wrestled with the possibility, but he didn't like it. How had Clip gotten inside Greg's house? There were no signs of forced entry. Had he picked the lock? Doubtful. Did he have a key? Doubtful. Did he hire a professional? Still doubtful. Clip hadn't even let a private investigator do a simple credit card check on Greg for fear word would get out. Whom would he trust to clean up the blood of a person he murdered?

And something else still jabbed at Myron with a sharpened, steel point: the woman's clothes in the bedroom. They had been packed away too. Why would Clip remove all traces of a secret girlfriend? Why would anybody?

The different scenarios swirled in Myron's head like rubber ducks in a whirlpool. He concentrated again on the mystery girlfriend. Could it have been Fiona White? She wasn't talking, but Myron firmly believed that she was not the one. How could Fiona have lived with Greg and kept it hidden from a husband as obsessively jealous as Leon? Perhaps there had been some entanglement between Greg and Fiona – a casual fling in a motel room or something – but Myron no longer believed even that. The more he thought about it, the 'greatest night of sexual ecstasy' epistle was more of a come-on than the talk of two familiar lovers. It seemed more logical that Greg was telling Leon the truth when he said he would never sleep with another man's wife. The thought gave Myron's old shame new life.

A commercial came on the radio. A very hip man and a very hip woman were enjoying a Molson's Golden far too much. They spoke in low voices and laughed at each other's lame jokes. Myron switched it off.

He still had more questions than answers. But when he

picked up his cellular phone to check Greg's answering machine, his fingers began to tremble. Something tightened his chest, making it hard to breathe. This feeling, however, was not like pregame jitters. In fact, it was the furthest thing from them.

Chapter 37

Myron rushed by Clip's secretary.

'He's not in there,' she cried.

Ignoring her, he opened the office door. The lights were off and the room was empty. He spun back toward the secretary. 'Where is he?'

The secretary, a classic battle-ax who had probably been with Clip since the Coolidge Administration, put her hands on her hips. 'I don't have the slightest idea,' she huffed.

Calvin Johnson came out of the adjoining office. Myron approached him. He waited until they were inside Calvin's office and the door was closed. 'Where is he?'

Calvin held up his hands. 'I don't know. I tried his house, but there was no answer.'

'Does he have a car phone?'

'No.'

Myron shook his head and began pacing. 'He lied to me,' Myron said. 'The son of a bitch lied.'

'What?'

'He met with the blackmailer.'

Calvin raised an eyebrow. He moved to the chair behind his desk and sat down. 'What are you talking about?'

'The night she was murdered,' Myron said, 'Clip went to her apartment.'

'But she wasn't supposed to meet with us until Monday,' Calvin said.

'Did you hear her say that?'

Calvin plucked at his chin with his thumb and pointer. The track lights from above his desk reflected off the receding forehead. His face remained the ever placid pool. 'No,' he said slowly. 'Clip told me.'

'He lied to you.'

'But why?'

'Because he's hiding something.'

'Do you know what?'

'No,' Myron said. 'But I intend to find out tonight.'

'How?'

'The blackmailer still wants to sell,' Myron said. 'I'm his new buyer.'

Calvin tilted his head. 'I thought you said the black-mailer was dead.'

'She had a partner.'

'I see,' Calvin said with a slow nod. 'And you're meeting tonight?'

'Yep. But I don't know when or where. He's supposed to call.'

'I see,' Calvin said again. He made a neat fist and coughed into it. 'If it's something damaging. I mean, something that could affect the outcome of the vote tomorrow . . .'

'I'll do whatever is right, Calvin.'

'Of course. I didn't mean to imply otherwise.'

Myron rose. 'Let me know when he gets here.'

'Sure.'

Myron entered the locker room. TC was in his pre-game pose – sprawled on a chair in the corner with a Walkman plugged into his ears, his eyes blazing straight ahead and unmoving. He did not acknowledge Myron. Leon was also there. He, too, studiously avoided Myron's gaze. Not surprising.

Audrey approached. 'How did it go with—?'

Myron shook his head to silence her. She nodded, understanding. 'You okay?' she asked.

'Fine.'

'You think they can hear us?'

'I'm not taking any chances.'

Audrey looked left, then right. 'You find something new?'

'Plenty,' Myron said. 'You should have your story tonight. And then some.'

The gleam in her eye expanded. 'You know where he is?'

Myron nodded. The locker room door opened. Calvin popped his head in. He leaned over and spoke to the Kipper for a moment. When he left, Myron noticed that he turned right, which led to the exit, as opposed to left which would have taken him back to his office.

The cellular phone in Myron's pocket rang. He looked up at Audrey. Audrey looked back. He moved closer to the corner and picked it up.

'Hello?'

An electronically altered voice said, 'You got the money?'

'You got lousy timing,' Myron said.

'Answer my question.'

Leon pulled up his gym shorts. TC stood and bobbed his head in rhythm to the music.

'I have it,' Myron said. 'I also have a game tonight.'

'Forget the game. Do you know Overpeck Park?'

'The one in Leonia? Yeah, I know it.'

'Turn in the right side off Route Ninety-five. Then go down a quarter mile and make another right. You'll see a cul-de-sac. Park there and look for a flashlight. Approach with both your hands raised.'

'Do I get to say a password?' Myron asked. 'I loves passwords.'

'Fifteen minutes. Don't be late. And for the record, I know your superhero partner is in his Park Avenue office. I have a man watching it. If he leaves between now and then, the deal is off.'

Myron turned off the phone. It was coming to a head now. In fifteen minutes it would all be over – one way or another. 'Could you hear?' he asked.

Audrey nodded. 'Most of it.'

'There's going to be some weird stuff going down,' Myron said. 'I need an unbiased journalist to record it. You want to come along?'

She smiled. 'That was a rhetorical question, right?'

'You'll have to keep on the floor in the backseat,' he went on. 'I can't risk having you spotted.'

'No problem,' she said. 'It'll remind me of my high school dates.'

Myron turned toward the door. His nerves were as frayed as an old horse whip. He tried to look nonchalant as they exited. Leon was lacing up his sneakers. TC remained still, but this time his eyes followed them out.

Chapter 38

Rain beat down, blackening the pavement. Cars were just starting to enter the arena lot in force. Myron took the back exit over the New Jersey Turnpike and onto the northbound lanes just past the final toll booth. He veered to the right, staying on Route 95.

'So what's going on?' Audrey asked.

'The man I am about to meet,' he said, 'killed Liz Gorman.'

'Who's Liz Gorman?'

'The blackmailer who was murdered.'

'I thought her name was Carla.'

'That was an alias.'

'Wait a minute. Isn't Liz Gorman the name of some sixties radical?'

Myron nodded. 'It's a long story; I don't have time to go into details. Suffice to say the guy we're about to meet was part of the blackmail scheme. Something went awry. She ended up dead.'

'Do you have evidence?' Audrey asked.

'Not really. That's what I need you for. You have your microcassette player?'

'Sure.'

'Let me have it.'

Audrey reached into her purse and handed it up front.

'I'm going to try to get him to talk,' Myron said.

'How?'

'By pushing the right buttons.'

She frowned. 'You think he'll fall for that?'

'Yeah, I do. If I push the right ones.' He picked up the car phone. 'I have two separate phones here: the car phone and the cellular in my pocket. I'm going to dial the car phone with the cellular and keep the line open. This way, you can listen in. I want you to take down every word. If something happens to me, go to Win. He'll know what to do.'

She leaned forward and nodded. The windshield wipers whipped shadows across her face. The rain picked up its tempo, glistening the road in front of them. Myron took the next exit. A sign reading Overpeck Park greeted them a quarter mile later.

'Get down,' he said.

She disappeared from view. He made the right turn. Another sign told him the park was closed. He ignored it and proceeded ahead. It was too dark to see anything, but he knew there were woods on his left and a horse stables straight ahead. He made the first right. The car's headlights danced across a picnic area, illuminating tables, benches, garbage cans, a swing set, a sliding board. He reached the cul-de-sac and stopped the car. He killed the lights, turned off the engine, and dialed the car's number on his cellular. He answered with the car's speakerphone so Audrey could listen in. Then he waited.

For several minutes nothing happened. The rain pelted down on the roof like tiny pebbles. Audrey remained still in the back. Myron put his hands back on the wheel and felt his grip tighten. He could hear his heart thumping in his chest.

Without warning, a beacon of light sliced through the night like a reaper's scythe. Myron shaded his eyes with his hand and squinted. He slowly opened the car door. The wind had picked up now, spraying the rain into his face. He hefted himself out of the car.

A male voice, distorted by the elements, shouted, 'Put your hands up.'

Myron raised them above his head.

'Open your coat. I know you're carrying a gun in a shoulder holster. Take it out with two fingers and toss it onto the seat of the car.'

Keeping one hand in the air, Myron unbuttoned his coat. He was already drenched from the rain, his hair matted against his forehead. He took out the gun and put it on his car seat.

'Close the door.'

Again Myron obeyed the voice.

'Do you have the money?'

'First I want to see what you brought,' Myron said.

'No.'

'Hey, be reasonable here. I don't even know what I'm buying.'

A brief hesitation. 'Come closer.'

Myron stepped toward the light, ignoring the symbolism. 'Whatever you're selling,' he said, 'how do I know you haven't made copies?'

'You don't,' the voice said. 'You'll have to trust me.'

'Who else knows about this?'

'I'm the only one,' the voice said, 'who is still alive.'

Myron picked up the pace. His hands were still in the air. The wind whipped into his face. His clothes were sopping. 'How do I know you won't talk?'

'Again, you don't. Your money buys my silence.'

'Until someone ups the bid.'

'No. I'm leaving after this. You won't hear from me again.' The flashlight flickered. 'Please stop.'

Ten feet in front of him stood a man wearing a ski mask. He had a flashlight in one hand and a box in the other. He nodded at Myron and lifted the box. 'Here.'

'What is it?'

'First, the money.'

'For all I know, the box is empty.'

'Fine. Go back to your car and leave then.' The man in the ski mask turned around.

'No, wait,' Myron said. 'I'll get the money.'

The ski mask faced Myron again. 'No games.'

Myron headed back to the car. He had moved about twenty paces when he heard the gunshots. Three of them. The noises did not startle him. He slowly turned around. The man with the ski mask was down. Audrey was running toward the still body. She was carrying Myron's gun.

'He was going to kill you,' Audrey cried. 'I had to shoot.'

Audrey kept running. When she reached the still body, she ignored it and scooped up the box. Myron slowly walked toward her.

'Open it,' he said.

'Let's get out of this rain first. The police—'

'Open it.'

She hesitated. No thunder bellowed. No lightning struck.

'You were right before,' Myron said.

Audrey looked puzzled. 'About what?'

'I was looking at this the wrong way.'

'What are you talking about?'

Myron took another step toward her. 'When I asked myself who knew about the blood in the basement,' he began, 'I only remembered Clip and Calvin. I forgot I told you. When I wondered why Greg's lover would have to keep her identity a secret, I thought about Fiona White and Liz Gorman. Again I forgot about you. It's hard enough for a woman to get respect as a female sports reporter. Your career would be ruined if anybody found out you were dating one of the players you covered. You had to keep it quiet.'

She looked at him, her face a wet, white blank.

'You're the only one who fits, Audrey. You knew about the blood in the basement. You had to keep a relationship with Greg a secret. You had a key to his house so access would be no problem. And you were the one who had a motive to clean up the blood in order to protect him. After all, you killed to protect him. What's cleaning up some blood?'

She brushed her hair away from her eyes and blinked into the rain. 'You can't seriously believe that I—'

'That night after TC's party,' Myron interrupted, 'when you told me how you had put it all together. I should have wondered then. Sure, my joining the team was unusual. But only somebody with a personal connection – somebody who truly knew that Greg had vanished and why – would have been able to come up with it so fast. You were the mystery lover, Audrey. And you don't know where Greg is either. You cooperated with me not because you wanted the story, but because you wanted to find Greg. You're in love with him.'

'That's ridiculous,' she said.

'The police will comb the house, Audrey. They'll find hairs.'

'That doesn't mean anything,' she said. 'I interviewed him a couple of times—'

'In his bedroom? In his bathroom? In his shower?' Myron shook his head. 'They'll also comb the murder scene now that they know about you. There'll be evidence there too. A hair or something.' He took another step toward her. Audrey raised the gun with a quivering hand.

'Beware the Ides of March,' Myron said.

'What?'

'You were the one who pointed it out to me. The ides are the fifteenth of March. Your birthday was the seventeenth. March seventeenth. Three-one-seven. The code Greg set on his answering machine.'

She pointed the gun at his chest. 'Turn off the tape recorder,' she said. 'And the phone.'

Myron reached into his pocket and did as she asked.

Tears and rain mixed together and cascaded down her cheeks. 'Why couldn't you just keep your mouth shut?' she wailed. She pointed to the still body on the wet grass. 'You heard what he said: no one else knows. All the blackmailers are dead. I could have destroyed this thing' – she held up the box – 'once and for all. I wouldn't have had to hurt you. It would have finally been over.'

'And what about Liz Gorman?'

Audrey made a scoffing noise. 'That woman was nothing more than a conniving blackmailer,' she said. 'She couldn't be trusted. I told Greg that. What was to stop her from making copies and bleeding him dry? I even went to her house that night and pretended I was an ex-girlfriend with an ax to grind. I told her I wanted to buy a copy. She said sure. Don't you see? Paying her off would do no good. There was only one way to keep her quiet.'

He nodded. 'You had to kill her.'

'She was just a low-life criminal, Myron. She'd robbed a bank, for chrissake. Greg and I . . . we were perfect together. You were right about my career. I had to keep our relationship a secret. But not much longer. I was going to get transferred to another beat. Baseball. The Mets or Yankees. Then we could be open about it. It was going so well, Myron, and then this low-life bitch comes along . . .' Her voice drifted off with a hard shake of the head. 'I had to think about our future,' she said. 'Not just Greg's. Not just mine. But our baby's too.'

Myron's eyes closed in pain. 'You're pregnant,' he said softly.

'Now do you see?' Her wide-eyed enthusiasm was back, though it took on a more twisted dimension now. 'She wanted to destroy him. Destroy us. What choice did I have? I'm not a killer but it was either us or her. And I know how it looks – Greg running off and not telling me. But it's just the way he is. We've been together for more than six months. I know he loves me. He just needed time.'

Myron swallowed. 'It's over now, Audrey.'

She shook her head and held the gun with both hands. 'I'm sorry, Myron. I don't want to do it. I'd almost rather die first.'

'It doesn't matter.' Myron took another step. She moved back. The gun trembled in her hand. 'They're blanks,' he said.

Her eyes squinted in confusion. The man in the ski mask sat up like Bela Lugosi in an old Dracula film. He pulled off the mask and showed his badge. 'Police,' Dimonte shouted. Win and Krinsky came over the crest. Audrey's mouth formed a perfect circle. Win had made the fake blackmailer call; Myron had set his cellular phone's volume on high to be sure Audrey overheard it. The rest was easy.

Dimonte and Krinsky made the arrest. Myron watched, no longer feeling the rain. After Audrey was put into the back of a cruiser, he and Win walked toward the car.

'Superhero partner?' Myron said.

Win shrugged.

Chapter 39

Esperanza was still in the office when the fax machine rang. She crossed the room and watched the machine begin to spew out paper. The facsimile was addressed to her attention, from the FBI:

Re: FIRST CITY NATIONAL BANK – TUCSON, ARIZONA
Subject: Renters of Safe-Deposit Boxes.

She'd been waiting for this transmission all day.

Esperanza's theory on the blackmail plot had gone something like this: The Raven Brigade robbed the bank. They hit the safe-deposit boxes. People keep all kinds of things in those. Money, jewelry, important documents. That was what hooked the timing together. Simply put, the Raven Brigade had found something in one of those boxes that was damaging to Greg Downing. Then they hatched their little blackmail scheme.

The names came out in alphabetical order. Esperanza read down the list while the paper was still being transmitted. The first page ended in the Ls. No name was familiar. The second page ended in the Ts. No name was familiar. On the third page, when she reached the Ws, her heart leaped into her throat. Her hand fluttered to her mouth, and for a moment she feared that she might scream.

It took several hours to sort through the mess. Statements had to be taken. Explanations made. Myron told Dimonte practically the whole story. He left out the videotape of Thumper and Emily. Again, it was nobody's business. He also left out the part about meeting up with Cole Whiteman. Myron somehow felt he owed him. For her part, Audrey would not talk at all, except to ask for a lawyer.

'Do you know where Downing is?' Dimonte asked Myron.

'I think so.'

'But you don't want to tell me.'

Myron shook his head. 'He's not your business.'

'Ain't that the truth,' Dimonte agreed. 'Go on. Get out of here.'

They were downtown at One Police Plaza. Myron and Win walked out in the city night. Large municipal structures consumed the neighboring area. Modern bureaucracy in its most extreme and intimidating form. Even this late at night, you could visualize lines of people heading out the door.

'It was a good plan,' Win said.

'Audrey is pregnant.'

'I heard.'

'Her baby will be born in jail.'

'Not your doing.'

'She thought it was her only way out,' Myron said.

Win nodded. 'She saw a blackmailer who stood in the way of all her dreams. I'm not so sure I would have behaved any differently.'

'You don't commit murder to stave off life's inconveniences,' Myron said.

Win didn't argue, but he didn't agree either. They kept walking. When they reached the car, Win said, 'So where does that leave us?'

'With Clip Arnstein,' Myron said. 'He has some explaining to do.'

'You want me to come along?'

'No. I want to talk to him alone.'

Chapter 40

By the time Myron arrived at the arena, the game was over. Cars tapped the exits, making it hard to go the opposite way. Myron managed to weave through. He showed his ID to the guard and drove into the players' lot.

He ran to Clip's office. Someone called his name. He ignored it. When he reached the outer office door, he tried the knob. It was locked. He was tempted to break it down.

'Yo, Myron.'

It was one of the towel boys. Myron forgot the kid's name. 'What's up?' he said.

'This came for you.'

The kid handed Myron a manila envelope.

'Who dropped this off?' Myron asked.

'Your uncle.'

'My uncle?'

'That's what the guy said.'

Myron looked at the envelope. His name was scrawled

across the front in giant block letters. He tore it open and turned it upside down. First, a letter slid out. He shook again and a black cassette tape fell into the palm of his hand. He put the cassette down and unfolded the letter:

Myron,

I should have given this to you at the cathedral. I'm sorry I didn't, but I got too caught up in Liz's murder. I wanted you to concentrate on catching the killer, not on this tape. I was afraid it would distract you. I still think it will, but that doesn't give me the right to keep it from you. I just hope you stay focused enough to find the bastard who killed Liz. She deserves justice.

I also wanted to tell you that I'm thinking about turning myself in. Now that Liz is gone, there's no reason to keep hiding. I spoke to some old lawyer buddies about it. They've already started reaching out to all the mercenaries Hunt's father hired. They're sure one of them will corroborate my story. We'll see.

Don't listen to this tape alone, Myron. Listen to it with a friend.

Cole

Myron folded the letter. He had no idea what to think. He glanced down the corridor. No sign of Clip. He jogged toward the exit. Most of the players had already left the arena. TC, of course. Last in, first out. Myron got in his car and turned the key. Then he stuck the tape into the car's player and waited.

Esperanza tried dialing Myron's car phone. No answer. Then his cellular. Same deal. He always carried his cellular. If he wasn't picking up, it was because he didn't want to. She quickly dialed Win's cellular. He picked up on the second ring.

'Do you know where Myron is?' she asked.

'He went to the arena.'

'Go find him, Win.'

'Why? What's wrong?'

'The Raven Brigade robbed the safe-deposit boxes. That's where they got the information they used to blackmail Downing.'

'What did they find?'

'I don't know,' she said, 'but I have a list of the people who rented the boxes.'

'So?'

'One was rented to a Mr and Mrs B. Wesson.'

Silence.

Win said, 'Are you sure it's the same B. Wesson who injured Myron?'

'I already checked,' she said. 'The B stands for Burt, listed on his application as a thirty-three-year-old high school basketball coach. It's him, Win. It's the same Burt Wesson.'

Chapter 41

Nothing.

Myron fiddled with the volume knob. Static feedback screeched through the car speakers. He turned it down a second, then back up. He heard muffled sounds, but he had no idea what they were. Then the sounds faded away.

Silence.

Two minutes of blank tape passed before Myron finally heard voices. His ears perked up, but he couldn't make out much. Then the voices grew a little louder, a little clearer. He leaned closer to the speaker and suddenly he heard a gruff voice with frightening clarity:

'*You have the money?*'

A hand reached into Myron's chest, grabbed his heart, and squeezed. He hadn't heard the voice in ten years, but recognition was instantaneous. It was Burt Wesson. What the hell—?

Then the second voice jarred him like a body blow:

'*I got half now. A thousand dollars now. You get the other half when he goes down . . .*'

Myron's entire body shuddered. A flash of rage unlike anything he had ever known warmed and then engulfed him. His hands tightened into fists. Tears forced their way forward. He remembered wondering why the black-mailers had contacted him to buy the dirt on Greg; he remembered Cole Whiteman's laugh and Marty Felder's ironic smile when they'd learned that he'd been hired to find Greg Downing; he remembered the voice on Greg's answering machine saying, 'He's willing to pay. Is that what you want?'; and most of all, he remembered Greg's pained face at the hospital all those years ago. It hadn't been a bond that brought Greg to Myron's bedside.

It'd been guilt.

'*Don't hurt him too bad, Burt. I just want Bolitar banged up for a few games . . .*'

Something in the deep recesses of Myron's mind snapped like a dry twig. Without conscious thought, Myron shifted into reverse.

'*Look, I really need the money. Can't you give me another five hundred? They're going to cut me soon. It's my last scrimmage and then I'm unemployed . . .*'

He straightened out his car and shifted into drive. His foot pressed down upon the pedal. The speedometer climbed. Myron's face twisted into a mask of incognizant fury. Tears sheeted down his cheeks but no sound came with them. He drove without really seeing.

When he reached the Jones Road exit, Myron wiped his face with his sleeve. He turned into TC's driveway. The security gate blocked his path.

The guard stepped out of his little hut. Myron waved

him closer to the car. When the guard was fully out of the box, Myron showed the gun.

'Move and I'll blow your head off.'

The guard's hands went up. Myron got out of the car and opened the gate. He ordered the guard inside the car. The car roared up the driveway. Myron slammed on the brake just feet before the front door. He jumped out on the run and without hesitating, he kicked in TC's front door. He ran into the den.

The television was on. TC looked up, startled. 'What the fuck—?'

Myron bounded across the room, grabbed TC's arm, twisted it behind his back.

'Hey—'

'Where is he?' Myron demanded.

'I don't know what—'

Myron pulled up on the arm. 'Don't make me break it, TC. Where is he?'

'What the fuck are you—?'

Myron silenced him by pushing the arm farther up his back. TC cried out, his huge frame bent at the waist to lessen the pressure. 'Last time I ask,' Myron said. 'Where's Greg?'

'I'm here.'

Myron let go and spun toward the voice. Greg Downing stood in the doorway. Myron did not hesitate. Letting out a guttural scream, he pounced.

Greg put up his hands, but it was like quieting a volcano with a squirt gun. Myron's fist landed square in Greg's face. Greg toppled back from the assault. Myron fell on him, his knee landing in his ribs. Something cracked. He straddled Greg's chest and threw another punch.

'Stop!' TC shouted, 'You're gonna kill him.'

Myron barely heard him.

He cocked his other fist, but TC was on him before he could throw it. Myron rolled with the tackle, digging his elbow into TC's solar plexus. When they hit the wall, the air whooshed out of TC, his eyes bulging as he gasped for air. Myron rose. Greg was scrambling away. Myron vaulted over the couch. He grabbed Greg by the leg and pulled him toward him.

'You fucked my wife!' Greg shouted. 'You think I didn't know? You fucked my wife!'

The words slowed Myron, but they didn't stop him. Through his tears, he threw another punch. Greg's mouth filled with blood. Myron cocked his fist again. A hand of iron reached out and grabbed his arm, holding it in place.

'Enough,' Win said.

Myron looked up, his face distorted by confusion and rage. 'What?'

'He's had enough.'

'But it's like you said,' Myron pleaded. 'Wesson did do it on purpose. Greg hired him.'

'I know,' Win said. 'But he's had enough.'

'What the hell are you talking about? If it was you—'

'I'd probably kill him,' Win finished for him. He looked down and something flickered in his eyes. 'But you wouldn't.'

Myron swallowed. Win nodded again and let go of Myron's wrist. Myron let his arm fall to his side. He got off Greg Downing.

Greg sat up, coughing blood into his hand. 'I followed Emily that night,' Greg managed through the hacks. 'I saw you two . . . I just wanted payback, that's all. You weren't supposed to get hurt that bad.'

Myron swallowed and breathed deeply. The adrenaline rush would soon ebb, but for now it was still there. 'You been hiding here since the beginning?'

Greg touched part of his face, winced, then nodded 'I was afraid they'd think I killed that woman,' he said. 'And I had the mob chasing me and the custody battle and my girlfriend is pregnant.' He looked up. 'I just needed some time.'

'Do you love Audrey?'

Greg said, 'You know?'

'Yes.'

'Yeah,' Greg said, 'I love her a lot.'

'Then give her a call,' Myron said. 'She's in jail.'

'What?'

Myron didn't elaborate. He'd hoped throwing that in Greg's face would give him some sort of perverse pleasure, but it didn't. All it did was remind him that he was far from blameless in this.

He turned and walked away.

Myron found Clip alone in that same corporate sky-box they'd met in when this all began. He was looking down at the empty court, his back to Myron. He didn't move when Myron cleared his throat.

'You knew all along,' Myron said.

Clip said nothing.

'You went to Liz Gorman's apartment that night,' Myron continued. 'She played the tape for you, didn't she?'

Clip clasped his hands behind his back. Then he nodded.

'That's why you hired me. This wasn't all a coincidence. You wanted me to find out the truth.'

'I didn't know how else to tell you.' Clip finally turned and faced Myron. His eyes were dazed and hazy. All color was gone from his face. 'It wasn't an act, you know. The emotion at the press conference . . .' He lowered his head, gathered himself, raised it again. 'You and I lost touch after your injury. I wanted to call you a thousand times, but I understood. You wanted to stay away. The injury never leaves the great ones, Myron. I knew it would never leave you.'

Myron opened his mouth but nothing came out. His entire being felt exposed and raw. Clip came closer. 'I thought this would be a way for you to learn the truth,' Clip said. 'I also hoped this would be something of a catharsis. Not a complete one. Like I said, it never leaves the great ones.'

For several moments, they both just stood and stared.

'You told Walsh to play me the other night,' Myron said.

'Yes.'

'You knew I wouldn't be able to match up.'

Clip nodded slowly.

Myron felt the tears come back to his eyes. He blinked them down.

Clip set his jaw. There were tiny tremors in his face, but he stood rigid. 'I wanted to help you,' he said, 'but my reasons for hiring you were not all altruistic. I knew, for example, that you'd always been a team player. You loved that aspect of basketball, Myron – being part of a team.'

'So?'

'My plan included making you feel like a member of the team. A real member. So much so that you would never hurt us.'

Myron understood. 'You figured that if I bonded with my teammates, I wouldn't blow the whistle when I learned the truth.'

'It's not in your nature,' Clip said.

'But it will come out,' Myron said. 'There's no way to avoid it now.'

'I know that.'

'You could lose the team.'

Clip smiled, shrugged. 'There are worse things,' he said. 'Just as you now know there are worse things than never being able to play again.'

'I always knew,' Myron said. 'I just maybe needed a reminder.'

Chapter 42

He and Jessica sat on the couch in her loft. He told her everything. Jess hugged her knees and rocked back and forth. Her eyes looked pained.

'She was my friend,' Jessica said.

'I know.'

'I wonder.'

'What?'

'What would I have done in the same situation? To protect you.'

'You wouldn't have killed.'

'No,' she said. 'I guess not.

Myron watched her. She looked on the verge of tears. He said, 'I think I learned something about us in all this.'

She waited for him to elaborate.

'Win and Esperanza didn't want me to play again. But you never tried to stop me. I was afraid that maybe you didn't understand me as well as they do. But that wasn't the case at all. You saw what they couldn't.'

Jessica studied his face with a penetrating gaze. She let go of her knees and slid her feet to the floor. 'We've never really talked about this before,' she said.

He nodded.

'The truth is, you never mourned the end of your career,' Jessica went on. 'You never showed weakness. You stuffed it all in some internal suitcase and moved on. You tackled everything else in your life with a smothering desperation. You didn't wait. You seized whatever was left and pressed it against you, afraid your whole world was as fragile as that knee. You rushed off to law school. You ran off and helped Win. You frantically clung to whatever you could.' She stopped.

'Including you,' he finished.

'Yes. Including me. Not just because you loved me. Because you were afraid of losing more than you already had.'

'I did love you,' he said. 'I still do.'

'I know. I'm not trying to put this all on you. I was an idiot. It was mostly my fault. I admit that. But your love back then bordered on the desperate. You channeled your grief into a grasping need. I was afraid of suffocating. I don't want to sound like an amateur shrink, but you needed to mourn. You needed to put it behind you, not suppress it. But you wouldn't face it.'

'You thought my playing again would make me face it,' he said.

'Yes.'

'It's not like this was a cure-all.'

'I know,' she said. 'But I think it helped you let go a little.'

'And that's why you think now is a good time for me to move in.'

Jessica swallowed hard. 'If you want,' she said. 'If you feel ready.'

He looked up in the air and said, 'I'll need more closet space.'

'Done,' she whispered. 'Whatever you want.'

She snuggled into him. He put his arms around her, pulled her close, and felt very much at home.

It was a sweltering morning in Tucson, Arizona. A big man opened his front door.

'Are you Burt Wesson?'

The big man nodded. 'Can I help you with something?'

Win smiled. 'Yes,' he said. 'I think you can.'

Back Spin

For the Armstrongs,
The World's Greatest In-Laws,
Jack and Nancy
Molly, Jane, Eliza, Sara, John and Kate
Thank you all for Anne

Acknowledgements

When an author is writing about an activity he enjoys about as much as sticking his tongue in a fan (golf), he needs help and lots of it. With that in mind the author wishes to thank the following: James Bradbeer, Jr, Peter Roisman, Maggie Griffin, Craig Coben, Larry Coben, Jacob Hoye, Lisa Erbach Vance, Frank Snyder, the rec.sports.golf board, Nitwit, Sparkle Hayter, Anita Meyer, the many golfers who regaled me with their scintillating tales (snore), and of course, Dave Bolt. While the US Open is a real golf tournament and Merion is a real golf club, this book is a work of fiction. I took some liberties, combined locales and tournaments, that kind of thing. As always, any errors – factual or otherwise – are totally the fault of these people. The author is not to blame. Myron and I tried. But we're still not sure we get it.

Chapter 1

Myron Bolitar used a cardboard periscope to look over the suffocating throngs of ridiculously clad spectators. He tried to recall the last time he'd actually used a toy periscope, and an image of sending in proof-of-purchase seals from a box of Cap'n Crunch cereal flickered in front him like headache-inducing sunspots.

Through the mirrored reflection, Myron watched a man dressed in knickers – knickers, for crying out loud – stand over a tiny white sphere. The ridiculously clad spectators mumbled excitedly. Myron stifled a yawn. The knickered man crouched. The ridiculously clad spectators jostled and then settled into an eerie silence. Sheer stillness followed, as if even the trees and shrubs and well-coiffed blades of grass were holding their collective breath.

Then the knickered man whacked the white sphere with a stick.

The crowd began to murmur in the indistinguishable

syllables of backstage banter. As the ball ascended, so did the volume of the murmurs. Words could be made out. Then phrases. 'Lovely golf stroke.' 'Super golf shot.' 'Beautiful golf shot.' 'Truly fine golf stroke.' They always said *golf* stroke, like someone might mistake it for a *swim* stroke, or – as Myron was currently contemplating in this blazing heat – a *sun*stroke.

'Mr Bolitar?'

Myron took the periscope away from his eyes. He was tempted to yell 'Up periscope,' but feared some at stately, snooty Merion Golf Club would view the act as immature. Especially during the US Open. He looked down at a ruddy-faced man of about seventy.

'Your pants,' Myron said.

'Pardon me?'

'You're afraid of getting hit by a golf cart, right?'

They were orange and yellow in a hue slightly more luminous than a bursting supernova. To be fair, the man's clothing hardly stood out. Most in the crowd seemed to have woken up wondering what apparel they possessed that would clash with, say, the free world. Orange and green tints found exclusively in several of your tackiest neon signs adorned many. Yellow and some strange shades of purple were also quite big – usually together – like a color scheme rejected by a Midwest high school cheerleading squad. It was as if being surrounded by all this God-given natural beauty made one want to do all in his power to offset it. Or maybe there was something else at work here. Maybe the ugly clothes had a more functional origin. Maybe in the old days, when animals roamed free, golfers dressed this way to ward off dangerous wildlife.

Good theory.

'I need to speak with you,' the elderly man whispered. 'It's urgent.'

The rounded, jovial cheeks belied his pleading eyes. He suddenly gripped Myron's forearm. 'Please,' he added.

'What's this about?' Myron asked.

The man made a movement with his neck, like his collar was on too tight. 'You're a sports agent, right?'

'Yes.'

'You're here to find clients?'

Myron narrowed his eyes. 'How do you know I'm not here to witness the enthralling spectacle of grown men taking a walk?'

The old man did not smile, but then again, golfers were not known for their sense of humor. He craned his neck again and moved closer. His whisper was hoarse. 'Do you know the name Jack Coldren?' he asked.

'Sure,' Myron said.

If the old man had asked the same question yesterday, Myron wouldn't have had a clue. He didn't follow golf that closely (or at all), and Jack Coldren had been little more than a journeyman over the past twenty years or so. But Coldren had been the surprise leader after the US Open's first day, and now, with just a few holes remaining in the second round, Coldren was up by a commanding eight strokes. 'What about him?'

'And Linda Coldren?' the man asked. 'Do you know who she is?'

This one was easier. Linda Coldren was Jack's wife and far and away the top female golfer of the past decade. 'Yeah, I know who she is,' Myron said.

The man leaned in closer and did the neck thing again. Seriously annoying – not to mention contagious. Myron found himself fighting off the desire to mimic the

3

movement. 'They're in deep trouble,' the old man whispered. 'If you help them, you'll have two new clients.'

'What sort of trouble?'

The old man looked around. 'Please,' he said. 'There are too many people. Come with me.'

Myron shrugged. No reason not to go. The old man was the only lead he'd unearthed since his friend and business associate Windsor Horne Lockwood III – Win, for short – had dragged his sorry butt down here. Being that the US Open was at Merion – home course of the Lockwood family for something like a billion years – Win had felt it would be a great opportunity for Myron to land a few choice clients. Myron wasn't quite so sure. As near as he could tell, the major component separating him from the hordes of other locust-like agents swarming the green meadows of Merion Golf Club was his naked aversion for golf. Probably not a key selling point to the faithful.

Myron Bolitar ran MB SportsReps, a sports representation firm located on Park Avenue in New York City. He rented the space from his former college roommate, Win, a Waspy, old-money, big-time investment banker whose family owned Lock-Horne Securities on the same Park Avenue in New York. Myron handled the negotiations while Win, one of the country's most respected brokers, handled the investments and finances. The other member of the MB team, Esperanza Diaz, handled everything else. Three branches with checks and balances. Just like the American government. Very patriotic.

Slogan: *MB SportsReps – the other guys are commie pinkos.*

As the old man ushered Myron through the crowd,

several men in green blazers – another look sported mostly at golf courses, perhaps to camouflage oneself against the grass – greeted him with whispered, 'How do, Bucky,' or 'Looking good, Buckster,' or 'Fine day for golf, Buckaroo.' They all had the accent of the rich and preppy, the kind of inflection where *mommy* is pronounced 'mummy' and summer and winter are verbs. Myron was about to comment on a grown man being called Bucky, but when your name is Myron, well, glass houses and stones and all that.

Like every other sporting event in the free world, the actual playing area looked more like a giant billboard than a field of competition. The leader board was sponsored by IBM. Canon handed out the periscopes. American Airlines employees worked the food stands (an airline handling food – what think tank came up with that one?). Corporate Row was jam-packed with companies who shelled out over one hundred grand a pop to set up a tent for a few days, mostly so that company executives had an excuse to go. Travelers Group, Mass Mutual, Aetna (golfers must like insurance), Canon, Heublein. Heublein. What the hell was a Heublein? They looked like a nice company. Myron would probably buy a Heublein if he knew what one was.

The funny thing was, the US Open was actually less commercialized than most tourneys. At least they hadn't sold their name yet. Other tournaments were named for sponsors and the names had gotten a little silly. Who could get up for winning the JC Penney Open or the Michelob Open or even the Wendy's Three-Tour Challenge?

The old man led him to a primo parking lot. Mercedeses, Caddies, limos. Myron spotted Win's Jaguar.

The USGA had recently put up a sign that read MEMBERS PARKING ONLY.

Myron said, 'You're a member of Merion.' Dr Deduction.

The old man twisted the neck thing into something approaching a nod. 'My family dates back to Merion's inception,' he said, the snooty accent now more pronounced. 'Just like your friend Win.'

Myron stopped and looked at the man. 'You know Win?'

The old man sort of smiled and shrugged. No commitment.

'You haven't told me your name yet,' Myron said.

'Stone Buckwell,' he said, hand extended. 'Everyone calls me Bucky.'

Myron shook the hand.

'I'm also Linda Coldren's father,' he added.

Bucky unlocked a sky-blue Cadillac and they slid inside. He put the key in the ignition. The radio played Muzak – worse, the Muzak version of 'Raindrops Keep Falling on My Head.' Myron quickly opened the window for air, not to mention noise.

Only members were allowed to park on the Merion grounds, so it wasn't too much of a hassle getting out. They made a right at the end of the driveway and then another right. Bucky mercifully flipped off the radio. Myron stuck his head back in the car.

'What do you know about my daughter and her husband?' Bucky asked.

'Not much.'

'You are not a golf fan, are you, Mr Bolitar?'

'Not really.'

'Golf is truly a magnificent sport,' he said. Then he

6

added, 'Though the word *sport* does not begin to do it justice.'

'Uh-huh,' Myron said.

'It's the game of princes.' Buckwell's ruddy face glowed a bit now, the eyes wide with the same type of rapture one saw in the very religious. His voice was low and awed. 'There is nothing quite like it, you know. You alone against the course. No excuses. No teammate. No bad calls. It's the purest of activities.'

'Uh-huh,' Myron said again. 'Look, I don't want to appear rude, Mr Buckwell, but what's this all about?'

'Please call me Bucky.'

'Okay. Bucky.'

He nodded his approval. 'I understand that you and Windsor Lockwood are more than business associates,' he said.

'Meaning?'

'I understand you two go back a long way. College roommates, am I correct?'

'Why do you keep asking about Win?'

'I actually came to the club to find him,' Bucky said. 'But I think it's better this way.'

'What way?'

'Talking to you first. Maybe after . . . well, we'll see. Shouldn't hope for too much.'

Myron nodded. 'I have no idea what you're talking about.'

Bucky turned onto a road adjacent to the course called Golf House Road. Golfers were so creative.

The course was on the right, imposing mansions on the left. A minute later, Bucky pulled into a circular drive-way. The house was fairly big and made of something called river rock. River rock was big in this area, though

7

Win always referred to it as 'Mainline Stone.' There was a white fence and lots of tulips and two maple trees, one on each side of the front walk. A large porch was enclosed on the right side. The car came to a stop, and for a moment neither of them moved.

'What's this all about, Mr Buckwell?'

'We have a situation here,' he said.

'What kind of situation?'

'I'd rather let my daughter explain it to you.' He grabbed the key out of the ignition and reached for the door.

'Why come to me?' Myron asked.

'We were told you could possibly help.'

'Who told you that?'

Buckwell started rolling his neck with greater fervor. His head looked like it'd been attached by a loose ball socket. When he finally got it under control, he managed to look Myron in the eyes.

'Win's mother,' he said.

Myron stiffened. His heart plummeted down a dark shaft. He opened his mouth, closed it, waited. Buckwell got out of the car and headed for the door. Ten seconds later, Myron followed.

'Win won't help,' Myron said.

Buckwell nodded. 'That's why I came to you first.'

They followed a brick path to a door slightly ajar. Buckwell pushed it open. 'Linda?'

Linda Coldren stood before a television in the den. Her white shorts and sleeveless yellow blouse revealed the lithe, toned limbs of an athlete. She was tall with short spunky black hair and a tan that accentuated the smooth, long muscles. The lines around her eyes and mouth placed her in her late thirties, and he could see instantly why she

8

was a commercial darling. There was a fierce splendor to this woman, a beauty derived from a sense of strength rather than delicacy.

She was watching the tournament on the television. On top of the set were framed family photographs. Big, pillowy couches formed a V in one corner. Tactfully furnished, for a golfer. No putting green, AstroTurf carpet. None of that golf artwork that seemed a step or two below the aesthetic class of, say, paintings of dogs playing poker. No cap with a tee and ball on the brim hanging from a moose head.

Linda Coldren suddenly swung her line of vision toward them, firing a glare past Myron before settling on her father. 'I thought you were going to get Jack,' she snapped.

'He hasn't finished the round yet.'

She motioned to the television. 'He's on eighteen now. I thought you were going to wait for him.'

'I got Mr Bolitar instead.'

'Who?'

Myron stepped forward and smiled. 'I'm Myron Bolitar.'

Linda Coldren flicked her eyes at him, then back to her father. 'Who the hell is he?'

'He's the man Cissy told me about,' Buckwell said.

'Who's Cissy?' Myron asked.

'Win's mother.'

'Oh,' Myron said. 'Right.'

Linda Coldren said, 'I don't want him here. Get rid of him.'

'Linda, listen to me. We need help.'

'Not from him.'

'He and Win have experience with this type of thing.'

'Win,' she said slowly, 'is psychotic.'

'Ah,' Myron said. 'Then you know him well?'

Linda Coldren finally turned her attention to Myron. Her eyes, deep and brown, met his. 'I haven't spoken to Win since he was eight years old,' she said. 'But you don't have to leap into a pit of flames to know it's hot.'

Myron nodded. 'Nice analogy.'

She shook her head and looked back at her father. 'I told you before: no police. We do what they say.'

'But he's not police,' her father said.

'And you shouldn't be telling anyone.'

'I only told my sister,' Bucky protested. 'She'd never say anything.'

Myron felt his body stiffen again. 'Wait a second,' he said to Bucky. 'Your sister is Win's mother?'

'Yes.'

'You're Win's uncle.' He looked at Linda Coldren. 'And you're Win's first cousin.'

Linda Coldren looked at him like he'd just peed on the floor. 'With smarts like that,' she said, 'I'm glad you're on our side.'

Everyone's a wiseass.

'If it's still unclear, Mr Bolitar, I could break out some poster board and sketch a family tree for you.'

'Could you use lots of pretty colors?' Myron said. 'I like pretty colors.'

She made a face and turned away. On the television, Jack Coldren lined up a twelve-foot putt. Linda stopped and watched. He tapped it; the ball took off and arched right into the hole. The gallery applauded with modest enthusiasm. Jack picked up the ball with two fingers and then tipped his hat. The IBM leader board flashed on the screen. Jack Coldren was up by a whopping nine strokes.

Linda Coldren shook her head. 'Poor bastard.'

Myron kept still. So did Bucky.

'He's waited twenty-three years for this moment,' she continued. 'And he picks now.'

Myron glanced at Bucky. Bucky glanced back, shaking his head.

Linda Coldren stared at the television until her husband exited to the clubhouse. Then she took a deep breath and looked at Myron. 'You see, Mr Bolitar, Jack has never won a professional tournament. The closest he ever came was in his rookie year twenty-three years ago, when he was only nineteen. It was the last time the US Open was held at Merion. You may remember the headlines.'

They were not altogether unfamiliar. This morning's papers had rehashed it a bit. 'He lost a lead, right?'

Linda Coldren made a scoffing sound. 'That's a bit of an understatement, but yes. Since then, his career has been completely unspectacular. There were years he didn't even make the tour.'

'He picked a hell of a time to snap his streak,' Myron said. 'The US Open.'

She gave him a funny look and folded her arms under her chest. 'Your name rings a bell,' she said. 'You used to play basketball, right?'

'Right.'

'In the ACC. North Carolina?'

'Duke,' he corrected.

'Right, Duke. I remember now. You blew out your knee after the draft.'

Myron nodded slowly.

'That was the end of your career, right?'

Myron nodded again.

'It must have been tough,' she said.

Myron said nothing.

She made a waving motion with her hand. 'What happened to you is nothing compared to what happened to Jack.'

'Why do you say that?'

'You had an injury. It may have been tough, but at least you weren't at fault. Jack had a six-stroke lead at the US Open with only eight holes left. Do you know what that's like? That's like having a ten-point lead with a minute left in the seventh game of the NBA finals. It's like missing a wide-open slam dunk in the final seconds to lose the championship. Jack was never the same man after that. He never recovered. He has spent his whole life since, just waiting for the chance of redemption.' She turned back to the television. The leader board was back up. Jack Coldren was still up by nine strokes.

'If he loses again . . .'

She did not bother finishing the thought. They all stood in silence. Linda staring at the television. Bucky craning his neck, his eyes moist, his face quivering near tears.

'So what's wrong, Linda?' Myron asked.

'Our son,' she said. 'Somebody has kidnapped our son.'

Chapter 2

'I shouldn't be telling you this,' Linda Coldren said. 'He said he'd kill him.'

'Who said?'

Linda Coldren took several deep breaths, like a child atop the high board. Myron waited. It took some time, but she finally took the plunge.

'I got a call this morning,' she said. Her large indigo eyes were wide and everywhere now, settling down on no one spot for more than a second. 'A man said he had my son. He said if I called the police, he would kill him.'

'Did he say anything else?'

'Just that he'd call back with instructions.'

'That's it?'

She nodded.

'What time was this?' Myron asked.

'Nine, nine-thirty.'

Myron walked over to the television and picked up one

of the framed photographs. 'Is this a recent photograph of your son?'

'Yes.'

'How old is he?'

'Sixteen. His name is Chad.'

Myron studied the photograph. The smiling adolescent had the fleshy features of his father. He wore a baseball cap with the brim curled the way kids like to nowadays. A golf club rested proudly on his shoulder like a minuteman with a bayonet. His eyes were squinted as though he were looking into the sun. Myron looked over Chad's face, as if it might give him a clue or some rare insight. It didn't.

'When did you first notice that your son was missing?'

Linda Coldren gave her father a quick glance, then straightened up, holding her head high as if she were readying himself for a blow. Her words came slow. 'Chad had been gone for two days.'

'Gone?' Myron Bolitar, Grand Inquisitor.

'Yes.'

'When you say gone—'

'I mean just that,' she interrupted. 'I haven't seen him since Wednesday.'

'But the kidnapper just called today?'

'Yes.'

Myron started to speak, stopped himself, softened his voice. Tread gently, fair Myron. Ever gently. 'Did you have any idea where he was?'

'I assumed he was staying with his friend Matthew,' Linda Coldren replied.

Myron nodded, as if this statement showed brilliant insight. Then nodded again. 'Chad told you that?'

'No.'

'So,' he said, aiming for casual, 'for the past two days, you didn't know where your son was.'

'I just told you: I thought he was staying with Matthew.'

'You didn't call the police.'

'Of course not.'

Myron was about to ask another follow-up question, but her posture made him rethink his words. Linda took advantage of his indecisiveness. She walked to the kitchen with an upright, fluid grace. Myron followed. Bucky seemed to snap out of a trance and trailed.

'Let me make sure I'm following you,' Myron said, approaching from a different angle now. 'Chad vanished before the tournament?'

'Correct,' she said. 'The Open started Thursday.' Linda Coldren pulled the refrigerator handle. The door opened with a sucking pop. 'Why? Is that important?'

'It eliminates a motive,' Myron said.

'What motive?'

'Tampering with the tournament,' Myron said. 'If Chad had vanished today – with your husband holding such a big lead – I might think that someone was out to sabotage his chances of winning the Open. But two days ago, before the tournament had begun . . .'

'No one would have given Jack a snowball's chance in hell,' she finished for him. 'Oddsmakers would have put him at one in five thousand. At best.' She nodded as she spoke, seeing the logic. 'Would you like some lemonade?' she asked.

'No, thanks.'

'Dad?'

Bucky shook his head. Linda Coldren bent down into the refrigerator.

'Okay,' Myron said, clapping his hand together, trying his best to sound casual. 'We've ruled out one possibility. Let's try another.'

Linda Coldren stopped and watched him. A gallon glass pitcher was gripped in her hand, her forearm bunching easily with the weight. Myron debated how to approach this. There was no easy way.

'Could your son be behind this?' Myron asked.

'What?'

'It's an obvious question,' Myron said, 'under the circumstances.'

She put the pitcher down on a wooden center block.

'What the hell are you talking about? You think Chad faked his own kidnapping?'

'I didn't say that. I said I wanted to check out the possibility.'

'Get out.'

'He was gone two days, and you didn't call the police,' Myron said. 'One possible conclusion is that there was some sort of tension here. That Chad had run away before.'

'Or,' Linda Coldren countered, her hands tightening into fists, 'you could conclude that we trusted our son. That we gave him a level of freedom compatible with his level of maturity and responsibility.'

Myron looked over at Bucky. Bucky's head was lowered. 'If that's the case—'

'That's the case.'

'But don't responsible kids tell their parents where they're going? I mean, just to make sure they don't worry.'

Linda Coldren took out a glass with too much care. She set it on the counter and slowly poured herself some lemonade. 'Chad has learned to be very independent,' she said as the glass filled. 'His father and I are both professional golfers. That means, quite frankly, that neither one of us is home very often.'

'Your being away so much,' Myron said. 'Has it led to tension?'

Linda Coldren shook her head. 'This is useless.'

'I'm just trying—'

'Look, Mr Bolitar, Chad did not fake this. Yes, he's a teenager. No, he's not perfect, and neither are his parents. But he did not fake his own kidnapping. And if he did – I know he didn't, but let's just pretend for the sake of argument that he did – then he is safe and we do not need you. If this is some kind of cruel deception, we'll learn it soon enough. But if my son is in danger, then following this line of thought is a waste of time I can ill afford.'

Myron nodded. She had a point. 'I understand,' he said.

'Good.'

'Have you called his friend since you heard from the kidnapper? The one you thought he might've been staying with?'

'Matthew Squires, yes.'

'Did Matthew have any idea where he was?'

'None.'

'They're close friends, right?'

'Yes.'

'Very close?'

She frowned. 'Yes, very.'

'Does Matthew call here a lot?'

'Yes. Or they talk by E-mail.'

'I'll need Matthew's phone number,' Myron said.

'But I just told you I spoke to him already.'

'Humor me,' Myron said. 'Okay, now let's back up a second. When was the last time you saw Chad?'

'The day he disappeared.'

'What happened?'

She frowned again. 'What do you mean, what happened? He left for summer school. I haven't seen him since.'

Myron studied her. She stopped and looked back at him a little too steadily. Something here was not adding up. 'Have you called the school,' he asked, 'to see if he was there that day?'

'I didn't think of it.'

Myron checked his watch. Friday. Five P.M. 'I doubt anyone will still be there, but give it a shot. Do you have more than one phone line?'

'Yes.'

'Don't call on the line the kidnapper called in on. I don't want the line tied up in case he calls back.'

She nodded. 'Okay.'

'Does your son have any credit cards or ATM cards or anything like that?'

'Yes.'

'I'll need a list. And the numbers, if you have them.'

She nodded again.

Myron said, 'I'm going to call a friend, see if I can get an override Caller ID put in on this line. For when he calls back. I assume Chad has a computer?'

'Yes,' she said.

'Where is it?'

'Up in his room.'

'I'm going to download everything on it to my office via his modem. I have an assistant named Esperanza. She'll comb through it and see what she can find.'

18

'Like what?'

'Frankly I have no idea. E-mails. Correspondence. Bulletin boards he participates in. Anything that might give us a clue. It's not a very scientific process. You check out enough stuff and maybe something will click.'

Linda thought about it for a moment. 'Okay,' she said.

'How about you, Mrs Coldren? Do you have any enemies?'

She sort of smiled. 'I'm the number one-rated woman golfer in the world,' she said. 'That gives me a lot of enemies.'

'Anyone you can imagine doing this?'

'No,' she said. 'No one.'

'How about your husband? Anybody who hates your husband enough?'

'Jack?' She forced out a chuckle. 'Everyone loves Jack.'

'What's that supposed to mean?'

She just shook her head and waved him off.

Myron asked a few more questions, but there was little left for him to excavate. He asked if he could go up to Chad's room and she led him up the stairs.

The first thing Myron saw when he opened Chad's door were the trophies. Lots of them. All golf trophies. The bronze figure on the top was always a man coiled in postswing position, the golf club over his shoulder, his head held high. Sometimes the little man wore a golf cap. Other times he had short, wavy hair like Paul Hornung in old football reels. There were two leather golf bags in the right corner, both jammed past capacity with clubs. Photographs of Jack Nicklaus, Arnold Palmer, Sam Snead, Tom Watson blanketed the walls. Issues of *Golf Digest* littered the floor.

'Does Chad play golf?' Myron asked.

Linda Coldren just looked at him. Myron met her gaze and nodded sagely.

'My powers of deduction,' he said. 'They intimidate some people.'

She almost smiled. Myron the Alleviator, Master Tension-Easer. 'I'll try to still treat you the same,' she said.

Myron stepped toward the trophies. 'Is he any good?'

'Very good.' She turned away suddenly and stood with her back to the room. 'Do you need anything else?'

'Not right now.'

'I'll be downstairs.'

She didn't wait for his blessing.

Myron walked in. He checked the answering machine on Chad's phone. Three messages. Two from a girl named Becky. From the sound of it, she was a pretty good friend. Just calling to say, like, hi, see if he wanted to, like, do anything this weekend, you know? She and Millie and Suze were going to, like, hang out at the Heritage, okay, and if he wanted to come, well, you know, whatever. Myron smiled. Times they might be a-changin', but her words could have come from a girl Myron had gone to high school with or his father or his father's father. Generations cycle in. The music, the movies, the language, the fashion – they change. But that's just outside stimuli. Beneath the baggy pants or the message-cropped hair, the same adolescent fears and needs and feelings of inadequacy remained frighteningly constant.

The last call was from a guy named Glen. He wanted to know if Chad wanted to play golf at 'the Pine' this week-end, being that Merion was off-limits because of the

Open. 'Daddy,' Glen's preppy taped voice assured Chad, 'can get us a tee time, no prob.'

No messages from Chad's close buddy Matthew Squires.

He snapped on the computer. Windows 95. Cool. Myron used it too. Chad Coldren, Myron immediately saw, used America Online to get his E-mail. Perfect. Myron hit FLASHSESSION. The modem hooked on and screeched for a few seconds. A voice said, 'Welcome. You have mail.' Dozens of messages were automatically downloaded. The same voice said, 'Good-bye.' Myron checked Chad's E-mail address book and found Matthew Squires's E-mail address. He skimmed the downloaded messages. None were from Matthew.

Interesting.

It was, of course, entirely possible that Matthew and Chad were not as close as Linda Coldren thought. It was also entirely possible that even if they were, Matthew had not contacted his friend since Wednesday – even though his friend had supposedly vanished without warning. It happens.

Still, it was interesting.

Myron picked up Chad's phone and hit the redial button. Four rings later a taped voice came on. 'You've reached Matthew. Leave a message or don't. Up to you.'

Myron hung up without leaving a message (it was, after all, 'up to him'). Hmm. Chad's last call was to Matthew. That could be significant. Or it could have nothing to do with anything. Either way, Myron was quickly getting nowhere.

He picked up Chad's phone and dialed his office. Esperanza answered on the second ring.

'MB SportsReps.'

'It's me.' He filled her in. She listened without interrupting.

Esperanza Diaz had worked for MB SportReps since its inception. Ten years ago, when Esperanza was only eighteen years old, she was the Queen of Sunday Morning Cable TV. No, she wasn't on any infomercial, though her show ran opposite plenty of them, especially that one with the abdominal exerciser that bore a striking resemblance to a medieval instrument of torture; rather, Esperanza had been a professional wrestler named Little Pocahontas, the Sensual Indian Princess. With her petite, lithe figure bedecked in only a suede bikini, Esperanza had been voted FLOW'S (Fabulous Ladies Of Wrestling) most popular wrestler three years running – or, as the award was officially known, the Babe You'd Most Like to Get in a Full Nelson. Despite this, Esperanza remained humble.

When he finished telling her about the kidnapping, Esperanza's first words were an incredulous, 'Win has a mother?'

'Yep.'

Pause. 'There goes my spawned-from-a-satanic-egg theory.'

'Ha-ha.'

'Or my hatched-in-an-experiment-gone-very-wrong theory.'

'You're not helping.'

'What's to help?' Esperanza replied. 'I like Win, you know that. But the boy is – what's the official psychiatric term again? – cuckoo.'

'That cuckoo saved your life once,' Myron said.

'Yeah, but you remember how,' she countered.

Myron did. A dark alley. Win's doctored bullets. Brain

22

matter tossed about like parade confetti. Classic Win. Effective but excessive. Like squashing a bug with a wrecking ball.

Esperanza broke the long silence. 'Like I said before,' she began softly, 'cuckoo.'

Myron wanted to change the subject. 'Any messages?'

'About a million. Nothing that can't wait, though.' Then she asked, 'Have you ever met her?'

'Who?'

'Madonna,' she snapped. 'Who do you think? Win's mother.'

'Once,' Myron said, remembering. More than ten years ago. He and Win had been having dinner at Merion, in fact. Win hadn't spoken to her on that occasion. But she had spoken to him. The memory made Myron cringe anew.

'Have you told Win about this yet?' she asked.

'Nope. Any advice?'

Esperanza thought a moment. 'Do it over the phone,' she said. 'At a very safe distance.'

Chapter 3

They got a quick break.

Myron was still sitting in the Coldrens' den with Linda when Esperanza called back. Bucky had gone back to Merion to get Jack.

'The kid's ATM card was accessed yesterday at 6:18 P.M.,' Esperanza said. 'He took out $180. A First Philadelphia branch on Porter Street in South Philly.'

'Thanks.'

Information like that was not difficult to obtain. Anybody with an account number could pretty much do it with a phone by pretending they were the account holder. Even without one, any semi-human who had ever worked in law enforcement had the contacts or the access numbers or at least the wherewithal to pay off the right person. It didn't take much anymore, not with today's overabundance of user-friendly technology. Technology did more than depersonalize; it ripped your life wide open, gutted you, stripped away any pretense of privacy.

A few keystrokes revealed all.

'What is it?' Linda Coldren asked.

He told her.

'It doesn't necessarily mean what you think,' she said. 'The kidnapper could have gotten the PIN number from Chad.'

'Could have,' Myron said.

'But you don't believe it, do you?'

He shrugged. 'Let's just say I'm more than a little skeptical.'

'Why?'

'The amount, for one thing. What was Chad's max?'

'Five hundred dollars a day.'

'So why would a kidnapper only take $180?'

Linda Coldren thought a moment. 'If he took too much, someone might get suspicious.'

Myron sort of frowned. 'But if the kidnapper was that careful,' he began, 'why risk so much for $180? Everyone knows that ATMs are equipped with security cameras. Everyone also knows that even the simplest computer check can yield a location.'

She looked at him evenly. 'You don't think my son is in danger.'

'I didn't say that. This whole thing may look like one thing and be another. You were right before. It's safest to assume that the kidnapping is real.'

'So what's your next step?'

'I'm not sure. The ATM machine was on Porter Street in South Philadelphia. Is that someplace Chad likes to hang out?'

'No,' Linda Coldren said slowly. 'In fact, it's a place I would never imagine him going.'

'Why do you say that?'

'It's a dive. One of the sleaziest parts of the city.'

Myron stood. 'You got a street map?'

'In my glove compartment.'

'Good. I'll need to borrow your car for a little while.'

'Where are you going?'

'I'm going to drive around this ATM.'

She frowned. 'What for?'

'I don't know,' Myron admitted. 'Like I said before, investigating is not very scientific. You do some leg-work and you push some buttons and you hope something happens.'

Linda Coldren reached into a pocket for her keys. 'Maybe the kidnappers grabbed him there,' she said. 'Maybe you'll see his car or something.'

Myron almost slapped himself in the head. A car. He had forgotten something so basic. In his mind, a kid disappearing on his way to or from school conjured up images of yellow buses or strolling sprightly with a book bag. How could he have missed something as obvious as a car trace?

He asked her the make and model. Gray Honda Accord. Hardly a car that stands out in a crowd. Pennsylvania license plate 567-AHJ. He called it in to Esperanza. Then he gave Linda Coldren his cellular phone number.

'Call me if anything happens.'

'Okay.'

'I'll be back soon,' he said.

The ride wasn't far. He traveled, it seemed, from green splendor to concrete crap instantaneously – like on *Star Trek* where they step through one of those time portals.

The ATM was a drive-through located in what would generously be labeled a business district. Tons of cameras. No human tellers. Would a kidnapper really risk this?

Very doubtful. Myron wondered where he could get a copy of the bank's videotape without alerting the police. Win might know somebody. Financial institutions were usually anxious to cooperate with the Lockwood family. The question was, would Win be willing to cooperate?

Abandoned warehouses – or at least, they looked abandoned – lined the road. Eighteen-wheelers hurried by like something out of an old convoy movie. They reminded Myron of the CB craze from his childhood. Like everyone else, his dad had bought one – a man born in the Flatbush section of Brooklyn who grew up to own an undergarment factory in Newark, barking 'breaker one nine' with an accent he had picked up watching the movie *Deliverance*. Dad would be driving on Hobart Gap Road between their house and the Livingston Mall – maybe a one-mile drive – asking his 'good buddies' if there was any sign of 'smokeys.' Myron smiled at the memory. Ah, CBs. He was sure that his father still had his someplace. Probably next to the eight-track player.

On one side of the ATM was a gas station so generic that it didn't even bother having a name. Rusted cars stood upon crumbling cinder blocks. On the other side, a dirt-bag, no-tell motel called the Court Manor Inn greeted customers with green lettering that read: $19.99 PER HOUR.

Myron Bolitar Traveling Tip #83: You may not be dealing with a five-star deluxe property when they prominently advertise hourly rates.

Under the price, in smaller black print, the sign read, MIRRORED CEILINGS AND THEME ROOMS SLIGHTLY EXTRA. Theme rooms. Myron didn't even want to know. The last line, back in the green big print: ASK ABOUT OUR FREQUENT VISITORS CLUB. Jesus.

Myron wondered if it was worth a shot and decided, why not? It probably wouldn't lead to anything, but if Chad was hiding out – or even if he'd been kidnapped – a no-tell was as good a place as any to disappear.

He parked in the lot. The Court Manor was a textbook two-level dump. The outer stairs and walkway terraces were made of rotting wood. The cement walls had that unfinished, swirling look that could cut your hand if you leaned against it wrong. Small chunks of concrete lay on the ground. An unplugged Pepsi machine guarded the door like one of the Queen's guards. Myron passed it and entered.

He'd expected to find the standard no-tell lobby interior – that is, an unshaven Neanderthal in a sleeveless, too-short undershirt chewing on a toothpick while sitting behind bullet-proof glass burping up a beer. Or something like that. But that was not the case. The Court Manor Inn had a high wooden desk with a bronze sign reading CONCIERGE on top of it. Myron tried not to snicker. Behind the desk, a well-groomed, baby-faced man in his late twenties stood at attention. He wore a pressed shirt, starched collar, dark tie tied in a perfect Windsor knot. He smiled at Myron.

'Good afternoon, sir!' he exclaimed. He looked and sounded like a John Tesh substitute on *Entertainment Weekly*. 'Welcome to the Court Manor Inn!'

'Yeah,' Myron said. 'Hi.'

'May I be of some service to you today, sir?'

'I hope so.'

'Great! My name is Stuart Lipwitz. I'm the new manager of the Court Manor Inn.' He looked at Myron expectantly.

Myron said, 'Congrats.'

'Well, thank you, sir, that's very kind. If there are any problems – if anything at the Court Manor does not meet your expectations – please let me know immediately. I will handle it personally.' Big smile, puffed-out chest. 'At the Court Manor, we guarantee your satisfaction.'

Myron just looked at him for a minute, waiting for the full-wattage smile to dim a bit. It didn't. Myron took out the photograph of Chad Coldren.

'Have you seen this young man?'

Stuart Lipwitz did not even look down. Still smiling, he said, 'I'm sorry, sir. But are you with the police?'

'No.'

'Then I'm afraid I can't help you. I'm very sorry.'

'Pardon me?'

'I'm sorry, sir, but here at the Court Manor Inn we pride ourselves on our discretion.'

'He's not in any trouble,' Myron said. 'I'm not a private eye trying to catch a cheating husband or anything like that.'

The smile did not falter or sway. 'I'm sorry, sir, but this is the Court Manor Inn. Our clientele use our services for a variety of activities and often crave anonymity. We at the Court Manor Inn must respect that.'

Myron studied the man's face, searching for some signal that this was a put-on. Nothing. His whole persona glowed like a performer in an *Up with People* halftime show. Myron leaned over the desk and checked out the shoes. Polished like twin mirrors. The hair was slicked back. The sparkle in the eye looked real.

It took Myron some time, but he finally saw where this was leading. He took out his wallet and plucked a twenty from the billfold. He slid it across the counter. Stuart Lipwitz looked at it but made no move.

'What's this for, sir?'

'It's a present,' Myron said.

Stuart Lipwitz did not touch it.

'It's for one piece of information,' Myron continued. He plucked out another and held it in the air. 'I have another, if you'd like.'

'Sir, we have a credo here at the Court Manor Inn: The guest must come first.'

'Isn't that a prostitute's credo?'

'Pardon me, sir?'

'Never mind,' Myron said.

'I am the new manager of the Court Manor Inn, sir.'

'So I've heard.'

'I also own ten percent.'

'Your mom must be the envy of her mah-jongg group.'

Still the smile. 'In other words, sir, I am in it for the long term. That's how I look at this business. Long term. Not just today. Not just tomorrow. But into the future. For the long term. You see?'

'Oh,' Myron said flatly. 'You mean long term?'

Stuart Lipwitz snapped his fingers. 'Precisely. And our motto is this: There are many places you can spend your adultery dollar. We want it to be here.'

Myron waited a moment. Then he said, 'Noble.'

'We at the Court Manor Inn are working hard to earn your trust, and trust has no price. When I wake up in the morning, I have to look at myself in the mirror.'

'Would that mirror be on the ceiling?'

Still smiling. 'Let me explain it another way,' he said. 'If the client knows that the Court Manor Inn is a place he can feel safe to commit an indiscretion, he or she will be more likely to return.' He leaned forward, his eyes wet with excitement. 'Do you see?'

30

Myron nodded. 'Repeat business.'

'Precisely.'

'Referrals too,' Myron added. 'Like, "Hey, Bob, I know a great place to get some ass on the side."'

A nod added to the smile. 'So you understand.'

'That's all very nice, Stuart, but this kid is fifteen years old. Fifteen.' Actually, Chad was sixteen, but what the hey. 'That's against the law.'

The smile stayed, but now it signaled disappointment in the favorite pupil. 'I hate to disagree with you, sir, but the statutory rape law in this state is fourteen. And secondly, there is no law against a fifteen-year-old renting a motel room.'

The guy was dancing too much, Myron thought. No reason to go through this rigmarole if the kid had never been here. Then again, let's face facts. Stuart Lipwitz was probably enjoying this. The guy was several french fries short of a Happy Meal. Either way, Myron thought, it was time to shake the tree a bit.

'It is when he is assaulted in your motel,' Myron said. 'It is when he claims that someone got an extra key from the front desk and used it to break into the room.' Mr Bluff Goes to Philadelphia.

'We don't have extra keys,' Lipwitz said.

'Well, he got in somehow.'

Still the smile. Still the polite tone. 'If that were the case, sir, the police would be here.'

'That's my next stop,' Myron said, 'if you don't cooperate.'

'And you want to know if this young man' – Lipwitz gestured to the photograph of Chad – 'stayed here?'

'Yes.'

The smile actually brightened a bit. Myron almost

shaded his eyes. 'But, sir, if you are telling the truth, then this young man would be able to tell if he was here. You wouldn't need me for that, correct?'

Myron's face remained neutral. Mr Bluff had just been outsmarted by the new manager of the Court Manor Inn. 'That's right,' he said, changing tactics on the fly. 'I already know he was here. It was just an opening question. Like when the police ask you to state your name even though they already know it. Just to get the ball rolling.' Mr Improvision Takes Over for Mr Bluff.

Stuart Lipwitz took out a piece of paper and began to scribble. 'This is the name and telephone number of the Court Manor Inn's attorney. He will be able to help you with any problems you may have.'

'But what about that handling it personally stuff? What about the satisfaction guarantee?'

'Sir.' He leaned forward, maintaining eye contact. Not a hint of impatience had crept into his voice or face. 'May I be bold?'

'Go for it.'

'I don't believe a word you're saying.'

'Thanks for the boldness,' Myron said.

'No, thank you, sir. And do come again.'

'Another prostitution credo.'

'Pardon me?'

'Nothing,' Myron said. 'May I too be bold?'

'Yes.'

'I may punch you in the face very hard if you don't tell me if you've seen this kid.' Mr Improvisation Loses His Cool.

The door swung open hard. A couple entwined about one another stumbled in. The woman was openly rubbing the man's crotch. 'We need a room pronto,' the man said.

Myron turned to them and said, 'Do you have your frequent visitor card?'

'What?'

Still the smile from Stuart Lipwitz. 'Good-bye, sir. And have a nice day.' Then he rejuvenated the smile and moved toward the writhing mound. 'Welcome to the Court Manor Inn. My name is Stuart Lipwitz. I'm the new manager.'

Myron headed out to his car. He took a deep breath in the parking lot and looked back behind him. The whole visit already had an unreal feeling, like one of those descriptions of alien abductions *sans* the anal probe. He got in the car and dialed Win's cellular. He just wanted to leave him a message on the machine. But to Myron's surprise, Win answered.

'Articulate,' he drolled.

Myron was momentarily taken aback. 'It's me,' he said.

Silence, Win hated the obvious. 'It's me,' was both questionable grammar (at best) and a complete waste. Win would know who it was by the voice. If he didn't, hearing 'It's me' would undeniably not help.

'I thought you didn't answer the phone on the course,' Myron said.

'I'm driving home to change,' Win said. 'Then I'm dining at Merion.' Mainliners never ate; they dined. 'Care to join me?'

'Sounds good,' Myron said.

'Wait a second.'

'What?'

'Are you properly attired?'

'I don't clash,' Myron said. 'Will they still let me in?'

'My, my, that was very funny, Myron. I must write that one down. As soon as I stop laughing, I plan on locating a

33

pen. However, I am so filled with mirth that I may wrap my precious Jag around an upcoming telephone pole. Alas, at least I will die with jocularity in my heart.'

Win.

'We have a case,' Myron said.

Silence. Win made this so easy.

'I'll tell you about it at dinner.'

'Until then,' Win said, 'it'll be all I can do to douse my mounting excitement and anticipation with a snifter of cognac.'

Click. Gotta love that Win.

Myron hadn't driven a mile when the cellular phone rang. Myron switched it on.

It was Bucky. 'The kidnapper called again.'

Chapter 4

'What did he say?' Myron asked.

'They want money,' Bucky said.

'How much?'

'I don't know.'

Myron was confused. 'What do you mean, you don't know? Didn't they say?'

'I don't think so,' the old man said.

There was noise in the background. 'Where are you?' Myron asked.

'I'm at Merion. Look, Jack answered the phone. He's still in shock.'

'Jack answered?'

'Yes.'

Doubly confused. 'The kidnapper called Jack at Merion?'

'Yes. Please, Myron, can you get back over here? It'll be easier to explain.'

'On my way.'

He drove from the seedy motel to a highway and then into green. Lots of green. The Philadelphia suburbs were lush lawns and high bushes and shady trees. Amazing how close it was – at least in a geographic sense – to the meaner streets of Philly. Like most cities, there was tremendous segregation in Philadelphia. Myron remembered driving with Win to Veterans Stadium for an Eagles game a couple of years back. They'd gone through an Italian block, a Polish block, an African American block; it was as if some powerful, invisible force field – again, like on *Star Trek* – isolated each ethnicity. The City of Brotherly Love could almost be called Little Yugoslavia.

Myron turned down Ardmore Avenue. Merion was about a mile away. His thoughts turned to Win. How, he wondered, would his old friend react to the maternal connection in this case?

Probably not well.

In all the years they had been friends, Myron had heard Win mention his mother on only one occasion.

It had been during their junior year at Duke. They were college roommates, just back from a wild frat party. The beer had flowed. Myron was not what you'd call a good drinker. Two drinks and he'd usually end up trying to French-kiss a toaster. He blamed this on his ancestry – his people had never handled spirits well.

Win, on the other hand, seemed to have been weaned on schnapps. Liquor never really affected him much. But at this particular party, the grain alcohol-laced punch made even his steps wobble a bit. It took Win three tries to unlock their dorm room door.

Myron quickly collapsed on his bed. The ceiling spun counterclockwise at a seemingly death-defying speed. He closed his eyes. His hands gripped the bed and held on in terror. His face had no color. Nausea clamped down painfully on his stomach. Myron wondered when he would vomit and prayed it would be soon.

Ah, the glamour of college drinking.

For a while neither of them said anything. Myron wondered if Win had fallen asleep. Or maybe Win was gone. Vanished into the night. Maybe he hadn't held on to his spinning bed tightly enough and the centrifugal force had hurled him out the window and into the great beyond.

Then Win's voice cut through the darkness. 'Take a look at this.'

A hand reached out and dropped something on Myron's chest. Myron risked letting go of the bed with one hand. So far, so good. He fumbled for whatever it was, found it, lifted it into view. A streetlight from outside – campuses are lit up like Christmas trees – cast enough illumination to make out a photograph. The color was grainy and faded, but Myron could still make out what looked to be an expensive car.

'Is that a Rolls-Royce?' Myron asked. He knew nothing about cars.

'A Bentley S Three Continental Flying Spur,' Win corrected, '1962. A classic.'

'Is it yours?'

'Yes.'

The bed spun silently.

'How did you get it?' Myron asked.

'A man who was fucking my mother gave it to me.'

The end. Win had shut down after that. The wall he put up was not only impenetrable but unapproachable, filled with land mines and a moat and lots of high-voltage

37

electric wires. Over the ensuing decade and a half, Win had never again mentioned his mother. Not when the packages came to the dorm room every semester. Not when the packages came to Win's office on his birthday even now. Not even when they saw her in person ten years ago.

The plain dark wood sign merely read MERION GOLF CLUB. Nothing else. No 'For Members Only.' No 'We're Elitist and We Don't Want You.' No 'Ethnics Use Service Entrance.' No need. It was just a given.

The last US Open threesome had finished a while back and the crowd was mostly gone now. Merion could hold only seventeen thousand for a tournament – less than half the capacity of most courses – but parking was still a chore. Most spectators were forced to park at nearby Haverford College. Shuttle buses ran constantly.

At the top of the driveway a guard signaled him to stop.

'I'm here to meet Windsor Lockwood,' Myron said.

Instant recognition. Instant wave-through.

Bucky ran over to him before he had the car in park. The rounded face was more jowly now, as if he were packing wet sand in his cheeks.

'Where is Jack?' Myron asked.

'The western course.'

'The what?'

'Merion has two courses,' the older man explained, stretching his neck again. 'The east, which is the more famous one, and the west. During the Open, the western course is used as a driving range.'

'And your son-in-law is there?'

'Yes.'

'Driving balls?'

'Of course.' Bucky looked at him, surprised. 'You always do that after a round. Every golfer on the tour knows that. You played basketball. Didn't you used to practice your shot after a game?'

'No.'

'Well, as I told you earlier, golf is very special. Players need to review their play immediately after a round. Even if they've played well. They focus in on their good strokes, see if they can figure out what went wrong with the bad strokes. They recap the day.'

'Uh-huh,' Myron said. 'So tell me about the kidnapper's call.'

'I'll take you to Jack,' he said. 'This way.'

They walked across the eighteen fairway and then down sixteen. The air smelled of freshly cut grass and pollen. It'd been a big year for pollen on the East Coast; nearby allergists swooned with greedy delight.

Bucky shook his head. 'Look at these roughs,' he said. 'Impossible.'

He pointed to long grass. Myron had no idea what he was talking about so he nodded and kept walking.

'Damn USGA wants this course to bring the golfers to their knees,' Bucky ranted on. 'So they grow the rough way out. Like playing in a rice paddy, for chrissake. Then they cut the greens so close, the golfers might as well be putting on a hockey rink.'

Myron remained silent. They two men kept walking.

'This is one of the famed stone-quarry holes,' Bucky said, calmer now.

'Uh-huh.' The man was babbling. People do that when they're nervous.

'When the original builders reached sixteen, seventeen,

39

and eighteen,' Bucky continued, sounding not unlike a tour guide in the Sistine Chapel, 'they ran across a stone quarry. Rather than giving up then and there, they plowed ahead, incorporating the quarry into the hole.'

'Gosh,' Myron said softly, 'they were so brave back then.'

Some babble when nervous. Some grow sarcastic.

They reached the tee and made a right, walking along Golf House Road. Though the last group had finished playing more than an hour ago, there were still at least a dozen golfers hitting balls. The driving range. Yes, professional golfers hit balls here – practicing with a wide array of woods and irons and big clubs, nay, warheads, they called Bertha and Cathy and the like – but that was only part of what went on. Most touring pros used the range to work out strategies with their caddies, check on equipment with their sponsors, network, socialize with fellow golfers, smoke a cigarette (a surprising amount of pros chain-smoke), even talk to agents.

In golf circles, the driving range was called the office.

Myron recognized Greg Norman and Nick Faldo. He also spotted Tad Crispin, the new kid on the block, the latest next Jack Nicklaus – in a phrase, the dream client. The kid was twenty-three, good-looking, quiet, engaged to an equally attractive, happy-just-to-be-here woman. He also did not yet have an agent. Myron tried not to salivate. Hey, he was as human as the next guy. He was, after all, a sports agent. Cut him some slack.

'Where is Jack?' Myron asked.

'Down this way,' Bucky said. 'He wanted to hit alone.'

'How did the kidnapper reach him?'

'He called the Merion switchboard and said it was an emergency.'

'And that worked?'

'Yes,' Bucky said slowly. 'Actually, it was Chad on the phone. He identified himself as Jack's son.'

Curious? 'What time did the call come in?'

'Maybe ten minutes before I called you.' Bucky stopped, gestured with his chin. 'There.'

Jack Coldren was a touch pudgy and soft in the middle, but he had forearms like Popeye's. His flyaway hair did just that in the breeze, revealing bald spots that had started off the day better covered. He whacked the ball with a wood club and an uncommon fury. To some this might all seem very strange. You have just learned your son is missing and you go out and hit golf balls. But Myron understood. Hitting balls was comfort food. The more stress Myron was under, the more he wanted to go in his driveway and shoot baskets. We all have something. Some drink. Some do drugs. Some like to take a long drive or play a computer game. When Win needed to unwind, he often watched videotapes of his own sexual exploits. But that was Win.

'Who's that with him?' Myron asked.

'Diane Hoffman,' Bucky said. 'Jack's caddie.'

Myron knew that female caddies were not uncommon on the men's pro tour. Some players even hired their wives. Saves money. 'Does she know what's going on?'

'Yes. Diane was there when the call came in. They're pretty close.'

'Have you told Linda?'

Bucky nodded. 'I called her right away. Do you mind

introducing yourself? I'd like to go back to the house and check up on her.'

'No problem.'

'How will I reach you if something comes up?'

'Call my cellular.'

Bucky nearly gasped. 'Cellular phones are forbidden at Merion.' Like it was a papal command.

'I walk on the wild side,' Myron said. 'Just call.'

Myron approached them. Diane Hoffman stood with her feet shoulder-width apart, her arms folded, her face intent on Coldren's backswing. A cigarette dangled from her lips almost vertically. She didn't even glance at Myron. Jack Coldren coiled his body and then let go, snapping like a released spring. The ball rocketed over the distant hills.

Jack Coldren turned, looked at Myron, smiled tightly, nodded a hello. 'You're Myron Bolitar, right?'

'Right.'

He shook Myron's hand. Diane Hoffman continued to study her player's every move, frowning as if she'd spotted a flaw in his hand-shaking technique. 'I appreciate your helping us out,' he said.

Face-to-face now – no more than a few feet away – Myron could see the devastation on the man's face. The jubilant glow after nailing the putt on eighteen had been snuffed out by something more pasty and sickly. His eyes had the surprised, uncomprehending look of a man who'd just been sucker punched in the stomach.

'You tried making a comeback recently,' Jack said. 'With New Jersey.'

Myron nodded.

'I saw you on the news. Gutsy move, after all these years.'

Stalling. Not sure how to begin. Myron decided to help. 'Tell me about the call.'

Jack Coldren's eyes swerved over the expanse of green. 'Are you sure it's safe?' he asked. 'The guy on the phone told me no police. To just act normal.'

'I'm an agent seeking clients,' Myron said. 'Talking to me is about as normal as it gets.'

Coldren thought about that for a moment then nodded. He still hadn't introduced Diane Hoffman. Hoffman didn't seem to mind. She remained about ten feet away, rock-still. Her eyes remained narrow and suspicious, her face weathered and pinched. The cigarette ash was incredibly long now, almost defying gravity. She wore a cap and one of those caddie vests that looked like a jogger's night reflector.

'The club president came up to me and whispered that there was an emergency call from my son. So I went inside the clubhouse and picked it up.'

He stopped suddenly and blinked several times. His breathing became heavier. He was wearing a tad-too-tight, yellow V-necked golf shirt. You could see his body expand against the cotton blend with each inhale. Myron waited.

'It was Chad,' he finally spat out. 'All he could say was "Dad," before someone grabbed the phone away from him. Then a man with a deep voice came on the line.'

'How deep?' Myron asked.

'Pardon?'

'How deep was the voice?'

'Very.'

'Did it sound funny to you? A little robotic?'

'Now that you mention it, yes, it did.'

Electronic altering, Myron guessed. Those machines

could make Barry White sound like a four-year-old girl. Or vice versa. They weren't hard to get. Even Radio Shack sold them now. The kidnapper or kidnappers could be any sex. Linda and Jack Coldren's description of a 'male voice' was irrelevant. 'What did he say?'

'That he had my son. He told me that if I called the police or anybody like that, Chad would pay. He told me that someone would be watching me all the time.' Jack Coldren accentuated the point by looking around again. No one suspicious lurked about, though Greg Norman waved and gave them a smiling thumbs-up. G'day, mate.

'What else?' Myron asked.

'He said he wanted money,' Coldren said.

'How much?'

'He just said a lot. He wasn't sure yet how much, but he wanted me to get it ready. He said he'd call back.'

Myron made a face. 'But he didn't tell you how much?'

'No. Just that it would be a lot.'

'And that you should get it ready.'

'Right.'

This made no sense. A kidnapper who wasn't sure how much ransom to extort? 'May I be blunt, Jack?'

Coldren stood a little taller, tucked in his shirt. He was what some would call boyishly and disarmingly handsome. His face was big and unthreatening with cottony, malleable features. 'Don't sugarcoat anything for me,' he said. 'I want the truth.'

'Could this be a hoax?'

Jack shot a quick glance at Diane Hoffman. She moved slightly. Might have been a nod. He turned back to Myron. 'What do you mean?'

'Could Chad be behind this?'

44

The longer flyaway hairs got caught up in a cross-breeze and fell down into his eyes. He pushed them away with his fingers. Something came across his face. Rumination, maybe? Unlike Linda Coldren, the idea had not snapped him into a defensive stance. He was pondering the possibility, or perhaps merely grasping at an option that meant safety for his son.

'There were two different voices,' Coldren said. 'On the phone.'

'It could be a voice changer.' Myron explained what that was.

More rumination. Coldren's face scrunched up. 'I really don't know.'

'Is it something you can imagine Chad doing?'

'No,' Coldren replied. 'But who can imagine anyone's kid doing something like this? I'm trying to remain objective here, hard as that is. Do I think my boy could do something like this? Of course not. But then again, I wouldn't be the first parent to be wrong about my kid; now, would I?'

Fair enough, Myron thought. 'Has Chad ever run away?'

'No.'

'Any trouble in the family? Anything that might make him want to do something like this?'

'Something like fake his own kidnapping?'

'It doesn't have to be that extreme,' Myron said. 'Maybe something you or your wife did that got him upset.'

'No,' he said, his voice suddenly faraway. 'I can't think of anything.' He looked up. The sun was low and not very strong anymore, but he still sort of squinted up at Myron, the side of his hand resting on his forehead in an

45

eye-shading salute. The posture reminded Myron of the photograph of Chad he'd seen at the house.

Jack said, 'You have a thought, Myron, don't you?'

'Barely.'

'I'd still like to hear it,' Coldren said.

'How badly do you want to win this tournament, Jack?'

Coldren gave a half-smile. 'You were an athlete, Myron. You know how badly.'

'Yes,' Myron said, 'I do.'

'So what's your point?'

'Your son is an athlete. He probably knows too.'

'Yes,' Coldren said. Then: 'I'm still waiting for the point.'

'If someone wanted to hurt you,' Myron said, 'what better way than to mess up your chance of winning the Open?'

Jack Coldren's eyes had that sucker punched look again. He took a step back.

'I'm only theorizing,' Myron added quickly. 'I'm not saying your son is doing that . . .'

'But you need to explore every avenue,' Jack Coldren finished for him.

'Yes.'

Coldren recovered, but it took him a little time. 'Even if what you're saying is true, it doesn't have to be Chad. Someone else could have done this to get at me.' Again he glanced over at his caddie. Still looking at her, he said, 'Wouldn't be the first time.'

'What do you mean?'

Jack Coldren didn't answer right away. He turned away from both of them and squinted out toward where he'd been hitting balls. There was nothing to see. His back was to Myron. 'You probably know I lost the Open a long time ago.'

'Yes.'

He didn't elaborate.

'Did something happen back then?' Myron asked.

'Maybe,' Jack Coldren said slowly. 'I don't know anymore. The point is, someone else might be out to get me. It doesn't have to be my son.'

'Maybe,' Myron agreed. He didn't go into the fact that he'd pretty much dismissed this possibility because Chad had vanished before Coldren had his lead. No reason to go into it now.

Coldren turned back to Myron. 'Bucky mentioned something about an ATM card,' he said.

'Your son's ATM card was accessed last night. At Porter Street.'

Something crossed his face. Not for long. Not for more than a second. A flash and then it was gone. 'On Porter Street?' he repeated.

'Yep. A First Philadelphia Bank on Porter Street in South Philadelphia.'

Silence.

'Are you familiar with that part of town?'

'No,' Coldren said. He looked over at his caddie. Diane Hoffman remained the statue. Arms still folded. Feet still shoulder-width apart. Ash finally gone.

'Are you sure?'

'Of course I am.'

'I visited there today,' Myron said.

His face remained steady. 'Did you learn anything?'

'No.'

Silence.

47

Jack Coldren gestured behind him. 'You mind if I take a few more swings while we talk?'

'Not at all.'

He put on his glove. 'Do you think I should play tomorrow?'

'That's up to you,' Myron said. 'The kidnapper said to act normal. Your not playing would certainly draw suspicion.'

Coldren bent down to put a ball on the tee. 'Can I ask you something, Myron?'

'Sure.'

'When you played basketball, how important was winning to you?'

Odd question. 'Very.'

Jack nodded like he'd been expecting that. 'You won the NCAA championship one year, right?'

'Yes.'

Coldren shook his head. 'Must have been something.'

Myron did not reply.

Jack Coldren picked up a club and flexed his fingers around the grip. He lined up next to the ball. Again the smooth coil-and-release movement. Myron watched the ball sail away. For a moment no one spoke. They just looked off into the distance and watched the final streaks of sun color the sky purple.

When Coldren finally spoke, his voice was thick. 'You want to hear something awful?'

Myron moved closer to him. Coldren's eyes were wet.

'I still care about winning this thing,' Coldren said. He looked at Myron. The pain on his face was so naked, Myron almost reached out and hugged him. He imagined that he could see the reflection of the man's past in his eyes, the years of torment, of thinking of what might have been, of finally having the chance at redemption, of having that chance suddenly snatched away.

'What kind of man still thinks about winning at a time like this?' Coldren asked.

Myron didn't say anything. He didn't know the answer. Or maybe he feared that he did.

Chapter 5

Merion's clubhouse was an expanded white farmhouse with black shutters. The only splash of color came from the green awnings shading the famed back porch and even that was muted by the surrounding green of the golf course. You expected something more awe-inspiring or intimidating at one of the country's most exclusive clubs, and yet the simplicity seemed to say, 'We're Merion. We don't need more.'

Myron walked past the pro shop. Golf bags were lined up on a metal stand. The men's locker room door was on his right. A bronze sign read that Merion had been designated a historic landmark. A bulletin board listed members' handicaps. Myron skimmed the names for Win's. Three handicap. Myron didn't know much about golfing, but he knew that was pretty damn good.

The outside porch had a stone floor and about two dozen tables. The legendary dining area did more than overlook the first tee – it actually seemed perched right over it. From here, members watched golfers tee off with the practiced glares of Roman senators at the Colosseum. Powerful businessmen and community leaders often crumbled under such century-old scrutiny. Even professionals were not immune – the porch's dining facility was kept open during the Open. Jack Nicklaus and Arnold Palmer and Ben Hogan and Bobby Jones and Sam Snead had all been subjected to the small restaurant noises, the grating tinkling of glass and silverware blending most disharmoniously with golf's hushed crowds and distant cheers.

The porch was packed with members. Most were men – elderly and red-faced and well fed. They wore blue or green blazers with different crests on them. Their ties were loud and usually striped. Many had floppy white or yellow hats on their heads. Floppy hats. And Win had been worried about Myron's 'attire.'

Myron spotted Win at a corner table with six chairs. He sat alone. His expression was both glacial and serene, his body completely at ease. A mountain lion patiently waiting for prey. One would think that the blond hair and patrician good looks would be life assets for Win. In many ways, they were; in many more ways, they branded him. His entire appearance reeked of arrogance, old money, and elitism. Most people did not respond well to that. A specific, seething hostility frothed and boiled over when people looked at Win. To look at such a person was to hate him. Win was used to it. People who judged purely on looks did not concern him. People who judged purely on looks were oft surprised.

Myron greeted his old friend and sat down.

'Would you care for a drink?' Win said.

'Sure.'

'If you ask for a Yoo-Hoo,' Win said, 'I'll shoot you in the right eye.'

'Right eye,' Myron repeated with a nod. 'Very specific.'

A waiter who must have been a hundred years old materialized. He wore a green jacket and pants – green, Myron surmised, so that even the help would blend into the famed milieu. Didn't work, though. The old waiter looked like the Riddler's grandfather. 'Henry,' Win said, 'I'll have an iced tea.'

Myron was tempted to ask for a 'Colt 45, like Billy Dee,' but decided against it. 'I'll have the same.'

'Very good, Mr Lockwood.'

Henry left. Win looked over at Myron. 'So tell me.'

'It's a kidnapping,' Myron said.

Win arched an eyebrow.

'One of the players' sons is missing. The parents have gotten two calls.' Myron quickly told him about them. Win listened in silence.

When Myron finished, Win said, 'You left something out.'

'What?'

'The name of the player.'

Myron kept his voice steady. 'Jack Coldren.'

Win's face betrayed nothing, but Myron still felt a cold gust blow across his heart.

Win said, 'And you've met Linda.'

'Yes.'

'And you know that she is related to me.'

'Yes.'

'Then you must have realized that I will not help.'

'No.'

Win sat back, steepled his fingers. 'Then you realize it now.'

'A boy might be in real danger,' Myron said. 'We have to help.'

'No,' Win said. 'I do not.'

'You want me to drop it?'

'What you do is your affair,' Win said.

'Do you want me to drop it?' Myron repeated.

The iced teas came. Win took a gentle sip. He looked off and tapped his chin with his index finger. His signal to end the topic. Myron knew better than to push it.

'So who are the other seats for?' Myron asked.

'I am mining a major lead.'

'A new client?'

'For me, almost definitely. For you, a barely remote possibility.'

'Who?'

'Tad Crispin.'

Myron's chin dropped. 'We're having dinner with Tad Crispin?'

'As well as our old friend Norman Zuckerman and his latest rather attractive ingenue.'

Norm Zuckerman was the owner of Zoom, one of the largest sneaker and sporting apparel companies in the country. He was also one of Myron's favorite people. 'How did you get to Crispin? I heard he was agenting himself.'

'He is,' Win said, 'but he still wants a financial adviser.' Barely in his mid-thirties, Win was already something of a Wall Street legend. Reaching out to Win made sense. 'Crispin is quite a shrewd young man, actually,' he went on. 'Unfortunately, he believes that all agents are thieves. That they have the morals of a prostitute practicing politics.'

'He said that? A prostitute practicing politics?'

'No, I came up with that one myself.' Win smiled. 'Pretty good, no?'

Myron nodded. 'No.'

'Anyway, the Zoom folks here are tailing him like a lapdog. They're introducing a whole new line of men's clubs and clothing on the back of young Mr Crispin.'

Tad Crispin was in second place, a goodly distance behind Jack Coldren. Myron wondered how happy Zoom was about Coldren possibly stealing their thunder. Not very, he supposed.

'So what do you make of Jack Coldren's good showing?' Myron asked. 'You surprised?'

Win shrugged. 'Winning was always very important to Jack.'

'Have you known him long?'

Flat eyes. 'Yes.'

'Did you know him when he lost here as a rookie?'

'Yes.'

Myron calculated the years. Win would have been in elementary school. 'Jack Coldren hinted that he thought someone tried to sabotage his chances back then.'

Win made a noise. 'Guff,' he said.

'Guff?'

'You don't recall what happened?'

'No.'

'Coldren claims his caddie gave him the wrong club on sixteen,' Win said. 'He asked for a six iron and supposedly his caddie handed him an eight. His shot landed short. More specifically, in one of the rock quarry bunkers. He never recovered.'

'Did the caddie admit the error?'

'He never commented, as far as I know.'

'What did Jack do?'

54

'He fired him.'

Myron chewed on that tidbit. 'Where is the caddie now?'

'I do not have the slightest idea,' Win said. 'He wasn't a young man at the time and this was more than twenty years ago.'

'Do you remember his name?'

'No. And this conversation is officially terminated.'

Before Myron could ask why, a pair of hands covered his eyes. 'Guess who?' came a familiar sing-song. 'I'll give you a couple of hints: I'm smart, good-looking, and loaded with talent.'

'Gee,' Myron said, 'before that hint, I would have thought you were Norm Zuckerman.'

'And with the hint?'

Myron shrugged. 'If you add "adored by women of all ages," I'd think it was me.'

Norman Zuckerman laughed heartily. He bent down and gave Myron a big, loud smack on the cheek. 'How are you, meshuggener?'

'Good, Norm. You?'

'I'm cooler than Superfly in a new Coupe de Ville.'

Zuckerman greeted Win with a loud hello and an enthusiastic handshake. Diners stared in distaste. The stares did not quiet Norman Zuckerman. An elephant gun could not quiet Norman Zuckerman. Myron liked the man. Sure, a lot of it was an act. But it was a genuine act. Norm's zest for everything around him was contagious. He was pure energy; the kind of person who made you examine yourself and left you feeling just a little wanting.

Norm brought forward a young woman who'd been standing behind him. 'Let me introduce you to Esme

Fong,' he said. 'She's one of my marketing vee-pees. In charge of the new golf line. Brilliant. The woman is absolutely brilliant.'

The attractive ingenue. Early-to-mid twenties, Myron guessed. Esme Fong was Asian with perhaps a hint of Caucasian. She was petite with almond eyes. Her hair was long and silky, a black fan with an earthy auburn tinge. She wore a beige business suit and white stockings. Esme nodded a hello and stepped closer. She wore the serious face of an attractive young woman who was afraid of not being taken seriously because she was an attractive young woman.

She stuck out her hand. 'A pleasure to meet you, Mr Bolitar,' she said crisply. 'Mr Lockwood.'

'Doesn't she have a firm handshake?' Zuckerman asked. Then turning to her: 'What's with all the *misters*? This is Myron and Win. They're practically family, for crying out loud. Okay, Win's a little goyish to be in my family. I mean, his people came over on the *Mayflower*, while most of mine fled a czar pogrom in a cargo ship. But we're still family, right, Win?'

'As rain,' Win said.

'Sit down already, Esme. You're making me nervous with all the seriousness. Try a smile, okay?' Zuckerman demonstrated, pointing at his teeth. Then he turned to Myron, spread his hands. 'The truth, Myron. How do I look?'

Norman was over sixty. His customary loud clothing, matching the man's personality, hardly stood out after what Myron had seen today. His skin was dark and rough; his eyes dropped inside black circles; his features jutted out in classical Semitism; his beard and hair were too long and somewhat unkempt.

'You look like Jerry Rubin at the Chicago Seven trial,' Myron said.

'Just the look I wanted,' Norm said. 'Retro. Hip. Attitude. That's what's in nowadays.'

'Hardly Tad Crispin's look,' Myron said.

'I'm talking about the real world, not golf. Golfers don't know from hip or attitude. Hasidim are more open to change than golfers, you know what I'm saying? I'll give you an example: Dennis Rodman is not a golfer. You know what golfers want? The same thing they've wanted since the dawn of sports marketing: Arnold Palmer. That's what they want. They wanted Palmer, then Nicklaus, then Watson – always good ol' boys.' He pointed a thumb at Esme Fong. 'Esme is the one who signed Crispin. He's her boy.'

Myron looked at her. 'Quite a coup,' he said.

'Thank you,' she said.

'We'll see how big a coup it is,' Zuckerman said. 'Zoom is moving into golf in a very big way. Huge. Humongous. Gigantic.'

'Enormous,' Myron said.

'Mammoth,' Win added.

'Colossal.'

'Titanic.'

'Bunyanesque.'

Win smiled. 'Brobdingnagian,' he said.

'Oooo,' Myron said. 'Good one.'

Zuckerman shook his head. 'You guys are funnier than the Three Stooges without Curly. Anyway, it's a helluva campaign. Esme is running it for me. Male and female lines. Not only have we got Crispin, but Esme's landed the numero uno female golfer in the world.'

'Linda Coldren?' Myron asked.

'Whoa!' Norm clapped his hands once. 'The Hebrew hoopster knows his golf! By the way, Myron, what kind of name is *Bolitar* for a member of the tribe?'

'It's a long story,' Myron said.

'Good, I wasn't interested anyway. I was just being polite. Where was I?' Zuckerman threw one leg over the other, leaned back, smiled, looked about. A ruddy-faced man at a neighboring table glared. 'Hi, there,' Norm said with a little wave. 'Looking good.'

The man made a huffing noise and looked away.

Norm shrugged. 'You'd think he never saw a Jew before.'

'He probably hasn't,' Win said.

Norm looked back over at the ruddy-faced man. 'Look!' Zuckerman said, pointing to his head. 'No horns!'

Even Win smiled.

Zuckerman turned his attention back to Myron. 'So tell me, you trying to sign Crispin?'

'I haven't even met him yet,' Myron said.

Zuckerman put his hand to his chest, feigning surprise. 'Well then, Myron, this is some eerie coincidence. You being here when we're about to break bread with him – what are the odds? Wait.' Norm stopped, put his hand to his ear. 'I think I hear *Twilight Zone* music.'

'Ha-ha,' Myron said.

'Oh, relax, Myron. I'm teasing you. Lighten up, for crying out loud. But let me be honest for a second, okay? I don't think Cripsin needs you, Myron. Nothing personal, but the kid signed the deal with me himself. No agent. No lawyer. Handled it all on his own.'

'And got robbed,' Win added.

Zuckerman put a hand to his chest. 'You wound me, Win.'

'Crispin told me the numbers,' Win said. 'Myron would have gotten him a far better deal.'

'With all due respect to your centuries of upper-crust inbreeding, you don't know what the hell you're talking about. The kid left a little money in the till for me, that's all. Is that a crime nowadays – for a man to make a profit? Myron's a shark, for crying out loud. He rips off my clothes when we talk. He leaves my office, I don't even have undies left. I don't even have furniture. I don't even have an office. I start out with this beautiful office and Myron comes in and I end up naked in some soup kitchen someplace.'

Myron looked at Win. 'Touching.'

'He's breaking my heart,' Win said.

Myron turned his attention to Esme Fong. 'Are you happy with how Crispin's been playing?'

'Of course,' she said quickly. 'This is his first major, and he's in second place.'

Norm Zuckerman put a hand on her arm. 'Save the spinning for those morons in the media. These two guys are family.'

Esme Fong shifted in her seat. She cleared her throat. 'Linda Coldren won the US Open a few weeks ago,' she said. 'We're running dual television, radio, and print ads – they'll both be in every spot. It's a new line, completely unknown to golf enthusiasts. Naturally, if we could introduce Zoom's new line with two US Open winners, it would be helpful.'

Norm pointed his thumb again. 'Ain't she something? *Helpful.* Nice word. Vague. Look, Myron, you read the sports section, am I right?'

'As rain.'

'How many articles did you see on Crispin before the tournament began?'

'A lot.'

'How much coverage has he gotten in the past two days?'

'Not much.'

'Try none. All anybody is talking about is Jack Coldren. In two days that poor son of a bitch is either going to be a miracle man of messianic proportions or the most pitiful loser in the history of the world. Think about it for a second. A man's entire life – both his past and his future – will be shaped by a few swings of a stick. Nuts, when you think about it. And you know what the worst part is?'

Myron shook his head.

'I hope like hell he messes up! I feel like a major son of a bitch, but that's the truth. My guy comes back and wins, you wait and see the way Esme spins it. The brilliant play of newcomer Tad Crispin forces a veteran to crack. The new kid stares down the pressure like Palmer and Nicklaus combined. You know what it'll mean to the launch of the new line?' Zuckerman looked over at Win and pointed. 'God, I wish I looked like you. Look at him, for crying out loud. He's beautiful.'

Win, in spite of himself, laughed. Several ruddy-faced men turned and stared. Norman waved at them, friendly-like. 'Next time I come,' Norm said to Win, 'I'm wearing a yarmulke.'

Win laughed harder. Myron tried to remember the last time he'd seen his friend laugh so openly. It'd been a while. Norm had that effect on people.

Esme Fong glanced at her watch and rose. 'I only

stopped by to say hello,' she explained. 'I really must be going.'

All three men stood. Norm bussed her cheek. 'Take care, Esme, okay? I'll see you tomorrow morning.'

'Yes, Norm.' She gave Myron and Win demure smiles accompanied by a shy lowering of the head. 'Nice meeting you, Myron. Win.'

She left. The three men sat. Win steepled his fingers. 'How old is she?' Win asked.

'Twenty-five. Phi Beta Kappa from Yale.'

'Impressive.'

Norm said, 'Don't even think it, Win.'

Win shook his head. He wouldn't. She was in the business. Harder to disentangle. When it came to the opposite sex, Win liked quick and absolute closure.

'I stole her from those sons of bitches at Nike,' Norm said. 'She was a bigwig in their basketball department. Don't get me wrong. She was making a ton of dough, but she smartened up. Hey, it's like I told her: There's more to life than money. You know what I'm saying?'

Myron refrained from rolling his eyes.

'Anyway, she works like a dog. Always checking and rechecking. In fact, she's on her way to Linda Coldren's right now. They're going to have a late-night tea party or something girly-girl.'

Myron and Win exchanged a glance. 'She's going to Linda Coldren's house?'

'Yeah, why?'

'When did she call her?'

'What do you mean?'

'Was this appointment made a long time ago?'

'What, now, I look like a receptionist?'

'Forget it.'

'Forgotten.'

'Excuse me a second,' Myron said. 'Do you mind if I go make a call?'

'Am I your mother?' Zuckerman made a shooing motion. 'Go already.'

Myron debated using his cellular phone but decided not to piss off the Merion gods. He found a phone booth in the men's locker room foyer and dialed the Coldrens' house. He used Chad's line. Linda Coldren answered.

'Hello?'

'Just checking in,' Myron said. 'Anything new?'

'No,' Linda said.

'Are you aware that Esme Fong is coming over?'

'I didn't want to cancel,' Linda Coldren explained. 'I didn't want to do anything that would draw attention.'

'You'll be okay, then?'

'Yes,' she said.

Myron watched Tad Crispin walk by in the direction of Win's table. 'Were you able to reach the school?'

'No; nobody was there,' she said. 'So what do we do next?'

'I don't know,' Myron said. 'I have the override Caller ID on your phone. If he calls again, we should be able to get the number.'

'What else?'

'I'll try to speak to Matthew Squires. See what he can tell me.'

'I already spoke to Matthew,' Linda said impatiently. 'He doesn't know anything. What else?'

'I could get the police involved. Discreetly. There's not much else I can do on my own.'

'No,' she said firmly. 'No police. Jack and I are both adamant on that point.'

'I have friends in the FBI—'

'No.'

He thought about his conversation with Win. 'When Jack lost at Merion, who was his caddie?'

She hesitated. 'Why would you want to know that?'

'I understand Jack blamed his caddie for the loss.'

'In part, yes.'

'And that he fired him.'

'So?'

'So I asked about enemies. How did the caddie feel about what happened?'

'You're talking about something that happened over twenty years ago,' Linda Coldren said. 'Even if he did harbor a deep hatred for Jack, why would he wait so long?'

'This is the first time the Open has been at Merion since then. Maybe that's reawakened dormant anger. I don't know. Chances are there's nothing to this, but it might be worth checking out.'

He could hear talking on the other end of the line. Jack's voice. She asked Myron to hold on a moment.

A few moments later, Jack Coldren came on the line. Without preamble, he said, 'You think there's a connection between what happened to me twenty-three years ago and Chad's disappearance?'

'I don't know,' Myron said.

His tone was insistent. 'But you think—'

'I don't know what I think,' he interrupted. 'I'm just checking out every angle.'

There was a stony silence. Then: 'His name was Lloyd Rennart,' Jack Coldren said.

'Do you know where he lives?'

'No. I haven't seen him since the day the Open ended.'

'The day you fired him.'

'Yes.'

'You never bumped into him again? At the club or a tournament or something?'

'No,' Jack Coldren said slowly. 'Never.'

'Where did Rennart live back then?'

'In Wayne. It's the neighboring town.'

'How old would he be now?'

'Sixty-eight.' No hesitation.

'Before this happened, were you two close?'

Jack Coldren's voice, when he finally spoke, was very soft. 'I thought so,' he said. 'Not on a personal level. We didn't socialize. I never met his family or visited his home or anything like that. But on the golf course' – he paused – 'I thought we were very close.'

Silence.

'Why would he do it?' Myron asked. 'Why would he purposely ruin your chances of winning?'

Myron could hear him breathing. When he spoke again, his voice was hoarse and scratchy. 'I've wanted to know the answer to that for twenty-three years.'

Chapter 6

Myron called in Lloyd Rennart's name to Esperanza. It probably wouldn't take much. Again modern technology would simplify the feat. Anyone with a modem could type in the address www.switchboard.com – a website that was virtually a telephone directory of the entire country. If that site didn't work, there were others. It probably wouldn't take long, if Lloyd Rennart was still among the living. If not, well, there were sites for that too.

'Did you tell Win?' Esperanza asked.

'Yes.'

'How did he react?'

'He won't help.'

'Not surprising,' she said.

'No,' he agreed.

Esperanza said, 'You don't work well alone, Myron.'

'I'll be fine,' he said 'You looking forward to graduation?'

Esperanza had been going to NYU Law School at night for the past six years. She graduated on Monday.

'I probably won't go.'

'Why not?'

'I'm not big on ceremony,' she said.

Esperanza's only close relative, her mother, had died a few months back. Myron suspected that her death had more to do with Esperanza's decision than not being big on ceremony.

'Well, I'm going,' Myron said. 'Sitting front row center. I want to see it all.'

Silence.

Esperanza broke it. 'Is this the part where I choke back tears because someone cares?'

Myron shook his head. 'Forget I said anything.'

'No, really, I want to get it right. Should I break down in loud sobs or just sniffle a little? Or better yet, I could get a little teary, like Michael Landon on *Little House on the Prairie*.'

'You're such a wiseass.'

'Only when you're being patronizing.'

'I'm not being patronizing. I care. Sue me.'

'Whatever,' she said.

'Any messages?'

'About a million, but nothing that I can't handle until Monday,' she said. 'Oh, one thing.'

'What?'

'The bitch asked me out to lunch.'

'The bitch' was Jessica, the love of Myron's life. Putting it kindly, Esperanza did not like Jessica. Many assumed that this had something to do with jealousy, with some sort of latent attraction between Esperanza and Myron. Nope. For one thing, Esperanza liked, er, flexibility in her love life. For a while she had dated a guy named Max, then a woman named Lucy, and now another woman named Hester. 'How many times have I asked you not to call her that?' Myron said.

'About a million.'

'So are you going?'

'Probably,' she said. 'I mean, it's a free meal. Even if I do have to look at her face.'

They hung up. Myron smiled. He was a bit surprised. While Jessica did not reciprocate Esperanza's animosity, a lunch date to thaw out their personal cold war was not something Myron would have anticipated. Perhaps now that they were living together, Jess figured it was time to offer an olive branch. What the hell. Myron dialed Jessica.

The machine picked up. He heard her voice. When the beep came on, he said, 'Jess? Pick up.'

She did. 'God, I wish you were here right now.' Jessica had a way with openings.

'Oh?' He could see her lying on the couch, the phone cord twisted in her fingers. 'Why's that?'

'I'm about to take a ten-minute break.'

'A full ten minutes?'

'Yup.'

'Then you'd be expecting extended foreplay?'

She laughed. 'Up for it, big guy?'

'I will be,' he said, 'if you don't stop talking about it.'

'Maybe we should change the subject,' she said.

Myron had moved into Jessica's Soho loft a few months ago. For most people, this would be a somewhat dramatic change – moving from a suburb in New Jersey to a trendy section of New York, moving in with a woman you love, etc. – but for Myron, the change rivaled puberty. He had spent his entire life living with his mom and dad in the classic suburban town of Livingston, New Jersey. Entire life. Age zero to six in the upstairs bedroom on the right. Age six to thirteen in the upstairs bedroom on the left. Age thirteen to thirty-something in the basement.

After that long, the apron strings become steel bands.

'I hear you're taking Esperanza out for lunch,' he said.

'Yup.'

'How come?'

'No reason.'

'No reason?'

'I think she's cool. I want to go to lunch. Stop being so nosy.'

'You realize, of course, that she hates you.'

'I can handle it,' Jessica said. 'So how's the golf tournament?'

'Very strange,' he said.

'How so?'

'Too long a story to tell now, sweetcakes. Can I call you later?'

'Sure.' Then: 'Did you say "sweetcakes"?'

When they hung up, Myron frowned. Something was amiss. He and Jessica had never been closer, their relationship never stronger. Moving in together had been the right move, and a lot of their past demons had been exorcised away of late. They were loving toward each other, considerate of each other's feelings and needs, and almost never fought.

So why did Myron feel like they were standing on the cusp of some deep abyss?

He shook it off. All of this was just the by-product of an overstimulated imagination. Just because a ship is sailing upon smooth waters, he surmised, does not mean it is heading for an iceberg.

Wow, that was deep.

By the time he got back to the table, Tad Crispin was sipping an iced tea too. Win made the introductions. Crispin was dressed in yellows, lots of yellows, kind of like the man with the yellow hat from the Curious George books. Everything was yellow. Even his golf shoes. Myron tried not to make a face.

As if reading his mind, Norm Zuckerman said, 'This isn't our line.'

'Good to hear,' Myron said.

Tad Crispin stood. 'Nice to meet you, sir.'

Myron offered up a great big smile. 'It's a true honor to meet you, Tad.' His voice reeked with the sincerity of, say, a chain-store appliance salesman. The two men shook hands. Myron kept on smiling. Crispin began to look wary.

Zuckerman pointed a thumb at Myron and leaned toward Win. 'Is he always this smooth?'

Win nodded. 'You should see him with the ladies.'

Everyone sat.

'I can't stay long,' Crispin said.

'We understand, Tad,' Zuckerman said, doing the shooing thing again with both hands. 'You're tired, you need to concentrate on tomorrow. Go already, get some sleep.'

Crispin sort of smiled a little and looked at Win. 'I want you to have my account,' he said.

'I don't "have" accounts,' Win corrected. 'I advise on them.'

'There's a difference?'

'Most definitely,' Win said. 'You are in control of your

money at all times. I will make recommendations. I will make them to you directly. No one else. We will discuss them. You will then make a final decision. I will not buy or sell or trade anything without you being fully aware of what is going on.'

Crispin nodded. 'That sounds good.'

'I thought it might,' Win said. 'From what I see, you plan on watching your money carefully.'

'Yes.'

'Savvy,' Win said with a nod. 'You've read about too many athletes retiring broke. Of being taken advantage of by unscrupulous money managers and the like.'

'Yes.'

'And it will be my job to help you maximize your return, correct?'

Crispin leaned forward a bit. 'Correct.'

'Very well, then. It will be my task to help maximize your investment opportunities *after* you earn it. But I would not be serving your best interests if I did not also tell you how to make more.'

Crispin's eyes narrowed. 'I'm not sure I follow.'

Zuckerman said, 'Win.'

Win ignored him. 'As your financial consultant, I would be remiss if I did not make the following recommendation: You need a good agent.'

Crispin's line of vision slid toward Myron. Myron remained still, looking back at him steadily. He turned back to Win. 'I know you work with Mr Bolitar,' Crispin said.

'Yes and no,' Win said. 'If you decide to use his services I do not make one penny more. Well, that's not exactly true. If you choose to use Myron's services, you will make more money and subsequently I will have more of your money to invest. So in that way, I will make more.'

'Thanks,' Crispin said, 'but I'm not interested.'

'That's up to you,' Win said, 'but let me just explain a little further what I meant by yes and no. I manage assets worth approximately four hundred million dollars. Myron's clients represent less than three percent of that total. I am not employed by MB SportsReps. Myron Bolitar is not employed by Lock-Horne Securities. We do not have a partnership. I have not invested in his enterprise and he is not invested in mine. Myron has never looked at, asked about, or in any way discussed the financial situation of any of my clients. We are totally separate. Except for one thing.'

All eyes were on Win. Myron, not famous for knowing when to keep his mouth shut, knew now.

'I am the financial consultant for every one of his clients,' Win said. 'Do you know why?'

Crispin shook his head.

'Because Myron insists upon it.'

Crispin looked confused. 'I don't understand. If he gets nothing out of it—'

'I didn't say that. He gets plenty out of it.'

'But you said—'

'He, too, was an athlete; did you know that?'

'I heard something about it.'

'He knows what happens to athletes. How they get cheated. How they squander their earnings, never fully accepting the fact that their careers can be over in a heartbeat. So he insists – insists, mind you – that he does not handle their finances. I've seen him refuse clients because of this. He further insists that I handle them. Why? For the same reason you sought me out. He knows

I am the best. Immodest but true. Myron further insists that they see me in person at least once every quarter. Not just phone calls. Not just faxes or E-mails or letters. He insists that I go over every item in the account personally with them.'

Win leaned farther back and steepled his fingers. The man loved to steeple his fingers. It looked good on him. Gave him an air of wisdom. 'Myron Bolitar is my best friend. I know he'd give his life for me and I for him. But if he ever thought that I was not doing what was in a client's best interest, he would take away their portfolios without a second thought.'

Norm said, 'Beautiful speech, Win. Got me right there.' He pointed to his stomach.

Win gave him the look. Norm stopped smiling.

'I made the deal with Mr Zuckerman on my own,' Crispin said. 'I could make others.'

'I won't comment on the Zoom deal,' Win said. 'But I will tell you this. You are a bright young man. A bright man knows not only his strengths but equally important, he knows his weaknesses. I do not, for example, know how to negotiate an endorsement contract. I may know the basics, but it is not my business. I'm not a plumber. If a pipe in my house broke, I would not be able to fix it. You are a golfer. You are one of the greatest talents I have ever seen. You should concentrate on that.'

Tad Crispin took a sip of iced tea. He crossed his ankle on his knee. Even his socks were yellow. 'You are making a hard sale for your friend,' he said.

'Wrong,' Win said. 'I would kill for my friend, but financially I owe him nothing. You, on the other hand, are my client, and thus I have a very serious fiscal respon-sibility with regard to you. Stripping it bare, you have

72

asked me to increase your portfolio. I will suggest several investment sources to you. But this is the best recommendation I can make.'

Crispin turned to Myron. He looked him up and down, studying him hard. Myron almost brayed so he could examine his teeth. 'He makes you sound awfully good,' Crispin said to Myron.

'I am good,' Myron said. 'But I don't want him to give you the wrong impression. I'm not quite as altruistic as Win might have made me sound. I don't insist clients use him because I'm a swell guy. I know that having him handle my clients is a major plus. He improves the value of my services. He helps keep my clients happy. That's what I get out of it. Yes, I insist on having clients heavily involved in the decision-making on money matters, but that's as much to protect me as them.'

'How so?'

'Obviously you know something about managers or agents robbing athletes.'

'Yes.'

'Do you know why so much of that occurs?'

Crispin shrugged. 'Greed, I suppose.'

Myron tilted his head in a yes-and-no gesture. 'The main culprit is apathy. An athlete's lack of involvement. They get lazy. They decide it's easier to fully trust their agent, and that's bad. Let the agent pay the bills, they say. Let the agent invest the money. That kind of thing. But that won't ever happen at MB SportsReps. Not because I'm watching. Not because Win's watching. But because you are watching.'

'I'm watching now,' Crispin said.

'You're watching your money, true. I doubt you're watching everything else.'

Crispin considered that for a moment. 'I appreciate the talk,' he said, 'but I think I'm okay on my own.'

Myron pointed at Tad Crispin's head. 'How much are you getting for that hat?' he asked.

'Excuse me?'

'You're wearing a hat with no company logo on it,' Myron explained. 'For a player of your ilk, that's a loss of at least a quarter of a million dollars.'

Silence.

'But I'm going to be working with Zoom,' Crispin said.

'Did they purchase hat rights from you?'

He thought about it. 'I don't think so.'

'The front of the hat is a quarter million. We can also sell the sides if you want. They'll go for less. Maybe we'll total four hundred grand. Your shirt is another matter.'

'Now just wait one minute here,' Zuckerman interjected. 'He's going to be wearing Zoom shirts.'

'Fine, Norm,' Myron said. 'But he's allowed to wear logos. One on the chest, one on either sleeve.'

'Logos?'

'Anything. Coca-Cola maybe. IBM. Even Home Depot.'

'Logos on my shirt?'

'Yep. And what do you drink out there?'

'Drink? When I play?'

'Sure. I can probably get you a deal with Powerade or one of the soda companies. How about Poland Spring water? They might be good. And your golf bag. You have to negotiate a deal for your golf bag.'

'I don't understand.'

'You're a billboard, Tad. You're on television. Lots of fans see you. Your hat, your shirt, your golf bag – those are all places to post ads.'

Zuckerman said, 'Now hold on a second. He can't just—'

A cell phone began to sound, but it never made it past the first ring. Myron's finger reached the ringer and turned it off with a speed that would have made Wyatt Earp retire. Fast reflexes. They came in handy every once in a while.

Still, the brief sound had drawn the ire of nearby club members. Myron looked around. He was on the receiving end of several dagger-glares, including one from Win.

'Hurry around behind the clubhouse,' Win said pointedly. 'Let no one see you.'

Myron gave a flippant salute and rushed out like a man with a suddenly collapsing bladder. When he reached a safe area near the parking lot, he answered the call.

'Hello.'

'Oh, God . . .' It was Linda Coldren. Her tone struck the marrow of his bone.

'What's wrong?'

'He called again,' she said.

'Do you have it on tape?'

'Yes.'

'I'll be right ov—'

'No!' she shouted. 'He's watching the house.'

'You saw him?'

'No. But . . . Don't come here. Please.'

'Where are you calling from?'

'The fax line in the basement. Oh God, Myron, you should have heard him.'

'Did the number come up on the Caller ID?'

'Yes.'

'Give it to me.'

75

She did, Myron took out a pen from his wallet and wrote the number down on an old Visa receipt.

'Are you alone?'

'Jack is right here with me.'

'Anybody else? What about Esme Fong?'

'She's upstairs in the living room.'

'Okay,' Myron said. 'I'll need to hear the call.'

'Hold on. Jack is plugging the machine in now. I'll put you on the speaker so you can hear.'

Chapter 7

The tape player was snapped on. Myron heard the phone ringing first. The sound was surprisingly clear. Then he heard Jack Coldren: 'Hello?'

'Who's the chink bitch?'

The voice was very deep, very menacing, and definitely machine-altered. Male or female, young or old, it was anyone's guess.

'I don't know what—'

'You trying to fuck with me, you dumb son of a bitch? I'll start sending you the fucking brat in little pieces.'

Jack Coldren said, 'Please—'

'I told you not to contact anyone.'

'We haven't.'

'Then tell me who that chink bitch is who just walked into your house.'

Silence.

'You think we're stupid, Jack?'

'Of course not.'

'So who the fuck is she?'

'Her name is Esme Fong,' Coldren said quickly. 'She works for a clothing company. She's just here to set up an endorsement deal with my wife, that's all.'

'Bullshit.'

'It's the truth, I swear.'

'I don't know, Jack . . .'

'I wouldn't lie to you.'

'Well, Jack, we'll just see about that. This is gonna cost you.'

'What do you mean?'

'One hundred grand. Call it a penalty price.'

'For what?'

'Never you fucking mind. You want the kid alive? It's gonna cost you one hundred grand now. That's in—'

'Now hold on a second.' Coldren cleared his throat. Trying to gain some footing, some degree of control.

'Jack?'

'Yes?'

'You interrupt me again and I'm going to stick your kid's dick in a vise.'

Silence.

'You get the money ready, Jack. One hundred grand. I'll call you back and let you know what to do. Do you understand?'

'Yes.'

'Don't fuck up, Jack. I enjoy hurting people.'

The brief silence was shattered by a sharp, sudden scream, a scream that jangled nerve endings and raised hackles. Myron's hand tightened on the receiver.

The phone disconnected. Then a dial tone. Then nothing.

Linda Coldren took him off the speaker. 'What are we going to do?'

'Call the FBI,' Myron said.

'Are you out of your mind?'

'I think it's your best move.'

Jack Coldren said something in the background. Linda came back on the line. 'Absolutely not. We just want to pay the ransom and get our son back.'

No point in arguing with them. 'Sit tight. I'll call you back as soon as I can.'

Myron disconnected the call and dialed another number. Lisa at New York Bell. She'd been a contact of theirs since the days he and Win had worked for the government.

'A Caller ID came up with a number in Philadelphia,' he said. 'Can you find an address for me?'

'No problem,' Lisa said.

He gave her the number. People who watch too much television think this sort of thing takes a long time. Not anymore. Traces are instantaneous now. No 'keep him on a little longer' or any of that stuff. The same is true when it comes to finding the location of a phone number. Any operator almost anywhere can plug the number into her computer or use one of those reverse directories, and whammo. Heck, you don't even need an operator. Computer programs on CD-ROM and websites did the same thing.

'It's a pay phone,' she said.

Not good news, but not unexpected either. 'Do you know where?'

'The Grand Mercado Mall in Bala-Cynwyd.'

'A mall?'

'Yes.'

'You're sure?'

'That's what it says.'

'Where in the mall?'

'I have no idea. You think they list it "between Sears and Victoria's Secret"?'

This made no sense. A mall? The kidnapper had dragged Chad Coldren to a mall and made him scream into a phone?

'Thanks, Lisa.'

He hung up and turned back toward the porch. Win was standing directly behind him. His arms were folded, his body, as always, completely relaxed.

'The kidnapper called,' Myron said.

'So I overheard.'

'I could use your help tracking this down.'

'No,' Win said.

'This isn't about your mother, Win.'

Win's face did not change, but something happened to his eyes. 'Careful,' was all he said.

Myron shook his head. 'I have to go. Please make my excuses.'

'You came here to recruit clients,' Win said. 'You claimed earlier that you agreed to help the Coldrens in the hopes of representing them.'

'So?'

'So you are excruciatingly close to landing the world's top golf protégé. Reason dictates that you stay.'

'I can't.'

Win unfolded his arms, shook his head.

'Will you do one thing for me? To let me know if I'm wasting time or not?'

Win remained still.

'You know how I told you about Chad using his ATM card?'

'Yes.'

'Get me the security videotape of the transaction,' he said. 'It may tell me if this whole thing is just a hoax on Chad's part.'

Win turned back to the porch. 'I'll see you at the house tonight.'

Chapter 8

Myron parked at the mall and checked his watch. Seven forty-five. It had been a very long day and it was still relatively early. He entered through a Macy's and immediately located one of those big table blueprints of the mall. Public telephones were marked with blue locators. Eleven altogether. Two at the south entrance downstairs. Two at the north entrance upstairs. Seven at the food court.

Malls were the great American geographical equalizer. Between shiny anchor stores and beneath excessively floodlit ceilings, Kansas equaled California, New Jersey equaled Nevada. No place was truly more Americana. Some of the stores inside might be different, but not by much. Athlete's Foot or Foot Locker, Rite Aid or CVS, Williams-Sonoma or Pottery Barn, the Gap or Banana Republic or Old Navy (all, coincidentally, owned by the same people), Waldenbooks or B. Dalton, several anonymous shoe stores, a Radio Shack, a Victoria's Secret, an art gallery with Gorman, McKnight, and Behrens, a museum store of some kind, two record stores – all wrapped up in some Orwellian, sleek-chrome neo-Roman Forum with chintzy fountains and overstated marble and dentist-office sculptures and unmanned information booths and fake ferns.

In front of a store selling electric organs and pianos sat an employee dressed in an ill-fitting navy suit and a sailor's cap. He played 'Muskrat Love' on an organ. Myron was tempted to ask him where Tenille was, but he refrained. Too obvious. Organ stores in malls. Who goes to the mall to buy an organ?

He hurried past the Limited or the Unlimited or the Severely Challenged or something like that. Then Jeans Plus or Jeans Minus or Shirts Only or Pants Only or Tank Top City or something like that. They all looked pretty much the same. They all employed lots of skinny, bored teenagers who stocked shelves with the enthusiasm of a eunuch at an orgy.

There were lots of high school kids draped about – just hanging, man – and looking very, er, rad. At the risk of sounding like a reverse racist, all the white boys looked the same to him. Baggie shorts. White T-shirts. Unlaced black hundred-dollar high-top sneakers. Baseball cap pulled low with the brim worked into a nifty curve, covering a summer buzzcut. Thin. Lanky. Long-limbed. Pale as a Goya portrait, even in the summer. Poor posture. Eyes that never looked directly at another human being. Uncomfortable eyes. Slightly scared eyes.

He passed a hair salon called Snip Away, which sounded more like a vasectomy clinic than a beauty parlor. The Snip Away beauticians were either reformed mall girls or guys named Mario whose fathers were named Sal. Two patrons sat in a window – one getting a perm, the other a bleach job. Who wanted that? Who wanted to sit in a window and have the whole world watch you get your hair done?

He took an escalator up past a plastic garden complete with plastic vines to the crowned jewel of the mall: the food court. It was fairly empty now, the dinner crowd long since gone. Food courts were the final outpost of the great American melting pot. Italian, Chinese, Japanese, Mexican, Middle Eastern (or Greek), a deli, a chicken place, one fast food chain like McDonald's (which had the biggest crowd), a frozen yogurt place, and then a few strange offshoots – the ones started by people who dream of franchising themselves into becoming the next Ray Kroc. Ethiopian Ecstasy. Sven's Swedish Meatballs. Curry Up and Eat.

Myron checked for numbers on the seven phones. All had been whited out. Not surprising, the way people abused them nowadays. No problemo either. He took out his cellular phone and punched in the number from the Caller ID. A phone starting ringing immediately.

Bingo.

The one on the far right. Myron picked it up to make sure. 'Hello?' he said. He heard the hello in his cellular phone. Then he said to himself through the cellular, 'Hello, Myron, nice to hear from you.' He decided to stop talking to himself, too early in the evening to be this goofy.

He hung up the phone and looked around. A group of mall girls inhabited a table not far away. They sat in a closed circle with the protectiveness of coyotes during mating season.

Of the food stands, Sven's Swedish Meatballs had the

best view of the phone. Myron approached. Two men worked the booth. They both had dark hair and dark skin and Saddam Hussein mustaches. One's name tag read Mustafa. The other Achmed.

'Which one of you is Sven?' he asked.

No smiles.

Myron asked about the phone. Mustafa and Achmed were less than helpful. Mustafa snapped that he worked for a living, and didn't watch phones. Achmed gestured and cursed him in a foreign tongue.

'I'm not much of a linguist,' Myron said, 'but that didn't sound like Swedish.'

Death glares.

'Bye now. I'll be sure to tell all my friends.'

Myron turned toward the table of mall girls. They all quickly looked down, like rats scurrying in the glare of a flashlight. He stepped toward them. Their eyes darted to and fro with what they must have thought were surreptitious glances. He heard a low cacophony of 'ohmygod! Ohmygod! Ohmygod! he'scomingover!'

Myron stopped directly at their table. There were four girls. Or maybe five or even six. Hard to say. They all seemed to blend into one another, into one hazy, indistinct mesh of hair and black lipstick and Fu Manchu-length fingernails and earrings and nose rings and cigarette smoke and too-tight halter tops and bare midriffs and popping gum.

The one sitting in the middle looked up first. She had hair like Elsa Lancaster in *The Bride of Frankenstein* and what looked like a studded dog collar around her neck. The other faces followed suit.

'Like, hi,' Elsa said.

Myron tried his most gentle, crooked smile. Harrison

85

Ford in *Regarding Henry*. 'Do you mind if I ask you a few questions?'

The girls all looked at one another. A few giggles escaped. Myron felt his face redden, though he wasn't sure why. They elbowed one another. No one answered. Myron proceeded.

'How long have you been sitting here?' he asked.

'Is this, like, one of those mall surveys?'

'No,' Myron said.

'Good. Those are, like, so lame, you know?'

'Uh-huh.'

'It's like, get away from me already, Mr Polyester Pants, you know?'

Myron said 'uh-huh' again. 'Do you remember how long you've been sitting here?'

'Nah. Amber, you know?'

'Like, we went to the Gap at four.'

'Right, the Gap. Fab sale.'

'Ultra sale. Love that blouse you bought, Trish.'

'Isn't it, like, the total package, Mindy?'

'Totally. Ultra.'

Myron said, 'It's almost eight now. Have you been here for the past hour?'

'Like, hello, anybody home? At least.'

'This is, like, our spot, you know?'

'No one else, like, sits here.'

'Except that one time when those gross lame-os tried to move in.'

'But, like, whoa, don't even go there, 'kay?'

They stopped and looked at Myron. He figured the answer to his prior question was yes, so he plowed ahead. 'Have you seen anybody use that pay phone?'

'Are you, like, a cop or something?'

86

'As if.'

'No way.'

'Way.'

'He's too cute to be a cop.'

'Oh, right, like Jimmy Smits isn't cute.'

'That's, like, TV, dumb wad. This is real life. Cops aren't cute in real life.'

'Oh, right, like Brad isn't totally cute? You, like, love him, remember?'

'As if. And he's not a cop. He's, like, some rent-a-uniform at Florsheim.'

'But he's so hot.'

'Totally.'

'Ultra buff.'

'He likes Shari.'

'Eeeuw. Shari?'

'I, like, hate her, you know?'

'Me too. Like, does she only shop at Sluts "R" Us, or what?'

'Totally.'

'It's, like, "Hello, Dial-a-Disease, this is Shari speaking."'

Giggles.

Myron looked for an interpreter. 'I'm not a cop,' he said.

'Told you.'

'As if.'

'But,' Myron said, 'I am dealing with something very important. Life-and-death. I need to know if you remember anyone using that phone – the one on the far right – forty-five minutes ago.'

'Whoa!' The one called Amber pushed her chair back.

'Clear out, because I'm, like, gonna barf for days, you know?'

'Like, Crusty the Clown.'

'He was, like, so gross!'

'Totally gross.'

'Totally.'

'He, like, winked at Amber!'

'As if!'

'Totally eeeuw!'

'Gag city.'

'Bet that slut Shari would have Frenched him.'

'At least.'

Giggles.

Myron said, 'You saw somebody?'

'Serious groatie.'

'Totally crusty.'

'He was, like, hello, ever wash your hair?'

'Like, hello, buy your cologne at the local Gas-N-Go?'

More giggles.

Myron said, 'Can you describe him to me?'

'Blue jeans from, like, "Attention, Kmart shoppers." '

'Work boots. Definitely not Timberland.'

'He was, like, so skinhead wanna-be, you know?'

Myron said, 'Skinhead wanna-be?'

'Like, a shaved head. Skanky beard. Tattoo of that thing on his arm.'

'That thing?' Myron tried.

'You know, that tattoo.' She kind of drew something in the air with her finger. 'It kinda looks like a funny cross from, like, the old days.'

Myron said, 'You mean a swastika?'

'Like, whatever. Do I look like a history major?'

'Like, how old was he?' Like. He'd said *like*. If he

stayed here much longer, he'd end up getting some part of him pierced. Way.

'Old.'

'Grampa-ville.'

'Like, at least twenty.'

'Height?' Myron asked. 'Weight?'

'Six feet.'

'Yeah, like six feet.'

'Bony.'

'Very.'

'Like, no ass at all.'

'None.'

'Was anybody with him?' Myron asked.

'As if.'

'Him?'

'No way.'

'Who would be with a skank like that?'

'Just him by that phone for like half an hour.'

'He wanted Mindy.'

'Did not!'

'Wait a second,' Myron said. 'He was there for half an hour?'

'Not that long.'

'Seemed a long time.'

'Maybe like fifteen minutes. Amber, like, always exaggerates.'

'Like, fuck you, Irish, all right? Just fuck you.'

'Anything else?' Myron asked.

'Beeper.'

'Right, beeper. Like anybody would ever call that skank.'

'Held it right up to the phone, too.'

Probably not a beeper. Probably a microcassette player.

That would explain the scream. Or a voice changer. They also came in a small box.

He thanked the girls and handed out business cards that listed his cellular phone number. One of the girls actually read it. She made a face.

'Like, your name is really Myron?'

'Yes.'

They all just stopped and looked at him.

'I know,' Myron said. 'Like, ultra lame-o.'

He was heading back to his car when a nagging thought suddenly resurfaced. The kidnapper on the phone had mentioned a 'chink bitch.' Somehow he had known about Esme Fong arriving at the house. The question was, how?

There were two possibilities. One, they had a bug in the house.

Not likely. If the Coldren residence was bugged or under some kind of electronic surveillance, the kidnapper would also have known about Myron's involvement.

Two, one of them was watching the house.

That seemed most logical. Myron thought a moment. If someone had been watching the house only an hour or so ago, it was fair to assume that they were still there, still hiding behind a bush or up a tree or something. If Myron could locate the person surreptitiously, he might be able to follow them back to Chad Coldren.

Was it worth the risk?

Like, totally.

Chapter 9

Ten o'clock.

Myron used Win's name again and parked in Merion's lot. He checked for Win's Jaguar, but it was nowhere to be seen. He parked and checked for guards. No one. They'd all been stationed at the front entrance. Made things easier.

He quickly stepped over the white rope used to hold back the galley and started crossing the golf course. It was dark now, but the lights from the houses across the way provided enough illumination to cross. For all its fame, Merion was a tiny course. From the parking lot to Golf House Road, across two fairways, was less than a hundred yards.

Myron trudged forward. Humidity hung in the air in a heavy blanket of beads. Myron's shirt began to feel sticky. The crickets were incessant and plenteous, their swarming tune as monotonous as a Mariah Carey CD, though not quite as grating. The grass tickled Myron's sockless ankles.

Despite his natural aversion to golf, Myron still felt the appropriate sense of awe, as if he were trespassing over sacred ground. Ghosts breathed in the night, the same way they breathed at any sight that had borne legends. Myron remembered once standing on the parquet floor at Boston Garden when no one else was there. It was a week after he had been picked by the Celtics in the first round of the NBA draft. Clip Arnstein, the Celtics' fabled general manager, had introduced him to the press earlier that day. It had been enormous fun. Everybody had been laughing and smiling and calling Myron the next Larry Bird. That night, as he stood alone in the famed halls of the Garden, the championship flags hanging from the rafters actually seemed to sway in the still air, beckoning him forward and whispering tales of the past and promises of what was to come.

Myron never played a game on that parquet floor.

He slowed as he reached Golf House Road and stepped over the white rope. Then he ducked behind a tree. This would not be easy. Then again, it would not be easy for his quarry either. Neighborhoods like this noted anything suspicious. Like a parked car where it didn't belong. That had been why Myron had parked in the Merion lot. Had the kidnapper done likewise? Or was his car out on the street? Or had someone dropped him off?

He kept low and darted to another tree. He looked, he assumed, rather doofy – a guy six-feet four inches tall and comfortably over two hundred pounds darting between bushes like something left on the cutting room floor of *The Dirty Dozen*.

But what choice did he have?

He couldn't just casually walk down the street. The kidnapper might spot him. His whole plan relied on the fact that he could spot the kidnapper before the kidnapper spotted him. How to do this? He really did not have a clue. The best he could come up with was to keep circling closer and closer to the Coldren house, looking out for, er, uh, something.

He scanned the surroundings – for what, he wasn't sure. Someplace for a kidnapper to use as a lookout spot, he guessed. A safe place to hide, maybe, or a perch where a man with binoculars could survey the scene. Nothing. The night was absolutely windless and still.

He circled the block, dashing haphazardly from one bush to another, feeling now very much like John Belushi breaking into Dean Wormer's office in *Animal House*.

Animal House and *The Dirty Dozen*. Myron watched too many movies.

As he continued to spiral closer to the Coldrens' residence, Myron realized that there was probably a good chance that he'd be the 'spottee' rather than the 'spotter.' He tried to hide himself better, to concentrate on making himself become part of the night, to blend in to the background and become invisible.

Myron Bolitar, Mutant Ninja Warrior.

Lights twinkled from spacious homes of stone and black shutters. They were all imposing and rather beautiful with a tutelary, stay-away coziness about them. Solid homes. The third-little-piggie homes. Settled and staying and proud homes.

He was getting very close to the Coldren house now. Still nothing – not even a single car parked on the roads. Sweat coated him like syrup on a stack of pancakes. God, he wanted to take a shower. He hunched down and watched the house.

Now what?

Wait. Be on the lookout for movement of some kind. Surveillance and the like was not Myron's forte. Win usually handled that kind of stuff. He had the body control and the patience. Myron was already getting fidgety. He wished he'd brought a magazine or something to read.

The three minutes of monotony was broken when the front door opened. Myron sat up. Esme Fong and Linda Coldren appeared in the door frame. They said their good-byes. Esme gave Linda the firm handshake and headed to her car. Linda Coldren shut the front door. Esme Fong started her car and left.

A thrill a second, this surveillance stuff.

Myron settled back behind a shrub. There were lots of shrubs around here. Everywhere one looked, there were shrubs of various sizes and shapes and purposes. Rich blue bloods must really like shrubs, Myron decided. He wondered if they had had any on the *Mayflower*.

His legs were beginning to cramp from all this crouching. He straightened them out one at a time. His bad knee, the one that ended his basketball career, began to throb. Enough. He was hot and sticky and in pain. Time to get out of here.

Then he heard a sound.

It seemed to be coming from the back door. He sighed, creaked to his feet, and circled. He found yet another comfy shrub and hid behind it. He peered out.

Jack Coldren was in the backyard with his caddie, Diane Hoffman. Jack held a golf club in his hands, but he wasn't hitting. He was talking with Diane Hoffman.

Animatedly. Diane Hoffman was talking back. Equally animated. Neither one of them seemed very pleased. Myron could not hear them, but they were both gesturing like mad.

An argument. A rather heated argument.

Hmm.

Of course, there probably was an innocent explanation. Caddies and players argue all the time, Myron guessed. He remembered reading how Seve Ballesteros, the Spanish former wunderkind, was always fighting with his caddie. Bound to happen. Routine stuff, a caddie and a pro having a little tiff, especially during such a pressure-filled tournament as the US Open.

But the timing was curious.

Think about it a second. A man gets a terrifying call from a kidnapper. He hears his son scream in apparent fright or pain. Then, a couple of hours later, he is in his backyard arguing about his backswing with his caddie.

Did that make sense?

Myron decided to move closer, but there was no straight path. Shrubs again, like tackle dummies at a football practice. He'd have to move to the side of the house and circle in behind them. He made a quick bolt to his left and risked another glance. The heated argument continued. Diane Hoffman took a step closer to Jack.

Then she slapped him in the face.

The sound sliced through the night like a scythe. Myron froze. Diane Hoffman shouted something. Myron heard the word *bastard*, but nothing else. Diane flicked her cigarette at Jack's feet and stormed off. Jack looked down, shook his head slowly, and went back inside.

Well, well, Myron thought. Must have been some trouble with that backswing.

Myron stayed behind the shrub. He heard a car start in the driveway. Diane Hoffman's, he assumed. For a moment, he wondered if she had a role in this. Obviously she had been in the house. Could she be the mysterious lookout? He leaned back and considered the possibility. The idea was just starting to soak in and settle when Myron spotted the man.

Or at least he assumed it was a man. It was hard to tell from where he was crouched. Myron could not believe what he was seeing. He had been wrong. Dead wrong. The perpetrator hadn't been hiding in the bushes or anything like that. Myron watched now in silence as someone dressed completely in black climbed out an upper-floor window. More specifically – if memory didn't fail him – Chad Coldren's bedroom window.

Hello there.

Myron ducked down. Now what? He needed a plan. Yes, a plan. Good thinking. But what plan? Did he grab the perp now? No. Better to follow him. Maybe he'd lead him back to Chad Coldren. That would be nice.

He took another peek out. The black-clad figure had scaled down a white lattice fence with entwined ivy. He jumped the last few feet. As soon as he hit the ground, he sprinted away.

Great.

Myron followed, trying to stay as far behind the figure as possible. The figure, however, was running. This made following silently rather difficult. But Myron kept back. Didn't want to risk being seen. Besides, chances were good that the perpetrator had brought a car or was getting picked up by someone. These streets barely had any traffic. Myron would be bound to hear an engine.

But then what?

What would Myron do when the perp got to the car? Run back to get his own? No, that wouldn't work. Follow a car on foot? Er, not likely. So what exactly was he going to do?

Good question.

He wished Win were here.

The perp kept running. And running. Myron was starting to suck air. Jesus, who the hell was he chasing anyway, Frank Shorter? Another quarter mile passed before the perp abruptly veered to the right and out of view. The turn was so sudden that for a moment Myron wondered if he'd been spotted. Impossible. He was too far back and his quarry had not so much as glanced over his shoulder.

Myron tried to hurry a bit, but the road was gravelly. Running silently would be impossible. Still, he had to make up ground. He ran high atop his tiptoes, looking not unlike Baryshnikov with dysentery. He prayed nobody would see him.

He reached the turn. The name of the street was Green Acres Road. Green Acres. The old TV show theme song started in his head, like someone had pressed buttons on a jukebox. He couldn't stop it. Eddie Albert rode a tractor. Eva Gabor opened boxes in a Manhattan penthouse. Sam Drucker waved from behind the counter of his general store. Mr Haney pulled his suspenders with both thumbs. Arnold the pig snorted.

Man, the humidity was definitely getting to him.

Myron wheeled to the right and looked ahead.

Nothing.

Green Acres was a short cul-de-sac with maybe five homes. Fabulous homes, or so Myron assumed. Towering shrub walls – again with the shrubs – lined either side of the street. Locked gates were on the driveways, the kind that worked by remote control or by pushing a combination in a keypad. Myron stopped and looked down the road.

So where was our boy?

He felt his pulse quicken. No sign of him. The only escape route was through the woods between two houses in the cul-de-sac. He must have gone in there, Myron surmised – if, that is, he was trying to escape and not, say, hide in the bushes. He might, after all, have spotted Myron. He might have decided to duck down somewhere and hide. Hide and then pounce when Myron walked by.

These were not comforting thoughts.

Now what?

He licked the sweat off his upper lip. His mouth felt terribly dry. He could almost hear himself sweat.

Suck it up, Myron, he told himself. He was six-four and two hundred and twenty pounds. A big guy. He was also a black belt in tae kwon do and a well-trained fighter. He could fend off any attack.

Unless the guy was armed.

True. Let's face it. Fight training and experience were helpful, but they did not make one bullet-proof. Not even Win. Of course, Win wouldn't have been stupid enough to get himself into this mess. Myron carried a weapon only when he thought it was absolutely necessary. Win, on the other hand, carried at least two guns and one bladed instrument at all times. Third world countries should be as well armed as Win.

So what to do?

He looked left and right, but there was no place much for anybody to hide. The shrub walls were thick and fully impenetrable. That left only the woods at the end of the road. But there were no lights down that way and the woods looked dense and forbidding.

Should he go in?

No. That would be pointless at best. He had no idea how big the woods were, what direction to head in, nothing. The odds of finding the perpetrator were frighteningly remote. Myron's best hope was that the perp was just hiding for a while, waiting for Myron to clear out.

Clear out. That sounded like a plan.

Myron moved back to the end of Green Acres. He turned left, traveled a couple of hundred yards, and settled behind yet another shrub. He and shrubs were on a first-name basis by now. This one he named Frank.

He waited an hour. No one appeared.

Great.

He finally stood up, said good-bye to Frank, and headed back to the car. The perpetrator must have escaped through the woods. That meant that he had planned an escape route or, more probably, he knew the area well. Could mean that it was Chad Coldren. Or it could mean that the kidnappers knew what they were doing. And if that was so, it meant there was a good chance that they now knew about Myron's involvement and the fact that the Coldrens had disobeyed them.

Myron hoped like hell it was just a hoax. But if it wasn't, if this was indeed a real kidnapping, he wondered about repercussions. He wondered how the kidnappers would react to what he had done. And as he continued on his way, Myron remembered their previous phone call and the harrowing, flesh-creeping sound of Chad Coldren' s scream.

Chapter 10

'*Meanwhile, back at stately Wayne Manor . . .*'

That voice-over from the TV *Batman* always came to Myron when he reached the steely gates of the Lockwood estate. In reality, Win's family home looked very little like Bruce Wayne's house, though it did offer up the same aura. A tremendous serpentine driveway wound to an imposing stone mansion on the hill. There was grass, lots of it, all the blades kept at a consistently ideal length, like a politician's hair in an election year. There were also lush gardens and hills and a swimming pool, a pond, a tennis court, horse stables, and a horse obstacle course of some kind.

All in all, the Lockwood estate was very 'stately' and worthy of the term 'manor,' whatever that meant.

Myron and Win were staying at the guest house – or as Win's father liked to call it, 'the cottage.' Exposed beams, hardwood floors, fireplace, new kitchen with a big island in the middle, pool room – not to mention five bedrooms, four and half baths. Some cottage.

Myron tried to sort through what was happening, but all he came up with was a series of paradoxes, a whole lot of 'which came first, the chicken or the egg?' Motive, for example. On the one hand, it might make sense to kidnap Chad Coldren to throw off Jack Coldren. But Chad had been missing since *before* the tournament, which meant the kidnapper was either very cautious or very prophetic. On the other hand, the kidnapper had asked for one hundred grand, which pointed to a simple case of kidnapping for money. A hundred grand was a nice, tidy sum – a little low for a kidnapping, but not bad for a few days' work.

But if this was merely a kidnapping to extort mucho dinero, the timing was curious. Why now? Why during the one time a year the US Open was played? More than that, why kidnap Chad during the one time in the last twenty-three years the Open was being played at Merion – the one time in almost a quarter of a century that Jack Coldren had a chance to revisit and redeem his greatest failing?

Seemed like a hell of a coincidence.

That brought it back to a hoax and a scenario that went something like this: Chad Coldren disappears before the tournament to screw around with his dad's mind. When that doesn't work – when, to the contrary, Dad starts winning – he ups the ante and fakes his own kidnapping. Taking it a step farther, one could assume that it had been Chad Coldren who had been climbing out of his own window. Who better? Chad Coldren knew the area. Chad Coldren probably knew how to go through those woods.

Or maybe he was hiding out at a friend's house who lived on Green Acres Road. Whatever.

It added up. It made sense.

All of this assumed, of course, that Chad truly disliked his father. Was there evidence of that? Myron thought so. Start off with the fact that Chad was sixteen years old. Not an easy age. Weak evidence for sure, but worth keeping in mind. Second – and far, far more important – Jack Coldren was an absent father. No athlete is away from home as much as a golfer. Not basketball players or football players or baseball players or hockey players. The only ones who come close are tennis players. In both tennis and golf, tournaments are taking place almost all year – there is little so-called off season – and there is no such thing as a home game. If you were lucky, you hit your home course once a year.

Lastly – and perhaps most crucial of all – Chad had been gone for *two* days without raising eyebrows. Forget Linda Coldren's discourse on responsible children and open child-raising. The only rational explanation for their nonchalance was that this had happened before, or at the very least, was not unexpected.

But there were problems with the hoax scenario too.

For example, how did Mr Total Grunge from the mall fit in?

There was indeed the rub. What role was the Crusty Nazi playing in all this? Did Chad Coldren have an accomplice? Possibly, but that really didn't fit in well with a revenge scenario. If Chad was indeed behind all this, Myron doubted that the preppy golfer would join forces with a 'skinhead wanna-be,' complete with a swastika tattoo.

So where did that leave Myron?

Baffled.

As Myron pulled up to the guest house, he felt his heart constrict. Win's Jag was there. But so was a green Chevy Nova.

Oh, Christ.

Myron got out of the car slowly. He checked the license plate on the Nova. Unfamiliar. As he expected. He swallowed and moved away.

He opened the cottage's front door and welcomed the sudden onslaught of air-conditioning. The lights were out. For a moment he just stood in the foyer, eyes closed, the cool air tingling his skin. An enormous grandfather clock ticked.

Myron opened his eyes and flicked on a light.

'Good evening.'

He pivoted to his right. Win was seated in a high-back leather chair by the fireplace. He cupped a brandy snifter in his hand.

'You were sitting in the dark?' Myron asked.

'Yes.'

Myron frowned. 'A bit theatrical, don't you think?'

Win switched on a nearby lamp. His face was a tad rosy from the brandy. 'Care to join me?'

'Sure. I'll be right back.'

Myron grabbed a cold Yoo-Hoo from the refrigerator and sat on the couch across from his friend. He shook the can and popped it open. They drank in silence for several minutes. The clock ticked. Long shadows snaked across the floor in thin, almost smoky tendrils. Too bad it was summertime. This was the kind of setting that begged for a roaring fire and maybe some howling wind. An air conditioner just didn't cut it.

Myron was just getting comfortable when he heard a toilet flush. He looked a question at Win.

'I am not alone,' Win said.

'Oh.' Myron adjusted himself on the couch. 'A woman?'

'Your gifts,' Win said. 'They never cease to amaze.'

'Anybody I know?' Myron asked.

Win shook his head. 'Not even somebody I know.'

The norm. Myron looked steadily at his friend. 'You want to talk about this?'

'No.'

'I'm here if you do.'

'Yes, I see that.' Win swished around the drink in the snifter. He finished it in one gulp and reached for the crystal decanter. There was a slight slur in his speech. Myron tried to remember the last time he had seen Win the vegetarian, the master of several martial arts, the transcendental meditator, the man so at ease and in focus with his surroundings, have too much to drink.

It had been a very long time.

'I have a golf question for you,' Myron said.

Win nodded for him to proceed.

'Do you think Jack Coldren can hang on to this lead?'

Win poured the brandy. 'Jack will win,' he said.

'You sound pretty sure.'

'I am sure.'

'Why?'

Win raised the glass to his mouth and looked over the rim. 'I saw his eyes.'

Myron made a face. 'What's that supposed to mean?'

'He has it back. The look in the eyes.'

'You're kidding, right?'

'Perhaps I am. But let me ask you something.'

'Go ahead.'

'What separates the great athletes from the very good? The legend from the journeyman? Simply put, what makes winners?'

'Talent,' Myron said. 'Practice. Skill.'

Win gave a slight shake of the head. 'You know better than that.'

'I do?'

'Yes. Many have talent. Many practice. There is more to the art of creating a true winner.'

'This look-in-the-eye thing?'

'Yes.'

Myron winced. 'You're not going to start singing "Eye of the Tiger," are you?'

Win cocked his head. 'Who sang that song?'

The continuing trivia game. Win knew the answer, of course. 'It was in *Rocky II*, right?'

'*Rocky III*,' Win corrected.

'That the one with Mr T?'

Win nodded. 'Who played . . . ?' he prompted.

'Clubber Lange.'

'Very good. Now who sang the song?'

'I don't remember.'

'The name of the group was Survivor,' Win said. 'Ironic name when you think of how quickly they vanished, no?'

'Uh-huh,' Myron said. 'So what is this great divider, Win? What makes a winner?'

Win took another swish and sip. 'Wanting,' he said.

'Wanting?'

'Hunger.'

'Uh-huh.'

'The answer isn't surprising,' Win said. 'Look in Joe DiMaggio's eyes. Or Larry Bird's. Or Michael Jordan's.

Look at pictures of John McEnroe in his prime, or Chris Evert. Look at Linda Coldren.' He stopped. 'Look in the mirror.'

'The mirror? I have this?'

'When you were on the court,' Win said slowly, 'your eyes were barely sane.'

They fell into silence. Myron took a swig of Yoo-Hoo. The cold aluminum felt good in his hand. 'You make the whole "wanting" thing sound like it's all foreign to you,' Myron said.

'It is.'

'Bull.'

'I am a good golfer,' Win said. 'Correction: I am a very good golfer. I practiced quite a bit in my youth. I have even won my share of tournaments. But I never wanted it bad enough to move up to that next level.'

'I've seen you in the ring,' Myron countered. 'In martial arts tournaments. You seemed plenty "wanting" to me.'

'That is very different,' Win said.

'How so?'

'I do not view a martial arts tournaments as a sporting contest, whereby the winner brings home a chintzy trophy and brags to colleagues and friends – nor do I view it as a competition that will lead to some sort of empty emotion that the insecure among us perceive as glory. Fighting is not a sport to me. It's about survival. If I could lose in there' – he motioned to an imaginary ring – 'I could lose in the real world.' Win looked up in the air. 'But . . .' His voice drifted off.

'But?' Myron repeated.

'But you may be on to something.'

'Oh?'

Win steepled his fingers. 'You see, fighting is life-and-death to me. That's how I treat it. But the athletes we've been talking about take it a step further. Every competition, even the most banal, is viewed by them as life-and-death – and losing is death.'

Myron nodded. He didn't buy it, but what the hell. Keep him talking. 'I don't get something,' he said. 'If Jack has this special "wanting," why hasn't he ever won a professional tournament?'

'He lost it.'

'The wanting?'

'Yes.'

'When?'

'Twenty-three years ago.'

'During the Open?'

'Yes,' Win said again. 'Most athletes lose it in a slow burnout. They grow weary or they win enough to quench whatever inferno rages in their bellies. But that was not the case with Jack. His fire was extinguished in one crisp, cold gust. You could almost see it. Twenty-three years ago. The sixteenth hole. The ball landing in the stone quarry. His eyes have never been the same.'

'Until now,' Myron added.

'Until now,' Win agreed. 'It took him twenty-three years, but he stoked the flames back to life.'

They both drank. Win sipped. Myron guzzled. The chocolaty coldness felt wonderful sliding down his throat. 'How long have you known Jack?' Myron asked.

'I met him when I was six years old. He was fifteen.'

'Did he have the "wanting" back then?'

Win smiled at the ceiling. 'He would sooner carve out his own kidney with a grapefruit spoon than lose to someone on the golf course.' He lowered his gaze to

Myron. 'Did Jack Coldren have the "wanting"? He was the pure definition.'

'Sounds like you admired him.'

'I did.'

'You don't anymore?'

'No.'

'What made you change?'

'I grew up.'

'Wow.' Myron took another swig of Yoo-Hoo. 'That's heavy.'

Win chuckled. 'You wouldn't understand.'

'Try me.'

Win put down the brandy snifter. He leaned forward very slowly. 'What is so great about winning?'

'Pardon?'

'People love a winner. They look up to him. They admire – nay, revere – him. They use terms like *hero* and *courage* and *perseverance* to describe him. They want to be near him and touch him. They want to be like him.'

Win spread his hands. 'But why? What about the winner do we want to emulate? His ability to blind himself to anything but the pursuit of empty aggrandizement? His ego-inflating obsession with wearing a hunk of metal around his neck? His willingness to sacrifice anything, including people, in order to best another human being on a lump of AstroTurf for a cheesy statuette?' He looked up at Myron, his always serene face suddenly lost. 'Why do we applaud this selfishness, this self-love?'

'Competitive drive isn't a bad thing, Win. You're talking about extremes.'

'But it is the extremists we admire most. By its nature, what you call "competitive drive" leads to extremism and destroys all in its path.'

'You're being simplistic, Win.'

'It is simple, my friend.'

They both settled back. Myron stared up at the exposed beams. After some time, he said, 'You have it wrong.'

'How so?'

Myron wondered how to explain it. 'When I played basketball,' he began, 'I mean, when I really got into it and reached these levels you're talking about – I barely thought about the score. I barely thought about my opponent or about beating somebody. I was alone. I was in the zone. This is going to sound stupid, but playing at the top of my game was almost Zen-like.'

Win nodded. 'And when did you feel this way?'

'Pardon?'

'When did you feel your most – to use your word – *Zen*?'

'I don't follow.'

'Was it at practice? No. Was it during an unimportant game or when your team was up by thirty points? No. What brought you to this sweat-drenched state of Nirvana, my friend, was competition. The desire – the naked need – to defeat a top-level opponent.'

Myron opened his mouth to counter. Then he stopped. Exhaustion was starting to take over. 'I'm not sure I have an answer to that,' he said. 'At the end of the day, I like to win. I don't know why. I like ice cream too. I don't know why either.'

Win frowned. 'Impressive simile,' he said flatly.

'Hey, it's late.'

Myron heard a car pull up front. A young blond entered the room and smiled. Win smiled back. She bent down and kissed him. Win had no problem with that. Win was never outwardly rude to his dates. He was not the type to rush them out. He had no problem with them staying the night, if it made them happier. Some might mistake this for kindness or a tender spot in the soul. They'd be wrong. Win let them stay because they meant so little to him. They could never reach him. They could never touch him. So why not let them stay?

'That's my taxi,' the blonde said.

Win's smile was blank.

'I had fun,' she said.

Not even a blink.

'You can reach me through Amanda if you want' – she looked at Myron, then back at Win – 'well, you know.'

'Yes,' Win said. 'I know.'

The young woman offered up an uncomfortable smile and left.

Myron watched, trying to keep his face from registering shock. A prostitute! Christ, she was a prostitute! He knew that Win had used them in the past – in the mid-eighties, he used to order in Chinese food from Hunan Grill and Asian prostitutes from the Noble House bordello for what he called 'Chinese Night' – but to still partake, in this day and age?

Then Myron remembered the Chevy Nova and his whole body went cold.

He turned to his friend. They looked at each other. Neither one of them said anything.

'Moralizing,' Win said. 'How nice.'

'I didn't say anything.'

'Indeed.' Win stood.

'Where are you going?'

'Out.'

Myron felt his heart pound. 'Mind if I go with you?'

'Yes.'

'What car are you taking?'

Win did not bother responding, 'Good night, Myron.'

Myron's mind raced for solutions, but he knew it was hopeless. Win was going. There was no way to stop him.

Win stopped at the door and turned back to him. 'One question, if I may.'

Myron nodded, unable to speak.

'Was Linda Coldren the one who first contacted you?' Win asked.

'No,' Myron said.

'Then who?'

'Your uncle Bucky.'

Win arched an eyebrow. 'And who suggested us to Bucky?'

Myron looked back at Win steadily, but he couldn't stop shaking. Win nodded and turned back to the door.

'Win?'

'Go to sleep, Myron.'

Chapter 11

Myron did not go to sleep. He didn't even bother trying.

He sat in Win's chair and tried to read, but the words never registered. He was exhausted. He leaned back against the rich leather and waited. Hours passed. Disjointed images of Win's potential handiwork wrested free in a heavy spray of dark crimson. Myron closed his eyes and tried to ride it out.

At 3:30 A.M., Myron heard a car pull up. The ignition died. A key clicked in the door and then it swung open. Win stepped inside and looked at Myron with nary a trace of emotion.

'Good night,' Win said.

He walked away. Myron heard the bedroom door close and let loose a held breath. Fine, he thought. He lifted himself into a standing position and made his way to his bedroom. He crawled under the sheets, but sleep still would not come. Black, opaque fear fluttered in his stomach. He had just begun to slide into true REM sleep when the bedroom door flew open.

'You're still asleep?' a familiar voice asked.

Myron managed to tear his eyes open. He was used to Esperanza Diaz barging into his office without knocking; he wasn't used to her doing it where he slept.

'What time is it?' he croaked.

'Six-thirty.'

'In the morning?'

Esperanza gave him one of her patented glares, the one road crews tried to hire out to raze large rock formations. With one finger she tucked a few spare strands of her raven locks behind her ear. Her shimmering dark skin made you think of a Mediterranean cruise by moonlight, of clear waters and puffy-sleeved peasant blouses and olive groves.

'How did you get here?' he asked.

'Amtrak red-eye,' she said.

Myron was still groggy. 'Then what did you do? Catch a cab?'

'What are you, a travel agent? Yes, I took a cab.'

'Just asking.'

'The idiot driver asked me for the address three times. Guess he's not used to taking Hispanics into this neighborhood.'

Myron shrugged. 'Probably thought you were a domestic,' he said.

'In *these* shoes?' She lifted her foot so he could see.

'Very nice.' Myron adjusted himself in the bed, his body still craving sleep. 'Not to belabor the point, but what exactly are you doing here?'

'I got some information on the old caddie.'

'Lloyd Rennart?'

Esperanza nodded. 'He's dead.'

'Oh.' Dead. As in dead end. Not that it had been much of a beginning. 'You could have just called.'

'There's more.'

'Oh?'

'The circumstances surrounding his death are' – she stopped, bit her lower lip – 'fuzzy.'

Myron sat up a bit. 'Fuzzy?'

'Lloyd Rennart apparently committed suicide eight months ago.'

'How?'

'That's the fuzzy part. He and his wife were on vacation in a mountain range in Peru. He woke up one morning, wrote a brief note, then he jumped off a cliff of some kind.'

'You're kidding.'

'Nope. I haven't been able to get too many details yet. The *Philadelphia Daily News* just had a brief story on it.' There was a hint of a smile. 'But according to the article, the body had not yet been located.'

Myron was starting to wake up in a big hurry. 'What?'

'Apparently Lloyd Rennart took the plunge in a remote crevasse with no access. They may have located the body by now, but I couldn't find a follow-up article. None of the local papers carried an obituary.'

Myron shook his head. No body. The questions that sprang to mind were obvious: could Lloyd Rennart still be alive? Did he fake his own death in order to plot out his revenge? Seemed a tad out there, but you never know. If he had, why would he have waited twenty-three years? True, the US Open was back at Merion. True, that could make old wounds resurface. But still. 'Weird,' he said. He looked up at her. 'You could have told me all this on the phone. You didn't have to come all the way down here.'

'What the hell is the big deal?' Esperanza snapped. 'I wanted to get out of the city for the weekend. I thought seeing the Open would be fun. You mind?'

'I was just asking.'

'You're so nosy sometimes.'

'Okay, okay.' He held up his hands in mock surrender. 'Forget I asked.'

'Forgotten,' she said. 'You want to fill me in on what's going on?'

He told her about the Crusty Nazi at the mall and about losing the black-clad perpetrator.

When he finished, Esperanza shook her head. 'Jesus,' she said. 'Without Win, you're hopeless.'

Ms Morale Booster.

'Speaking of Win,' Myron said, 'don't talk to him about the case.'

'Why?'

'He's reacting badly.'

She watched him closely. 'How badly?'

'He went night visiting.'

Silence.

'I thought he stopped doing that,' she said.

'I thought so too.'

'Are you sure?'

'There was a Chevy parked in the driveway,' Myron said. 'He took it out of here last night and didn't get back till three-thirty.'

Silence. Win stored a bunch of old, unregistered Chevys. Disposable cars, he called them. Completely untraceable.

Esperanza's voice was soft. 'You can't have it both ways, Myron.'

'What are you talking about?'

'You can't ask Win to do it when it suits you, then get pissed off when he does it on his own.'

'I never ask him to play vigilante.'

'Yeah, you do. You involve him in violence. When it suits your needs, you unleash him. Like he's a weapon of some kind.'

'It's not like that.'

'It is like that,' she said. 'It is exactly like that. When Win goes out on these night errands, he doesn't hurt the innocent, does he?'

Myron considered the question. 'No,' he said.

'So what's the problem? He is just attacking a different type of guilty. He picks out the guilty instead of you.'

Myron shook his head. 'It's not the same thing.'

'Because you judge?'

'I don't send him out to hurt people. I send him out to watch people or to back me up.'

'I'm not sure I see the difference.'

'Do you know what he does when he night visits, Esperanza? He walks through the worst neighborhoods he can find in the middle of the night. Old FBI buddies tell him where drug dealers or child pornographers or street gangs hang out – alleyways, abandoned buildings, whatever – and he goes strolling through those hellholes no cop would dare tread.'

'Sounds like Batman,' Esperanza countered.

'You don't think it's wrong?'

'Oh, I think it's wrong,' she replied steadily. 'But I'm not sure you do.'

'What the hell is that supposed to mean?'

'Think about it,' she said. 'About why you're really upset.'

Footsteps approached. Win stuck his head in the doorway. He was smiling like a guest star on the opening credits of the *Love Boat*. 'Good morning, all,' he said with far too much cheer. He bussed Esperanza's cheek. He was decked out in classic, though fairly understated, golf clothes. Ashworth shirt. Plain golf cap. Sky-blue pants with pleats.

'Will you be staying with us, Esperanza?' he asked in his most solicitous tone.

Esperanza looked at him, looked at Myron. Nodded.

'Wonderful, You can use the bedroom down the hall on the left.' Win turned to Myron. 'Guess what?'

'I'm all ears, Mr Happy Face,' Myron said.

'Crispin still wants to meet with you. It appears that your walking out last night actually made something of an impression on him.' Big smile, spread hands. 'The reluctant suitor approach. I must try it sometime.'

Esperanza said, 'Tad Crispin? *The* Tad Crispin?'

'The very,' Win replied.

She gave Myron an approving look. 'Wow.'

'Indeed,' Win said. 'Well, I must be going. I'll see you at Merion. I'll be at the Lock-Horne tent most of the day.' Renewing the smile. 'Ta-ta.'

Win started to leave, stopped, snapped his fingers. 'I almost forgot.' He tossed Myron a videotape. 'Maybe this will save you some time.'

The videotape landed on the bed. 'Is this . . . ?'

'The bank security tape from First Philadelphia,' Win said. 'Six-eighteen on Thursday afternoon. As per your request.' One more smile, one more wave. 'Have a great day.'

Esperanza watched him go. ' "Have a great day"?' she repeated.

Myron shrugged.

'Who the hell was that guy?' she asked.

'Wink Martindale,' Myron said. 'Come on. Let's go downstairs and watch this.'

Chapter 12

Linda Coldren opened the door before Myron knocked.

'What is it?' she asked.

Linda's face was drawn, accentuating the already high cheekbones. Her eyes had a lost and hollow look. She hadn't slept. The pressure was growing unbearable. The worrying. The not knowing. She was strong. She was trying to stand up to it. But her son's disappearance was beginning to gnaw away at her core.

Myron held up the videotape. 'Do you have a VCR?' he asked.

In something of a daze, Linda Coldren led him to the same television he had seen her watching yesterday when they first met. Jack Coldren appeared from a back room, his golf bag on his shoulder. He, too, looked worn. There were sacks under his eyes, fleshy pouches like soft cocoons. Jack tried to toss up a welcoming smile, but it sputtered up like a lighter low on fluid.

'Hey, Myron.'

'Hey, Jack.'

'What's going on?'

Myron slid the tape into the opening. 'Do you know anybody who lives on Green Acres Road?' he asked.

Jack and Linda looked each other.

'Why do you want to know that?' Linda asked.

'Because last night I watched your house. I saw somebody crawl out a window.'

'A window?' It was Jack. He lowered his eyebrows. 'What window?'

'Your son's.'

Silence.

Then Linda asked, 'What does that have to do with Green Acres Road?'

'I followed whoever it was. He turned down Green Acres Road and disappeared – either into a house or into the woods.'

Linda lowered her head. Jack stepped forward and spoke. 'The Squires live on Green Acres Road,' he said. 'Chad's best friend Matthew.'

Myron nodded. He was not surprised. He flicked on the television. 'This is a bank security tape from First Philadelphia.'

'How did you get it?' Jack asked.

'It's not important.'

The front door opened and Bucky entered. The older man, dressed today in checked pants with a yellow-and-green top, stepped into the den doing his customary neck craning bit. 'What's going on here?' he demanded.

Nobody replied.

'I said—'

'Just watch the screen, Dad,' Linda interrupted.

'Oh,' Bucky said softly, moving in closer.

Myron turned the channel to Three and hit the PLAY button. All eyes were on the screen. Myron had already seen the tape. He studied their faces instead, watching for reactions.

On the television, a black-and-white image appeared. The bank's driveway. The view was from up high and a bit distorted, a concave fish-eye effect to capture as much space as possible. There was no sound. Myron had the tape all cued up on the right spot. Almost immediately a car pulled into view. The camera was on the driver's side.

'It's Chad's car,' Jack Coldren announced.

They watched in rapt silence as the car window lowered. The angle was a bit odd – above the car and from the machine's point of view – but there was no doubt. Chad Coldren was the driver. He leaned out the window and put his card in the ATM machine slot. His fingers tripped across the buttons like an experienced stenographer's.

Young Chad Coldren's smile was bright and happy.

When his fingers finished their little rumba, Chad settled back into the car to wait. He turned away from the camera for a moment. To the passenger seat. Someone was sitting next to Chad. Again Myron watched for a reaction. Linda, Jack, and Bucky all squinted, all trying to make out a face, but it was impossible. When Chad finally turned back to the camera, he was laughing. He pulled the money out, grabbed his card, leaned back into the car, closed the window, and drove off.

Myron switched off the VCR and waited. Silence flooded the room. Linda Coldren slowly lifted her head. She kept her expression steady, but her jaw trembled from being so set.

'There was another person in the car,' Linda offered. 'He could have had a gun on Chad or—'

'Stop it!' Jack shouted. 'Look at his face, Linda! For crying out loud, just look at his goddamn smirking face!'

'I know my son. He wouldn't do this.'

'You don't know him,' Jack countered. 'Face it, Linda. Neither one of us knows him.'

'It's not what it looks like,' Linda insisted, speaking more to herself than anyone in the room.

'No?' Jack gestured at the television, his face reddening. 'Then how the hell do you explain what we just saw? Huh? He was laughing, Linda. He's having the time of his life at our expense.' He stopped, struggled with something. 'At my expense,' he corrected himself.

Linda gave him a long look. 'Go play, Jack.'

'That's exactly what I am going to do.'

He lifted his bag. His eyes met Bucky's. Bucky remained silent. A tear slid down the older man's cheek. Jack tore his gaze away and started for the door.

Myron called out, 'Jack?'

Coldren stopped.

'It still might not be what it looks like,' Myron said.

Again with the eyebrows. 'What do you mean?'

'I traced the call you got last night,' Myron explained. 'It was made from a mall pay phone.' He briefly filled them in on his visit to the Grand Mercado Mall and the Crusty Nazi. Linda's face kept slipping from hope to heartbreak and mostly confusion. Myron understood. She wanted her son to be safe. But at the same time, she did not want this to be some cruel joke. Tough mix.

'He is in trouble,' Linda said as soon as he'd finished. 'That proves it.'

'That proves nothing,' Jack replied in tired exasperation. 'Rich kids hang out at malls and dress like punks too. He's probably a friend of Chad's.'

Again Linda looked at her husband hard. Again she said in a measured tone, 'Go play, Jack.'

Jack opened his mouth to say something, then stopped. He shook his head, adjusted the bag on his shoulder, and left. Bucky crossed the room. He tried to hold his daughter, but she stiffened at his touch. She moved away, studying Myron's face.

'You think he's faking too,' she said.

'Jack's explanation makes sense.'

'So you're going to stop looking?'

'I don't know,' Myron said.

She straightened her back. 'Stay with it,' she began, 'and I promise to sign with you.'

'Linda . . .'

'That's why you're here in the first place, right? You want my business. Well, here's the deal. You stay with me and I'll sign whatever you want. Hoax or no hoax. It'll be quite a coup, no? Signing the number one-ranked female golfer in the world?'

'Yes,' Myron admitted. 'It would be.'

'So there you go.' She stuck out her hand. 'Do we have a deal?'

Myron kept his hands by his side. 'Let me ask you something.'

'What?'

'Why are you so sure it's not a hoax, Linda?'

'You think I'm being naive?'

'Not really,' he said. 'I just want to know what makes you so certain.'

She lowered her hand and turned away from him. 'Dad?'

Bucky seemed to snap out of a daze. 'Hmm?'

'Would you mind leaving us alone for a minute?'

'Oh,' Bucky said. Neck crane. Then another. Two of them back-to-back. Good thing he wasn't a giraffe. 'Yes, well, I wanted to get to Merion anyway.'

'You go ahead, Dad. I'll meet you there.'

When they were alone, Linda Coldren began to pace the room. Myron was again awed by her looks – the paradoxical combination of beauty, strength and now delicacy. The strong, toned arms, yet the long, slender neck. The harsh, pointed features, yet the soft indigo eyes. Myron had heard beauty described as 'seamless'; hers was quite the opposite.

'I'm not big on' – Linda Coldren made quote marks in the air with her fingers – 'woman's intuition or any of that mother-knows-her-boy-best crap. But I know that my son is in danger. He wouldn't just disappear like this. No matter how it looks, that's not what happened.'

Myron remained silent.

'I don't like asking for help. It's not my way – to depend on someone else. But this is a situation . . . I'm scared. I've never felt fear like this in all of my life. It's all-consuming. It's suffocating. My son is in trouble and I can't do anything to help him. You want proof that this is not a hoax. I can't provide that. I just know. And I'm asking you to please help me.'

Myron wasn't sure how to respond. Her argument came straight from the heart, *sans* facts or evidence. But that didn't make her suffering any less real. 'I'll check out Matthew's house,' he said finally. 'Let's see what happens after that.'

Chapter 13

In the light of day, Green Acres Road was even more imposing. Both sides of the street were lined with ten-foot-high shrubs so thick that Myron couldn't tell how thick. He parked his car outside a wrought iron gate and approached an intercom. He pressed a button and waited. There were several surveillance cameras. Some remained steady. Some whirred slowly from side to side. Myron spotted motion detectors, barbed wire, Dobermans.

A rather elaborate fortress, he thought.

A voice as impenetrable as the shrubs came through the speaker. 'May I help you?'

'Good morning,' Myron said, offering up a friendly-but-not-a-salesman smile to the nearest camera. Talking to a camera. He felt like he was on *Nightline*. 'I'm looking for Matthew Squires.'

Pause. 'Your name, sir?'

'Myron Bolitar.'

'Is Master Squires expecting you?'

'No.' *Master* Squires?

'Then you do not have an appointment?'

An appointment to see a sixteen-year-old? Who is this kid, Doogie Howser? 'No, I'm afraid I don't.'

'May I ask the purpose of your visit?'

'To speak to Matthew Squires.' Mr Vague.

'I am afraid that will not be possible at this time,' the voice said.

'Will you tell him it involves Chad Coldren?'

Another pause. Cameras pirouetted. Myron looked around. All the lenses were aiming down from up high, glaring at him like hostile space aliens or lunchroom monitors.

'In what way does it involve Master Coldren?' the voice asked.

Myron squinted into a camera. 'May I ask with whom I am speaking?'

No reply.

Myron waited a beat, then said, 'You're supposed to say, "I am the great and powerful Oz."'

'I am sorry, sir. No one is admitted without an appointment. Please have a nice day.'

'Wait a second. Hello? Hello?' Myron pressed the button again. No reply. He leaned on it for several seconds. Still nothing. He looked up into the camera and gave his best caring-homespun-family-guy smile. Very Tom Brokaw. He tried a small wave. Nothing. He took a small step backward and gave a great big Jack Kemp fake-throwing-a-football wave. Nada.

He stood there for another minute. This was indeed odd. A sixteen-year-old with this kind of security? Something was not quite kosher. He pressed the button one more time. When no one responded he looked into the camera, put a thumb in either ear, wiggled his fingers and stuck out his tongue.

When in doubt, be mature.

Back at his car, Myron picked up the car phone and dialed his friend Sheriff Jake Courter.

'Sheriff's office.'

'Hey, Jake. It's Myron.'

'Fuck. I knew I shouldn't have come in on Saturday.'

'Ooo, I'm wounded. Seriously, Jake, do they still call you the Henny Youngman of law enforcement?'

Heavy sigh. 'What the fuck do you want, Myron? I just came in to get a little paperwork done.'

'No rest for those vigilantly pursuing peace and justice for the common man.'

'Right,' Jake said. 'This week, I went out on a whole twelve calls. Guess how many of them were for false burglar alarms?'

'Thirteen.'

'Pretty close.'

For more man twenty years, Jake Courier had been a cop in several of the country's meanest cities. He'd hated it and craved a quieter life. So Jake, a rather large black man, resigned from the force and moved to the picturesque (read: lily-white) town of Reston, New Jersey. Looking for a cushy job, he ran for sheriff. Reston was a college (read: liberal) town, and thus Jake played up his – as he put it – 'blackness' and won easily. The white man's guilt, Jake had told Myron. The best vote-getter this side of Willie Horton.

'Miss the excitement of the big city?' Myron asked.

'Like a case of herpes,' Jake countered. 'Okay, Myron, you've done the charm thing on me. I'm like Play-Doh in your paws now. What do you want?'

'I'm in Philly for the US Open.'

'That's golf, right?'

'Yeah, golf. And I wanted to know if you've heard of a guy name Squires.'

Pause. Then: 'Oh, shit.'

'What?'

'What the fuck are you involved in now?'

'Nothing. It's just that he's got all this weird security around his house—'

'What the fuck are you doing by his house?'

'Nothing.'

'Right,' Jake said. 'Guess you were just strolling by.'

'Something like that.'

'Nothing like that.' Jake sighed. Then: 'Ah what the hell, it ain't on my beat anymore. Squires. Reginald Squires aka Big Blue.'

Myron made a face. 'Big Blue?'

'Hey, all gangsters need a nickname. Squires is known as Big Blue. Blue, as in blue blood.'

'Those gangsters,' Myron said. 'Pity they don't channel their creativity into honest marketing.'

' "Honest marketing," ' Jake repeated. 'Talk about your basic oxymoron. Anyway Squires got a kiloton of family dough and all this blue-blood breeding and schooling and shit.'

'So what's he doing keeping such bad company?'

'You want the simple answer? The son of a bitch is a serious wacko. Gets his jollies hurting people. Kinda like Win.'

'Win doesn't get his jollies hurting people.'

'If you say so.'

'If Win hurts someone, there's a reason. To prevent them from doing it again or to punish or something.'

'Sure, whatever,' Jake said. 'Kinda touchy though, aren't we, Myron?'

'It's been a long day.'

'It's only nine in the morning.'

Myron said, 'For what breeds time but two hands on a clock?'

'Who said that?'

'No one. I just made it up.'

'You should consider writing greeting cards.'

'So what is Squires into, Jake?'

'Want to hear something funny? I'm not sure. Nobody is. Drugs and prostitution. Shit like that. But very upscale. Nothing very well organized or anything. It's more like he plays at it, you know? Like he gets involved in whatever he thinks will give him a thrill, then dumps it.'

'How about kidnapping?'

Brief pause. 'Oh shit, you are involved in something again, aren't you?'

'I just asked you if Squires was into kidnapping.'

'Oh. Right. Like it's a hypothetical question. Kinda like, "If a bear shits in the forest and no one is around, does it still reek"?'

'Precisely. Does kidnapping reek like his kind of thing?'

'Hell if I know. The guy is a major league loon, no question. He blends right into all that snobbish bullshit – the boring parties, the shitty food, the laughing at jokes that aren't remotely funny, the talking with the same boring people about the same boring worthless bullshit—'

'It sounds like you really admire them.'

'Just my point, my friend. They got it all, right? On the outside. Money, big homes, fancy clubs. But they're all so fucking boring – shit, I'd kill myself. Makes me wonder if maybe Squires feels that way too, you know?'

'Uh-huh,' Myron said. 'And Win is the scary one here, right?'

Jake laughed. 'Touché. But to answer your question, I don't know if Squires would be into kidnapping. Wouldn't surprise me though.'

Myron thanked him and hung up. He looked up. At least a dozen security cameras lined the top of the shrubs like tiny sentinels.

What now?

For all he knew, Chad Coldren was laughing his ass off, watching him on one of those security cameras. This whole thing could be an exercise in pure futility. Of course, Linda Coldren had promised to be a client. Much as he didn't want to admit it to himself, the idea was not wholly unpleasant. He considered the possibility and started to smile. If he could also somehow land Tad Crispin . . .

Yo, Myron, a kid may be in serious trouble.

Or, more likely, a spoiled brat or neglected adolescent – take your pick – is playing hooky and having some fun at his parents' expense.

So the question remained: What now?

He thought again about the videotape of Chad at the ATM machine. He didn't go into details with the Coldrens, but it bothered him. Why there? Why that particular ATM machine? If the kid was running away or hiding out, he might have to pick up money. Fine and dandy, that made sense.

But why would he do it at Porter Street?

Why not do it at a bank closer to home? And equally important, what was Chad Coldren doing in that area in the first place? There was nothing there. It wasn't a stop between highways or anything like that. The only thing in

131

that neighborhood that would require cash was the Court Manor Inn. Myron again remembered *motelier extraordinaire* Stuart Lipwitz's attitude and wondered.

He started the car. It might be something. Worth looking into, at any rate.

Of course, Stuart Lipwitz had made it abundantly clear that he would not talk. But Myron thought he had just the tool to make him change his mind.

Chapter 14

'Smile!'

The man did not smile. He quickly shifted the car in reverse and backed out. Myron shrugged and lowered the camera. It was on a neck strap and bounced lightly against his chest. Another car approached. Myron lifted the camera again.

'Smile!' Myron repeated.

Another man. Another no smile. This guy managed to duck down before shifting his car into reverse.

'Camera shy,' Myron called out to him. 'Nice to see in this age of paparazzi overkill.'

It didn't take long. Myron had been on the sidewalk in front of the Court Manor Inn for less than five minutes when he spotted Stuart Lipwitz sprinting toward him. Big Stu was in full custom – gray tails, wide tie, a concierge key pin in the suit's lapel. Gray tails at a no-tell motel. Like a maître d' at Burger King. Watching Stu move closer, a Pink Floyd song came to mind: *Hello, hello,*

hello, is there anybody out there? David Bowie joined in: *Ground control to Major Tom.*

Ah, the seventies.

'You there,' he called out.

'Hi, Stu.'

No smile this time. 'This is private property,' Stuart Lipwitz said, a little out of breath. 'I must ask you to remove yourself immediately.'

'I hate to disagree with you, Stu, but I am on a public sidewalk. I got every right to be here.'

Stuart Lipwitz stammered, then flapped his arms in frustration. With the tails, the movement kind of reminded Myron of a bat. 'But you can't just stand there and take pictures of my clientele,' he semi-whined.

'"Clientele,"' Myron repeated. 'Is that a new euphemism for *john*?'

'I'll call the police.'

'Oooo. Stop scaring me like that.'

'You are interfering with my business.'

'And you are interfering with mine.'

Stuart Lipwitz put his hands on his hips and tried to look threatening. 'This is the last time I'll ask you nicely. Leave the premises.'

'That wasn't nice.'

'Excuse me?'

'You said it was the last time you'd ask me nicely,' Myron explained. 'Then you said, "Leave the premises." You didn't say *please*. You didn't say, "Kindly leave the premises." Where's the nice in that?'

'I see,' Lipwitz said. Beads of sweat dotted his face. It was hot and the man was, after all, in tails. 'Please kindly leave the premises.'

'Nope. But now, at least, you're a man of your word.'

Stuart Lipwitz took several deep breaths. 'You want to know about the boy, don't you? The one in the picture.'

'You bet.'

'And if I tell you if he was here, will you leave?'

'Much as it would pain me to leave this quaint locale, I would somehow tear myself away.'

'That, sir, is blackmail.'

Myron looked at him. 'I would say "*blackmail* is such an ugly word," but that would be too cliché. So instead I'll just say "Yup." '

'But' – Lipwitz started stammering – 'that's against the law!'

'As opposed to, say, prostitution and drug dealing and whatever other sleazy activity goes on in this fleabag?'

Stuart Lipwitz's eyes widened. 'Fleabag? This is the Court Manor Inn, sir. We are a respectable—'

'Stuff it, Stu. I got pictures to take.' Another car pulled up. Gray Volvo station wagon. Nice family car. A man about fifty years old was neatly attired in a business suit. The young girl in the passenger seat must have shopped – as the mall girls had recently taught him – at Sluts 'R' Us.

Myron smiled and leaned toward the window. 'Whoa, sir, vacationing with your daughter?'

The man splashed on a classic deer-caught-in-the headlights look. The young prostitute whooped with laughter. 'Hey, Mel, he thinks I'm your daughter!' She whooped again.

Myron raised the camera. Stuart Lipwitz tried to step in his way, but Myron swept him away with his free hand. 'It's Souvenir Day at the Court Manor,' Myron said. 'I can put the picture on a coffee mug if you'd like. Or maybe a decorative plate?'

The man in the business suit reversed the car. They were gone several seconds later.

Stuart Lipwitz's face reddened. He made two fists. Myron looked at him. 'Now Stuart . . .'

'I have powerful friends,' he said.

'Ooooo. I'm getting scared again.'

'Fine. Be that way.' Stuart turned away and stormed up the drive. Myron smiled. The kid was a tougher nut to crack than he'd anticipated, and he really didn't want to do this all day. But let's face it: There were no other leads and besides, playing with Big Stu was fun.

Myron waited for more customers. He wondered what Stu was up to. Something frantic, no doubt. Ten minutes later, a canary yellow Audi pulled up and a large black man slid out. The black man was maybe an inch shorter than Myron, but he was built. His chest could double as a jai alai wall and his legs resembled the trunks of redwoods. He glided when he moved – not the bulky moves one usually associated with the overmuscled.

Myron did not like that.

The black man had sunglasses on and wore a red Hawaiian shirt with blue jean shorts. His most noticeable feature was his hair. The kinks had been slicked straight and parted on the side, like old photographs of Nat King Cole.

Myron pointed at the top of the man's head. 'Is that hard to do?' he asked.

'What?' the black man said. 'You mean the hair?'

Myron nodded. 'Keeping it straight like that.'

'Nah, not really. Once a week I go to a guy named Ray. In an old-fashioned barbershop, as a matter of fact. The kind with the pole in front and everything.' His smile was almost wistful. 'Ray takes care of it for me. Also gives me a great shave. With hot towels and everything.' The man stroked his face for emphasis.

'Looks smooth,' Myron said.

'Hey, thanks. Nice of you to say. I find it relaxing, you know? Doing something just for me. I think it's important. To relieve the stress.'

Myron nodded. 'I hear you.'

'Maybe I'll give you Ray's number. You could stop by and check it out.'

'Ray,' Myron repeated. 'I'd like that.'

The black man stepped closer. 'Seems we have a little situation here, Mr Bolitar.'

'How did you know my name?'

He shrugged. Behind the sunglasses, Myron sensed that he was being sized up. Myron was doing the same. Both were trying to be subtle. Both knew exactly what the other was doing.

'I'd really appreciate it if you would leave,' he said very politely.

'I'm afraid I can't do that,' Myron said. 'Even though you did ask nicely.'

The black man nodded. He kept his distance. 'Let's see if we can work something out here, okay?'

'Okeydokey.'

'I got a job to do here, Myron. You can appreciate that, can't you?'

'Sure can,' Myron said.

'And so do you.'

'That's right.'

The black man took off his sunglasses and put them in his shirt pocket. 'Look, I know you won't be easy. And you know I won't be easy. If push comes to shove, I don't know which one of us will win.'

'I will,' Myron said. 'Good always triumphs over evil.'

The man smiled. 'Not in this neighborhood.'

'Good point.'

'I'm also not sure it's worth it to either one of us to find out. I think we're both probably past the proving-himself, macho-bullshit stage.'

Myron nodded. 'We're too mature.'

'Right.'

'It seems then,' Myron continued, 'that we've hit an impasse.'

'Guess so,' the black man agreed. 'Of course, I could always take out a gun and shoot you.'

Myron shook his head. 'Not over something this small. Too many repercussions involved.'

'Yeah. I didn't think you'd go for it, but I had to give it a whirl. You never know.'

'You're a pro,' Myron agreed. 'You'd feel remiss if you didn't at least try. Hell, I'd have felt cheated.'

'Glad you understand.'

'Speaking of which,' Myron said, 'aren't you a tad high-level to be dealing with this situation?'

'Can't say I disagree.' The black man walked closer to Myron. Myron felt his muscles tighten; a not-unpleasant anticipatory chill steeled him.

'You look like a guy who can keep his mouth shut,' the man said.

Myron said nothing. Proving the point.

'The kid you had in that picture, the one that got Leona Helmsley's panties in a bunch? He was here.'

'When?'

The black man shook his head. 'That's all you get. I'm being very generous. You wanted to know if the kid was here. The answer is yes.'

'Nice of you,' Myron said.

'I'm just trying to make it simple. Look, we both know that Lipwitz is a dumb kid. Acts like this urinal is the Beverly Wilshire. But the people who come here, they don't want that. They want to be invisible. They don't even want to look at themselves, you know what I'm saying?'

Myron nodded.

'So I gave you a freebie. The kid in the picture was here.'

'Is he still here?'

'You're pushing me, Myron.'

'Just tell me that.'

'No. He only stayed that one night.' He spread his hands. 'Now you tell me, Myron. Am I being fair with you?'

'Very.'

He nodded. 'Your turn.'

'I guess there's no way you'll tell me who you're working for.'

The black man made a face. 'Nice meeting you, Myron.'

'Same here.'

They shook hands. Myron got into his car and drove away.

He had almost reached Merion when the cellular rang. He picked up and said hello.

'Is this, like, Myron?'

Mall girl. 'Hi, yes. Actually this is Myron, not just like him.'

'Huh?'

'Never mind. What's up?'

'That skank you were, like, looking for last night?'

'Right.'

'He's, like, back at the mall.'

'Where at the mall?'

'The food court. He's on line at the McDonald's.'

Myron spun the car around and hit the gas pedal.

Chapter 15

The Crusty Nazi was still there.

He sat at a corner table by himself, downing a burger of some sort like it had personally offended him. The girls were right. *Skank* was the only word to describe him, even though Myron didn't know what the word meant or if it even existed. The punk's face was aiming for tough-guy-unshaven, but a lack of testosterone made it land far closer to upkempt-adolescent-Hasid. He wore a black baseball cap with a skull and crossbones decal. His ripped white T-shirt was rolled all the way up to reveal milky, reedy arms, one with a swastika tattoo. Myron shook his head. Swastika. The kid was too old to be so utterly clueless.

The Crusty Nazi took another vicious bite, clearly furious with his burger now. The mall girls were there, pointing toward Crusty like Myron might not know which guy they'd been talking about. Myron signaled them to stop with a shushing finger at his lips. They obeyed, overcompensating by engaging in a too-loud, too-casual conversation, sliding furtive-to-the-point-of-totally-obvious glances in his direction. Myron looked away.

The Crusty Nazi finished his burger and stood. Good timing. As advertised, Crusty was very skinny. The girls were, right – the boy had no ass. None at all. Myron couldn't tell if the kid was going for that too-big-jeans look or if it was because he lacked a true backside, but every few steps, Crusty paused to hitch up the pants. Myron suspected a bit of both.

He followed him outside into the blazing sun. Hot. Damn hot. Myron felt almost a nostalgic longing for the omnipresent mall air-conditioning. Crusty strutted cool-like into the lot. Going to his car, no doubt. Myron veered to the right so as to get ready to follow. He slid into his Ford Taurus (read: Chick Trawler) and started up the engine.

He slowly cruised the lot and spotted Crusty heading way out to the last row of cars. Only two vehicles were parked out there. One was a silver Cadillac Seville. The other was a pickup truck with those semi-monster wheels, a Confederate flag decal, and the words BAD TO THE BONE painted on the side. Using his years of investigative know-how, Myron deduced that the pickup truck was probably Crusty's vehicle. Sure enough, Crusty opened the door and hopped up and in. Amazing. Sometimes Myron's powers of deduction bordered on the psychic. Maybe he should get a 900 line like Jackie Stallone.

Tailing the pickup truck was hardly a challenge. The vehicle stuck out like a golfer's clothing in a monastery, and El Crust-ola wasn't heavy on the gas pedal. They drove for about half an hour. Myron had no idea where they were going, but up ahead he recognized Veterans Stadium. He'd gone with Win to several Eagles games there. Win always had seats on the fifty-yard line, lower tier. Being an old stadium, the 'luxury' skyboxes at the Vet were too high up; Win did not care for them. So he chose instead to sit with the masses. Big of him.

About three blocks before the stadium, Crusty pulled down a side road. He threw his pickup into park and got out running. Myron once again debated calling Win for backup, but it was pointless. Win was at Merion. His phone would be off. He wondered again about last night and about Esperanza's accusations this morning. Maybe she was right. Maybe he was, at least partially, responsible for what Win did. But that wasn't the point. He knew that now. The truth, the one that scared Esperanza too, was far clearer:

Maybe Myron didn't care so much.

You read the papers and you watch the news and you see what Myron has seen and your humanity, your basic faith in human beings, begins to look frighteningly Pollyanna. That was what was really eating away at him – not that he was repulsed by what Win did, but that it really didn't bother him that much.

Win had an eerie way of seeing the world in black and white; lately, Myron had found his own gray areas blackening. He didn't like that. He did not like the change that experience – seeing the cruelty man inflicts on man – was forcing upon him. He tried to hold on to his old values, but the rope was getting awfully slick. And why was he holding on, anyway? Was it because he truly believed in these values, or because he liked himself more as a person who believed?

He didn't know anymore.

He should have brought a gun. Stupid. Still he was only following some grunge-ball. Of course, even a grunge-ball could fire a gun and kill him. But what choice did he have? Should he call the police? Well, that would appear a bit extreme based on what he had. Come back later with a firearm of some sort? By that time, Crusty could be gone – along with Chad Coldren maybe.

Nope, he had to follow. He'd just be careful.

Myron was not sure what to do. He stopped the car at the end of the block and got out. The street was crowded with low-rise brick dwellings that all looked the same. At one time, this might have been a nice area, but now the neighborhood looked like a man who'd lost his job and stopped bathing. There was an overgrown, faded quality to it, like a garden that no one bothered to tend anymore.

Crusty turned down an alleyway. Myron followed. Lots of plastic garbage bags. Lots of rusted fire escapes. Four legs stuck out of a refrigerator box. Myron heard snoring. At the end of the alley, Crusty turned right. Myron trailed slowly. Crusty had gone into what looked like an abandoned building through a fire door. There was no knob or anything, but the door was slightly ajar. Myron reached in with his fingers and pried it open.

As soon as he crossed the musty threshold, Myron heard a primal scream. Crusty. Right in front of him. Something swung toward Myron's face. Fast reflexes paid off. Myron managed to duck enough so that the iron bar only clipped his shoulder blade. A quick flash of pain bolted down his arm. Myron dropped to the ground. He rolled across the cement floor and stood back up.

There were three of them now. All armed with crowbars or tire irons. All with shaved heads and tattooed swastikas. They were like sequels to the same awful movie. The Crusty Nazi was the original. Beneath the Planet of Crusty Nazi – the one on his left – was smiling with idiotic glee. The one on his right – Escape from the Planet of Crusty Nazi – looked a bit more frightened. The weak link, Myron thought.

'Changing a tire?' Myron asked.

The Crusty Nazi slapped the tire iron against his palm for emphasis. 'Gonna flatten yours.'

Myron raised his hand in front of him with the palm facing down. He shook it back and forth and said, 'Eh.'

'Why the fuck you following me, asshole?'

'Me?'

'Yeah, you. Why the fuck you following me?'

'Who says I'm following you?'

There was momentary confusion on Crusty's face. Then: 'You think I'm fucking stupid or something?'

'No, I think you're Mr Mensa.'

'Mister what?'

Beneath the Planet of Crusty Nazi said, 'He's just fucking with you, man.'

'Yeah,' Escape chimed in. 'Fucking with you.'

Crusty's wet eyes bulged out. 'Yeah? Is that what you're doing, asshole? You fucking with me, huh? Is that what you're doing? Fucking with me?'

Myron looked at him. 'Can we move on please?'

Beneath said, 'Let's fuck him up a little. Soften his ass up.'

Myron knew that three of them were probably not experienced fighters, but he also knew that three armed men beat one good man on almost any given day. They were also a bit too jittery, their eyes as glazed as morning doughnuts. They were constantly sniffing and rubbing their noses.

145

Two words: Coked up. Or Nose Candy. Or Toot Sweet. Take your pick.

Myron's best chance was to confuse and strike. Risky. You wanted to piss them off, to upset their already-tipsy equilibrium. But at the same time, you wanted to control it, to know when to back off a bit. A delicate balance requiring Myron Bolitar, darling of the high wire, to perform high above the crowd without the benefit of a safety net.

Once again Crusty asked, 'Why the fuck you following me, asshole?'

'Maybe I'm just attracted to you,' Myron said. 'Even if you don't have an ass.'

Beneath started cackling. 'Oh man, oh man, let's fuck him up. Let's fuck him up good.'

Myron tried to give them the tough-guy look. Some mistook this for constipation, but he was getting better at it. Practice. 'I wouldn't do that if I were you.'

'Oh no?' It was Crusty. 'Give me one good reason why we don't just fuck you up. Give me one good reason why I don't break every fucking rib in your body with this.' He raised the tire iron. In case Myron thought he was being too subtle.

'You asked before if I thought you were stupid,' Myron said.

'Yeah, so?'

'So do you think I'm stupid? Do you think somebody who meant you harm would be dumb enough to follow you in here – knowing what was about to go down?'

That made all three of them pause.

'I followed you,' Myron continued, 'as a test.'

'What the fuck you talking about?'

'I work for certain people. We won't mention names.'

146

Mostly, Myron thought, because he didn't know what the hell he was talking about. 'Let's just say they are in a business you guys frequent.'

'Frequent?' More nose rubbing. Toot, sweet, toot, sweet.

'Frequent,' Myron repeated. 'As in occurring or appearing quite often or at close intervals. Frequent.'

'What?'

Jesus. 'My employer,' Myron said, 'he needs someone to handle certain territory. Somebody new. Somebody who wants to make ten percent on sales and get all the free blow they can.'

Eyes went buggy.

Beneath turned to Crusty. 'You hear that, man?'

'Yeah, I hear him.'

'Shit, we don't get no commission from Eddie,' Beneath went on. 'The fucker is so small-time.' He gestured at Myron with the tire iron. 'This guy, man, look how fucking old he is. He's gotta be working for somebody with juice.'

'Got to be,' Escape added.

The Crusty One hesitated, squinted suspicion. 'How did you find out about us?'

Myron shrugged. 'Word gets around.' Shovel, shovel.

'So you was just following me for some kinda fucking test?'

'Right.'

'Just came to the mall and decided to follow me?'

'Something like that.'

Crusty smiled. He looked at Escape and at Beneath. His grip on the tire iron tightened. Uh-oh. 'Then how the fuck come you were asking about me last night, huh? How come you want to know about a call I made?'

Uh-oh.

Crusty stepped closer, eyes aglow.

Myron raised his hand. 'The answer is simple.' They all hesitated. Myron took advantage. His foot moved like a piston, shooting out and landing squarely on the knee of the unprepared Escape. Escape fell. Myron was already running.

'Get the fucker!'

They chased, but Myron had already slammed his shoulder into the fire door. The 'macho-bullshit' part of him, as his friend at the Court Manor Inn had described it, wanted to try to take them on, but he knew that would be foolhardy. They were armed. He wasn't.

By the time Myron reached the end of the alley, his lead was only about ten yards. He wondered if he'd have enough time to open his car door and get in. No choice. He'd have to try.

He grabbed the handle and swung the door open. He was sliding in when a tire iron whacked his shoulder. Pain erupted. He kept rolling, closing the door. A hand grabbed it, offered resistance. Myron used his weight and leaned into the pull.

His window exploded.

Glass tinkled down into his face. Myron kicked his heel through the open window and hit face. The grip on the door released. He already had the key out and in the ignition. He turned it as the other car window exploded. Crusty leaned into the car, his eyes blazing with fury.

'Motherfucker, you're gonna die!'

The tire iron was heading toward his face again. Myron blocked it. From behind him, he felt a sharp blow connect with his lower neck. Numbness ensued. Myron shifted into reverse and flew out of the spot, tires squealing.

Crusty tried to leap into the car through the broken window. Myron elbowed him in the nose and Crusty's grip eased. He fell hard to the pavement, but then he jumped right back up. That was the problem with fighting cokeheads. Pain often does not register.

All three men ran for the pickup, but Myron already had too big a lead. The battle was over. For now.

Chapter 16

Myron called in the pickup truck's license plate number, but that was a dead end. The plate had expired four years ago. Crusty must have taken it off a car in a dump or something. Not uncommon. Even petty crooks knew enough not to use their real plates when committing a traceable crime.

He circled back and checked the inside of the building for clues. Bent syringes and broken vials and empty bags of Doritos lay scattered about the cement. There was also an empty garbage can. Myron shook his head. Bad enough being a drug dealer. But a litterbug?

He looked around a bit more. The building was abandoned and half-burned out. There was no one inside. And no clues.

Okay, so what did this all mean? Were the three cokeheads the kidnappers? Myron had a hard time picturing it. Cokeheads break into houses. Cokeheads jump people in alleyways. Cokeheads attack with tire irons. Coke-heads, by and large, do not plan elaborate kidnappings.

But on the other hand, how elaborate was this kidnap-ping? The first two times the kidnapper called, he didn't even know how much money to extort. Wasn't that a little odd? Could it be that all this was merely the work of some out-of-their-league crusty cokeheads?

Myron got into his car and headed toward Win's house. Win had plenty of vehicles. He'd switch for a car without smashed windows. The residual damage to his body seemed to be clearing up. A bruise or two but noth-ing broken. None of the blows had landed flush, except the ones to his car windows.

He ran several possibilities through his head and even-tually managed to come up with a pretty decent scenario. Let's say that for some reason Chad Coldren decided to check into the Court Manor Inn. Maybe to spend some time with a girl. Maybe to buy some drugs. Maybe because he enjoyed the friendly service. Whatever. As per the bank surveillance camera, Chad grabbed some dough at a local ATM. Then he checked in for the night. Or the hour. Or whatever.

Once at the Court Manor Inn, something went awry. Stu Lipwitz's denials notwithstanding, the Court Manor is a sleazy joint patronized by sleazy people. It wouldn't be hard to get in trouble there. Maybe Chad Coldren tried to buy drugs from Crusty. Maybe he witnessed a crime. Maybe the kid just talked too much and some nasty people realized that he came from money. Whatever. The life orbits of Chad Coldren and the Crusty Nazi's crew dovetailed. The end result was a kidnapping.

It kinda fit.

The key word here: *kinda*.

On the road toward Merion, Myron helped deflate his own scenario with several well-placed puncture holes. First of all, the timing. Myron had been convinced that the kidnapping had something to do with Jack's return to playing the US Open at Merion. But in his Crusty-orbit scenario, the nagging timing question had to be written off as mere coincidence. Okay, maybe Myron could live with that. But then how, for example, had the Crusty Nazi – stationed at a mall pay phone – known that Esme Fong was in the Coldren house? How did the man who climbed out the window and disappeared on Green Acres Road – a person Myron had been sure was either Matthew Squires or Chad Coldren – fit into all this? Was the well-shielded Matthew Squires in cahoots with the Crusties? Or was it just a coincidence that the window man disappeared down Green Acres Road?

The scenario balloon was going *sssss* in a very big way.

By the time Myron got to Merion, Jack Coldren was on the fourteenth hole. His partner for today's round was none other than Tad Crispin. No surprise there. First place and second place were normally the final twosome of the day.

Jack was still playing well, though not spectacularly. He'd lost only one stroke off his lead, remaining a very comfortable eight strokes ahead of Tad Crispin. Myron trudged toward the fourteenth green. Green – that word again. Everything was so dang green. The grass and trees, naturally, but also tents, overhangs, scoreboards, the many television towers and scaffolds – everything was lush green to blend in with the picturesque natural sur-roundings, except, of course, for the sponsors' boards, which drew the eye with all the subtlety of Vegas hotel signs. But hey, the sponsors paid Myron's salary. Be kinda hypocritical to complain.

'Myron, sweetheart, get your wiggly ass over here.'

Norm Zuckerman beckoned Myron forward with a big wave. Esme Fong stood next to him. 'Over here,' he said.

'Hey, Norm,' Myron said. 'Hi, Esme.'

'Hi, Myron,' Esme said. She was dressed a bit more casual today, but she still clutched at her briefcase like it was a favorite stuffed animal.

Norm threw his arm around Myron's back, draping the hand over the sore shoulder. 'Myron, tell me the truth here. The absolute truth. I want the truth, okay?'

'The truth?'

'Very funny. Just tell me this. Nothing more, just this. Am I not a fair man? The truth, now. Am I a fair man?'

'Fair,' Myron said.

'Very fair, am I right? I am a very fair man.'

'Let's not push it, Norm.'

Norm put up both hands, palms out. 'Fine, be that way. I'm fair. Good enough, I'll take it,' He looked over toward Esme Fong. 'Keep in mind, Myron is my adversary. My worst enemy. We're always on opposite sides. Yet he is willing to admit that I'm a fair man. We straight on that?'

Esme rolled her eyes. 'Yes, Norm, but you're preaching to the converted. I already told you that I agreed with you on this—'

'Whoa,' Norm said, as though reining in a frisky pony. 'Just hold the phone a sec, because I want Myron's opinion too. Myron, here's the deal. I bought a golf bag. Just one. I wanted to test it out. Cost me fifteen grand for the year.'

Buying a golf bag meant pretty much what it said.

Norm Zuckerman had bought the rights to advertise on a golf bag. In other words, he put a Zoom logo on it. Most of the golf bags were bought by the big golf companies – Ping, Titleist, Golden Bear, that kind of thing. But more and more often, companies that had nothing to do with golf advertised on the bags. McDonald's, for example. Spring-Air mattresses. Even Pennzoil oil. Pennzoil. Like someone goes to a golf tournament, sees the Pennzoil logo, and buys a can of oil.

'So?' Myron said.

'So, look at it!' Norm pointed at a caddie. 'I mean, just look at it!'

'Okay, I'm looking.'

'Tell me, Myron, do you see a Zoom logo?'

The caddie held the golf bag. Like on every golf bag, there were towels draped over the top in order to clean off the clubs.

Norm Zuckerman spoke in a first-grade-teacher sing-song. 'You can answer orally, Myron, by uttering the syllable "no." Or if that's too taxing on your limited vocabulary, you can merely shake your head from side to side like this.' Norm demonstrated.

'It's under the towel,' Myron said.

Norm dramatically put his hand to his ear. 'Pardon?'

'The logo is under the towel.'

'No shit it's under the towel!' Norm railed. Spectators turned and glared at the crazy man with the long hair and heavy beard. 'What good does that do me, huh? When I film an advertisement for TV, what good would it do me if they stick a towel in front of the camera? When I pay all those schmucks a zillion dollars to wear my sneakers, what good would it do me if they wrapped their feet in towels? If every billboard I had was covered with a great big towel—'

'I get the picture, Norm.'

'Good. I'm not paying fifteen grand for some idiot caddie to cover my logo. So I go over to the idiot caddie and I kindly tell him to move the towel away from my logo and the son of a bitch gives me this look. This look, Myron. Like I'm some brown stain he couldn't rinse out of the toilet. Like I'm this little ghetto Jew who's gonna take his goy crap.'

Myron looked over at Esme. Esme smiled and shrugged.

'Nice talking to you, Norm,' Myron said.

'What? You don't think I'm right?'

'I see your point.'

'So if it was your client, what would you do?'

'Make sure the caddie kept the logo in plain view.'

'Exactamundo.' He swung his arm back around Myron's shoulder and lowered his head conspiratorially. 'So what's going on with you and golf, Myron?' he whispered.

'What do you mean?'

'You're not a golfer. You don't have any golf clients. All of a sudden I see you with my very own eyes closing in on Tad Crispin – and now I hear you're hanging out with the Coldrens.'

'Who told you that?'

'Word gets around. I'm a man with tremendous sources. So what's the deal? Why the sudden interest in golf?'

'I'm a sports agent, Norm. I try to represent athletes. Golfers are athletes. Sort of.'

'Okay, but what's up with the Coldrens?'

'What do you mean?'

'Look, Jack and Linda are lovely people. Connected, if you know what I mean.'

'I don't know what you mean.'

'LBA represents Linda Coldren. Nobody leaves LBA. You know that. They're too big. Jack, well, Jack hasn't done anything in so long, he hasn't even bothered with an agent. So what I'm trying to figure out is, why are the Coldrens suddenly hot to trot with you?'

'Why do you want to figure that out?'

Norm put his hand on his chest. 'Why?'

'Yeah, why would you care?'

'Why?' Norm repeated, incredulous now. 'I'll tell you why. Because of you, Myron. I love you, you know that. We're brothers. Tribe members. I want nothing but the best for you. Hand to God, I mean that. You ever need a recommendation, I'll give it to you, you know that.'

'Uh-huh.' Myron was less than convinced. 'So what's the problem?'

Norm threw up both hands. 'Who said there's a problem? Did I say there was a problem? Did I even use the word *problem*? I'm just curious, that's all. It's part of my nature. I'm a curious guy. A modern-day *yenta*. I ask a lot of questions. I stick my nose in where it doesn't belong. It's part of my makeup.'

'Uh-huh,' Myron said again. He looked over at Esme Fong, who was now comfortably out of earshot. She shrugged at him. Working for Norm Zuckerman probably meant you did a lot of shrugging. But that was part of Norm's technique, his own version of good-cop, bad-cop. He came across as erratic, if not totally irrational, while his assistant – always young, bright, attractive –

was the calming influence you grabbed on to like a life preserver.

Norm elbowed him and nodded toward Esme. 'She's a looker, huh? Especially for a broad from Yale. You ever see what that school matriculates? No wonder they're known as the Bulldogs.'

'You're so progressive, Norm.'

'Ah, screw progressive. I'm an old man, Myron. I'm allowed to be insensitive. On an old man, insensitive is cute. A cute curmudgeon, that's what they call it. By the way, I think Esme is only half.'

'Half?'

'Chinese,' Norm said. 'Or Japanese. Or whatever. I think she's half white too. What do you think?'

'Good-bye, Norm.'

'Fine, be that way. See if I care. So tell me, Myron, how did you hook up with the Coldrens? Win introduce you?'

'Good-bye, Norm.'

Myron walked off a bit, stopping for a moment to watch a golfer hit a drive. He tried to follow the ball's route. No go. He lost sight of it almost immediately. This shouldn't be a surprise really – it is, after all, a tiny white sphere traveling at a rate of over one hundred miles per hour for a distance of several hundred yards – except that Myron was the only person in attendance who couldn't achieve this ophthalmic feat of hawklike proportions. Golfers. Most of them can't read an exit sign on an interstate, but they can follow the trajectory of a golf ball through several solar systems.

No question about it. Golf is a weird sport.

The course was packed with silent fans, though *fan* didn't exactly feel like the right word to Myron. *Parishioners* was a hell of a lot closer. There was a constant

157

reverie on a golf course, a hushed, wide-eyed respect. Every time the ball was hit, the crowd release was nearly orgasmic. People cried sweet bliss and urged the ball with the ardor of *Price Is Right* contestants: Run! Sit! Bite! Grab! Grow teeth! Roll! Hurry! Get down! Get up! – almost like an aggressive mambo instructor. They lamented over a snap hook and a wicked slice and a babied putt and goofy greens and soft greens and waxed greens and the rub of the green and the pursuit of a snowman and being stymied and when the ball traveled off the fairway and on the fringe and in the rough and deep lies and rough lies and bad lies and good lies. They showed admiration when a player got all of that one or ripped a drive or banged it home and gave dirty looks when someone loudly suggested that a certain tee-shot made a certain player 'da man.' They accused a putter who did not reach the hole of hitting the ball 'with your purse, Alice.' Players were constantly playing shots that were 'unplayable.'

Myron shook his head. All sports have their own lexicons, but speaking golfese was tantamount to mastering Swahili. It was like rich people's rap.

But on a day like today – the sun shining, the blue sky unblemished, the summer air smelling like a lover's hair – Myron felt closer to the chalice of golf. He could imagine the course free of spectators, the peace and tranquillity, the same aura that drew Buddhist monks to mountaintop retreats, the double-cut grass so rich and green that God Himself would want to run barefoot. This did not mean Myron got it – he was still a nonbeliever of heretic proportions – but for a brief moment he could at least envision what it was about this game that ensnared and swallowed so many whole.

When he reached the fourteenth green, Jack Coldren was lining up for a fifteen-foot putt. Diane Hoffman took the pin out of the hole. At almost every course in the world, the 'pin' had a flag on the top. But that would just not do at Merion. Instead, the pole was topped with a wicker basket. No one seemed to know why. Win came up with this story about how the old Scots who invented golf used to carry their lunch in baskets on sticks, which could then double as hole markers, but Myron smelled the pungent odor of lore in Win's rationale rather than fact. Either way, Merion's members made a big fuss over these wicker baskets on the end of a big stick. Golfers.

Myron tried to move in closer to Jack Coldren, looking for Win's 'eye of the tiger.' Despite his protestations, Myron knew very well what Win had meant the previous night, the intangibles that separated raw talent from on-field greatness. Desire. Heart. Perseverance. Win spoke about these things as though they were evil. They were not. Quite the opposite, in fact. Win, of all people, should know better. To paraphrase and completely abuse a famous political quote: Extremism in the pursuit of excellence is no vice.

Jack Coldren's expression was smooth and unworried and distant. Only one explanation for that: the zone. Jack had managed to squeeze his way into the hallowed zone, that tranquil room in which no crowd or big payday or famous course or next hole or knee-bending pressure or hostile opponent or successful wife or kidnapped son may reside. Jack's zone was a small place, comprising only his club, a small dimpled ball, and a hole. All else faded away now like the dream sequence in a movie.

This, Myron knew, was Jack Coldren stripped to his purest state. He was a golfer. A man who wanted to win.

Needed to. Myron understood. He had been there – his zone consisting of a large orange ball and a metallic cylinder – and a part of him would always be enmeshed in that world. It was a fine place to be – in many ways, the best place to be. Win was wrong. Winning was not a worthless goal. It was noble. Jack had taken life's hits. He had striven and battled. He had been battered and bloodied. Yet here he stood, head high, on the road to redemption. How many people are awarded this opportunity? How many people truly get the chance to feel this vibrant, to reside for even a short time on such a plateau, to have their hearts and dreams stirred with such unquenchable inner passion?

Jack Coldren stroked the putt. Myron found himself watching the ball slowly arc toward the hole, lost in that vicarious rush that so fiercely drew spectators to sports. He held his breath and felt something like a tear well up in his eye when the ball dropped in. A birdie. Diane Hoffman made a fist and pumped it. The lead was back up to nine strokes.

Jack looked up at the applauding gallery. He acknowledged them with a tip of his hat, but he saw nothing. Still in the zone. Fighting to stay there. For a moment, his eyes locked on Myron's. Myron nodded back, not wanting to nudge him back to reality. Stay in that zone, Myron thought. In that zone, a man can win a tournament. In that zone, a son does not purposely sabotage a father's lifelong dream.

Myron walked past the many portable toilets – they'd been provided by a company with the semiaccurate name Royal Flush – and headed toward Corporate Row. Golf matches had an unprecedented hierarchy for ticket holders. True, at most sporting arenas there was a grading of one sort or another – some had better seats, obviously, while some had access to skyboxes or even courtside seats. But in those cases, you handed a ticket to an usher or ticket collector and took your place. In golf, you displayed your entrance pass all day. The general-admission folk (read: serfs) usually had a sticker plastered on their shirt, not unlike, say, a scarlet letter. Others wore a plastic card that dangled from a metal chain wrapped around their neck. Sponsors (read: feudal lords) wore either red, silver, or gold cards, depending on how much money they spent. There were also different passes for players' family and friends, Merion club members, Merion club officers, even steady sports agents. And the different cards gave you different access to different places. For example, you had to have a colored card to enter Corporate Row. Or you needed a gold card if you wanted to enter one of those exclusive tents – the ones strategically perched on hills like generals' quarters in an old war movie.

Corporate Row was merely a row of tents, each sponsored by one enormous company or another. The theoretical intention of spending at least one hundred grand for a four-day tent rental was to impress corporate clients and gain exposure. The truth, however, was that the tents were a way for the corporate bigwigs to go to the tournament for free. Yes, a few important clients were invited, but Myron also noticed that the company's major officers always managed to show too. And the hundred grand rental fee was just a start. It didn't include the food, the drinks, the employees – not to mention the first-class flights, the deluxe hotel suites, the stretch limos, et cetera, for the bigwigs and their guests.

Boys and girls, can you say, 'Chu-ching goes the cash register'? I thought you could.

Myron gave his name to the pretty young woman at the Lock-Horne tent. Win was not there yet, but Esperanza was sitting at a table in the corner.

'You look like shit,' Esperanza said.

'Maybe. But at least I feel awful.'

'So what happened?'

'Three crackheads adorned with Nazi memorabilia and crowbars jumped me.'

She arched an eyebrow. 'Only three?'

The woman was constant chuckles. He told her about his run-in and narrow escape. When he was finished, Esperanza shook her head and said, 'Hopeless. Absolutely hopeless.'

'Don't get all dewy-eyed on me. I'll be fine.'

'I found Lloyd Rennart's wife. She's an artist of some kind, lives on the Jersey shore.'

'Any word on Lloyd Rennart's body?'

Esperanza shook her head. 'I checked the NVI and Treemaker websites. No death certificate has been issued.'

Myron looked at her. 'You're kidding.'

'Nope. But it might not be on the Web yet. The other offices are closed until Monday. And even if one hasn't been issued, it might not mean anything.'

'Why not?' he asked.

'A body is supposed to be missing for a certain amount of time before the person can be declared dead,' Esperanza explained. 'I don't know – five years or something. But what often happens is that the next of kin files a motion in order to settle insurance claims and the estate. But Lloyd Rennart committed suicide.'

'So there'd be no insurance,' Myron said.

'Right. And assuming everything was held jointly between Rennart and his wife, then there would be no need for her to press it.'

Myron nodded. It made sense. Still it was yet another nagging hangnail that needed to be clipped. 'You want something to drink?' he asked.

She shook her head.

'I'll be right back.' Myron grabbed a Yoo-Hoo. Win had made sure the Lock-Horne tent stocked them. What a pal. A television monitor in the upper corner had a Scoreboard. Jack had just finished the fifteenth hole. Both he and Crispin had parred it. Barring a sudden collapse, Jack was going to take a huge lead into tomorrow's final round.

When Myron got settled again, Esperanza said, 'I want to talk to you about something.'

'Shoot.'

'It's about my graduating law school.'

'Okay,' Myron said, dragging out the word.

'You've been avoiding the subject,' she said.

'What are you talking about? I'm the one who wants to go to your graduation, remember?'

'That's not what I mean.' Her fingers found and began to fiddle with a straw wrapper. 'I'm talking about what happens *after* I graduate. I'm going to be a full-fledged attorney soon. My role in the company should change.'

Myron nodded. 'Agreed.'

'For one thing, I'd like an office.'

'We don't have the space.'

'The conference room is too large,' she countered. 'You can slice a little out of there and a little out of the waiting room. It won't be a huge office, but it'll be good enough.'

Myron nodded slowly. 'We can look into that.'

'It's important to me, Myron.'

'Okay, it sounds possible.'

'Second, I don't want a raise.'

'Don't?'

'That's right.'

'Odd negotiating technique, Esperanza, but you convinced me. Much as I might like to give you a raise, you will not receive one penny more. I surrender.'

'You're doing it again.'

'Doing what?'

'Joking around when I'm serious. You don't like change, Myron. I know that. It's why you lived with your parents until a few months ago. It's why you still keep Jessica around when you should have forgotten about her years ago.'

'Do me a favor,' he said wearily. 'Spare me the amateur analysis, okay?'

'Just stating the facts. You don't like change.'

'Who does? And I love Jessica. You know that.'

'Fine, you love her,' Esperanza said dismissively. 'You're right, I shouldn't have brought it up.'

'Good. Are we done?'

'No.' Esperanza stopped playing with the straw wrapper. She crossed her legs and folded her hands in her lap. 'This isn't easy for me to talk about,' she said.

'Do you want to do it another time?'

She rolled her eyes. 'No, I don't want to do it another time. I want you to listen to me. Really listen.'

Myron stayed silent, leaned forward a little.

'The reason I don't want a raise is because I don't want to work for someone. My father worked his whole life doing menial jobs for a variety of assholes. My mother spent hers cleaning other people's houses.' Esperanza stopped, swallowed, took a breath. 'I don't want to do that. I don't want to spend my life working for anyone.'

'Including me?'

'I said *anyone*, didn't I?' She shook her head. 'Jesus, you just don't listen sometimes.'

Myron opened his mouth, closed it. 'Then I don't see where you're going with this.'

'I want to be a part owner,' she said.

He made a face. 'Of MB SportsReps?'

'No, of AT&T. Of course MB.'

'But the name is MB,' Myron said 'The M is for Myron. B for Bolitar. Your name is Esperanza Diaz. I can't make it MBED. What kind of name is that?'

She just looked at him. 'You're doing it again. I'm trying to have a serious conversation.'

'Now? You pick now when I just got hit over the head with a tire iron—'

'Shoulder.'

'Whatever. Look, you know how much you mean to me—'

'This isn't about our friendship,' she interrupted. 'I don't care what I mean to you right now. I care about what I mean to MB SportsReps.'

'You mean a lot to MB. A hell of a lot.' He stopped.

'But?'

'But nothing. You just caught me a little off balance, that's all. I was just jumped by a group of neo-Nazis. That does funny things to the psyche of people of my persuasion. I'm also trying to solve a possible kidnapping. I know things have to change. I planned on giving you more to do, letting you handle more negotiations, hiring someone new. But a partnership . . . that's a different kettle of gefilte.'

Her voice was unyielding. 'Meaning?'

'Meaning I'd like to think about it, okay? How do you plan on becoming a partner? What percentage do you want? Do you want to buy in or work your way in or what? These are things we'll have to go over, and I don't think now is the time.'

'Fine.' She stood up. 'I'm going to hang around the players' lounge. See if I can strike up a conversation with one of the wives.'

'Good idea.'

'I'll see you later.' She turned to leave.

'Esperanza?'

She looked at him.

'You're not mad, right?'

'Not mad,' she repeated.

'We'll work something out,' he said.

She nodded. 'Right.'

'Don't forget. We're meeting with Tad Crispin an hour after they finish. By the pro shop.'

'You want me there?'

'Yes.'

She shrugged. 'Okay.' Then she left.

Myron leaned back and watched her go. Great. Just what he needed. His best friend in the world as a business partner. It never worked. Money screwed up relationships; it was simply one of life's givens. His father and his uncle – two closer brothers you never saw – had tried it. The outcome had been disastrous. Dad finally bought Uncle Morris out, but the two men didn't speak to each other for four years. Myron and Win had labored painstakingly to keep their businesses separate while maintaining the same interests and goals. It worked because there was no cross-interference or money to divide up. With Esperanza things had been great, but that was because the relationship had always been boss and employee. Their roles were well defined. But at the same time, he understood. Esperanza deserved this chance. She had earned it. She was more than an important employee to MB. She was a part of it.

So what to do?

He sat back and chugged the Yoo-Hoo, waiting for an idea. Fortunately, his thoughts were waylaid when someone tapped his shoulder.

Chapter 17

'Hello.'

Myron turned around. It was Linda Coldren. Her head was wrapped in a semi-babushka and she wore dark sunglasses. Greta Garbo circa 1984. She opened her purse. 'I forwarded the home phone here,' she whispered, pointing to a cellular phone in the purse. 'Mind if I sit down?'

'Please do,' Myron said.

She sat facing him. The sunglasses were big, but Myron could still see a hint of redness around the rims of her eyes. Her nose, too, looked like it had been rubbed raw by a Kleenex overdose. 'Anything new?' she asked.

He told her about the Crusty Nazis jumping him. Linda asked several follow-up questions. Again the internal paradox tore at her: she wanted her son to be safe, yet she did not want it all to be a hoax. Myron finished by saying, 'I still think we should get in touch with the feds. I can do it quietly.'

She shook her head. 'Too risky.'

'So is going on like this.'

Linda Coldren shook her head again and leaned back. For several moments they sat in silence. Her gaze was cast somewhere over his shoulder. Then she said, 'When Chad was born, I took off nearly two years. Did you know that?'

'No,' Myron said.

'Women's golf,' she muttered, 'I was at the height of my game, the top female golfer in the world, and yet you never read about it.'

'I don't follow golf much,' Myron said.

'Yeah, right,' she snorted. 'If Jack Nicklaus took two years off, you would have heard about it.'

Myron nodded. She had a point. 'Was it tough coming back?' he asked.

'You mean in terms of playing or leaving my son?'

'Both.'

She took a breath and considered the question. 'I missed playing,' she said. 'You have no idea how much. I regained the number one spot in a couple of months. As for Chad, well, he was still an infant. I hired a nanny to travel with us.'

'How long did that last?'

'Until Chad was three. That's when I realized that I couldn't drag him around anymore. It wasn't fair to him. A child needs some sort of stability. So I had to make a choice.'

They fell into silence.

'Don't get me wrong,' she said. 'I'm not into the self-pity thing and I'm glad women are given choices. But what they don't tell you is that when you have choices, you have guilt.'

'What kind of guilt?'

'A mother's guilt, the worst kind there is. The pangs are constant and ceaseless. They haunt your sleep. They point accusatory ringers. Every joyous swing of the golf club made me feel like I was forsaking my own child. I flew home as often as I could. I missed some tournaments that I really wanted to play in. I tried damn hard to balance career and motherhood. And every step of the way, I felt like a selfish louse.' She looked at him. 'Do you understand that?'

'Yes, I think so.'

'But you don't really sympathize,' she added.

'Of course I do.'

Linda Coldren gave him a skeptical glance. 'If I had been a stay-at-home mother, would you have been so quick to suspect that Chad was behind this? Didn't the fact that I was an absent mother sway your thinking?'

'Not an absent mother,' Myron corrected. 'Absent parents.'

'Same thing.'

'No. You were making more money. You were by far the more successful parent business-wise. If anyone should have stayed home, it was Jack.'

She smiled. 'Aren't we politically correct?'

'Nope. Just practical.'

'But it's not that simple, Myron. Jack loves his son. And during the years he didn't qualify for the tour, he did stay home with him. But let's face facts: Like it or not, it's the mother who bears that burden.'

'Doesn't make it right.'

'Nor does it let me off the hook. Like I said, I made my choices. If I had to do it all over again, I still would have toured.'

'And you still would have felt guilty.'

She nodded. 'With choice comes guilt. No escaping it.'

Myron took a sip of his Yoo-Hoo. 'You said that Jack stayed home some of the time.'

'Yes,' she said. 'When he failed Q school.'

'Q school?'

'Qualifying school,' she said. 'Every year the top 125 moneymakers get their PGA Tour card automatically. A couple of other players get sponsor exemptions. The rest are forced to go to Q school. Qualifying school. If you don't do well there, you don't play for the year.'

'One tournament decides all that?'

She tilted the glass at him as though making a toast. 'That's right.'

Talk about pressure. 'So when Jack failed Q school, he'd stay home for the year?'

She nodded.

'How did Jack and Chad get along?'

'Chad used to worship his father,' Linda said.

'And now?'

She looked off, her face vaguely pained. 'Now Chad is old enough to wonder why his father keeps losing. I don't know what he thinks anymore. But Jack is a good man. He tries very hard. You have to understand what happened to him. Losing the Open that way – it might sound overly melodramatic, but it killed something inside him. Not even having a son could make him whole.'

'It shouldn't matter so much,' Myron said, hearing the echo of Win in his words. 'It was just one tournament.'

'You were involved in a lot of big games,' she said. 'Ever choke away a victory like Jack did?'

'No.'

'Neither have I.'

Two gray-haired men sporting matching green ascots made their way down the buffet table. They leaned over each food selection and frowned like it had ants. Their plates were still piled high enough to cause the occasional avalanche.

'There's something else,' Linda said.

Myron waited.

She adjusted the sunglasses and put her hands on the table palms down. 'Jack and I are not close. We've haven't been close in many years.'

When she didn't continue, Myron said, 'But you've stayed married.'

'Yes.'

He wanted to ask why, but the question was so obvious, just hanging out there within easy view, that to voice it would be redundant.

'I am a constant reminder of his failures,' she continued. 'It's not easy for a man to live with that. We're supposed to be life partners, but I have what Jack longs for most.' Linda tilted her head. 'It's funny.'

'What?'

'I never allow mediocrity on the golf course. Yet I allowed it to dominate my personal life. Don't you find that odd?'

Myron made a noncommittal motion with his head. He could feel Linda's unhappiness radiating off her like a breaking fever. She looked up now and smiled at him. The smile was intoxicating, nearly breaking his heart. He found himself wanting to lean over and hold Linda Coldren. He felt this almost uncontrollable urge to press her against him and feel the sheen of her hair in his face. He tried to remember the last time he had held such thought for any woman but Jessica; no answer came to him.

'Tell me about you,' Linda suddenly said.

The change of subject caught him off guard. He sort of shook his head. 'Boring stuff.'

'Oh, I doubt that,' she said, almost playfully. 'Come on now. It'll distract me.'

Myron shook his head again.

'I know you almost played pro basketball. I know you hurt your knee. I know you went to law school at Harvard. And I know you tried to make a comeback a few months ago. Want to fill in the blanks?'

'That's pretty much it.'

'No, I don't think so, Myron. Aunt Cissy didn't say that you could help us because you were good at basketball.'

'I worked a bit for the government.'

'With Win?'

'Yes.'

'Doing what?'

Again he shook his head.

'Top secret, huh?'

'Something like that.'

'And you date Jessica Culver?'

'Yes.'

'I like her books.'

He nodded.

'Do you love her?'

'Very much.'

'So what do you want?'

'Want?'

'Out of life. What are your dreams?'

He smiled. 'You're kidding, right?'

'Just getting to the heart of the matter,' Linda said. 'Humor me. What do you want, Myron?' She looked at him with keen interest. Myron felt flushed.

'I want to marry Jessica. I want to move to the suburbs. I want to raise a family.'

She leaned back as though satisfied. 'For real?'

'Yes.'

'Like your parents?'

'Yes.'

She smiled. 'I think that's nice.'

'It's simple,' he said.

'Not all of us are built for the simple life,' she said, 'even if it's what we want.'

Myron nodded. 'Deep, Linda. I don't know what it means, but it sounded deep.'

'Me neither.' She laughed. It was deep and throaty and Myron liked the sound of it. 'Tell me where you met Win.'

'At college,' Myron said. 'Freshman year.'

'I haven't seen him since he was eight years old.' Linda Coldren took a swallow of her seltzer. 'I was fifteen then. Jack and I had already been dating a year, believe it or not. Win loved Jack, by the way. Did you know that?'

'No,' Myron said.

'It's true. He followed Jack everywhere. And Jack could be such a prick back then. He bullied other kids. He was mischievous as all hell. At times he was downright cruel.'

'But you fell for him?'

'I was fifteen,' she said, as if that explained everything. And maybe it did.

'What was Win like as a kid?' Myron asked.

She smiled again, the lines in the corners of her eyes and lips deepening. 'Trying to figure him out, eh?'

'Just curious,' Myron said, but the truth in her words stung. He suddenly wanted to withdraw the question, but it was too late.

'Win was never a happy kid. He was always' – Linda stopped, searching for the word – 'off. I don't know how else to put it. He wasn't crazy or flaky or aggressive or anything like that. But something was not right with him. Always. Even as a child, he had this strange ability to detach.'

Myron nodded. He knew what she meant.

'Aunt Cissy is like that too.'

'Win's mother?'

Linda nodded.' 'The woman can be pure ice when she wants to be. Even when it comes to Win. She acts as though he doesn't exist.'

'She must talk about him,' Myron said. 'To your father, at least.'

Linda shook her head. 'When Aunt Cissy told my father to contact Win, it was the first time she'd mentioned his name to him in years.'

Myron said nothing. Again the obvious question hung in the air unasked: What had happened between Win and his mother? But Myron would never voice it. This conversation had already gone too far. Asking would be an unforgivable betrayal; if Win wanted him to know, he'd tell him.

Time passed, but neither one of them noticed. They talked, mostly about Chad and the kind of son he was. Jack had held on and still led by eight strokes. A gigantic lead. If he blew it this time, it would be worse than twenty-three years ago.

The tent began to empty out, but Myron and Linda stayed and talked some more. A feeling of intimacy began to warm him; he found it hard to breathe when he looked at her. For a moment he closed his eyes. Nothing, he realized, was really going on here. If there was an attraction of some sort, it was simply a classic case of damsel-in-distress syndrome – and there was nothing less politically correct (not to mention Neanderthal) than that.

The crowd was gone now. For a long time nobody came into view. At one point, Win stuck his head into the tent. Seeing them together, he arched an eyebrow and then slipped back out.

Myron checked his watch. 'I have to go. I have an appointment.'

'With whom?'

'Tad Crispin.'

'Here at Merion?'

'Yes.'

'Do you think you'll be long?'

'No.'

She started fiddling with her engagement ring, studying it as though making an appraisal. 'Do you mind if I wait?' she asked. 'We can catch dinner together.' She took off her glasses. The eyes were puffy, but they were also strong and focused.

'Okay.'

He met up with Esperanza at the clubhouse. She made a face at him.

'What?' he said.

'You thinking about Jessica?' Esperanza asked suspiciously.

'No, why?'

'Because you're making your nauseating, lovesick-puppy face. You know. The one that makes me want to throw up on your shoes.'

'Come on,' he said. 'Tad Crispin is waiting.'

*

The meeting ended with no deal. But they were getting close.

'That contract he signed with Zoom,' Esperanza said. 'A major turkey.'

'I know.'

'Crispin likes you.'

'We'll see what happens,' Myron said.

He excused himself and walked quickly back to the tent. Linda Coldren was in the same seat, her back to him, her posture still queenlike.

'Linda?'

'It's dark now,' she said softly. 'Chad doesn't like the dark. I know he's sixteen, but I still leave the hall light on. Just in case.'

Myron remained still. When she turned toward him – when he first saw her smile – it was like something cork-screwed into his heart. 'When Chad was little,' she began, 'he always carried around this red plastic golf club and Wiffle ball. It's funny. When I think about him now, that's how I see him. With that little red club. For a long time I hadn't been able to picture him like that. He's so much like a man now. But since he's been gone, all I see is that little, happy kid in the backyard hitting golf balls.'

Myron nodded. He stretched out his hand toward hers. 'Let's go, Linda,' he said gently.

She stood. They walked together in silence. The night sky was so bright it looked wet. Myron wanted to reach out and hold her hand. But he didn't. When they got to her car, Linda unlocked it with a remote control. Then she opened the door as Myron began circling for the passenger side. He stopped suddenly.

The envelope was on her seat.

For several seconds, neither of them moved. The

envelope was manila, big enough for an eight-by-ten photograph. It was flat except for an area in the middle that puffed up a bit.

Linda Coldren looked up at Myron. Myron reached down, and using his palms, he picked up the envelope by the edges. There was writing on the back. Block letters:

I WARNED YOU NOT SEEK HELP
NOW CHAD PAYS THE PRICE
CROSS US AGAIN AND IT WILL GET MUCH WORSE.

Dread wrapped Myron's chest in tight steel bands. He slowly reached out and tentatively touched the puffy part with just a knuckle. It felt claylike. Carefully, Myron slit the seal open. He turned the envelope upside down and let the contents fall to the car seat.

The severed finger bounced once and then settled onto the leather.

Chapter 18

Myron stared, unable to speak.

Ohmygodohmygodohmygodohmygod . . .

Raw terror engulfed him. He started shivering, and his body went numb. He looked down at the note in his hand. A voice inside his head said, *Your fault, Myron. Your fault.*

He turned to Linda Coldren. Her hand fluttered near her mouth, her eyes wide.

Myron tried to step toward her, but he staggered like a boxer who didn't take advantage of a standing eight count. 'We have to call someone,' he managed, his voice sounding distant even to him. 'The FBI. I have friends—'

'No.' Her tone was strong.

'Linda, listen to me . . .'

'Read the note,' she said.

'But—'

'Read the note,' she repeated. She lowered her head grimly. 'You're out of this now, Myron.'

'You don't know what you're dealing with.'

'Oh no?' Her head snapped up. Her hands tightened into fists. 'I'm dealing with a sick monster,' she said. 'The kind of monster who maims at the slightest provocation.' She stepped closer to the car. 'He cut off my son's finger just because I talked to you. What do you think he'd do if I went directly against his orders?'

Myron's head swirled. 'Linda, paying off the ransom doesn't guarantee—'

'I know that,' she interrupted.

'But . . .' His mind flailed about helplessly and then said something exceedingly dumb. 'You don't even know if it's his finger.'

She looked down now. With one hand, she held back a sob. With the other, she caressed the finger lovingly, without a trace of repulsion on her face. 'Yes,' Linda said softly. 'I do.'

'He may already be dead.'

'Then it makes no difference what I do, does it?'

Myron stopped himself from saying any more. He had sounded asinine enough. He just needed a moment or two to gather himself, to figure out what the next step should be.

Your fault, Myron. Your fault.

He shook it off. He had, after all, been in worse scrapes. He had seen dead bodies, taken on some very bad people, caught and brought killers to justice. He just needed—

All with Win's help, Myron. Never on your own.

Linda Coldren lifted the finger into view. Tears streamed down her cheeks, but her face remained a placid pool.

'Good-bye, Myron.'

'Linda . . .'

'I'm not going to disobey him again.'

'We have to think this through—'

She shook her head. 'We should never have contacted you.'

Cupping her son's severed finger like a baby chick, Linda Coldren slid into the car. She put the finger down carefully and started the car. Then she shifted it into gear and drove away.

Myron made his way to his car. For several minutes he sat and took deep breaths, willing himself to calm down. He had studied martial arts since Win had first introduced him to tae kwon do when they were college freshmen. Meditation was a big part of what they'd learned, yet Myron never quite grasped the critical nuances. His mind had a habit of drifting. Now he tried to practice the simple rules. He closed his eyes. He breathed in through the nose slowly, forcing it down low, letting only his stomach, not his chest, expand. He released it through the mouth, even slower, draining his lungs fully.

Okay, he thought, what is your next step?

The first answer to float to the surface was the most basic: Give up. Cut your losses. Realize that you are very much out of your element. You never really worked for the feds. You only accompanied Win. You were way out of your league on this and it cost a sixteen-year-old boy his finger and maybe more. As Esperanza had said, 'Without Win, you're hopeless.' Learn your lesson and walk away.

And then what? Let the Coldrens face this crisis alone?

If he had, maybe Chad Coldren would still have ten fingers.

The thought made something inside of him crumble. He opened his eyes. His heart started trip-hammering again. He couldn't call the Coldrens. He couldn't call the feds. If he pursued this on his own, he would be risking Chad Coldren's life.

He started up the car, still trying to regain his balance. It was time to be analytical. It was time to be cold. He had to look at this latest development as a clue for a moment. Forget the horror. Forget the fact that he might have screwed up. The finger was just a clue.

One: The placement of the envelope was curious – inside Linda Coldren's locked (yes, it had been locked – Linda had used the remote control to open it) car. How had it gotten there? Had the kidnapper simply broken into the vehicle? Good possibility, but would he have had time in Merion's parking lot? Wouldn't someone have reported it? Probably. Did Chad Coldren have a key that the kidnapper could have used? Hmm. Very good possibility, but one he couldn't confirm unless he spoke to Linda, which was out of the question.

Dead end. For now.

Two: More than one person was involved in this kidnapping. This hardly took brilliant detective work. First off, you have the Crusty Nazi. The phone call at the mall proved that he had something to do with this – not to mention his subsequent behavior. But there was no way a guy like Crusty could sneak into Merion and plant the envelope in Linda Coldren's car. Not without drawing suspicion. Not during the US Open. And the note had warned the Coldrens not to 'cross' them again. Cross. Did that sound like a Crusty word?

Okay, good. What else?

Three: The kidnappers were both vicious and dumb.

Vicious was again obvious – the dumb part maybe less so. But look at the facts. For example, making a large ransom demand over a weekend when you know that the banks won't be open until Monday – was that bright? Not knowing how much to ask for the first two times they called – didn't that say ding-a-ling? And lastly, was it really prudent to cut off a kid's finger just because his parents happened to talk to a sports agent? Did that even make sense?

No.

Unless, of course, the kidnappers knew that Myron was more than a sports agent.

But how?

Myron pulled into Win's long driveway. Unfamiliar people were taking horses out of the stable. As he approached the guest house, Win appeared in the doorway. Myron pulled into a spot and got out.

'How did your meeting with Tad Crispin go?' Win asked.

Myron hurried over to him. 'They chopped off his finger,' he managed, breathy to the point of almost hyperventilating. 'The kidnappers. They cut off Chad's finger. Left it in Linda's car.'

Win's expression did not change. 'Did you discover this before or after your meeting with Tad Crispin?'

Myron was puzzled by the question. 'After.'

Win nodded slowly. 'Then my original question remains: How did your meeting go with Tad Crispin?'

Myron stepped back as though slapped. 'Jesus Christ,' he said in an almost reverent tone. 'You can't be serious.'

'What happens to that family does not concern me. What happens to your business dealings with Tad Crispin does.'

Myron shook his head, stunned. 'Not even you could be that cold.'

'Oh please.'

'Please what?'

'There are far greater tragedies in this world than a sixteen-year-old boy losing his finger. People die, Myron. Floods wipe out entire villages. Men do horrible things to children every day.' He paused. 'Did you, for example, read this afternoon's paper?'

'What are you rambling about?'

'I'm just trying to make you understand,' Win continued in too slow, too measured a voice. 'The Coldrens mean nothing to me – no more than any other stranger and perhaps less. The newspaper is filled with tragedies that hit me on a more personal level. For example . . .'

Win stopped and looked at Myron very steadily.

'For example what?' Myron asked.

'There was a new development in the Kevin Morris case,' Win replied. 'Are you familiar with that one?'

Myron shook his head.

'Two seven-year-old boys – Billy Waters and Tyrone Duffy – have been missing for nearly three weeks. They disappeared while riding their bikes home from school. The police questioned one Kevin Morris, a man with a long record of perversion, including molestation, who had been hanging around the school. But Mr Morris had a very sharp attorney. There was no physical evidence and despite a fairly convincing circumstantial case – they found the boys' bikes in a Dumpster not far from his home – Mr Morris was set free.'

Myron felt something cold press against his heart. 'So what was the new development, Win?'

'The police received a tip late last night.'

'How late?'

Again Win looked at him steadily. 'Very late.'

Silence.

'It seems,' Win went on, 'that someone had witnessed Kevin Morris burying the bodies off a road in the woods near Lancaster. The police dug them up last night. Do you know what they found?'

Myron shook his head again, afraid to even open his mouth.

'Billy Waters and Tyrone Duffy were both dead. They'd been sexually molested and mutilated in ways that even the media couldn't report. The police also found enough evidence at the burial site to arrest Kevin Morris. Fingerprints on a medical scalpel. Plastic bags that matched ones in his kitchen. Semen samples that offer a preliminary match in both boys.'

Myron flinched.

'Everyone seems quite confident that Mr Morris will be convicted,' Win finished.

'What about the person who called in the tip? Will he be a witness?'

'Funny thing,' Win said. 'The man called from a pay phone and never gave his name. No one, it seems, knows who he was.'

'But the police captured Kevin Morris?'

'Yes.'

The two men stared at each other.

'I'm surprised you didn't kill him,' Myron said.

'Then you really don't know me.'

A horse whinnied. Win turned and looked at the magnificent animal. Something strange came across his face, a look of loss.

'What did she do to you, Win?'

Win kept staring. They both knew whom Myron was talking about.

'What did she do to make you hate so much?'

'Don't engage in too much hyperbole, Myron. I am not that simple. My mother is not solely responsible for shaping me. A man is not made up of one incident, and I am a far cry from crazy, as you suggested earlier. Like any other human being, I choose my battles. I battle quite a bit – more than most – and usually on the right side. I battled for Billy Waters and Tyrone Duffy. But I do not wish to battle for the Coldrens. That is my choice. You, as my closest friend, should respect that. You should not try to prod or guilt me into a battle I do not wish to fight.'

Myron was not sure what to say. It was scary when he could understand Win's cold logic. 'Win?'

Win wrested his gaze from the horse. He looked at Myron.

'I'm in trouble,' Myron said, hearing the desperation in his tone. 'I need your help.'

Win's voice was suddenly soft, his face almost pained. 'If that were true, I'd be there. You know that. But you are not in any trouble from which you cannot easily disentangle. Just back away, Myron. You have the option of ending your involvement. To draw me into this against my will – using our friendship in that way – is wrong. Walk away this time.'

'You know I can't do that.'

Win nodded and headed toward his car. 'Like I said, we all choose our battles.'

When he entered the guest house, Esperanza was screaming, 'Bankrupt! Lose a turn! Bankrupt!'

Myron came up behind her. She was watching *Wheel of Fortune*.

'This woman is so greedy,' Esperanza said, gesturing at the screen. 'She's got over six thousand dollars and she keeps spinning. I hate that.'

The wheel stopped, landing on the glittery $1,000. The woman asked for a *B*. There were two of them. Esperanza groaned. 'You're back early,' she said. 'I thought you were going out to dinner with Linda Coldren.'

'It didn't work out.'

Esperanza finally turned around and looked at his face. 'What happened?'

He told her. Her dark complexion lost a bit of color along the way. When he finished, Esperanza said, 'You need Win.'

'He won't help.'

'Time to swallow your macho pride and ask him. Beg him if you have to.'

'Been there, done that. He's out.' On the television, the greedy woman bought a vowel. This always baffled Myron. Why do contestants who clearly know the puzzle's solution still buy vowels? To waste money? To make sure their opponents know the answer too?

'But,' he said, 'you're here.'

Esperanza looked at him. 'So?'

It was, he knew, the real reason she had come down in the first place. On the phone she had told him that he didn't work well alone. The words spoke volumes about her true motivation for fleeing the Big Apple.

'Do you want to help?' he asked.

The greedy woman leaned forward, spun the wheel, and then started clapping and shouting, 'Come on, a thousand!' Her opponents clapped too. Like they wanted her to do well. Right.

'What do you want me to do?' Esperanza asked.

'I'll explain on the way. If you want to come.'

They both watched the wheel decelerate. The camera moved in for a close-up. The arrow slowed and slowed before settling on the word BANKRUPT. The audience groaned. The greedy woman kept the smile, but now she looked like someone had just punched her hard in the stomach.

'That's an omen,' Esperanza said.

'Good or bad?' Myron asked.

'Yes.'

Chapter 19

The girls were still at the mall. Still at the food court. Still at the same table. It was amazing, when you thought about it. The long summer days beckoned with sunny skies and chirping birds. School was out, and yet so many teenagers spent all their time inside a glorified school cafeteria, probably lamenting the day they would have to return to school.

Myron shook his head. He was complaining about teenagers. A sure sign of lost youth. Soon he'd be screaming at someone for turning up the thermostat.

As soon as he entered the food court, the girls all turned in his direction. It was like they had people-we-know detectors at every entrance. Myron did not hesitate. Making his expression as stern as possible, he rushed toward them. He studied each face as he approached. These were, after all, just teenagers. The guilty one, Myron was sure, would show it.

And she did. Almost instantly.

She was the one that had been teased yesterday, the one they taunted for being the recipient of a Crusty smile. Missy or Messy or something. It all made sense now. Crusty hadn't spotted Myron's tail. He'd been tipped off. In fact, the whole thing had been arranged. That was how Crusty had known that Myron had been asking questions about him. That explained the seemingly fortuitous timing – that is, Crusty hanging around the food court just long enough for Myron to arrive.

It had all been a big setup.

The one with Elsa Lancaster hair screwed up her face and said, 'Like, what's the matter?'

'That guy tried to kill me,' Myron said.

Lots of gasps. Faces lit up with excitement. To most of them, this was like a television show come to life. Only Missy or Messy or some name with an *M* remained rock-still.

'Not to worry though,' Myron continued. 'We've just about got him. In an hour or two, he'll be under arrest. The police are on their way to find him right now. I just wanted to thank you all for your cooperation.'

The *M* girl spoke: 'I thought you weren't a cop.'

A sentence without the word *like*. Hmm. 'I'm undercover,' Myron said.

'Oh. My. God.'

'Get out!'

'Whoa!'

'You mean like on *New York Undercover*?'

Myron, no stranger to TV, had no idea what she was talking about. 'Exactly,' he said.

'This is *so* cool.'

'Are we, like, going to be on TV?'

'The six o'clock news?'

'That guy on Channel Four is *so* cute, you know?'

'My hair totally sucks.'

'No way, Amber. But mine is like a total rat nest.'

Myron cleared his throat. 'We have this pretty much all wrapped up. Except for one thing. The accomplice.'

Myron waited for one of them to say, 'Accomplice?' No one did. Myron elaborated. 'Someone in this very mall helped that creep set me up.'

'In, like, here?

'In *our* mall?'

'Not *our* mall. No way.'

They said the word *mall* like some people said the word *synagogue*.

'Someone helped that skank?'

'*Our* mall?'

'Eeeuw.'

'I can't, like, believe it.'

'Believe it,' Myron said. 'In fact, he or she is probably here right now. Watching us.'

Heads swirled about. Even *M* managed to get into the act, though it was an uninspired display.

Myron had shown the stick. Now the carrot. 'Look, I want you ladies to keep your eyes and ears open. We'll catch the accomplice. No question about it. Guys like that always talk. But if the accomplice was just a hapless dupe . . .'

Blank faces.

'If she, like, didn't really know the score' – not exactly hip-hop lingo, but they nodded now – 'and she came to me right away, before the cops nail her, well, then I'd probably be able to help her out. Otherwise, she could be charged with attempted murder.'

Nothing. Myron had expected that. *M* would never

admit this in front of her friends. Jail was a great fear-inducer, but it was little more than a wet match next to the bonfire that was teenage peer pressure.

'Good-bye, ladies.'

Myron moved to the other side of the food court. He leaned against a pillar, putting himself in the path between the girls' table and the bathroom. He waited, hoping she'd make an excuse and come over. After about five minutes, M stood up and began walking toward Myron. Just as he planned. Myron almost smiled. Maybe he should have been a high school guidance counselor. Mold young minds, change lives for the better.

The M girl veered away from him and toward the exit. Damn.

Myron quickly trotted over, the smile on full blast. 'Mindy?' He had suddenly remembered her name.

She turned to him but said nothing.

He put on the soft voice and the understanding eyes. A male Oprah. A kinder, gentler Regis. 'Whatever you say to me is confidential,' he said. 'If you're involved in this—'

'Just stay away from me, okay? I'm not, like, involved in anything.'

She pushed past him and hurried past Foot Locker and the Athlete's Foot – two stores Myron had always assumed were the same, alter egos if you will, like you never saw Batman and Bruce Wayne in the same room.

Myron watched her go. She hadn't cracked, which was a bit of a surprise. He nodded and his backup plan went into action. Mindy kept hurrying away, glancing behind her every few steps to make sure Myron wasn't following her. He wasn't.

Mindy, however, did not notice the attractive, jean-clad Hispanic woman just a few feet to her left.

Mindy found a pay phone by the record store that looked exactly like every other mall record store. She glanced about, put a quarter into the slot, and dialed a number. Her finger had just pressed the seventh digit when a small hand reached over her shoulder and hung up the phone.

She spun toward Esperanza. 'Hey!'

Esperanza said, 'Put down the phone.'

'Hey!'

'Right, hey. Now put down the phone.'

'Like, who the fuck are you?'

'Put down the phone,' Esperanza repeated, 'or I'll shove it up a nostril.'

Wide-eyed with confusion, Mindy obeyed. Several seconds later, Myron appeared. He looked at Esperanza. 'Up a nostril?'

She shrugged.

Mindy shouted, 'You can't, like, do that.'

'Do what?' Myron said.

'Like' – Mindy stopped, struggled with the thought – 'like, make me hang up a phone?'

'No law against that,' Myron said. He turned to Esperanza. 'You know any law against that?'

'Against hanging up a phone?' Esperanza emphatically shook her head. 'No, señor.'

'See, no law against it. On the other hand, there is a law against aiding and abetting a criminal. It's called a felony. It means jail time.'

'I didn't aid nothing. And I don't bet.'

Myron turned to Esperanza. 'You get the number?'

She nodded and gave it to him.

'Let's trace it.'

Again, the cyber-age made this task frightening easy. Anybody can buy a computer program at their local software store or hop on certain websites like Biz, type in the number, and voilà, you have a name and address.

Esperanza used a cellular phone to dial the home number of MB SportsReps' new receptionist. Her name was, fittingly, Big Cyndi. Six-five and over three hundred pounds, Big Cyndi had wrestled professionally under the moniker Big Chief Mama, tag-team partner of Esperanza 'Little Pocahontas' Diaz. In the ring, Big Cyndi wore makeup like Tammy Faye on steroids; spiked hair that would have been the envy of Sid and Nancy; ripped muscle-displaying T-shirts; and an awful, sneering glare complete with a ready growl. In real life, well, she was exactly the same.

Speaking Spanish, Esperanza gave Cyndi the number.

Mindy said, 'Hey, I'm, like, outta here.'

Myron grabbed her arm. ' 'Fraid not.'

'Hey! You can't, like, hold me here.'

Myron maintained his grip.

'I'll scream rape.'

Myron rolled his eyes. 'At a mall pay phone. In broad fluorescent light. When I'm standing here with my girlfriend.'

Mindy looked at Esperanza. 'She's your girlfriend?'

'Yes.'

Esperanza began whistling 'Dream Weaver.'

'But you can't, like, make me stay with you.'

'I don't get it, Mindy. You look like a nice girl.' Actually, she was wearing black leggings, too-high pumps, a red halter top, and what looked like a dog choker around her neck. 'Are you trying to tell me that this guy is worth going to jail over? He deals drugs, Mindy. He tried to kill me.'

Esperanza hung up. 'It's a bar called the Parker Inn.'

'You know where it is?' he asked Mindy.

'Yeah.'

'Come on.'

Mindy pulled away. 'Let go,' she said, stretching out the last word.

'Mindy, this isn't fun and games here. You helped someone try to kill me.'

'So you say.'

'What?'

Mindy put her hands on her hips, chewed gum. 'So, like, how do I know that you're not the bad one, huh?'

'Excuse me?'

'You, like, come up to us yesterday, right, all mysterious and stuff, right? You don't, like, have a badge or nothing. How do I know that you aren't, like, after Tito? How do I know that you aren't another drug dealer trying to take over his turf?'

' "Tito?" ' Myron repeated, looking at Esperanza. 'A neo-Nazi named Tito?'

Esperanza shrugged.

'None of his friends, like, call him Tito,' Mindy went on. 'It's way too long, you know? So they call him Tit.'

Myron and Esperanza exchanged a glance, shook their heads. Too easy.

'Mindy,' Myron said slowly, 'I wasn't kidding back there. Tito is not a nice fellow. He may, in fact, be involved in kidnapping and maiming a boy about your age. Somebody cut off the boy's finger and sent it to his mother.'

Her face pinched up. 'Oh, that's, like, so gross.'

'Help me, Mindy.'

'You a cop?'

'No,' Myron said. 'I'm just trying to save a boy.'

She waved her hands dismissively. 'Then, like, go. You don't need me.'

'I'd like you to come with us.'

'Why?'

'So you don't try to warn Tito.'

'I won't.'

Myron shook his head. 'You also know how to get to Parker Inn. It'll save us time.'

'Uh-uh, no way. I'm not going with you.'

'If you don't,' Myron said, 'I'll tell Amber and Trish and the gang all about your new boyfriend.'

That snared her attention. 'He's not my boyfriend,' she insisted. 'We just, like, hung out a couple of times.'-

Myron smiled. 'So I'll lie,' he said. 'I'll tell them you slept with him.'

'I did not!' she screamed. 'That's, like, so unfair.'

Myron shrugged helplessly.

She crossed her arms and chewed her gum. Her version of defiance. It didn't last long. 'Okay, okay, I'll go.' She pointed a finger at Myron. 'But I don't want Tit to see me, okay? I stay in the car.'

'Deal,' Myron said. He shook his head. Now they were after a man named Tit. What next?

The Parker Inn was a total redneck, biker, skeezer bar. The parking lot was packed with pickup trucks and motorcycles. Country music blared from the constantly opening door. Several men in John Deere baseball caps were using the side of the building as a urinal. Every once in a while one would turn and piss on another. Curses and laughter spewed forward. Fun city.

From his car parked across the street, Myron looked at Mindy and said, 'You used to hang out here?'

She shrugged. 'I, like, came here a couple of times,' she said. 'For excitement, you know?'

Myron nodded. 'Why didn't you just douse yourself with gasoline and light matches?'

'Fuck you, all right? You my father now?'

He held his hands up. She was right. None of his business. 'Do you see Tito's truck?' Myron just couldn't call him Tit. Maybe if he got to know him better.

Mindy scanned the lot. 'No.'

Neither did Myron. 'Do you know where he lives?'

'No.'

Myron shook his head. 'He deals drugs. He wears a swastika tattoo. And he has no ass. But don't tell me . . . underneath all that, Tito is really sweet.'

Mindy shouted, 'Fuck you, all right? Just fuck you.'

'Myron,' Esperanza said by way of warning.

Again Myron put his hands up. They all sat back and watched. Nothing happened.

Mindy sighed as audibly as possible. 'So, like, can I go home now?'

Esperanza said, 'I have a thought.'

'What?' Myron asked.

Esperanza pulled the tail of her blouse out of her jeans. She tied it up, making a knot under her rib cage and revealing plenty of flat, dark stomach. Then she unbuttoned her top to a daring low. A black bra was now visible, Myron noticed, trained detective that he was. She pulled down the visor mirror and began to apply makeup. Lots of makeup. Far too much makeup. She mussed up her hair a bit and rolled up her jeans cuffs. When she finished she smiled at Myron.

'How do I look?' she asked.

Even Myron felt a little weak at the knees. 'You're going to walk in there looking like that?'

'That's how everyone in there dresses.'

'But everyone doesn't look like you,' he said.

'Oh, my, my,' Esperanza said. 'A compliment.'

'I meant, like a chorus dancer in *West Side Story*.'

' "A boy like that," ' Esperanza sang, ' "he keel your brother, forget that boy, go find another—" '

'If I do make you a partner,' Myron said, 'don't dress like this at board meetings.'

'Deal,' Esperanza said. 'Can I go now?'

'First call me on the cellular now. I want to make sure I can hear everything that goes on.'

She nodded, dialed the phone. He picked it up. They tested the connection.

'Don't go playing hero,' he said. 'Just find out if he's there. Something gets out of hand, you get out of there pronto.'

'Okay.'

'And we should have a code word. Something you say if you need me.'

Esperanza nodded, feigning seriousness. 'If I say the words premature ejaculation, it means I want you to come.'

'So to speak.'

Esperanza and even Mindy groaned.

Myron reached into his glove compartment. He snapped it open and pulled out a gun. He was not going to be caught unprepared again. 'Go,' he said.

Esperanza hopped out of the car and crossed the street.

A black Corvette with flame decals on the hood and an extra-*vrooming* engine pulled up. A gold-chain-enmeshed primate raced the engine and leaned his head out the window. He smiled greasily at Esperanza. He hit the gas again, giving off a few more deep *vrooms*. Esperanza looked at the car, then at the driver. 'Sorry to hear about your penis,' she deadpanned.

The car drove off. Esperanza shrugged and waved at Myron. It wasn't an original line, but it never failed her.

'God, I love that woman,' Myron said.

'She's, like, totally hot,' Mindy agreed. 'I wish I looked like her.'

'You should wish to be like her,' he corrected.

'What's the difference? She must, like, really work out, right?'

Esperanza entered the Parker Inn. The first thing that hit her was the smell – a pungent combination of dried vomit and body odor, only less olfactorily pleasing. She wrinkled her nose and continued inside. The floor was hardwood with lots of sawdust. The light was dingy, coming off the pool table ceiling fixtures that were supposed to look like imitation Tiffany lamps. The crowd was probably two-to-one men over women. Everyone was dressed – in a word – cheesy.

Esperanza looked around the room. Then she spoke out loud so that Myron would hear her through the phone. 'About a hundred guys in here fit your description,' she said. 'It's like asking me to find an implant in a strip club.'

Myron's phone was on mute, but she'd bet he was laughing. An implant at a strip club. Not bad, she thought. Not bad at all.

So now what?

People were staring at her, but she was used to that. Three seconds passed before a man approached her. He had a long, kinky beard; bits of coagulated food were lodged in it. He smiled toothlessly, looked her up and down unapologetically.

'I've got a great tongue,' he said to her.

'Now all you need is some teeth.'

She pushed past him and made her way to the bar. Two seconds later, a guy jumped toward her. He wore a cowboy hat. Cowboy hat. Philadelphia. What's wrong with this picture?

'Hey, sweetheart, don't I know you?'

Esperanza nodded. 'Another line that smooth,' she said, 'and I may start to undress.'

The cowboy whooped it up like it was the funniest thing he had ever heard. 'No, little darling, I'm not handing you a line. I'm serious here . . .' His voice sort of drifted off. 'Holy shit!' the man cried. 'It's Little Pocahontas! The Indian Princess! You're Little Pocahontas, right? Don't deny it now, darling. It's you! I can't believe it!'

Myron was probably laughing his ass off right now.

'Nice to see you,' Esperanza said. 'Thank you very much for remembering.'

'Shit, Bobby, take a lookie here. It's Little Pocahontas! Remember? That hot little vixen on FLOW?'

FLOW, of course, stood for the 'Fabulous Ladies Of Wrestling.' The organization's original name had been the 'Beautiful Ladies Of Wrestling,' but once they became popular enough for television, the networks insisted on a new acronym.

'Where?' Another man approached, eyes wide and

drunk and happy. 'Holy shit, you're right! It's her! It's really her!'

'Hey, thanks for the memories, fellas, but—'

'I remember this one time, you were fighting Tatiana the Siberian Husky? Remember that one? Shit, my hard-on nearly poked a hole clean through my bedroom window.'

Esperanza hoped to file that little tidbit under Too Much Information.

An enormous bartender came over. He looked like the pullout centerfold for *Leather Biker Monthly*, Extra big and extra scary. He had long hair, a long scar, and tattoos of snakes slithering up both arms. He shot the two men a glare and – poof – they were gone. Like the glare had evaporated them. Then he turned his eyes toward Esperanza. She met the glare and gave him one back. Neither backed down.

'Lady, what the fuck are you?' he asked.

'Is that a new way of asking what I'm drinking?'

'No.' The mutual glaring continued. He leaned two massive snake-arms on the bar. 'You're too good-looking to be a cop,' he said. 'And you're too good-looking to be hanging out in this toilet.'

'Thanks, I guess,' Esperanza said. 'And you are?'

'Hal,' he said. 'I own this toilet.'

'Hi, Hal.'

'Hi back. Now what the fuck do you want?'

'I'm trying to score some blow,' she said.

'Nah,' Hal said with a shake of his head. 'You'd go to Spic City for that. Buy it from one of your own kind, no offense.' He leaned even closer now. Esperanza couldn't help but wonder if Hal would be a good match for Big

Cyndi. She liked big biker guys. 'Let's cut the crap, sweetheart. What do you want?'

Esperanza decided to try the direct approach. 'I'm looking for a sliver of scum named Tito. People call him Tit. Skinny, shaved head—'

'Yeah, yeah, I *might* know him. How much?'

'Fifty bucks.'

Hal made a scoffing sound. 'You want me to sell out a customer for fifty bucks?'

'A hundred.'

'Hundred and fifty. The deadbeat sack of shit owes me money.'

'Deal,' she said.

'Show me the money.'

Esperanza took the bills out of her wallet. Hal reached it for it, but she pulled back. 'You first,' she said.

'I don't know where he lives,' Hal said. 'He and his goose-stepping faggots come in every night except Wednesdays and Saturdays.'

'Why not Wednesdays and Saturdays?' she asked.

'How the fuck am I supposed to know? Bingo night and Saturday night mass maybe. Or maybe they all do a circle jerk crying "Heil, Hitler" when they shoot off. How the fuck do I know?'

'What's his real name?'

'I don't know.'

She looked around the bar. 'Any of the boys here know?'

'Nah,' Hal said. 'Tit always comes in with the same limp-dicked crew and they leave together. They don't talk to no one else. It's *verboten*.'

'Sounds like you don't like him.'

'He's a stupid punk. They all are. Assholes who blame the fact that they're genetic mutations on other people.'

'So why do you let them hang out here?'

'Because unlike them, I know that this is the US of A. You can do what you want. Anyone is welcome here. Black, white, Spic, Jap, whatever. Even stupid punks.'

Esperanza almost smiled. Sometimes you find tolerance in the strangest places. 'What else?'

'That's all I know. It's Saturday night. They'll be here tomorrow.'

'Fine,' Esperanza said. She ripped the bills in half. 'I'll give you the other half of the bills tomorrow.'

Hal reached out his big hand and closed it over her forearm. His glare grew a little meaner. 'Don't be too smart, hot legs,' he said slowly. 'I can yell *gang bang* and have you on your back on a pool table in five seconds. You give the hundred and fifty now. Then you rip another hundred in half to keep my mouth shut. You got it?'

Her heart was beating wildly in her chest. 'Got it,' she said. She handed him the other half of the bills. Then she took out another hundred, ripped it, and handed it to him.

'Get out, sweet buns. Like now.'

He didn't have to tell her twice.

Chapter 20

There was nothing else they could do tonight. To approach the Squires estate would be foolhardy, at best. He couldn't call or contact the Coldrens. It was too late to try to reach Lloyd Rennart's widow. And lastly – and perhaps most important – Myron was bone-tired.

So he spent the evening at the guest house with his two best friends in the world. Myron, Win, and Esperanza lay sprawled on separate couches like Dalí clocks. They wore T-shirts and shorts and buried themselves deep within puffy pillows. Myron drank too much Yoo-Hoo; Esperanza drank too much diet Coke; Win drank almost enough Brooklyn Lager (Win drank only lager, never beer). There were pretzels and Fritos and Ruffles and freshly delivered pizza. The lights were out. The big-screen television was on. Win had recently taped a whole bunch of *Odd Couple* episodes. They were on the fourth in a row. The best thing about the *Odd Couple*, Myron surmised, was the consistency. They never had a weak episode – how many shows could say that?

Myron bit into a slice of pizza. He needed this. He had barely slept in the millennium since he'd first encountered the Coldrens (in reality, it only had been yesterday). His brain was fried; his nerves were fraying like overused floss. Sitting with Win and Esperanza, their faces blue-lit by the picture tube, Myron felt true contentment.

'It's simply not true,' Win insisted.

'No way,' Esperanza agreed, tossing down a Ring-Ding.

'I'm telling you,' Myron said. 'Jack Klugman is wearing a hairpiece.'

Win's voice was firm. 'Oscar Madison would never wear a rug. Never, I say. Felix, maybe. But Oscar? It simply cannot be.'

'It is,' Myron said. 'That's a hairpiece.'

'You're still thinking of the last episode,' Esperanza said. 'The one with Howard Cosell.'

'Yes, that's it,' Win agreed with a snap of his fingers. 'Howard Cosell. He wore a hairpiece.'

Myron looked up the ceiling, exasperated. 'I'm not thinking of Howard Cosell. I know the difference between Howard Cosell and Jack Klugman. I'm telling you. Klugman is sporting a rug.'

'Where's the line?' Win challenged, pointing at the screen. 'I cannot see a break or a line or a discoloration. And I'm usually quite good at spotting lines.'

'I don't see it either,' Esperanza added, squinting.

'That's two against one,' Win said.

'Fine,' Myron said. 'Don't believe me.'

'He had his own hair on *Quincy*,' Esperanza said.

'No,' Myron said, 'he didn't.'

'Two against one,' Win repeated. 'Majority rules.'

'Fine,' Myron repeated. 'Wallow in ignorance.'

On the screen, Felix fronted for a band called Felix Unger and the Sophisticates. They rambled through an up-tempo number with the repeated phrase 'Stumbling all around.' Kinda catchy.

'What makes you so sure it's a rug?' Esperanza asked.

'*The Twilight Zone*,' Myron said.

'Come again?'

'*The Twilight Zone*. Jack Klugman was in at least two episodes.'

'Ah, yes,' Win said. 'Now, don't tell me, let me see if I remember.' He paused, tapping his lip with his index finger. 'The one with the little boy Pip. Played by . . . ?' Win knew the answer. Life with his friends was an ever-continuing game of Useless Trivia.

'Bill Mumy.' It was Esperanza.

Win nodded. 'Whose most famous role was . . . ?'

'Will Robinson,' Esperanza said. '*Lost in Space*.'

'Remember Judy Robinson?' Win sighed. 'Quite the Earth babe, no?'

'Except,' Esperanza interjected, 'what was up with her clothes? Kmart velour sweaters for space travel? Who came up with that one?'

'And we cannot forget the effervescent Dr Zachery Smith,' Win added. 'The first gay character on series TV.'

'Scheming, conniving, gutless – with a hint of pedophilia,' Esperanza said with a shake of her head. 'He set back the movement twenty years.'

Win grabbed another slice of pizza. The pizza box was white with red-and-green lettering and had the classic caricature of a heavy-set chef twirling a thin mustache with his finger. The box read – and this is absolutely true:

206

> *Whether it's a pizza or submarine,*
> *We buy the best,*
> *To prepare the best,*
> *And leave it to you for the rest.*

Wordsworth.

'I don't recall Mr Klugman's second *Twilight Zone*,' Win said.

'The one with the pool player,' Myron answered. 'Jonathan Winters was in it too.'

'Ah, yes,' Win said with a serious nod. 'Now I remember. Jonathan Winters's ghost shoots pool against Mr Klugman's character. For bragging rights or some such thing.'

'Correct answer.'

'So what do those two *Twilight Zone* episodes have to do with Mr Klugman's hair?'

'You got them on tape?'

Win paused. 'I believe that I do. I taped the last *Twilight Zone* marathon. One of those episodes is bound to be on it.'

'Let's find it,' Myron said.

It took the three of them almost twenty minutes of sifting through his vast video collection before they finally found the episode with Bill Mumy. Win put it in the VCR and reclaimed his couch. They watched in silence.

Several minutes later, Esperanza said, 'I'll be damned.'

A black-and-white Jack Klugman was calling out 'Pip,' the name of his dead son, his tormented cries chasing a tender apparition from his past. The scene was quite moving, but also very much beside the point. The key factor, of course, was that even though this episode predated the *Odd Couple* by some ten years, Jack Klugman's hairline was in a serious state of retreat.

Win shook his head. 'You are good,' he said in a hushed voice. 'So very good.' He looked at Myron. 'I am truly humbled to be in your presence.'

'Don't feel bad,' Myron said. 'You're special in your own way.'

This was about as heavy as the conversation got.

They laughed. They joked. They made fun of one another. No one talked about a kidnapping or the Coldrens or business or money matters or landing Tad Crispin or the severed finger of a sixteen-year-old boy.

Win dozed off first. Then Esperanza. Myron tried to call Jessica again, but there was no answer. No surprise. Jessica often didn't sleep well. Taking walks, she claimed, inspired her. He heard her voice on the machine and felt something inside him plunge. When the beep came on, he left a message:

'I love you,' he said. 'I will always love you.'

He hung up. He crawled back onto the couch and pulled the cover up to his neck.

Chapter 21

When Myron arrived at Merion Golf Club the next morning, he wondered briefly if Linda Coldren had told Jack about the severed finger. She had. By the third hole, Jack had already dropped three strokes off his lead. His complexion was cartoon Casper. His eyes were as vacant as the Bates Motel, his shoulders slumped like bags of wet peat moss.

Win frowned. 'Guess that finger thing is bothering him.'

Mr Insight.

'That sensitivity workshop,' Myron said, 'it's really starting to pay off.'

'I did not expect Jack's collapse to be so total.'

'Win, his son's finger was chopped off by a kidnapper. That's the kind of thing that could distract someone.'

'I guess.' Win didn't sound convinced. He turned away and started heading up the fairway. 'Did Crispin show you the numbers in his Zoom deal?'

'Yes,' Myron said.

'And?'

'And he got robbed.'

Win nodded. 'Not much you can do about it now.'

'Plenty I can do about it,' Myron said. 'It's called renegotiate.'

'Crispin signed a deal,' Win said.

'So?'

'Please do not tell me that you want him to back out of it.'

'I didn't say I wanted him to back out. I said I wanted to renegotiate.'

'"Renegotiate,"' Win repeated as though the word tasted vinegary. He continued trudging up the fairway. 'How come an athlete who performs poorly never renegotiates? How come you never see a player who has a terrible season restructure his deal downward?'

'Good point,' Myron said. 'But, you see, I have this job description. It reads something like this: Get the most money I can for a client.'

'And ethics be damned.'

'Whoa, where did that come from? I may search for legal loopholes, but I always play by the rules.'

'You sound like a criminal defense attorney,' Win said.

'Ooo, now that's a low blow,' Myron said.

The crowd was getting caught up in the unfolding drama in an almost disturbing way. The whole experience was like watching a car crash in super slow motion. You were horrified; you stared; and part of you almost cheered the misfortune of a fellow human being. You gaped, wondering about the outcome, almost hoping the crash would be fatal. Jack Coldren was slowly dying. His heart was crumbling like brown leaves caught in a closed fist. You saw it all happening. And you wanted it to continue.

On the fifth hole Myron and Win met up with Norm Zuckerman and Esme Fong. They were both on edge, especially Esme, but then again she had a hell of a lot riding on this round. On the eighth hole they watched Jack miss an easy putt. Stroke by stroke, the lead shrank from insurmountable to comfortable to nail-biting.

On the back nine Jack managed to control the hemorrhaging a bit. He continued to play poorly, but with only three holes left to play, Jack was still hanging on to a two-stroke lead. Tad Crispin was applying pressure, but it would still take a fairly major gaffe on Jack Coldren's part for Tad to win.

Then it happened.

The sixteenth hole. The same hazard that had laid waste to Jack's dream twenty-three years ago. Both men started off fine. They hit good tee-shots to what Win called 'a slightly offset fairway.' Uh-huh. But on Jack's second shot, disaster struck. He came over the top and left the sucker short. Way short.

The ball landed in the stone quarry.

The crowd gasped. Myron watched in horror. Jack had done the unthinkable. Again.

Norm Zuckerman nudged Myron. 'I'm moist,' he said giddily. 'Swear to God, I'm moist in my nether regions. Go ahead, feel for yourself.'

'I'll take your word for it, Norm.'

Myron turned to Esme Fong. Her face lit up. 'Me too,' she said.

A more intriguing proposal but still no sale.

Jack Coldren barely reacted, as if some internal wiring

had shorted out. He was not waving a white flag, but it looked like he should have been.

Tad Crispin took advantage. He hit a fine approach shot and was left with an eight-foot putt that would give him the lead. As young Tad stood over the ball, the silence in the gallery was overwhelming – not just the crowd, but it was as if the nearby traffic and overhead planes and even the grass, the trees, the very course had all aligned themselves against Jack Coldren.

This was big-time pressure. And Tad Crispin responded in a big way.

When the putt dropped into the cup, there was no polite golf clap. The crowd erupted like Vesuvius in the last days. The sound spilled forward in a powerful wave, warming the young newcomer and sweeping aside the dying warhorse. Everyone seemed to want this. Everyone wanted to crown Tad Crispin and behead Jack Coldren. The young handsome man against the ruffled veteran – it was like the golf equivalent of the Nixon-Kennedy debates.

'What a yip master,' someone said.

'A major case of the yips,' another agreed.

Myron looked a question at Win.

'Yip,' Win said. 'The latest euphemism for *choke.*'

Myron nodded. There was nothing worse you could call an athlete. It was okay to be untalented or to screw up or to have an off day – but not to choke. Never to choke. Chokers were gutless. Chokers had their very manhood questioned. Being called a choker was tantamount to standing naked in front of a beautiful woman while she pointed and laughed.

Er, or so Myron imagined.

He spotted Linda Coldren in a private grandstand tent

overlooking the eighteenth hole. She wore sunglasses and a baseball cap pulled low. Myron looked up at her. She did not look back. Her expression was one of mild confusion, like she was working on a math word problem or trying to recall the name behind a familiar face. For some reason, the expression troubled Myron. He stayed in her line of vision, hoping she'd signal to him. She didn't.

Tad Crispin took a one-stroke lead into the final hole. The other golfers were finished for the day, many coming out and standing around the eighteenth green to watch the final act of golf's greatest collapse.

Win started playing Mr Merion. 'The eighteenth hole is a four hundred and sixty-five yard, par four,' he began. 'The tee is in the stone quarry. You need to hit it up the hill – a two-hundred yard carry.'

'I see,' Myron said. Huh?

Tad was up first. He hit what looked like a good, solid drive. The gallery did that polite golf-clap thing. Jack Coldren took his turn. His shot climbed higher, seemingly pulling itself against the elements.

'Very nice golf shot,' Win said. 'Super.'

Myron turned to Esme Fong. 'What happens if it ends in a tie? Sudden death?'

Esme shook her head. 'Other tournaments, yes. But not at the Open. They make both players come back tomorrow and play a whole round.'

'All eighteen holes?'

'Yes.'

Tad's second shot left him just short of the green.

'A solid golf shot,' Win informed him. 'Sets him up nicely for the par.'

Jack took out an iron and approached the ball.

Win smiled at Myron. 'Recognize this?'

213

Myron squinted. Déjà vu swarmed in. He was no golf fan, but from this angle even he recognized the spot. Win kept the picture on his credenza at the office. Almost every golf book or golf pub or golf whatever had the photograph. Ben Hogan had stood exactly where Jack Coldren now stood. In 1950 or thereabouts. Hogan had stroked the famous one-iron that had made him the US Open champion. It was the golf equivalent of 'Havlicek stole the ball!'

As Jack took his practice swing, Myron could not help but wonder about old ghosts and strange possibilities.

'He has an almost impossible task,' Win said.

'Why's that?'

'The pin placement is brutal today. Behind that yawning bunker.'

A yawning bunker? Myron did not bother asking.

Jack fired a long iron at the green. He reached it, but as Win had predicted, he still left himself a good twenty-plus feet away. Tad Crispin took his third shot, a beautiful little chip that came to rest within six inches of the hole. Tad tapped it in for par. That meant that Jack had no chance of winning in regulation. The best he could do was force a tie. If he made this putt.

'A twenty-two-foot putt,' Win said with a grim shake of the head. 'No chance.'

He had said twenty-two feet – not twenty-one feet or twenty-three feet. Twenty-two feet. Win could tell from a quick glance from over fifty yards away. Golfers. Go figure.

Jack Coldren strolled to the green. He bent down, picked up his ball, put down a marker, picked up the marker, put down the ball again in the exact same spot. Myron shook his head. Golfers.

Jack looked very far away, like he was putting from New Jersey. Think about it. He was twenty-two feet away from a hole four-and-a-quarter inches in diameter. Break out a calculator. Do the math.

Myron, Win, Esme, and Norm waited. This was it. The coup de grâce. The part where the matador finally drives the long, thin blade home.

But as Jack studied the break in the green, some sort of transformation seemed to take place. The fleshy features hardened. The eyes became focused and steely and – though it was probably Myron's imagination – a hint of yesterday's 'eye' seemed to flint up in them. Myron looked behind him. Linda Coldren had spotted the change too. For a brief moment she let her attention slip and her eyes sought out Myron's, as if for confirmation. Before Myron could do more than meet her gaze, she looked away.

Jack Coldren took his time. He read the green from several angles. He squatted down, his club pointing in front of him the way golfers do. He talked to Diane Hoffman at some length. But once he addressed the ball, there was no hesitation. The club went back like a metronome and kissed the ball hard on the way down.

The tiny white sphere carrying all of Jack Coldren's dreams circled toward the hole like an eagle seeking its prey. There was no question in Myron's mind. The pull was almost magnetic. Several seemingly infinite seconds later, the tiny white sphere dropped to the bottom of the hole with an audible clink. For a moment there was silence and then another eruption, this one more from surprise than exhilaration. Myron found himself applauding wildly.

Jack had done it. He'd tied the score.

Over the crowd's cacophony, Norm Zuckerman said, 'This is beautiful, Esme. The whole world will be watching tomorrow. The exposure will be incredible.'

Esme looked stunned. 'Only if Tad wins.'

'What do you mean?'

'What if Tad loses?'

'Hey, second place at the US Open?' Norm said, palms up to the sky. 'Not bad, Esme. Not bad at all. That's where we were this morning. Before all this happened. Nothing lost, nothing gained.'

Esme Fong shook her head. 'If Tad loses now, he doesn't come in second place. He's just a loser. He would have gone one-on-one with a famed choke-artist and lost. Outchoked the ultimate choker. It'll be worse than the Buffalo Bills.'

Norm made a scoffing noise. 'You worry too much, Esme,' he said, but his usual bluster had tapered off.

The crowd began to dissipate, but Jack Coldren just stood in the same position, still holding his putter. He did not celebrate. He did not move, even when Diane Hoffman began to pound his back. His features seemed to lose their tone again, his eyes suddenly more glazed than ever. It was as if the effort of that one stroke had drained every ounce of energy, karma, strength, life force right out of him.

Or maybe, Myron wondered, there was something else at work here. Something deeper. Maybe that last moment of magic had given Jack some new insight – some new life clarity – as to the relative, long-term importance of this tournament. Everyone else saw a man who had just sunk the most important putt of his life. But maybe Jack Coldren saw a man standing alone wondering what the big deal was and if his only son was still alive.

Linda Coldren appeared on the fringe of the green. She tried to look enthusiastic as she approached her husband and dutifully kissed him. A television crew followed her. Long-lensed cameras clicked and their flashes strobed. A sportscaster came up to them, microphone at the ready. Linda and Jack both managed to smile.

But behind the smiles, Linda looked almost wary. And Jack looked positively terrified.

Chapter 22

Esperanza had come up with a plan. 'Lloyd Rennart's widow's name is Francine. She's an artist.'

'What kind?'

'I don't know. Painting, sculpture – what's the difference?'

'Just curious. Go ahead.'

'I called her up and said that you were a reporter for the *Coastal Star*. It's a local paper in the Spring Lake area. You are doing a lifestyle piece on several local artists.'

Myron nodded. It was a good plan. People rarely refuse the chance to be interviewed for self-promoting puff pieces.

Win had already gotten Myron's car windows fixed. How, Myron had no idea. The rich. They're different.

The ride took about two hours. It was eight o'clock Sunday night. Tomorrow Linda and Jack Coldren would drop off the ransom money. How would it be done? A meeting in a public place? A go-between? For the ump-teenth time, he wondered how Linda and Jack and Chad were faring. He took out the photograph of Chad. He imagined what Chad's young, carefree face must have looked like when his finger was being severed off. He wondered if the kidnapper had used a sharp knife or a cleaver or an axe or a saw or what.

He wondered what it felt like.

Francine Rennart lived in Spring Lake Heights, not Spring Lake. There was a big difference. Spring Lake was on the Atlantic Ocean and about as beautiful a shore town as you could hope to find. There was plenty of sun, very little crime, and almost no ethnics. It was a problem, actually. The wealthy town was nicknamed the Irish Riviera. That meant no good restaurants. None. The town's idea of *haute cuisine* was food served on a plate rather than in a basket. If you craved exotic, you drove to a Chinese take-out place whose eclectic menu included such rare delicacies as chicken chow mein, and for the especially adventurous, chicken *lo* mein. This was the problem with some of these towns. They needed some Jews or gays or something to spice things up, to add a bit of theater and a couple of interesting bistros.

One man's opinion.

If Spring Lake was an old movie, then Spring Lake Heights would be the other side of the tracks. There weren't slums or anything like that. The area where the Rennarts lived was a sort of tract-house suburbia – the middle ground between a trailer park and circa 1967 split-level colonials. Solid Americana.

Myron knocked on the door. A woman he guessed was Francine Rennart pushed open the screen. Her ready smile was shadowed by a daunting beak of a nose. Her burnt-auburn hair was wavy and undisciplined, like she'd just taken out her curlers but hadn't had time to comb it out.

'Hi,' Myron said.

'You must be from the *Coastal Star*.'

'That's right.' Myron stuck out his hand. 'I'm Bernie Worley.' Scoop Bolitar uses a disguise.

'Your timing is perfect,' Francine said. 'I've just started a new exhibit.'

The living room furniture didn't have plastic on it, but it should have. The couch was off-green. The Barca-Lounger – a real, live BarcaLounger – was maroon with duct tape mending rips. The console television had rabbit ears on top. Collectors plates Myron had seen advertised in *Parade* were neatly hung on a wall.

'My studio's in the back,' she said.

Francine Rennart led him to a big addition off the kitchen. It was a sparsely furnished room with white walls. A couch with a spring sticking out of it sat in the middle of the room. A kitchen chair leaned against it. So did a rolled-up carpet. There was something that looked like a blanket draped over the top in a triangular pattern. Four bathroom wastepaper baskets lined the back wall. Myron guessed that she must have a leak.

Myron waited for Francine Rennart to ask him to sit down. She didn't. She stood with him in the entranceway and said, 'Well?'

He smiled, his brain stuck in a cusp where he was not dumb enough to say, 'Well what?' but not smart enough to know what the hell she was talking about. So Myron froze there with his anchorman-waiting-to-go-to-commercial grin.

'You like it?' Francine Rennart asked.

Still the grin. 'Uh-huh.'

'I know it's not for everybody.'

'Hmm.' Scoop Bolitar engages in sparkling repartee.

She watched his face for a moment. He kept up the idiot grin. 'You don't know anything about installation art, do you?'

He shrugged. 'Got me.' Myron shifted gears on the fly. 'Thing is, I don't do features normally. I'm a sports writer. That's my beat.' Beat. Note the authentic reporter lingo. 'But Tanya – she's my boss – she needed somebody to handle a lifestyle piece. And when Jennifer called in sick, well, the job fell to me. It's a story on a variety of local artists – painters, sculptors . . .' He couldn't think of any other kind of artist, so he stopped. 'Anyway, maybe you could explain a little bit about what it is you do.'

'My art is about space and concepts. It's about creating a mood.'

Myron nodded. 'I see.'

'It's not art, per se, in the classic sense. It goes beyond that. It's the next step in the artistic evolutionary process.'

More nods. 'I see.'

'Everything in this exhibit has a purpose. Where I place the couch. The texture of the carpeting. The color of the walls. The way the sunlight shines in through the windows. The blend creates a specific ambience.'

Oh, boy.

Myron motioned at the, uh, art. 'So how do you sell something like this?'

She frowned. 'You don't sell it.'

'Pardon?'

'Art is not about money, Mr Worley. True artists do

not put a monetary value on their work. Only hacks do that.'

Yeah, like Michelangelo and Da Vinci, those hacks. 'But what do you do with this?' he asked. 'I mean, do you just keep the room like this?'

'No. I change it around. I bring in other pieces. I create something new.'

'And what happens to this?'

She shook her head. 'Art is not about permanence. Life is temporary. Why shouldn't art be the same?'

Oooookay.

'Is there a name for this art?'

'Installation art. But we do not like labels.'

'How long have you been an, uh, installation artist?'

'I've been working on my masters at the New York Art Institute for two years.'

He tried not to look shocked. 'You go to school for this?'

'Yes. It's a very competitive program.'

Yeah, Myron thought, like a TV/VCR repair course advertised by Sally Struthers.

They finally moved back into the living room. Myron sat on the couch. Gently. Might be art. He waited to be offered a cookie. Might be art too.

'You still don't get it, do you?'

Myron shrugged. 'Maybe if you threw in a poker table and some dogs.'

She laughed. Mr Self-Deprecation strikes again. 'Fair enough,' she said.

'Let me shift gears for a moment, if I may,' Myron said. 'How about a little something on Francine Rennart, the person?' Scoop Bolitar mines the personal angle.

She looked a bit wary, but she said, 'Okay, ask away.'

'Are you married?'

'No.' Her voice was like a slamming door.

'Divorced?'

'No.'

Scoop Bolitar loves an garrulous interviewee. 'I see,' he said. 'Then I guess you have no children.'

'I have a son.'

'How old is he?'

'Seventeen. His name is Larry.'

A year older than Chad Coldren. Interesting. 'Larry Rennart?'

'Yes.'

'Where does he go to school?'

'Right here at Manasquan High. He's going to be a senior.'

'How nice.' Myron risked it, nibbled on a cookie. 'Maybe I could interview him too.'

'My son?'

'Sure. I'd love a quote from the prodigal son on how proud he is of his mom, of how he supports what she's doing, that kinda thing.' Scoop Bolitar grows pathetic.

'He's not home.'

'Oh?'

He waited for her to elaborate. Nothing.

'Where is Larry?' Myron tried. 'Is he staying with his father?'

'His father is dead.'

Finally. Myron put on the big act. 'Oh, sheesh, I'm sorry. I didn't . . . I mean, you being so young and all. I just didn't consider the possibility that . . .' Scoop Bolitar as Robert DeNiro.

'It's okay,' Francine Rennart said.

'I feel awful.'

'No need to.'

'Have you been widowed long?'

She tilted her head. 'Why do you ask?'

'Background,' he said.

'Background?'

'Yes. I think it's crucial to understanding Francine Rennart the artist. I want to explore how being widowed affected you and your art.' Scoop Bolitar shovels it good.

'I've only been a widow a short time.'

Myron motioned toward the, uh, studio. 'So when you created this work, did your husband's death have any bearing on the outcome? On the color of the wastebaskets maybe. Or the way you rolled up that rug.'

'No, not really.'

'How did your husband die?'

'Why would you—'

'Again, I think it's important for digesting the entire artistic statement. Was it an accident, for example? The kind of death that makes you ponder fickle fate. Was it a long illness? Seeing a loved one suffer—'

'He committed suicide.'

Myron feigned aghast. 'I'm so sorry,' he said.

Her breathing was funny now, her chest giving off short hitches. As Myron watched her, an awful pang struck him deep in the chest. Slow down, he told himself. Stop focusing solely on Chad Coldren and remember that this woman, too, has suffered. She had been married to this man. She had loved him and lived with him and built a life with him and had a child with him.

And after all that, he had chosen to end his life rather than spend it with her.

Myron swallowed. Fiddling with her pathos like this was, at best, unfair. Belittling her artistic expression

224

because he did not understand it was cruel. Myron did not like himself much right now. For a moment he debated just going away – the odds that any of this had anything to do with the case were so remote – but then again, he couldn't simply forget a sixteen-year-old boy with a missing finger, either.

'Were you married long?'

'Almost twenty years,' she said softly.

'I don't mean to intrude, but may I ask you his name?'

'Lloyd,' she said. 'Lloyd Rennart.'

Myron narrowed his eyes as though scanning for a memory. 'Why does that name ring a bell?'

Francine Rennart shrugged. 'He co-owned a tavern in Neptune City. The Rusty Nail.'

'Of course,' Myron said. 'Now I remember. He hung out there a lot, right?'

'Yes.'

'My God, I met the man. Lloyd Rennart. Now I remember. He used to teach golf, right? Was in the big time for a while.'

Francine Rennart's face slid closed like a car window. 'How do you know that?'

'The Rusty Nail. And I'm a huge golf fan. A real duffer, but I follow it like some people follow the Bible.' He was flailing, but maybe he was getting somewhere. 'Your husband caddied Jack Coldren, right? A long time ago. We talked about it a bit.'

She swallowed hard. 'What did he say?'

'Say?'

'About being a caddie.'

'Oh, not much. We mostly talked about some of our favorite golfers. Nicklaus, Trevino, Palmer. Some great courses. Merion mostly.'

'No,' she said.

'Ma'am?'

Her voice was firm. 'Lloyd never talked about golf.'

Scoop Bolitar steps in it in a big way.

Francine Rennart skewered him with her eyes. 'You can't be from the insurance company. I didn't even try to make a claim.' She pondered that for a moment. Then: 'Wait a second. You said you're a sports writer. That's why you're here. Jack Coldren is making a comeback, so you want to do a where-are-they-now story.'

Myron shook his head. Shame flushed his face. Enough, he thought. He took a few deep breaths and said, 'No.'

'Then who are you?'

'My name is Myron Bolitar. I'm a sports agent.'

She was confused now. 'What do you want with me?'

He searched for the words, but they all sounded lame. 'I'm not sure. It's probably nothing, a complete waste of time. You're right. Jack Coldren is making a comeback. But it's like . . . it's like the past is haunting him. Terrible things are happening to him and his family. And I just thought—'

'Thought what?' she snapped. 'That Lloyd came back from the dead to claim vengeance?'

'Did he want vengeance?'

'What happened at Merion,' she said. 'It was a long time ago. Before I met him.'

'Was he over it?'

Francine Rennart thought about that for a while. 'It took a long time,' she said at last. 'Lloyd couldn't get any golf work after what happened. Jack Coldren was still the fair-haired boy and no one wanted to cross him. Lloyd lost all his friends. He started drinking too much.' She hesitated. 'There was an accident.'

Myron stayed still, watching Francine Rennart draw breaths.

'He lost control of his car.' Her voice was robot-like now. 'It slammed into another car. In Narberth. Near where he used to live.' She stopped and then looked at him. 'His first wife died on impact.'

Myron felt a chill rush through him. 'I didn't know,' he said softly.

'It was a long time ago, Mr Bolitar. We met not long after that. We fell in love. He stopped drinking. He bought the tavern right away – I know, I know, it sounds weird. An alcoholic owning a bar. But for him, it worked. We bought this house too. I – I thought everything was okay.'

Myron waited a beat. Then he asked, 'Did your husband give Jack Coldren the wrong club on purpose?'

The question did not seem to surprise her. She plucked at the buttons on her blouse and took her time before answering. 'The truth is, I don't know. He never talked about this incident. Not even with me. But there was something there. It may have been guilt, I don't know.' She smoothed her skirt with both hands. 'But all of this is irrelevant, Mr Bolitar. Even if Lloyd did harbor ill feelings toward Jack, he's dead.'

Myron tried to think of a tactful way of asking, but none came to him. 'Did they find his body, Mrs Rennart?'

His words landed like a heavyweight's hook. 'It-it was a deep crevasse,' Francine Rennart stammered. 'There was no way . . . the police said they couldn't send anyone down there. It was too dangerous. But Lloyd couldn't have survived. He wrote a note. He left his clothes there. I still have his passport . . .' Her voice faded away.

Myron nodded. 'Of course,' he said. 'I understand.'

But as he showed himself out, he was pretty sure that he understood nothing.

Chapter 23

Tito the Crusty Nazi never showed at the Parker Inn.

Myron sat in a car across the street. As usual, he hated surveillance. Boredom didn't set in this time, but the devastated face of Francine Rennart kept haunting him. He wondered about the long-term effects of his visit. The woman had been privately dealing with her grief, locking her private demons in a back closet, and then Myron had gone and blown the hinges off the door. He had tried to comfort her. But in the end what could he say?

Closing time. Still no sign of Tito. His two buddies – Beneath and Escape – were another matter. They'd arrived at ten-thirty. At 1 A.M. they both exited. Escape was on crutches – the aftertaste, Myron was sure, of the nasty side kick to the knee. Myron smiled. It was a small victory, but you take them where you can.

Beneath had his arm slung around a woman's neck. She had a dye job from the planet Bad Bottle and basically looked like the type of woman who might go for a tattoo-infested skinhead – or to say the same thing in a slightly different way, she looked like a regular on *The Jerry Springer Show*.

Both men stopped to urinate on the outside wall. Beneath actually kept his arm around the girl while emptying his bladder. Jesus. So many men peed on that wall that Myron wondered if there was a bathroom inside. The two men broke off. Beneath got into the passenger side of a Ford Mustang. Bad Bleach drove. Escape hobbled onto his own chariot, a motorcycle of some kind. He strapped the crutches onto the side. The two vehicles drove off in separate directions.

Myron decided to follow Escape. When in doubt, tail the one that's lame.

He kept far back and remained extra careful. Better to lose him than risk in the slightest way the possibility of being spotted. But the tail didn't last long. Three blocks down the road, Escape parked and headed into a shabby excuse for a house. The paint was peeling off in flakes the size of manhole covers. One of the support columns on the front porch had completely given way, so the front lip of the roof looked like it'd been ripped in half by some giant. The two upstairs windows were shattered like a drunk's eyes. The only possible reason that this dump hadn't been condemned was that the building inspector had not been able to stop laughing long enough to write up a summons.

Okay, so now what?

He waited an hour for something to happen. Nothing did. He had seen a bedroom light go on and off. That was it. The whole night was fast turning into a complete waste of time.

So what should he do?

He had no answer. So he changed the question around a bit.

What would Win do?

Win would weigh the risks. Win would realize that the situation was desperate, that a sixteen-year-old boy's finger had been chopped off like a bothersome thread. Rescuing him imminently was paramount.

Myron nodded to himself. Time to play Win.

He got out of the car. Making sure he kept out of sight, Myron circled around to the back of the dump. The yard was bathed in darkness. He trampled through grass long enough to hide Viet Cong, occasionally stumbling across a cement block or rake or a garbage can top. His shin got whacked twice; Myron had to bite down expletives.

The back door was boarded up with plywood. The window to its left, however, was open. Myron looked inside. Dark. He carefully climbed into the kitchen.

The smell of spoilage assaulted his nostrils. Flies buzzed about. For a moment, Myron feared that he might find a dead body, but this stink was different, more like the odor of a Dumpster at a 7-Eleven than anything in the rotting flesh family. He checked the other rooms, walking on tiptoes, avoiding the several spots on the floor where there was no floor. No sign of a kidnap victim. No sixteen-year-old boy tied up. No one at all. Myron followed the snoring to the room he had seen the light in earlier. Escape was on his back. Asleep. Without a care.

That was about to change.

Myron leapt into the air and landed hard on Escape's bad knee. Escape's eyes widened. His mouth opened in a scream that Myron cut off with a snap punch in the mouth. He moved quickly, straddling Escape's chest with his knees. He put his gun against the punk's cheek.

'Scream and die,' Myron said.

Escape's eyes stayed wide. Blood trickled out of his mouth. He did not scream. Still, Myron was disappointed in himself. Scream and die ? He couldn't come up with anything better than scream and die?

'Where is Chad Coldren?'

'Who?'

Myron jammed the gun barrel into the bleeding mouth. It hit teeth and nearly gagged the man. 'Wrong answer.'

Escape stayed silent. The punk was brave. Or maybe, just maybe, he couldn't talk because Myron had stuck a gun in his mouth. Smooth move, Bolitar. Keeping his face firm, Myron slowly slid the barrel out.

'Where is Chad Coldren?'

Escape gasped, caught his breath. 'I swear to God, I don't know what you're talking about.'

'Give me your hand.'

'What?'

'Give me your hand.'

Escape lifted his hand into view. Myron grabbed the wrist, turned it, and plucked out the middle finger. He curled it inward and flattened the folded digit against the palm. The kid bucked in pain. 'I don't need a knife,' Myron said. 'I can just grind it into splinters.'

'I don't know what you're talking about,' the kid managed. 'I swear!'

Myron squeezed a little harder. He did not want the bone to snap. Escape bucked some more. Smile a little, Myron thought. That's how Win does it. He has just a hint of a smile. Not much. You want your victim to think you are capable of anything, that you are completely cold, that you might even enjoy it. But you don't want him thinking you are a complete lunatic, out of control, a nut who would hurt you no matter what. Mine that middle ground.

'Please . . .'

'Where is Chad Coldren?'

'Look, I was there, okay? When he jumped you. Tit said he'd give me a hundred bucks. But I don't know no Chad Coldren.'

'Where is Tit?' That name again.

'At his crib, I guess. I don't know.'

Crib? The neo-Nazi was using dated urban street lingo. Life's ironies. 'Doesn't Tito usually hang out with you guys at the Parker Inn?'

'Yeah, but he never showed.'

'Was he supposed to?'

'I guess. It's not like we talk about it.'

Myron nodded. 'Where does he live?'

'Mountainside Drive. Right down the street. Third house on the left after you make the turn.'

'If you're lying to me, I will come back here and slice your eyes out.'

'I ain't lying. Mountainside Drive.'

Myron pointed at the swastika tattoo with the barrel of the gun. 'Why do you have this?'

'What?'

'The swastika, moron.'

'I'm proud of my race, that's why.'

'You want to put all the "kikes" in gas chambers? Kill all the "niggers"?'

'That ain't what we're about,' he said. More confidence in his voice now that he was on well-rehearsed ground. 'We're for the white man. We're tired of being overrun by niggers. We're sick of being trampled on by the Jews.'

Myron nodded. 'Well, by this Jew anyway,' he said. In

life, you take satisfaction where you can. 'You know what duct tape is.'

'Yeah.'

'Gee, and I thought all neo-Nazis were dumb. Where is yours?'

Escape's eyes kinda narrowed. Like he was actually thinking. You could almost hear rusty gears churning. Then: 'I don't have none.'

'Too bad. I was going to use it to tie you up, so you couldn't warn Tito. But if you don't have any, I'll just have to shoot both your kneecaps.'

'Wait!'

Myron used up almost the entire roll.

Tito was in the driver's seat of his pickup truck with the monster wheels.

He was also dead.

Two shots in the head, probably from very close range. Very bloody. There wasn't much of a head left anymore. Poor Tito. No head to match his no ass. Myron didn't laugh. Then again, gallows humor was not his forte.

Myron remained calm, probably because he was still in Win mode. No lights were on in the house. Tito's keys were still in the ignition. Myron took them and unlocked the front door. His search confirmed what he'd already guessed: no one was there.

Now what?

Ignoring the blood and brain matter, Myron went back to the truck and did a thorough search. Talk about not his forte. Myron reclicked the Win icon. Just protoplasm, he told himself. Just hemoglobin and platelets and enzymes and other stuff he'd forgotten since ninth-grade biology. The blocking worked enough to allow him to dig his hands under the seats and into the cushion crevices. His fingers located lots of crud. Old sandwiches. Wrappers from Wendy's. Crumbs of various shapes and sizes.

Fingernail clippings.

Myron looked at the dead body and shook his head. A little late for a scolding, but what the hell.

Then he hit pay dirt.

It was gold. It had a golf insignia on it. The initials *C.B.C.* were engraved lightly on the inside – Chad Buckwell Coldren.

It was a ring.

Myron's first thought was that Chad Coldren had cleverly taken it off and left it behind as a clue. Like in a movie. The young man was sending a message. If Myron was playing his part correctly, he would shake his head, toss the ring in the air, and mutter admiringly, 'Smart kid.'

Myron's second thought, however, was far more sobering.

The severed finger in Linda Coldren's car had been the ring finger.

Chapter 24

What to do?

Should he contact the police? Just leave? Make an anonymous call? What?

Myron had no idea. He had to think first and foremost of Chad Coldren. What risk would calling the police put the kid in?

No idea.

Christ, what a mess. He wasn't even supposed to be involved in this anymore. He was supposed to have – should have – stayed out. But now the proverbial doo-doo was hitting a plethora of proverbial fans. What should he do about finding a dead body? And what about Escape? Myron couldn't just leave him tied and gagged indefinitely. Suppose he vomited into the duct tape, for chrissake?

Okay, Myron, think. First, you should not – repeat, not – call the police. Someone else will discover the body. Or maybe he should make an anonymous call from a pay phone. That might work. But don't the police tape all incoming calls nowadays? They'd have his voice on tape. He could change it maybe. The rhythm and tempo. Make the tone a little deeper. Add an accent or something. Oh, right, like Meryl Streep. Tell the dispatcher to hurry because 'the dingo's got ma baby.'

Wait, hold the phone.

Think about what had just happened. Rewind to about an hour ago and see how it looks. Without provocation, Myron had broken into a man's house. He had physically assaulted the man, threatened him in terrible ways, left him tied and gagged – all in the pursuit of Tito. Not long after this incident, the police get an anonymous call. They find Tito dead in his pickup.

Who is going to be the obvious suspect?

Myron Bolitar, sports agent of the terminally troubled. Damn.

So now what? No matter what Myron did at this stage – call or not call – he was going to be a suspect. Escape would be questioned. He would tell about Myron, and then Myron would look like the killer. Very simple equation when you thought about it.

So the question remained: What to do?

He couldn't worry about what conclusions the police might leap upon. He also couldn't worry about himself. The focus must be on Chad Coldren. What would be best for him? Hard to say. The safest bet, of course, would be to upset the apple cart as little as possible. Try not to make his presence in all this known.

Okay, good, that made sense.

So the answer was: Don't report it. Let the body lay where it was. Put the ring back in the seat cushion in case the police need it as evidence later. Good, this looked like a plan – a plan that seemed the best way of keeping the kid safe and also obeying the Coldrens' wishes.

Now, what about Escape?

Myron drove back to Escape's shack. He found Escape right where he left him – on his bed, hog-tied and gagged with gray duct tape. He looked half dead. Myron shook him. The punk started to, his face the green of seaweed. Myron ripped off the gag.

Escape retched and did a few dry heaves.

'I have a man outside,' Myron said, removing more duct tape. 'If he sees you move from this window, you will experience an agony very few have been forced to endure. Do you understand?'

Escape nodded quickly.

Experience an agony very few have been forced to endure. Jesus.

There was no phone in the house, so he didn't have to worry about that. With a few more harsh warnings lightly sprinkled with torture clichés – including Myron's personal favorite, 'Before I'm finished, you'll beg me to kill you' – he left the neo-Nazi alone to quake in his goose-stepping black boots.

No one was outside. The proverbial coast was clear. Myron got in the car, wondering yet again about the Coldrens. What was going on with them right now? Had the kidnapper already called? Had he given them instructions? How did Tito's death affect what was happening? Had Chad suffered more bloodshed or had he escaped? Maybe he'd gotten hold of the gun and shot someone.

Maybe. But doubtful. More likely, something had gone awry. Someone had lost control. Someone had gone nuts.

He stopped the car. He had to warn the Coldrens.

Yes, Linda Coldren had clearly instructed him to stay

away. But that was before he'd found a dead body. How could he sit back now and leave them blind? Someone had chopped off their son's finger. Someone had murdered one of the kidnappers. A 'simple' kidnapping – if there is such a thing – had spun off its axis. Blood had been splattered about freely.

He had to warn them. He had to contact the Coldrens and let them know what he had learned.

But how?

He pulled onto Golf House Road. It was very late now, almost two in the morning. Nobody would be up. Myron flicked off his lights and cruised silently. He glided the car into a spot on the property line between two houses – if by some chance one of the occupants was awake and looked out the window, he or she might believe the car belonged to someone visiting a neighbor. He stepped out and slowly made his way on foot toward the Coldren house.

Keeping out of sight, Myron moved closer. He knew, of course, that there was no chance the Coldrens would be asleep. Jack might give it a token effort; Linda wouldn't even sit down. But right now, that didn't much matter.

How was he going to contact them?

He couldn't call on the phone. He couldn't walk up and knock on the door. And he couldn't throw pebbles at the window, like some clumsy suitor in a bad romantic comedy. So where did that leave him?

Lost.

He moved from shrub to shrub. Some of the shrubs were familiar from his last sojourn into these parts. He said hello to them, chatted, offered up his best cocktail-party banter. One shrub gave him a stock tip. Myron ignored it. He circled closer to the Coldren house, slowly, still careful not to be seen. He had no idea what he was going to do, but when he got close enough to see a light on in the den, an idea came to him.

A note.

He would write a note, telling them of his discovery, warning them to be extra careful, offering up his services. How to get the note close to the house? Hmm. He could fold the note into a paper airplane and fly it in. Oh, sure, with Myron's mechanical skills, that would work. Myron Bolitar, the Jewish Wright Brother. What else? Tie the note to a rock maybe? And then what? Smash a window?

As it happened, he didn't have to do any of that.

He heard a noise to his right. Footsteps. On the street. At two in the morning.

Myron quickly dove back down behind a shrub. The footsteps were moving closer. Faster. Someone approaching. Running.

He kept down, his heart beating wildly in his chest. The footsteps grew louder and then suddenly stopped. Myron peeked around the side of the shrub. His view was blocked by still more hedges.

He held his breath. And waited.

The footsteps started up again. Slower this time. Unhurried. Casual. Taking a walk now. Myron craned his neck around the other side of the shrub. Nothing. He moved into a crouch now. Slowly he raised himself, inch by inch, his bad knee protesting. He fought through the pain. His eyes reached the top of the shrub. Myron looked out and finally saw who it was.

Linda Coldren.

She was dressed in a blue sweat suit with running sneakers. Out for a jog? Seemed like a very strange time for it. But you never know. Jack drove golf balls. Myron shot baskets. Maybe Linda was into late-night jogging.

He didn't think so.

She neared the top of the driveway. Myron had to reach her. He clawed a rock out of the dirt and skimmed it toward her. Linda stopped and looked up sharply, like a deer interrupted while drinking. Myron threw another rock. She looked toward the bush. Myron waved a hand. Christ, this was subtle. But if she had felt safe enough to leave the house – if the kidnapper had not minded her taking a little night stroll – then walking toward a bush shouldn't cause a panic either. Bad rationale, but it was getting late.

If not out for a jog, why was Linda out so late?

Unless . . .

Unless she was paying off the ransom.

But no, it was still Sunday night. The banks wouldn't be open. She couldn't raise one hundred grand without going to a bank. She had made that clear, hadn't she?

Linda Coldren slowly approached the bush. Myron was almost tempted to light the bush on fire, deepen his voice, and say, 'Come forward, Moses.' More gallows humor. More not-funny.

When she was about ten feet away, Myron raised his head into view. Linda's eyes nearly leaped out of their sockets.

'Get out of here!' Linda whispered.

Myron wasted no time. Whispering back, he said, 'I found the guy from the pay phone dead. Shot twice in the head. Chad's ring was in his car. But no sign of Chad.'

'Get out!'

'I just wanted to warn you. Be careful. They're playing for keeps.'

241

Her eyes darted about the yard. She nodded and turned away.

'When's the drop-off?' Myron tried. 'And where's Jack? Make sure you see Chad with your own eyes before you hand over anything.'

But if Linda heard him, she gave no indication. She hurried down the driveway, opened the door, and disappeared from sight.

Chapter 25

Win opened the bedroom door. 'You have visitors.'

Myron kept his head on the pillow. Friends not knocking hardly fazed him anymore. 'Who is it?'

'Law enforcement officials,' Win said.

'Cops?'

'Yes.'

'Uniformed?'

'Yes.'

'Any idea what it's about?'

'Oooo, sorry. That would be a no. Let's move on to Kitty Carlisle.'

Myron picked the sleep out of his eyes and threw on some clothes. He slipped into a pair of Top-Siders without socks. Very Win-like. A quick brush of the teeth, for the sake of breath rather than long-term dental health. He opted for a baseball cap rather than taking the time to wet his hair. The baseball cap was red and said TRIX CEREAL in the front and SILLY RABBIT on the back. Jessica had bought it for him. Myron loved her for it.

The two uniforms waited with cop-patience in the living room. They were young and healthy-looking. The taller one said, 'Mr Bolitar?'

'Yes.'

'We'd appreciate it if you would accompany us.'

'Where?'

'Detective Corbett will explain when we arrive.'

'How about a hint?'

Two faces of stone. 'We'd rather not, sir.'

Myron shrugged. 'Let's go then.'

Myron sat in the back of the squad car. The two uniforms sat in the front. They drove at a pretty good clip but kept their siren off. Myron's cell phone rang.

'Do you guys mind if I take a call?'

Taller said, 'Of course not, sir.'

'Polite of you.' Myron hit the *on* switch. 'Hello.'

'Are you alone?' It was Linda Coldren.

'Nope.'

'Don't tell anyone I'm calling. Can you please get here as soon as possible? It's urgent.'

'What do you mean you can't deliver it until Thursday?' Mr Throw Them Off Track.

'I can't talk right now either. Just get here as soon as you can. And don't say anything until you do. Please. Trust me on this.'

She hung up.

'Fine, but then I better get free bagels. You hear me?'

Myron turned off the cell phone. He looked out the window. The route the cops were taking was overly familiar. Myron had taken the same one to Merion. When they reached the club entranceway on Ardmore

Avenue, Myron saw a plethora of media vans and cop cars.

'Dang,' the taller cop said.

'You knew it wouldn't stay quiet for long,' Shorter added.

'Too big a story,' Taller agreed.

'You fellas want to clue me in?'

The shorter cop twisted his head toward Myron. 'No, sir.' He turned back around.

'Okeydokey,' Myron said. But he didn't have a good feeling about this.

The squad car drove steadily through the press gauntlet. Reporters pushed against the windows, peering in. Flashes popped in Myron's face. A policeman waved them through. The reporters slowly peeled off the car like dandruff flakes. They parked in the club lot. There were at least a dozen other police cars, both marked and unmarked, nearby.

'Please come along,' Taller said.

Myron did so. They walked across the eighteenth fairway. Lots of uniformed officers were walking with their heads down, picking up pieces of lord-knows-what and putting them in evidence bags.

This was definitely not good.

When they reached the top of the hill, Myron could see dozens of officers making a perfect circle in the famed stone quarry. Some were taking photos. Crime scene photos. Others were bent down. When one stood up, Myron saw him.

He felt his knees buckle. 'Oh no . . .'

In the middle of the quarry – sprawled in the famed hazard that had cost him the tournament twenty-three years ago – lay the still, lifeless body of Jack Coldren.

The uniforms watched him, gauging his reaction. Myron showed them nothing. 'What happened?' he managed.

'Please wait here, sir.'

The taller cop walked down the hill; the shorter stayed with Myron. Taller spoke briefly to a man in plainclothes Myron suspected was Detective Corbett. Corbett glanced up at Myron as the man spoke. He nodded to the shorter cop.

'Please follow me, sir.'

Still dazed, Myron trudged down the hill into the stone quarry. He kept his eye on the corpse. Coagulated blood coated Jack's head like one of those spray-on toupees. The body was twisted into a position it was never supposed to achieve. Oh, Christ. Poor, sad bastard.

The plainclothes detective greeted him with an enthusiastic handshake. 'Mr Bolitar, thank you so much for coming. I'm Detective Corbett.'

Myron nodded numbly. 'What happened?'

'A groundskeeper found him this morning at six.'

'Was he shot?'

Corbett smiled crookedly. He was around Myron's age and petite for a cop. Not just short. Plenty of cops were on the short side. But this guy was small-boned to the point of being almost sickly. Corbett covered up the small physique with a trench coat. Not a great summer look. Too many episodes of *Columbo*, Myron guessed.

'I don't want to be rude or anything,' Corbett said, 'but do you mind if I ask the questions?'

Myron glanced at the still body. He felt light-headed. Jack dead. Why? How did it happen? And why had the police decided to question him? 'Where is Mrs Coldren?' Myron asked.

Corbett glanced at the two officers, then at Myron. 'Why would you want to know that?'

'I want to make sure she's safe.'

'Well then,' Corbett began, folding his arms under his chest, 'if that's the case, you should have asked, "How is Mrs Coldren?" or "Is Mrs Coldren all right?" – not "Where is Mrs Coldren?" I mean, if you're really interested in how she is.'

Myron looked at Corbett for several seconds. 'God. You. Are. Good.'

'No reason for sarcasm, Mr Bolitar. You just seem very concerned about her.'

'I am.'

'You a friend?'

'Yes.'

'A close friend?'

'Pardon me?'

'Again, I don't want to appear rude or anything,' Corbett said, spreading his hands, 'but have you been – you know – porking her?'

'Are you out of your mind?'

'Is that a yes?'

Calm down, Myron. Corbett was trying to keep him off balance. Myron knew the game. Dumb to let it get to him. 'The answer is no. We've had no sexual contact whatsoever.'

'Really? That's odd.'

He wanted Myron to bite with a 'What's odd?' Myron did not oblige him.

'You see, a couple of witnesses saw you two together several times over the past few days. At a tent in Corporate Row, mostly. You sat alone for several hours. Very snuggly. Are you sure you weren't playing a little kissy-face?'

Myron said, 'No.'

'No, you weren't playing a little kissy-face, or no—'

'No, we weren't playing kissy-face or anything like that.'

'Uh-huh, I see.' Corbett feigned chewing over this little tidbit. 'Where were you last night, Mr Bolitar?'

'Am I a suspect, Detective?'

'We're just chatting amicably, Mr Bolitar. That's all.'

'Do you have an estimated time of death?' Myron asked.

Corbett offered up another cop-polite smile. 'Once again, far be it from me to be obtuse or rude, but I would rather concentrate on you right now.' His voice gathered a little more muster. 'Where were you last night?'

Myron remembered Linda's call on the cell phone. Undeniably the police had already questioned her. Had she told them about the kidnapping? Probably not. Either way, it was not his place to mention it. He didn't know where things stood. Speaking out of turn could jeopardize Chad's safety. Best to get out of here pronto.

'I'd like to see Mrs Coldren.'

'Why?'

'To make sure she's okay.'

'That's sweet, Mr Bolitar. And very noble. But I'd like you to answer my question.'

'I'd like to see Mrs Coldren first.'

Corbett gave him the narrow cop-eyes. 'Are you refusing to answer my questions?'

'No. But right now my priority is my potential client's welfare.'

248

'Client?'

'Mrs Coldren and I have been discussing the possibility of her signing on with MB SportsReps.'

'I see,' Corbett said, rubbing his chin. 'So that explains your sitting together in the tent.'

'I'll answer your questions later, Detective. Right now I'd like to check up on Mrs Coldren.'

'She's fine, Mr Bolitar.'

'I'd like to see for myself.'

'You don't trust me?'

'It's not that. But if I am going to be her agent, then I must be at her disposal first and foremost.'

Corbett shook his head and raised his eyebrows. 'That's some crock of shit you're peddling, Bolitar.'

'May I go now?'

Corbett gave the big hand spread again. 'You're not under arrest. In fact' – he turned to the two officers – 'please escort Mr Bolitar to the Coldren residence. Make sure nobody bothers him on the way.'

Myron smiled. 'Thank you, Detective.'

'Think nothing of it.' As Myron began to walk away, Corbett called out, 'Oh, one more thing.' The man had definitely watched too much *Columbo*. 'That call you got in the squad car just now. Was that from Mrs Coldren?'

Myron said nothing.

'No matter. We can check the phone records.' He gave the Columbo wave. 'Have a special day.'

Chapter 26

There were four more cop cars outside the Coldren house. Myron walked to the door on his own and knocked. A black woman Myron did not recognize opened it.

Her eyes flicked at the top of his head. 'Nice hat,' she said without inflection. 'Come on in.'

The woman was about fifty years old and wore a nicely tailored suit. Her coffee skin looked leathery and worn. Her face was kind of sleepy, her eyes half-closed, her expression perpetually bored. 'I'm Victoria Wilson,' she said.

'Myron Bolitar.'

'Yes, I know.' Bored voice too.

'Is anybody else here?'

'Just Linda.'

'Can I see her?'

Victoria Wilson nodded slowly; Myron half expected her to stifle a yawn. 'Maybe we should talk first.'

'Are you with the police?' Myron asked.

'The opposite,' she said. 'I'm Mrs Coldren's attorney.'

'That was fast.'

'Let me put this plainly,' she ho-hummed, sounding like a diner waitress reading off the specials in the last hour of a double shift. 'The police believe that Mrs Coldren killed her husband. They also think that you're involved in some way.'

Myron looked at her. 'You're kidding, right?'

The same sleepy expression. 'Do I look like a prankster, Mr Bolitar?'

Rhetorical question.

'Linda does not have a solid alibi for late last night,' she went on, still with the flat tone. 'Do you?'

'Not really.'

'Well, let me tell you what the police already know.' The woman took blasé and raised it to an art form. 'First' – raising a finger in the air seemed to take great effort – 'they have a witness, a groundskeeper, who saw Jack Coldren enter Merion at approximately one in the morning. The same witness also saw Linda Coldren do likewise thirty minutes later. He also saw Linda Coldren leave the grounds not long after that. He never saw Jack Coldren leave.'

'That doesn't mean—'

'Second' – another finger in the air, making a peace sign – 'the police received a report last night at approximately two in the morning that your car, Mr Bolitar, was parked on Golf House Road. The police will want to know what you were doing parking in such a strange spot at such a strange time.'

'How do you know all this?' Myron asked.

'I have good connections with the police,' she said. Again bored. 'May I continue?'

'Please.'

'Third' – yep, another finger – 'Jack Coldren had been seeing a divorce attorney. He had, in fact, begun the process of filing papers.'

'Did Linda know this?'

'No. But one of the allegations Mr Coldren made concerned his wife's recent infidelity.'

Myron put both hands to his chest. 'Don't look at me.'

'Mr Bolitar?'

'What?'

'I am just stating facts. And I'd appreciate it if you didn't interrupt. Fourth' – final finger – 'on Saturday, at the US Open golf tournament, several witnesses described you and Mrs Coldren as being a bit more than chummy.'

Myron waited. Victoria Wilson lowered the hand, never showing the thumb.

'Is that it?' Myron asked.

'No. But that's all we'll discuss for now.'

'I met Linda for the first time on Friday.'

'And you can prove that?'

'Bucky can testify to it. He introduced us.'

Another big sigh. 'Linda Coldren's father. What a perfect, unbiased witness.'

'I live in New York.'

'Which is less than two hours by Amtrak from Philadelphia. Go on.'

'I have a girlfriend. Jessica Culver. I live with her.'

'And no man has ever cheated on his girlfriend before. Stunning testimony.'

Myron shook his head. 'So you're suggesting—'

'Nothing,' Victoria Wilson interrupted him with the monotone. 'I am suggesting absolutely nothing. I am telling you what the police believe – that Linda killed

Jack. The reason why there are so many police officers surrounding this house is because they want to make sure that we do not remove anything before a search warrant is issued. They have made it crystal clear that they want no Kardashians on this one.'

Kardashian. As in O.J. The man had changed law lexicon forever. 'But . . .' Myron stopped. 'This is ridiculous. Where is Linda?'

'Upstairs. I've informed the police that she is too grief-stricken to speak to them at this time.'

'You don't understand. Linda shouldn't even be a suspect. Once she tells you the whole story, you'll see what I mean.'

Another near yawn. 'She has told me the whole story.'

'Even about . . . ?'

'The kidnapping,' Victoria Wilson finished for him. 'Yes.'

'Well, don't you think that kind of exonerates her?'

'No.'

Myron was confused. 'Do the police know about the kidnapping?'

'Of course not. We are saying nothing at this time.'

Myron made a face. 'But once they hear about the kidnapping, they'll focus on that. They'll know Linda couldn't be involved.'

Victoria Wilson turned away. 'Let's go upstairs.'

'You don't agree?'

She didn't respond. They began to climb the staircase. Victoria said, 'You are an attorney.'

It didn't sound like a question, but Myron still said, 'I don't practice.'

'But you passed the bar.'

'In New York.'

'Good enough. I want you to be co-counsel in this case. I can get you an immediate dispensation.'

'I don't do criminal law,' Myron said.

'You don't have to. I just want you to be an attorney of record for Mrs Coldren.'

Myron nodded. 'So I can't testify,' he said. 'So everything I hear falls under privilege.'

Still bored. 'You are a smart one.' She stopped next to a bedroom door and leaned against a wall. 'Go in. I'm going to wait out here.'

Myron knocked. Linda Coldren told him to come in. He opened the door. Linda stood by the far window looking out onto her backyard.

'Linda?'

Her back still faced him. 'I'm having a bad week, Myron.' She laughed. It was not a happy sound.

'Are you okay?' he asked.

'Me? Never better. Thanks for asking.'

He stepped toward her, unsure what to say. 'Did the kidnappers call about the ransom?'

'Last night,' Linda said. 'Jack spoke to them.'

'What did they say?'

'I don't know. He stormed out after the call. He never told me.'

Myron tried to picture this scene. A call comes in. Jack answers it. He runs out without saying anything. It didn't exactly mesh.

'Have you heard from them again?' he tried.

'No, not yet.'

Myron nodded, even though she wasn't facing him. 'So what did you do?'

'Do?'

'Last night. After Jack stormed out.'

Linda Coldren folded her arms across her chest. 'I waited a few minutes for him to calm down,' she said. 'When he didn't come back, I went out looking for him.'

'You went to Merion,' Myron said.

'Yes. Jack likes to stroll the grounds. To think and be alone.'

'Did you see him there?'

'No. I looked around for a while. Then I came back here. That's when I ran into you.'

'And Jack never came back,' Myron said.

With her back still to him, Linda Coldren shook her head. 'What tipped you off, Myron? The dead body in the stone quarry?'

'Just trying to help.'

She turned to him. Her eyes were red. Her face was drawn. She was still incredibly beautiful. 'I just need someone to take it out on.' She shrugged, tried a smile. 'You're here.'

Myron wanted to step closer. He refrained. 'You've been up all night?'

She nodded. 'I've been standing right here, waiting for Jack to come home. When the police knocked on the door, I thought it was about Chad. This is going to sound awful, but when they told me about Jack, I was almost relieved.'

The phone rang.

Linda spun around with enough speed to start up a wind tunnel. She looked at Myron. He looked at her.

'It's probably the media,' he said.

Linda shook her head. 'Not on that line.' She reached for the phone, pressed the lit-up button, picked up the receiver.

'Hello,' she said.

A voice replied. Linda gasped and bit down in mid-scream. Her hand flew to her mouth. Tears pushed their way out of her eyes. The door flew open. Victoria Wilson stepped into the room, looking like a bear stirred from a power nap.

Linda looked up at them both. 'It's Chad,' she said. 'He's free.'

Chapter 27

Victoria Wilson took control. 'We'll go pick him up,' she said. 'You stay on the line with him.'

Linda started shaking her head. 'But I want—'

'Trust me on this, honey. If you go, every cop and news reporter will follow. Myron and I can lose them if we have to. I don't want the police talking to your son until I have. You just stay here. You say nothing. If the police come in with a warrant, you let them in. You don't say a word. No matter what. Do you understand?'

Linda nodded.

'So where is he?'

'On Porter Street.'

'Okay, tell him Aunt Victoria is on the way. We'll take care of him.'

Linda grabbed her arm, her face pleading. 'Will you bring him back here?'

'Not right away, hon.' The voice was still matter-of-fact.

'The police will see. I can't have that. It'll raise too many questions. You'll see him soon enough.'

Victoria Wilson turned away. There was no debate with this woman.

In the car, Myron asked, 'How do you know Linda?'

'My mother and father were servants for the Buckwells and Lockwoods,' she replied. 'I grew up on their estates.'

'But somewhere along the line you went to law school?'

She frowned. 'You writing my biography?'

'I'm just asking.'

'Why? You surprised that a middle-aged black woman is the attorney for rich WASPs?'

'Frankly,' Myron said, 'yes.'

'Don't blame you. But we don't have time for that now. You got any important questions?'

'Yes,' Myron said. He was doing the driving. 'What aren't you telling me?'

'Nothing that you need to know.'

'I'm an attorney of record on the case. I need to know everything.'

'Later. Let's concentrate on the boy first.'

Again the no-argument monotone.

'Are you sure we're doing the right thing?' Myron continued. 'Not telling the police about the kidnapping?'

'We can always tell them later,' Victoria Wilson replied. 'That's the mistake most defendants make. They think they have to talk their way out of it right away. But that's dangerous. There is always time to talk later.'

'I'm not sure I agree.'

'Tell you what, Myron. If we need some expertise on negotiating a sneaker deal, I'll put you in charge. But while this thing is still a criminal case, let me take the lead, okay?'

'The police want to question me.'

'You say nothing. That is your right. You don't have to say a word to the police.'

'Unless they subpoena me.'

'Even then. You are Linda Coldren's attorney. You don't say anything.'

Myron shook his head. 'That only works for what was said *after* you asked me to be co-counsel. They can ask me about anything that happened before.'

'Wrong.' Victoria Wilson gave a distracted sigh. 'When Linda Coldren first asked you to help, she knew you were a bar-appointed attorney. Therefore everything she told you fell under attorney-client.'

Myron had to smile. 'That's reaching.'

'But that's the way it is.' He could feel her eyes on him now. 'No matter what you might want to do, morally and legally you are not allowed to talk to anyone.'

She was good.

Myron drove a bit faster. No one was tailing them; the police and the reporters had stuck to the house. The story was all over the radio. The anchorman kept repeating a one-line statement issued by Linda Coldren: 'We are all saddened by this tragedy. Please allow us to grieve in peace.'

'You issue that statement?' Myron asked.

'No. Linda did it before I got there.'

'Why?'

'She thought it would keep the media off her back. She knows better now.'

They pulled up on Porter Street. Myron scanned the sidewalks.

'Up there,' Victoria Wilson said.

Myron saw him. Chad Coldren was huddled on the

ground. The telephone receiver was still gripped in one hand, but he wasn't talking. The other hand was heavily bandaged. Myron felt a little queasy. He hit the gas pedal. The car jerked forward. They pulled up to the boy. Chad stared straight ahead.

Victoria Wilson's indifferent expression finally melted a bit. 'Let me handle this,' she said.

She got out of the car and walked over to the boy. She bent down and cradled him. She took the receiver away from him, talked into it, hung up. She helped Chad to his feet, stroking his hair, whispering comforts. They both got into the backseat, Chad leaned his head against her. She made soothing shushing noises. She nodded at Myron. Myron put the car in drive.

Chad did not speak during the drive. Nobody asked him to. Victoria gave Myron directions to her office building in Bryn Mawr. The Coldren family doctor – a gray-haired, old family friend named Henry Lane – had his office there too. He unwrapped Chad's bandage and examined the boy while Myron and Victoria waited in another room. Myron paced. Victoria read a magazine.

'We should take him to a hospital,' Myron said.

'Dr Lane will decide if that's necessary.' Victoria yawned and flipped a page.

Myron tried to take it all in. With all the activity surrounding the police accusation and Chad's safe recovery, he had almost forgotten about Jack Coldren. Jack was dead. It was almost impossible for Myron to comprehend. The irony did not escape him: the man finally has the chance at redemption and he ends up dead in the same hazard that altered his life twenty-three years ago.

Dr Lane appeared in the doorway. He was everything you wanted a doctor to look like – Marcus Welby without the receding hairline. 'Chad is better now. He's talking. He's alert.'

'How's his hand?' Myron asked.

'It'll need to be looked at by a specialist. But there's no infection or anything like that.'

Victoria Wilson stood. 'I'd like to talk to him.'

Lane nodded. 'I would warn you to go easy on him, Victoria, but I know you never listen.'

Her mouth almost twitched. Not a smile. Not even close. But there was a sign of life. 'You'll have to stay out here, Henry. The police may ask you what you heard.'

The doctor nodded again. 'I understand.'

Victoria looked at Myron. 'I'll do the talking.'

'Okay.'

When Myron and Victoria entered the room, Chad was staring down at his bandaged hand like he expected the missing finger to grow back.

'Chad?'

He slowly looked up. There were tears in his eyes. Myron remembered what Linda had said about the kid's love of golf. Another dream lay in ashes. The kid did not know it, but right now he and Myron were kindred spirits.

'Who are you?' Chad asked Myron.

'He's a friend,' Victoria Wilson replied. Even with the boy, the tone was completely detached. 'His name is Myron Bolitar.'

'I want to see my parents, Aunt Vee.'

Victoria sat across from him. 'A lot has happened, Chad. I don't want to go into it all now. You'll have to trust me, okay?'

Chad nodded.

'I need to know what happened to you. Everything. From the beginning.'

'A man car-jacked me,' Chad said.

'Just one man?'

'Yeah.'

'Go on. Tell me what happened.'

'I was at a traffic light, and this guy just opens the passenger door and gets in. He's wearing a ski mask and sticks this gun in my face. He told me to keep driving.'

'Okay. What day was this?'

'Thursday.'

'Where were you Wednesday night?'

'At my friend Matt's house.'

'Matthew Squires?'

'Yes.'

'Okay, fine.' Victoria Wilson's eyes did not wander from the boy's face. 'Now where were you when this man got into your car?'

'A couple of blocks from school.'

'Did this happen before or after summer school?'

'After. I was on my way home.'

Myron kept quiet. He wondered why the boy was lying.

'Where did the man take you?'

'He told me to drive around the block. We pulled into this parking lot. Then he put something over my head. A burlap bag or something. He made me lie down in the back. Then he started driving. I don't know where we went. I never saw anything. Next thing I knew I was in a room someplace. I had to keep the bag on my head all the time so I didn't see anything.'

'You never saw the man's face?'

'Never.'

'Are you sure it was a man? Could it have been a woman?'

'I heard his voice a few times. It was a man. At least, one of them was.'

'There was more than one?'

Chad nodded. 'The day he did this . . .' He lifted his bandaged hand into view. His face went totally blank. He looked straight ahead, his eyes unfocused. 'I had that burlap bag over my head. My hands were handcuffed behind my back.' His voice was as detached as Victoria's now. 'That bag was so itchy. I used to rub my chin against my shoulder. Just for relief. Anyway, the man came in and unlocked the handcuffs. Then he grabbed my hand and put it flat on the table. He didn't say anything. He didn't warn me. The whole thing took less than ten seconds. He just put my hand on the table. I never saw a thing. I just heard a whack. Then I felt this weird sensation. Not even pain at first. I didn't know what it was. Then I felt a warm wetness. From the blood, I guess. The pain came a few seconds later. I passed out. When I woke up, my hand was wrapped. The throbbing was awful. The burlap bag was back over my head. Someone came in. Gave me some pills. It dulled the pain a little. Then I heard voices. Two of them. It sounded like they were arguing.'

Chad Coldren stopped as though out of breath. Myron watched Victoria Wilson. She did not go over and comfort him.

'Were the voices both male?'

'Actually, one sounded like a female. But I was pretty out of it. I can't say for sure.'

Chad looked back down at his bandages. He moved his fingers a bit. Testing them out.

'What happened next, Chad?'

He kept his eyes on the bandages. 'There's not a lot to tell, Aunt Vee. They kept me that way for a few days. I don't know how many. They fed me mostly pizza and soda. They brought a phone in one day. Made me call Merion and ask for my dad.'

The ransom call at Merion, Myron thought. The kidnapper's second call.

'They also made me scream.'

'Made you scream?'

'The guy came in. He told me to scream and to make it scary. Otherwise, he would make me scream for real. So I tried different screams for, like, ten minutes. Until he was satisfied.'

The scream from the call at the mall, Myron thought. The one where Tito demanded a hundred grand.

'That's about it, Aunt Vee.'

'How did you escape?' Victoria asked.

'I didn't. They let me go. A little while ago someone led me to a car. I still had the burlap bag on my head. We drove a little. Then the car stopped. Someone opened the door and pulled me out. Next thing I knew, I was free.'

Victoria looked over at Myron. Myron looked back. Then she nodded slowly. Myron took that as his cue.

'He's lying.'

Chad said, 'What?'

Myron turned his attention to him. 'You're lying, Chad. And worse, the police will know you're lying.'

'What are you talking about?' His eyes sought Victoria's. 'Who is this guy?'

'You used your ATM card at 6:18 P.M. on Thursday on Porter Street,' Myron said.

Chad's eyes widened. 'That wasn't me. It was the asshole who grabbed me. He took my wallet—'

'It's on videotape, Chad.'

He opened his mouth, but nothing came out. Then: 'They made me.' But his voice was weak.

'I saw the tape, Chad. You were smiling. You were happy. You were not alone. You also spent an evening at the sleazy motel next door.'

Chad lowered his head.

'Chad?' It was Victoria. She did not sound pleased. 'Look at me, boy.'

Chad slowly raised his eyes.

'Why are you lying to me?'

'It has nothing to do with what happened, Aunt Vee.'

Her face was unyielding. 'Start talking, Chad. And now.'

He looked down again, studying the bandaged hand. 'It's just like I said – except the man didn't grab me in my car. He knocked on my door at that motel. He came in with a gun. Everything else I told you is the truth.'

'When was this?'

'Friday morning.'

'So why did you lie to me?'

'I promised,' he said. 'I just wanted to keep her out of this.'

'Who?' she asked.

Chad looked surprised. 'You don't know?'

'I have the tape,' Myron said, giving a little bluff here. 'I haven't shown it to her yet.'

'Aunt Vee, you have to keep her out of it. This could really hurt her.'

'Honey, listen to me now. I think it's sweet that you're trying to protect your girlfriend. But I don't have time for that.'

Chad looked from Myron to Victoria. 'I want to see my mom please.'

'You will, honey. Soon. But first you have to tell me about this girl.'

'I promised that I would keep her out of it.'

'If I can keep her name out of this, I will.'

'I can't, Aunt Vee.'

'Forget it, Victoria,' Myron said. 'If he won't tell, we can all just watch the tape together. Then we can call the girl on her own. Or maybe the police will find her first. They'll have a copy of the tape too. They won't be so worried about her feelings.'

'You don't understand,' Chad said, looking from Victoria Wilson to Myron, then back at Victoria again. 'I promised her. She can get in serious trouble.'

'We'll talk to her parents, if need be,' Victoria said. 'We'll do what we can.'

'Her parents?' Chad looked confused. 'I'm not worried about her parents. She's old enough . . .' His voice died away.

'Who were you with, Chad?'

'I swore I'd never say anything, Aunt Vee.'

'Fine,' Myron said. 'We can't waste time on this, Victoria. Let the police track her down.'

'No!' Chad looked down. 'She had nothing to do with it, okay? We were together. She went out for a little while and that's when they grabbed me. It wasn't her fault.'

Victoria shifted in her seat. 'Who, Chad?'

His words came out slow and grudging. But they were also quite clear. 'Her name is Esme Fong. She works for a company called Zoom.'

Chapter 28

It was all starting to make awful, horrible sense.

Myron did not wait for permission. He stormed out of the office and down the corridor. It was time to confront Esme.

A scenario was fast taking shape in Myron's mind. Esme Fong meets Chad Coldren while negotiating the Zoom deal with his mother. She seduces him. Why? Hard to say. For kicks maybe. Not important.

Anyway, Chad spends Wednesday night with his buddy Matthew. Then on Thursday he meets up with Esme for a romantic tryst at the Court Manor Inn. They pick up some cash at an ATM. They have their fun. And then things get interesting.

Esme Fong has not only signed Linda Coldren, but she has managed to land wunderkind Tad Crispin. Tad is playing wonderfully well in his first US Open. After one round, he is in second place. Amazing. Great publicity. But if Tad could somehow win – if he could catch the veteran with a gigantic lead – it would give Zoom's launch into the golf business a nuclear boost. It would be worth millions.

Millions.

And Esme had the leader's son right in front of her.

So what does the ambitious Esme Fong do? She hires Tito to grab the boy. Nothing complicated. She wants to distract Jack big-time. Make him lose that edge. What better way than kidnapping his kid?

It all kinda fit together.

Myron turned his attention to some of case's more bothersome aspects. First of all, the not demanding the ransom for so long suddenly made sense. Esme Fong is no expert at this and she doesn't want a payoff – that would just complicate manners – so the first few calls are awkward. She forgets to demand a ransom. Second, Myron remembered Tito's 'chink bitch' call. How had he known Esme was there? Simple. Esme had told him when she would be there – to scare the hell out of the Coldrens and make them think they were being watched.

Yep. It fit. Everything had been going according to Esme Fong's plan. Except for one thing.

Jack continued to play well.

He maintained his insurmountable lead through the next round. The kidnapping may have stunned him a bit, but he had regained his footing. His lead was still huge. Drastic action was necessary.

Myron got into the elevator and headed down to the ground-floor lobby. He wondered how it had happened. Maybe it had been Tito's idea. Maybe that was why Chad had heard two voices arguing. Either way, someone decided to do something that was guaranteed to throw Jack off his game.

Cut off Chad's finger.

Like it or not – Tito's idea or hers – Esme Fong took advantage. She had Linda's car keys. She knew what her car looked like. It wouldn't take much. Just a turn of the key, a quick drop on the car seat. Easy for her. Nothing suspicious. Who would notice an attractive, well-dressed woman unlocking a car with a key?

The severed finger did the trick, too. Jack's game was left in shambles. Tad Crispin stormed back. It was everything she wanted. But, alas, Jack had one more trick up his sleeve. He managed to land a big putt on the eighteenth hole, forcing a tie. This was a nightmare for Esme. She could not take the risk of Tad Crispin losing to Jack, the ultimate choker, in a one-on-one situation.

A loss would be disastrous.

A loss would cost them millions. Maybe destroy her entire campaign.

Man, did it fit.

When Myron thought about it, hadn't he heard Esme voice that very viewpoint with Norm Zuckerman? Her Buffalo Bill analogy – hadn't he been standing right there when she said it? Now that she was trapped, was it so hard to believe that she'd go the extra mile? That she would call Jack on the phone last night? That she would set up a rendezvous at the course? That she would insist he come alone – right now – if he wanted to see his son alive?

Ka-bang.

And once Jack was dead, there was no reason to hold on to the kid anymore. She let him go.

The elevator slid open. Myron stepped out. Okay, there were holes. But maybe after confronting Esme, he would be able to plug a few of them up. Myron pushed open the glass door. He headed into the parking lot. There were taxis waiting near the street. He was midway through the lot when a voice reached out and pulled him to a stop.

'Myron?'

An icy nerve-jangle punctured a hole through his heart. He had heard the voice only once before. Ten years ago. At Merion.

Chapter 29

Myron froze.

'I see you've met Victoria,' Cissy Lockwood said.

He tried a nod, but it wouldn't happen.

'I called her as soon as Bucky told me about the murder. I knew she'd be able to help. Victoria is the best lawyer I know. Ask Win about her.'

He tried the nod again. Got a little motion going this time.

Win's mother stepped closer. 'I'd like a word with you in private, Myron.'

He found his voice. 'It's not a good time, Ms Lockwood.'

'No, I imagine not. Still, this won't take long.'

'Really, I should go.'

She was a beautiful woman. Her ash-blond hair was streaked with gray, and she had the same regal bearing as her blood niece Linda. The porcelain face, however, she had given almost verbatim to Win. The resemblance was uncanny.

She took one more step forward, her eyes never off him. Her clothes were a bit odd. She wore a man's over-size shirt, untucked, and stretch pants. Annie Hall goes maternity shopping. It was not what he'd have expected, but then again, he had bigger worries than fashion right now.

'It's about Win,' she said.

Myron shook his head. 'Then it's none of my business.'

'True enough. But that does not make you immune to responsibility, does it? Win is your friend. I count myself lucky that my son has a friend who cares like you do.'

Myron said nothing.

'I know quite a bit about you, Myron. I've had private investigators keep tabs on Win for years now. It was my way of staying close. Of course, Win knew about it. He never said anything, but you can't keep something like that from Win, now can you?'

'No,' Myron said. 'You can't.'

'You're staying at the Lockwood estate,' she said. 'In the guest cottage.'

He nodded.

'You've been there before.'

Another nod.

'Have you ever seen the horse stables?'

'Only from a distance,' Myron said.

She smiled Win's smile. 'You've never been inside?'

'No.'

'I'm not surprised. Win doesn't ride anymore. He used to love horses. More than golf even.'

'Ms Lockwood—'

'Please call me Cissy.'

273

'I really don't feel comfortable hearing this.'

Her eyes hardened a bit. 'And I do not feel comfortable telling you this. But it must be done.'

'Win wouldn't want me to hear it,' Myron said.

'That's too bad, but Win cannot always have what he wants. I should have learned that long ago. He did not want to see me as a child. I never forced it. I listened to the experts, who told me that my son would come around, that compelling him to see me would be counter-productive. But they did not know Win. By the time I stopped listening to them it was too late. Not that it mattered. I don't think ignoring them would have changed anything.'

Silence.

She stood proud and tall, her slender neck high. But something was going on. Her fingers kept flexing, as if she were fighting off the desire to make fists. Myron's stomach knotted up. He knew what was coming next. He just didn't know what to do about it.

'The story is simple,' she began, her voice almost wistful. She was no longer looking at Myron. Her gaze rose above his shoulder, but he had no idea what she was actually seeing. 'Win was eight years old. I was twenty-seven at the time. I married young. I never went to college. It was not as though I had a choice. My father told me what to do. I had only one friend – one person I could confide in. That was Victoria. She is still my dearest friend, not unlike what you are to Win.'

Cissy Lockwood winced. Her eyes closed.

'Ms Lockwood?'

She shook her head. The eyes slowly opened. 'I am getting off track,' she said, catching her breath. 'I apologize. I'm not here to tell you my life story. Just one incident in it. So let me just state it plainly.'

A deep breath. Then another.

'Jack Coldren told me that he was taking Win out for a golf lesson. But it never happened. Or perhaps they had finished far earlier than expected. Either way, Jack was not with Win. His father was. Somehow Win and his father ended up going into the stables. I was there when they entered. I was not alone. More specifically, I was with Win's riding instructor.'

She stopped. Myron waited.

'Do I need to spell this out for you?'

Myron shook his head.

'No child should see what Win saw that day,' she said. 'And worse, no child should ever see his father's face under those circumstances.'

Myron felt tears sting his eyes.

'There is more to it, of course. I won't go into it now. But Win has never spoken to me since that moment. He also never forgave his father. Yes, his father. You think he hates only me and loves Windsor the Second. But it is not so. He blames his father, too. He thinks that his father is weak. That he allowed it to happen. Utter nonsense, but that is the way it is.'

Myron shook his head. He didn't want to hear any more. He wanted to run and find Win. He wanted to hug his friend and shake him and somehow make him forget. He thought of the lost expression on Win's face as he watched the horse stables yesterday morning.

My God. Win.

When Myron spoke, his voice was sharper than he'd expected. 'Why are you telling me this?'

'Because I am dying,' she replied.

Myron slumped against a car. His heart ripped anew.

'Again, let me put this simply,' she said in too calm a voice. 'It has reached the liver. It is eleven centimeters long. My abdomen is swelling from liver and kidney failure.' That explained the wardrobe – the untucked, oversize shirt and the stretch pants. 'We are not talking months. We are talking perhaps weeks. Probably less.'

'There are treatments,' Myron tried lamely. 'Procedures.'

She simply dismissed this with a shake of her head. 'I am not a foolish woman. I do not have delusions of engaging in a moving reunion with my son. I know Win. That will not happen. But there is still unfinished business here. Once I am dead, there will be no chance for him to disentangle himself again. It will be over. I do not know what he will do with this opportunity. Probably nothing. But I want him to know. So that he can decide. It is his last chance, Myron. I do not believe he will take it. But he should.'

With that, she turned away and left. Myron watched her walk away. When she was out of sight, Myron hailed a taxi. He got in the back.

'Where to, bud?'

He gave the man the address where Esme Fong was staying. Then he settled back in the seat. His eyes stared blankly out the window. The city passed by in a misty, silent blur.

Chapter 30

When he thought that his voice would not betray him, Myron called Win on the cell phone.

After a quick hello, Win said, 'Bummer about Jack.'

'From what I hear, he used to be your friend.'

Win cleared his throat. 'Myron?'

'What?'

'You know nothing. Remember that.'

True enough. 'Can we have dinner tonight?'

Win hesitated. 'Of course.'

'At the cottage. Six-thirty.'

'Fine.'

Win hung up. Myron tried to put it out of his mind. He had other things to worry about.

Esme Fong paced the sidewalk outside the entrance to the Omni Hotel on the corner of Chestnut Street and Fourth. She wore a white suit and white stockings. Killer legs. She kept wringing her hands.

Myron got out of the taxi. 'Why are you waiting out here?' he asked.

'You insisted on talking privately,' Esme answered. 'Norm is upstairs.'

'You two live in the same room?'

'No, we have adjoining suites.'

Myron nodded. The no-tell motel was making more sense now. 'Not much privacy, huh?'

'No, not really.' She gave him a tentative smile. 'But it's okay. I like Norm.'

'I'm sure you do.'

'What's this about, Myron?'

'You heard about Jack Coldren?'

'Of course. Norm and I were shocked. Absolutely shocked.'

Myron nodded. 'Come on,' he said. 'Let's walk.'

They headed up Fourth Street. Myron was tempted to stay on Chestnut Street, but that would have meant strolling past Independence Hall and that would have been a tad too cliché for his liking. Still, Fourth Street was in the colonial section. Lots of brick. Brick sidewalk, brick walls and fence, brick buildings of tremendous historical significance that all looked the same. White ash trees lined the walk. They turned right into a park that held the Second Bank of the United States. There was a plaque with a portrait of the bank's first president. One of Win's ancestors. Myron looked for a resemblance but could not find one.

'I've tried to reach Linda,' Esme said. 'But the phone is busy.'

'Did you try Chad's line?'

Something hit her face, then fled. 'Chad's line?'

278

'He has his own phone in the house,' he said. 'You must have known that.'

'Why would I know that?'

Myron shrugged. 'I thought you knew Chad.'

'I do,' she said, but her voice was slow, careful. 'I mean, I've been over to the house a number of times.'

'Uh-huh. And when was the last time you saw Chad?'

She put her hand to her chin. 'I don't think he was there when I went over Friday night,' she said, the voice still slow. 'I don't really know. I guess a few weeks ago.'

Myron made a buzzing noise. 'Incorrect answer.'

'Excuse me?'

'I don't get it, Esme.'

'What?'

Myron continued walking, Esme stayed in step. 'You're what,' he said, 'twenty-four years old?'

'Twenty-five.'

'You're smart. You're successful. You're attractive. But a teenage boy – what's up with that?'

She stopped. 'What are you talking about?'

'You really don't know?'

'I don't have the slightest idea.'

His eyes bore into hers. 'You. Chad Coldren. The Court Manor Inn. That help?'

'No.'

Myron gave her skeptical. 'Please.'

'Did Chad tell you that?'

'Esme . . .'

'He's lying, Myron. My God, you know how teenage boys are. How could you believe something like that?'

'Pictures, Esme.'

Her face went slack. 'What?'

'You two stopped at an ATM machine next door to the

motel, remember? They have cameras. Your face was clear as day.' It was a bluff. But it was a damn good one. She caved a little piece at a time. She looked around and then collapsed on a bench. She turned and faced a colonial building with a lot of scaffolding. Scaffolding, Myron thought, ruined the effect – like armpit hair on a beautiful woman. It shouldn't really matter, but it did.

'Please don't tell Norm,' she said in a faraway voice. 'Please don't.'

Myron said nothing.

'It was dumb. I know that. But it shouldn't cost me my job.'

Myron sat next to her. 'Tell me what happened.'

She looked back at him. 'Why? What business is this of yours?'

'There are reasons.'

'What reasons?' Her voice was a little sharper now. 'Look, I'm not proud of myself. But who appointed you my conscience?'

'Fine. I'll go ask Norm then. Maybe he can help me.'

Her mouth dropped. 'Help you with what? I don't understand. Why are you doing this to me?'

'I need some answers. I don't have time to explain.'

'What do you want me to say? That I was dumb? I was. I could tell you that I was lonely being in a nice place. That he seemed like a sweet, handsome kid and that at his age, I figured there'd be no fear of disease or attachments. But at the end of the day, that does not change much. I was wrong. I'm sorry, okay?'

'When was the last time you saw Chad?'

'Why do you keep asking me that?' Esme insisted.

'Just answer my questions or I'll go to Norm, I swear it.'

She studied his face. He put on his most impermeable face, the one he'd learned from really tough cops and toll collectors on the New Jersey Turnpike. After a few seconds she said, 'At that motel.'

'The Court Manor Inn?'

'Whatever it was called. I don't remember the name.'

'What day was that?' Myron asked.

She thought a moment. 'Friday morning. Chad was still sleeping.'

'You haven't seen or spoken to him since?'

'No.'

'You didn't have any plans to rendezvous for another tryst?'

She made an unhappy face. 'No, not really. I thought he was just out for some fun, but once we were there, I could see he was developing a crush. I didn't count on that. Frankly I was worried.'

'Of what exactly?'

'That he'd tell his mother. Chad swore he wouldn't, but who knew what he'd do if I hurt him? When I didn't hear from him again, I was relieved.'

Myron searched her face and her story for lies. He couldn't find one. Didn't mean they weren't there.

Esme shifted on the bench, crossing her legs. 'I still don't understand why you're asking me all this.' She thought about it a moment and then something seemed to spark in her eyes. She squared her shoulders toward Myron. 'Does this have something to do with Jack's murder?'

Myron said nothing.

'My God.' Her voice quaked. 'You can't possibly think that Chad has something to do with it.'

Myron waited a beat. All-or-nothing time. 'No,' he said. 'But I'm not so sure about you.'

Confusion set camp on her face. 'What?'

'I think you kidnapped Chad.'

She raised both hands. 'Are you out of your mind? Kidnapped? It was completely consensual. Chad was more than willing, believe me. Okay, he was young. But do you think I took him to that motel at gunpoint?'

'That's not what I mean,' Myron said.

Confusion again. 'Then what the hell do you mean?'

'After you left the motel on Friday. Where did you go?'

'To Merion. I met you there that night, remember?'

'How about last night? Where were you?'

'Here.'

'In your suite?'

'Yes.'

'What time?'

'From eight o'clock on.'

'Anybody who can verify that?'

'Why would I need someone to verify that?' she snapped. Myron put on the impermeable face again – not even gases could get through. Esme sighed. 'I was with Norm until midnight. We were working.'

'And after that?'

'I went to bed.'

'Would the hotel's nightman be able to verify that you never left your suite after midnight?'

'I think so, yes. His name is Miguel. He's very nice.'

Miguel. He'd have Esperanza track down that one. If her alibi stuck, his neat little scenario went down the toilet. 'Who else knew about you and Chad Coldren?'

'No one,' she said. 'At least, I told no one.'

'How about Chad? Did he tell anyone?'

'It sounds to me like he told you,' she said pointedly. 'He might have told someone else, I don't know.'

Myron thought about it. The black-clad man crawling out Chad's bedroom window. Matthew Squires. Myron remembered his own teenage years. If he had somehow managed to bed an older woman who looked like Esme Fong, he would have been busting to tell someone – especially if he'd been staying at his best friend's house the night before.

Once again, things circled back to the Squires kid.

Myron asked, 'Where will you be if I need to reach you?'

She reached into her pocket and pulled out a card. 'My cell phone number is on the bottom.'

'Good-bye, Esme.'

'Myron?'

He turned to her.

'Are you going to tell Norm?'

She seemed only worried about her reputation and her job, not a murder rap. Or was this just a clever diversion? No way of knowing for sure.

'No,' he said. 'I won't tell.'

At least, not yet.

Chapter 31

Episcopal Academy. Win's high school alma mater.

Esperanza had picked him up in front of Esme Fong's and driven him here. She parked across the street. She turned off the ignition and faced him.

'Now what?' she asked.

'I don't know. Matthew Squires is in there. We can wait for a lunch break. Try to get in then.'

'Sounds like a plan,' Esperanza said with a nod. 'A really bad one.'

'You have a better idea?'

'We can go in now. Pretend we're touring parents.'

Myron thought about it. 'You think that'll work?'

'Better than hanging out here doing nothing.'

'Oh, before I forget. I want you to check out Esme's alibi. The hotel nightman named Miguel.'

'Miguel,' she repeated. 'It's because I'm Hispanic, right?'

'Pretty much, yeah.'

She had no problem with that. 'I put a call in to Peru this morning.'

'And?'

'I spoke to some local sheriff. He says Lloyd Rennart committed suicide.'

'What about the body?'

'The cliff is called *El Garganta del Diablo* – in English, Throat of the Devil. No bodies are ever located. It's actually a fairly common suicide plunge.'

'Great. Think you can do a little more background stuff on Rennart?'

'Like what?'

'How did he buy the bar in Neptune? How did he buy the house in Spring Lake Heights? Stuff like that.'

'Why would you want know that?'

'Lloyd Rennart was a caddie for a rookie golfer. That isn't exactly loads of dough.'

'So?'

'So maybe he had a windfall after Jack blew the US Open.'

Esperanza saw where he was going. 'You think somebody paid Rennart off to throw the Open?'

'No,' Myron said. 'But I think it's a possibility.'

'It's going to be hard to trace after all this time.'

'Just give it a shot. Also, Rennart got into a serious car accident twenty years ago in Narberth. It's a small town right around here. His first wife was killed in the crash. See what you can find out about it.'

Esperanza frowned. 'Like what?'

'Like was he drunk. Was he charged with anything. Were there other fatalities.'

'Why?'

'Maybe he pissed off someone. Maybe his first wife's family wants vengeance.'

Esperanza kept the frown. 'So they – what? – waited twenty years, followed Lloyd Rennart to Peru, pushed him off a cliff, came back, kidnapped Chad Coldren, killed Jack Coldren . . . Are you getting my point?'

Myron nodded. 'And you're right. But I still want you to run down everything you can on Lloyd Rennart. I think there's a connection somewhere. We just have to find what it is.'

'I don't see it,' Esperanza said. She tucked a curl of black hair behind her ear. 'Seems to me that Esme Fong is still a much better suspect.'

'Agreed. But I'd still like you to look into it. Find out what you can. There's also a son, Larry Rennart. Seventeen years old. See if we can find out what he's been up to.'

She shrugged. 'A waste of time, but okay.' She gestured toward the school. 'You want to go in now?'

'Sure.'

Before they moved, a giant set of knuckles gently tapped on Myron's window. The sound startled him. Myron looked out his window. The large black man with the Nat King Cole hair – the one from the Court Manor Inn – was smiling at him. 'Nat' made a cranking motion with his hand, signaling Myron to lower the window. Myron complied.

'Hey, I'm glad we ran into you,' Myron said. 'I never got the number of your barber.'

The black man chuckled. He made a frame with his large hands – thumbs touching, arms outstretched – and tilted it back and forth the way a movie director does.

'You with my doo,' he said with a shake of his head. 'Somehow I just don't see it.'

He leaned into the car and stuck his hand across Myron toward Esperanza. 'My name is Carl.'

'Esperanza.' She shook his hand.

'Yes, I know.'

Esperanza squinted at him. 'I know you.'

'Indeed you do.'

She snapped her fingers. 'Mosambo, the Kenyan Killer, the Safari Slasher.'

Carl smiled. 'Nice to see Little Pocahontas remembers.'

Myron said, 'The Safari Slasher?'

'Carl used to be a professional wrestler,' Esperanza explained. 'We were in the ring together once. In Boston, right?'

Carl climbed into the backseat of the car. He leaned forward so his head was between Esperanza's right shoulder and Myron's left. 'Hartford,' he said. 'At the Civic Center.'

'Mixed tag-team,' Esperanza said.

'That's right,' Carl said with his easy smile. 'Be a sweetheart, Esperanza, and start up the car. Head straight until the third traffic light.'

Myron said, 'You mind telling us what's going on?'

'Sure thing. See that car behind you?'

Myron used the passenger-side mirror. 'The one with the two goons?'

'Yep. They're with me. And they are bad men, Myron. Young. Far too violent. You know how the kids are today. *Bam, bam*, no talk. The three of us are supposed to escort you to an unknown destination. In fact, I'm supposed to be holding a gun on you now. But hell, we're all friends here, right? No need, the way I see it. So just start heading straight. The goons will follow.'

'Before we take off,' Myron said, 'do you mind if we let Esperanza go?'

Carl chuckled. 'Kinda sexist, don't you think?'

'Excuse me?'

'If Esperanza were a man – like, say, your buddy Win – would you be making this gallant gesture?'

'I might,' he said. But even Esperanza was shaking her head.

'Me thinks not, Myron. And trust me here: it would be the wrong move. The young goons back there, they'd want to know what's up. They'd see her get out of the car and they got those itchy fingers and those crazy eyes and they like hurting people. Especially women. And maybe, just maybe, Esperanza here is an insurance policy. Alone, you might try something dumb; with Esperanza right there, you might not be so inclined.'

Esperanza glanced at Myron. Myron nodded. She started the car.

'Make a left at the third light,' Carl said.

'Tell me something,' Myron said. 'Is Reginald Squires as big a nut-job as I hear?'

Still leaning forward, Carl turned to Esperanza. 'Am I supposed to be wowed by his sharp deductive reasoning skills?'

'Yes,' Esperanza replied. 'He'll be terribly disappointed if you aren't.'

'Figured that. And to answer your question, Squires is not that big a nut-job – when he stays on his medication.'

'Very comforting,' Myron said.

The young goons stayed right on their tail for the entire fifteen-minute drive. Myron was not surprised when Carl told Esperanza to turn down Green Acres Road. When they approached the ornate front entrance, the iron gates swung open like on the closing credits of *Get Smart*. They continued up a windy driveway through the heavily wooded property. After about a half mile, they hit a clearing with a building. The building was big and plain and rectangular, like a high school gym.

The only entrance Myron could see was a garage door. As if on cue, the door slid open. Carl told Esperanza to pull into it. Once far enough inside, he told her to park and kill the engine. The goon car came in behind them and did likewise.

The garage door came back down, slowly slicing out the sun. No lights were on inside; the room was submerged in total darkness.

'This is just like the haunted house at Six Flags,' Myron said.

'Give me your gun, Myron.'

Carl had his game face on. Myron handed him the gun.

'Step out of the car.'

'But I'm afraid of the dark,' Myron said.

'You too, Esperanza.'

They all stepped out the car. So did the two goons behind them. Their movements echoed off the cement floor, hinting to Myron that they were in a very large room. The interior car lights provided a modicum of illumination, but that didn't last long. Myron made out nothing before the doors were closed.

Absolute blackness.

Myron made his way around the car and found Esperanza. She took his hand in hers. They remained still and waited.

A beacon, the kind used at a lighthouse or a movie

premiere, snapped on in their faces. Myron's eyes slammed shut. He shaded them with his hand and slowly squinted them open. A man stepped in front of the bright light. His body cast a giant shadow on the wall behind Myron. The effect reminded Myron of the Bat Signal.

'No one will hear your screams,' the man said.

'Isn't that a line from a movie?' Myron asked. 'But I think the line was, "No one will hear you scream." I could be wrong about that.'

'People have died in this room,' the voice boomed. 'My name is Reginald Squires. You will tell me everything I want to know. Or you and your friend will be next.'

Oh, boy. Myron looked at Carl. Carl's face remained stoic. Myron turned back toward the light. 'You're rich, right?'

'Very rich,' Squires corrected.

'Then maybe you could afford a better scriptwriter.'

Myron glanced back at Carl. Carl slowly shook his head no. One of the two young goons stepped forward. In the harsh light, Myron could see the man's psychotic, happy smile. Myron tensed, waited.

The goon cocked a fist and threw it at Myron's head. Myron ducked, and the punch missed. As the fist flew by him, Myron grabbed the goon's wrist. He put his forearm against the back of the man's elbow and pulled the joint back in a way it was never intended to bend. The goon had no choice. He dropped to the ground. Myron added a bit more pressure. The goon tried to squirm free. Myron snapped his knee straight into the goon's nose. Something splattered. Myron could actually feel the nose cartilage give way and fan out.

The second goon took out his gun and pointed it at Myron.

'Stop,' Squires shouted.

Myron let the goon go. He slid to the floor like wet sand through a torn bag.

'You will pay for that, Mr Bolitar.' Squires liked to project his voice. 'Robert?'

The goon with the gun said, 'Yes, Mr Squires.'

'Hit the girl. Hard.'

'Yes, Mr Squires.'

Myron said, 'Hey, hit me. I'm the one who smarted off.'

'And this is your punishment,' Squires said calmly. 'Hit the girl, Robert. Now.'

Goon Robert moved toward Esperanza.

'Mr Squires?' It was Carl.

'Yes, Carl.'

Carl stepped into the light. 'Allow me to do it.'

'I did not think you were the type, Carl.'

'I'm not, Mr Squires. But Robert might do serious damage to her.'

'But that's my intent.'

'No, I mean, he'll leave bruising or break something. You want her to feel pain. That's my area of expertise.'

'I realize that, Carl. It's why I pay you what I do.'

'So then let me do my job. I can hit her without leaving a mark or permanent injury. I know control. I know the right spots.'

The shadowy Mr Squires considered this a moment. 'Will you make it painful?' he asked. 'Very painful?'

'If you insist.' Carl sounded reluctant but resolved.

'I do. Right now. I want it to hurt her a great deal.'

Carl walked up to Esperanza. Myron start to move toward him, but Robert placed the gun against his head.

There was nothing he could do. He tried fire-throwing a warning glare at Carl.

'Don't,' Myron said.

Carl ignored him. He stood in front of Esperanza now. She looked at him defiantly. Without preamble he punched her deep in the stomach.

The power of the blow lifted Esperanza off her feet. She made an oofing noise and folded at the waist like an old wallet. Her body landed on the floor. She curled up into a protective ball, her eyes wide, her chest heaving for air. Carl looked down at her without emotion. Then he looked at Myron.

'You son of a bitch,' Myron said.

'It's your fault,' Carl said.

Esperanza continued to roll on the ground in obvious agony. She still couldn't get any air into her lungs. Myron's whole body felt hot and red. He moved toward her, but Robert again stopped him by pressing the gun hard against his neck.

Reginald Squires did the big voice-projection again. 'You will listen now, won't you, Mr. Bolitar?'

Myron took deep breaths. His muscles bunched. Every part of him fumed. Every part of him craved vengeance. He watched in silence as Esperanza writhed on the floor. After a while she managed to get to all fours. Her head was down. Her body heaved. A retching noise came out of her. Then another retching noise.

The sound made Myron pause.

Something about the sound . . . Myron searched his memory banks. Something about the whole scenario, the way she doubled up, the way she rolled on the floor – it was strangely familiar. As though he'd seen it before. But that was impossible. When would he . . . ? He stopped as the answer came to him.

In the wrestling ring.

My God, Myron thought. She was faking it!

Myron looked over at Carl. There was a hint of a smile on his face.

Son of a bitch. It was an act!

Reginald Squires cleared his throat. 'You have taken an unhealthy interest in my son, Mr. Bolitar,' he continued, voice thundering. 'Are you some sort of pervert?'

Myron almost flew off another wisecrack, but he bit it back. 'No.'

'Then tell me what you want with him.'

Myron squinted into the light. He still couldn't see anything but the shadowy outline of Squires. What should he say? The guy was a major loony tune. No question about that. So how to play this . . . ?

'You've heard about Jack Coldren's murder,' Myron said.

'Of course.'

'I'm working on the case.'

'You're trying to find out who murdered Jack Coldren?'

'Yes.'

'But Jack was murdered last night,' Squires countered. 'You were asking about my son Saturday.'

'It's a long story,' Myron said.

The shadow's hands spread. 'We have all the time in the world.'

How did Myron know he was going to say that?

With nothing much to lose, Myron told Squires about the kidnapping. Most of it anyway. He emphasized several times that the actual abduction had happened at the

Court Manor Inn. There was a reason for that. It had to do with the egocentricity. Reginald Squires – the ego in question – reacted in predictable fashion.

'Are you telling me,' he shouted, 'that Chad Coldren was kidnapped at *my* motel?'

His motel. Myron had figured that out by now. It was the only explanation for why Carl had run interference for Stuart Lipwitz.

'That's right,' Myron said.

'Carl?'

'Yes, Mr Squires?'

'Did you know anything about this kidnapping?'

'No, Mr Squires.'

'Well, something has to be done,' Squires shouted. 'No one does something like that on my turf. You hear me? No one.'

This guy had seen waaaaaay too many gangster films.

'Whoever did this is dead,' he ranted on. 'Do you hear me? I want them dead. D-E-A-D. Do you understand what I'm saying, Mr Bolitar?'

'Dead,' Myron said with a nod.

The shadow pointed a long finger at Myron. 'You find him for me. You find who did this and then you call me. You let me handle it. Do you understand, Mr Bolitar?'

'Call you. You handle.'

'Go then. Find the wretched bastard.'

Myron said, 'Sure thing, Mr Squires. Sure thing.' Hey, two can play the Bad Movie Dialogue game. 'But the thing is, I need some help.'

'What sort of help?'

'With your permission, I'd like to speak with your son Matthew. Find out what he knows about all this.'

'What makes you think he knows anything?'

'He's Chad's best friend. He may have heard or seen something. I don't know, Mr Squires, but I'd like to check it out.'

There was a brief silence. Then Squires snapped, 'Do it. Carl will take you back to the school. Matthew will speak freely to you.'

'Thank you, Mr Squires.'

The light went off, bathing them again in thick darkness. Myron felt his way to the car door. The 'recovering' Esperanza managed to do likewise. So did Carl. The three of them got in.

Myron turned around and looked at Carl. Carl shrugged his shoulders and said, 'Guess he forgot to take his medication.'

Chapter 32

'Chad, like, told me he was hooking up with an older babe.'

'Did he tell you her name?' Myron asked.

'Nah, man,' Matthew Squires said. 'Just that she was take-out.'

'Take-out?'

'You know. Chinese.'

Jesus.

Myron sat facing Matthew Squires. The kid was pure Yah Dude. His long, stringy hair was parted in the middle and hung past his shoulders. The coloring and texture reminded Myron of Cousin It from the *Addams Family*. He had acne, a fair amount of it. He was over six feet and weighed maybe one hundred twenty pounds. Myron wondered what it had been like for this kid growing up with Mr Spotlight as a father.

Carl was on his right. Esperanza had taken a taxi to

check out Esme Fong's alibi and look into Lloyd Rennart's past.

'Did Chad tell you where he was meeting her?'

'Sure, dude. That hot sheet is, like, my dad's haunt, you know.'

'Did Chad know your father owned the Court Manor?'

'Nah. We don't, like, talk daddy's dinero or anything. Not righteous, you know what I'm saying?'

Myron and Carl exchanged a glance. The glance bemoaned today's youth.

'Did you go with him to the Court Manor?'

'Nah. I went later, you know. I figured the dude would want to party after getting a little, you know. Kinda celebrate and shit.'

'So what time did you go to the Court Manor?'

'Ten-thirty, eleven, something like that.'

'Did you see Chad?'

'Nah. Things got, like, so weird right away. Never got the chance.'

'What do you mean, weird?'

Matthew Squires hesitated a bit. Carl leaned forward. 'It's okay, Matthew. Your father wants you to tell him the whole story.'

The kid nodded. When the chin went down, the stringy hair slid across the face. It was like a tasseled curtain opening and closing in rapid succession. 'Okay, like, here's the deal: When I pulled my Benz into the parking lot, I saw Chad's old man.'

Myron felt a queasy surge. 'Jack Coldren? You saw Jack Coldren? At the Court Manor Inn?'

Squires nodded. 'He was just, like, sitting in his car,' he said. 'Next to Chad's Honda. He looked really pissed off, man. I wanted no part of it, you know? So I took a hike.'

Myron tried not to look too stunned. Jack Coldren at the Court Manor Inn. His son inside a room screwing Esme Fong. The next morning Chad Coldren would be kidnapped.

What the hell was going on?

'Friday night,' Myron continued, 'I saw someone climb out the window of Chad's room. Was that you?'

'Yeah.'

'You want to tell me what you were doing?'

'Seeing if Chad was home. That's what we do. I climb through his window. Like Vinny used to do with Doogie Howser. Remember that show?'

Myron nodded. He did know. Kinda sad when you thought about it.

There was not much more to extract from young Matthew. When they finished up, Carl walked Myron to his car.

'Strange shit,' Carl said.

'Yep.'

'You'll call when you learn something?'

'Yep.' Myron didn't bother telling him that Tito was already dead. No point. 'Nice move, by the way. The fake punch with Esperanza.'

Carl smiled. 'We're professionals. I'm disappointed you spotted it.'

'If I hadn't seen Esperanza in the ring, I wouldn't have. It was very nice work. You should be proud.'

'Thanks.' Carl stuck out his hand. Myron shook it. He got in the car and drove away. Now where?

Back to the Coldren house, he guessed.

His mind still reeled from this latest revelation: Jack Coldren had been at the Court Manor Inn. He had seen his son's car there. How the heck did that fit into this?

Was Jack Coldren following Chad? Maybe. Was he just there by coincidence? Doubtful. So what other options were there? Why would Jack Coldren be following his own son? And where had he followed him from – Matthew Squires's house? Did that make sense? The man plays in the US Open, has a great opening round, and then goes parking in front of the Squires estate waiting for his kid to pull out?

Nope.

Hold the phone.

Suppose Jack Coldren had not been following his son. Suppose he had been following Esme Fong.

Something in his brain went 'click.'

Maybe Jack Coldren had been having an affair with Esme Fong too. His marriage was on the rocks. Esme Fong was probably a bit of a kinkster. She had seduced a teenage boy – what would have stopped her from seducing his father? But did this make sense either? Was Jack stalking her? Had he somehow found out about the tryst? What?

And the larger question: What does any of this have to do with Chad Coldren's kidnapping and Jack Coldren's murder?

He pulled up to the Coldren house. The media had been kept back, but there were now at least a dozen cops on hand. They were hauling out cardboard boxes. As Victoria Wilson had feared, the police had gotten a search warrant.

Myron parked around the corner and walked toward the house. Jack's caddie, Diane Hoffman, sat alone on the curb across the street. He remembered the last time he had seen her at the Coldren house: in the backyard, fighting with Jack. He also realized that she had been one of the very few people who knew about the kidnapping – hadn't she been standing right there when Myron first talked about it with Jack at the driving range?

She was worth a conversation.

Diane Hoffman was smoking a cigarette. The several stubs by her feet indicated that she had been there for more than a few minutes. Myron approached.

'Hi,' he said. 'We met the other day.'

Diane Hoffman looked up at him, took a deep drag of the cigarette, released it into the still air. 'I remember.' Her hoarse voice sounded like old tires on rough pavement.

'My condolences,' Myron said. 'You and Jack must have been very close.'

Another deep drag. 'Yeah.'

'Caddy and golfer. Must be a tight relationship.'

She looked up at him, squinting suspiciously. 'Yeah.'

'Almost like husband and wife. Or business partners.'

'Uh-huh. Something like that.'

'Did you two ever fight?'

She glared at him for a second, then she broke into a laugh that ended in a hacking cough. When she could talk again, she asked, 'Why the hell do you want to know that?'

'Because I saw you two fighting.'

'What?'

'Friday night. You two were in the backyard. You called him names. You threw down your cigarette in disgust.'

Diane Hoffman crushed out the cigarette. There was the smallest smile on her face. 'You some kinda Sherlock Holmes, Mr Bolitar?'

'No. I'm just asking you a question.'

'And I can tell you to go mind your own fucking business, right?'

'Right.'

'Good. Then you go do that.' The smile became fuller now. It was not a particularly pretty smile. 'But first – to save you some time – I'll tell you who killed Jack. And also who kidnapped the kid, if you like.'

'I'm all ears.'

'The bitch in there.' She pointed to the house behind her with a thumb. 'The one you got the hots for.'

'I don't have the hots for her.'

Diane Hoffman sneered. 'Right.'

'What makes you so sure it was Linda Coldren?'

'Because I know the bitch.'

'That's not much of an answer.'

'Tough luck, cowpoke. Your girlfriend did it. You want to know why Jack and me was fighting? I'll tell you. I told him he was being an asshole for not calling the police about the kidnapping. He said he and Linda thought it best.' She sneered. 'He and Linda, my ass.'

Myron watched her. Something wasn't meshing again.

'You think it was Linda's idea not to call the police?'

'Damn straight. She's the one who grabbed the kid. The whole thing was a big setup.'

'Why would she do that?'

'Ask her.' An awful smile. 'Maybe she'll tell you.'

'I'm asking you.'

She shook her head. 'Not that easy, cowpoke. I told you who did it. That's enough, don't you think?'

Time to approach from another angle. 'How long have you been Jack's caddie?' he asked.

'A year.'

'What's your qualifications, if I may ask? Why did Jack choose you?'

She snorted a chuckle. 'Don't matter none. Jack didn't listen to caddies. Not since ol' Lloyd Rennart.'

'Did you know Lloyd Rennart?'

'Nope.'

'So why did Jack hire you?'

She did not answer.

'Were you two sleeping together?'

Diane Hoffman gave another cough-laugh. A big one. 'Not likely.' More hacking laughter. 'Not likely with ol' Jack.'

Somebody called his name. Myron turned around. It was Victoria Wilson. Her face was still sleepy, but she beckoned him with some urgency. Bucky stood next to her. The old man looked like a window draft would send him skittering.

'Better head on down there, cowpoke,' she mocked. 'I think your girlfriend is gonna need some help.'

He gave her a last look and turned toward the house. Before he moved three steps, Detective Corbett was on him. 'Need a word with you, Mr Bolitar.'

Myron brushed past him. 'In a minute.'

When he reached Victoria Wilson, she made herself very clear: 'Do not talk to the cops,' she said. 'In fact, go to Win's and stay put.'

'I'm not crazy about taking orders,' Myron said.

'Sorry if I'm bruising your male ego,' she said in a tone that made it clear she was anything but. 'But I know what I'm doing.'

'Have the police found the finger?'

Victoria Wilson crossed her arms. 'Yes.'

'And?'

302

'And nothing.'

Myron looked at Bucky. Bucky looked away. He turned his attention back to Victoria Wilson. 'They didn't ask you about it?'

'They asked. We refused to answer.'

'But the finger could exonerate her.'

Victoria Wilson sighed and turned away. 'Go home, Myron. I'll call you if anything new turns up.'

Chapter 33

It was time to face Win.

Myron rehearsed several possible approaches in the car. None felt right, but that really did not matter much. Win was his friend. When the time came, Myron would deliver the message and Win would adhere to it or not.

The trickier question was, of course, should the message be delivered at all? Myron knew that repression was unhealthy and all that – but did anybody really want to risk unbottling Win's suppressed rage?

The cell phone rang. Myron picked it up. It was Tad Crispin.

'I need your help,' Tad said.

'What's up?'

'The media keep hounding me for a comment. I'm not sure what to say.'

'Nothing,' Myron told him. 'Say nothing.'

'Yeah, okay, but it's not that easy. Learner Shelton – he's the Commissioner of the USGA – called me twice. He wants to have a big trophy ceremony tomorrow. Name me US Open champion. I'm not sure what to do.'

Smart kid, Myron thought. He knows that if this is handled poorly, it could seriously wound him. 'Tad?'

'Yes?'

'Are you hiring me?' Business was still business. Agenting was not charity work.

'Yeah, Myron, you're hired.'

'Okay then, listen up. There'll be details to work out first. Percentages, that kinda thing. Most of it is fairly standard.' Kidnapping, limb-severing, murder – nothing stopped the almighty agent from trying to turn a buck. 'In the meantime, say nothing. I'll have a car come by to pick you up in a couple of hours. The driver will call up to your room before he gets there. Go straight to the car and say nothing. No matter what the press yells at you, keep silent. Do not smile or wave. Look grim. A man has just been murdered. The driver will bring you to Win's estate. We'll discuss strategy then.'

'Thanks, Myron.'

'No, Tad, thank you.'

Profiting from a murder. Myron had never felt so much like a real agent in all his life.

The media had set up camp outside Win's estate.

'I've hired extra guards for the evening,' Win explained, empty brandy snifter in hand. 'If anybody approaches the gate, they've been instructed to shoot to kill.'

'I appreciate that.'

Win gave a quick head bow. He poured some Grand Marnier into the snifter. Myron grabbed a Yoo-Hoo from the fridge. The two men sat.

'Jessica called,' Win said.

'Here?'

'Yes.'

'Why didn't she call me on the cellular?'

'She wanted to speak with me,' Win said.

'Oh.' Myron shook his Yoo-Hoo, just like the side of the can said. SHAKE! IT'S GREAT! Life is poetry. 'What about?'

'She was worried about you,' Win said.

'Why?'

'For one thing, Jessica claimed that you left a cryptic message on the answering machine.'

'Did she tell you what I said?'

'No. Just that your voice sounded strained.'

'I told her that I loved her. That I'd always love her.'

Win took a sip and nodded as though that explained everything.

'What?'

'Nothing,' Win said.

'No, tell me. What?'

Win put down the snifter and steepled his fingers. 'Who were you trying to convince?' he asked. 'Her or you?'

'What the hell does that mean?'

Bouncing the fingers now instead of steepling. 'Nothing.'

'You know how much I love Jessica.'

'Indeed I do,' Win said.

'You know what I've gone through to get her back.'

'Indeed I do.'

'I still don't get it,' Myron said. 'That's why Jess called you? Because my voice sounded strained?'

'Not entirely, no. She'd heard about Jack Coldren's

306

murder. Naturally, she was upset. She asked me to watch your back.'

'What did you tell her?'

'No.'

Silence.

Win lifted the snifter in the air. He swirled around the liquid and inhaled deeply. 'So what did you wish to discuss with me?'

'I met your mother today.'

Win took a slow sip. He let the liquid roll over his tongue, his eyes studying the bottom of the glass. After he swallowed, he said, 'Pretend I just gasped in surprise.'

'She wanted me to give you a message.'

A small smile came to Win's lips. 'I assume that dear ma-ma told you what happened.'

'Yes.'

A bigger smile now. 'So now you know it all, eh, Myron?'

'No.'

'Oh come, come, don't make it so easy. Give me some of that pop psychology you're so fond of expounding. An eight-year-old boy witnessing his grunting mother on all fours with another man – surely that scarred me emotionally. Can we not trace back everything I've become to that one dastardly moment? Isn't this episode the reason why I treat women the way I do, why I build an emotional fortress around myself, why I choose fists where others choose words? Come now, Myron. You must have considered all this. Tell me all. I am sure it will all be oh-so-insightful.'

Myron waited a beat. 'I'm not here to analyze you, Win.'

'No?'

'No.'

Win's eyes hardened. 'Then wipe that pity off your face.'

'It's not pity,' Myron said. 'It's concern.'

'Oh please.'

'It may have happened twenty-five years ago, but it had to hurt. Maybe it didn't shape you. Maybe you would have ended up the exact same person you are today. But that doesn't mean it didn't hurt.'

Win relaxed his jaw. He picked up the snifter. It was empty. He poured himself more. 'I no longer wish to discuss this,' he said. 'You know now why I want nothing to do with Jack Coldren or my mother. Let us move on.'

'There's still the matter of her message.'

'Ah, yes, the message,' Win repeated. 'You are aware, are you not, that dear ma-ma still sends me presents on my birthday and assorted holidays?'

Myron nodded. They had never discussed it. But he knew.

'I return them unopened,' Win said. He took another sip. 'I think I will do the same with this message.'

'She's dying, Win. Cancer. She has maybe a week or two.'

'I know.'

Myron sat back. His throat felt dry.

'Is that the entire message?'

'She wanted you to know that it's your last chance to talk to her,' Myron said.

'Well, yes, that's true. It would be very difficult for us to chat after she's dead.'

Myron was flailing now. 'She's not expecting any kind of big reconciliation. But if there are any issues you want to resolve . . .' Myron stopped. He was being redundant and obvious now. Win hated that.

'That's it?' Win asked. 'That's your big message?'

Myron nodded.

'Fine, then. I'm going to order some Chinese. I hope that will be suitable with you.'

Win rose from his seat and strolled toward the kitchen.

'You claim it didn't change you,' Myron said. 'But before that day, did you love her?'

Win's face was a stone. 'Who says I don't love her now?'

Chapter 34

The driver brought Tad Crispin in through the back entrance.

Win and Myron had been watching television. A commercial came on for Scope. A married couple in bed woke up and turned their heads in disgust. Morning breath, the voice-over informed them. You need Scope. Scope cures morning breath.

Myron said, 'So would, say, brushing your teeth?'

Win nodded.

Myron opened the door and led Tad into the living room. Tad sat on a couch across from Myron and Win. He glanced about, his eyes searching for a spot to settle on but not having any luck. He smiled weakly.

'Would you care for a beverage?' Win asked. 'A croissant or a Pop Tart perhaps?' The Host with the Most.

'No, thank you.' Another weak smile.

Myron leaned forward. 'Tad, tell us about Learner Shelton's call.'

The kid dove right in. 'He said that he wanted to congratulate me on my victory. That the USGA had officially declared me the US Open champion.' For a moment, Tad stopped. His eyes hazed over, the words hitting him anew. Tad Crispin, US Open champion. The stuff of dreams.

'What else did he say?'

Crispin's eyes slowly cleared. 'He's holding a press conference tomorrow afternoon. At Merion. They'll give me the trophy and a check for $360,000.'

Myron did not waste time. 'First of all, we tell the media that you do not consider yourself the US Open champion. If they want to call you that, fine. If the USGA wants to call you that, fine. You, however, believe that the tournament ended in a tie. Death should not rob Jack Coldren of his magnificent accomplishment or his claim to the title. A tie it ended. A tie it is. From your vantage point, you two are co-winners. Do you understand?'

Tad was hesitant. 'I think so.'

'Now, about that check.' Myron strummed the end table with his fingers. 'If they insist on giving you the full winner's purse, you'll have to donate Jack's portion to charity.'

'Victims' rights,' Win said.

Myron nodded. 'That would be good. Something against violence—'

'Wait a second,' Tad interrupted. He rubbed the palms of his hands on his thighs. 'You want me to give away $180,000?'

'It'll be a tax write-off,' Win said. 'That knocks the value down to half that.'

'And it'll be chicken feed compared to the positive press you'll get,' Myron added.

'But I was charging back,' Tad insisted. 'I had the momentum. I would have won.'

Myron leaned in a little closer. 'You're an athlete, Tad. You're competitive and confident. That's good – heck, that's great. But not in this situation. This murder story is huge. It transcends sports. For most of the world's population, this will be their first look at Tad Crispin. We want them to see someone likable. Someone decent and trustworthy and modest. If we brag now about what a great golfer you are – if we dwell on your comeback rather than this tragedy – people are going to see you as cold, as another example of what's wrong with today's athletes. Do you see what I'm saying?'

Tad nodded. 'I guess so.'

'We have to present you in a certain light. We have to control the story as much as possible.'

'So we do interviews?' Tad asked.

'Very few.'

'But if we want publicity—'

'We want carefully orchestrated publicity,' Myron corrected. 'This story is so big, the last thing we need to do is create more interest. I want you to be reclusive, Tad. Thoughtful. You see, we have to maintain the right balance. If we toot our horn, it looks like we're grandstanding. If we do a lot of interviews, it looks like we're taking advantage of a man's murder.'

'Disastrous,' Win added.

'Right. What we want to do is control the flow of information. Feed the press a few tiny morsels. No more.'

'Perhaps one interview,' Win said. 'One where you will be at your most contrite.'

'With Bob Costas maybe.'

'Or even Barbara Walters.'

'And we don't announce your big donation.'

'Correct, no press conference. You are far too magnanimous for such bravado.'

That confused Tad. 'How are we supposed to get good press if we don't announce it?'

'We leak it,' Myron said. 'We get someone at the charity to tell a nosy reporter, maybe. Something like that. The key is, Tad Crispin must remain far too modest a fellow to publicize his own good deeds. Do you see what we're aiming for here?'

Tad's nod was more enthusiastic now. He was warming up. Myron felt like a heel. Spin-doctoring – just another hat today's sports representative must wear. Being an agent was not always pretty. You had to get dirty sometimes. Myron did not necessarily like it, but he was willing. The media would portray events one way; he would present them another. Still he felt like a grinning political strategist after a debate, and you cannot get much lower than that.

They discussed details for a few more minutes. Tad started to look off again. He was rubbing the famed palms against the pants again. When Win left the room for a minute, Tad whispered, 'I saw on the news that you're Linda Coldren's attorney.'

'I'm one of them.'

'Are you her agent?'

'I might be,' Myron said. 'Why?'

'Then you're a lawyer too, right? You went to law school and everything?'

Myron was not sure he liked where this was going. 'Yes.'

'So I can hire you to be my lawyer too, right? Not just my agent?'

Myron really didn't like where this was going. 'Why would you need a lawyer, Tad?'

'I'm not saying I do. But if I did—'

'Whatever you tell me is confidential,' Myron said.

Tad Crispin stood. He put his arms out straight and gripped an imaginary golf club. He took a swing. Air golf. Win played it all the time. All golfers do. Basketball players don't do that. It's not like Myron stops at every store window and checks the reflection of his shot in the mirror.

Golfers.

'I'm surprised you don't know about this already,' Tad said slowly.

But the creeping feeling in the pit of Myron's stomach told him that maybe he did. 'Don't know about what, Tad?'

Tad took another swing. He stopped his movement to check his backswing. Then his expression changed to one of panic. He dropped the imaginary club to the floor. 'It was only a couple of times,' he said, his words pouring out like silver beads. 'It was no big deal really. I mean, we met while we were filming those ads for Zoom.' He looked at Myron, his eyes pleading. 'You've seen her, Myron. I mean, I know she's twenty years older than me, but she's so good-looking and she said her marriage was dead . . .'

Myron did not hear the rest of his words; the ocean was crashing in his ears. Tad Crispin and Linda Coldren. He could not believe it, yet it made perfect sense. A young guy obviously charmed by a stunning older woman. The mature beauty trapped in a loveless marriage finding escape in young, handsome arms. Nothing really wrong with it.

Yet Myron felt his cheeks go scarlet. Something inside of him began to fume.

Tad was still droning on. Myron interrupted him.

'Did Jack find out?'

Tad stopped. 'I don't know,' he said. 'But I think maybe he did.'

'What makes you say that?'

'It was just the way he acted. We played two rounds together. I know we were competitors and that he was trying to intimidate me. But I kind of got the impression he knew.'

Myron lowered his head into his hands. He felt sick to his stomach.

Tad asked, 'Do you think it'll get out?'

Myron held back a chuckle. This would be one of the biggest news stories of the year. The media would attack like old women at a Loehmann's clearance sale. 'I don't know, Tad.'

'What do we do?'

'We hope it doesn't get out.'

Tad was scared. 'And if it does?'

Myron faced him. Tad Crispin looked so damn young – check that, he was young. Most kids his age are happily pulling fraternity pranks. And when you thought about it, what had Tad really done that was so bad? Slept with an older woman who for some odd reason remained in a dead marriage. Hardly unnatural. Myron tried to picture himself at Tad's age. If a beautiful older woman like Linda Coldren had come on to him, would he have stood a chance?

Like, duh. He probably did not stand a chance now.

But what about Linda Coldren? Why did she stay in this dead marriage? Religion? Doubtful. For the sake of her son? The kid was sixteen years old. It might not be easy, but he'd survive.

'Myron, what'll happen if the media find out?'

But Myron was suddenly no longer thinking about the media. He was thinking about the police. He was thinking about Victoria Wilson and reasonable doubt. Linda Coldren had probably told her ace attorney about her affair with Tad Crispin. Victoria would have seen it too.

Who is declared US Open champion now that Jack Coldren is dead?

Who doesn't have to worry about out-choking the choker in front of a massive audience?

Who has all the same motives to kill Jack Coldren that Myron had earlier assigned to Esme Fong?

Whose squeaky-clean image might get soiled by a Coldren divorce, especially one where Jack Coldren would name his wife's indiscretion?

Who was having an affair with the deceased's wife?

The answer to all the above was sitting in front of him.

Chapter 35

Tad Crispin left not long after that.

Myron and Win settled into the couch. They put on Woody Allen's *Broadway Danny Rose*, one of Woody's most underrated masterpieces. What a flick. Rent it sometime.

During the scene where Mia drags Woody to the fortune-teller, Esperanza arrived.

She coughed into her fist. 'I, ahem, don't want to sound didactic or fictitious in any manner,' she began, doing a great Woody impression. She had his timing, the speech delay tactics. She had the hand mannerisms. She had the New York accent. It was her best work. 'But I may have some important information.'

Myron looked up. Win kept his eyes on the screen.

'I located the man Lloyd Rennart bought the bar from twenty years ago,' Esperanza said, returning to her own voice. 'Rennart paid him in cash. Seven grand. I also checked on the house in Spring Lake Heights. Bought at the same time for $21,000. No mortgage.'

'Lots of expenses,' Myron said, 'for a washed-up caddie.'

'Sí, señor. And to make matters more interesting, I also found no indication that he worked or paid taxes from the time he was fired by Jack Coldren until he purchased the Rusty Nail bar.'

'Could be an inheritance.'

'I would doubt it,' Esperanza said. 'I managed to go back to 1971 and found no record of him paying any inheritance tax.'

Myron looked at Win. 'What do you think?'

Win's eyes were still on the screen. 'I'm not listening.'

'Right, I forgot.' He looked back at Esperanza. 'Anything else?'

'Esme Fong's alibi checks out. I spoke to Miguel. She never left the hotel.'

'Is he solid?'

'Yeah, I think so.'

Strike one. 'Anything else?'

'Not yet. But I found the office for the local paper in Narberth. They have the back editions in a storage room. I'll go through them tomorrow, see what I can dig up on the car accident.'

Esperanza grabbed a take-out container and a pair of chopsticks from the kitchen and then she plopped down on the open couch. A mafioso hit man was calling Woody a cheesehead. Woody commented that he had no idea what that meant, but he was confident it wasn't a good thing. Ah, the Woodman.

Ten minutes into *Love and Death*, not long after Woody wondered how old Nahampkin could be younger than young Nahampkin, exhaustion overtook Myron. He fell asleep on the couch. A deep sleep. No dreams. No stirring. Nothing but the long fall down the deep well.

He woke up at eight-thirty. The television was off. A clock ticked and then chimed. Someone had laid a comforter over Myron while he'd been sleeping. Win probably. He checked the other bedrooms. Win and Esperanza were both gone.

He showered and dressed and put on some coffee. The phone rang. Myron picked it up and said, 'Hello.'

It was Victoria Wilson. She still sounded bored. 'They arrested Linda.'

Myron found Victoria Wilson in an attorney waiting area.

'How is she?'

'Fine,' Victoria replied. 'I brought Chad home last night. That made her happy.'

'So where is Linda?'

'In a holding cell awaiting arraignment. We'll see her in a few minutes.'

'What do they have?'

'Quite a bit, actually,' Victoria said. She sounded almost impressed. 'First, they have the guard who saw her entering and leaving an otherwise abandoned golf course at the time of the murder. With the exception of Jack, nobody else was seen going in or out all night.'

'Doesn't mean nobody did. It's an awfully big area.'

'Very true. But from their standpoint it gives Linda opportunity. Second, they found hairs and fibers on Jack's body and around the murder scene that preliminary tests link to Linda. Naturally, this one should be no problem to discredit. Jack is her husband; of course he'd have hair and fibers from her on his body. He could have spread them around the scene.'

'Plus she told us she went to the course to look for Jack,' Myron added.

'But we're not telling them that.'

'Why not?'

'Because right now we are saying and admitting to nothing.'

Myron shrugged. Not important. 'What else?'

'Jack owned a twenty-two-caliber handgun. The police found it in a wooded area between the Coldren residence and Merion last night.'

'It was just sitting out?'

'No. It was buried in fresh dirt. A metal detector picked it up.'

'They're sure it's Jack's gun?'

She nodded. 'The serial numbers match. The police ran an immediate ballistics test. It's the murder weapon.'

Myron's veins iced up.

'Fingerprints?' he asked.

Victoria Wilson shook her head. 'Wiped clean.'

'Are they running a powder test on her?' The police run a test on the hands, see if there are any powder burns.

'It'll take a few days,' Victoria said, 'and it'll probably be negative.'

'You had her scrub her hands?'

'And treat them, yes.'

'Then you think she did it.'

Her tone remained unruffled. 'Please don't say that.'

She was right. But it was starting to look bad. 'Is there more?' he asked.

'The police found your tape machine still hooked up to

the phone. They were obviously curious as to why the Coldrens found it necessary to tape all incoming calls.'

'Did they find any tapes of the conversations with the kidnapper?'

'Just the one where the kidnapper refers to the Fong woman as a "chink bitch" and demands one hundred grand. And to answer your next two questions, no, we did not elaborate on the kidnapping and yes, they are pissed off.'

Myron pondered that for a moment. Something was not right. 'That was the only tape they found?'

'That's it.'

He frowned. 'But if the machine was still hooked up, it should have taped the last call the kidnapper made to Jack. The one that got him to storm out of the house and head to Merion.'

Victoria Wilson looked at him steadily. 'The police found no other tapes. Not in the house. Not on Jack's body. Nowhere.'

Again the ice in the veins. The implication was obvious: The most reasonable explanation for there being no tape was that there was no call. Linda Coldren had made it up. The lack of a tape would have been viewed as a major contradiction *if* she had said anything to the cops. Fortunately for Linda, Victoria Wilson had never let her tell her story in the first place.

The woman was good.

'Can you get me a copy of the tape the police found?' he asked.

Victoria Wilson nodded. 'There is still more,' she said.

Myron was almost afraid to hear it.

'Let's take the severed finger for a moment,' she

continued as though ordering it as an appetizer. 'You found it in Linda's car in a manila envelope.'

Myron nodded.

'The envelope is the type sold only at Staples – their brand, the number ten size. The writing was done by a red Flair pen, medium-point. Three weeks ago, Linda Coldren visited Staples. According to the receipt found at her house yesterday, she purchased numerous office supplies, including a box of Staples' number ten manila envelopes and a red Flair medium-point pen.'

Myron could not believe what he was hearing.

'On the positive side, their handwriting analyst could not tell if the writing on the envelope came from Linda.'

But something else was dawning on Myron. Linda had waited around for him at Merion. The two of them had gone to the car together. They had found the finger together. The district attorney would pounce upon that story. Why had she waited for Myron? The answer, the DA would claim, was obvious: she needed a witness. She had planted the finger in her own car – she could certainly do that without drawing suspicion – and she needed a hapless dupe to be with her when she found it.

Enter Myron Bolitar, the dupe du jour.

But of course, Victoria Wilson had neatly arranged it so that the DA would never hear that story. Myron was Linda's attorney. He could not tell. No one would ever know.

Yep, the woman was good – except for one thing.

'The severed finger,' Myron said. 'That has to be the kicker, Victoria. Who is going to believe that a mother would cut off her own son's finger?'

Victoria looked at her watch. 'Let's go talk to Linda.'

'No, hold up here. That's the second time you blew this off. What aren't you telling me?'

She slung her purse over her shoulder. 'Come on.'

'Hey, I'm getting a little tired of getting jerked around here.'

Victoria Wilson nodded slowly, but she did not speak or stop walking. Myron followed her into a holding room. Linda Coldren was already there. She was decked out in a bright orange prison jumpsuit. Her hands were still manacled. She looked up at Myron through hollow eyes. There were no hellos or hugs or even pleasantries.

Without preamble, Victoria said, 'Myron wants to know why I don't think the severed finger helps us.'

Linda faced him. There was a sad smile on her face. 'I guess that's understandable.'

'What the hell is going on here?' Myron said. 'I know you didn't cut off your own son's finger.'

The sad smile remained. 'I didn't do it,' Linda said. 'That part is true.'

'What do you mean, that part?'

'You said I didn't cut off my son's finger,' she continued. 'But Chad is not my son.'

Chapter 36

Something in Myron's head clicked again.

'I'm infertile,' Linda explained. She said the words with great ease, but the pain in her eyes was so raw and naked that Myron almost flinched. 'I have this condition where my ovaries cannot produce eggs. But Jack still wanted a biological child.'

Myron spoke softly. 'You hired a surrogate?'

Linda looked toward Victoria. 'Yes,' she said. 'Though it was not quite so aboveboard.'

'It was all done to the letter of the law,' Victoria interjected.

'You handled it for them?' Myron asked.

'I did the paperwork, yes. The adoption was completely legal.'

'We wanted to keep it a secret,' Linda said. 'That's why I took off from the tour so early. I went into seclusion. The birth mother was never even supposed to know who we were.'

Something else in his head went click. 'But she found out.'

'Yes.'

Another click. 'It's Diane Hoffman, isn't it?'

Linda was too exhausted to look surprised. 'How did you know?'

'Just an educated guess.' Why else would Jack hire Diane Hoffman as his caddie? Why else would she have gotten upset at the way they were handling the kidnapping? 'How did she find you?'

Victoria answered that one. 'As I said, it was all done legally. With all the new disclosure laws, it wasn't that hard to do.'

Another click. 'That's why you couldn't divorce Jack. He was the biological parent. He'd have the upper hand in a custody battle.'

Linda slumped her shoulders and nodded.

'Does Chad know about all this?'

'No,' Linda said.

'At least, not to your knowledge,' Myron said.

'What?'

'You don't know for sure. Maybe he found out. Maybe Jack told him. Or Diane. Maybe that's how this whole thing got started.'

Victoria crossed her arms. 'I don't see it, Myron. Suppose Chad did find out. How would that have led to his own kidnapping and his father's murder?'

Myron shook his head. It was a good question. 'I don't know yet. I need time to think it through. Do the police know all this?'

'About the adoption? Yes.'

It was beginning to make sense now. 'This gives the DA

their motive. They'll say that Jack's suing for divorce worried Linda. That she killed him to keep her son.'

Victoria Wilson nodded. 'And the fact that Linda is not the biological mother could play one of two ways: either she loved her son so much that she killed Jack to keep him – or because Chad was not her own flesh and blood, she could indeed be driven to cut off his finger.'

'Either way, finding the finger doesn't help us.'

Victoria nodded. She did not say 'I told you so,' but she might as well have.

'Can I say something?' It was Linda. They turned and looked at her.

'I didn't love Jack anymore. I told you that straight out, Myron. I doubt I would have, if I'd been planning on killing him.'

Myron nodded. Made sense.

'But I do love my son – *my* son – more than life itself. The fact that it's more believable that I'd maim him because I'm an adoptive mother rather than a biological one is sick and grotesque in the extreme. I love Chad as much as any mother could love a child.'

She stopped, her chest heaving. 'I want you both to know that.'

'We know,' Victoria said. Then: 'Let's all sit down.'

When they were settled in their seats, Victoria continued to take charge. 'I know it's early, but I want to start thinking about reasonable doubt. Their case will have holes. I'll be sure to exploit them. But I'd like to hear some alternative theories on what happened.'

'In other words,' Myron said, 'some other suspects.'

Victoria caught something in his tone. 'That's exactly what I mean.'

'Well, you already have one ace in the hole, don't you?'

Victoria nodded coolly. 'I do.'

'Tad Crispin, right?'

This time, Linda did indeed look surprised. Victoria remained unfazed. 'Yes, he's a suspect.'

'The kid hired me last night,' Myron said. 'Talking about him would be a conflict of interest.'

'Then we won't talk about him.'

'I'm not sure that's good enough.'

'Then you'll have to dump him as a client,' Victoria said. 'Linda hired you first. Your obligation must be to her. If you feel that there is a conflict, then you'll have to call Mr Crispin and tell him that you cannot represent him.'

Trapped. And she knew it.

'Let's talk about other suspects,' Myron said.

Victoria nodded. Battle won. 'Go ahead.'

'First off, Esme Fong.' Myron filled them in on all the reasons that she made a good suspect. Again Victoria looked sleepy; Linda looked semi-homicidal.

'She seduced my son?' Linda shouted. 'The bitch came into my house and seduced my son?'

'Apparently so.'

'I can't believe it. That's why Chad was at that sleazy motel?'

'Yup—'

'Okay,' Victoria interrupted. 'I like it. This Esme Fong has motive. She has means. She was one of the few people who knew where Chad was.'

'She also has an alibi for the killing,' Myron added.

'But not a great one. There must be other ways in and out of that hotel. She could have worn a disguise. She could have sneaked out when Miguel took a bathroom break. I like her. Who else?'

'Lloyd Rennart.'

'Who?'

'Jack's former caddie,' Myron explained. 'The one who helped throw the Open.'

Victoria frowned. 'Why him?'

'Look at the timing. Jack returns to the site of his greatest failure and suddenly all this happens. It can't be a coincidence. Firing Rennart ruined his life. He became a drunk. He killed his own wife in a car crash.'

'What?' It was Linda.

'Not long after the Open, Lloyd totaled his car while DWI. His wife was killed.'

Victoria asked, 'Did you know her?'

Linda shook her head. 'We never met his family. In fact, I don't think I ever saw Lloyd outside of our home or the golf course.'

Victoria crossed her arms and leaned back. 'I still do not see what makes him a viable suspect.'

'Rennart wanted vengeance. He waited twenty-three years to get it.'

Victoria frowned again.

'I admit that it's a bit of a stretch.'

'A bit? It's ridiculous. Do you know where Lloyd Rennart is now?'

'That's a little complicated.'

'Oh?'

'He may have committed suicide.'

Victoria looked at Linda, then at Myron. 'Would you please elaborate?'

'The body was never found,' Myron said. 'But everyone thinks he jumped off a cliff in Peru.'

Linda groaned. 'Oh, no . . .'

'What is it?' Victoria asked.

'We got a postcard from Peru.'

'Who did?'

'It was addressed to Jack, but it was unsigned. It arrived last fall or winter.'

Myron's pulse raced. Last fall or winter. About the time Lloyd allegedly jumped. 'What did it say?'

'It only had two words on it,' Linda said. ' "Forgive me." '

Silence.

Victoria broke it. 'That doesn't sound like the words of a man out for revenge.'

'No,' Myron agreed. He remembered what Esperanza had learned about the money Rennart had used to buy his house and bar. This postcard now confirmed what he had already suspected: Jack had been sabotaged. 'But it also means that what happened twenty-three years ago was no accident.'

'So what good does that do us?' Victoria asked.

'Someone paid Rennart off to throw the US Open. Whoever did that would have motive.'

'To kill Rennart maybe,' Victoria countered. 'But not Jack.'

Good point. Or was it? Somebody had hated Jack enough twenty-three years ago to destroy his chances of winning the Open. Maybe that hatred had not died. Or maybe Jack had learned the truth and thus had to be quieted. Either way, it was worth looking into.

'I do not want to go digging into the past,' Victoria said. 'It could make things very messy.'

'I thought you liked messy. Messy is fertile land for reasonable doubt.'

'Reasonable doubt, I like,' she said. 'But the unknown, I don't. Look into Esme Fong. Look into the Squires family. Look into whatever. But stay away from the past, Myron. You never know what you might find back there.'

Chapter 37

On the car phone: 'Mrs Rennart? This is Myron Bolitar.'

'Yes, Mr Bolitar.'

'I promised that I'd call you periodically. To keep you updated.'

'Have you learned something new?'

How to proceed? 'Not about your husband. So far, there is no evidence that suggests Lloyd's death was anything other than a suicide.'

'I see.'

Silence.

'So why are you calling me, Mr Bolitar?'

'Have you heard about Jack Coldren's murder?'

'Of course,' Francine Rennart said. 'It's on every station.' Then: 'You don't suspect Lloyd—'

'No,' Myron said quickly. 'But according to Jack's wife, Lloyd sent Jack a postcard from Peru. Right before his death.'

'I see,' she said again. 'What did it say?'

'It had only two words on it: "Forgive me." He didn't sign it.'

There was a brief pause and then she said, 'Lloyd is dead, Mr Bolitar. So is Jack Coldren. Let it lie.'

'I'm not out to damage your husband's reputation. But it is becoming clear that somebody either forced Lloyd to sabotage Jack or paid him to do it.'

'And you want me to help you prove that?'

'Whoever it was may have murdered Jack and maimed his son. Your husband sent Jack a postcard asking for forgiveness. With all due respect, Mrs Rennart, don't you think Lloyd would want you to help?'

More silence.

'What do you want from me, Mr Bolitar? I don't know anything about what happened.'

'I realize that. But do you have any old papers of Lloyd's? Did he keep a journal or a diary? Anything that might give us a clue?'

'He didn't keep a journal or a diary.'

'But there might be something else.' Gently, fair Myron. Tread gently. 'If Lloyd did receive compensation' – a nice way of saying a bribe – 'there may be bank receipts or letters or something.'

'There are boxes in the basement,' she said. 'Old photos, some papers maybe. I don't think there are any bank statements.' Francine Rennart stopped talking for a moment. Myron kept the receiver pushed against his ear. 'Lloyd always did have a lot of cash,' she said softly. 'I never really asked where it came from.'

Myron licked his lips. 'Mrs Rennart, can I look through those boxes?'

'Tonight,' she said. 'You can come by tonight.'

*

Esperanza was not back at the cottage yet. But Myron had barely sat down when the intercom buzzed.

'Yes?'

The guard manning the front gate spoke with perfect diction. 'Sir, a gentleman and a young lady are here to see you. They claim that they are not with the media.'

'Did they give a name?'

'The gentleman said his name is Carl.'

'Let them in.'

Myron stepped outside and watched the canary-yellow Audi climb the drive. Carl pulled to a stop and got out. His flat hair looked freshly pressed, like he'd just gotten it 'martinized,' whatever that was. A young black woman who couldn't have been twenty years old came out of the passenger door. She looked around with eyes the size of satellite dishes.

Carl turned to the stables and cupped his big hand over his eyes. A female rider decked out in full gear was steering a horse through some sort of obstacle course.

'That what they call steeplechasing?' Carl asked.

'Got me,' Myron said.

Carl continued to watch. The rider got off the horse. She unstrapped her black hat and patted the horse. Carl said, 'You don't see a lot of brothers dressed like that.'

'What about lawn jockeys?'

Carl laughed. 'Not bad,' he said. 'Not great, but not bad.'

Hard to argue. 'You here to take riding lessons?'

'Not likely,' Carl said. 'This is Kiana. I think she may be of help to us.'

'Us?'

'You and me together, bro.' Carl smiled. 'I get to play your likable black partner.'

Myron shook his head. 'No.'

'Excuse me?'

'The likable black partner always ends up dead. Usually early on, too.'

That stopped Carl a second. 'Damn, I forgot about that.'

Myron shrugged a what-can-you-do. 'So who is she?'

'Kiana works as a maid at the Court Manor Inn.'

Myron looked at her. She was still out of earshot. 'How old is she?'

'Why?'

Myron shrugged. 'Just asking. She looks young.'

'She's sixteen. And guess what, Myron? She's not an unwed mother, she's not on welfare, and she's not a junkie.'

'I never said she was.'

'Uh-huh. Guess none of that racist shit ever seeps into your color-blind cranium.'

'Hey, Carl, do me a favor. Save the racial-sensitivity seminar for a less active day. What does she know?'

Carl beckoned her forward with a tight nod. Kiana approached, all long limbs and big eyes. 'I showed her this photo' – he handed Myron a snapshot of Jack Coldren – 'and she remembered seeing him at the Court Manor.'

Myron glanced at the photograph, and then at Kiana. 'You saw this man at the motel?'

'Yes.' Her voice was firm and strong and belied her years. Sixteen. She was the same age as Chad. Hard to imagine.

'Do you remember when?'

'Last week. I saw him there twice.'

'Twice?'

334

'Yes.'

'Would that have been Thursday or Friday?'

'No.' Kiana kept up with the poise. No ringing hands or happy feet or darting eyes. 'It was Monday or Tuesday. Wednesday at the latest.'

Myron tried to process this tidbit. Jack had been at the Court Manor twice *before* his son. Why? The reason was fairly obvious: If the marriage was dead for Linda, it was probably dead for Jack. He, too, would be engaging in extramarital liaisons. Maybe that was what Matthew Squires witnessed. Maybe Jack had pulled in for his own affair and spotted his son's car. It kinda made sense . . .

But it was also a hell of a coincidence. Father and son end up at the same hot sheets at the same time? Stranger things have happened, but what were the odds?

Myron gestured to Jack's photograph. 'Was he alone?'

Kiana smiled. 'The Court Manor doesn't rent out a lot of single rooms.'

'Did you see who was with him?'

'Very briefly. The guy in the photograph checked them in. His partner stayed in the car.'

'But you saw her? Briefly anyway.'

Kiana glanced at Carl, then back at Myron. 'It wasn't a her.'

'Excuse me?'

'The guy in the photograph,' she said. 'He wasn't there with a woman.'

A large boulder fell from the sky and landed on Myron's head. It was his turn now to glance at Carl. Carl nodded. Another click. A big click. The loveless marriage. He had known why Linda Coldren stayed in it – she was afraid of losing custody of her son. But what about Jack? Why hadn't he left? The answer was suddenly transparent: Being married to a beautiful, constantly traveling woman was the perfect cover. He remembered Diane Hoffman's reaction when he asked her if she'd been sleeping with Jack – the way she laughed and said, 'Not likely with ol' Jack.'

Because ol' Jack was gay.

Myron turned his focus back to Kiana. 'Could you describe the man he was with?'

'Older – maybe fifty or sixty. White. He had this long dark hair and a bushy beard. That's about all I can tell you.'

But Myron did not need more.

It was starting to come together now. It wasn't there. Not yet anyway. But he was suddenly a quantum leap closer.

Chapter 38

As Carl drove out, Esperanza drove in.

'Find anything?' Myron asked her.

Esperanza handed him a photocopy of an old newspaper clipping. 'Read this.'

The headline read: CRASH FATALITY

Economy of words. He read on:

> Mr Lloyd Rennart of 27 Darby Place crashed his automobile into a parked car on South Dean Street near the intersection of Coddington Terrace. Mr Rennart was taken into police custody under suspicion of driving while intoxicated. The injured were rushed to St. Elizabeth's Medical Center, where Lucille Rennart, Mr Lloyd Rennart's wife, was pronounced dead. Funeral services are to be arranged.

Myron reread the paragraph twice. ' "The injured were rushed," ' he read out loud. 'As in more than one.'

Esperanza nodded.

'So who else was hurt?'

'I don't know. There was no follow-up article.'

'Nothing on the arrest or the arraignment or the court case?'

'Nothing. At least, nothing I could find. There was no further mention of any Rennarts. I also tried to get something from St Elizabeth's, but they wouldn't help. Hospital-patient confidentiality, they claimed. I doubt their computers go back to the seventies anyway.'

Myron shook his head. 'This is too weird,' he said.

'I saw Carl heading out,' Esperanza said. 'What did he want?'

'He came by with a maid from the Court Manor. Guess who Jack Coldren was linking up with for a little afternoon delight?'

'Tonya Harding?'

'Close. Norm Zuckerman.'

Esperanza tilted her head back and forth, as though sizing up an abstract work at the Met. 'I'm not surprised. About Norm anyway. Think about it. Never married. No family. In public, he always surrounds himself with young, beautiful women.'

'For show,' Myron said.

'Right. They're beards. Camouflage. Norm is the front man for a major sports fashion business. Being a known gay could destroy him.'

'So,' Myron said, 'if it got out that he was gay . . .'

'It would hurt a lot,' Esperanza said.

'Is that a motive for murder?'

'Sure,' she said. 'It's millions of dollars and a man's reputation. People kill for a lot less.'

Myron thought about it. 'But how did it happen? Let's

say Chad and Jack meet up at the Court Manor by accident. Suppose Chad figures out what Daddy and Norm are up to. Maybe he mentions it to Esme, who works for Norm, Maybe she and Norm . . .'

'They what?' Esperanza finished. 'They kidnap the kid, cut off his finger, and then let him go?'

'Yeah, it doesn't mesh,' Myron agreed, 'Not yet anyway. But we're getting close.'

'Oh sure, we're really narrowing down the field. Let's see. It could be Esme Fong. It could be Norm Zuckerman. It could be Tad Crispin. It could be a still-alive Lloyd Rennart. It could be his wife or his kid. It could be Matthew Squires or his father or both. Or it could be a combination plan of any of the above – the Rennart family perhaps, or Norm and Esme. And it could be Linda Coldren. How does she explain the gun from her house being the murder weapon? Or the envelopes and the pen she bought?'

'I don't know,' Myron said slowly. Then: 'But you may be on to something here.'

'What?'

'Access. Whoever killed Jack and cut off Chad's finger had access to the Coldren house. Barring a break-in, who could have gotten hold of the gun and the stationery supplies?'

Esperanza barely hesitated. 'Linda Coldren, Jack Coldren, maybe the Squires kid, since he liked to crawl in through the window.' She paused. 'I guess that's it.'

'Okay, good. Now let's move on a little. Who knew that Chad Coldren was at the Court Manor Inn? I mean, whoever kidnapped him had to know where he was, right?'

'Right. Okay, Jack again, Esme Fong, Norm Zuckerman, Matthew Squires again. Boy, Myron, this is really helpful.'

'So what names show up on both lists?'

'Jack and Matthew Squires. And I think we can leave Jack's name off – his being the victim and all.'

But Myron stopped for a moment. He thought about his conversation with Win. About the naked desire to win. How far would Jack go to guarantee victory? Win had said that he would stop at nothing. Was he right?

Esperanza snapped her fingers in his face. 'Yo, Myron?'

'What?'

'I said, we can eliminate Jack Coldren. Dead people rarely bury murder weapons in nearby woods.'

That made sense. 'So that leaves Matthew Squires,' Myron said, 'and I don't think he's our boy.'

'Neither do I,' Esperanza said. 'But we're forgetting someone – someone who knew where Chad Coldren was and had complete access to the gun and stationery supplies.'

'Who?'

'Chad Coldren.'

'You think he cut off his own finger?'

Esperanza shrugged. 'What about your old theory? The one where the kidnapping was a hoax that went out of control. Think about it. Maybe he and Tito had a falling-out. Maybe it was Chad who killed Tito.'

Myron considered the possibility. He thought about Jack. He thought about Esme. He thought about Lloyd Rennart. Then he shook his head. 'This is getting us nowhere. Sherlock Holmes warned that you should never theorize without all the facts because then you twist facts to suit theories rather than theories to suit facts.'

'That never stopped us before,' Esperanza said.

'Good point.' Myron checked his watch. 'I gotta go see Francine Rennart.'

'The caddie's wife.'

'Yup.'

Esperanza went sniff, sniff.

'What?' Myron asked.

One more big sniff. 'I smell a complete waste of time,' she said.

She smelled wrong.

Chapter 39

Victoria Wilson called on the car phone. What, Myron wondered, did people do before the car phone, before the cell phone, before the beeper?

Probably had a lot more fun.

'The police found the body of your neo-Nazi friend,' she said. 'His last name is Marshall.'

'Tito Marshall?' Myron frowned. 'Please tell me you're joking.'

'I don't joke, Myron.'

Of that he had little doubt. 'Do the police have any idea he's tied into this?' Myron asked.

'None whatsoever.'

'And I assume he died of a gunshot wound.'

'That's the preliminary finding, yes. Mr Marshall was shot twice in the head at close range with a thirty-eight.'

'A thirty-eight? But Jack was killed with a twenty-two.'

'Yes, Myron, I know.'

'So different guns killed Jack Coldren and Tito Marshall.'

Victoria did the bored thing again. 'Hard to believe you're not a professional ballistics expert.'

Everyone's a smart-ass. But this new development threw a whole bunch of scenarios out of whack. If two different guns had killed Jack Coldren and Tito Marshall, did that mean there were two different killers? Or was the killer smart enough to use different weapons? Or had the killer disposed of the thirty-eight after killing Tito and was thus forced to use the twenty-two on Jack? And what kind of warped mind names a kid Tito Marshall? Bad enough to go through life with a moniker like Myron. But Tito Marshall? No wonder the kid had turned out as a neo-Nazi. Probably started out as a virulent anti-Communist.

Victoria interrupted his thoughts. 'I called for another reason, Myron.'

'Oh?'

'Did you pass on the message to Win?'

'You set that up, didn't you? You told her I'd be there.'

'Please answer the question.'

'Yes, I delivered the message.'

'What did Win say?'

'I delivered the message,' Myron said. 'But that doesn't mean I'm giving out reports on my friend's reaction.'

'She's getting worse, Myron.'

'I'm sorry.'

Silence.

'Where are you right now?' she asked.

'I just hit the New Jersey Turnpike. I'm on my way to Lloyd Rennart's house.'

'I thought I told you to leave that path alone.'

'So you did.'

More silence.

'Good-bye, Myron.'

She hung up. Myron sighed. He suddenly longed for the days before the car phone, the cell phone, the beeper. Reaching out and touching someone was getting to be a real pain in the ass.

An hour later, Myron parked again in front of the Rennarts' modest home. He knocked on the door. Mrs Rennart opened it immediately. She studied his face for a few long seconds. Neither of them spoke. Not even a greeting or salutation.

'You look tired,' she said at last.

'I am.'

'Did Lloyd really send that postcard?'

'Yes.'

The answer had been automatic. But now he wondered – had Lloyd Rennart sent a postcard? For all he knew, Linda was simply sizing him for the title role in *Big Sap: The Musical*. Take the missing taped phone call, for example. If indeed the kidnapper had called Jack before his death, where was the tape of the call? Maybe the call had never occurred. Maybe Linda had lied about it. Maybe she was lying about the postcard too. Maybe she was lying about everything. Maybe Myron was simply being semi-seduced, like the hormone-driven male in one of those cheesy, unrated, direct-to-video, *Body Heat* rip-offs co-starring women with names like Shannon or Tawny.

Not a pleasant thought.

Francine Rennart silently led him into a dark basement. When they hit bottom, she reached up and switched on one of those swinging lightbulbs like something out of

344

Psycho, The room was pure cement. There was a water heater, a gas heater, a washer and dryer, and storage containers of various sizes, shapes, and material. Four boxes lay on the floor in front of him.

'That's his old stuff,' Francine Rennart said without looking down.

'Thank you.'

She tried, but she could not make herself look at the boxes. 'I'll be upstairs,' she said. Myron watched her feet disappear from view. Then he turned to the boxes and squatted down. The boxes were taped shut. He took out his key-chain penknife and slit the packing tape.

The first box had golf memorabilia. There were certificates and trophies and old tees. A golf ball was mounted to a wooden base with a rusty plaque that read:

HOLE IN ONE – 15TH HOLE AT HICKORY PARK
JANUARY 17, 1972

Myron wondered what life had been like for Lloyd on that clear, crisp golf afternoon. He wondered how often Lloyd had replayed the shot in his mind, how many times he'd sat alone in that BarcaLounger and tried to recapture that pure, cold rush. Had he remembered the feel of the club's grip, the tightness in his shoulders as he began the backswing, the clean, solid stroke of the ball, the floating follow-through.

In the second box, Myron found Lloyd's high school diploma. He found a yearbook from Penn State. There was a picture of the golf team. Lloyd Rennart had been captain. Myron's finger touched upon a large, felt *P.* Lloyd's varsity letter. There was a recommendation letter from his golf coach at Penn State. The words *bright future* jumped out at Myron. Bright future. The coach may have been a great motivator, but he made a lousy soothsayer.

The third box started off with a photograph of Lloyd in Korea. It was a casual group photo, a dozen or so boys/men in unbuttoned fatigues, arms dangling loosely around neighboring necks. Lots of smiles, seemingly happy smiles. Lloyd was thinner there, but he saw nothing gaunt or drawn in the eyes.

Myron put the picture down. In the background, Betty Buckley was not singing 'Memory,' but maybe she should have been. These boxes were a life – a life that in spite of these experiences and dreams and wants and hopes had chosen to terminate itself.

From the bottom of the box Myron pulled out a wedding album. The faded gold leaf read: *Lloyd and Lucille, November 17, 1968, Now and Forever.* More irony. The fake-leather cover was crusted with what looked like drink ringlets. Lloyd's first marriage, neatly wrapped and packed away in the bottom of a box.

Myron was about to put the album to the side when his curiosity got the better of him. He sat all the way down, his legs splayed like a kid with a new pack of baseball cards. He placed the photo album on the cement floor and began to open it. The binding made a cracking noise from the years of disuse.

The first photograph almost made Myron scream out loud.

Chapter 40

Myron's accelerator foot never eased.

Chestnut Street near Fourth is a no-parking zone, but that did not even make Myron pause. He was out of the car before it had come to a complete stop, ignoring the chorus of honking horns. He hurried through the Omni's lobby and into an open elevator. When he got off on the top floor, he found the right room number and knocked hard.

Norm Zuckerman opened the door. '*Bubbe*,' he said with a big smile. 'What a nice surprise.'

'Can I come in?'

'You? Of course, sweetheart, anytime.'

But Myron had already pushed by him. The suite's outer room was – to use hotel brochure lingo – spacious and elegantly appointed. Esme Fong sat on a couch. She looked up at him with the cornered-rabbit face. Posters and blueprints and advertisements and similar paraphernalia carpeted the floor and cascaded off the coffee table. Myron spotted blown-up images of Tad Crispin and Linda Coldren. Zoom logos were everywhere, inescapable, like vengeful ghosts or telemarketers.

'We were just doing a little strategizing,' Norm said. 'But hey, we can always take a break, right, Esme?'

Esme nodded.

Norm made his way behind a wet bar. 'You want something, Myron? I don't think they have any Yoo-Hoo in here, but I'm sure—'

'Nothing,' Myron interrupted.

Norm did the mock surrender thing with his hands. 'Sheesh, Myron, relax,' he said. 'What's twisting your nipple?'

'I wanted to warn you, Norm.'

'Warn me about what?'

'I don't want to do this. As far as I'm concerned, your love life should be personal. But it's not that easy. Not anymore. It's going to get out, Norm. I'm sorry.'

Norm Zuckerman did not move. He opened his mouth as though readying to protest. Then he stopped. 'How did you find out?'

'You were with Jack. At the Court Manor Inn. A maid saw you.'

Norm looked at Esme, who kept her head high. He turned back to Myron. 'Do you know what will happen if words gets out that I'm a *faygeleh*?'

'I can't help that, Norm.'

'I am the company, Myron. Zoom is about fashion and image and sports – which just so happens to be the most blatantly homophobic entity on this planet. Perception is everything in this business. If they find out I'm an old queen, you know what happens? Zoom goes plop down the septic tank.'

348

'I'm not sure I agree,' Myron said, 'but either way, it can't be helped.'

'Do the police know?' Norm asked.

'No, not yet.'

Norm threw up his hands. 'So why does it have to come out? It was just a fling, for crying out loud. Okay, so I met Jack. So we were attracted to each other. So we both had a ton to lose if either of us opened our traps. No big whup. It's got nothing to do with his murder.'

Myron stole a glance at Esme. She looked back at him with eyes that urged him to keep silent. 'Unfortunately,' Myron said, 'I think it does.'

'You think? You're going to destroy me on an "I think"?'

'I'm sorry.'

'I can't talk you out of it?'

'I'm afraid not.'

Norm moved away from the bar and half-collapsed into a chair. He put his face in the palms of his hands, his fingers sliding toward the back, meeting up in the hair, interweaving. 'I've spent my entire life with lies, Myron,' he began. 'I spent my childhood in Poland pretending I wasn't a Jew. Can you believe that? Me, Norm Zuckerman, pretending I was some slack-jawed *goy*. But I survived. I came here. And then I spent my adult life pretending I was a real man, a Casanova, a guy who always had a beautiful girl on his arm. You get used to lying, Myron. It gets easier, you know what I mean? The lies become a sort of second reality.'

'I'm sorry, Norm.'

He breathed deeply and forced up a tired smile. 'Maybe it's for the best,' Norm said. 'Look at Dennis Rodman.

He cross-dresses, for crying out loud. Hasn't hurt him any, has it?'

'No. It hasn't.'

Norm Zuckerman lifted his eyes toward Myron. 'Hey, once I got to this country, I became the most in-your-face Jew you ever saw. Didn't I? Tell me the truth. Am I not the most in-your-face Jew you've ever met, or what?'

'In my face,' Myron said.

'Bet your skinny *melinka* of a butt I am. And when I first started out, everyone told me to tone it down. Stop being so Jewish, they said. So ethnic. You'll never be accepted.' His face had true hope now. 'Maybe I can do the same for us closet *faygelehs*, Myron. Be in the world's face again, you know what I'm saying?'

'Yes, I do,' Myron said softly. Then he asked, 'Who else knew about you and Jack?'

'Knew?'

'Did you tell anybody?'

'No, of course not.'

Myron gestured toward Esme. 'How about one of those beautiful girlfriends on your arm? How about someone who practically lived with you? Wouldn't it have been easy for her to find out?'

Norm shrugged. 'I suppose so. You get this close to someone, you trust them. You drop your guard. So maybe she knew. So what?'

Myron looked at Esme. 'You want to tell him?'

Esme's voice was cool. 'I don't know what you're talking about.'

'Tell me what?'

Myron kept his eyes on hers. 'I wondered why you'd seduce a sixteen-year-old boy. Don't get me wrong. You gave a bravo performance – all that talk about being lonely and Chad being sweet and disease-free. You waxed quite eloquent. But it still rang hollow.'

Norm said, 'What the hell are you talking about, Myron?'

Myron ignored him. 'And then there was the matter of the bizarre coincidence – you and Chad showing up at the same motel at the same time as Jack and Norm. Too weird. I just couldn't buy it. But of course, we both know that it wasn't a coincidence. You planned it that way, Esme.'

'What plan?' Norm interjected. 'Myron, will you tell me what the hell is going on?'

'Norm, you mentioned that Esme used to work on Nike's basketball campaign. That she quit that job to come to you.'

'So?'

'Did she take a cut in salary?'

'A little.' Norm shrugged. 'Not much.'

'When exactly did she hook up with you?'

'I don't know.'

'Within the past eight months?'

Norm thought a moment. 'Yeah, so?'

'Esme seduced Chad Coldren. She set up a liaison with him at the Court Manor Inn. But she wasn't bringing him there for sex or because she was lonely. She brought him there as part of a setup.'

'What kind of setup?'

'She wanted Chad to see his father with another man.'

'Huh?'

'She wanted to destroy Jack. It was no coincidence. Esme knew your routine. She learned about your affair

351

with Jack. So she tried to set it up so Chad would see what his father was really about.'

Esme remained silent.

'Tell me something, Norm. Were you and Jack supposed to meet Thursday night?'

'Yeah,' Norm said.

'What happened?'

'Jack called it off. He pulled into the lot and got spooked. He said he saw a familiar car.'

'Not just familiar,' Myron said. 'His son's. That's where Esme screwed up. Jack spotted the car. He left before Chad had a chance to see him.'

Myron stood and walked toward Esme. She remained still. 'I almost had it right from the beginning,' he told her. 'Jack took the lead at the Open. His son was there, right in front of you. So you kidnapped Chad to throw Jack's game off. It was just like I thought. Except I missed your real motive. Why would you kidnap Chad? Why would you crave such vengeance against Jack Coldren? Yes, money was part of the motive. Yes, you wanted Zoom's new campaign to succeed. Yes, you knew that if Tad Crispin won the Open, you'd be heralded as the marketing genius of the world. All that played into it. But, of course, that never explained why you brought Chad to the Court Manor Inn in the first place – *before* Jack had the lead.'

Norm sighed. 'So tell us, Myron. What possible reason could she have for wanting to hurt Jack?'

Myron reached into his pocket and pulled out a grainy photograph. The first page of the wedding album. Lloyd and Lucille Rennart. Smiling. Happy. Standing side by side. Lloyd in a tux. Lucille holding a bouquet of flowers. Lucille looking stunning in a long white gown. But that wasn't what had shocked Myron to the core. What shocked him had nothing to do with what Lucille wore or held; rather, it was what she was.

Lucille Rennart was Asian.

'Lloyd Rennart was your father,' Myron said. 'You were in the car that day when he crashed into a tree. Your mother died. You were rushed to the hospital too.'

Esme's back was rod-straight, but her breathing was coming out in hitches.

'I'm not sure what happened next,' he continued. 'My guess would be that your father had hit rock bottom. He was a drunk. He had just killed his own wife. He felt washed-up, useless. So maybe he realized that he couldn't raise you. Or he didn't deserve to raise you. Or maybe an arrangement was reached with your mother's family. In return for not pressing charges, Lloyd would give Lucille's family custody of you. I don't know what happened. But you ended up being raised by your mother's family. By the time Lloyd straightened himself out, he probably felt it would be wrong to tear you out by the roots. Or maybe he was afraid that his daughter wouldn't take back the father who'd been responsible for killing her mother. Whatever, Lloyd kept quiet. He never even told his second wife about you.'

Tears were streaming down Esme's cheeks now. Myron felt like crying too.

'How close am I, Esme?'

'I don't even know what you're talking about.'

'There'll be records,' Myron said. 'Birth certificates, for certain. Probably adoption papers. It won't take the police long to trace.' He held up the photograph, his voice soft.

353

'The resemblance between you and your mother is almost enough.'

Tears continued to flow, but she was not crying. No sobs. No hitching. No quivering facial muscles. Just tears. 'Maybe Lloyd Rennart was my father,' Esme said. 'But you still have nothing. The rest is pure conjecture.'

'No, Esme. Once the police confirm your parentage, the rest will be easy. Chad will tell them that it was you who suggested you go to the Court Manor Inn. They'll look closely into Tito's death. There'll be a connection there. Fibers. Hairs. It'll all come together. But I have one question for you.'

She remained still.

'Why did you cut off Chad's finger?'

Without warning, Esme broke into a run. Myron was caught off guard. He jumped over the couch to block her path. But he had misjudged her. She had not been heading for an exit; she was going into a bedroom. Her bedroom. Myron hurdled back over the couch. He reached her room, but he was a little late.

Esme Fong had a gun. She pointed it at Myron's chest. He could see in her eyes that there'd be no confession, no explanations, no talk. She was ready to shoot.

'Don't bother,' Myron said.

'What?'

He pulled out his cell phone and handed it to her. 'This is for you.'

Esme did not move for a moment. Then, with her hand still on the gun, she reached out and took the phone. She pressed it against her ear, but Myron could hear just fine.

A voice said, 'This is Detective Alan Corbett from the Philadelphia Police Department. We are standing outside your door listening to every word that has been said. Put down the gun.'

Esme looked back at Myron. She still had the gun aimed at his chest. Myron felt a bead of sweat run down his back. Looking into the barrel of a gun was like staring into the cavern of death. Your eyes saw the barrel, only the barrel, as though it were growing impossibly larger, preparing to swallow you whole.

'It would be dumb,' he said.

She nodded then and lowered the gun. 'And pointless.'

The weapon dropped to the floor. Doors burst open. Police swarmed in.

Myron looked down at the gun. 'A thirty-eight,' he said to Esme. 'That the gun you killed Tito with?'

Her expression gave him the answer. The ballistics tests would be conclusive. She would be prosecutorial toast.

'Tito was a lunatic,' Esme said. 'He chopped off the boy's finger. He started making money demands. You have to believe that.'

Myron gave a noncommittal nod. She was testing out her defense, but it sort of sounded like the truth to Myron.

Corbett snapped handcuffs onto her wrists.

Her words were spilling out fast now. 'Jack Coldren destroyed my entire family. He ruined my father and killed my mother. And for what? My father did nothing wrong.'

'Yes,' Myron said, 'he did.'

'He pulled the wrong club out of a golf bag, if you

believe Jack Coldren. He made a mistake. An accident. Should it have cost him so much?'

Myron said nothing. It was no mistake, no accident. And Myron had no idea what it should have cost.

Chapter 41

The police cleaned up. Corbett had questions, but Myron was not in the mood. He left as soon as the detective was distracted. He sped to the police station where Linda Coldren was about to be released. He took the cement steps three or four at a clip, looking like a spastic Olympian timing the triple jump.

Victoria Wilson almost – the key word being *almost* – smiled at him, 'Linda will be out in a few minutes.'

'Do you have that tape I asked you to get?'

'The phone call between Jack and the kidnapper?'

'Yes.'

'I have it,' she said. 'But why—'

'Please give it to me,' Myron said.

She heard something in his tone. Without argument, she reached into her handbag and pulled it out. Myron took it. 'Do you mind if I drive Linda home?' he said.

Victoria Wilson regarded him. 'I think maybe that would be a good idea.'

A policeman came out. 'She's ready to leave,' he said.

Victoria was about to turn away, when Myron said, 'I guess you were wrong about digging into the past. The past ended up saving our client.'

Victoria held his eye. 'It's like I said before,' she began. 'You never know what you will find.'

They both waited for the other to break the eye contact. Neither did until the door behind them opened.

Linda was back in civilian clothes. She stepped out tentatively, like she'd been in a dark room and wasn't sure her eyes could handle the sudden light. Her face broke into a wide smile when she saw Victoria. They hugged. Linda dug her face into Victoria's shoulder and rocked in her arms. When they released, Linda turned and hugged Myron. Myron closed his eyes and felt his muscles unbunch. He smelted her hair and felt the wondrous skin of her cheek against his neck. They embraced for a long time, almost like a slow dance, neither wanting to let go, both perhaps a little bit afraid.

Victoria coughed into her fist and made her excuses. With the police leading the way, Myron and Linda made it to the car with a minimum of press fuss. They strapped on their seat belts in silence.

'Thank you,' she said.

Myron said nothing. He started the car. For a while neither of them spoke. Myron switched on the air-conditioning.

'We have something here, don't we?'

'I don't know,' Myron said. 'You were worried about your son. Maybe that's all it was.'

Her face said that she was not buying. 'How about you?' Linda asked. 'Did you feel anything?'

'I think so,' he said. 'But part of that might be fear, too.'

'Fear of what?'

'Of Jessica.'

She gave a weary grin. 'Don't tell me you're one of those guys who fears commitment.'

'Just the opposite. I fear how much I love her. I fear how much I want to commit.'

'So what's the problem?'

'Jessica left me once before. I don't want to be exposed like that again.'

Linda nodded. 'So you think that's what it was? Fear of abandonment?'

'I don't know.'

'I felt something,' she said. 'For the first time in a very long time. Don't get me wrong. I've had affairs. Like with Tad. But that's not the same thing.' She looked at him. 'It felt nice.'

Myron said nothing.

'You're not making this very easy,' Linda said.

'We have other things to talk about.'

'Like what?'

'Victoria filled you in on Esme Fong?'

'Yes.'

'If you remember, she had a solid alibi for Jack's murder.'

'A night clerk at a big hotel like the Omni? I doubt that will hold up on scrutiny.'

'Don't be so sure,' Myron said.

'Why do you say that?'

Myron did not answer. He turned right and said, 'You know what always bothered me, Linda?'

'No, what?'

'The ransom calls.'

'What about them?' she asked.

'The first one was made on the morning of the kidnapping. You answered. The kidnappers told you that they had your son. But they made no demands. I always found that odd, didn't you?'

She thought about it. 'I guess so.'

'Now I understand why they did that. But back then, we didn't know what the real motive for the kidnapping was.'

'I don't understand.'

'Esme Fong kidnapped Chad because she wanted revenge on Jack. She wanted to make him lose the tournament. How? Well, I'd thought that she'd kidnapped Chad to fluster Jack. Make him lose his focus. But that was too abstract. She wanted to make sure Jack lost. That was her ransom demand right from the beginning. But you see, the ransom call came in a little late. Jack was already at the course. You answered the phone.'

Linda nodded. 'I think I see what you're saying. She had to reach Jack directly.'

'She or Tito, but you're right. That's why she called Jack at Merion. Remember the second call, the one Jack got after he finished the round?'

'Of course.'

'That was when the ransom demand was made,' Myron said. 'The kidnapper told Jack plain and simple – you start losing or your son dies.'

'Hold up a second,' Linda said. 'Jack said they didn't make any demands. They told him to get some money ready and they'd call back.'

'Jack lied.'

'But . . . ?' She stopped, and then said, 'Why?'

'He didn't want us – or more specifically, you – to know the truth.'

Linda shook her head. 'I don't understand.'

Myron took out the cassette Victoria had given him. 'Maybe this will help explain.' He pushed the tape into the cassette player. There were several seconds of silence and then he heard Jack's voice like something from beyond the grave:

'*Hello?*'

'*Who's the chink bitch?*'

'*I don't know what—*'

'*You trying to fuck with me, you dumb son of a bitch? I'll start sending you the fucking brat in little pieces.*'

'*Please—*'

'What's the point of this, Myron?' Linda sounded a little annoyed.

'Just hold on another second. The part I'm interested in is coming up.'

'*Her name is Esme Fong. She works for a clothing company. She's just here to set up an endorsement deal with my wife, that's all.*'

'*Bullshit.*'

'*It's the truth, I swear.*'

'*I don't know, Jack. . . .*'

'*I wouldn't lie to you.*'

'*Well, Jack, we'll just see about that. This is gonna cost you.*'

'*What do you mean?*'

'*One hundred grand. Call it a penalty price.*'

'*For what?*'

Myron hit the STOP button. 'Did you hear that?'

'What?'

' "Call it a penalty price." Clear as day.'

'So?'

'It wasn't a ransom demand. It was a penalty.'

'This is a kidnapper, Myron. He's probably not all that caught up in semantics.'

' "One hundred grand," ' Myron repeated. ' "Call it a penalty price." As if a ransom demand had already been made. As if the hundred grand was something he'd just decided to tack on. And what about Jack's reaction? The kidnapper asks for one hundred grand. You would figure he would just tell him fine. But instead he says, "For what?" Again, because it's in addition to what he's already been told. Now listen to this.' Myron pushed the PLAY button.

'Never you fucking mind. You want the kid alive? It's gonna cost you one hundred grand now. That's in—'

'Now hold on a second.'

Myron hit the STOP button again. ' "It's gonna cost you one hundred grand *now*." ' Myron repeated. '*Now*. That's the key word. *Now*. Again as if it's something new. As if before this call there was another price. And then Jack interrupts him. The kidnapper says, "That's in—" when Jack jumps in. Why? Because Jack doesn't want him to finish the thought. He knew that we were listening. "That's in addition." I'd bet anything that was the next word he was about to say. "That's in addition to our original demand." Or, "that's in addition to losing the tournament." '

Linda looked at him. 'But I still don't get it. Why wouldn't Jack just tell us what they wanted?'

'Because Jack had no intention of complying with their demand.'

That stopped her. 'What?'

'He wanted to win too badly. More than that – he

362

needed to win. Had to. But if you learned the truth – you who had won so often and so easily – you would never understand. This was his chance at redemption, Linda. His chance of going back twenty-three years and making his life worth living. How badly did he want to win, Linda? You tell me. What would he have sacrificed?'

'Not his own son,' Linda countered. 'Yes, Jack needed to win. But not badly enough to forfeit his own son's life.'

'But Jack didn't see it that way. He was looking through his own rose-tinted prism of desire. A man sees what he wants to, Linda. What he has to. When I showed you and Jack the bank videotape, you both saw something different. You didn't want to believe your son could do something so hurtful. So you looked for explanations that would counter that evidence. Jack did just the opposite. He wanted to believe that his son was behind it. That it was only a big hoax. That way he could continue to try his hardest to win. And if by some chance he was wrong – if Chad had indeed been kidnapped – well, the kidnappers were probably bluffing anyway. They'd never really go through with it. In other words, Jack did what he had to do: he rationalized the danger away.'

'You think his desire to win clouded his thinking that much?'

'How much clouding did he need? We all had doubts after watching that bank tape. Even you. So how hard would it be for him to go the extra step?'

Linda sat back. 'Okay,' she said. 'Maybe I buy it. But I still don't see what this has to do with anything.'

'Bear with me a little while longer, okay? Let's go back to when I showed you the bank videotape. We're at your house. I show the tape. Jack storms out. He is upset, of course, but he still plays well enough to keep the big lead.

This angers Esme. He's ignoring her threat. She realizes that she has to up the ante.'

'By cutting off Chad's finger.'

'It was probably Tito, but that's not really relevant right now anyway. The key thing is, the finger is severed, and Esme wants to use it to show Jack she's serious.'

'So she plants it in my car and we find it.'

'No,' Myron said.

'What?'

'Jack finds it first.'

'In my car?'

Myron shook his head. 'Remember that Chad's key chain has Jack's car keys on it as well as yours. Esme wants to warn Jack, not you. So she puts the finger in Jack's car. He finds it. He's shocked, of course, but he's in the lie too deep now. If the truth came out, you'd never forgive him. Chad would never forgive him. And the tournament would be over for him. He has to get rid of the finger. So he puts the finger in an envelope and writes that note. Remember it? "I warned you not to seek help." Don't you see? It's the perfect distraction. It not only draws attention away from him, but it also gets rid of me.'

Linda chewed on her lower lip. 'That would explain the envelope and pen,' she said. 'I bought all the office supplies. Jack would have had some in his briefcase.'

'Exactly. But here is where things get really interesting.'

She arched an eyebrow. 'They're not interesting now?'

'Just hold on. It's Sunday morning. Jack is about to head into the final round with an insurmountable lead. Bigger than he had twenty-three years ago. If he loses now, it would be the greatest golf collapse in history. His name would forever be synonymous with choking – the

364

one thing Jack hated more than anything else. But on the other hand, Jack was not a complete ogre. He loved his son. He knew now that the kidnapping was not a hoax. He was probably torn, not sure what to do. But in the end he made a decision. He was going to lose the tournament.'

Linda said nothing.

'Stroke by stroke, we watched him die. Win understands the destructive side of wanting to win far better than I. He also saw that Jack had the fire back, that old need to win. But despite all that, Jack still tried to lose. He didn't completely collapse. That would have looked too suspicious. But he started dropping strokes. He made it close. And then he purposely fumbled big-time in the stone quarry and lost his lead.

'But imagine what was going on in his head. Jack was fighting against everything that he was. They say a man can't drown himself. Even if it means saving his own child's life, a man cannot keep himself under water until his lungs burst. I'm not so sure that's any different than what Jack was trying to do. He was literally killing himself. His sanity was probably ripping away like divots on the course. On the eighteenth green, the survival instinct took over. Maybe he started rationalizing again – or more likely, he just couldn't help himself. But we both saw the transformation, Linda. We saw his face suddenly crystallize on eighteen. Jack stroked that putt home and tied the score.'

Linda's voice was barely audible. 'Yes,' she said. 'I saw him change.' She sat up in her seat and let loose a long breath. 'Esme Fong must have been in a panic by then.'

'Yes.'

'Jack had left her no choice. She had to kill him.'

365

Myron shook his head. 'No.'

She looked contused again. 'But it adds up. Esme was desperate. You said so yourself. She wanted vengeance for her father, and on top of that she was now worried about what would happen if Tad Crispin lost. She had to kill him.'

'One problem,' Myron said.

'What?'

'She called your house that night.'

'Right,' Linda said. 'To set up the meeting at the course. She probably told Jack to come alone. To not tell me anything.'

'No,' Myron said. 'That's not what happened.'

'What?'

'If that was what happened,' Myron continued, 'we'd have the call on tape.'

Linda shook her head. 'What are you talking about?'

'Esme Fong did call your house. That part is true. My bet is that she just threatened him some more. Let him know that she meant business. Jack probably begged forgiveness. I don't know. I'll probably never know. But I'd bet he ended the call by promising to lose the next day.'

'So?' Linda said. 'What does that have to do with the call being taped?'

'Jack was going through hell,' Myron went on. 'The pressure was too much. He was probably close to a breakdown. So he ran out of the house – just as you said – and ended up at his favorite place in the world. Merion. The golf course. Did he go out there just to think? I don't know. Did he bring the gun with him, maybe even contemplating suicide? Again, I don't know. But I do know that the tape machine was still hooked up to your phone.

The police confirmed that. So where did the tape of that last conversation go?'

Linda's tone was suddenly more measured. 'I don't know.'

'Yes, Linda, you do.'

She gave him a look.

'Jack might have forgotten the call was recorded,' Myron continued. 'But you didn't. When he ran out of the house, you went down to the basement. You played the tape. And you heard everything. What I'm telling you in this car is not new to you. You knew why the kidnappers had taken your child. You knew what Jack had done. You knew where he liked to go when he took his walks. And you knew you had to stop him.'

Myron waited. He missed the turnoff, took the next one, U-turned back onto the highway. He found the right exit and put on his blinker.

'Jack did bring the gun,' Linda said too calmly. 'I didn't even know where he kept it.'

Myron gave a slight nod, silently trying to encourage.

'You're right,' she continued. 'When I played back the tape, I realized that Jack couldn't be trusted. He knew it too. Even with the threat of his own son's death, he had nailed that putt on eighteen. I followed him out to the course. I confronted him. He started to cry. He said he would try to lose. But' – she hesitated, weighed her words – 'that drowning man example you gave. That was Jack.'

Myron tried to swallow, but his throat was too dry.

'Jack wanted to kill himself. And I knew he had to. I'd listened to the tape. I'd heard the threats. And I had no doubts: If Jack won, Chad was dead. I also knew something else.'

She stopped and looked at Myron.

'What?' he said.

'I knew Jack would win. Win was right – the fire was back in Jack's eyes. But it was a raging inferno now. One that even he couldn't control anymore.'

'So you shot him,' Myron said.

'I struggled to get the gun from him. I wanted to injure him. Seriously injure him. If there was the possibility he could play again, I was afraid the kidnapper might just hold on to Chad indefinitely. The voice on the phone sounded that desperate. But Jack wouldn't surrender the gun – nor would he pull it away from me. It was weird. He just held on and looked at me. Almost like he was waiting. So I curled my finger around the trigger and pulled.' Her voice was very clear now. 'It didn't go off accidentally. I had hoped to wound him seriously, not kill him. But I fired. I fired to save my son. And Jack ended up dead.'

More silence.

'Then you headed back to the house,' Myron said. 'You buried the gun. You saw me in the bushes. When you got inside, you erased the tape.'

'Yes.'

'And that was why you released that press announcement so early. The police wanted to keep it quiet, but you needed the story to go public. You wanted the kidnappers to know that Jack was dead, so they'd let Chad go.'

'It was my son or my husband,' Linda said. She turned her body to face him. 'What would you have done?'

'I don't know. But I don't think I would have shot him.'

' "Don't think"?' she repeated with a laugh. 'You talk about Jack being under pressure, but what about me? I hadn't slept. I was stressed and I was confused and I was more scared than I had ever been in my entire life – and yes, I was enraged that Jack had sacrificed our son's chance of playing the game we all so loved. I didn't have the luxury of an I-don't-know, Myron. My son's life was hanging in the balance. I only had time to react.'

They turned up Ardmore Avenue and drove in silence past the Merion Golf Club. They both looked out the window at the course's gently sloping sea of green broken up only by the clean, white faces of sand. It was, Myron had to admit, a magnificent sight.

'Are you going to tell?' she asked.

She already knew the answer. 'I'm your attorney,' Myron said. 'I can't tell.'

'And if you weren't my attorney?'

'It wouldn't matter. Victoria would still be able to offer up enough reasonable doubt to win the case.'

'That's not what I meant.'

'I know,' Myron said. He left it at that. She waited, but no answer was coming.

'I know you don't care,' Linda continued, 'but I meant what I said before. My feelings for you were real.'

Neither of them spoke again. Myron pulled into the driveway. The police kept the media back. Chad was outside, waiting. He smiled at his mother and ran toward her. Linda opened the car door and got out. They might have embraced, but Myron did not see it. He was already backing out the drive.

Chapter 42

Victoria opened the door.

'In the bedroom. Follow me.'

'How is she?' Myron asked.

'She's been sleeping a lot. But I don't think the pain is that bad yet. We have a nurse and a morphine drip ready if she needs it.'

The decor was far simpler and less opulent than Myron had expected. Solid-colored furniture and pillows. Uncluttered white walls. Pine bookcases with artifacts gathered from vacations to Asia and Africa. Victoria had told him that Cissy Lockwood loved to travel.

They stopped in front of a doorway. Myron looked inside. Win's mother lay in bed. Exhaustion emanated from her. Her head was back on the pillow as though it were too heavy to lift. An IV bag was attached to her arm. She looked at Myron and mustered a gentle smile. Myron smiled back. With his peripheral vision, he saw Victoria signal to the nurse. The nurse stood and moved past him. Myron stepped inside. The door closed behind him.

Myron moved closer to the bed. Her breathing was labored and constricted, as though she was being slowly strangled from inside. Myron did not know what to say. He had seen people die before, but those had been quick, violent deaths, the life force snuffed out in one big, powerful gust. This was different. He was actually watching a human being die, her vitality dripping out of her like the liquid in her IV bag, the light in her eyes almost imperceptibly dimming, the grinding whir of tissues and sinews and organs eroding under the onslaught of whatever manic beast had lain claim to her.

She lifted a hand and put it on his. Her grip was surprisingly strong. She was not bony or pale. Her muscles were still toned, her summer tan only slightly faded.

'You know,' she said.

Myron nodded.

She smiled. 'How?'

'A lot of little things,' he said. 'Victoria not wanting me to dig into the past. Jack's mischievous past. Your too-casual comment about how Win was supposed to be playing golf with Jack that day. But mostly it was Win. When I told him about our conversation, he said that I now knew why he wanted nothing to do with you and Jack. You, I could understand. But why Jack?'

Her chest heaved a bit. She closed her eyes for a moment. 'Jack destroyed my life,' she said. 'I realize that he was only a teenager pulling a prank. He apologized profusely. He told me that he had not realized that my husband was on the premises. He said that he was certain I would hear Win coming and hide. It was all a joke, he said. Nothing more. But none of that made him less liable. I lost my son forever because of what he did. He had to face the consequences.'

Myron nodded. 'So you paid off Lloyd Rennart to sabotage Jack at the Open.'

'Yes. It was an inadequate punishment for what he had done to my family, but it was the best I could do.'

The bedroom door opened, and Win stepped into the room. Myron felt the hand release his. A sob came out of Cissy Lockwood. Myron did not hesitate or say good-bye. He turned away and walked out the door.

She died three days later. Win never left her side. When the last pitiful breath was drawn, when the chest mercifully stopped rising and falling and her face froze in a final, bloodless death mask, Win appeared in the corridor.

Myron stood and waited. Win looked at him. His face was serene, untroubled.

'I did not want her to die alone,' he said.

Myron nodded. He tried to stop shaking.

'I am going to take a walk.'

'Is there anything I can do?' Myron asked.

Win stopped. 'Actually,' he said, 'there is.'

'Name it.'

They played thirty-six holes at Merion that day. And thirty-six more the next. And by the third day, Myron was starting to get it.

Drop Shot

A young woman is shot in cold blood, her lifeless body dumped outside the stadium at the height of the US Open. Once her tennis career had skyrocketed. Now the headlines were being made by another young player from the wrong side of the tracks.

When Myron Bolitar investigates the killing he uncovers a connection between the two players and a six-year old murder at an exclusive club. Suddenly Myron is in over his head. And with a dirty senator, a jealous mother, and the mob all drawn into the case, he finds himself playing the most dangerous game of all . . .

'Bolitar is a glorious character' *Guardian*

'The twists and turns in the plots continue right to the very last page . . . These are very vivid books' *Independent*

ALSO BY HARLAN COBEN

Darkest Fear

Life isn't going well for Myron Bolitar. His business is struggling, and his father has recently suffered a heart attack when, out of the blue, Myron's college sweetheart, Emily, appears. Her thirteen-year-old son Jeremy is gravely ill and can be saved only by a bone marrow transplant from a donor who has vanished without trace. Then Emily reveals even more shocking news: Jeremy is Myron's son, conceived the night before Emily's wedding to another man.

Staggered by the revelation, Myron plunges into a search for the missing donor – and gets caught up un a brutal kidnapping and a cat-and-mouse game between an ambitious reporter and the FBI.

'Coben's genius – and his most frustrating trick – is that he makes it all seem so obvious, then kicks your legs away at the end' *FHM*

Also by Harlan Coben

No Second Chance

When the first bullet hit my chest, I thought of my daughter . . .

Marc Seidman wakes up in ICU to find his wife has been murdered and his baby daughter, Tara, has vanished. Then something arrives to give Marc new hope: a ransom note. *We are watching. If you contact the authorities you will never see your daughter again. There will be no second chance.*

The note is chilling, but Marc sees only one thing: the chance to save his daughter. And, haunted by deception and deadly secrets – about his wife, about an old life, and about his own past – he vows to bring Tara home . . . at any cost.

'Exciting and moving . . . *No Second Chance* is a consummate and thrilling piece of storytelling' *Observer*

All Orion/Phoenix titles are available at your local bookshop or from the following address:

> Mail Order Department
> Littlehampton Book Services
> FREEPOST BR535
> Worthing, West Sussex, BN13 3BR
> *telephone* 01903 828503, *facsimile* 01903 828802
> *e-mail* MailOrders@lbsltd.co.uk
> (Please ensure that you include full postal address details)

Payment can be made either by credit/debit card (Visa, Mastercard, Access and Switch accepted) or by sending a £ Sterling cheque or postal order made payable to *Littlehampton Book Services*.
DO NOT SEND CASH OR CURRENCY.

Please add the following to cover postage and packing

UK and BFPO:
£1.50 for the first book, and 50p for each additional book to a maximum of £3.50

Overseas and Eire:
£2.50 for the first book plus £1.00 for the second book and 50p for each additional book ordered

---

BLOCK CAPITALS PLEASE

name of cardholder _____

address of cardholder _____

_____

_____

postcode _____

delivery address
(if different from cardholder)

_____

_____

_____

postcode _____

☐ I enclose my remittance for £_____

☐ please debit my Mastercard/Visa/Access/Switch (delete as appropriate)

card number ☐☐☐☐ ☐☐☐☐ ☐☐☐☐ ☐☐☐☐

expiry date ☐☐☐☐   Switch issue no. ☐☐

signature _____

prices and availability are subject to change without notice